The Faces
Of
The Damned

Book 4
Of The Warrior Series

By
Sandra J Yearman

Seraphim Publishing LLC

We Will Bring Light To All The Dark Places

Registered trademark-Sandra J Yearman

Seraphim Publishing
438 Water St
Cambridge, WI 53523
sandrajyearman@gmail.com

Library of Congress Catalog Number: 2014913976

ISBN: 978-0-9890263-2-1

First Edition

About The Author

Sandra J Yearman is a native of Wisconsin, where she currently resides. She graduated from the University of Wisconsin with a Bachelor of Arts degree in Journalism. Sandra was a member of the United States Army Reserves for over twenty years. She retired from the Dane County Sheriff's Office in Madison Wisconsin as a sergeant.

Sandra is a cancer survivor. And it is on this journey that she says she found her voice and began to write. She established Seraphim Publishing LLC in 2008. Sandra has spent decades supporting and working with rescued domestic animals.

Books written by Sandra:

Novels
Brother Kings
The Scroll And The Sword
Song Of The Second Son
The Faces Of The Damned
A Single Lion Roars
Stand Before The Children
Tyrants, Dictators And Kings

Politicians And Kings
Armada Of The Dead

Poetry

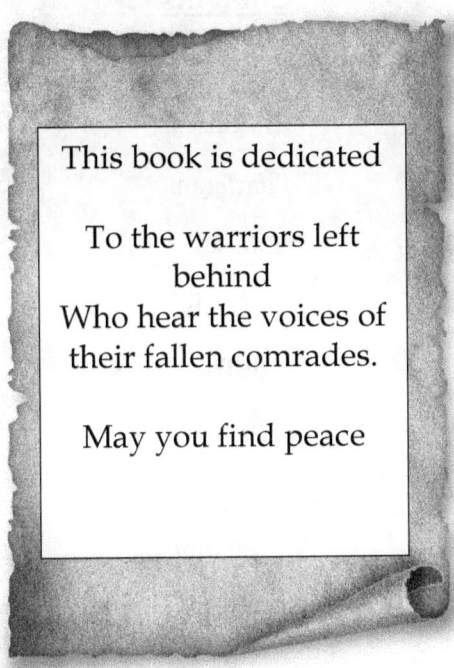

This book is dedicated

To the warriors left
behind
Who hear the voices of
their fallen comrades.

May you find peace

Contents

7

Chapter I
Recupero

"Archetenus," yelled the soldier. "You're free to go."

Archetenus looked up from his hand of cards when he heard the lock to the cell door loudly click. "What did the judge have a change of heart?" Archetenus asked sarcastically as he stood up from his seat on the floor. "I thought I had another six months in here."

"Apparently you have a friend who paid your way out," the soldier said.

"Well, boys, I can't say it's been fun," said Archetenus with a huge grin as he walked out of the prison cell he had been living in for the last ten months.

"You can pick up your things at the front desk," the soldier said as he unlocked another heavy metal door.

"Any idea who paid for me to get out?" Archetenus asked as he followed the soldier down a long, cold stone hallway.

"Nope, I was just told to fetch ya."

The soldier escorted Archetenus through three more hallways, each of which was secured with a heavy metal door. "Go up to that desk over there," the soldier said and pointed. "James has your paperwork and your stuff."

"I'm missing two daggers," Archetenus said irritably as he sorted through the pile of belongings that James had placed on the table.

"Are you sure you came in with them?" James asked with a grin. "If I remember right you were pretty damn drunk when they hauled you in here."

"You're probably right," Archetenus replied. "So where do I sign?" James pushed a sheet of paper in front of Archetenus and handed him a pen. "So who paid to get me out?"

"Don't know; I don't take the money," said James.

"Well, is there a note or anything?"

"Nope," James spit a big wad of tobacco on the floor then grinned. "Guess it's gonna to be a surprise."

"Never been much for surprises," Archetenus said as he finished strapping on the last of his weapons and turned towards the door.

Roch was starving. This was the third sunrise since his escape through the hole in the wall of the hell dimension. His surroundings looked familiar although Roch was so disorientated he no longer trusted his own senses. He had no weapons or clothes for that matter and his body, what was happening to his body?

Roch felt a constant pulsing through his entire being and he did not understand what it was. Sometimes when he looked at his arms or legs they appeared as a normal human's would look but other times and it was these other times that filled the madman with utter terror. Was he imagining all of this?

There were times when Roch thought that his body was transparent, sometimes it seemed to glow and then there were times that his limbs appeared gnarled and black like the tar that had surrounded him in the hell dimension.

Roch had run hysterically for two days after escaping from Ahriman's prison. Roch didn't know where he was going; he was driven to run by the terror within him. Now he lay on the floor of a forest that was but miles from the castle of his reign; although Roch did not realize that. The once mighty dictator and king was grabbing beetles from a rotten log and devouring them.

"You know the King and Queen said you could have your own room," Hannah said as she entered Jared's room and once again saw Zoya sleeping in a large overstuffed chair.

"I just don't feel right taking a room in the castle," Zoya said modestly as she sat up in the chair.

9

"Honestly Zoya, King Sudfad and Queen Renya are two of the most charitable people you will ever meet," Hannah said as she pulled the covers back so she could check Jared's wound. "There are plenty of rooms here and you won't be much good for your friend here if you get sick yourself."

"How does it look?" Zoya asked as she stood up and walked to the side of the bed where Hannah was standing.

"He's healing but he lost a lot of blood."

"He never would have been hurt if it wasn't for me," Zoya said guiltily.

"What do you mean?" asked Hannah as she replaced the wet cloth on Jared's head.

"Eight Taperian soldiers stopped us from crossing the border. Jared was fighting with them all and winning until one of them grabbed me. In the moment that Jared looked at me, he got stabbed."

"Zoya it is not your fault," Hannah said as she turned around and gave Zoya a long hard look. "Zoya I think you have lost weight and you look exhausted. I am going to be your physician now and take you to a room to get some rest and a meal. Why are you looking at me so strangely?"

"Hannah you have been so kind to me and I don't want to scare you," Zoya said almost apologetically. "But did your husband tell you about me?"

"Gabriel said you are a seer, honestly I have never met a seer before," Hannah said then she paused. "Zoya you are seeing something about me aren't you? Tell me please."

"Hannah it's not so much what I am seeing as what I am hearing from the spirits. Was there great conflict between your parents before they died?"

"Yes," gasped Hannah as fear ran through her body.

"I think it is your mother who has been contacting me; was her name Harriet?"

"Yes," Hannah said in a whisper.

"She sends you great love and I can feel the warmth but she also shows me a cold hatred that I believe is aimed at your father. Your mother says she is happy that you married and moved from Nora but she wants you to tell Gabriel that they did not find everything at your house."

"What does she mean?"

"I'm not really sure," Zoya said as if she was looking at something that Hannah could not see. "She is showing me rocks, huge rocks as if in a mountain. The moon is rising and as it comes up over these rocks there is a beam of light that points at a hill or mountain. She keeps showing me the same scene over and over. Does that have meaning for you?"

"No but Gabriel is here for his morning meeting with the King and the others, we need to tell them this," Hannah grabbed Zoya's hand and they walked out of Jared's bedroom and down the hallway. Hannah boldly knocked on the door to Sudfad's study. The Sanuri was sitting the closest to the door and opened it. "I am sorry to disturb you but Zoya has something she needs to tell you."

The two women walked into the room and joined the Sanuri, Sudfad, Raul, Simon, Matthew, Mathas, Sorren, Gabriel and Raphael. Once again Zoya felt intimidated by the presence of men of such importance. She started to stammer as she repeated her words to the men in the room.

"So Zoya are you saying that spirits contact you without you requesting them to?" Raphael asked.

"Oh yes My Lord," Zoya said earnestly. "Most of my life my visions and the voices I hear have terrified me. It wasn't until the voices protected me a couple of times that I felt safe to try and talk with them. I truly don't know why these things happen to me. I'll be honest I wish I was just a normal person."

"Zoya may I look into your mind?" the Sanuri asked. "I will not hurt you."

"Yes My Lord, what do you need me to do?"

11

"Nothing," replied the Sanuri as he placed the palms of both of his hands on Zoya's head. After several minutes the Sanuri let go of her head. "Zoya have you prayed to The Great Ruler that He use your gifts for good?"

"Well, I am not sure that they are really gifts but yes I have, did you see that?"

The Sanuri addressed the others in the room. "Zoya is not a charlatan and it is no accident that she is here. Think of Zoya as a window into other worlds. I believe Zoya has been sent to us to help in this great battle that lies before us." Now the Sanuri looked at Zoya. "Zoya, I saw that you are very powerful but your fears of your abilities are limiting you. Your abilities are a gift and you will need to overcome your fears in order to help us."

"My Lord I would be more than honored to help you however I can but I think overcoming my fears, well, will not be that easy," Zoya said sincerely.

"Zoya ask The Great Ruler to help you," the Sanuri said. "Because I believe you will have a significant role to play."

"Zoya is too humble to accept a room and honestly I don't know the last time she ate," Hannah said. "She needs some rest and a hot meal."

"Of course," Sudfad said. "I will call Marie."

"If you don't mind I will take Zoya to Marie to make sure she eats," Hannah said and took Zoya's hand.

The two women started to walk towards the door when Zoya stopped and turned to the Sanuri. "Did you see the vision that Hannah's mother was showing me?"

"No," the Sanuri said. "After you have eaten and gotten some rest, you should return to us and contact Harriet."

After Hannah made sure that Zoya had a meal, she walked with Zoya and Marie as Marie showed Zoya to her room. Zoya's room was in the same hallway as Jared's.

Marie left first and as Hannah was turning to leave Zoya stopped her. "Hannah do you think it is possible that what the Sanuri said is true?"

"About you having a gift?"

"No the part about me coming here to help them," Zoya said. "Because if it is, what a strange chain of events brought me here."

Hannah smiled. "I'm sure what the Sanuri said was true. I have to tell you I haven't known Gabriel very long. He and Prince Raul were in Nora searching for some very evil men and well, it's a long story but it too was a strange chain of events that brought many of us together. Many of us who now consider each other close friends and family. It is strange how things work out sometimes. So does this mean you will be staying in Wetpr?"

"I never wanted to return to Stordt it is such an evil place. I was frightened all of the time. I was married to a good man, his name was Thomas. One day Thomas was bringing groceries home and these men just came out of a tavern and started to beat him with bullwhips. They killed him in the middle of the street and no one did anything to help him," Zoya paused.

"It was after Thomas died that I had to use my visions to make money, I had no other skills. When Jared came into my shop, I know this may sound awful because I believe he is a dangerous man. But I jumped at the chance to leave Taperia. Jared is so big and looks so mean, I thought if anyone could get me past the border guards it would be him."

Hannah sat down on the edge of Zoya's bed as she listened to Zoya talk. "And now to have a holy man tell me I was meant to come here, it is all so hard to believe. Hannah I know everyone here believes Jared is a really bad man and perhaps he is. But I tell you the truth, he showed me great kindness always and he was honest with me. And he really was trying to warn the Sanuri. So he can't be all bad can he?"

"I'm not telling you anything!" screamed High Priest Meekos as he sat bound to a chair in the underground torture room that Hannah's father had built under their home in Nora.

"I haven't asked you any questions," High Priest Tyrus said as he, High Priest Ephraim and High Priest Gideon entered the cold stone room.

"Then why am I here and who the hell are you?" Meekos screamed.

"Meekos you have been calling yourself a high priest for over three hundred years, surely you know who we are," Tyrus replied.

Meekos now stared at the three high priests who were standing before him in their white robes with green armbands. "Are you the Patronus?" he asked fearfully.

"For a high priest there is such fear in your voice; Meekos is that because you are realizing that The Great Ruler and the Church know of your crimes?" Tyrus asked in a calm and soothing voice.

"I don't know what you are talking about," Meekos snapped. "I demand that you untie me at once."

"We found your underground chambers at the monastery in Malga," Tyrus said. "We know you were sacrificing humans to demons. We have been intercepting your correspondence. We are aware that you are a member of the Recupero sect of the Insidiae and that you have been trying to help the demon Omnibus escape from his prison in The Abyss."

The blood drained from Meekos' face as he listened to Tyrus. Meekos had always prided himself on his careful and detailed planning of every mission. But never had it occurred to him that the Church would investigate and spy on him. Meekos had heard about the Patronus, the protectors of the Church. But never had he met a member of this organization and never did he think they would uncover his work for the Insidiae. "So what are you going to do with me?" Meekos asked fearfully.

"If you were in my place what would you do?" Tyrus asked. Meekos did not answer but sweat started to run down his face. "I assume by now you realize that your spells and dark magics will not work in here. This building has been reclaimed for The Great Ruler and is protected by holiness."

"You cannot call to your demons for help. But know that if you decide to talk with us, the demons cannot hear your words," Tyrus said.

"And why would I ever talk to you?" Meekos asked with a sneer.

Archetenus walked out of his prison at Fort Friada and stood for a few moments enjoying the warmth of the morning sun, something he had not felt in many months. He looked around at the soldiers and civilians who were going through their morning routines within the walls of the massive fort. Archetenus did not see anyone who he recognized, nor did he see anyone who was watching him. He walked to the front gate and showed the soldiers his release papers. The massive gate was opened and Archetenus once again knew freedom.

No one was waiting for Archetenus outside of the fort and he had no idea where his horse was, so he started the long walk to the City of Port Friada. He needed to get to the room he had rented at the Sea's End Hotel because he had hidden a fortune in gold coins under the floorboards.

As he walked, Archetenus was thinking about who would have paid for his release from prison and why this mysterious person did not leave a note or show up at the fort. Archetenus had few friends, except for the men who he drank with at The Ghost Ship Tavern and as he thought about them; he realized none of these men were really his friends.

Archetenus tried to remember the night that he was put into prison. That night, like every other started with him going to The Ghost Ship Tavern to play cards. He clearly remembered buying a bottle of whiskey before he joined a card game but after that everything seemed to be in fragments.

Archetenus was told that he killed three men that night. He was never told their names and he didn't know why he killed them. Actually he didn't really remember killing the men but he would get brief memories of fighting and being really angry. Archetenus had killed many men in his life; these three would not be his last.

"And how is my favorite patient?" Hannah asked as she walked into the parlor of Matthew's and Angelina's home in the castle at Wetpr. All the men were still in the morning meeting in the King's study. Vitomas, Annabelle, Rosa, Shara, Laurel and Renya were all visiting Angelina and her new baby daughter Alexas Rose. Rosa was holding the baby and now handed her to Hannah.

"She is such a beautiful baby," Hannah said as she examined Alexas. "Tell me when do you plan to return to Lentz?"

"Fahron and Isadore left yesterday," Angelina said. "Fahron and Claudius will run the kingdom while Mathas stays here with us. The rest of our families will all travel home at the same time, although I don't know when that will be yet."

"Did you notice the change in Isadore and Fahron?" Rosa asked everyone but looked at Renya.

"Rosa this was the first time I have met your friends," Renya said. "I don't know them well enough to answer that."

"You know Sudfad allowed them to go to the dungeons to visit Timothy," Rosa said then turned to Annabelle. "Honey we all know that Timothy is a monster and what he tried to do to you is unforgiveable but you have to believe me when I tell you that Timothy's parents are truly wonderful people. They were so wounded and horrified by what Timothy did that they rarely came out of their home and they stopped talking with friends."

"Well, Mathas told me that he went with them when they visited Timothy and Timothy said such horrible things that both Fahron and Isadore could no longer think of him as their son. Mathas said it was like their bond had been severed and a great weight had been lifted from them."

"What in the world could Timothy have said that would cause his mother to sever her bond with him?" Renya asked.

"Well, among other things he was bragging that he had raped other girls."

"My Lord," Marie called as she knocked on the door to Sudfad's study. "I am sorry to interrupt you but there are Enrops here with messages for both of the high priests and the Sanuri. They say the messages are very important."

Within moments the door to the study opened and Gabriel, Raphael and the Sanuri all walked out, heading for the front door. "Thank you Marie," the Sanuri said as he walked past her.

"Marie," Sudfad called "Would you bring Zoya here?" He paused for a moment then added. "But if she is sleeping do not wake her."

"They have Meekos," Gabriel said as the three men walked back into Sudfad's study. "Our men have him as a prisoner in the basement of Hannah's home. Of course he refuses to talk to them." Gabriel was obviously overjoyed by the information. "I am leaving at once to interrogate him."

"Now let's wait for a moment," the Sanuri said. "We need to have a plan here because this too could be another trap. Meekos cannot perform any black magics because the home is protected by holiness but you know Ahriman and others know your men have him."

"And I want him," Sudfad said sternly. "He was behind the attempted murder of two of my sons and the kidnapping of a third. I want to execute him."

"Old friend do not let your anger cloud your judgment," the Sanuri said. "Meekos is the most important piece to the puzzle that we have so far. There is much information that we need to get from him, which is why I will also be going to Nora. But you know there are many who will try and silence Meekos and the men who are holding him are in grave danger." As the Sanuri spoke there was a delicate knock on the door.

"Gabriel would you open that?" Sudfad asked. "It's Zoya."

"You requested my presence?" Zoya asked meekly as she entered the room.

"Zoya I am sorry to disturb you," Sudfad said. "But I feel we need you to try and talk with the spirit who was giving you messages this morning."

"I've never tried to contact a spirit with this many people in the room before," Zoya said as she was looking around the study. "When the spirits talk to me, they do it whenever they choose. But when I try to contact them I usually sit at a table and have it quiet so I can concentrate."

Mathas, Matthew, Sorren and Simon were sitting around a table in the study; all four men now stood up and moved so Zoya could sit down. "Sanuri and Gabriel I feel like you should sit at the table with me. First let me explain some things," Zoya said with more confidence in her voice. "All of you have been so kind to me but you know I am greatly intimidated because you are all such powerful men. But perhaps other than the Sanuri, the spirit world is one in which I walk. You must understand that sometimes things can be dangerous. If I am to do this for you, you must let me be in control of this and you must do as I say."

"I believe we all understand that," Sudfad said.

"Now what is it that you want me to ask?"

"Try to get more clarification on the images she was showing you this morning," said Sudfad.

"Before you start," Raul said. "I will take notes." He stood up and took paper and pen from his father's desk.

Zoya sat at the table with the Sanuri on her right side and Gabriel sitting across from her. The room was silent as all eyes were now on Zoya. She closed her eyes and appeared to be going into a trance. Zoya did not speak for several minutes and when she did it was not to any of the men in the room.

"Wait, one voice at a time I can't understand you," Zoya said then she was silent again for a few moments. Zoya kept her eyes closed as she spoke. "Sanuri I think because you are here many spirits want to talk. I had to call Harriet to come forward and her message is mostly for Gabriel."

"Gabriel, Harriet is very happy that you make Hannah so happy and that you have taken her from Nora. But she wants to warn you that you have no idea how diabolical Hannah's father was."

"Harriet says she knows more now than when she was alive. She says the images she was showing me this morning points to a secret temple that the Insidiae have. She said it is a place of great horrors and many will die if you don't stop them. She says the temple is inside of a mountain but there does not appear to be an opening in the mountain."

"Harriet says I didn't understand what she was showing me before. She says there is an unusual rock; it is tall and thin and stands by itself hundreds of yards from the opening to the mountain. Then closer to the mountain is another rock formation but this looks like an archway. When the moon is full and it rises at one point a beam of light will come forth from the lone rock and shoot through the archway and this beam will show you the opening to the mountain."

"Is the mountain near Nora?" Gabriel asked.

"No, she says it is in Ryed," Zoya paused for a moment. "Harriet says you found the safe in Arthur's office. But the back wall of the safe is false. She says you must open it because the things her husband really wanted to hide are in a compartment behind the safe."

Zoya paused again and a look of compassion appeared on her face. "Harriet is very sad and ashamed. She says I must tell Hannah that Harriet had no knowledge of what Arthur was doing and if she had she would have tried to stop him. Now she is showing me a small cemetery that is surrounded by old trees. It looks like the cemetery lies between the house and the area of the river you crossed to get to Nora every day."

"She is showing me a large stone mausoleum with 'Eaidisni' carved in the front. Harriet says this mausoleum conceals hidden underground chambers. You must feel along the walls for the levers to open the secret doors. Harriet says there are thirteen doors," Zoya paused again. "She doesn't know what is behind the doors but there is a great presence of evil, she warns you to be very careful."

"Who is Eaidisni?" Sorren asked.

"Harriet just turned the word around and it is Insidiae spelled backwards," Zoya explained.

"When Gabriel, Natasha and I had our experiences when the demons were trying to pull us into hell, we all kept seeing the number 'thirteen' everywhere. During my experience I had a vision of The Lion and he said 'thirteen levels, thirteen doors.' Then he asked me if we were willing to stand up to what we found behind those doors," Simon said. "I told him we were. Then I was returned to this world."

"The Lion has said similar things to me also," the Sanuri said.

"Could this be another trap?" asked Matthew.

"I did not feel any darkness from Harriet," Zoya said. "She is so horrified and ashamed of what her husband did when they were both alive that she is trying to make up for it now. I think she would have told you what was behind those doors if she knew. Oh, by The Great Ruler," Zoya gasped as she put her hand over her mouth. Tears started to run down Zoya's cheeks.

"What do you see?" Sudfad asked earnestly.

Zoya did not speak for a few moments and when she did it was haltingly. "Harriet showed me her husband holding her back as a crowd of people watched Roch rape and murder their little girl. Harriet said Arthur stopped being her husband that night and she wants those monsters stopped. Harriet said she will try to help us as she can."

"What she showed you is true," Gabriel said solemnly. "Please don't share that part with Hannah because she is still trying to heal from it all."

"I won't describe that to Hannah," Zoya said. "I could feel Harriet's anger and pain. Wait something is happening."

"What do you mean?" asked Gabriel.

"Many spirits are coming to me and all talking at once," Zoya's eyes grew wide. "They say the demon released Roch back into this world days ago but they could not tell it was him because something is very wrong with him."

"Is he a man or a demon?" Raul asked.

"The spirits say it is too early to tell. They are saying he is constantly changing shapes; there is something very wrong with his body. They are telling me that sometimes it is as if he is a spirit and sometimes a man and other times he looks like a monster but they can't tell if he is a demon at those times. The spirits that are talking to me say they have never seen anything like this before."

Chapter II
Disguises

"Calen what are you thinking?" yelled Natasha. "You aren't well enough yet to fly to Nora, you will never make it."

"Natasha you are right, that is why I will be riding in the boca with the Sanuri," Calen said as he packed a few items from their bedroom in Gabriel and Hannah's new house. "Didn't you hear what Gabriel said, they have Meekos."

"Then I am coming too!" Natasha said angrily.

"Natasha you are pregnant. You stay here with Hannah. We won't be gone that long."

"Calen I have been working on missions since I was a child, you can't predict how long you will be gone. You need someone to take care of you."

"Honey I got wounded a couple of times before I got married and I made it through," Calen said and kissed Natasha on the forehead. "I have been working too long with Gabriel on this mission to sit it out when we finally have Meekos. Simon is staying here, he will watch over you and Hannah."

"Calen I think Hannah and I are pretty safe in Salar," Natasha said sarcastically. "This isn't fair. I agreed not to work on the missions when I was pregnant but you and Gabriel both said I could still come along and cook and take care of you. I am really mad at you!"

"Honey why don't you help Hannah fix up this house and if it looks like Gabriel and I will be gone more than two weeks then we will talk about you joining us."

Natasha angrily stomped her right foot on the floor and put her hands on her hips. "Calen I love you with all my heart and I want to be a good wife and mother to our children but I want more out of life. I have trained all my life for these missions. You told me the women of your tribe are wives and mothers and yet still warriors. Why do you treat me differently?"

Calen stared at Natasha as he now realized how angry she was. "Natasha I think it is because I love you so much that I don't want you to get hurt. You almost died twice on this mission and it tore me apart. I don't know what I would do if I lost you."

Natasha stared angrily at Calen with the tears streaming down her face but she did not speak. She knew how scared Calen had been when her life was threatened; Natasha remembered the terror in his eyes. Natasha marched over to the bedroom door and flung it open but before she could speak she heard Hannah yell, "Gabriel this isn't fair."

That night as Archetenus sat before his campfire he removed his boots and rubbed his aching feet. Ten months in prison had softened him. He had walked all day and figured he was only about halfway to Port Friada. Fortunately for Archetenus he was able to kill a rabbit which he had cooking on a skewer over the fire. Ten months without whiskey, all Archetenus was thinking about was how badly he wanted a drink.

A cold wind was blowing which made Archetenus huddle closer to his fire. He was remembering the last time he sat before an open fire; he was heading for Port Friada then too. A pang of sadness stabbed Archetenus in the heart as he thought about how long he had planned to kidnap Vitomas; how he loved her and how angry he became when he realized she did not feel the same.

Then for just a moment Archetenus was filled with regret when he remembered the vision that Miranda had showed him, the vision of him murdering Vitomas because she did not love him. Miranda, he had not thought of her or spoken to her since he arrived at Port Friada.

"Miranda would be so mad at me," thought Archetenus as he remembered his life in Port Friada. "It's funny," Archetenus thought to himself with a laugh. "She haunted me and angered me and yet somehow she seemed like my only friend."

As Roch wandered aimlessly in the forest near his castle he heard the sound of running water. Once a man of strength and dexterity, Roch now crashed throw the underbrush like a wounded animal. He tripped and fell and tripped and fell because his feet and legs were having difficulty keeping their form. Sometimes when Roch fell he had difficulty standing because he could not always push himself up with his arms because they too would lose their substance.

Thirst was consuming Roch's thoughts as he crawled along the ground towards the sound of running water. Suddenly he stopped moving as the sound of a panther screaming echoed through the forest. He quickly looked around him for something that he could use as a weapon. But night had fallen and although Roch's eyes were accustomed to the darkness he could not make out the outlines of anything close to him. Roch tried to slow down his breathing as he listened to the sounds of the night.

Roch lay motionless for several minutes; he did not hear movement or the scream of the panther again. So he tried to stand but fell back to the earth. He cursed as his fall made noise, for Roch was not the only creature in the forest that was trying to avoid detection by the huge predator. Once again he lay motionless, listening to the sounds of the night. After several minutes he slowly crawled on his stomach towards the sound of running water. Roch had only moved a few feet when he sensed a presence.

Quickly Roch rolled onto his back just as the huge cat leaped upon him. He grabbed the neck of the creature trying to keep it's fangs from tearing into his throat. Roch should have been afraid but every fiber of his body was focused on survival at that moment. "You will not kill me!" He screamed.

Then the black panther screamed and jumped back from Roch. The two predators stared at each other. Roch slowly stood up when the panther lunged at him again. He took the full force of the mighty animal which threw him on his back again. Roch felt like the wind had been knocked out of him. He could not breathe.

Roch saw the panther bite his forearm but he felt no pain because his arm was in a state of transitioning. Suddenly the cat screamed and jumped back again. The panther turned and ran back into the forest. Roch grabbed his arm but there was no blood, his arm had no substance; just a pulsating form. He did not understand what was happening to him. He quickly ran his hands over his body but did not feel any blood, nor could he if he was bleeding because both of his hands were changing shape. Roch rolled over onto his stomach and slowly moved along the forest floor.

Neither Stephan nor Thaos had returned to their jobs in the military in the few weeks that followed the vicious attack on Ingr and the birth of Thaos' son. Although Nikki and Ingr were not used to having their husbands home during the day, they enjoyed the companionship. Both Stephan and Thaos the mighty warriors; were overcoming their fears of holding their young infants.

Thaos bonded with his son Titus more quickly than Stephan bonded with the twins Marcus and Sicily. Because Stephan chose to keep his attention on Ingr's recovery. The sight of her stomach cut open and blood gushing from her body haunted him often; as did the guilt that he did not protect his young wife from that mad man.

While Ingr was recovering, the homes that Bella and Claudius were having built inside of the castle for the two young couples were completed. Bella had the homes furnished and decorated and when everything was prepared, Stephan carried Ingr to their new home. Both Stephan and Ingr were pleased and relieved to move into their new quarters, since remaining in their old chambers was a constant reminder of the attack.

Bella and Claudius were floating on air, having three young grandbabies in the castle. Stephan would often smile when he saw how radiant both of his parents seemed when they were holding the babies. Sorren, Shara and their sons had not yet returned from Wetpr; where they were celebrating the birth of their first grandchild. But even without Sorren and Shara the castle was always full of activity now. Ryan came over every night when he completed his duties in the military. And Nikki's mother Gladys and many others from the Nordes Tribe visited daily.

"I've never seen your mother so happy," Claudius said as he handed both of his sons glasses of whiskey. Although Stephan and Thaos had spent several weeks at home, they still attended the regular morning meetings, which now included only Fahron and Claudius, since King Mathas and Matthew were still in Wetpr. And every night Claudius met with his sons in his study. It was during these meetings that Stephan and Thaos told Claudius of all that had happened at the battle at the hills of Sendra.

"So this nightmare may not be over," Claudius said angrily. "It is truly hard to imagine the enormity of Juleta's hatred that her plans of revenge seem unending."

"A few days after the attack I remembered about the letter and map that Lazo had in his shirt pocket," Thaos said. "I found what was left of his body since the animals had been pulling it around but I was able to find the papers. They're blood stained but you can still read them." Thaos handed the letter and map that Lazo had stolen from Juleta's castle to Claudius.

"That letter is signed by King Douma telling Juleta where to leave his payment," Stephan explained. "And that map is all of the water ways from the Schenomi Sea."

"I have never heard of King Douma," Claudius said gruffly.

"Neither had we," continued Stephan. "But Sorren and Thedes had. It is said that Douma ruled over a kingdom that lay west of the Kingdoms of Norkv and Xepoltr in what is now the Waste Lands of Manod. The stories differ a little about the destruction of the kingdom but Thedes and Sorren said that Douma is said to have made a pact with a powerful demon that saved Douma's people by allowing them to breathe underwater. Douma is said to have built a kingdom on the floor of the Schenomi Sea. Sorren said that Douma still owes the demon, so he sends his tribe into the kingdoms in Opots at times to do the bidding of the demon."

"That entire story sound preposterous," said Claudius.

"And yet we have that letter and map," Thaos said gravely.

26

That night Archetenus tossed and turned as he slept on the hard ground without a blanket. Periodically he would wake and throw more wood onto the fire. It was during one of these times that Archetenus realized he had a visitor. As he put a small log on the fire, Archetenus saw a beautiful woman with flowing raven hair and a blue dress standing on the other side of the fire.

"Miranda I was thinking about you tonight and here you are," Archetenus said with a smile.

"You have been busy since we last spoke, it seems that you should have thought of me more often," Miranda said coldly.

"I knew you were going to say that," Archetenus said as he straightened himself up to a sitting position. "Miranda scold me all you want but I have to tell you I am happy to see you."

"Why?" asked Miranda.

"I guess I really don't know," Archetenus said with a grin. "I think I missed your company."

"You could have called to me anytime and yet you always chose to call to darkness. If you would have called to me those three men would still be alive."

"Yeah about that, I'll tell you I was so drunk I really don't remember much about that."

"Then let me give you back your memories," Miranda said and in an instant she was standing near Archetenus and softly touched the side of his head with her hand. Suddenly Archetenus and Miranda were transported back in time. They both stood as outsiders watching a scene unfold before them. Archetenus watched himself stumbling around in The Ghost Ship Tavern. He saw himself fall on top of a table where four men were playing cards. The table broke under his weight and he fell onto the floor. Many men in the tavern started to laugh which appeared to anger Archetenus.

One of the men who had been playing cards at the table started to yell at Archetenus but never got a chance to finish his sentence before Archetenus slit his throat and quickly killed two of the other men at the table before the bar patrons could stop him. In an instant Miranda and Archetenus were back at his campfire.

"Those men did not deserve to die," Archetenus said guiltily.

"I agree," said Miranda. "Archetenus I gave you a great gift, I allowed you to see the patterns of your life and the consequences of your choices. Although you released Vitomas, you have done little of value since I showed you these things. Why is that?"

Archetenus was shocked by her question. "I don't know," he said after a few moments.

"Oh you can do better than that."

"I really am not sure but I think I just went back to the life I knew."

"A life filled with violence and great darkness, and yet you are happy to see an Angel. Why is that Archetenus?"

This time Archetenus thought seriously about Miranda's question before he answered and when Archetenus spoke his voice was hoarse. "Miranda I usually don't like what you tell me but I just realized you are the only one I trust."

"And that is something you should seriously think about Archetenus. A handsome, powerful and wealthy man, yet you have no friends or family. No one came to see you in prison because no one realized you were gone. It was as if you never existed. That in itself would scare many men. Tell me Archetenus does it scare you?"

Archetenus did not answer but the blood drained from his face as he listened to Miranda's words. "Archetenus you have always had the power to change your life but you prefer to roll in the mud of hell because you are too lazy to take any action. I warned you about the plans the Insidiae have for you, your time is coming Archetenus. You must start to carefully consider your decisions."

Suddenly a realization struck him. "Miranda who paid for my release from prison? That's why you are here isn't it?"

"The men who paid for your release are not friends although they will wear that as a disguise. You will not recognize their faces but you will recognize the darkness in their hearts."

"Miranda what should I do?"

"I cannot tell you what to do. But you must remember that if they go through with their plans for you; they will turn your body into a monster of great proportions and your essence will be tortured in hell. Then I can no longer come to your aid."

"What if I can't change Miranda?"

"Archetenus the Brave, fears no man or beast yet he is afraid to change his behavior, do you see the irony in that?"

"Miranda your words are true; I will not argue with any of them. I don't know if I can change, I will not lie to you. But whatever you think of me I still have some honor left. You saved my life and you were a friend to me when there were no others. I owe you for that. How can I repay you?"

"It is not me you owe for your life, but even if your words are hollow they are good to hear."

"Miranda my words are sincere; cannot you tell that?"

"Archetenus what are you willing to do?"

"What do you mean?"

"I mean I may ask of you something that is hard work or that is dangerous, would you be willing to do that since you are not so willing to try and change your behavior?"

"I am not afraid of hard work or danger," Archetenus replied indignantly.

"Archetenus remember how you felt when you fought in the Gefrey Games and all of the people of Stordt would praise you for your courage? You were a hero to many."

"Yes, I enjoyed that very much."

"Archetenus you have gone from being a hero and a threat to powerful men to being that stumbling drunk that you saw in that bar. I may ask you to be a hero again. But you are no fool; you know it will not be an easy road. I want you to seriously think about this Archetenus. I will not force you to do anything but if you once make that choice to be a hero again, there is no turning back. Because the arena you will be fighting in is much more dangerous than what you faced in the Gefrey Games."

Before dawn the next morning the Sanuri, Raul, Gabriel, Raphael, Calen and three hundred Wetprian soldiers left for Nora. Prior to this morning, King Sudfad of Wetpr and King Hamond of Stordt had worked out a treaty which gave the soldiers of Wetpr safe passage to Nora, which was located in the southwestern portion of the Kingdom of Stordt.

This treaty was entered into under duress, as King Hamond was forced to recognize King Sudfad's rights to that throne and the fact that Sudfad now owned the rights to the richest gold mines and many of the waterways in that kingdom. But even with the treaty in place, no one really trusted Hamond or his men.

"I was surprised we crossed the border so easily," Raul said to the Sanuri as he rode next to the boca.

"Hamond will not give up those riches so easily," the Sanuri said as he drove his boca with Calen sitting next to him in the front seat. "He just hasn't figured out a plan yet. And I don't believe he is aware of all the troops your father has in Nora."

"It will be interesting to see how far they have gotten on the building of Fort Nora," said Raul.

"The people of Nora want the protection of your troops badly. The entire city was helping with the construction of that fort, I would not be surprised if it isn't near completion," the Sanuri said.

"I hope you are right," said Raul. "They may need it."

"Sanuri did you send word to Prince Lakin that Meekos is our prisoner?" Calen asked. "I'll bet he and Luca come to Nora."

"I did send him a message and I also asked if some of his warriors would be available if we needed them," the Sanuri said.

Calen chuckled, "Well, it will be interesting to see if Zada gets as mad at Lakin for leaving again as Natasha and Hannah got at us." Then Calen looked at Gabriel, who was riding on the passenger side of the boca. "I never realized how much alike our wives are before last night. They were even yelling the same things at us," Calen said with a grin.

"Oh I knew they were alike," Gabriel said. "You and Natasha have been so in love you just hadn't seen that side of her yet. She can be very strong willed."

"How about you Raul," Calen asked. "Is Vitomas mad at you too?"

"Vitomas isn't much for yelling, which I would almost prefer because the crying tears me apart."

"Hopefully we won't be gone long, this time," Gabriel said. "Because I have to admit I do miss the girls already."

"What is the meaning of this?" yelled Erebus as he was pushed down on the cold hard floor of a cave. "Sophie are you alright?" he yelled as he saw two of their masked attackers push her into the cave.

"There is no need to act like barbarians," Sophie said indignantly. "I know who you are. Untie us."

There were already ten men in the cave, all of whom were wearing masks, now Erebus and Sophie faced them. One of the men started to laugh then said, "Sophie you have a lot of explaining to do."

"Malik, take that damned mask off and have your men untie us," Sophie said. "You are right, there is much to tell you and I will bet that the messages that Meekos and I sent to you were intercepted just as ours were."

31

"Intercepted. What are you talking about?" the masked man asked.

"Malik, we do have a great deal to discuss, in fact you may want to pour us all some wine," Sophie said.

The masked man laughed then took off his mask which exposed a middle aged man with gray hair and a large gray handlebar mustache. "Untie them," Malik ordered. "And let's go into the next room." Malik stood up and led the others down a narrow tunnel that opened into another cavern that was lavishly decorated with fine rugs and furniture. As soon as the men entered this room they all took off their masks.

"Erebus, this is Malik and all of these men are members of the Insidiae," said Sophie. Then she turned to Malik. "Before you say anything Erebus has been helping Meekos and me, he knows about Roch and he has valuable information for you."

Chapter III
Charlatans

Miranda disappeared before she told Archetenus how he could pay her back or how he could become a hero again. Archetenus would never admit to Miranda that he always thought about her words, although he did not heed them most of the time. But he believed Miranda when she told him about the plans of the Insidiae, after all she had shown him that image of his body in a stone tub next to that of the demon Omnibus.

Miranda had told Archetenus that she was not just trying to save him but all of the people who would fall victim to him if the Insidiae succeeded with their plans. She told Archetenus this when he was travelling with Vitomas and his mind was consumed with thoughts of owning and controlling Vitomas. Archetenus did not have much interest in Miranda's words then, but now on this cold night, he sat before his fire and contemplated the words of his most unlikely companion.

Before Archetenus realized it the sun was rising, he had sat up all night contemplating his future; something he had not done for a very long time. But the hours did not give way to decisions. He put out his fire and started the long walk to Port Friada.

This morning when Hannah arrived at the castle at Wetpr to check on her patients, Natasha came with her. The woman arrived at the castle earlier than Hannah's normal routine. When they entered the castle they walked past the dining room where the Royal Family was eating breakfast.

"Hannah, Natasha," Simon called out. "Come in and join us."

"Thank you but we have already eaten," Hannah said.

"Then just come in and talk with us for a while," said Renya.

As soon as Natasha and Hannah sat down Simon asked with a grin, "So did you two fight with Gabriel and Calen all night?"

"Simon how did you know?" Natasha asked with surprise.

"I lived with you long enough. You know they had to go," Simon said.

"We weren't stopping them from going," said Hannah. "We wanted to go with them."

"Simon they said they would not be gone long," Natasha said. "But I have been working on these missions since I was ten years old and I will tell you that you can't anticipate how long things will go; especially once you start uncovering evidence."

"Oh I don't want to hear that," Vitomas said. "I was crying all night because I didn't want Raul to leave again."

Natasha turned to Vitomas but she also looked at Annabelle as she spoke. "Your families have been through so much that I can't imagine what you must be going through. And I don't know if Raul and Simon have shared with you all of the horrors we all faced on this mission. But you have to understand what is at stake if the Insidiae and demons are allowed to go through with their plans. I do not exaggerate when I say this world will change and it will not be a place that you want to raise your children. If we lose this battle perhaps you should move to the Ice Caves, because this world will be destroyed."

Everyone at the table stared at Natasha as she spoke. Then Annabelle turned to Simon and asked, "Is everything she says true?"

"Actually Natasha has understated the situation. Vitomas you know how much Raul loves you and Annabelle I hope you know how much I love you and the children," Simon said sincerely. "But we would not be leaving you so much if it wasn't necessary."

"Simon, perhaps it is time you really told us about this mission," Vitomas said softly.

"Vitomas a lot of this involves Roch and you know the horrors he has inflicted," Hannah explained. "Imagine a world with many Rochs whose cruelty and power is greatly intensified. The group that created Roch has created others and they plan to unleash them on this world. That is what all of our husbands have been trying to stop."

"I don't understand, created Roch?" Vitomas said. Then she saw the looks on the faces of Sudfad, Renya and Matthew. "You all know about this don't you?"

"Yes dear but we didn't want to worry you and Annabelle any more than you already were," Sudfad said.

"Simon you need to tell us," said Vitomas.

"You may not want to hear the details," Natasha said to Vitomas. As Natasha spoke an Enrop landed on the dining room windowsill. "Hannah I have an idea," Natasha said with a grin. "I am going to send a message to Luca and the others and see if they will take us to our husbands."

"Oh I like that," said Hannah.

"My dears, I know I am an old woman," Laurel said. "But why would you want to go back on this awful mission?"

Before either Natasha or Hannah could answer Simon said. "Because they both were invaluable at getting information and saving lives and they know it. They have skills the others do not possess. I understand why you want to go but you know that I promised Gabriel and Calen that I would watch over you."

Natasha gave Simon a coy smile, "Well, then Simon I guess you will have to either tie us to our chairs or come with us."

Angelina had been sitting quietly listening to the conversation as had her family. "I like you two," Angelina said. "If I hadn't just given birth I would gladly go with you. My family has come to understand the death and destruction that dark lords and demons can bring upon us." Sorren smiled proudly as he listened to the words of his daughter.

"Hannah and Natasha I understand why you want to leave but do you understand how dangerous this is?" Sudfad asked.

"We know full well what is going on and that is why we want to stand beside our husbands," Hannah said boldly.

"What do you mean?" Annabelle asked.

"They have captured High Priest Meekos," Hannah explained. "He is a powerful dark lord and member of the Insidiae. He is the one who orchestrated the attacks on Raul and Simon and the kidnapping of Petra. The place they are keeping him has been blessed with holiness so he cannot use his dark magics and demons cannot come to his aid. But if they transport Meekos here for execution it will be difficult for our husbands because there are probably as many who want to shut Meekos up as there are who want to help him. That is why the Sanuri is with them."

"I know you two," Simon said as he leaned back in his chair. "If Luca and the others refuse to take you to Nora, what do you have planned?"

Natasha accompanied Hannah as she checked on Jared, who still had not regained consciousness. As usual Zoya was sitting in Jared's room watching over him.

"You are worried because he has not woken up," Zoya said.

"Yes and I will admit I am not sure why he hasn't," Hannah replied. "He doesn't seem to be running a fever and his wound looks good. I really don't understand what is going on here. Perhaps I missed something." Hannah lifted the covers from Jared and carefully examined his body again. "Natasha and Zoya will you help me roll him over?"

After examining Jared's back Hannah said "I don't see any other wounds. Zoya have you had any visions that could help me figure out what is happening with Jared?"

"No Hannah, he seems to be sleeping peacefully when you are gone."

"Something is not right here," Hannah said. Then she walked out of the room and knocked on the door to Sudfad's study where the men were having their morning meeting. Sorren opened the door. "I am sorry to disturb you but something is not right with Jared. I can't put my finger on it so I was wondering if I could borrow Simon's crystal."

Simon and Sudfad looked at each other. "Hannah is Natasha in Jared's room?" Sudfad asked.

"Yes both she and Zoya are in there, why?"

"Why don't you get Natasha and we have something to discuss with you," Sudfad continued.

Within moments, Natasha and Hannah joined, Simon, Matthew, Mathias, Sorren and Sudfad in the study. "I'll be honest Hannah, there are some things that we have been trying to decide if we want to share with you but after listening to you and Natasha talk about leaving Salar, well, we've decided to tell you," Sudfad said. "The reason Simon is still here as well as the others in this room is because of Jared."

"I don't understand," Hannah said suspiciously. "Zoya said he is a hired killer but he is in no shape to hurt anyone."

"He is more than a hired killer," Simon said. "He is one of the second sons, like Roch is."

"What! How do you know this?" asked Hannah.

"Because Jared and Zoya brought a book to the Sanuri that Jared had stolen from Pravis and Tenebrae. It listed the names of the men who have been created to be the vessels for demons and Jared's name is in the book. That was one of the reason's they came here, to give the Sanuri the book and to warn him that Ahriman was setting traps for him."

"Ok I don't understand why Jared would warn the Sanuri if he is evil," said Natasha.

"From what we gathered," Sudfad explained. "Zoya is a sweet girl who believes in The Great Ruler and she talked Jared into coming here. Jared went to Zoya because he thought Roch was trying to contact him but Zoya believed it was not Roch but a demon. No matter how dangerous Jared is as a man it sounds like he was unnerved by his experience with the demon and then finding his name in that book."

"Hannah we would like you to stay here at least a few more days," Simon said. "Perhaps you could do some tests on Jared and see what you can find out. I mean it is almost like a gift that he has been put into our laps."

"I take it you haven't said anything to the women here," Hannah said.

"That is true, none of our wives have been told," Sudfad said. "Why do you ask?"

"Sometimes keeping secrets is a disservice," said Hannah. "There are tests that I can do but I will be honest, for the answers that you want we need Lakin here, or one of the other Ruala healers. Their medicine is very different from mine and most amazing."

"Actually I have already sent a message to Lakin," Sudfad said.

"Hannah you initially came in here to get my crystal, why?" asked Simon.

"Because Jared has not regained consciousness and I can find no logical reason for that. I thought I would see if your crystal reacted against his skin. Except that from what you just told me, I think I should wait until Lakin is here. Because if I encounter a demon, I don't have the tools to make it leave."

"I do," said Natasha.

"Ladies, I really did promise your husbands I would watch over you," Simon said sternly. "We will wait until Lakin gets here."

"There is something else," Hannah said. "Of course I don't know either Zoya or Jared very well but she seems very attached to him. Does she know he is a monster?"

"It sounds like she knows as much about his situation as he does," Sudfad said. "I know they seem like a very unlikely pair but she seems to be a positive influence on him and she couldn't have gotten across the border without him."

"She was terrified and alone and Jared protected her and made her feel safe," Hannah said. "That tells you a lot about Stordt, when a monster makes a young girl feel safe."

38

Archetenus walked all day and arrived in Port Friada after dark. He went straight to The Sea's End Hotel where no one recognized him because his beard and hair had grown long while he was in prison. Fortunately for Archetenus, The Sea's End was not a popular hotel and they had not rented his former room to a lot of people during the ten months he was gone.

"Well, there's a fellar in there now," the old clerk said. "I suppose I could ask him if he wants to move to another room, we do have a few open. But tell me what is so special about that room?"

"I left some things in there," Archetenus replied. "I will go with you when you ask him to move."

"Now, I don't want no trouble or nothing here," the clerk said with concern.

"I just want my things," said Archetenus.

The two men walked up one flight of stairs and stopped at room 201. The clerk meekly knocked on the door but there was no answer, then Archetenus knocked, a loud and powerful knock.

"What ya want?" a male voice called out from the other side of the door.

"Just to talk," Archetenus said.

A frail man, who looked to be about sixty years old came to the door wearing only his trousers, it was obvious to both the clerk and Archetenus that the man had been sleeping.

"This feller here," explained the clerk. "Used to live in this room permanent and left some things behind, he was wondering if you would move to another room."

The old man stepped to the side to allow Archetenus and the clerk to enter the room. "You are more than welcome to look around but I didn't see any belongings."

"These aren't the kind of belongings you leave out in the open," Archetenus replied. "Would you be willing to move?"

"Well, I guess so if I don't get charged no extra," the man said as he pulled his suspenders up over his shirtless arms.

As Archetenus looked around the room he remembered his conversation with Miranda. Although Archetenus could afford a much nicer hotel, he chose the Sea's End because it was near to the bars that he liked to frequent. "I'll tell you what," Archetenus said with a sudden change of heart. "Just let me see if my things are in here and I will leave."

"Either way is fine by me," the old man replied.

Archetenus proceeded to move around several pieces of furniture, including the bed so that he could roll back the old and tattered carpet on the floor. He lifted two boards out of the floor and pulled out two bulging sets of saddlebags.

"Well I'll be," the clerk said as he watched Archetenus put the furniture back.

Archetenus threw both saddlebags over his shoulder and walked out of the room, "Sorry to disturb you," he said to the old man. Archetenus walked eight blocks north and entered the business area of the city. Port Friada was a city that was alive all day and night. The streets were filled with people and the lights were on in all of the businesses on the streets. There were several hotels on the street. Archetenus chose one called The Captain's Retreat. It was not extravagant but it had a dining room and a sign that offered baths.

"Are you the captain?" Archetenus asked sarcastically when he walked up to the hotel clerk.

"No but a real captain owns this hotel," the young clerk said enthusiastically. "Want a room?"

"Yeah, with a view of the front street and I need a bath and a hot meal," Archetenus said as he watched the people in the lobby.

"The kitchen is open all night and I have three rooms that have views of the street. One on the second floor, the fourth floor and the fifth floor, they all cost the same so you can have your pick."

Archetenus decided on the room on the fifth floor. He was expecting trouble and thought that being on the top floor might give him an advantage. "There is a bathing area on each floor," the clerk said. "Of course a bath is extra. How long you planning on staying?"

"Not sure yet, it might be a while," Archetenus replied and took the key for his room.

"You say we aren't prisoners yet we are not allowed to leave," Erebus said angrily as he and Sophie were once again escorted to the lavishly decorated cavern where Malik and the others had questioned them earlier in the day.

"Let's just say you are temporary visitors," Malik said with a grin. "There are still so many unanswered questions."

"We agree and that is why Sophie and I were in that field performing spells."

"Malik we have told you everything that we know," Sophie said with annoyance. "You may not have received our messages but you cannot tell me you didn't have any idea of the problems. Perhaps it is time that you gave me and Erebus some answers."

"Very well," Malik said. "Sophie I always admired your direct approach."

"Do you know where Meekos is?" Sophie asked.

"All I know is that he rented a carriage in Taperia then disappeared. He has not been seen in Nora," Malik said.

"Are you absolutely sure?" Sophie asked with fear in her voice. "And what of Pravis and Tenebrae?"

"We believe they were killed in Nora when the cave blew up."

"Where is Roch?" asked Erebus.

"Actually we were hoping that Meekos would lead us to him," Malik said.

"You think Meekos is the spy?" Erebus asked accusingly.

"Oh Malik, you pompous fool!" Sophie said loudly. "Meekos is not the spy and while you are thinking that you should be searching for the real spy. You have been acting so superior and condescending so now tell us what are you going to do about this mess?"

"As you know, although Roch was the preferred vessel he certainly was not the only one," Malik said. "Our men are locating them now."

"So you think the ascension can still go as planned?" Erebus asked incredulously. "What about the chambers?"

"We have other areas that we are preparing," Malik said.

"And what about Ahriman's interference?" Sophie asked.

"Now that can be blamed on your brother, Pravis and Tenebrae," Malik said angrily.

"We can argue all night whether that is true or not," Sophie said. "But that won't change the fact that Ahriman is interfering with the ascension. Have you got a plan?"

"Well, since we didn't know about Ahriman's interference until you told us, no we don't have a plan in place yet," Malik replied.

"How can that be?" Erebus asked. "I mean you are all dark lords aren't you? Don't you ever talk to the underworlds to get information or are you being blocked too?"

Archetenus tore up some floor boards in his room, hid his saddlebags of money and went down to the dining room to eat. Archetenus knew he looked dirty and disheveled but he didn't care. He ordered two dinners and devoured them quickly. As Archetenus ate he could feel many eyes upon him but he wasn't sure if that was because of his appearance. No one and yet everyone in the dining room looked suspicious to him. He left the dining room and bought a bath. Archetenus shaved for the first time in ten months and cut his hair so it hung just above his shoulders.

Having eaten and bathed made Archetenus feel much better so he decided to see what shops were open at that time of night. He was not surprised that all of the shops on the street were open. He bought himself several sets of new clothes, one he wore out of the shop. He bought new boots, a jacket, a rain poncho, a new sword, two knives and three daggers. Archetenus returned to his hotel, but as he started to walk up the stairs the desk clerk called to him. "I have a message for you."

"From who?" Archetenus asked suspiciously.

"A couple of men were here they said to give it to you."

"Did they know my name?"

"No, they pointed you out in the dining room but then I got busy and when I looked for you, you were gone."

"What did these men look like?"

The young clerk tried to remember. "They were very well dressed, they even wore jewels. One was really big with marks on his face, his skin was reddish like he had a rash and the other guy was short and stocky with spectacles and lighter hair. They were both wearing hats so I really couldn't see their hair."

Archetenus handed the clerk a gold coin, "Thanks if you see them again let me know."

"Why yes My Lord, thank you My Lord."

When Archetenus got to the door of his room he checked the door to see if it had been forced open, then he listened before he entered the room. The room was empty with no signs that he had visitors. Archetenus opened the note and read three words *You are welcome.*

Now that Hannah and Natasha knew that Jared was one of the men created to be a vessel for a demon, they decided to postpone their idea of joining their husbands in Nora. They returned to Hannah's house and unpacked all of the medical equipment and set up a medical office in one of the rooms on the first floor.

Hannah and Natasha were surprised that this task took them the rest of the day and into the night. They were both up before sunrise. They hitched two horses to the small boca that Gabriel had bought them and drove into Salar with a long shopping list of needed supplies.

"Hannah you might want to buy more bedding now, in case any of the Ruala warriors stay with us," Natasha said. "Also I was thinking; we really should furnish a weapons room in the house. You certainly have plenty of rooms; you would just have to hire a carpenter to build the shelves and holders. Hannah you are so quiet is anything wrong?"

"No, I am sorry Natasha; you are right about everything you said. Let's fill the boca this morning, then I am going to the castle and get samples of Jared's skin, blood and hair and return home and run some tests. If he really was created by some black magics I am not sure I will be able to find anything with my tests. I so wish Lakin was here. He offered to teach me his medicines, if Gabriel ever takes a break from these missions I want to go to the Ice Caves so I can learn their secrets."

"Hannah, there are three powerful healers at the castle now, let's ask Simon if we can talk with them, they might have something that you don't."

"That is not a bad idea," Hannah replied. "But I think we need to speak with Sudfad. I am concerned about this because Simon is right, it's like Jared is a gift, I just don't, actually I don't really know what is bothering me. I just have a bad feeling about this."

Archetenus slept a few hours then walked down to the dining room for breakfast. He did not sleep well because for some reason he did not feel safe.

"My Lord," said the young night clerk who was still on duty. "Please come here." As soon as Archetenus was at the desk the young man said in a low voice.

"Those men are back, they are sitting at a table in the dining room in front of the windows and they have a third man with them."

"Did they ask for me?"

"No, we weren't busy when they came in so I could watch them," the clerk explained. "They looked around the lobby and dining room then sat at a table. I don't know if this is important My Lord but when these men were looking around, well, they acted like they were expecting to get attacked."

"What is your name boy?"

"Calvin My Lord."

"Calvin you are doing well, thank you," Archetenus said and handed the young man another gold coin.

Archetenus walked into the dining room and chose a table on the far side of the room, so he could sit with his back against the wall and watch the three men who were seated at a table in front of the window. Calvin had done a good job describing the men, who looked at Archetenus when he entered the room. One man was seated with his back to Archetenus and the other two men were seated on either side of this man.

The third man that Calvin did not describe from the night before, was wearing an expensive suit but he had the demeanor and build of a hired killer. He had dark curly hair and penetrating eyes. This was the one man at the table who kept looking at Archetenus. Because these men wore suits, no weapons were exposed, although Archetenus believed they carried weapons.

Archetenus was an experienced soldier and fighter, he surveyed the area to see if others were watching him. When he was convinced that the three men were alone, Archetenus walked over to their table. The three men stayed in their seats as he walked up to them although Archetenus noticed that the man who looked like a hired killer was tensing up.

Archetenus swaggered as he walked; something he often did before a fight. He walked up to the table so he was standing directly behind the man who had his back to Archetenus. This man was the one who Archetenus had already determined was the leader of the group.

Archetenus threw the note he had received the night before onto the table and asked gruffly, "What is the meaning of this."

"Why don't you take a seat," said the man with his back to Archetenus.

"Tell your men to put their weapons on top of the table or I will snap your neck."

"Do as he says," the man said to his partners who each put several knives and daggers on top of the table. "Archetenus we aren't here to fight; please take a seat," the same man said.

Archetenus picked up all of the weapons from the table and dropped them on the floor behind the chair he sat in. Archetenus was now sitting with his back to the window, facing the man who had been speaking. "So talk!" Archetenus said.

"First introductions," continued the man who was doing all of the talking. "My name is Dieter, this is Romale." Dieter indicated the man with the red pock marked face. "And this is Sabot," Dieter nodded towards the man who looked like a hired killer. "We are not your enemies Archetenus," Dieter continued. "I paid for your release from prison because I would like to hire you."

Archetenus stared boldly at each man, "Keep talking."

"I am a man with many enemies and I hire only the best to work for me. I pay very well."

"How do you know my name and what do you know about me?" Archetenus asked suspiciously.

"A few years ago I attended the Gefrey Games in the Kingdom of Stordt. You Archetenus were the featured fighter, you killed a panther with your bare hands. I was quite impressed with your performance. So imagine my surprise when I open a new office in Port Friada and I hear a story about a man who murdered three other men in a matter of seconds. You killed those men the same day I bought my business. You do not have a common name, I had some of my people ask around and I heard that you were from Stordt."

"So if you heard I was here ten months ago, why did you wait until now to contact me?"

"Because I didn't have an opening until now," Dieter replied.
Dieter made the hair on the back of Archetenus' neck stand up, he knew Dieter was lying to him but he wanted to find out who Dieter really was. "So what kind of business do you have?"

"Actually I have a number of businesses," Dieter replied. "I own mines in various kingdoms, I own refineries and transportation companies. And here in Port Friada I just bought a ship which I hope to expand into a more lucrative import and export business."

"So why do you have so many enemies?" asked Archetenus as he eyed Romale and Sabot.

"Let's just say I am a man who takes what he wants and well; one can gain many enemies with that philosophy."

"So you want to hire me for protection?" Archetenus asked.

"Protection yes; and the occasional odd job," said Dieter and smiled for the first time, exposing his teeth which were made of gold.

Chapter IV
Meekos

"We've got company," Raul said as he pointed at a large group of Ruala warriors who were flying towards their campsite. The setting sun made a magnificent background for the two hundred winged warriors. As the warriors landed they initially sought out the campfire where the Sanuri, Raul, Gabriel, Raphael and Calen were sitting.

"I wondered if you could keep away," Gabriel said with a smile when he saw Luca, Dagon and Misha walking towards them.

"After all we have been through to hunt down Meekos, we weren't going to miss this," Luca said. "Rabi didn't want to leave Marcia at the Ice Caves so he stayed back and Koby is still healing from all of his knife wounds. Misha here refused to stay home even though he isn't strong enough to fly yet."

"You can ride in the boca with me," Calen said with a grin to his cousin and good friend.

"I am surprised that Lakin didn't come," the Sanuri said.

"He is going to Sudfad's castle to help Hannah do some tests on that man who is one of the vessels," said Luca.

"Jared," Gabriel said. "Why did Sudfad tell Hannah about Jared, I would prefer she not spend so much time around that man he is very dangerous."

"Well, it sounds like he is unconscious," Luca said then he got a big smile across his face. "I don't know for sure but I suspect that Sudfad told Hannah and Natasha that Jared was one of the potential vessels to keep them in Salar."

"What do you mean?" growled Calen.

"Your wife sent several of us messages asking us to bring her and Hannah to Nora," Luca said then started to laugh. "Personally I would think she would enjoy a break from you."

"Gabriel what are we going to do with those two?" Calen asked then started to laugh.

"I really am not that surprised," Gabriel said. "I hate to admit it but I miss them both."

"Yeah, so do I," replied Calen. "So let's change the subject. From what we know, Meekos hired a private carriage in Taperia to take him to Nora. Two men who work with the Patronus were driving that carriage. They drugged Meekos and took him to Hannah's old house, which as you know, is now a headquarters for the Patronus."

"Have they gotten any information from him?" Dagon asked.

"The priests cleansed that house and grounds and claimed them in the name of The Great Ruler, by doing so not only are they preventing Ahriman and any other demons from entering but the holiness blocks Meekos from performing any of his dark magics," the Sanuri explained. "To my knowledge they have not obtained any useful information from him yet. But I will tell you I am concerned for everyone involved because I suspect there will be demons and dark lords who want to either release Meekos or kill him before he can talk to us."

"And Father wants Meekos brought back to Salar so we can execute him," Raul said. "And there is something else, a seer told us that Roch had been released by the demon that held him captive. Roch is back in this world but the seer said there is something wrong with him and she couldn't tell if he was a man or a demon."

Roch spent almost two days lying in the shade near a pool that was created by a water fall. He thought that he recognized the site but his thoughts were so confused that he did not trust them. He was still unaware that he was on the royal grounds of his own castle. There were fish in the pond but Roch could not catch them because he could not grasp the fish with his hands that were constantly changing form.

Roch ate bugs, berries and grass when he could grasp such things. But to Roch's own amazement he was not often hungry. His body seemed in a constant state of transition but his body was not alone. Roch's brain, his memories, his very essence were constantly pulsating and changing.

Roch had always been a strong willed and driven man. He was now trying desperately to gain control of his body and his memories. Roch's thoughts were often fragmented which caused him great frustration; for Roch's entire being was consumed with the idea that he needed to remember something, something that was eluding him in the vast regions of his mind, something that was of great importance, something that terrified him.

"Lakin I am so glad to see you," Hannah said and hugged the Ruala Prince when she saw him in Sudfad's castle.

"Where is Natasha?" Lakin asked and grinned. "I heard she sent messages to many of my warriors asking them to take you two to Nora. You know none of them are going to go against the wishes of Gabriel and Calen."

"All of you men stick together," Hannah said with a coy smile. "But you can ask Simon here we have rather had a change of heart. Having one of the vessels so close to our home made me realize that I should prepare our house for the type of work we do, as well as making it our home. Simon and Sudfad have been gracious enough to loan me a crew of carpenters."

"Natasha is home now with these men, we are building a weapons room, expanding the medical office, making many changes to Gabriel's study and adding to the wine cellar and building a smoke house. And Simon is going to take Natasha shopping later for weapons. I told all of the men I would double their pay if they could complete these projects in two weeks. I am hoping everything is completed before Gabriel returns home."

"Hannah I believe Gabriel will be very pleased with what you are doing," said Lakin.

"Well, I am sure that if we finish these projects before our husbands return that Simon will find another distraction for us," Hannah smiled at Simon as she said this.

"As much as I love you and Natasha I don't want to go against Calen's and Gabriel's wishes either. Honestly Hannah there may be times when Raul and I ask them to watch over our families and we would expect that they would honor their word," Simon said.

"I know," Hannah replied. "It's just that I have a bad feeling about this whole thing with Meekos. It just seems like a trap to me. But back to the matter at hand, Jared. He was stabbed in the ribs with a dagger by the Taperian border guards. He lost a great deal of blood before I saw him. He no longer has a fever and his wound is healing nicely but he has not regained consciousness and I have no idea why."

"Simon and Raul said the Taperian soldiers do not put poisons on the tips of their weapons, so that was ruled out. I took some samples of his hair, blood and skin but I could not find any differences in them from any normal human nor could I find any disease or infection in his body. I believe my medical skills are now useless here, this is in your realm."

"I am glad that you did not try anything further because it could be very dangerous for you," Lakin said. "I did not come alone and to repay you for all of the medical supplies that you sent to the Ice Caves, I have brought you many of our supplies and plants. We will start your training while I am here."

"Wonderful, I am anxious to get started," Hannah said happily. "Lakin, our home is not as lavish as the castle but you and your men are welcome to stay with us. Natasha and I have already prepared rooms."

"There are six of us; do you have room for all?"

"Yes, if two of you don't mind sharing a room, several of the rooms have more than one bed."

"That will be fine," Lakin said. "Before I forget Marcia sent you a letter, she misses you greatly."

With the light of a new day, the Sanuri and the others headed out for Nora. They expected to arrive at the headquarters of the Patronus around noon.

The Sanuri had sent several Enrops ahead to announce their arrival to the Patronus priests. About midmorning the great birds returned.

"Sanuri stop!" yelled Oja. "Something is wrong." Raul stopped the troops as the leaders of the group gathered around the Enrops. "There is a large circle that surrounds the headquarters it is black and appears as smoke but it is not. We were able to fly through it. The priests are alright because their buildings are protected by holiness but this great ring of darkness starts exactly at the boundaries of their land."

"Have any of my men been hurt?" Raphael asked.

"We were told they have not tried to cross it," Oja continued. "They know you are coming so they were going to wait for the Sanuri."

"Did you see anything else, any demons or Hutas?" asked Raul.

"No just this dark ring."

"It sounds like a trap to me," Raul said. "So no one has actually ridden through the ring?"

"No," Oja answered.

"I will take some warriors and we will drop rocks or something onto the ring to see what happens," Luca said.

"I am not surprised by this," said the Sanuri. "The demons are going to try and intimidate the priests."

Luca and ten other Rualas grabbed rocks and small logs from the ground and flew ahead of the advancing army; several of the Enrops accompanied them. Within the hour the Rualas saw the massive ring of darkness which resembled the smoke from a huge forest fire. Luca ordered two of his warriors to fly high above the dark clouds and to drop a rock and a log, to see if there were different effects. He told the remaining Rualas to ready their bows. The two warriors did as they were ordered then returned to Luca and the others.

The Ruala warriors waited for several minutes but nothing happened, just as they were going to return to the Sanuri and others, Ciao, one of the female warriors yelled out. Suddenly lightning bolts appeared within the dark clouds, then shapes started to form and come alive within the darkness.

Four Huta warriors ran out of the dark cloud. While the Rualas were shooting their arrows at the Hutas, Luca's eyes widened as he saw two giant beasts flying towards them. These creatures appeared as some kind of birds, their bodies resembled skeletons and their enormous heads were elongated with huge beaks that exposed rows of long fangs.

Luca yelled to his warriors who turned their attention to the flying creatures. The Rualas shot arrow after arrow into the hell beasts but the birds were not fazed by the weapons of man. Luca ordered his warriors to return to the Sanuri. Several of the Enrops flew ahead of the Rualas. The Ruala warriors and the remaining Enrops flew in staggered erratic patterns to make it more difficult for the hell beasts to grasp their prey.

Suddenly there was a bloodcurdling scream as one of the hell beasts latched onto the leg of a Ruala warrior. Luca and three others returned to their comrade as the other warriors distracted the second beast. Luca landed on top of the demonic bird and pulled a huge knife from the sheath on his belt. He plunged the knife into the brain and spinal cord of the beast without getting it to release its hold on the warrior.

Luca instantly had an idea. He tore his crystal necklace off and pushed it into one of the wounds of the great bird. The bird's movements became erratic as the holiness from the crystal poisoned its being. Within moments the bird started to smoke. The hell beast released its hold on the warrior as two of his comrades caught him. Luca jumped off the beast as it started to propel towards the ground in a fiery blaze.

Ratri carried his wounded comrade as Ciao put her crystal necklace into one of the wounds made by the beast. Ratri and Ciao flew back towards the Sanuri as quickly as they could. Now the other Rualas turned towards the remaining hell beast. While two warriors continued to distract the bird, Dagon jumped on its back and plunged his knife into its head.

Dagon pulled his crystal necklace off and forced it into the wound, within moments the creature started to smoke and spun out of control as is burst into flames.

Natasha heard her name called and walked to the front door where she saw five Ruala warriors. Natasha paused for a moment when she saw the man who was calling her name. "Excuse me for staring but you look so much like Calen," Natasha said as she opened the door for them to enter.

"I am Elan, Calen is my cousin. Hannah said you were here alone with workmen so we came to stay with you."

"I welcome the company but I am in no danger here," Natasha said with a laugh. "Will you all be staying with us?"

"Yes, Lakin is at the castle with Hannah," Elan said. "I saw you at the ceremonies that King Sudfad held but I did not get a chance to meet you. When I unpack I have a letter for you from Emeral and Maxwell." As Elan spoke the other Ruala warriors entered the house. "Natasha this is Dack, Joao, Bekka and Fala, this is Calen's wife Natasha," Elan said.

All Rualas were tall, both the men and the women. Dack was an extremely muscular man with short brown hair and large brown eyes. Joao wore his blonde hair pulled back in a ponytail. He had electric blue eyes and dimples. Bekka and Fala were female warriors; both were beautiful and graceful, characteristics that Natasha was finding as common among the Ruala women. Bekka had long curly auburn hair and hazel eyes. Fala appeared to be the youngest of the group; she had long straight black hair and blue eyes.

"We have rooms prepared but two of you will have to share one," Natasha said, then she paused. "Are you couples?" This comment brought smiles among the warriors.

"No," Bekka said. "We are all friends. Fala and I can share a room. And Natasha we would like to help you while we are here so put us to work."

"You are starting to show," Elan said. "How long does it take for a human to carry a baby?"

"Nine months," Natasha said. "My, I never thought it might be different for Rualas, how long is it for you?"

"Usually twelve months but since this baby is both races, you will just have to wait and see," Bekka said.

"Twelve months!" Natasha gasped. Then she composed herself and asked, "Do many Rualas marry humans?"

"Well, so far you and Marcia are the only two," Elan said. "So it will be interesting to see what your children are like."

Natasha's eyes grew wide as she listened to Elan speak. "I never realized we would be starting a new race."

As soon as the Enrops returned to the Sanuri and told him that the Rualas were under attack, Gad, a Ruala warrior picked up the Sanuri and followed the Enrops back to Luca and his warriors.

Half of the remaining Ruala warriors flew with Gad and the Sanuri while the others stayed with Raul and his men. After almost twenty minutes Ratri and Ciao saw the Sanuri and called to him. "They are killing the beasts but Nabi is badly hurt," Ratri yelled. Gad and the Sanuri landed with Ratri and Ciao as the other Ruala warriors continued forward.

"What sort of beast did this?" asked the Sanuri as he looked at the deep wounds on Nabi's legs. Ratri quickly described the demon birds as the Sanuri examined Nabi. "I will need silence now," the Sanuri said as he placed one of his hands on each of Nabi's legs. The three Ruala warriors watched in awe as the Sanuri used his own life force to heal the wounded warrior. "There is bedding in the back of my boca," the Sanuri said. "Put Nabi back there and someone should stay with him."

"I will, he is my brother," Ciao said.

"Wash the blood from his legs and make him drink some water when he wakes," as the Sanuri was speaking Luca and the other Rualas joined him. Luca described in great detail everything that had occurred with their encounter with the dark cloud. The Sanuri advised that they should all return to Raul and the others as this may have been a distraction for another attack.

Lakin carefully examined Jared and he too could not initially determine a reason for Jared not to have regained consciousness. After the examination Lakin turned to Zoya who had been quietly sitting in a chair near the bed. "Is he your husband?" Lakin asked.

"No, a friend, he got hurt helping me. We were bringing a book and a message to the Sanuri."

Lakin looked quizzically at Zoya then at Hannah. "I'll explain later," Hannah said.

"You are wondering why someone who is named in that book would bring it to the Sanuri," Zoya said. "I don't know yet if Jared is totally evil."

"Zoya I am a healer of my tribe. Neither Hannah nor I can find a cause why Jared has not woken up. I am going to try some remedies to see if black magics are involved and if they are, sometimes it can get dangerous. I would prefer that you leave the room," Lakin said.

"What do you mean dangerous?" asked Zoya.

"Well, sometimes demons come forth," Lakin explained.

"And you can stop the demons?"

"I can make them leave," Lakin said.

"Lakin the Sanuri said that Zoya is a very powerful seer, perhaps she should stay," said Hannah.

"Zoya it is your choice but if you stay, you must not interfere in any way," Lakin said. "And you must do exactly as I tell you."

"I will admit I am a little frightened but perhaps I can be of service," Zoya said meekly. "I will stay."

"In that case Zoya, will you go across the hall and knock on the door to the King's study, Simon wanted to be here too?" Lakin asked. Then he turned and started taking items out of a large pouch. Lakin placed a silk cloth on top of the table near Jared's bed. He then placed a variety of small containers and crystals on the cloth.

Sudfad, Simon, Matthew, Mathas and Sorren all crowded into the bedroom and shut the door. "I will tell you all the same thing that I told Zoya, once I start do not interfere under any circumstances and if I tell you to do something you must obey me. I have never performed these rituals on someone like Jared before, who knows what evil we will call forth."

Then Lakin turned to Hannah, "I want you to watch at first and I will explain later what I am doing. Under circumstances like this, when so much darkness could be involved I always pray first to The Great Ruler to protect us and to guide us and I would strongly suggest that you do the same." After Lakin said these words he pulled the blankets back from Jared and sprinkled blessed water on him. As soon as the drops touched Jared's body they began to smoke.

"What does that mean?" asked Sudfad.

"That happens when blessed water touches the skin of a demon," Lakin replied. Lakin raised Jared's head and poured blessed water down his throat. Jared instantly screamed in pain. "Be gone demon you have no power here," Lakin said sternly and proceeded to place crystals on top of Jared's body. Lakin was chanting as he placed each crystal upon the body. Suddenly Jared started to shake uncontrollably.

"This is like what happened with Gabriel," Hannah gasped.

"This castle is surrendered to The Great Ruler your darkness cannot exist here," Lakin said loudly. "Be gone demon, you are powerless here."

"I can hear him," Zoya yelled. "He is screaming for help. I am seeing the chamber that he saw in his visions, the one with all of the stone tubs. I cannot see the faces of the men in the tubs but the room is filled with shadows. Jared these people are trying to help you," Zoya screamed. "Can you show them how?"

Jared continued to shake and thrash around the bed; suddenly he started to cough up blood. "That necklace he is wearing, tear it off and put it in the blessed water," Zoya said frantically. "It's a vial of demon blood."

"Simon grab that glass from the dresser and pour one of these bottles into it," Lakin said as he pulled a knife out of his sheath and cut Jared's necklace from around his throat. "Put that glass near the window and every one stand back," Lakin ordered as he ran around the bed and dropped the necklace into the glass of blessed water. Instantly a cloud of dark smoke formed and the glass began to shake. The glass moved around the windowsill then shattered in dozens of pieces.

"Is anyone cut?" Lakin asked. When no one answered he turned his attention back to Jared, who was starting to moan. "Zoya come over here and hold his hand," Lakin said. "He knows you; it will help to bring him back." Jared stopped shaking but he was doing little besides moaning for several minutes.

"He's squeezing my hand," said Zoya.

Suddenly Jared's eyes opened and he sat up in bed. He looked wildly at everyone in the room but calmed down as Zoya was speaking to him. Jared looked at his own hands and legs with a look of amazement then he looked at Lakin and Hannah. "Thank you, I don't know how you did it but I think you pulled me out of hell."

"Jared hold out your arm," Lakin said as he sprinkled some blessed water on the arm. This time the water did not smoke.

"Jared this is important," Simon said. "Do you remember anything about where you were?"

"Hell ya, it was a nightmare."

"If I get some paper and a pen, can you tell me about your experiences, while we get you something to eat?"

"Sure but why?"

"Because there are three of us who were pulled into hell worlds and when we came back we realized we had been sent messages," Simon said. "I'll explain more later."

"I don't like this at all," Raul said. "You know it's a trap of some kind. Ahriman or whoever made that dark ring knows you have the power to destroy it, so it must be a diversion from something else." Raul said to the Sanuri.

"I agree," said Raphael. "Perhaps you should talk to The Lion."

The Sanuri smiled, "I see you are taking your lessons to heart. I too feel this is a trap. Raphael and Gabriel why don't the two of you walk into the forest together and request an audience with The Lion." Although both of these powerful high priests had spoken with The Lion, they still did not feel comfortable or worthy to call upon such a holy messenger. Gabriel and Raphael stopped when they were in a secluded area; they both looked at each other then Gabriel spoke.

"We request the presence of The Great Lion, the holy messenger of The Great Ruler."

"I hope there will be a time when it feels natural for you to call upon me," The Lion said as he appeared before them. "And once again you are both speechless."

"We are simply in awe," Gabriel said. "And we will try to do better. We need your guidance now about that demonic ring that surrounds the Patronus headquarters. We feel it is a trap, possibly for the Sanuri. And we suspect it is a diversion for something else."

"You are right about everything except that you forget what grand prizes both of you and Raul are for the demons also. Raphael and Gabriel, the Sanuri and I are trying to teach you that you need to think outside of the limitations of your humanity. Because then and only then will you be able to conquer the darkness that seeks to destroy you. Now tell me what do you think that hellish ring is a diversion for?"

"An attack on the headquarters to liberate Meekos," Raphael said.

"Or perhaps to kill him before he has a chance to give us information," The Lion said. "How do you think the demons plan to get past the holiness that surrounds those buildings?"

"Suck Meekos into the earth," suggested Gabriel.

"That would be one way," The Lion said. "What about having the Patronus walk Meekos to the dark ring?"

"They would never do such a thing," Raphael said.

"They might if they were trading him for hostages."

"What hostages?" asked Gabriel.

"You two and the Sanuri."

"The Rualas were able to fly to the ring of darkness, so does that mean there are no traps between us and the ring?"

"It does not, there are multiple traps between here and the ring of darkness and between the ring and the headquarters. What are you going to do?"

"Ask that you consume everything, all of the traps and all of us with holiness," Gabriel said.

"I am pleased with that answer," The Lion said. "But I am going to test your faith. I will engulf you and your small army with a holy white light so that you can walk through those traps. Gabriel and Raphael there will be men in your army who do not believe or have your faith. You will have to lead them through the darkness. Go back and tell the others what I have said. And prepare to continue your journey in twenty minutes."

Marie brought Jared a second tray of food as he sat up in bed and recounted his experiences to Simon who wrote down every word. No one left the room as they were captivated with the story, so Jared had an audience.

"I remember being carried into the castle," Jared said. "And I remember seeing you looking over me," Jared said to Hannah.

"I knew Zoya was near me because I could feel her and sometimes hear her voice. Then I remember feeling like something grabbed me and was pulling me through the earth. Everything was thick blackness and I felt like I was falling very fast."

"I don't know how long I was falling but when I stopped I was in that cave; the one I had visions about before. There was a large stone tub with the name Omnibus carved into it and thirteen smaller tubs in a row to the left of the big one. In my visions I always saw Roch in the first tub, the one closest to the demon, but this time I was in that first tub."

"I was standing there," Jared continued. "Looking at myself dead. Then I heard whispering and laughing but I couldn't see who was making the sounds. Suddenly shadows appeared on the walls of the cave. I could see them because there were lit torches on the walls. The shadows were all sizes and shapes but I could not see what was making them."

"Then it seemed like all of the shadows were laughing and somehow I knew there was an auction and I was being auctioned off; that is when I started screaming for help. Then I remember hearing your voices and it was like you were pulling me out of the hell world but the demons were hanging on to me trying to keep me there. Then I heard Zoya tell me to help you and I somehow knew about the necklace. I owe you all so much; tell me how I can repay you."

"Jared do you really mean that?" Simon asked sternly.

"Yes, I am not lying to you; why do you ask like that?"

"Because we are hunting the men who created men like you to be vessels for demons. We are trying to stop them," Simon said. "Those priests who hired you, Meekos, Pravis and Tenebrae were some of the men. They were going to use Roch as a vessel for a demon but another demon took Roch, we don't know why. But those priests probably hired you so they could use you instead of Roch."

"I had a feeling they were setting me up for something," Jared said angrily.

"If you truly want to thank us, you can help us," Simon said. "And if you don't want to help us, well, you just experienced what will happen to you if we don't stop them."

"You mean that can happen again?" Jared asked with fear in his voice.

"As far as we know it can," Simon replied.

"Jared these people here are good people; they have been very kind and generous to both you and me and they certainly didn't have to be," Zoya said. "Jared the reason Simon said the men who created you is that a group of dark lords has spent generations creating men who are so evil that they can house the essence of a demon."

"So these people brought you into their home knowing that you could be that evil. Jared I have not known you long but I have only seen the kindness in you. If you truly want to escape your destiny you will have to fight the evil within you. Do you think you can do that?"

Jared's face turned white as he listened to both Simon and Zoya. "It is true, I have led a violent life and honestly I don't know if I can fight the evil within me. But I will tell you I never want to go back to that hell world and I want to fight those damn demons and dark lords for doing this to me. What do you need me to do?"

"Giving us information will be a good start," Simon said. "Where did you get that necklace?"

"I don't know honestly, I think I have been wearing it all my life."

"No Sanuri, The Lion said it had to be me and Gabriel who led the warriors through the traps," Raphael said. "He said it was a test of faith and I really doubt if your faith needs to be tested."

"Can I ride with you?" Raul asked.

Both Gabriel and Raphael looked at the Sanuri who smiled and nodded. Raul lined the soldiers up in a formation, then Gabriel, Raphael and Raul proceeded to the headquarters on horseback. The three men had not traveled more than ten yards before they heard screeching and yelling of hell beasts that fell back from the holiness that surrounded the three men.

Gabriel, Raphael and Raul did not stop but proceeded forward as their path was made clear for them. The army of Wetprian soldiers followed, many who had fear gripping their hearts. The Ruala warriors and Enrops flew overhead and the Sanuri drove his boca in the rear of the formation with Misha and Calen sitting in the front seat next to him. Ciao was tending to her wounded brother Nabi in the back of the boca. The Sanuri smiled when he heard The Lion's voice, although no one else heard it.

"The children are doing well."

As this small band of warriors proceeded forward they got glimpses of Hutas and hell beasts but they all fell away as if being pulled back into another world. After almost an hour of travelling, they came to the dark ring that surrounded the headquarters. When Raphael, Gabriel and Raul started to ride through the ring, lightning bolts materialized within the dark clouds, which startled their horses.

The three men maintained their course and the others followed. The screams of the demons and hell beasts were considerably louder within the dark clouds, but none of the soldiers broke formation. In less than an hour they stopped in front of the Nora headquarters of the Patronus.

High Priests Rueben, Tyrus and Gideon met their guests. "We are glad to see you," Rueben said. "That demonic ring appeared yesterday. All day and night we have been listening to the screams of hell beasts. So tell me how did you get through it?"

"The Lion engulfed us in holiness," Raphael said. "But is anyone with Meekos, this could all be a diversion?"

"Ephraim, Silas and Amos are with him," Rueben said.

Within moments the Sanuri pulled up in front of the headquarters. "Rueben I don't mean to be rude but we need to see Meekos right away."

"Certainly, follow us," Rueben said as he, Tyrus and Gideon turned and proceeded through the kitchen and down the cellar steps. They walked through the wine cellar to the hidden door then entered the room that once was the torture chamber of Arthur Marcus. Meekos was bound to a chair with his head slumped forward.

"Is he still alive?" the Sanuri asked as he moved quickly towards the prisoner.

"He was cursing us just a few moments ago," High Priest Amos said.

The Sanuri placed his hands on either side of Meekos' head which caused the dark lord to scream in pain. The Sanuri did not speak but concentrated on the many images and sounds that were in Meekos' memories. Meekos skin began to smoke from the touch of the Sanuri.

"Get him off from me," Meekos screamed over and over.

The Sanuri did not speak but kept staring into the eyes of the infamous dark lord for over thirty minutes. When the Sanuri stepped back from Meekos the men in that room heard anger in the voice of the Sanuri; something they had not heard before."

"Your deeds and actions bring tears to my heart for the horror you have inflicted upon this world. But to know that you danced with demons and committed these atrocities while claiming to be an emissary of The Great Ruler enrages me."

"Before this is through you will join your friends Pravis and Tenebrae in Ahriman's hell dimension. But you are like a rabid dog," said the Sanuri as his voice became louder. "You are too dangerous to allow in this world as you are. You consorted with beasts so shall you become."

Meekos started to scream, "No." But the entire word did not come forth for Meekos started to snort as a pig. His eyes became dull and his body movements exaggerated.

The Sanuri turned to the men who filled the small chamber. "He is an animal now. He is no longer a threat for us to transport. I am sure the demons and dark lords will feel that Meekos' power is gone."

"What did you see?" Raul asked.

"Evil of unimaginable proportion."

Chapter V
Eternity

"It looks like the dark ring is dissolving," Luca said after they returned to the first floor. "How can that be? How can the demons know that you stopped Meekos this quickly?"

"They are all connected by blood," the Sanuri answered. "Everyone swears a blood allegiance to the demons and I suspect that is how we will take them down."

"I still don't understand," said Luca.

"And I am not sure that I can explain it well," the Sanuri said to the kitchen full of men who were listening to him. "This blood allegiance doesn't allow them to communicate in the sense that you would think of but it does allow them to sense the rise or fall of powerful energies."

"Wait," said Gabriel. "We had confiscated many correspondences between Pravis, Tenebrae and Meekos, in which they said they kept trying to contact the underworld to find out what had happened to Roch. As powerful as these dark lords were, shouldn't they have sensed something?"

"Yes," replied the Sanuri. "That's why they were so fearful; they felt cut off from their lifeline so to speak."

"Was The Great Ruler stopping them from getting this information?" Raphael asked.

"No, other demons, very powerful demons," said the Sanuri.

"Why would they do that?" Raul asked.

"Demons are as jealous and cruel to each other as they are to humans. Think of different groups of humans who go to war for power and greed. There were two groups of thirteen original Old Ones that came to this world because the humans called to them. There are other worlds that also have demons and some of them want to take over this world because it is such a ripe feeding ground," explained the Sanuri.

"Ahriman is the strongest Old One in this world but he is being challenged by demons of great proportions from other worlds. The wars have already begun and I suspect that is why Ahriman is taking such an active role in this world; something that has never been done before," the Sanuri continued.

"What do you mean the demons don't take an active role in this world, we are fighting them all of the time?" Raul asked.

"The Old Ones are held in the same regard as the ancient kings of your people. They sit on their thrones and have their underlings do all of their work for them. Most of the demons you have encountered are the underlings, so to speak. The Old Ones themselves rarely get actively involved with humans. But many of you in this room have been attacked by Ahriman and have actually heard his voice, in each case The Great Ruler saved you. This is all of great significance; I just don't fully understand how all of the pieces are falling yet," said the Sanuri.

Simon asked Jared questions for hours. Questions about his life, his experiences with what he thought was Roch's spirit, his visions and his interaction with Pravis, Tenebrae and Meekos.

"Jared you are going to be very angry with me but you should tell them the rest," Zoya said.

Jared gave Zoya a stern look. "I waited for Pravis and Tenebrae to return to their rooms when they didn't show for a couple of days and after I heard about the battle between the Hutas and Rualas I figured they weren't coming back. So I stole everything out of their rooms. Which was a lot."

"What sort of things?" asked Sudfad.

"Mostly lots of gold coins but also jewelry, some books and strange candles and things."

"And where are these things now?" asked Sudfad.

"I brought all of Jared's things in here," Zoya said. She stood up and opened the door to an attached room and showed the men all of Jared's saddlebags and other possessions that were piled on the floor."

"Do you know where they got the money from?" Sorren asked.

"No."

"We aren't interested in the money," Sudfad said. "But we would like the books and any papers they had."

"Help yourselves; I can't get them for you." Zoya and Sudfad proceeded to search through Jared's belongings as he watched them.

"You might want to look at the jewelry and see if there is anything else that contains demon blood," Lakin suggested. "Because that seemed to give the demons a strong hold on him."

"I wonder if the priests took all these rings off from the people they sacrificed," Sudfad said.

"Oh my god! I wore one of them," Zoya gasped.

"I told her it might be easier to get past the border guards if we pretended to be married," Jared said then he looked at Hannah and Lakin. "Any idea when I will be able to get out of this bed?"

"Not for a couple of days at least," Lakin replied. "And even then you aren't going to be able to lift a saddle or fight."

"Well, it looks like you are stuck with me for a couple of more days," Jared said with a laugh. "What else do you need?"

"Actually Jared, I would like you to stay until the Sanuri returns," Sudfad said. "He will have more insight into this matter and how we can help you."

"Jared, I think that is a good idea," Zoya said. "The Sanuri is very nice and you won't be in any shape to travel for a while."

"If you are done here, Jared really needs to get some rest," Hannah said.

Sudfad, Lakin, Mathis, Sorren, Matthew and Simon returned to Sudfad's study and closed the door.

"I really don't like having him under the same roof as our wives and children," Matthew said. "I mean when he was unconscious it was one thing but now."

"I agree," said Simon but he is really valuable to us.

"Boys, did you see his face when you told him the demons could pull him back to hell?" Sorren asked. "For all that he is, that man was terrified. You could see it in his eyes. At least for now, I don't think he is much of a threat."

"Zoya seems to have a great influence over him," Mathas said. "Did you see how he reacts to her? He listens to her like she is his wife. Are they romantically involved?"

"I don't believe so," Sudfad said. "But that doesn't mean there aren't attractions between them. They are a strange pair but it seems like neither of them had anyone in their lives until they met each other."

"She seems like a nice girl," Matthew said. "How could she be interested in him?"

"From what Hannah says," Sudfad replied. "It sounds like Jared is the first man to protect her in a while. They have been taking care of each other since they started this journey."

"She is a nice girl, I've talked to her a couple of times," Sorren said. "Perhaps she is exactly what he needs."

"Something isn't right here, I can feel it in my bones," the Sanuri said as he looked out of the windows of the headquarters. "This was really too easy. I feel there is more to come."

"Demons can't pass through the field of holiness but humans can is that correct?" Raul asked as he too looked out the windows.

"Yes, just so you know the field of holiness extends over these buildings," the Sanuri said.

"I believe we need to prepare for battle," Raul said and walked outside to talk with his soldiers and the Ruala warriors.

"I will prepare our men," High Priest Tyrus said and he also walked out of the headquarters.

"Sound the Horn of Cass," the Sanuri instructed. "I believe we are going to need help from Fort Nora."

"But will they hear it from this far away?" Gabriel asked as he took the horn off from the knob it was tied to on the wall.

"Oh they will hear it," said the Sanuri. "I am going to the roof." Gabriel walked outside and blew the horn three times then waited thirty seconds and blew it three more times, he repeated this pattern seven times.

"There are huge dust clouds in every direction," Raul said as he entered the house. "We have company coming. Where is the Sanuri?"

"He went to the roof," Raphael said. "Rueben you and some men stay with Meekos, this whole thing seems to be about him."

"Do you think the girls left any of those bombs around here?" Calen joked.

"If there still are all those bottles of whiskey in the wine cellar, can't we put rags in those and ignite them?" Misha asked as he started for the wine cellar. He returned to the kitchen a few moments later. "There are shelves full of bottles of whiskey."

"Misha you and Calen start tearing up some blankets or sheets," Luca said. Then he turned to a couple of the priests in the room. "Would you help me bring the bottles up?"

As the Sanuri stood on the roof of the house that now was the headquarters for the Patronus he saw men of all sorts riding towards their location. Evil men, who had answered the call of darkness. Hutas who listened to their demon masters and demons themselves. So much dust was raised by the hoofs of thousands of horses that the sky darkened.

"Great Ruler protect these men who stand in your name," the Sanuri prayed.

"What are you doing?" Raul asked as he, Gabriel and Raphael walked into the kitchen and saw all of the tables filled with bottles of whiskey that had long rags hanging out of them.

"We're making bombs," Calen replied. "Of course they aren't as good as the ones the girls make but they should help. Luca is getting some of our warriors now."

"You're not going to be able to fly far with these," Luca was explaining to twenty Ruala warriors who were following him into the kitchen. "So you will have to wait until they are close to us."

"All total we have maybe eight hundred men here," Raphael said. "I was on the roof with the Sanuri; the armies surrounding us number many more. I asked him if I should call to The Lion and he said, 'No.'"

"It's time," called the Sanuri as his voice seemed to reverberate so all of the warriors could hear him. "Archers prepare!" The Patronus priests and Wetprian soldiers formed a large circle around the headquarters. "Release!" yelled the Sanuri. The first row of archers shot their arrows at the attacking armies, then immediately fell to one knee as they strung more arrows into their bows.

"Release!" yelled the Sanuri and the second group of archers released their arrows. The first group of archers stood up. "Release!" The arrows soared. "Release! Release! Release!" With every order the sky filled with arrows and the arrows seemed to multiple in numbers as if unseen archers were assisting them in battle.

"Rualas stand ready!" shouted the Sanuri. "Now!" Two hundred Rualas warriors flew over the advancing armies and dropped their primitive bombs on them. Men and demons screamed and horses reared and threw their riders as the fire rained upon them. Each Ruala was told to return to the headquarters as soon as they had dropped their bombs.

"Archers stand ready!" yelled the Sanuri as he waited for the last of the Rualas to return. "Release!" arrows soared through the air. "Release! Release! Release! Rualas stand ready!"

"These are the last of our bombs," Luca said as he flew up to the Sanuri.

"Have your warriors drop them and return," the Sanuri said.

"What is happening?" yelled High Priest Silas as the ground under Meekos' chair began to shake violently. High Priest Tyrus started to move towards Meekos.

"No stay back," ordered High Priest Rueben. "If the demons take him they cannot reverse what the Sanuri has done. Meekos is of no use to them. This was the trap for the Sanuri. It is time for us to pray." The three high priests stood shoulder to shoulder and all repeated the same prayer as the Sanuri had instructed. The house shook violently as the ground beneath Meekos started to collapse. Meekos' mind was no more and he seemed unaware of the turmoil beneath him.

General Colter was leading four thousand troops from Fort Nora. He could see the smoke and dust clouds in the distance as they neared the headquarters. Suddenly Colter and no one else heard the voice of the Sanuri. "We are surrounded, have your men circle behind them."

The Wetprian soldiers and Patronus priests now took to their horses and rode towards the advancing armies. The Ruala warriors flew overhead and proceeded to shoot arrows into the throngs from hell. Gabriel, Raul and Raphael were fighting on the ground because they stood closest to the headquarters. Misha and Calen although still injured from a previous battle grabbed their swords and ran out of the door.

Calen jumped on the back of a Huta who was grabbing Gabriel from behind. Gabriel, Raul and Raphael were greatly outnumbered. Misha grabbed a sword off from a body and flew towards his friends. He plunged the sword in his left hand through the back of a man fighting with Raul.

Misha quickly turned and with the sword in his right hand he cut the head off from a Huta who was running towards Raphael. Gabriel grabbed a battle axe off from a man he had just killed and swung it with such force that he cracked the skull of a Huta who was on top of Raphael.

The Horn of Cass was heard as General Colter's men attacked the dark armies from the rear. His men rode through the attacking mobs, stabbing them with swords and breaking their skulls with battleaxes. Men were falling from their horses only to be trampled by others. So focused was Ahriman's army on attack that many of the men did not realize they now were surrounded. Horses screamed and ran hysterically through the battlefield adding to the chaos.

The ground shook violently but no one seemed to notice except for the three priests who were in the cellar with Meekos and the Sanuri who was still on the roof of the building. Suddenly deafening screams were heard. Screams that brought many of the combatants to their knees. Screams that caused men to cover their ears and their noses to bleed. Screams from the powerful demon Ahriman as he was burned with holy energy.

Ahriman grabbed Meekos and quickly retreated into the tunnel he had created under the cellar. The prayers of the three high priests caused the holy energy to follow Ahriman as he traveled through dark worlds trying to escape his demise.

The hole in the floor of the cellar disappeared as quickly as it had opened. The three high priests quickly grabbed their swords and ran out to the battlefield. Raul lunged forward with his sword when his adversary suddenly disappeared. When the screams could no longer be heard in this world, the battle ceased because the legions of hell were no longer empowered by the great demon.

Ahriman's focus now was to return to his realm before the holy energy engulfed him. Ahriman the creator of fears was now filled with terror. Never before had The Great Ruler come after him with such fury. The demon knew he would be imprisoned in The Great Abyss for all eternity if he allowed the holiness to engulf him.

Still grasping Meekos, Ahriman mustered all of his power and lunged forward forcing a tear in the fabric of space. Ahriman sped towards his hell dimension. He yelled and a door was opened before him, half of Ahriman's being shot through the door before the holy energy attacked him. Ahriman screamed in pain as the holiness set his being on fire. Ahriman pulled the rest of his wounded body through the door to his hell dimension. And the powerful lord of demons cried and whimpered as the burning pain surged through his being. A punishment that would remain with him throughout all time.

That night during dinner Lakin and Hannah told Natasha, Elan, Dack, Joao, Bekka and Fala about their experiences with Jared and Zoya.

"I can't believe they allow him to live in the castle," Elan said. "He is a threat to their families."

"He is a threat yes," Lakin explained. "I find it interesting. When we were in Nora we read a book that Sophie had written, she was documenting everything that Roch did to make sure he was worthy of his role as a vessel. Natasha you read that book and it upset you greatly, did it not?"

"Yes, I couldn't make it through even a few pages without crying and Calen, well, he would get so angry, especially when she talked about any of Simon's family members."

"Jared certainly looks like a monster but his friend said she has never seen anything but kindness from him and he seemed normal and cooperative with us. It was obvious he was terrified by his ordeal," Lakin said. "As bad as Jared probably is as a person he doesn't seem to come close to the type of evil displayed by Roch. I am wondering how these men were chosen and if there is some kind of bond or blood or something that links them all. Hannah you have spent more time with him, what do you think?"

"I wasn't as courageous as you and Natasha, I couldn't read that book," Hannah said. "But I certainly heard what everyone was saying about it and I agree with what you said. You know I don't think anyone has looked into the men who were created to be vessels. You might be onto something very important."

"Jared stole a book from Pravis and Tenebrae and in the back were the names of people who had been created for vessels. He and Zoya brought it to the Sanuri," Natasha said. "Tomorrow let's ask Simon if we can read it to at least get the names of these men, then perhaps we can do some research into them."

"Do you think the Insidiae are still creating these men?" Elan asked.

"I don't think anyone has thought about that," Hannah gasped.

"Zoya why did you stay?" Jared asked as they were eating dinner in his room. "I mean you could have taken the gold and left."

"What did you just say to me?" Zoya yelled angrily. "I can't believe you said that Jared. You make me so mad." Zoya got out of her chair and marched up to his bed. "I don't steal Jared. I'm not like you. I thought you were my friend. I would not leave you when you needed help."

Jared smiled at how angry Zoya was. "Oh so now you are laughing at me," Zoya yelled. "Perhaps I should go. You will be well enough to take care of yourself soon."

"Zoya, please don't leave," Jared said as she was heading towards the door. "I am sorry I didn't mean to offend you. I really appreciate that you stayed with me. I just meant a lot of people would have taken the gold and left me to die. Zoya please come over here so we can talk." Zoya turned and looked at Jared, then slowly started to walk towards him. "Here sit on the bed, I won't hurt you," he said.

"Jared right now I would be more concerned with me hurting you," Zoya said as she sat on the edge of his bed.

"I know what I said didn't come out right but why are you so mad?"

Zoya was surprised by his question. "I don't know. Jared I have been so worried about you and I have been praying for you, then you make it sound like I am some kind of criminal."

"I don't think anyone has ever prayed for me before."

"Well, that is just sad and maybe if someone did you wouldn't be in so much danger now."

"Are you worried about me?" Jared asked seriously.

"Jared we haven't known each other long but we have been through a lot together. I don't know you well but I consider you my friend and yes I am worried about you."

"And I worry about you. Zoya if something happens to me, take that money and make yourself a new life."

"Jared I can't take your money."

"If I'm dead I won't need it, so promise me that you will take it."

"Jared do you have a feeling like you are going to die soon?" Zoya asked with concern.

"Well, I almost did today if these people hadn't saved me. And who knows what could happen next."

"That's why I think we need to stay here until the Sanuri returns; he can help us."

"Why did you say us?"

"I don't know," Zoya said and blushed.

"Zoya are you planning on staying here in Wetpr?"

"Yes, I like it here and the Sanuri said he thought I was meant to come here, to be of help."

"How are you going to live?"

"I don't know yet. I have a little money. I haven't gone into the city yet to see if they have any shops like the one I was working in. I know you plan to go to Port Friada but if you can be of help to King Sudfad and the others who are trying to stop the men that created you; I think you should stay here for a while too."

"Zoya would you get mad at me if I gave you some money? You could get yourself a little house and at least I would know you would be able to buy food."

"Jared, that is really sweet of you but I don't know if I could take your money, Jared, Jared, Jared," Zoya screamed as his eyes rolled back in his head and Jared started to foam at the mouth. Zoya ran out of the room yelling, help him please help him."

The Royal Family and guests were eating in the dining room; all of the men ran out of the dining room and towards Zoya.

"What is going on?" Simon asked.

"I think the demons are trying to get him again."

"Matthew send someone to get Hannah and Lakin," Simon said. "Father give me your crystal," Simon said as he tore his necklace off."

When they entered the room they found Jared convulsing in bed. "Son what are you going to do?" Sudfad asked.

"I don't know, buy time until Lakin gets here," Simon said. "Zoya I may need your help."

Simon opened each of Jared's clenched fists and put one of the necklaces that contained tiny crystals from the Ice Caves of Mordv into each of his hands. "Jared these crystals are blessed by The Great Ruler, don't let go of them. You can fight the demons; refuse to let them take you. Zoya say something to him."

"Jared, we will help you with your fight, let us know how we can help you. Jared come back, don't let them take you."

Matthew returned to the room, "I sent a soldier for them."

"Matthew give me your crystal," Simon said then he put Matthew's necklace around Jared's neck. "Jared hang on to these because the darkness cannot tolerate holiness."

Jared continued to flail around on the bed. His eyes were rolled back in his head and a green foam was coming from his mouth. Zoya kept talking to him but Jared did not respond.

"I'm not getting anything," Zoya cried in frustration. The minutes moved slowly as everyone in the room was watching a man being pulled into hell.

"We're here," Lakin said as he, Hannah, Natasha and the other Ruala warriors ran into the room. "Please get back from him."

"I put crystals in his hands and around his neck," Simon said. "I couldn't think of anything else to do."

"Hannah get back from him," Natasha said. "I have seen that green foam before." Natasha stood over Jared and prayed to The Great Ruler to help Jared fight the demons that were trying to take him. She repeated her prayer over and over and Lakin joined in. As Lakin prayed with Natasha he sprinkled blessed water on Jared, but this time it did not smoke when it touched his skin. Lakin tried to pour blessed water down Jared's throat but the green foam which was now covering his chest and bedding was preventing the water from going down his throat.

"Release this man," Lakin ordered as he covered Jared with crystals. "Release him, you have no power here." Meanwhile Natasha continued to pray. Hannah stood next to Natasha and started to repeat the same prayer.

Suddenly Jared started thrashing around more violently and blood started to come out of his nose and mouth. The bed started moving around the floor and an intense energy filled the room. Elan tried to pull Natasha away from Jared but she would not move. A picture crashed to the floor and the candles were flickering as if a wind was in the room. A scream pierced the night but it was not made by anyone in the room. Jared was thrashing more violently. Another scream was heard. Natasha, Lakin and Hannah continued to pray.

"Where are those screams coming from?" Sudfad asked.

"Hell, Jared is battling the demons," said Lakin.

"Is there anything we can do to help him?" Bekka asked.

"Hand him a sword," Zoya said. "I can see him now. The demons are screaming because he is tearing into them." One by one each warrior placed their sword on Jared.

The room started to tremble, more screams were heard. Natasha, Lakin and Hannah kept praying. Suddenly Jared lunged forward and fell onto the floor.

"I'm alright," Jared growled as Lakin and Simon helped him up. "Those stinking bastards, you were right they came for me again. But this time I fought them and here," Jared handed a large pouch to Simon.

"What is this?" Simon asked.

"I don't know but it was sitting on a sort of pedestal and once the fight started they were trying to protect it. I thought it might help you. And if not maybe they will think twice before they grab me again."

Hannah grabbed some water and a cloth and started to wash the blood and foam off from Jared so she could check him for injuries. Simon loosened the strings on the pouch and poured the contents on the foot of Jared's bed.

"What is that?" Sorren asked as they looked at a large black orb.

"It looks like it's polished," said Matthew.

"Where were you?" Simon asked Jared.

"They pulled me back to that auction block again. Those bastards were going to auction me off like a piece of meat. There were those shadows on the walls again but there were these huge ugly bastards standing around so I grabbed a couple and the fight was on. Don't know how you knew to give me a sword but when you did one appeared in my hand. I stabbed a couple, grabbed the pouch and ran back here."

"Something has happened," screamed Sophie as she jumped up in bed. "Erebus I can feel it, something has happened to Meekos."

"Honey what are you talking about?" Erebus asked as he tried to wake up. Sophie started to cry. Erebus put his arms around her. "Are you sure it wasn't a bad dream?" he asked.

Sophie continued crying for several minutes then she tried to compose herself enough to talk. "Erebus, in the Insidiae we are all connected by our blood; we have to give a blood offering when we join the society. I don't really understand how it works but it somehow keeps us connected."

"Sophie I really don't understand what you are saying."

"You know how you can feel power shifts when you are connecting with the underworld?"

"Yes."

"Well it's like that for us. And I just felt a major loss of power in the connection but the feeling was so overpowering I think it was Meekos since we are related by blood."

"If that is true what does that mean?" Erebus asked. "Do you think he is dead?"

"I don't know but tomorrow I am going to have a talk with Malik."

"Sophie are you going back to those caves?" Erebus asked with concern.

"No, Malik owns the Taperian Fortress Bank, when he is not trying to play cloak and dagger. I will visit him at his work."

Chapter VI
Through Their Eyes

"I think it is time you explained what is going on here," Renya said sternly as all of the men returned to the dining room after Jared's episode. Hannah, Lakin and Zoya remained in the bedroom with Jared as they cleaned him up and checked his wounds. Zoya changed the bedding which had been soiled with green foam and blood. Natasha and the five Ruala warriors were walking past the dining room when Renya called to them.

"Natasha would you and your friends please come in here," Renya asked. "I am just asking the men to explain to the rest of the family what is going on with the secret patient you have."

Natasha's eyes grew wide and she looked at Simon for help. Simon looked at Sudfad. Sudfad looked at Natasha and the Rualas. "You might as well take a seat this is going to take a while," then Sudfad addressed all of the women at the table.

"We have a patient and we are not sure if he is dangerous which is why we have been keeping all of you away from this area of the castle except for at meal times. This patient is very valuable to our work in trying to stop the Insidiae from raising a demon and that is why Lakin and these other Ruala warriors have arrived here. They are helping us to study him."

"Study him?" Rosa asked. "Is he human?"

"Well we think so," Sudfad said as Marie walked into the dining room with plates for the Rualas.

Marie started to laugh, excuse me for interrupting but not too long ago I was walking into that room to get their trays and that little Zoya had her hands on her hips just giving Jared hell and that monster of a man just sat in bed apologizing like he was a little kid, I think he is human." Marie's comments brought smiles to everyone's faces.

"And who is she?" Renya asked. "You won't let us near her either."

"This really is going to be a long story so I suggest you all fill your glasses with wine," Sudfad said. "Rosa and Angelina I don't know how much of this you know so I will go back a little further. We have discovered that the attacks on this castle when our children were married, the attacks against Raul and Simon that almost killed them and Petra's kidnapping were all orchestrated by a group of men called the Insidiae."

"They are a secret society that worships demons. And they are busy doing many things besides attacking our family. They have been trying to raise a very powerful demon from its prison in The Abyss."

"Sudfad that sounds rather outlandish," Rosa said.

"Aunt Rosa, Natasha here and her brother Gabriel are demon hunters. Hannah, Lakin, Raul and I were working with them for months and let me tell you, Raul and I now understand that real demons exist," Simon said.

"Natasha and Hannah," Rosa gasped. "Those two sweet little girls."

"Those two girls are both vicious and courageous warriors," Simon said with admiration.

"I knew I liked them," Angelina said as she looked across the table at Natasha.

"Well, let me continue with this story or we will all still be sitting here until breakfast," Sudfad said. "What these insane men have been doing is and this is hard to explain, they worked with demons to plant seeds in some men. These seeds of pure evil are passed down through the second sons of each generation. They did this to create men so evil that their bodies could be used to house powerful demons. For the demon Omnibus to escape his prison, he has to leave his form behind so he would need a new body, or as the Insidiae calls them vessels for the demon to exist in." Now Sudfad turned to Vitomas.

"Vitomas we all understand how upset you have been that Raul is leaving all of the time for these missions. I am going to tell you why. It is because he loves you so much," Sudfad explained.

"We are finding the names of some of the men who are intended vessels. Of course these men have no idea of what is happening to them. Vitomas both Roch and Archetenus are such men. And both of these evil men are obsessed with you. That is what Raul is trying to stop."

Vitomas gasped loudly, then she looked at Annabelle then back at Sudfad. "As horrible and outrageous as that story is, it actually explains a lot about Roch and Archetenus. But Roch seems so much more evil."

"Roch is apparently the worse of the bunch from what we seem to know so far," Sudfad said. "We are working with the Patronus to try and stop all of this. Now for Jared, he too is one of these men."

"What!" yelled Renya.

"Please dear let me finish," Sudfad said. "Simon, Gabriel and Raul saw Jared a few times in Nora. He had been hired by the men behind the attacks on our family. But he was hired by them to deliver messages over great distances nothing more. When some of these men were killed Jared stole their things and found a book about the Insidiae that named some of the men that are meant to be vessels and his name was in the book, which scared him greatly. During all of this Jared is being, for lack of a better word haunted by a spirit. He goes to a shop in Taperia were Zoya worked."

"Now before you jump to conclusions let me tell you about Zoya. Sorren and others here can tell you that she is a very nice young girl whose husband was brutally murdered in Taperia and she had been living there in fear. Zoya is a seer and the Sanuri says she is very powerful but she doesn't realize it because her own fears of her abilities block her."

"Zoya told Jared that a demon was talking to him and to shorten the story the two of them believed the demon was setting a trap for the Sanuri. So they both risked their lives to come here and warn the Sanuri and to give him the book that Jared stole, the one with the names," Sudfad continued.

"Jared and Zoya were attacked by Taperian border guards," Simon said. "Raul and I found them on one of our morning rides."

"Both Zoya and Jared have given us a great deal of information to help us. So far Jared is acting like a normal person and Zoya says he has been very kind to her; but we don't know him or understand what he is, enough to let you near him."

"Well, what happened when all of you ran into his room just now?" Renya said.

"Demons have been trying to get him, they are pulling him into hell," Sudfad said. "I don't know how else to explain it. We have been trying to help Jared fight them."

"Why are the demons doing that?" Annabelle asked.

"Maybe to stop him from helping us," Simon said. "We don't know."

"Mathias, Matthew all of us have been in that room when Jared is attacked and let me tell you it is like something we have never seen before," Sorren said.

"We don't like him in the castle with all of you here," Simon said. "But not only is Jared in danger but Hannah and Lakin hope to do some tests on him to see if they can find any information that might help us."

"It breaks my heart to say this," King Mathas said sadly. "But these men that Sudfad has been talking about. They are part of the same evil society that Juleta belonged to. That is why we all have been so involved."

Angelina looked at her mother Shara, then she looked at Laurel who was sitting next to her. "Laurel would you please hold Alexas for a moment?" Angelina asked as she handed her infant to Laurel. Angelina stood up with the presence and authority of a warrior princess. Sorren sat back and smiled.

"First of all I hope you all know how much I truly love this family and how honored I am to be a part of it. Yet the men in this family make me so angry I can barely contain myself."

"We just went through this in Lentz when our husbands kept secrets from us to protect us and they blinded us to our enemies. Renya, Vitomas and Annabelle, are not trained as I am but they are mighty warriors who need to protect their families."

Angelina continued with her voice rising, "You allow the wives of others to fight for this family and you keep us in the dark. My mother and Gala are two very powerful healers that know the old medicines and they have taught me also. There are old medicines that are used effectively for demon possessions and other things not of this world. If you would have bothered to tell us this before, we could have helped you."

"Angelina I don't want you near Jared," Matthew said.

"And yet you have no problem with Natasha, who is pregnant, being near Jared," Angelina said angrily. "And that Zoya, why are you keeping her locked in that room is she a prisoner?"

"No," Sudfad said. "She knows that none of you understood her role here."

Vitomas stood up from the table. "Where are you going?" Simon asked.

"Angelina is right. Annabelle and I have spent most of our lives being prisoners of such monsters. I am going in to see Jared for myself and to ask Zoya to join us." Annabelle and Angelina both left the table and the three young Princesses walked to Jared's room and knocked on the door.

"You can come in," Hannah said as she was putting new bandages on Jared's wounds. Everyone in the room stared as Vitomas, Annabelle and Angelina entered the room.

"The men of our family finally told the rest of us what is going on here," Vitomas said. "I am Vitomas, Raul's wife, this is Annabelle, Simon's wife and this is Angelina, Matthew's wife. Our husbands and fathers have been keeping you both locked in here to protect us. You are not prisoners here; you can certainly join the rest of us."

Vitomas walked up to Jared and stared into his eyes. "Annabelle and I were prisoners of Roch's for many years. And there is another name in that book you gave the Sanuri, a person that Annabelle and I know well. We were mistreated greatly at their hands and that is why our families are so protective of us."

"My mother is a great healer as is another woman here, Gala, and they have taught me the old medicines," Angelina said as she looked at Jared. "We might be able to help you, would you let us?"

"How could you help me?" Jared asked.

"The old medicines treat all the aspects of a person, not just the physical wounds; but also the things you can't see like demon possessions. Perhaps we could help you close that door to the other world so the demons can't come for you."

"Hell ya, give it a try," Jared said. "I don't want to be a vessel for a damn demon."

"He has really been through a lot today," Hannah said. "Could you do this tomorrow? And I would like to watch."

"Actually, you all have helped me fight the demons twice today," Jared said. "If these ladies can help me even a little I would like to try. Could you do it now?"

"Let me talk to my mother and Gala and see if we have the herbs and things we need," Angelina said as she started to turn and saw that most of the family was standing in the doorway. Matthew walked into the room holding Jacob; as he walked next to Angelina, Zoya yelled "Wait." Everyone in the room and doorway looked at Zoya who now was walking up to Jacob.

"I can give you the answers you need to calm your fears," Zoya said as she touched Jacob's hand. "As soon as the three of you walked in here the spirits were clamoring around me, they were talking so much that I had to sort through it. There are connections here. Your child has no demon in him. He found your camp because an Angel protected him and led him to you. The same Angel who protected Vitomas when Archetenus kidnapped her."

Zoya paused as if listening to a voice, "The same Angel who protected Jacob's mother when Roch tried to rape her and kill her with the baby in the room. The Angel scared Roch and he tripped and his blood ring fell from his hand as he ran from their house. Jacob's father put on the ring and became a monster. The blood rings, they contain demon blood."

"Was it Jacob's parents that were killed in that cabin?" Matthew asked.

"Yes, Jacob's father stole treasures belonging to a dark lord, who sent demons after them. I don't know how but the boy is special that is why the Angel saved him and brought him to you. The demons are not after the boy, they never saw him because the Angel concealed him. Jacob was always meant to be with you." Zoya said then paused. "But, they are all talking so much, so many voices, wait." Zoya turned to Vitomas.

"Archetenus was taking you to Port Friada is that right?"

"Yes, he kept saying that it was a good place to start over."

Zoya quickly turned to Jared, "You keep saying the same thing and you too are going to Port Friada. Jared the spirits are telling me this is not a coincidence. There is something calling the men like you to that place."

"Zoya everything you have said about Archetenus is true," Vitomas said. "Tell me, is the Angel's name Miranda?"

"That is the name she takes when she is in this world, I am being shown."

Vitomas spoke to the room full of people, "Archetenus would have arguments with an imaginary person. I thought he was crazy and at the end he said he was bringing me to Raul because Miranda told him to."

Angelina touched Zoya's arm and said, "Thank you, we have been so worried about Jacob."

"He is safe with you and I can see that he will make you very proud one day but I can't see why," Zoya said.

Renya had been listening from the hallway and now entered the room, she first walked up to Zoya, "I am Sudfad's wife Renya." Before Renya could continue talking, Zoya curtsied and became flustered.

"Oh you are the Queen, I am sorry I did not know," Zoya said.

"Zoya you do not need to curtsy, I want to apologize for you being kept in this room, please come out and join the rest of us."

"Oh My Lady, I am not a prisoner here; I have been watching over Jared."

Renya smiled at Zoya's comment, then she walked up to Jared, "My husband and I have never turned our backs on anyone who needed help. And the fact that you want us to help you fight the demons gives me hope that you are not as bad as Roch. Jared you are welcome to stay here and we all will help you. But our children and our grandchildren are in this castle. Can you look me in the eyes and tell me you are no threat to them?"

Jared stared boldly at Renya. "My Lady I will not lie to you. I am a hired fighter. I have killed more men than I can remember but I swear to you I have never hurt a woman or a child and I have no intention to. The danger I bring to you is the demons that are after me. I don't think any of your family should be around me because I don't know what can happen."

"I believe you Jared, which gives me relief," Renya said. "Jared we have fought demons before, we will help you the best that we can."

"Shara left a while ago to get Gala and their medicine bags," Sorren announced then he looked at Jared. "If I were you I would want to get this done tonight too."

Later that evening after the wounded were taken care of and the dead were buried many of the high priests of the Patronus met in the study of the headquarters with the Sanuri, Raul, Gabriel, Raphael, Luca, Calen and Misha. Raul waited until everyone had a drink and was seated before he spoke. "Sanuri I don't think I am the only one here who is wondering what happened today and where is Meekos?"

"As many of you already know, Ahriman has been involved in many aspects of our investigations. He ordered Petra's kidnapping to set up a trap for me. He has been setting traps for almost everyone in this room, and if it wasn't for The Great Ruler most of us here would be dead. Few demons have so boldly gone after the emissaries of The Great Ruler. So The Lion set a trap for Ahriman."

"So this battle was a distraction set up by The Lion?" High Priest Amos asked.

"Oh no, Ahriman meant to kill you all and he sent a lot more beasts than the ones you battled," the Sanuri explained. "For every arrow we sent into that army, thousands more rained from the sky against our enemies. Most of the demons were destroyed leaving the humans for you to fight."

"The trap was set when I read the mind of Meekos. Because Meekos is so closely linked with so many aspects of darkness I was not only able to receive a great deal of information but The Lion allowed Ahriman to see an image of me through Meekos' eyes. It wasn't Meekos Ahriman was coming for it was me."

The Sanuri continued, "High Priests Rueben, Tyrus and Silas were instructed to repeat a very powerful prayer in unison. Because of this prayer holy energy attacked Ahriman when he opened the floor under Meekos. Ahriman should have sensed the holiness but he was so filled with rage when he realized that he had been tricked that he hesitated long enough for the holiness to affect him. Once he realized what was happening he attempted to get back to his hell dimension as quickly as he could. Those were his screams you heard as the holiness burned the evil within him."

"Did he make it?" asked Luca.

"I was told that he is back in his hell dimension with Meekos, but he is greatly damaged from the holy energy and will suffer the effects through eternity."

"What of Meekos?" Gabriel asked. "You took his mind; did he even realize what was happening to him?"

"He received his mind back as soon as Ahriman grabbed him. Meekos is now getting the punishment he deserves. He is a prisoner of Ahriman's along with Pravis and Tenebrae. And I would suspect Ahriman is taking his anger out on them because of the rage and pain he is feeling now."

"It sounds like justice but Father will be disappointed, he wanted to punish Meekos too," Raul said.

"Sudfad will realize that the punishment he could inflict is but a grain of sand compared to what Meekos is receiving now," said the Sanuri.

"Why hasn't anyone asked about the disappearing armies?" asked Calen. "That actually seems more incredible to me."

"They were conjured up by Ahriman, as his power weakened he could no longer support that illusion," the Sanuri replied.

"Well, for illusions they sure could fight," said Misha with a grin.

"I used that term because those men were not born into this world they were, created so to speak for the purpose of attacking us."

"And what were those demon birds that attacked us before we got here?" Luca asked.

"They are called Durisks and they literally are creatures that dwell in hell dimensions. Ahriman has been ripping holes in the dimensions, for what purpose I do not know," said the Sanuri.

"So does this mean we don't have to worry about Ahriman anymore?" Gabriel asked.

"I don't know," replied the Sanuri. "But I believe he will think twice before coming after any of us again. You have to understand, Ahriman is also battling other Old Ones from this world and he is being attacked by Old Ones from other worlds. The damage done by the holy energy is not only inflicting eternal pain upon him but has greatly weakened his power. If he has not realized that now he soon will."

"Why are the Old Ones at war?" asked High Priest Tyrus.

"Why do men go to war?" asked the Sanuri. "To seize wealth, power and control. Only instead of battling over land these powerful demons are battling over worlds filled with victims, such as ours."

"So how will you know if it is effective?" Lakin asked.

"It's complicated," Shara said. "If someone is possessed by a demon it is much easier to tell if the demon has vacated the person; for example sprinkling blessed water on them. Then we pray that the patient is blocked from the demons having access to them. But Jared is not possessed; but he may have evil in him that was planted. And the demons have a powerful doorway if they can try to drag him into hell."

"There has to be something that connects him to the demons," Gala said. "You broke the hold that the necklace has but there has to be something else. It might be the seed that was planted generations ago or it might be something very obvious."

"Jared you said you didn't remember where you got that necklace filled with demon's blood. Do you have any other jewelry, a talisman or anything that you keep on your person?" Shara asked.

"Just this earring," Jared said and took it out of his ear and handed it to Shara. As Shara examined the earring, Gala was mixing herbs and tonics and Angelina was carefully examining the many tattoos that Jared had on his body. Lakin and Hannah stood near the bed with the three healers and most of the Royal Family members and Zoya either stood farther back in the bedroom or stood in the doorway.

"Jared, if you aren't comfortable with all of these people watching, I can ask them to leave," Shara said softly.

"Let them stay," Jared said. "Besides after the last couple of attacks on me, you ladies might need some help."

"Jared can you lean forward so I can look at the tattoos on your back?" Angelina asked. As she knelt on the bed next to him."

"Sure, but the only one I have is my wife's name with flowers. She was murdered by the Hutas."

"Jared, you have another tattoo under your ponytail," Angelina said.

"No I don't," Jared said with surprise.

"Yes you do and it's the Mark of Satan." Angelina said. "We found the connection. Jared I am going to pin your hair up so we can work on this."

"I have crystals that are blessed by The Great Ruler," Lakin said. "You may need them."

Natasha started to push through the crowd but Elan pulled her back. "Elan," she snapped. "Did Calen send you here to watch me?"

"He sent me here to take care of you," Elan replied with a grin. "And I see why, you are always getting in the middle of things."

"Well, then come with me," Natasha said as she grabbed his hand. "Because this is important. Don't anyone touch that tattoo before I see it, because it might not be a tattoo." Natasha looked at the tattoo for a few moments. "Lakin hand me one of your crystals," Natasha said. "I have seen Gabriel do this. If I touch it with a crystal and it moves, it is not a tattoo."

"You're not touching it," said Elan.

"Then you do it," Natasha said and handed him the crystal. "Just touch the tip of the crystal against the tattoo." Elan followed Natasha's directions and jumped back when the tattoo started to move.

"What is that?" Elan asked.

"I'm not sure but it's alive," Natasha said. "Now the question is can we kill it without killing Jared."

"Jared could you feel that moving?" asked Hannah.

"No, what did it do?"

"It jumped when touched with the crystal," Hannah replied. "We could cut it out."

"Not while it is still alive, it may be attached to his entire system," Natasha said. "I wish Gabriel or the Sanuri were here."

"Just cut it out of me," said Jared.

"No Jared really it would probably kill you," Natasha said.

"Perhaps if we covered it with crystals it would shrink back," Lakin suggested.

"Or it might strike at you too," Natasha said.

"Give me a handful of those crystals," Jared said. "Then everyone get away from this bed I will hold the crystals against it so we can see what happens." Lakin handed Jared the crystals. "Get back farther; I don't want anyone getting hurt on a count of me."

"Wait," Simon said and he walked up to Jared and placed his sword on Jared's bed. "You might need this." Simon returned to the doorway, where he was standing with Annabelle and Vitomas.

Jared pressed the crystals against the back of his neck and instantly his body started to jerk. The more violently his body moved, the harder Jared pressed the crystals against the Mark of Satan.

"That snake might come out of him," Natasha said. "Some of you be prepared to kill it." Sorren, Elan, Lakin and Matthew were standing the closest to the bed and they all drew their swords from their sheaths.

"Jared can you feel it?" Hannah asked.

"It feels like the damn thing is alive and biting me. Don't anyone come near me."

"If the snake comes out, you have to wait until it is out of his body before you kill it," said Natasha.

"Look, there's a bulge in his back," Zoya cried.

Jared was having difficulty keeping the crystals pressed against the back of his neck. He was in a great deal of pain and his body was jerking violently.

"Jared you are a strong man," Angelina said. "Keep the crystals pressed against it; that bulge has moved up to the back of your neck.

Jared screamed in pain as his skin burst open. Blood splattered on the bedding and the wall behind the bed as a giant red serpent forced its way out of his body. The eyes of everyone in the room grew wide as a snake of incredible proportions emerged. Jared slumped forward and appeared unconscious. Elan readied his sword. The snake saw the movement and sprang towards the Ruala warrior. Sorren stepped forward and cut the head off the beast with one powerful downward stroke.

Lakin quickly pushed the body of the snake off from the bed and grabbed Jared. "He's still breathing," Lakin said. "Hannah pour the blessed water into his wound while I hold him." When Jared became unconscious he released his hold on the crystals which now fell onto the bedding.

"Look at those crystals, they are black now," Rosa gasped.

"I'm getting this thing out of here," said Sorren as he picked up the pieces of the snake and walked out of the room.

"Please everyone out of here," Lakin said. "We have a lot of work to do. Shara, Gala and Angelina you can stay and help if you want."

"I'm not leaving," Zoya said with tears in her eyes.

"That's fine," Lakin said. "But we don't know how much damage that beast did."

Chapter VII
Finding Their Way Home

Jared was unconscious for three days. He suffered no demon attacks during that time; but he suffered greatly from the damage the giant serpent had done inside of his body. Zoya never left his side, although various people asked her to join them at their gatherings for meals. Zoya was fearful, not only for the welfare of her friend, but the voices she always heard were silent. The voices of the spirits that Zoya had learned to live with and often found annoying were speaking no more and Zoya found that terrifying.

"Renya, Sudfad, we will all be leaving tomorrow," Mathas said as they sat around the breakfast table. "Angelina and Alexas should be able to make the journey home now. Although Claudius and Fahron have assured me there are no problems I feel I must get back to our kingdom."

"We understand," Renya said. "Although I will miss you, this has been such a gift, our families spending so much time together."

"Renya we feel the same way," Rosa said. "We have to make the time to do this again."

"Actually I would feel better waiting until Raul was back," Matthew said. "There are so many strange things going on."

"While we appreciate your concern," Sudfad said with a warm smile. "I do believe we can handle whatever is thrown at us."

"Well, don't let your guards down with Jared," Matthew said. "I know the snake is gone but I just don't trust him."

"Matthew you have seen him," Shara said. "He may not live through this. All of us have done everything we can; now we just have to wait."

With the Sanuri's help many of the warriors wounded in the battle at Nora were healing quickly. During the next few days Raul spent a great deal of time at Fort Nora. He was amazed that the construction of the huge installation was almost completed. Every day hundreds of people from Nora went to the construction site to help the soldiers. Although a large kitchen had been built at the fort, daily women drove bocas to the site with food for the workman.

The Sanuri too, was impressed with the progress of the construction of the monastery. He joined Padre Thomas and Padre Bartholomew during some of their classes, which they taught three times a day. The people of Nora eagerly embraced their new lives, as free men and women. Hundreds of young men from Nora flocked to the fort to join the military. And dozens of Wetprian soldiers were courting or marrying girls from Nora.

"This is getting embarrassing," Misha said as he, Calen and Luca walked in the business district of Nora.

"I know," replied Calen. "All these people coming up to us and shaking our hands, makes me uncomfortable."

"It makes you wonder how much fear they lived in," Luca said as the three men stopped in front of a jewelry store. "Are you getting something for Natasha?"

"Actually I came here the other day and the jeweler is designing something for me. I want to see if it's done," Calen said.

Charles was a short, rotund man with gray curly hair and spectacles. His face lit up when he saw the three Ruala warriors enter his store. "Calen I hope you like them, now if you don't you just tell me and I will make any changes." Charles reached under one of the counters and pulled out a large velvet lined tray. On the tray were two golden necklaces, one was petite and feminine and the other large and considerably longer. Each necklace had links in the chains that would support the insertion of golden hoops. Two golden hoops on each necklace attached small golden disks.

"Is this what you are naming the baby?" Luca asked as he picked up the smaller necklace and saw that one of the disks had Calen's name inscribed and the other disk had the name *Lily Irena* inscribed.

"Yes, you know Lily is Mother's middle name and Irena was the name of Natasha's mother," Luca said as he inspected the two pieces.

"And yours has Natasha's name and Lily's?" Misha asked as he moved closer to the counter.

"Yes and there are many links here for all of our future children," Calen said with a smile then he turned to Charles. "I am very pleased with these. I will be back each time we have a child. How much do I owe you?"

"Nothing, please just take them, it is the least I can do," Charles said happily.

"Really Charles all of you have done so much for us, please let me pay for them." After several minutes of arguing, Charles named a price that Calen believed was too low but he paid it to end the argument.

"Natasha is going to love that," Luca said. "But I think you should have gotten something for Elan too."

"Why?" asked Misha.

"Because he is supposed to keep Natasha out of trouble while I am gone," Calen said and all three men broke into laughter.

The morning of the fourth day Jared regained consciousness although he was disoriented and weak. Lakin and Hannah had visited him several times every day and were relieved that Jared finally showed some sign of improvement. Mathas and his family had just left for Lentz when Hannah walked up to Simon. "Simon, Jared is awake and would like to speak with you, he says it is important."

When Simon entered the bedroom Jared was sitting up in bed. "You better get a pen and some paper," Jared said.

Simon went to his father's study to get some paper and returned to Jared's room.

"Do you want us to leave?" Hannah asked.

"No you all can stay," Jared said weakly. "First things first. Simon if I don't make it I want you to take that gold in the other room and buy Zoya a place to live and make sure she has food and what she needs. Will you do that?"

"Yes," Simon said. "I promise."

"Ok now for the rest," Jared said. "My head is still foggy, so I am trying to remember. When I put those crystals against that thing on my neck, well, I felt like my whole body was being torn apart but I also felt something else and I don't know how to explain it. I somehow felt like I was connected to others, many others and don't ask me I don't know if they were humans or demons or what." Jared paused to take a drink of water.

"Lakin and Hannah told me about the snake that came out of me. It's the damndest thing. Spent my whole life fighting Hutas and men and it's a demon snake that's gonna kill me."

"Jared, don't talk like that," Zoya said. "You'll get better."

"Zoya I'm a betting man and I wouldn't bet on it. Anyways back to the snake. Course I couldn't see what it was crawling around in me when it was happening but I swear I heard screaming. At first I thought it was the snake but then I realized I heard more than one voice screaming. The voices were screaming like they were in pain. It was like what was happening to me was affecting others. Then I started seeing things. Thought it was my life flashing before my eyes at the time."

"But now I don't know because I don't know what I saw. It was like pieces of pictures were being flashed before me really fast. I saw multiple pictures of caves but they were all different. I think all of them had altars in them, those altars for worshiping demons."

"In some of the pictures there were those shadows against the wall. Then I think I was looking at a kind of temple, it was huge and there were paintings on the walls and golden statues of snakes."

"And although I couldn't see people I felt like there were people in the temple that were somehow seeing what was happening to me. I could feel anger, but it wasn't mine. Then I saw a room that was filled with babies, they were laying in rows of little beds."
"I heard chanting and I saw what looked like men with hoods bowing down before someone they call Emeric. Does that name mean anything to you?"

Angelina, Rosa and Shara all rode in the carriage on their return trip to Lentz. These three women from such different backgrounds and lives, broke barriers once thought unbreakable and formed a loving family. The carriage was filled with activity as Margarit, Jacob, Sarah and Alexas Rose were all awake and acting their ages. Sorren's young sons, Nathanial and Peter rode horses as was befitting young warriors.

"Something doesn't seem right," Matthew said as he rode along side of his father King Mathas and his father-in-law Chief Sorren.

"What do you mean son?" Mathas asked.

"Can't really explain it, just a bad feeling."

The Royal Family of Lentz were riding in the company of two hundred soldiers. "Well, if it would make you feel better send extra scouts ahead," Mathas said.

"I'm going to do that," said Matthew and rode to the front of the military formation.

"Matthew has good instincts," Sorren said. "But I think being a new father is making him really protective."

"And we were so different," Mathas said with a grin and the two old warriors broke into laughter.

Five days after the battle at Nora Raul, the Sanuri and the others started their journey back home. Although they had extra scouts during the days and posted extra guards during the nights the trip to Wetpr was uneventful.

"I don't know if I should appreciate the fact that we haven't been attacked yet or if this is a really bad sign," Raul said as he sat around the evening campfire with his friends.

"I'm surprised that none of us have received messages from our wives," Gabriel said. "I am thinking that is a really bad sign."

"I know, this is the first time that Vitomas has not written to me every day," Raul said. "She has been so upset about me going on these missions."

"Perhaps if you told her why, it would help," the Sanuri suggested.

"I don't want to scare her," Raul said. "She and Annabelle have had such horrible lives that Simon and I want them to just enjoy life now."

"But keeping secrets just fuels their imaginations, which can be much worse than knowing the truth," the Sanuri said.

"Changing the subject," Raphael said. "Now that I am staying in Wetpr I need to find a place to live and a place to set up a headquarters for my men. They can't stay in the army barracks forever. Raul if you know of any real estate for sale I would appreciate the help."

"Why don't you just live with me and Hannah?" Gabriel asked.

"That was fine when we were growing up but you have a wife now. I would think the two of you would like your privacy."

"Actually Hannah was alone for so long that she likes a house full of people. I will speak with her when we get home."

"There's an abandoned mansion just north of Cicero College. It faces Lake Petz and backs up to the River Toba. The family that built the college lived there but they died and the place is sitting empty. It's a huge estate."

"And no one owns it?" Raphael asked.

"Not that I am aware of," Raul said. "I can take you there after we return. It is secluded and yet only an hour's ride from Salar."

"That sounds perfect," said Gabriel.

"The place probably needs some work. I think it has been empty for a couple of years," Raul added.

"That will not be a problem," said Raphael. "My men have many abilities."

"Come in," Jared called weakly as there was a knock on his door.

"We are sorry to disturb you," Laurel said as she, Gala and Alexander entered the bedroom. "Oh good Zoya is here too."

"That's fine," said Jared.

"Simon told us that you wanted to get Zoya a place to live," Laurel said. "We were just out for one of our morning rides and we came across the nicest little farm house. It's empty but Alexander said it's in good shape. It's only five miles from here, if you would like to see it, Zoya."

"Oh I don't know," Zoya said hesitantly.

"Tell me about this place," said Jared.

"There is a barn, a smoke house and a chicken house and they are all in good shape," Alexander said. "I don't think the place has been empty long. The house is all on one floor, looks like three bedrooms. And there is a large garden in back."

"And you are sure it is empty?" asked Jared.

"Not a piece of furniture in the place, just some curtains on the windows," Alexander said.

Jared tried to straighten himself up to a better sitting position. "Alexander go into the next room and grab a bag of gold coins. Zoya I want you to go with them and look at this place."

"But Jared, I can't let you pay for a home."

"Yes you can, I would probably just lose that money playing cards anyways."

"Alexander, if Zoya likes it will you buy it for her?"

"Of course."

"In fact take two bags of gold," Jared said. "If you get it she is going to need a lot of things and you can see how reluctant she is to take anything."

"Jared I don't know if I should leave you."

"Hannah and Lakin are here and besides those damn demons haven't come for me since their snake ripped me up."

Alexander took two pouches of gold and showed Jared what he had taken. "Come on Zoya," Gala said sweetly. "We think you will really like this place." Zoya reluctantly stood up and walked over to the door.

As they were all turning to leave Jared called to Alexander, "Thank you, this will make me feel better."

Although Matthew had a nagging feeling that they were being watched, the Royal Family of Lentz and Sorren's family returned to Lentz without encountering any difficulties. They arrived home mid-morning and found Claudius, Fahron, Thaos and Stephan still in their morning meeting.

"Did you start late or is there something wrong?" Mathas asked as he, Matthew and Sorren walked into the King's study.

"Both," Claudius said. "You better pour yourselves some coffee. Mathas before we get started did Matthew explain to you about the letter that Lazo found in Juleta's castle? The one where the King of Ogg is telling her where to leave the payment."

"Yes, he and Sorren told me. But I have to admit I have never heard of Ogg or King Douma."

"You're not alone there," Fahron replied. "Did they show you the letter and map?"

"No, they just told me about it when we were in Wetpr."

Fahron handed Mathas two pieces of paper and waited to speak until the King had finished reviewing the documents. "It all sounds so damn absurd that Claudius and I didn't know what to think about it. Then this morning some of the miners from the diamond mines, flag down our soldiers while they were on patrol. The miners found the bodies of three men. Looks like someone was trying to hide the bodies in the mines. The three were stripped naked, so we have no idea who they are and from the looks of them they put up one hell of a fight."

"One of the bodies had his fists clenched and when a soldier tried to open the man's hands he found a crumpled up piece of paper," Claudius said as he handed the paper to Mathas.

"What is it Father?" asked Matthew as he walked closer to Mathas.

"It looks like the same map that was in the letter," Mathas replied and handed the map to Matthew.

"We all know how cunning Juleta was," Fahron said. "This could just be another one of her elaborate tricks."

"Or we could be under attack again," Matthew said.

"That's a really nice thing you are doing for Zoya," Hannah said as she cleaned Jared's wound in the back of his neck.

"That poor girl almost starved after her husband was murdered," Jared said. "She had to sell her wedding rings for food. And she's just so damn proud she won't take a cent."

Hannah smiled at Jared's comment. "Jared I think you and Zoya care about each other more than either of you will admit."

"We are just friends."

"Jared I've seen the way you look at her; you think of her as more than just a friend."

"Hannah look at me, hell I scare people just the way I look and now, if I live, maybe I will be a cripple. And then there is the whole demon thing," Jared paused. "Hannah I have done some awful things in my life. I don't want to take a chance that I will turn into a demon and hurt her."

"I think you should talk to her about these things. It's only fair to both of you. Jared, Zoya strikes me as a very smart woman. Let her make up her own mind."

"Maybe you're right but I don't even know how to bring it up because..." Jared did not complete his sentence because the bedroom door opened and Zoya, Gala, Laurel and Alexander walked in. Zoya walked up to the bed and hugged Jared.

"Jared wait until you see this place it is wonderful," Zoya gushed. "I've always dreamed about a little home like this. And we didn't even have to pay for it. They took me into Salar and we found out the home was abandoned," Zoya was so excited that she was talking very fast which made everyone in the room smile. "And Alexander has a friend who owns a furniture store. We bought all the furniture for the house and the owner's sons are delivering it for us, can you believe that? They are coming tomorrow morning so I'll have to be at the house."

Jared looked at Alexander, Laurel and Gala, "Would you go with her?"

"Of course," Laurel said. "Besides we promised to help her clean the house and fix it up."

"What else did you buy?" Jared asked.

"Cleaning supplies, bedding, some dishes and material," Zoya said happily.

"I want you to stock that place with food and I mean really stock it. I don't want you going hungry. And buy everything you need, the seeds for your garden and some animals and chickens," Jared said. "You should probably get a small boca too."

Zoya sat down on the bed and stared at Jared for a few moments and when she spoke to him it was in a scolding tone. "Now listen to me Jared, stop acting like you are going to die. You're not, I can just feel it. But it is going to take you a long time to get better. As soon as you are able to travel, Alexander said he will move you out to the house so I can take care of you. And don't even think about arguing with me about it. I love that house but I don't want to live out there by myself. So stop acting like you are ready for the grave; those demons didn't beat you. And we have a lot of work to do."

Everyone in the room smiled at the shocked look on Jared's face. After a few moments he managed to say in a hoarse whisper, "Ok."

"Now I would like to go back to the house and start cleaning, if you think you will be alright," Zoya said.

"We're going with her," said Gala.

"No go ahead, I'm fine," Jared said as he was still taken back by Zoya's words.

Zoya kissed Jared on the cheek and left with Gala, Alexander and Laurel. Hannah waited until the door closed before she spoke. "Jared as your physician I am telling you I think Zoya is the best medicine you could have," Hannah said and smiled.

"I can't believe what she said. Hannah why would she want me, a crippled fighter?"

"Jared she sees much more than that in you."

No sooner had Zoya and the others left then there was another knock on Jared's door. "Come in," Jared said.

"I'm looking for my wife," Gabriel said as he opened the door.

"Gabriel," Hannah gasped and flew into his arms. "I have missed you so." Gabriel and Hannah kissed and hugged for several moments. Then Gabriel looked at Jared, "Simon and Sudfad told me what's been happening with you. You're lucky to be alive."

"Well, if it wasn't for your wife and Lakin and the others I would still be in hell. I owe them all a great debt."

"I know you talked to Simon but when you are up to it I would like to go over your experiences with you. I have been working on this mission longer than Simon and may discover something that he didn't."

"Any time is fine with me but I am sure you want to spend some time with Hannah first."

"Gabriel, where is Raphael?" Hannah asked excitedly.

"He's with the Sanuri looking at that orb Jared brought back from hell. Why did you ask it like that?"

"Because I don't want either of you going back to the house without me; I have got all kinds of surprises for you."

Gabriel said, "Calen went to the house because Simon told him Natasha was there. Is that alright?"

Hannah laughed, "You know how those two are when they get together he will never notice anything besides her."

"Natasha," Calen called as he and Luca walked into the house.

"What is all that pounding?" Luca asked as they could hear the carpenters working.

"Calen," screamed Natasha as she came out of the kitchen and ran to him. Calen picked Natasha up and kissed her passionately.

"I missed you so much," Natasha said as Calen set her on the floor.

"I missed you too," he said and kissed her again. "Now let me say hi to the baby," Calen said as he patted Natasha's stomach.

"Calen you have new wounds, did you get into a fight?" Natasha asked disapprovingly.

"The demons set a lot of traps for us," Calen said. "And Luca here figured out how to kill some giant demon birds."

"Luca you're hurt too, are you alright?"

"Yes," Luca replied with a smile.

"I worried about you so much," Natasha said and stretched up and kissed Calen again. Then she suddenly pushed away from him and said in a scolding tone, "You got me a baby sitter. How could you?" Calen started to grin.

"And she needed one," Elan said with a laugh, as he had followed Natasha to the foyer. "She's always getting in the middle of everything."

"And you wrote to my friends and asked them to bring you to Nora after I told you to stay here," Calen said with a laugh.

"They told you!" Natasha gasped.

"Of course they told me."

"Luca!" Natasha tried to pretend that she was angry but she started to laugh.

"Come on," Calen said and took Natasha's hand.

"Where are we going?"

"To our room," Calen replied with a grin.

"Oh," Natasha said with a coy smile. Then as an afterthought she turned to Elan. "Elan can you finish that thing?"

"Don't worry I will take care of it," Elan said smiling.

"Elan you might want to take care of lunch too," Calen said with a loud laugh. "We might be a while."

"Have you figured out what that thing is?" Gabriel asked as he and Hannah entered Sudfad's study. Before anyone could answer there was a knock on the door.

"I am sorry to disturb you," Marie said. "But I have a note for Raul."

"It must be a good note," Simon said. "Did you see the grin on Marie's face?"

"Vitomas wants me to come home in exactly thirty minutes and I am to come alone," Raul said with a grin. "From the amount of perfume on this note I hope it is a good surprise."

"She knows about Roch and Archetenus," Sudfad said. "Sorry son I told her. It's a long story that I will tell you later."

"I'm sorry," Raul said. "Back to the orb."

"I have never seen one of these before, only heard about them," the Sanuri said as he carefully examined the orb. "I believe this is a scio. You have heard stories about crystal balls well here is the real thing."

"But it is black," Raphael said. "Is there a way to unlock its powers?"

"That I will have to figure out. What I find curious is that Jared saw this on a pedestal at what he thought was an auction block," the Sanuri said. "I will need to speak with him."

"Jared has been very cooperative," Simon said. "You should have seen what the guy went through. I'll tell you he as guts. We were all shocked when he brought that back."

"Sanuri, could this just be another one of Ahriman's tricks?" Sudfad asked.

"That is always possible, but I don't think this is," the Sanuri said. "But I do need to study this. And the rest of you all have families to return to. Go to your homes, we can discuss this at the meeting tomorrow morning."

Gabriel tied his horse to the back of the boca and drove Hannah home. Raphael rode alongside on his horse. "Raphael, Hannah said that you and I aren't allowed in the house without her," Gabriel said with a grin.

"Natasha and I have been very busy while you were gone," Hannah said as she hugged Gabriel's arm.

"We know you tried to get some of the Rualas to bring you to Nora," Gabriel said grinning.

"Yes, we were both so mad at you for leaving us. But then Simon and Sudfad told us about Jared and besides that it was fascinating trying to figure out how to help him. It struck me that the family business as you call it is everywhere. So I hired a team of carpenters to work on the house and Natasha and I have been buying out Salar," Hannah said happily.

Gabriel pulled the boca to a stop in front of their house as Hannah finished speaking. They could all hear pounding and sawing as they entered the home. "I told the carpenters that I would pay them extra to get the work done in two weeks but then I kept adding projects," Hannah said as she proudly opened a door. "Here is your weapons room. Simon, Elan and the others helped us choose the weapons."

"This is wonderful," Gabriel said as he and Raphael looked at the huge room that held hundreds of different kinds of weapons.

"And over here is my medical room," Hannah said. "Once I started working on this I had the carpenters build all those shelves and enlarge the room."

Gabriel put his arm around Hannah, "I will say dear I am impressed."

"Now for your study," Hannah opened the door and found Elan, Dack, Joao, Bekka and Fala all arranging books on the newly built bookshelves that now lined every wall.

"Did my wife put you to work?" Gabriel kidded.

"We have been having a lot of fun here," Fala said. "Actually we spend more time in Salar than we have here."

"That's because Dack and Joao found girlfriends," Bekka said teasingly.

"Yes we have enjoyed our visit," Joao said. "In fact we may stay a while, if that is alright."

"That's fine with us," Gabriel said and started to walk around the newly remodeled room. "I love this Hannah."

"I thought about all the work you did in Nora, so I bought extra tables and chairs for this room. And brighter carpets. And the wall behind your desk is actually a closet that contains a safe. I thought you might need something like that."

"I really do love this, thank you," Gabriel said and kissed Hannah. "This is perfect."

"Now follow me," Hannah said as she led Gabriel and Raphael upstairs. "Raphael, your things were in that other room but that was too small for you. I had the carpenters take a few walls out to combine two rooms but then that still seemed too small so I hope you like this." Hannah said proudly as she opened the door to newly built chambers.

Raphael was the first to enter the beautifully decorated sitting room. "Hannah this is beautiful," he started to say but Hannah interrupted him in her excitement.

"Natasha and I both decorated it. You have a large study, a small library and a couple of bedrooms.

"A couple of bedrooms?" Raphael asked.

"We thought you might want to have guests stay," Hannah said as Gabriel squeezed her hand. "Natasha picked out the colors but if you don't like anything you let me know and I will change it."

"Hannah I am so touched I really don't know what to say," Raphael said genuinely.

Gabriel hugged Hannah appreciatively. "I asked Raphael to live here with us and he was afraid he would be a bother."

"Nonsense Raphael you are like Gabriel's brother, of course we want you to live here. Oh I almost forgot that chest by your bed is a gift from Natasha, it's for weapons."

Raphael walked up to Hannah and kissed her on the cheek. "Thank you, you make me feel very welcomed."

"Hannah you have done a wonderful job, I am very proud of you and Natasha," Gabriel said. "But can I asked why neither of you wrote to us?"

"Because we are still mad at you for leaving us behind," Hannah said with a coy smile.

"Hannah, Gabriel you should come down here," Elan called.

"Is something wrong," Hannah asked as they came down the stairs.

"The carpenters that are working in the cellar found a tunnel," Elan said as he led the way into the wine cellar.

"I am having more shelves built down here," Hannah explained as they descended the steps.

Luca was waiting for them at the bottom of the stairs, he was holding two lit torches and handed one to Gabriel. Luca opened a wooden door that exposed a tunnel that was large enough for the men to stand in. As they walked through the tunnel they noticed metal holders fastened to the walls for torches.

"I wonder if this was some type of escape route," Gabriel said as they continued to walk. After almost fifteen minutes they came to the end of the tunnel and Luca and Raphael pushed the door open, the hinges squeaked loudly. They walked out of the tunnel and found themselves in the small boat house that was next to the pier on their property.

When Raul walked into his parlor he was immediately struck by how quiet it was. "Vitomas," he called.

"Are you alone?"

"Yes."

Vitomas walked out of the bedroom and towards Raul, wearing a beautiful sapphire lace nightgown. "The girls have the children, I thought we could have some time alone," she said as she stretched up and kissed him.

Then Vitomas took Raul's hand and led him to their bathing room, which was filled with lit candles and bottles of oils. There was a small table on the tile floor that held a bottle of wine and two glasses. Raul took Vitomas into his arms and kissed her passionately.

Chapter VIII
To See

The Sanuri spent the entire afternoon talking with Jared. He examined Jared's body and looked into his mind. "So what's the verdict? Am I gonna turn into a demon?" Jared asked.

"Do you want to?"

"Of course not; but I am serious about asking this. Zoya is preparing a house for us to move into and well, I'm afraid I will turn into a monster and hurt her."

The Sanuri sat down on the edge of Jared's bed and stared into his eyes. "Jared you know everyone is born with free will. Many of the things you did in the past were because of your choices as a human. You made the choice to fight those demons and you did something no human has ever done before. You took a powerful object and escaped from hell."

"And you didn't consider keeping it for your own power; you immediately gave it to Simon. I'm going to let you in on a little secret. The demons can't control you if you refuse to let them. You don't have to be a mind reader to see that you are in love with Zoya. Love is a very powerful thing. If you want to have a happy life with that girl, you will."

"Thank you," Jared said with a sign of great relief. "Although I still can't understand why a beautiful young girl like that would want me."

"Jared I think you started changing the moment you met her. It takes a strong person to change the course of their life. I believe that Zoya is worth it."

"So I'm gonna live?"

"Yes but it will be a while before you have your old strength back."

"I know that I am like a specimen for everyone here," Jared said. "Yet, everyone has been so good to both Zoya and me, even though they fear I could turn into a demon."

"And I will be damned if I will let those demons sell me on an auction block. I guess what I am trying to say is I would like to help all of you with your mission. I understand you may not trust me but let me know what I can do."

"Jared the choice you just made will change your life for the better," the Sanuri said. "The people in this castle do not hate you; they feared for their children as any parents would. But after seeing what you have gone through to fight the demons instead of giving into them, well, I know you have gained the respect of many. We welcome your help."

"I just keep thinking about all the other poor bastards out there that are in the same boat I am and could be pulled into hell any minute."

"Jared do you understand the demons can't do that to you anymore. You battled your demons and won."

That evening over the dinner table, everyone at the home of Hannah and Gabriel shared the stories of all the events that had occurred while they were separated.

"I love having everyone together again," Natasha said. "Luca I really missed you and I am so happy that Raphael is moving in here."

"I truly appreciate the chambers you two prepared for me. I already feel very much at home," said Raphael.

"Natasha you are acting like this is our permanent home," Calen said. "As soon as I can travel that far we will be moving to the Ice Caves."

"Oh Calen, no don't misunderstand me," Natasha said. "It's just that we agreed to have a home in the Ice Caves and one in this world and Gabriel I have to admit I like your new home here much better than our castle. It just seems like more of a home. And Salar is a wonderful city to live near."

"Which brings up a subject that I was planning on talking with you two about later," Gabriel said. "You know Hannah and I plan to build living quarters for you here and at the castle."

"Do you feel up to working on some designs of what you want? Make it as big as you want, I am sure you will have a great deal of company."

"I appreciate that Gabriel," Calen said. "We will start working on them tomorrow."

"I think we should add a few more bedrooms for guests," Hannah said. "I really love having a house full of people."

Gabriel turned to Hannah, "I know you haven't seen our castle yet but I agree with Natasha. I love this home and with the work that Raphael and I are going to be doing for Sudfad. I believe we will be spending much more time here than I originally thought. I am thinking about having some of my things shipped here from the castle."

Hannah smiled and kissed Gabriel. "I love this home too and I am happy to stay here."

"Well, if you are going to do that, I am making a list of things," Natasha said. "All of my clothes and jewelry are at the castle and there are some things of our parents that I would like to have."

"Give me your list when you're done and I will have everything shipped here," Gabriel said. "Raphael you make a list too."

"That reminds me," Raphael said. "All of you left that hotel in Taperia so quickly that you left many things behind. A couple of my men are bringing them here."

"Are they still using that hotel as a hide out?" asked Gabriel.

"Yes, it works out well. From what they tell me, Sophie and one of the warlocks seem to be romantically involved. They are living together in her hotel room and they have often been seen going to a field outside of Taperia to practice spells," Raphael explained. "Sophie does not seem to have altered her behavior since Meekos left Taperia."

"She probably thinks he is coming back," Natasha said.

"Zoya said the spirits told her that Roch was released by the demon," Gabriel said. "Have your men seen any sign of him?"

"No but it is difficult for them to get onto the royal grounds. So I asked the Sanuri if we could have an entire flock of Enrops work with my men. He said he sent a flock out this afternoon. He also told the Enrops that we aren't really sure what Roch looks like right now."

"Gabriel, I know Calen, Koby, Dagon, Luca and Misha have been working with you for a long time," Elan said. "And now especially with Koby, Calen and Misha injured; I was wondering if I could volunteer to work with you."

"But you're just a baby," Luca said kiddingly to his cousin.

"I'm older than Natasha," Elan said with a grin.

"It's fine with me," Gabriel said. "As long as your cousins here approve."

"Elan will be good," Calen said with pride.

"Calen are you just saying that so you will have Elan around to babysit me?" Natasha joked. Calen looked at Natasha and grinned.

Archetenus took the job that Dieter offered him, not because he needed the money but because he felt it was better to keep his enemies close at hand. The first couple of weeks were actually boring for Archetenus. Dieter did not expect him to show up at a work location every day, he merely wanted Archetenus to be available if needed; which meant Dieter always had to know where Archetenus was.

Archetenus was sure that Dieter was having him watched, so he decided to turn the tables and started following Dieter. Fortunately for Archetenus he was considerably more skilled at covert surveillance than was Sabot, the man Dieter ordered to follow Archetenus. Dieter lived in Port Friada in a mansion on the shoreline of the Inlet of the Sea of Grevtd.

From Archetenus' observations, Dieter had no children but a beautiful wife who was half his age. Archetenus wondered why two people lived in a house that covered an entire city block.

The house was surrounded by a high fence and armed guards; it was the only mansion in Port Friada to have these extra security measures.

The first two weeks Archetenus followed Dieter to what appeared to be business meetings and luncheons; once he recognized Dieters routines, Archetenus turned his attention on the house. Dieter and his wife did not often have visitors and when they did the armed security guards checked each person before allowing them to enter the house. Archetenus' curiosity was peaked one morning when a large boca arrived at the mansion.

As soon as the guards allowed it through the gates, they changed their routine, by doubling the number of men who were standing guard. Two hours later the boca exited the gate to Dieter's house and slowly drove down the main business street of Port Friada. Archetenus followed the boca for several blocks before he saw it pull up in front of the Old Saddle Tavern. Archetenus got a good look at both the driver and passenger as they entered the tavern. He waited a few minutes before following them in.

That morning after breakfast, Simon, Raul, Lakin, Gabriel, Raphael, Luca, Calen and Misha joined the Sanuri and Sudfad in the King's study for the morning meeting. "I apologize that it is such a small room," Sudfad said, "But I wanted to ensure our privacy since the Sanuri will be telling us about that orb that Jared stole from hell."

"I did research all night without finding any information about the orb," the Sanuri said as he stood in front of the room of warriors. "I do not believe anyone has ever returned from a hell dimension with such an object, or any objects for that matter. So I called upon The Lion to give us guidance."

The Sanuri smiled broadly and continued, "It appears that Jared has brought us quite a gift. This is not just an orb, it is the Sundra Templer it is as old as time itself."

"It was once a gift from The Great Ruler to His children but it was stolen by dark lords many hundreds of years ago."

"It is a very powerful object that allowed the demons to pull Jared into their world."

"Are you saying it opens doors to different worlds?" Gabriel asked in amazement.

"Think of it more as breaking through walls," the Sanuri replied. "But the victim, such as Jared has to have an attachment to evil. For example a demon could not use this to pull one of us into hell. But it has other purposes also, which The Lion told me The Great Ruler blocked while it was in the possession of the demons. We have all heard stories about crystal balls showing people images; well this is the real thing. The images are not conjured by men but a gift from The Great Ruler."

"Have you seen images with it?" asked Simon.

"No," replied the Sanuri. "But The Lion said that it was returned to us at a time when we will need it most."

"So how do you see an image?" Raul asked.

"At this point I believe you simply pray for an answer and The Great Ruler can use this gift to give you the information that you need," the Sanuri said.

"So was Jared meant to bring that to us?" asked Raphael.

"That I do not know. But don't you think it a miracle that at a time of such darkness, one of the last men in this world that you would expect to help us; gives us so much information and in the journey redeems himself," the Sanuri said. "I spoke with Jared for a long time yesterday. He allowed me to look into his mind. He is not our enemy. But he is very afraid that he will turn into a monster. I explained to him that as long as he resists the demons they have no power over him."

The Sanuri continued, "Jared is in love with Zoya and wants to change his life and take care of her. He said that he would like to help us on our mission but he expects that most of you are afraid of him and do not trust him; and he believes you have every reason to feel this way."

"Jared's body has a great deal of healing to do, but I believe he will be very valuable to us. But understand that none of you are obligated to work with him," the Sanuri said.

"I'll be the first to say that I didn't want him in the castle," Simon said. "But what that guy went through fighting those demons, unless you were there I don't think I can even explain it. Guess I am trying to say, I would rather have him on our side and I have no problems working with him."

"I agree with Simon," Lakin said. "And from my experience with him, he has been honest, forthcoming and descent. Actually I would like to study him a little more before he moves out to his home with Zoya."

"I have been wondering about that," Sudfad said. "Once he leaves the castle will he and Zoya be in danger of retaliation by demons and dark lords? After all he seems to have destroyed some of Arhiman's plans to trap you, besides escaping his destiny. He certainly isn't in any shape to fight and Zoya isn't a warrior."

"They have risked a great deal to help us, I will help to keep them safe," the Sanuri said. "But this is something that I need to discuss with them."

"They will only be living a few miles from here, we can certainly have our men ride past their place on patrols," Raul said.

"I would like that," Sudfad said. "I think they both deserve a chance to start over, and I think Zoya's gift could be useful to us also."

"I have a question for the Sanuri," Lakin said. "When Jared was putting the crystals on the Mark of Satan that had been placed on the back of his neck, he was severing his cords to the darkness. He was in extreme pain and that creature came alive in him. For a few moments several of us heard screaming but it was not coming from anyone in the room. It was coming from hell. First of all how could we hear it and secondly, was that demons screaming or is Jared connected to the other men who were created like him?"

"I don't know the exact answers to those questions," the Sanuri said. "I would venture to guess that you heard demons screaming with rage. I think it is very possible that Jared is connected to the other men like him but whether it was their screams you heard I do not know. And as for how you could hear them, I will have to ask for guidance on that question."

Towards the end of the two hour meeting there was a hesitant knock on the door to Sudfad's study. Misha was seated closest to the door and opened it. Zoya hesitated when she saw all of the men in the room.

"Zoya please come in," the Sanuri said.

"I am so sorry to interrupt your meeting but I thought I should tell you some things," Zoya meekly walked into the room and towards the Sanuri; suddenly she turned and looked at each man in the room. Then she walked up to Misha and Calen who were seated near each other. "Please let me touch your hands, I am a seer, I will not hurt you." Both Calen and Misha smiled and extended their hands.

"I see you both looking down a hole at thousands of Hutas who are dancing and wearing war paint. There are two priests standing on a ledge above the Hutas. There are shadows appearing on the walls but they aren't the shadows of men but of demons. I don't know how the demons can appear as just shadows. Some of the shadows saw you but they did not try to stop you because something is happening. The priests are very frightened."

Zoya was silent for a few moments and stared past the two Ruala warriors as she tried to sort through what she was seeing. Zoya quickly turned around without letting go of Calen's and Misha's hands. "Sanuri, I am seeing through their eyes. They saw something important but I can't figure out what it is. Can you place your hands on my head, and maybe you will understand what I am seeing."

In the moments that it took for the Sanuri to reach Zoya; she looked at Calen and said, "You are going to have a baby and you were feeling sad that you might not see your wife and baby again." Calen stared at Zoya in astonishment.

"Everything you have said is true," Calen stammered.

As soon as the Sanuri placed his hands on Zoya's head she said, "If you can see the images in that cave; look in the same direction that the priests are looking. There is some type of movement on the walls of the cave. The Hutas don't seem to notice. There the movement happened again. Can you see it? I can feel such evil coming from that movement, even more than from the Hutas. Sanuri now do you see that? What is it?"

The Sanuri remained quiet for several moments, then he took his hands away from Zoya's head. "Calen's and Misha's brains recorded something they did not remember. Zoya what you saw was an opening between worlds. It was like a circular doorway that opened for a second, then closed and reopened. I believe there were demons from other worlds attempting to enter that cave but something seemed to be preventing them. Zoya tell me, how did you know to go up to Calen and Misha?"

"That is strange, usually when the spirits talk to me it is like I am surrounded by a group of children who are all talking at the same time and trying to get my attention. But as soon as I walked in here I heard one voice that told me to turn around and pointed these two men out. Wait there is something else," Zoya continued. "Now it is how the spirits usually talk to me." Zoya looked at Luca then at Lakin and back at Calen and Misha. "There is a connection between you more than your tribe, are you all brothers?"

"We're all cousins," Luca said.

"There's another here but he is younger. Do you have another cousin close by?"

"Elan is at Gabriel's house with our wives," Calen said.

"Was he the boy with Natasha when they discovered the tattoo on Jared?" Zoya asked.

"Yes," Lakin said.

"The spirits are saying that he desperately wants to prove himself to the four of you, he wants to join you in something. And he will put himself in a dangerous situation very soon."

Zoya paused and smiled. "Someone named Melinda said you have to watch out for him."

"Melinda was my grandmother," Misha said in awe. "How can the spirits know these things?"

"I don't know," Zoya said. "But I can tell you that the information I get usually comes true, especially when it is meant to protect someone. The voice of Melinda seemed urgent about the danger, so I would guess it is very close."

"If you will excuse me I am going home," Calen said and stood up. Misha and Luca also stood up and the three men walked towards the door. Luca turned around and asked. "Zoya when you first came in here was it to tell the Sanuri something else?"

"Oh yes," Zoya said. "The spirits have been quiet for days; that has never happened to me before. Normally it is like my head is so noisy with their voices that I have to ignore them. Then this morning they started to talk again. They said the demons are at war with each other. Ahriman was weakened and others are after his territory. Was that not the demon that was trying to trick you?"

Archetenus sat at a table near the bar so he could watch and listen to the two men who drove the boca. At that time of the morning, most of the patrons were eating breakfast; none of them were drunk and boisterous so conversations could easily be heard. One of the men slammed a handful of gold coins on the bar and ordered a bottle of whiskey.

"Jake could you believe the guards in that place?" one of the men asked. "You would have thought we were going to the King's castle."

"I'll tell ya, as itchy as some of those guys seemed, I wondered if we was gonna get out of there without a fight," Jake replied as he gulped down a glass of whiskey. "Makes ya wonder what the hell was in those crates."

"I wondered the same damn thing," the man replied. "And that one guy, did you see him? Nothing but tattoos, he kept looking at us like he wanted to tear our heads off. They pay well but I'm not so sure I want to take any more jobs for them."

Archetenus ordered breakfast so he wouldn't look conspicuous. He listened as the two men talked about their families, their job and women. As soon as Archetenus thought the two men were drunk, he joined them at the bar. "Can I buy you a drink fellas?" Archetenus asked. "I won big last night and feel like sharing the luck."

"No one can ever says I turns down a free drink," Jake said with a grin. "Thanks; didn't get ya name."

"Tyron and yours?" Archetenus was not going to reveal his true identity

"I's Jake and this here is Louie."

"So Jake and Louie what brings you to Port Friada?"

"We lives here," Jake said. "We work for Talverson Transportation Company. We just moved a load from the docks to some rich guy's house."

"We never seen nothing like it," Louie said. "There was a damn army at that place and high fences, looked like a prison."

"Yeah me and Louie was just glad to get out of there with our hides, those was a bunch of mean looking bastards."

"I felt sorry for that girl," Louie said as he poured himself another drink.

"A girl," Archetenus said nonchalantly.

"Yeah pretty little thing but she had bruises all over her face and arms, looked like someone beat the hell out of her. She was picking flowers when we drove in and one of those big guys made her go into the house."

"What did she look like?" Archetenus asked as he filled their glasses with whiskey.

"Young, I'm no good at guessing women's ages but I would say she was close to twenty years old. And long curly blonde hair. She was a looker even with all those bruises."

"So what did you say that cargo was?" Archetenus asked.

"Don't know," Jake said. Just a lot of big heavy crates and a couple of barrels. But these were big damn crates. Took more'n eight of those big fellas to move each one."

"And you said you picked the load up from the Mermaid?" asked Archetenus.

"No, no the Mermaid ain't even in dock, we got it from the Tygrus," Louie replied.

"Do you take deliveries there often?" asked Archetenus.

"Why're you so interested in that cargo?" Louie asked suspiciously.

"Just making conversation," Archetenus replied as he filled their glasses with whiskey.

"Where's Elan?" Calen asked as he, Misha and Luca entered the kitchen of Gabriel's house.

"He's upstairs helping Natasha pack," Hannah said. "Is something wrong? All of you look troubled?"

"No," Luca replied as the three men quickly walked up the stairs. Hannah followed them because she did not believe Luca's answer. When Calen opened the door to his and Natasha's chambers all three men started to laugh at the sight before them.

"I hope all of your children are girls," Elan kidded. "Look at all the baby clothes Natasha and Hannah bought." Piles of pink clothing were stacked on the floor, tables and chairs. "And not one thing has holes for the wings."

"We may have gotten a little carried away," Natasha said with a sweet smile as she walked up to Calen and kissed him.

"Elan thinks I should send some of the clothes ahead so your mother can adjust them. I never learned to sew." Luca walked over to one pile of clothing and picked up a little pink lace dress and showed Calen with a grin on his face.

"Don't laugh," Calen said. "You and Misha are going to be the godfathers." Then he turned back to Natasha. "I think Elan is right. Mother will love working on those things. But we are here because we need to talk to Elan for a moment in private."

"Is everything alright?" Natasha asked because of the tone of Calen's voice.

"Yes, it's just a family thing," Luca said.

"Well, be nice to him, he's been helping me a lot," said Natasha as she walked out of the chambers.

"What's going on?" Elan asked when he saw the serious looks on the faces of his cousins.

"We were at a meeting at the castle when Zoya joined us," Luca said. "You know she is a seer?"

"Yes, I have met her," said Elan.

"Well, she told Calen and me all kinds of things and every word she said was true," Misha said. "Then she said the spirits were talking to her about all of us and then she said Grandma Melinda was speaking to her."

"Elan, Zoya said that you want desperately to prove yourself to us and that you will put yourself in a dangerous situation soon. Melinda told us to protect you," Calen said. "Elan we tease you, just like we tease each other but you have nothing to prove to any of us. We know you are a courageous warrior. If I didn't think so, I wouldn't have asked you to watch over Natasha for me."

Elan stared at his cousins in disbelief. "I don't know what situation she is talking about but you are right. The three of you have fought in so many battles together and you have had so many adventures."

"And the work you do is so important, I want to be just like you; that is why I asked Gabriel if I could join the mission."

"Elan, you know us," Luca said. "If we didn't think you could work on the mission we would have told you and Gabriel. And we know you are intelligent but what we are concerned about is that you don't have the experience with these demons that we do. They are cunning and will trick you and ambush you every chance they get. We want you to always work with one of us until you are trained. Don't go off doing anything by yourself. Do you promise me?"

"I am really glad to hear that all of you have faith in me," Elan said sincerely. "I promise I won't do anything stupid." Then Elan smiled. "I think Natasha feels the same way, she has been teaching me about demons and dark lords."

"That's my girl," Calen said.

After Calen, Luca and Misha left the meeting, Sudfad and the others walked across the hallway to Jared's room. "Is something going on?" Jared asked when he saw the men and Zoya walk into his room.

"No," the Sanuri said. "We have a few things to discuss with you. That orb that you brought back from hell, turns out to be a powerful gift that The Great Ruler gave to His children hundreds of years ago. Dark lords stole it and thanks to you it has been recovered. The demons used the power of this object to pull you into hell, so you don't have to worry about that happening to you again."

"Well, that is a load off my mind," Jared said with relief.

"Also, we are concerned that the demons and dark lords may come after you once you leave the castle," said Sudfad.

"I've been thinking about that myself," Jared said with concern. "It's Zoya that I am worried about."

"Well we are worried about both of you," Sudfad continued. "Your place is only a few miles from here, so we are going to have our soldiers patrol by your land every day. If you have any concerns please tell them."

"And I will have Enrops and Hengers, watching over you," the Sanuri said.

"What are Hengers?" asked Zoya.

"They are ancient birds of war," the Sanuri explained. "They look like giant blue eagles."

Jared stared at the group of men for a moment before speaking. "Don't think that I am not grateful but I have a king, a holy man, three princes and two high priests in my room telling me they want to protect us. What is really going on?"

Gabriel smiled. "The Sanuri told us that you offered to work on our mission and we are going to take you up on that offer. This mission is dangerous and many of us have been personally attacked. Simon, my sister Natasha and I were all pulled into hell but our experiences were different from yours."

"If you are really willing to help us; you need to understand the dangers. Jared to our knowledge you are the first of the men created to be vessels that has changed his destiny. The demons may not want the others to know that is possible, so even if you change your mind to help us you might still be in danger."

Jared looked at Zoya then at the others before he spoke again. "I've been fighting my whole life and I thought the things I did, no matter how bad, were by my choice. Now I find out I have been manipulated and set up my entire life. Don't get me wrong I'm not saying I would have been a great man but the way I figure it I've got an axe to grind with those damn demons. And the little bit you all have told me about this mission it sounds like a lot of people could get hurt if we don't stop them. My only concern is Zoya. I will do whatever you need me to do but I want you to promise me that you will protect her and take care of her."

Simon stepped closer to the bed. "Jared, I believe I have spent more time with you than the others have. I hope you know I am a man of my word. I promise you that we will protect Zoya and take care of her."

"Do I get to say something?" Zoya asked as she gave Jared an angry look. "Jared I am proud of you for the way you have fought the demons and I am proud that you want to help them. But don't make it sound like a suicide mission because I don't want to lose you. Do you understand me? Please don't do anything foolish."

Jared smiled and held his hand out to Zoya. She walked closer to the bed and took his hand then turned to the others. "There is something I should tell you. I didn't understand what it meant until now. When Jared first walked into my shop, the spirits were all talking so much I could barely understand what they were saying."

"Jared sat down and I took both of his hands into mine. At that moment I could see that he was a dangerous man but I could also see that he was himself in great danger. I saw that he and I would take a journey together and a voice kept telling me that I had to find the Sanuri."

"Sometimes when the spirits talk to me I only understand or see pieces of the information. This much I told Jared." Zoya continued, "What I didn't tell him is that I saw images of men, including Jared that looked like they were all connected by long ropes. These images were floating in the air almost like they were dolls and most of the images appeared to be in great pain."

"Then I saw these men again and they were still connected but they were dressed for battle and riding black horses. There were great armies of them and they were all riding from the left of my vision and facing forward. Although I have seen this vision several times, until today I could not see what this army was riding towards."

"As Gabriel was speaking I saw that image again and this time I saw that army was riding to do battle with another army. This new army was vast also and it scares me to tell you that many of the faces in that army I have seen in this castle and in this room."

"There are both male and female warriors of different tribes and different races riding towards the army of demons but they ride as one. And a voice said they are led by the seven. I am sorry but I don't know what that means."

"We do," the Sanuri said. "Matthew has visions also and several years ago he had a similar vision. There is a prophesy as old as time that says there will be Seven Sons of Light that fight the armies of the night, of course there is much more to it than I have said."

"The voice is talking again," Zoya said. "It said the seventh son will come to you soon and you will know him when you see him and he will bear the scars from the demons."

The Sanuri smiled. "Gentlemen, there is a hidden message in what Zoya just told us. The Lion told me those exact same words some time ago. Zoya's gift has always frightened her greatly. But she prayed every night for The Great Ruler to find a good use for her gifts. I believe we were just told to listen to Zoya and to take her words seriously."

"Did you see anything that could tell you where or when this battle was taking place?" Raphael asked.

"No but your faces look like they do now." Zoya paused. "I am being shown another vision, which the voice says for you to remember. It looks like a prison, many men and women are in chains and the guards are creatures I have never seen before. I don't think this is in hell, for some reason I think it is in this world but there is something so strange. It is like a world within this world. A world that exists under water." Zoya suddenly jumped backwards. "The word *Juleta* was just thrust at me."

Chapter IX
Expectations

Three days later at the morning meeting of the ruling families of Lentz, an Enrop flew through an open window as Claudius was talking. "What is this?" Claudius asked as the giant bird landed in the middle of Mathas' desk. Mathas took the note that the bird was carrying in his beak. A solemn look consumed the King's face as he read the note from his brother-in-law King Sudfad.

"This is from Sudfad," Mathas said to Claudius, Fahron, Matthew, Stephan and Thaos. "Do you remember Matthew and me telling you about Zoya, the seer who brought a book to the Sanuri?"

"She was the friend of Jared," Matthew added.

"Well, she had a vision of a prison of sorts," Mathas explained. "There were humans chained and strange creatures guarding them. Zoya said it was not a hell dimension but a world within a world. A world that was under water. As Zoya was telling Sudfad and the others about this vision, she said a voice in her head said to tell them they must remember her words. Then Sudfad says that Zoya suddenly jumped back and said the word 'Juleta' was thrust at her."

Everyone in the room sat in silence for several moments before Mathas continued. "Matthew and I did not give credence to seers until we met Zoya. The Sanuri said she is very powerful, although you would not guess it because she is such a humble young girl. The Sanuri believes Zoya was sent to Sudfad's castle to help us."

"Father after the meeting I am going to write to Sudfad and tell him everything we know about King Douma and the Kingdom of Ogg. Perhaps Zoya or Gabriel or some of the others working with Sudfad can provide us with more information," Matthew said. "I know you keep telling me that I am acting overprotective because of the baby but I really have a bad feeling about all of this."

"Did either of you tell the Sanuri about any of this?" Claudius asked.

Matthew and his father looked at each other. "I didn't," Matthew said.

"Neither did I," Mathas stated. "I believe the Sanuri is still in Wetpr but in case he is travelling send a second letter to him."

"I think it is time to tell our wives everything about this," Stephan said. "After Ingr was attacked, I don't want to keep them in the dark about anything anymore."

"I agree," Claudius said. "Tonight why don't all of you bring your families to our home and we will discuss this over dinner."

"We should invite Sorren and Shara too," Matthew said.

"Of course, I will send a messenger right after the meeting," Claudius said.

"I think we should also send a message to Thedes," Thaos said. "Some of his tribe crossed the Waste Lands of Manod looking for refugees. These men have never been heard of since. If the Kingdom of Ogg is real, perhaps the Shettees are there."

"I hate to give him false hope," Stephan said. "But he did say that part of their coming of age rituals required the young boys to survive in the Waste Lands for days. And as tough as the Shettees are, you would think someone would have survived from that group."

"Matthew, in your letter ask Zoya to describe the creatures she saw in her vision," Mathas said. "And ask if she can describe any other details. We need all of the information that we can get."

The door to Jared's room opened and Zoya, Alexander and Laurel walked in. "Jared you are sitting in a chair," Zoya gasped.

"Yeah, Gabriel and Simon helped me," Jared said and smiled. "Hannah wants me to try just sitting up for periods of time for a couple of days then she wants me walking short distances."

Zoya threw her arms around Jared's neck and hugged him. "This is wonderful. You are improving much faster than I expected."

"Well you said we have a lot of work to do on our place," Jared said with a bright smile.

"Alexander may have most of it done by time you come home," Zoya said. "He fixed all the fences so we can put some animals in the pastures if you want."

"Alexander how will I repay you and Laurel for all you have done?" Jared asked sincerely.

"It's our pleasure and we are enjoying it," said Laurel.

"Jared, if you want any cows, horses or pigs let me know," Alexander said. "I can get you a fair price. Zoya said she would like to have at least one milking cow."

"Tell me what the pastures will reasonably hold," said Jared.

"There are two fenced pastures and a corral. The pastures are about five to ten acres each but there is plenty of room to expand them if you want. You don't have an area that is good for pigs but I can certainly build one for you," Alexander said.

"How much land is there for expanding?" asked Jared.

"I don't think anyone owns the land around your property for miles in each direction," Alexander said. "If you and Zoya plan to stay here, you should file a claim for the land that you want."

"I was thinking the same thing," Jared said. "Why don't you get a few milk cows for now. I am going to ask Hannah if maybe by the end of the week I can ride out there with you. I am looking forward to seeing the place."

"Did you draw this?" Gabriel asked as Calen handed him several sheets of paper.

"Yes," Calen replied.

"I must say you have a talent for building plans," Gabriel said as he looked over the blueprints that Calen drew of the wing that he and Natasha would live in.

"Now the question is, do you want the carpenters to start on this while you are still here to give them directions or do you want me to have it built while you are in the Ice Caves?"

"Actually I would like to start it now, if that is alright with you," Calen said. "It will probably be at least a couple of more weeks until I am strong enough to fly Natasha home." Calen paused. "I don't know if she has said anything to you or Hannah, but Natasha really wants both of you with us when the baby is born."

"And we would like that also," Gabriel said. "I do have to admit, I am still getting use to the idea that my little sister is married and now she is going to be a mother. It seems like yesterday she was a little girl with long braids."

"Gabriel, you were not only Natasha's brother but her mother and father also. In a way it is like your child is growing up. And Natasha loves Hannah but she has taken care of you for so long, it is also difficult for her to give that role up."

"I did wonder if there would be any conflict between Hannah and Natasha when we got married. Unless I have missed something they seem to be very close."

"Gabriel the two of them act like sisters and they are alike in so many ways that I am not sure if that is good or bad for us," Calen said and started to laugh.

Archetenus took great delight in evading the men that Dieter sent to follow him. To Archetenus it was becoming a game of cat and mouse. On this morning Archetenus was sneaking around the back of Dieter's house when he heard a door open. He hid in the shrubbery that was near a patio and watched Dieter's young wife walk into one of the gardens. The young woman was slender with long blonde curly hair that cascaded down the back of her light blue dress.

The young woman had her back to Archetenus as she picked a basket of flowers. Archetenus had seen this woman several times but always from a distance. His curiosity was getting the better of him as Archetenus carefully looked around the grounds for any sign of Dieter's men.

"Good morning My Lady," Archetenus said as he boldly walked up to her. The woman was startled and not only jumped but dropped her basket of flowers. "I am sorry I did not mean to scare you," Archetenus said as he knelt down to help her pick up the flowers.

"Thank you," the woman said shyly and smiled. Her dimples and bright blue eyes captivated Archetenus.

"Are you Dieter's wife?"

The woman glanced fearfully towards the house then whispered, "Yes. My husband doesn't like me talking to other men."

"But I work for your husband."

"It doesn't matter, he will still become angry," as the woman reached for some of the fallen flowers Archetenus saw dark bruises on her arm.

"Is that what Dieter does when he becomes angry?" The woman did not answer but pulled on the sleeve of her dress to cover the bruises. "What is your name?"

"Delilah," she replied and once again glanced fearfully towards the house. "You should go he will punish both of us if he sees us talking."

"Delilah do you need help?" Archetenus asked sincerely.

Delilah stared imploringly into Archetenus eyes and suddenly tears started to run down her cheeks. "I don't think anyone can help me," Delilah said in a hopeless whisper. As they were talking they finished picking up the flowers and returned them to the basket. Archetenus took Delilah's hand and they both stood up.

"Can you leave here?" Archetenus asked.

"I am allowed to go shopping but there are always guards."

"Can you go shopping this afternoon?"

"Yes but why are you asking?"

"Do the guards come into the store with you or stand out front?"

"They usually stand in front of the shop, why?"

"I would like to talk to you some more," Archetenus said as he still held her hand in his.

"You have no idea how evil Dieter is," Delilah said fearfully. "He will kill you."

"Give me the name of the store you will be at."

Delilah paused for a moment. Fear filled her being as she looked up at this handsome stranger who was boldly holding her hand. "Madame Bular's I will be there at two."

"I will see you then, My Lady," Archetenus said with a smile and turned to leave.

"What is your name?"

"I will tell you if you meet me," Archetenus said with a grin and disappeared into the shrubbery but he did not leave Dieter's property because he wanted to see what would happen when Delilah returned to the house.

Delilah walked into the kitchen to get a vase for the flowers. As she was arranging the flowers Dieter walked up behind her and put his arms around her waist and kissed her neck. "Dieter would it be alright if I went shopping today?" Delilah asked sweetly and turned so she could face him.

"That would be fine," Dieter replied. "In fact, stop at the tailor's and order me three more silk shirts."

"Is there anything else that you want?" Delilah was trying to be nonchalant but she was fearful that Dieter may have seen her talking to the man in the garden.

"You should get yourself a new ball gown," Dieter said as he caressed her hair. "Martin Froush and his wife are throwing a celebration because they just launched another ship."

"I thought you hated him."

"I do," Dieter replied. "But we have appearances to keep." He kissed Delilah on the cheek and walked out of the kitchen.

Delilah waited for a few minutes then walked to the parlor and watched as Dieter and his body guards got into a carriage. She suddenly felt like crying. She was filled with relief that Dieter had not seen her talking with that man. And Delilah was filled with fear as she had been every day since Dieter bought her.

Delilah's father owned one of the largest shipping yards in Port Friada; her marriage to Dieter was a business arrangement between Dieter and her father to increase their holdings. Delilah was horrified when she met Dieter, she found him repulsive and she cringed every time he touched her. Delilah had hoped that she would learn to love Dieter but his controlling nature and his fits of rage were destroying her.

Delilah felt like a shadow of a person; sometimes she would try to remember the last time she felt happy or unafraid. The memories of her life before her marriage to Dieter seemed distant and illusive. Sometimes Delilah felt like her memories belonged to someone else.

Delilah had come to know the sinister side of her husband. She suspected Dieter was a criminal and involved in horrible things but she had no idea that Dieter was a leader of the Insidiae and a dark lord. Delilah had no idea that her husband was sacrificing humans to demons in the chambers he had built beneath their mansion. Delilah had no idea that many of the men who Dieter had hired as body guards were intended vessels for demons to enter this world. And Delilah had no idea that Dieter was amassing an army of the damned.

"Luca can I speak with you for a moment?" Hannah asked as Luca and Calen were going to meet with the carpenters who were starting to work on the wing of the house that Calen designed.

Luca glanced at Calen then replied, "Yes."

Hannah turned and walked into the kitchen and Luca followed her, closing the door behind them. "Luca you have been acting so strangely. Are you mad at me? Have I done something to offend you? Because if I have I am very sorry."

Luca stared at Hannah. This was the moment that he dreaded. Gabriel was Luca's closest friend and Luca had been in love with Hannah from the moment he met her. When Luca realized that Hannah and Gabriel were falling in love with each other, Luca told Gabriel about his feelings for Hannah.

Gabriel knew that Luca was a man of integrity and would not act on his feelings. In fact Gabriel had asked Luca to care for Hannah in the event that Gabriel was killed during one of the missions. Luca's feelings for Hannah were detected by many of the men who stayed at Hannah's house in Nora, before the infamous battle between the Rualas and the Hutas. But Hannah, herself, was oblivious to Luca's feelings.

"Hannah you have done nothing wrong, why do you ask such a thing?"

"Because we used to spend so much time together in Nora and now that we are in Salar it seems like you are avoiding me. Please tell me what has changed. I miss our talks."

"Hannah you are imagining things. We have all just been busy."

"No Luca I am not imagining things. We are family and I don't want any bad feelings. Something is different. What has happened?"

Calen was well aware of his cousin's feelings for Hannah and was listening to their conversation through the kitchen door. "Luca are you coming?" Calen called out. "We are going to be late." Calen was trying to help Luca out of an uncomfortable situation.

"Hannah nothing is wrong and I have to go," Luca said and stepped forward and kissed Hannah on the cheek.

"Luca I am not stupid, something is wrong," Hannah said. "And now I feel worse because you won't even tell me."

"Hannah some things are better left unsaid," Luca said then turned and walked out of the kitchen.

Delilah felt extremely nervous as she entered the front door of Madam Bular's dress shop. Her two body guards took their positions in front of the store. Delilah always felt that Dieter's guards were meant to watch her more than to protect her and she resented their presence. Madam Bular greeted Delilah as she entered the store. "There is a handsome man waiting for you in the dressing room," Madam Bular whispered. "No one else is back there."

"This is not what it may look like," Delilah said with embarrassment.

"It doesn't look like anything to me my dear," Madam Bular said and smiled warmly. "That young man is really quite charming. I wish he was waiting for me."

"I don't even know his name," said Delilah.

"Well don't keep him waiting," Madam Bular said. "I will warn you if the guards come in."

Delilah walked into the back of the shop which was divided into three small changing areas that were separated by long, heavy drapes. Delilah found Archetenus sitting in the second changing area drinking coffee. She stood in the doorway, hesitant to enter.

"I mean you no harm, My Lady," Archetenus said as he stood up. "Come in and pull the curtain."

"I don't usually do this sort of thing," Delilah said fearfully as she pulled the drapes shut behind her.

"What sort of thing? We are merely going to talk," said Archetenus.

"I meant I don't meet strange men," Delilah said as she walked up to him.

"Why did you come then?"

"I don't know," Delilah said then she paused. "That is not true. I came because you offered to help me, when no one else has. But I am afraid to even hope because Dieter and his men seem to be everywhere."

"Why did you marry him?"

"I had no choice, my father gave me to him as part of a business arrangement," Delilah said sadly.

Archetenus smiled as he remembered Miranda's words. "A friend of mine once told me we always have a choice in every situation. Do you want to stay with him?"

"No," Delilah whispered.

"If I would help you to escape," Archetenus said as he moved closer to Delilah. "Where would you like to go?"

"I don't know," Delilah said with anguish. "All of my family is in Port Friada but I could never stay here."

"Do you know how to ride?"

"Of course," Delilah said with a hint of indignation. "I was not always a prisoner."

"We will have to plan this carefully. Think about where you would like me to take you."

Delilah gently put her hand on Archetenus' forearm. "My Lord, I still do not know your name or why you would risk your life to help me. What price must I pay for your services?"

"Delilah can I trust you not to speak of this to Dieter?"

"Yes, he would beat me severely if he knew I was even talking with you."

"My name is Archetenus. And I believe your husband is involved in something that must be stopped."

"I believe my husband is involved in many horrible things, although I don't know the details of his businesses."

139

"I would ask of you only information," Archetenus said.

Late that evening after Gabriel and Hannah made love, she lay in his arm and they talked about their day. "Calen said that Natasha wants us to be with them when the baby is born. How do you feel about a trip to the Ice Caves?" Gabriel asked.

"Gabriel, of course I want to be with her," Hannah replied as she propped herself up on one arm so she could look at Gabriel's face. "Besides she confided to me that she is a little scared of giving birth. Elan told her that that she and Marcia are the only human women to marry Ruala men. This is making her more anxious because their baby will essentially be starting a new race and she doesn't know what to expect."

"She hasn't said anything to me about that and I doubt if she has said anything to Calen either."

"I'm not surprised. First of all when was the last time Natasha admitted to you that she was afraid of anything?" Hannah asked. "And she doesn't want you and Calen to worry."

"I am going to mention it to Calen. He should know this." Hannah got a strange look on her face. "Don't you want me to say anything to Calen?" asked Gabriel.

"No it's not that. I just have been feeling guilty because I must have done something to upset Luca. I asked him today why he always avoids me now and he wouldn't even tell me. Gabriel he is one of your closest friends. Do you know what I did because I just feel awful about this?"

Gabriel started to stroke Hannah's hair but he did not answer her question. "You do know," she said. "Please tell me what I did so I can apologize."

"Hannah you didn't do anything wrong."

"That's what Luca said too but he is so cold to me now, I just don't understand it. We all have been living under the same roof for so long; it is uncomfortable to feel like someone is angry with me."

"Hannah do you really not know what is going on?"

Hannah now looked at Gabriel suspiciously. "No Gabriel I don't and I want you to tell me."

"Like me, Luca fell in love with you the first time he met you. He didn't pursue you because he saw that you and I had feelings for each other."

"What!" gasped Hannah. "And he told you this? Why he has never said anything to me."

"He did tell me. Luca is a man of great honor; he would never do anything to jeopardize our marriage."

"But he talked to me when we lived in Nora, why the change now?"

"Now he is in our home; perhaps that is making him feel uncomfortable."

"I should talk to him."

"And what would you say?" Gabriel asked sincerely.

Hannah paused again. "Gabriel I don't know. But he is Calen's cousin and your close friend. I don't want us to spend the rest of our lives with this uncomfortable silence. What do you think I should say?"

"Hannah I can't tell you what to say but I do agree that you two should probably talk."

"Calen knows doesn't he?"

"Honey, everyone that lived with us in Nora could tell, except for you."

"Natasha knows?"

"Yes."

"How could I have not seen this?" Hannah asked, then smiled. "I know the answer to that, because once I met you I only had eyes for you Gabriel."

Archetenus was lying on his bed in his hotel room. He was still fully clothed and was lying on his back staring at the ceiling.

"What are you thinking about?" Miranda asked as she suddenly appeared in his room.

Archetenus sat up and smiled. "I don't know how you do that, I was just thinking about you. I believe that Dieter is a member of the Insidiae and that he is building some type of chambers in the basement of his house. How can I stop him?"

"Why do you want to stop him?"

Archetenus was surprised by Miranda's question. "You showed me the plans that the Insidiae have for me and others. I don't want to be a vessel for a damn demon."

"So you have made that choice?"

"Yes."

"Good. I will say Archetenus I am proud of the choices you have been making. You stopped drinking and you have not gone back to the Ghost Ship Tavern. Why have you done these things?"

"Miranda you know me so well. I loved being the hero of Stordt. I guess I hadn't realized how much I had fallen until you showed me that image of me drunk when I killed those men. You said I could be a hero again."

"And Delilah has nothing to do with these changes?"

"I just met her."

"She looks at you as a hero but you have put her in even greater danger by asking her to spy on Dieter."

"Miranda when I help her escape I will have to leave Port Friada too but I want to stop Dieter first. What should I do?"

142

"You Archetenus should call upon me more often," Miranda said. "You are right about Dieter and he needs to be stopped. But I am telling you now you cannot stop him by yourself. You are a powerful man but Dieter has engaged forces beyond this world. If you truly want to stop him you will need my help and the help of The Great Ruler. Are you prepared to ask for this help?"

Archetenus stared at Miranda for a moment before he said, "Yes."

"Good, now let's talk about Delilah. She is in a very dangerous situation and you are the only glimmer of light in her dark prison. She looks at you the way you fantasized that Vitomas would when you kidnapped her from Roch. There are some great similarities between the situations between these two women." Archetenus remained silent. "Do you desire her?"

"She is very beautiful," Archetenus said. "Of course I desire her; why do you ask?"

"Because we have been talking about choices." Miranda said. "You wanted Vitomas to think of you as her hero but when she looked at you she saw the face of Roch and that angered you enough to murder her. Do you want Delilah to see the face of Dieter in you?"

"Of course not," Archetenus snapped.

"Archetenus the demons are still within you, it is your choice whether you continue to feed them and allow them to exist. I will not tell you if Delilah is the woman for you. But I will tell you that right now, you are her only hope and her life depends on the choices you make. Would you save her from Dieter only to kill her yourself?"

"I don't want to hurt her," Archetenus replied in a hoarse whisper.

"Then you have a great deal to think about and some important choices to make. Now back to Dieter. As you have guessed, many of the men that Dieter has hired as body guards are men like you, men created to be vessels. That should tell you that these men have above human strength and great evil within them. How do you think Dieter controls these savage men?"

"Is he a dark lord?"

"Yes and what does that tell you?"

Archetenus thought about this question for a few moments before answering. "Is his place protected by dark magics?"

"Yes and what else?"

"Is he having me watched by dark magics?"

"No, but you will have to be very careful."

"What about Delilah?"

"She has no idea that the monster she married is a dark lord, but she will not be surprised when she finds out. He is very cruel to her."

"Has he done anything to her with his magics?"

"Are you worried about her?"

"Yes, she is a sweet girl and so helpless."

Miranda smiled at Archetenus' words. "When you decide to stop feeding your demons, take off that necklace and crush it because it contains demon blood and helps the Insidiae to control you. We will talk again then."

"Miranda you will not leave," Archetenus yelled as he jumped up from the bed. He tore the necklace from his neck and crushed it with the heel of his boot. "We will talk now. You only come to me when something is important, why have you come this night?"

"There is another man as you; created from evil to be a vessel. He too was told his destiny. He made the decision to change his future. He literally battled demons and he won. He is the first of his kind to stand up to the demons and dark lords, like all darkness they don't want the rest of you to know you have choices."

"The dark ones will retaliate; Dieter has been calling many of your kind here to form an army. The dark ones will be taking more control of men like you. Make your choices now Archetenus for the hour is coming when they intend to drag you into hell."

Archetenus listened intently to Miranda's words. "Miranda am I supposed to stop Dieter or save Delilah?"

"If those are your choices you can do both and be a hero again but you will have to change your plans. If you leave Delilah in that house she will be killed before she can get the information you want."

"Miranda where can I take her that she will be safe?"

"How will you get her away from her guards and Dieter?"

"I haven't figured out a plan yet."

"Tell me Archetenus do you really want to save this girl from a dark lord?"

"You are insinuating that I should be asking you for help."

"You are finally listening to me. Archetenus you do not have the power to defy a dark lord as powerful as Dieter."

"Then will you help me?"

"Of course but I am going to test you also, since most of the time you make poor choices after our conversations."

"What do you mean?"

"Do you trust me?"

"I usually don't like what you tell me but I do trust you Miranda."

"Then you will have to prove it."

"How?"

"Because for once you will not be controlling the situation. Archetenus you will need to follow my lead; do you agree to do this? Do you think you can do this to save that girl?"

"Yes."

"Early tomorrow morning return to Madam Bular's shop. Ask her to go to Dieter's home and bring Delilah back to her shop. She will help you. For she too has seen the bruises on Delilah. Have two horses behind the store and packed for a trip. Take the girl to the monastery at Leven; she will be safe there until you return for her. You will be coming back to Port Friada."

"That sounds too easy. What about the guards that will be at the store and it is a two day ride to that monastery, won't they follow us?"

"This is your test Archetenus; you must have faith."

The next morning as they were all finishing breakfast, Hannah mustered up all of her courage and asked, "Luca can I speak in private with you for a moment?"

Luca looked at Gabriel then back at Hannah. "I really have a lot to do today."

"It will only take a moment, please."

"All right," Luca said reluctantly and stood up. Hannah and Luca walked into Gabriel's study and closed the door.

"What's going on?" whispered Natasha.

"She has been so upset about how Luca has been acting that I told her," Gabriel said.

"Do you think that was wise?" Lakin asked.

"Do you think she was going to stop asking?" Gabriel replied. "She cares for him and it upsets her that he won't talk to her anymore."

"What is she going to say to him?" asked Calen.

"I don't know. But she wants them both to feel comfortable living under the same roof."

"Well, I am glad she is going to talk to him," Natasha said. "Maybe he won't seem so sad anymore."

"Luca it has been killing me that you have been acting so upset around me," Hannah said soothingly. "So last night I made Gabriel tell me what is going on."

"He had no right to do that," Luca said angrily.

"Luca he knew I was not going to stop until I found out. Luca I never meant to hurt you, I really had no idea that you cared for me more than just a friend. I don't know how I, well, I really don't know what to say except that I care about you a great deal and I don't want us to feel uncomfortable around each other. Please tell me what I can do to make you feel better."

Luca grabbed Hannah and hugged her tightly. "I don't know, I'm not sure there is anything you can do that you aren't already," Luca said.

Hannah started to cry as she hugged him. "Luca I really treasure your friendship and I miss our talks. Can we go back to the way things were before we came to Salar?"

"Hannah the reason I have been avoiding you is that I didn't want you to figure out that I cared for you. Apparently everyone else was able to tell from the way I looked at you."

"Luca I don't understand; what did you think I was going to do, get mad?"

"I don't know," Luca said as he continued to hold Hannah in his arms. "I guess I thought you would stop talking to me."

"So you decided to stop talking to me first? That doesn't make any sense."

Luca laughed, "I guess it doesn't."

"So we can go back to being friends? Or is that too upsetting for you?"

"I have missed spending time with you too Hannah. Yes we can go back to being friends."

"Well promise me you will tell me if anything upsets you and don't do this to me again."

"I promise," Luca said. He was surprised at how relieved he felt that Hannah knew the truth although it wasn't going to change the situation.

Hannah and Luca walked back into the dining room with their arms around each other. Everyone had remained seated at the table and now watched Hannah and Luca as they returned to their seats. "We worked things out," Luca said. "Actually I am relieved that she knows." Hannah sat down next to Gabriel, who put his arm around her. Gabriel could see that Hannah had been crying.

"Well, we're all glad too," Calen said with a grin. "This has been hard on all of us."

"I have no idea what is going on here," Elan said with a confused look on his face.

"I'll tell you later," whispered Natasha.

"No, we can tell him now," Luca said. "I think keeping all these secrets has been hard on all of us." Luca turned to Elan. "Gabriel and I both fell in love with Hannah at the same time. And apparently you and Hannah are the only two who didn't know that."

"What!" yelled Elan.

Chapter X
Choices

"What is happening?" Delilah asked as she closed the curtains to one of the changing rooms in Madam Bular's shop.

Archetenus quickly walked up to Delilah and took her hand in both of his. "We are leaving now."

"Now!" She said. "But I haven't prepared anything. Where will we go?"

"Delilah I know you don't know me but you have to trust me on this. Some things will be happening that will make it even more dangerous for you to stay in that house. I will buy you what you need, but we have to leave now."

Delilah stared into Archetenus' eyes and felt that he was being sincere. "Alright," she whispered. Archetenus led Delilah out of the back of the shop and helped her onto one of his horses. They rode north through the back streets of Port Friada, both of them were filled with fear that Dieter's men would see them. Suddenly they heard a horn blow; the type of horn that was used by warriors who were calling for help.

"Just keep riding," Miranda's voice whispered into Archetenus' ear.

No sooner had Gabriel and his friends and family stood up from the breakfast table when an Enrop scratched on the window of the dining room. Bekka was the closest to the window and opened it allowing the bird to enter. The bird flew over to Raphael and handed him an envelope.

"The priests in Nora have located the mausoleum that Zoya told of. Hannah it was in a small private cemetery only five miles from your home," Raphael said. "Rueben is having his men watch the mausoleum until he hears from us. I must speak with the Sanuri at once."

"We will all go with you," Gabriel said then he looked at Hannah who was grabbing her shawl.

"I have a patient at the castle," Hannah responded when she saw the disapproving look on Gabriel's face. "I visit Jared every morning. Don't tell me we are going to fight already about your leaving."

"No," Gabriel said.

Natasha grabbed Calen's arm. "You better not be thinking about leaving me behind again. I want to go with you Calen. I won't do anything dangerous I will cook for you, I promise."

Calen put his arm around Natasha's shoulder and said with a grin, "Honey we can fight about this later."

Gabriel hitched up the boca and drove Hannah and Natasha to Sudfad's castle as the Ruala warriors flew ahead of them.

Unbeknown to Delilah, Dieter's men were forcing slaves to build additional caverns underneath their mansion. There were parts of the mansion that Dieter never allowed Delilah to go into and the basement was one such place. The caverns were so deep within the earth that Delilah never heard the commotion of the slaves breaking through stone walls; or their cries as Dieter's men beat them.

Dieter was getting dressed when Madam Bular arrived at the mansion earlier that morning. Madam Bular told Dieter that the material that Delilah had chosen for her gown for the ball had been damaged. Dieter was a man of great pride and insisted that Delilah be dressed in a manner befitting their standing in the community, so he did not protest when Delilah left to choose new material.

Dieter was humming to himself as he greased back his hair and opened one of his jewelry chests to choose his rings for the day. He did not hear the screams of his men or the slaves as they fought with hundreds of Rogetts that were storming the caverns. As the slaves broke through an area in the stone walls they unleashed a colony of Rogetts upon the mansion.

The Rogetts showed no mercy as they savagely attacked the slaves and Dieter's men. While some of the Rogetts stayed in the caverns to feast upon the dead and dying the majority of the colony stormed through all the underground chambers and climbed up the stairs into the mansion.

The master bedroom was on the second floor of the mansion. Dieter was choosing his cologne for the day when he heard a blood chilling scream. He grabbed his sword which was propped against the wall and ran into the hallway. Dieter hesitated at the horror before him. Everything that he could view of the first floor was drenched in blood. One of his men was fighting with four Rogetts that were tearing pieces of his face away and eating the man alive.

The powerful dark lord started to mumble an enchantment when he was knocked to the floor by three Rogetts that attacked him from behind. Dieter could feel their sharp fangs as they bit the back of his neck and his arms. Enraged the dark lord spat an ancient incantation of control to stop the Rogetts but his words of darkness had no effect on the monsters. Dieter quickly mumbled a second enchantment to make the Rogetts disappear, but this too had no effect on them.

Dieter quickly rolled onto his back, freeing his arms. The rage welled within him as he managed to push two of the Rogetts off from him by throwing the weight of his body to his right. Dieter quickly ran his sword through one of the demonic creatures. Then he threw himself against a wall in an effort to dislodge the Rogett that was clinging to his back. The maneuver worked but the Rogett was stunned only for a moment, Dieter quickly turned and plunged his sword into the Rogett.

As Dieter turned the third Rogett that had been circling Dieter and growling now jumped on his back. The creature sunk his teeth into Dieter's shoulder, as Dieter screamed in pain. Suddenly the Rogett stopped biting Dieter and fell to the floor, when Dieter turned he saw that one of his men had cut the throat of the creature. Dieter could hear the screams of his men, then he heard someone blow the Horn of Cornwall, to summon help.

"What is going on here?" Dieter demanded breathlessly.

"The place is overrun with these monsters," the man yelled as he ran back down the stairs towards the battle. Dieter picked his sword up from the floor and he too ran down the stairs. As Dieter ran he repeated several incantations but nothing happened. Fear gripped his heart. Dieter was more afraid of losing his powers than he was of fighting an army of Rogetts.

Archetenus and Delilah did not speak as they rode through Port Friada. As soon as they were north of the city Archetenus headed to the western tributary of the River Toba. They rode across a bridge and once they were on the eastern side of the river, they rode their horses in the shallow water along the shore line to hide their trail. They rode north for almost three miles before Delilah spoke.

"I can't believe this is really happening," she gasped. "Archetenus please tell me that I am not dreaming."

"Oh you aren't dreaming My Lady," Archetenus replied as he looked behind them to see if they were being followed.

"Please call me Delilah." He did not speak. "You are worried that we will be followed," she said as she too looked behind them.

"Yes, Dieter is not a stupid man and from what you said he has a small army at his command."

"Archetenus whatever happens to us I, well, I have to tell you. No one has ever dared to defy Dieter before. You are the bravest man I know." Archetenus was riding ahead of Delilah and he now turned and looked at her.

"If they catch us we will both be killed," he said as he was not sure Delilah understood the seriousness of their situation.

"I died the day that monster took me as his wife. You are setting me free and if it is for but a short time, it is freedom. Archetenus if they come upon us, you go save yourself, I would rather be killed then to return to that life. I don't want you to suffer because of me."

"Delilah I'm not leaving you behind."

"Where are we going?"

"I am taking you to the monastery at Leven," Archetenus replied. "You will be safe there."

"You are leaving me alone?" Delilah gasped. "Why?"

Archetenus again turned and looked at Delilah who was riding behind him, as the tone of her voice surprised him. "I will come back for you. I have some things I must do."

"You are going to try and stop Dieter aren't you? Archetenus you will be killed. Please stay with me. I have never traveled alone and, I don't know where I will go. Please don't leave me. I will find a way to pay you for your help."

"I will be fine and I will come back for you," Archetenus said as he could hear the fear in her voice. "I promised that I would take you wherever you wanted to live. And I will, you do not have to pay me."

Delilah was quiet for a few moments before she spoke again, "Archetenus why are you risking your life to help me?"

Archetenus turned and looked at her again and smiled, "What can I say you are a beautiful woman who needed help."

"Then you are not only brave, you are the most gallant man I have ever met," Delilah said sincerely. "Even more reason why you should not be hurt because of me."

Archetenus slowed down his horse so that Delilah could catch up and ride along side of him. "Delilah this is all very hard to explain but when I saw you I was spying on your home. The business I have to take care of is separate from me helping you. I really can't give you details I am just asking you to trust me."

Delilah looked into Archetenus' eyes. "I do trust you, although I don't know why I would trust a strange man who I just met. There is something about you; oh I don't know how to explain it. I hope you don't think that I am the kind of girl who would run off with just any man."

Archetenus laughed loudly, "I don't think that at all. Delilah I am no threat to you, I simply want to help you."

"And is that what you do Archetenus, you travel the world helping women in distress?" Delilah asked teasingly as she tried to find out more about her traveling companion.

"I wish I could say yes," Archetenus said with a laugh.

"Then why me?"

"You aren't going to let up until I tell you that you are one of the most beautiful women I have ever seen, are you?" he asked grinning.

Delilah blushed, "I wasn't trying to get compliments; I am just trying to get to know the man I am running off with."

Archetenus looked at Delilah and for the first time realized that she might be afraid of him and what she was doing. "Delilah, I wish I had better answers for you. Yesterday when I saw you and started to talk to you, I don't know; I just wanted to protect you. I can't explain it better than that."

"Then you really are my hero," she said with a smile.

Hannah and Natasha were in Jared's room helping him to walk. "I hope you ladies know that if I fall neither of you will be able to pull me up," he said with a chuckle.

"I think we are just helping you balance for now," Hannah teased. "And besides Jared don't underestimate us."

"Simon told me that both you girls are demon hunters. I don't underestimate anything you can do," Jared said and laughed. "Do you know why Gabriel asked Zoya to join their meeting?"

"Zoya says that the spirit of Hannah's mother has been giving her information and showing her visions," Natasha explained. "There was a mausoleum that Zoya saw in her visions and we just received word that some of the Patronus found it. Hannah's mother said it was the doorway to a very dangerous place, so I assume they are asking for more information."

"You know a year ago I would have thought someone was crazy if they talked about ghosts and demons," Jared said. "Now it is all we talk about."

"Oh Jared," Hannah teased. "Don't you and Zoya talk about your home and your future?"

"Actually we haven't talked much about our future, except that we are going to live together. I want to ask her to marry me but I don't want to do it while I am a cripple. Hannah I am really anxious to see the house. Alexander said he would drive me out in a boca. What do you say? When can I go?"

As they talked they had walked several laps around the bedroom. "Why don't you sit in this chair," Hannah suggested. After Jared was seated Hannah stood so she could look into his eyes. "Jared the new life you have is greatly motivating you to heal. I believe you can take a ride out there anytime. But listen to your body. If you feel weak or dizzy, sit down. You aren't going to be any good to Zoya if you have a relapse. And speaking of Zoya, if you want to marry her I think you should ask her now." Hannah looked at Natasha and asked, "What do you think?"

"Jared, Zoya loves you; trust me it won't matter to her what condition you are in when you ask her. What will matter is that you asked her," Natasha said.

"I don't have a ring yet," said Jared.

"I really doubt if that matters," Hannah said warmly.

"Send Rueben a message and tell him I don't want anyone going into that mausoleum or even near it until I get there," the Sanuri said to Raphael. "We have been getting messages about thirteen doors, thirteen levels for a long time. This may be a trap; either a trap for those of us who enter the mausoleum or it may be a distraction to get us to leave other areas vulnerable. I believe we should think this through before we all run to Nora."

"When Gabriel, Natasha and I had our visions of hell, we saw the number thirteen everywhere," Simon said. "And we believed it was Ahriman who was taunting us. And Sanuri it seemed that it was you, who he really wanted to trap."

"Ahriman's power has been greatly weakened and he is being attacked on many fronts, he is fighting for his power and his existence," the Sanuri said. "I think there is much more to this than one demon's quest for power. I want to confer with The Lion before we make any decisions. There is something about this situation which bothers me greatly."

"In the meantime the rest of us will strategize this as if it was a pending battle," Raul said. "Why don't we all move to the Great Hall where we will have more room."

"I think we should have Natasha and Hannah join us," Gabriel said.

"Perhaps Jared might have some insight," Simon suggested.

"Zoya you have been so quiet," Sudfad said. "Yet you have such a quizzical look on your face."

"None of the spirits have been talking to me while you were discussing this matter, and you have to understand that the spirits are always talking to me. Have you ever walked into a room filled with children and they all run up to you and try to get your attention at the same time. That is how the spirits act when they know someone can hear them."

"Are you saying the spirits are listening to our conversation?" asked Raphael.

"I really don't know if they can hear you talk but the fact that they aren't talking to me is curious. And the entire time you have been discussing this mausoleum I have been seeing a strange image. I see hundreds of pieces that look like they are part of a puzzle and I see hands trying to put the pieces together but they aren't being very successful," Zoya said.

Delilah found herself stealing glances of Archetenus as they rode away from Port Friada. He was the most handsome man she had ever met. She liked his powerful and muscular build, so unlike that of Dieter. Delilah blushed as she realized she was admiring Archetenus' body. She felt passions stirring within her, something she had never felt with Dieter.

Suddenly Delilah realized that Archetenus was watching her looking at him and she blushed. Archetenus laughed. "Should I ask what you were thinking?"

"No," Delilah said as she was filled with embarrassment. "I am sorry it was rude of me to stare."

"That's alright," Archetenus said with a grin. "I like it when beautiful women look at me the way you just did."

Delilah was both embarrassed and annoyed by Archetenus' statement. "Well, I am sure that a man as handsome as you are is used to women staring at him," she said with an edge to her voice.

"Delilah are you mad?" he asked with a large grin.

"No, why would I be mad?"

Archetenus laughed loudly, "Jealous then?"

"Jealous," Delilah repeated incredulously. "I don't know you well enough to be jealous. You are certainly full of yourself."

"Well, your voice changed when we talked about other women," Archetenus said as he continued to laugh.

"Well, I don't know what to say about that," Delilah said in a huff. She did not speak for several minutes, then she said, "I don't think my voice changed." Archetenus roared with laughter.

Four hours after the attack began; Dieter's men had rounded up the remaining Rogetts and herded them into one of the underground caverns. Dieter ordered his men to douse the Rogetts with oil and to set them on fire. The screams were deafening as Dieter watched the Rogetts burned alive.

Dieter had every physician in Port Friada brought to his mansion to care for his wounded men. Forty of Dieter's men had been killed and many were wounded or still unaccounted for. Of the dead, twenty one of the men had been created as vessels for demons.

Dieter's men had stopped the vicious Rogetts from entering the City of Port Friada. But the story of the battle at Dieter's mansion created fear and panic within the city.

Dieter was a suspicious and paranoid man. He might have considered the attack by the Rogetts a matter of fate had his magics not been useless against the monsters. He knew he had many enemies among demons and dark lords as well as humans. A man like Dieter did not gain power without making enemies. As the chaos slowly subsided, he sent messages to other members of the Insidiae, ordering them to his house to discuss the attack. It was not until late afternoon that Dieter realized Delilah and both of her guards were missing.

"We're making camp now," Archetenus announced. "Because we can't take a chance of a fire giving away our location once it gets dark."

Delilah was exhausted; they had been riding all day with little rest. It was late afternoon and Archetenus chose a secluded location east of the river. "Do you know how to cook?" Archetenus asked as he helped Delilah down from her horse.

"Yes," she replied wearily.

Archetenus set two sets of saddlebags on the ground. "There are supplies in there," he said. "I will take care of the horses and gather wood." Within the hour they were sitting before a fire eating biscuits, beans and fried bacon. "It's nothing fancy," Archetenus said. "I didn't have a lot of time to get things."

"This is just fine," said Delilah. "I am just so grateful for what you are doing that everything seems wonderful."

"So have you given any thought to where you want to live?"

"I really haven't been to many places outside of Port Friada," Delilah said shyly. "Maybe you could help me think of a place."

"I don't think you would want to live in most of the places I have been," Archetenus replied. When he saw the look on Delilah's face he added, "Sure I will help you find something."

"Archetenus what was that horn that we heard blowing when we were leaving Port Friada?"

"Horns like that are usually used by soldiers to signal that they are under attack and need help. I did wonder if it was Dieter's men sounding the horn because you were missing."

"I don't think so," she said. "I have never heard his men use something like that." Delilah paused for a moment. "You know I still don't really understand why you are helping me and I don't know how I am ever going to repay you."

Archetenus stared at Delilah as many different thoughts rushed through his mind. There was a time when he would have said she could pay him back with sex. But as Archetenus stared at Delilah his thoughts were filled with how beautiful and vulnerable she was. Archetenus fought the urge to grab her and kiss her.

"Now who is staring? What were you thinking?"

"You don't want to know," he said with a grin. "And you don't owe me anything."

"What do you mean I don't want to know?" she asked her question with such seriousness that Archetenus wasn't sure if she was naïve or being coy.

"Delilah how long were you with Dieter?"

"It's been almost two years since my father sold me to him," Delilah said sadly. "And I still can't believe that Papa would do such a horrible thing."

"Perhaps he thought you would be happy," Archetenus said trying to cheer her up.

"No, it was part of a business agreement, Papa made a great deal of money."

"Did you have any suitors before Dieter?"

"How come you can ask me questions but you won't answer mine?"

"Ok, I will answer yours after you answer my question."

"There were some boys, nothing serious. I was more serious about my studies. Why do you ask?"

"Because you've said a couple of things today that I didn't know how to take. I wasn't sure if you were being flirtatious or if you are just too innocent to know what you are saying. I've decided you are innocent."

"I'm not stupid," Delilah said angrily.

"I never said you were, there is nothing wrong with being innocent." Delilah stared at Archetenus angrily. "Do you even know what it is you said?" he asked.

Delilah looked down at the ground. "No," she said with a pout.

"If I tell you don't get mad at me, alright?"

"Tell me," she said.

"When a woman, especially as beautiful as you are says things like 'I don't know how I would ever pay you back.' Well the first thing a man thinks is you can pay him back with your body. You might want to be careful how you say some things." Delilah stared at Archetenus but did not speak. "You don't owe me anything."

"And what does that mean?" Delilah asked softly. "That you don't want to sleep with me? Do you have a wife?"

Archetenus was shocked at the directness of Delilah's question. "I don't have a wife or a girl for that matter. If you have to know I haven't even been with a woman for a while."

"But you wouldn't want to be with me?"

"Delilah I have been fighting the urge to kiss you ever since I met you. Of course I want to make love to you. But I am trying to tell you that you don't owe me anything for helping you."

"You are so different from anyone I have ever met," Delilah said and stood up. She looked at Archetenus for a moment then walked over to him and sat down very close to him. "When you caught me staring at you this morning I was thinking about kissing you."

Archetenus put both of his massive arms around Delilah and pulled her close to him. He kissed her on the lips, gently at first. A kiss that she passionately reciprocated. They kissed hungrily, devouring each other for several moments as the sweat poured down Archetenus' body. He momentarily broke their embrace. "Delilah I hope you want to make love."

"I do," she whispered into his ear and stretched up and kissed Archetenus on the lips.

Archetenus took her arms from around his neck and said, "I'm going to lay out the blankets." He quickly grabbed the bedrolls and laid their blankets on the ground near the campfire. When he turned around, he saw Delilah standing behind him wearing only a thin pale pink slip which clung to her body. She took two steps towards Archetenus and he gently lifted the slip over her head.

Archetenus took a deep breath and said, "You are even more beautiful naked." He pulled Delilah tightly against him and kissed her hard on the lips. She started to unbutton his shirt and opened it, then she gently kissed his chest. Archetenus tore his shirt off, then his boots and pants. He picked Delilah up and she wrapped her legs around him.

That night after dinner Gabriel and all his family and guests sat around the dining room table and discussed the day's events. After their morning meeting that day, Raul led another meeting in the Great Hall of the castle. Hannah, Natasha, Jared and Zoya joined the men as they strategized the possible situations that could arise if they went to the mausoleum in Nora. The Sanuri had reminded the group that many of them were considered prizes for the demons and dark lords so traps could be set for any of them.

"Remember in Simon's experience with the demon snake," Lakin reiterated, "The Lion asked him if we were willing to do battle with the demons, then he said thirteen doors, thirteen levels. I think we should view this as preparing for a major battle and we should have adequate troops available."

"I agree with Lakin," Raphael said. "But I also feel that there is a high probability that this is a distraction. Sudfad and his family are likely targets as is Gabriel's family, and any of the locations of the Patronus."

"This also could be a ruse to keep us distracted while they try to raise a demon," Calen suggested.

"I found it curious that the maps that Jared stole from Pravis and Tenebrae did not have the location of the mausoleum on them," Gabriel said. "That in itself makes me think this is a trap."

"But didn't Endleson tell you that many factions of the Insidiae work independently of each other and in secret?" Luca asked. "Endleson and other members of the Insidiae didn't want Pravis and Tenebrae to raise Omnibus or unleash the Huta army. It is likely they were keeping many secrets from those crazy priests."

"Tomorrow morning when we meet I am going to suggest to the Sanuri that we send Ruala warriors ahead to watch the area," Lakin stated. "Our warriors can see so much more than the men on the ground."

Before Lakin finished speaking Elan, Bekka, Fala, Joao and Dack all stood up from the table as a sign that they wanted to volunteer for the mission. Luca, Calen, Misha and Lakin were all seasoned warriors and laughed at the enthusiasm of the young Rualas. "I will lead the mission," Luca said. "Calen and Misha are still healing from their injuries and you Lakin are needed here with Sudfad."

"I agree," Lakin replied but I am not sending the six of you out there. I will send for more warriors."

"We'll I don't agree," Calen said. "Misha and I are mending nicely."

"Calen you aren't even strong enough to fly your wife home," Luca said. "You two need to stay here."

"See how you like it," Natasha said sarcastically to Calen.

"And that brings up another point," Misha said. "Now Natasha don't start yelling at me," he said with a grin. "Perhaps we should fly Natasha and Hannah to the Ice Caves if we are concerned there may be an attack here."

"Misha!" Natasha said angrily.

"Honey look at you," Misha said sweetly. "You are bigger than Annabelle and she is at least a month farther along than you. You are carrying the first Ruala and human baby of our tribe; we don't really know what to expect. There isn't a person at this table who doesn't respect you for being a powerful warrior but things are different now and you have to accept that."

Natasha did not speak but stared at Misha angrily. "Now why do you yell at me when I say the same things?" Calen joked.

"Natasha I know this is going to make you mad but Misha does have a point," Hannah said. "But I don't understand why I have to go."

"Are you going to let Natasha go through all of this by herself?" Misha asked. "She's moving to a new world where she really doesn't know anyone and she is having her first baby. Natasha may not admit it but she needs you Hannah. Hopefully we will all live long lives and participate in many battles but the reality of it is that sometimes we have to sit one out. Besides the two of you are so damn smart and cunning I am sure you will find some other ways to help the mission."

Both Hannah and Natasha sat in silence. Calen and Gabriel looked at their wives then at each other and grinned. "Misha when Gabriel and I say these same things the girls yell and fight with us, when you say them they listen. From now on you are in-charge of talking to our wives," Calen said then laughed heartedly.

"Good Morning," Delilah said with a warm smile when she opened her eyes and saw Archetenus watching her. He leaned down and kissed her on the lips. Neither Archetenus nor Delilah had gotten much sleep as their passions had taken control. And now with the first light of dawn, Archetenus again lowered his body onto Delilah.

The fears had fallen away during the night as Delilah was consumed with feelings of love for Archetenus, feelings she was unaccustomed to. And Archetenus too, was consumed with feelings and thoughts that were both overwhelming and conflicting. He was well aware that his experiences with Delilah were almost identical to the fantasies he had for so many years about Vitomas. Archetenus did not believe in coincidences and fear surged through him that this relationship was not real.

After an hour, Delilah lay in Archetenus' arm as the two young lovers were catching their breath. "Archetenus please don't go back to Port Friada, you will be killed and I don't want to lose you."

"I have to go back for a while," he said and kissed Delilah on the forehead. "But I will be fine and I promise I will come back for you." Tears started to run down her cheeks. Archetenus stared at her then wiped away her tears. He could not remember the last time someone cried because they cared about him.

Dieter's men finally located the bodies of the two guards who were with Delilah the morning of her escape. When they heard the horn of Cornwell, both men had run to the grounds of the mansion and were attacked by groups of Rogetts. Both bodies were greatly mutilated. Dieter himself went to talk with Madam Bular who lied and told him that Delilah had left her shop to return to the mansion with the two guards. Dieter was enraged. He regarded Delilah as one of his valuable possessions and he did not like to lose things.

"I'm so excited," Zoya said as she helped Jared to get dressed. "I do hope you like the place; we have put so much work in it."

When Zoya got excited she spoke very fast; Jared laughed at how fast she was now talking. It made him happy that Zoya was so excited for him to see their new home.

There was a knock on the door then Alexander and Simon walked into Jared's room. "Simon is coming with us so he can help if you have difficulty walking," Alexander said.

"I really appreciate what you both have done for me," Jared said sincerely. "I know I keep saying it but I don't know how I will repay you. You see I'm not really used to people helping me out."

"Don't worry, we are going to put you to work when you're up to it," said Simon as he and Alexander helped Jared to a standing position. "We're taking two bocas," Simon continued. "Annabelle and Laurel are coming too and they said Marie has packed some treats for all of us."

"Oh this is going to be so much fun," said Zoya.

Jared was so excited to leave the confines of his bedroom that he tried to walk quickly down the hallway and out the door. He stopped and looked up at the sun for several moments, enjoying the warmth. He never before thought he would miss the sun. Alexander and Simon helped Jared down the many steps into the courtyard and into the first boca.

"How are you doing?" asked Alexander.

"That took a little more out of me than I expected," Jared said. "But I can't tell you how good it feels to be in fresh air and to feel the sun again. Guess I kind of took those things for granted."

Alexander drove the first boca and Simon drove the second. Zoya's and Jared's excitement was contagious and the entire group was happy and joking as they drove the short distance to the small farm.

"Let me just sit here a minute and take this all in," Jared said as he was overwhelmed with feelings.

Everything that Jared looked at was in perfect shape. There was a covered front porch to the house which was decorated with furniture and plants. There was a newly painted chicken house and dozens of chickens running around. The barn too, looked as if it had just been painted and there were Jared's two horses in the attached corral. Laurel, Zoya and Gala had planted two large flower gardens in the front of the house.

"The smoke house and vegetable garden are behind the house," Alexander said. "But while we have you in the boca I am going to drive behind the barn and show you the pastures." There were four milk cows in one of the fenced pastures. Jared sat quietly as Alexander drove him behind the farm house so he could see the huge vegetable garden and the smokehouse. "That smoke house is full of meat," Alexander said and smiled as he saw the look of awe on Jared's face.

Alexander stopped the boca in front of the house and Simon and Alexander helped Jared out of the boca. "So what do you think?" Simon asked.

"I really can't believe this," Jared said. "It's beautiful and you must have done so much work."

"Wait until you see the inside," Zoya said with excitement and the group walked into the little house.

There were curtains on the windows and rugs on the floors. Every room was furnished and the walls were decorated with pictures and mirrors. There were bouquets of flowers in every room.

"Jared you're so quiet," Zoya said with concern. "Don't you like it?"

"I like it very much," he said. "I just didn't expect all of this. It's, I mean look at all the work you put into this place. It looks like we've lived here for years." Zoya hugged him.

"Why don't you boys come over here," Laurel said as she and Annabelle were setting the table with the food that Marie had sent along.

"I just don't know what to say," Jared said as he took a seat at the table.

"The barn is pretty empty," Alexander said. "You are going to have to stock up on hay. I don't know if Zoya has said anything to you yet but she would like some sheep and I can help you build an area for pigs if you want. And if you are feeling up to it after we eat, Simon and I can show you some of the land that surrounds your farm if you want to put a claim to it. Of course it would be better if we were on horseback."

Jared stared at the people who were seated at the table eating cold fried chicken and potato salad. "I know I'm not saying much, it's never been my way to gush about things. But don't think I don't really appreciate all that you have done. All of you live as a family. Me, well, I've been on my own for a long time. A hired fighter can't afford to make a lot of friends, besides I was moving around all of the time. So all of this is new to me. I guess I've been, well, I guess what I am trying to say is I forgot how kind people can be."

Chapter XI
Discoveries

For weeks Roch lived the life of an animal. He slept near the small pond that was fed by a waterfall. He ate insects, plants anything he could grasp and he hid in the underbrush from predators. Slowly, very slowly Roch's memories were returning to him. As he gained control of his mind, he increased his control over his body. And as he gained control over his mind he cursed all that existed for the pain and agony he was experiencing.

Nightly Roch was plagued by nightmares but these were no longer the nightmares of holy messengers sending him warnings or dark lords enticing him. Now his nightmares were flashbacks of his time in Ahriman's hell dimension. Roch had been tortured for his deeds, Roch had been tortured because he was a vessel for Ahriman's rival Omnibus and Roch had been tortured for Ahriman's amusement.

A weaker man may have crumbled from these experiences. A holier man may have learned lessons or decided to change his behavior. But Roch, the man created by dark lords, the human version of a demon became darker and more hateful. Roch had an incredibly strong will to survive. He had always been a resourceful and self-reliant individual and his personality did not change as he was enduring the tortures of hell.

After what seemed like years of torture to Roch, Ahriman Lord of the Demons gave him a choice. Roch could become the demon and torture others or he could continue to be the victim. Without hesitation Roch made his choice. Ahriman had laughed and called Roch 'soulless' as Roch inflicted great pain and torment on the others in the hell dimension. For Roch's cruelty and mercilessness, Ahriman rewarded him by returning Roch to the World of Nunc.

But Roch thought he would be returned in his former body, vital and strong. Roch did not understand the transformations he was undergoing. As he endured the weakness and pain, Roch plotted against Ahriman, the demon that had tortured and betrayed him.

"I am moving to Ryed," Sophie said boldly. "And I want out of the Insidiae."

"It's not that easy," Malik said. "And please keep your voice down Sophie; I don't want the customers to hear." Sophie was meeting with Malik in his office at the bank he owned in Taperia.

"Malik, I sacrificed my life for the Insidiae. I lived in that deplorable castle with Roch for years, while the rest of you enjoyed your lives and riches," Sophie said. "Now Meekos is gone, so I have lost my family to the mission. Malik all I want is a chance to enjoy the things that you and the others have enjoyed for years."

"What will it cost to get her out of this?" Erebus asked.

Malik sat back in his chair, stroking his large handlebar mustache and stared at Sophie and Erebus. "Sophie what you say is true. You have sacrificed much more than the rest of us and you have always been a loyal member of the group. But because of this you are also extremely useful to us. Let's do this, you and Erebus move to Ryed and have a happy life together. But you remain a member of the Insidiae."

"But Malik," Sophie said loudly. She did not finish her sentence because Malik held up his hand to silence her.

"Sophie I was not finished. All the members of the Insidiae enjoy life, they take vacations; you get my point. I will tell the others that you are on a well-deserved vacation for a very long time. There may be times when we contact you for help; you do not have to accept assignments."

"Can't she just get out?" Erebus asked with frustration

"Erebus, I am trying to keep Sophie alive. Once the blood oath is taken, no one is allowed to leave the Insidiae. But we have many members who have done little in our organization. Sophie deserves to reap the benefits. I can sell this to the others without raising suspicion."

"Erebus, Malik is right," Sophie said.

"Sophie you and I have had our moments but know that I have always respected you and the work you do. But once you move to Ryed you are outside of my jurisdiction of protection. Cedrick Teivel rules that area and he may not be as accommodating as me. Erebus I know you have a home there but you might want to consider living someplace else."

"What is he talking about?" Erebus asked Sophie.

"Like any organization the continents are divided into regions, and every region has a Master who rules it. The regional masters are very powerful and they answer only to the Grand Masters of the Insidiae. Malik is the ruler of this region, which is the Kingdom of Stordt and Teivel rules the Kingdom of Ryed and a small portion of western Wetpr. The Insidiae is a highly organized and regimented organization."

"You said other continents?" Erebus asked.

"Well yes, the Insidiae exist in the entire world," replied Sophie.

"Sophie I tell you what," Malik said. "Return in two days and I will have a letter for you to present to Teivel, of course you can read it. My hopes will be that the letter will cause him to leave you alone but I cannot force him to do anything, you understand."

Malik saw the look of concern on Erebus' face and now directed his words to Erebus. "Every Insidiae Master is allowed to rule his region as he sees fit. And as different as people are, so are the Masters. Teivel has a reputation, how shall I say it politely? He has a reputation as a barbarian, which is why I would suggest you consider living in another region. And of course I will do what I can to assist you."

"Thank you Malik," Sophie said as she stood up. "You have been more than generous."

"Sophie know that you are always welcomed to remain in Stordt," Malik said.

As soon as Erebus and Sophie walked out onto the street Erebus said, "Well, I feel considerably worse about this now."

"Let's have lunch and you can explain the hierarchy of the Insidiae to me."

Sophie could hear both the fear and the anger in Erebus' voice so she decided not to argue with him. "Alright but let's go to that little café, the tables are more secluded," Sophie said and the two of them walked down the street in silence. When they reached the Attic Café they asked for a secluded table in one of the gardens.

"Erebus I know you are worried but you must understand that I have been sworn to secrecy about the Insidiae."

"And I am your husband now and the only one who is trying to protect you Sophie. I feel like you are sending me into battle without a weapon. You know I am not going to tell anyone else what you say," Erebus said with frustration.

"Then do a quick protection spell so that no one hears our conversation," Sophie said. Erebus mumbled his words for several minutes. When Sophie could feel the energy around them changing she spoke.

"Every continent in this world is divided into regions, before you ask I don't know how they determine the regions. Each region is ruled by a Master. The Masters are extremely powerful men as you heard Malik say. In Opots Malik rules all of Stordt and as you know Teivel rules Ryed and a small portion of Wetpr. Dieter rules the Kingdoms of Marba and Ganz. Molach rules the Kingdoms of Gandt and Puntd and Esteban rules the Kingdoms of Lentz and Zorta."

Sophie continued, "There are no working Insidiae groups in most of Wetpr, the Kingdoms of Norkv, Xepoltr and Ogg, and of course the Ice Caves where the Rualas live."

Erebus reached across the table and gently took Sophie's hand. "My first question is will you be safer in a kingdom that does not have Insidiae?"

"I don't know," Sophie said. "You have to understand that the Masters are like war lords and they are very protective of their boundaries. I might have more protection if I lived in an area where the Master accepted me."

171

"Honey we are both very powerful beings, don't you think we can figure out a way to stay safe? I'm just thinking that if we live in an area with the Insidiae that they will be asking you to be of service to them."

"Erebus that could happen no matter where we live."

"Well, perhaps we could plead our case to one of the Grand Masters that you and Malik mentioned."

Sophie's face turned white as she listened to Erebus' suggestion. "Erebus the Grand Masters are like the Old Ones. In fact they are the ones who called to the Old Ones and brought them here. Most members of the Insidiae never come close to the presence of a Grand Master and to bring someone in from the outside, such as you, would mean certain death for us both."

"Can you at least tell me their names, I might know one," Erebus said.

"Know one!" gasped Sophie.

"My dear do you forget that I have worked in the dark arts for many years; you might be surprised who I know."

Sophie stared at Erebus with a mixture of fear and awe in her eyes, then she leaned forward and whispered. "I don't even know who they all are," she said fearfully. "Or even how many of them exist."

"You don't even know if they exist and you are this afraid?" Erebus asked incredulously. "Sophie I have never seen you this frightened before."

"Oh they exist," Sophie said with conviction.

"Sophie you are acting more frightened of the Grand Masters than you are of the Old Ones."

"The Old Ones pretty much stay in their regions but the Grand Masters walk among us."

"Well, who do you think they are?"

"Erebus I have never met any of them that I know of but Meekos did."

Erebus interrupted Sophie, "What do you mean that you know of?"

"Erebus the Grand Masters have been around since this world began, they still retain the physical appearances they had when they sold their souls, like we all do but names have changed greatly over the centuries. They don't go around advertising who they are."

"So they are in disguise?"

"In a way, I told you they live among us and it's not like you are going to be able to recognize one of them when you see them," Sophie said. "Meekos wanted greatly to be an Insidiae Master. He told me once that he had an audience with a Grand Master named Emeric. Meekos said he was surprised because Emeric looked like such a young man, but that he embodied pure evil."

"The other names I have heard, now remember these are their ancient names are: Zadok, Aaryan, Emon, Fadil, Imad, Jerik and Radnor as men," Sophie continued. "The women are: Banaka, Mab, Tahira, Zeni, and Rahi. I have heard that some of these ancients are married to each other but I don't know who the couples are. And I don't know where they live or what names they are using now."

"Father I received a letter from Zoya," Matthew said as he walked into Mathas' study. "She describes the creatures that she saw in her vision in the underwater prison. I was thinking of showing the letter to Ingr, she is a remarkable artist, perhaps she can draw these creatures for us."

"Sounds like a good idea," Mathas said as he took the letter from his son. "By the heavens these creatures sound hideous. The way she has described them they sound like they are part human and part fish."

"That may be to our benefit," Matthew said. "If they are on land, they will stand out, unless they have their heads and arms covered."

"Take this to Ingr and ask her to make several pictures so we can each have one," Mathas said as he continued to read the letter. "Did you read this? She and that Jared fellow are going to live on a farm just a few miles from the castle. Zoya said she and Jared will be able to help us with our missions. I certainly hope that poor girl knows what she is getting into."

"You mean getting into a relationship with Jared?" Matthew asked. "I thought you were convinced he had turned good."

"I do believe so but I wouldn't want my daughter to marry him. Zoya is nice and although she has been through a lot she still seems naïve."

"That is what I have been saying all along," Matthew said as he sat down in a chair across from his father's desk. "There is another page to this letter Father," Matthew said as he handed the last page to Mathas.

Mathas' eyes widened as he read the letter. "We have to tell the family about this. In fact Matthew when you go to Claudius' tell him that our families need to meet at his home. It is easier for us to go there than for them to transport three little babies here. I will send a soldier to Sorren so he and Shara can join us."

Archetenus and Delilah continued their journey northbound until late afternoon, then they turned east, from this point of their trek it was a three hour ride to the monastery at Leven. Although they talked as they rode, both Archetenus and Delilah where overwhelmed with thoughts and emotions flooding through them.

"We are going to make camp now," Archetenus said as he turned and looked at Delilah. "I know there is a lot of daylight left but I would like to spend another night with you before I have to leave you at the monastery." His words brought a smile to her face.

"I was thinking the same thing," Delilah said as she followed Archetenus to a secluded area in the forest.

Archetenus dismounted first then walked to Delilah's horse and helped her dismount. As soon as her feet touched the ground, Archetenus kissed her passionately on the lips. She put her arms around him and returned his fervor. After a few moments Archetenus quickly took care of the horses as Delilah spread their bedding on the ground. They tore each other's clothing off and fell on top of the blankets. Their passions and their needs consumed them. These two broken people who had led such lonely and horrible lives were being healed in the arms of the other.

"Are you sure you are up to it?" Simon asked.

"I think I can take care of him," Zoya said happily. "And if I can't I will come and get you."

"Simon you and your family have done so much for me but now that I am home I would like to stay here," Jared said as he put his arm around Zoya. "Besides Zoya and I have some things to discuss."

"Honey, let's leave them alone," Annabelle said with a sly smile as she took Simon's arm.

"Jared, I don't doubt that you and Zoya need some time together but I will be honest I am concerned for your safety," Simon said. "Annabelle and I will stay with you while Alexander and Laurel return to the castle and tell the Sanuri and Raul that you need protection."

"Jared after I talk to the Sanuri and Raul I will bring your things out here," Alexander said.

"This just doesn't feel right," Jared said as he shook his head. "I've never needed protection my whole life."

"You never turned hell upside down before either," Simon said as he sat back down at the table. "Want another piece of cake?" Simon asked as he helped himself to a chocolate layer cake that Marie had sent with them.

"So Annabelle, have you picked out any names yet?" Zoya asked as she filled their cups with coffee.

"Simon really liked the name Timothy but since that is the name of the man who attacked me we won't use it. So his second choice is David if it's a boy and we haven't really decided on a girl's name yet."

"How far along are you?" asked Zoya.

"I'm not really sure, I think about seven months," Annabelle said happily. "Natasha and I were trying to figure out our due dates. We think our babies may be born just a few weeks apart which would be fun."

"Honey I am sure they will have moved to the Ice Caves by then," Simon said. "Calen really wants her to have the baby at his home, with his family around."

"She's a little scared," Annabelle said. "Did you know they are having the first baby that is part human and part Ruala? I told her that they are both such beautiful people that the baby will be beautiful whether it has wings or not."

"Rualas are part human," Simon said. "So I don't think it will look that different. Now it will be interesting to see what Ibula's and Thedes' baby looks like. She's a couple of months behind you." Simon looked at Jared and Zoya. "The friends I am speaking of are Ruala and Shettee so their baby will be a new race also."

"I thought all of the Shettees had been wiped out," Jared said.

"The Sanuri saved them and they live in the Ice Caves with the Rualas."

"Simon do you think we could go to the Ice Caves and visit them all sometime?" Annabelle asked.

"I am sure we could get some of the Rualas to fly us; I'm just not sure I want to fly with all of the children," Simon said. "The Ice Caves are a long ways from here. I'll talk to Calen about it."

"What is that sound?" Jared asked as they all heard a loud squawking.

"Hengers," Simon said. "You really have to see them." All four people stood up from the table. Jared leaned on furniture but was able to walk to the door by himself.

"Oh Simon they're beautiful," Annabelle gasped as they watched a dozen giant blue eagles flying over the farm.

"They are incredible," Zoya said with awe. "And here comes some Enrops too."

"Our soldiers will be stopping by on a regular basis," Simon said. "And you can always send us messages with the Enrops."

"You really think all of this is necessary?" Jared asked.

"I guess we will see," said Simon.

Archetenus was lying on his back and Delilah was lying next to him with her head on his chest, both were lost in their thoughts.

"Delilah when I come back for you," Archetenus said softly. "Would you like to stay together?"

Delilah quickly propped herself up on her arm so she could look Archetenus in the face. "Oh yes, I was trying to get up the nerve to ask you the same thing. I know this is all so crazy but I, well I, I think I am falling in love with you."

Archetenus pulled Delilah to him and kissed her on the lips. "I feel the same way," he said. "Are you and Dieter really married or did he just take you for a wife?"

"He put on a huge wedding celebration for show. He told everyone that we had a small private ceremony but we never did."

"So you aren't legally married to him?"

"No."

"Then we could be married," Archetenus said almost more to himself than to Delilah.

"Archetenus are you asking me to marry you?" she asked with a mixture of excitement and disbelief.

A sly smile crossed his face. "What would you say if I did ask you?"

"Well, considering the fact that we don't really know each other," Delilah said teasingly. "I would say yes."

"We could have one of the priests at the monastery marry us tomorrow," Archetenus said with a smile that lit up his face.

"Archetenus ask me, say the words."

"Delilah will you marry me?"

"Yes," Delilah said and started to giggle. She kissed him on the lips. "Archetenus I feel like I have dreamt all of this. A brave handsome warrior saves me and we fall in love. Does that sound crazy to you?"

"No, I feel like I have dreamed this too."

When Alexander and Laurel returned to Jared's farm they brought all of his belongings that were at the castle. Alexander carried everything into the house then left almost immediately. Jared picked up several bags of gold coins. "I usually hide my valuables under floorboards, but you have everything looking so nice I hate to tear up the floor."

"I know; there is a small cupboard of sorts in the back of the closet in our room. I'm sure it will all fit," Zoya said and grabbed an armload of bags. Jared followed her without assistance but his steps were slow and painful. Zoya led him into a large bedroom with a huge bed. "I had the bed specially made for you because you are such a big man," she said proudly. Zoya opened the closet and shoved a couple of pieces of clothing to the side and showed Jared a small door in the back wall of the closet.

"I don't think I can bend down, can you put the bags in there?"

"Of course," Zoya said happily and returned to the kitchen several more times to get more armloads of bags. When she put the last of the bags into the hiding place, Zoya turned and saw that Jared was sitting on the bed.

"Zoya come over here and sit with me," he said and held his hand out to her. "All that money I gave you didn't you buy yourself any clothes?"

"Why no, I told you everything I bought, it was all for this place."

"Honey we have plenty of money, I want you to buy yourself a wardrobe. In fact I will need to get some things too, especially if I am going to be working on our farm." Jared was smiling as he spoke. He took Zoya's hand and looked into her eyes.

"All that time I spent in bed I kept thinking of all the different ways I could ask you to marry me. I had hoped to be well, hell I had hoped to have the ring bought but now feels like the right time. I would get down on one knee but I probably can't get back up," he said with a grin.

Zoya was smiling as tears were running down her cheeks. "But first there is something else I have to ask you Zoya. You are such a beautiful girl and I am almost twice your age. I'm an aging, crippled fighter I don't understand why you want to be with me."

Zoya stared at Jared; she was momentarily speechless by his question. "Jared I know you must have been a bad man once for your name to have been in that book but since I have known you all I have seen is your kindness and generosity. You have been my protector since the moment I met you. And you truly are the bravest man I know." Then Zoya started to giggle, "And you don't even mind that I see visions and talk with spirits. Jared I fell in love with you because of your goodness."

Jared was squeezing Zoya's hand as she spoke. "Zoya I told you about my first marriage and what a bad husband I was. I am older now and I know what I want. I love you and this little place and I promise to take good care of you." He cleared his throat. "Zoya will you be my wife?" Jared asked softly.

179

"Yes," she said enthusiastically and threw her arms around Jared's neck. They kissed for the first time and both of them were overwhelmed with the emotions that consumed them.

"You want to try out our new bed?" Jared asked smiling.

"Are you sure you are up to it?" Zoya asked sincerely.

"I think we can figure something out," he said with a grin.

"Claudius I hope you don't feel put upon that I wanted to hold another meeting at your home?" Mathas asked.

"Of course not, we all feel that it is very considerate on your part," Claudius said with a smile that had not left his face since his grandchildren were born. "In fact until all the babies are a little older, just plan to have all the family meetings here."

"Ingr you are walking so well," Angelina said as she ran up to her friend and hugged her tightly.

"I am feeling stronger every day," Ingr said with a laugh. "It really is a miracle how well I am healing."

"Ingr where are the babies?" asked Margarit.

"They are still taking a nap," Ingr said. "As soon as they wake you can hold one of them."

"I like the girl the best," Margarit said with a coy smile which made both Angelina and Ingr laugh.

The sound of a baby crying made them turn and look towards the door to the parlor. Thaos and Nikki walked into the room. Thaos was cuddling the baby that was becoming quiet.

"Every time he takes Titus he stops crying," Nikki said with a laugh. "So now Thaos is getting up with me all night."

"Thaos can I see your baby?" Margarit asked as she ran up to them.

"Do you want to hold him?" asked Thaos.

"No, I just want to look at him."

Thaos kneeled down so Margarit could look at Titus' face. Margarit looked at Titus then at Thaos then back at Titus. "He looks just like you," Margarit said in awe. Both Thaos and Nikki laughed.

"This one isn't even sleeping through the night yet and Thaos is already talking about the next baby," Nikki said and laughed. "Where's Alexas?"

"Father has her," Angelina said. "He and Matthew are still outside talking. And mother has Jacob. I'm afraid Jacob will forget how to walk, what with Mother, Father and Matthew always carrying him," Angelina said and laughed.

"Well look at this," Nikki said as Stephan walked into the parlor carrying both his babies.

"They always wake up at the same time," Stephan said as Ingr took Sicily from him.

"Margarit you go sit in a chair and I will put Sicily in your arms," Ingr said.

"Where's your mother?" asked Claudius.

"Changing her dress," Stephan said with a grin. "Marcus puked on her."

Towards evening, Roch was feeling stronger and was in the pool trying to catch a fish with his hands. The water was clear so he could easily see the fish swimming beneath him. He made several vain attempts to catch a particularly large fish which kept eluding his grasp. Frustrated, Roch lunged at the fish; in doing so he submersed himself in the water. He could see what appeared to be an underwater cave, he swam towards it and when he came up for air he was in a small cavern behind the waterfall.

Roch pulled himself up on a rocky ledge and looked around in amazement. The cavern had several small chests and small barrels inside of it and each was filled with jewels and gold coins.

Little did Roch know that he once owned the treasures that were before him. When Cerephus was planning on taking the throne from Roch, Cerephus was slowly stealing Roch's riches and hiding them in this cave.

The sight of these riches brought fragmented pieces of Roch's memories to the forefront of his mind. The sun was starting to set which made it difficult for him to see, in the darkening cavern. He grabbed several handfuls of jewels and smelled them as he rolled them between his fingers. The pleasure Roch felt surged through him as his sense of greed again became familiar to him.

Archetenus walked back to their campsite with another arm load of wood for the fire. Delilah was preparing their meal. He stopped and watched her; he was always overwhelmed by her beauty. After a few moments Archetenus set the wood down and walked farther into the forest.

"Miranda," Archetenus called.

"Congratulations."

Archetenus turned around and saw Miranda standing behind him. "Thank you for coming. I am doing everything that you told me to."

"But you are troubled because everything that has happened with Delilah is like the fantasies you had about Vitomas."

"Yes, is what I have with Delilah real? Is she real?"

"Yes and perhaps all this is so similar to your fantasies to prove a point," Miranda said. "Have you noticed how your life has changed for the better once you started to make the right choices?"

"Thank you," Archetenus said with relief. "But I am concerned that I might turn into a monster and hurt her."

"Archetenus take control of your life. You have always given control to your demons. I will help you."

"I don't want to hurt her."

"You should get back to her soon," Miranda said with a smile. "After your wedding, when you leave the monastery I will come to you again. Archetenus you are realizing that you have a reason to live now. But both you and Delilah and the baby you created last night are in great danger."

"Baby!"

"Yes, Archetenus you will be a father before the year is through so it is very important that you follow what I say. In the coming weeks I will be asking you to do things which may confuse you but you have to have faith that I am trying to protect you and your new family. Do you still trust me Archetenus?"

He smiled and said, "Yes Miranda, I do trust you. And thank you for Delilah. Guess I owe you two favors now." Miranda smiled and in an instant she was gone.

As everyone took their seats in the parlor in Claudius' castle, Mathas stood up and addressed the group, which included the families of Fahron, Sorren, Claudius and Mathas. "As all of you know from an earlier meeting, Zoya, the seer in Wetpr, had a vision of an underwater prison. Matthew wrote to her and asked her to describe the creatures she saw in her vision. He received a letter from Zoya today. Matthew asked Ingr to draw pictures of the creatures based on Zoya's descriptions. I am handing one picture to every family and Ingr will draw more for us.

"They're hideous," Bella gasped as she stared at one of the drawings.

"Actually they rather look like men until you get to the head," Fahron said as he handed his picture to Isadore.

"As you can see Ingr drew these pictures with a pen, but Zoya describes the creatures as having green skin. They look like they have Mohawk haircuts but Zoya said that is not hair but some kind of tentacles that protrude from their heads."

"She also said those circles that you see around their eyes are bright red. Zoya said she thinks those markings on them are tattoos and she said to look at the ones on their necks. She does not understand their meanings but she feels they are important."

"They would have to cover their heads and arms to be able to walk among humans without being recognized," Matthew said. "I'm thinking that something like a priest's robe would be what they probably would wear. We have seen other demons wear such robes."

"If we fight them we should make sure the battle is on ground," Claudius said as he studied one of the pictures. "I fear they would have a great advantage in the water."

"Zoya said she saw humans as their prisoners," Mathas said. "I am curious how they would transport the humans underwater. Does anyone have anything they want to say about these creatures before I move onto the next subject?" Everyone in the room remained quiet. "Zoya said that when we were all visiting in Wetpr she was seeing fragments of images but she did not understand their significance until she was talking with Vitomas a few days ago."

Mathas paused and looked at Rosa who was sitting near him holding baby Sarah. "Zoya thought that Sarah was Rosa's and my daughter. So she didn't understand when she kept seeing images of Sarah changing to images of a man. Then she would see images of this man change and in some he was wearing an eye patch and others he wasn't. I will let you all read the letter but the description sounds like Thaos."

Before Mathas could say anything else Thaos blurted out "Hector! But I didn't see him around her place until she was planning to steal Margarit." As soon as the words came out of his mouth Thaos looked at Margarit. The little girl was sitting in an overstuffed chair holding baby Sicily.

To everyone's surprise Margarit did not seem upset; she said in a nonchalant manner, "One of the men who stole me looked like Thaos but he wasn't cuz Thaos is nice."

"But you were gone a lot," Stephan said. "You really don't know when Juleta met him or hired him."

184

"I let the men go that we took as prisoners," Claudius said. "I think we would have noticed if he was among them."

"If Hector is the father, he is a hired fighter with no compassion for children; it seems unlikely that he would want to claim Sarah as his daughter," Angelina said.

"Angelina, Sarah is heir to the throne," Sorren said. "That is quite a motivation. I wonder if he knows the child exists."

"The only public ceremony you have taken Sarah to; was in Salar," Matthew said. "I think we should keep her presence quiet."

"Mathas, Matthew you are overlooking the obvious," Fahron said. "Adopt Sarah. We can draw the papers up tonight. You have everyone here that you would need for signatures."

"Mathas I think Fahron is right," Sorren said. "But remember how much you and I talked with Zoya. It seems like when the spirits talked to her it was to help or protect someone. Anyone who helps in such a diabolical plot as Hector did is without conscious. I think you have more to fear from him then trying to claim the throne."

"Can I add something," Ingr said and stood up so she could address the room. "We all hated Juleta but that doesn't mean Hector did. Let's say he was her lover and the father of her child. Nikki, Angelina you and I know we would do anything for our husbands. If Hector had some feelings for Juleta he might continue carrying out her revenge against our families."

"There you are," Delilah said as she walked up to Archetenus and stretched up to kiss him. "I was getting worried about you."

"I was just making sure we didn't have any unwanted visitors," Archetenus said as he kissed her.

"Always my protector," Delilah said with a proud smile. "Come, dinner is ready. Honey why are you looking at me so strangely?"

Archetenus wanted to burst with the news that he and Delilah were going to have a baby but he knew he couldn't tell her. She would never believe him when he said an Angel told him the news. "I was just thinking that by this time tomorrow you will be my wife," Archetenus said as he continued to smile.

"Archetenus sit down and eat, I have some things I want to give you," Delilah said as she walked over to her saddlebags. Delilah walked up to Archetenus and handed him two handfuls of jewelry. "You have to understand I was nothing more to Dieter than a showpiece. He was very concerned with his image in Port Friada and he wanted everyone to know how rich and powerful he was."

"Dieter always made me wear lots of jewels. These are the things I was wearing yesterday when we left. I took them off because I don't want anything to remind me of Dieter. If I had to start over some place by myself I was going to sell them. But now that we are getting married, you take them. They are very expensive; we could sell them and buy a house."

Archetenus looked at a diamond necklace with matching earrings. There was a gold and diamond bracelet and a broach with diamond and pearls. "I don't even remember seeing these on you. Guess all I could focus on was your face," he said with a smile. "Are these your wedding rings?" Archetenus looked at a gold band that was filled with diamonds and a huge diamond ring. "Are these the kind of rings that you like?" he asked as he realized he needed to buy rings.

"Yes, they are supposed to be my wedding rings," Delilah said. "And no I don't like them. Dieter never asked me what I liked he just told me what he wanted me to wear."

"Well when we leave here, you can pick out the rings you want; but we won't have them in time for the wedding."

Delilah put her arms around Archetenus' neck and kissed him. "I think we are going to be so happy together."

Chapter XII
Gifts

Archetenus and Delilah arrived at the monastery at Leven midmorning. "Can I speak to whoever is in-charge?" Archetenus asked as they dismounted.

"Certainly, come with us," a young priest said as he led Archetenus and Delilah to one of the older buildings in the monastery. "High Priest Barnabas will be with you in just a moment," the priest said as he opened a door to a room that was decorated like a parlor. As soon as the door closed Delilah put her arms around Archetenus.

"I am so excited," Delilah gushed about their pending marriage.

Within moments the door opened and an elderly man entered the room. He wore the crimson robes of a high priest and carried himself with stature. "What can I do for you?" he asked in a kindly manner.

"My name is Archetenus and this is Delilah, first we would like you to marry us this morning and secondly I would like to leave her in your care for a few days. I won't lie to you, we are probably being pursued by some dangerous men, I will take care of them but I need to know that she is safe. I will pay you for your services."

High Priest Barnabas stared first at Archetenus then at Delilah as if he was reading their faces. "Why are these men after you, have you committed a crime?"

"I was a prisoner of a powerful and cruel man," Delilah said. "Archetenus saved me. If this man catches us he will surely kill us both."

"And why were you a prisoner?" High Priest Barnabas asked.

"Because she is a beautiful young woman, nothing more," Archetenus replied. "We have committed no crimes."

"Very well, you both seem sincere in your statements. When would you like to marry?"

"Now if we could," Archetenus said as he took Delilah's hand.

"Thaos; Bella and Ingr are here," Nikki said as she escorted the two women into the kitchen of their home. Thaos was sitting at the table holding baby Titus. "Bella has something to speak with you about and before she begins I want you to know that Ingr and I both agree with what she is proposing."

"This could be serious," Thaos said with a grin.

Bella and Ingr sat down at the kitchen table as Nikki poured two more cups of coffee. "It's about Ryan," Bella said. "He is such a sweet boy and don't take this the wrong way Thaos but he is nothing like you and Stephan. I don't think he has it in him to be a soldier and that concerns me for his safety. You know I had a woodshop built for him and he has such creative talents. The girls say he just comes alive when he is working on a project."

"Well, so far I do agree with everything you have said Bella but why are you saying this?"

"Tonight when we give Claudius his gifts I am hoping that he realizes what a talented artist Ryan is."

"And?" Thaos asked.

"And I am going to ask Claudius to release Ryan from his military duties and help Ryan open up a shop of his own."

"Have you talked to Ryan about this?" Thaos asked.

"No," Bella replied. "He is so humble I fear he would turn down anything I want to do for him."

"You love helping us poor souls don't you Bella?" Thaos said warmly. "I like your idea. Nikki and I have money; we can help Ryan with his shop."

"My dear boy, Claudius has more money than he knows what to do with. But like you and Stephan, Claudius is such a warrior that I don't know if he would understand a boy like Ryan."

"Bella, Claudius is one of the most perceptive and intelligent men I have ever met. I will bet you anything he already knows that Ryan is not cut out to be a soldier. But he is not going to kick Ryan out of the army. The boy hasn't done anything wrong and he has no place to go. I will go with you when you speak with Claudius," Thaos said.

"We were planning on going with Bella too, to give her support," said Nikki.

"Have you told any of this to Stephan?" Thaos asked.

"No, I came to you first because you are the closest thing that Ryan has to family," Bella said.

"Ingr go get Stephan," said Thaos. "We might as well make this a family decision."

Archetenus stayed with Delilah for one hour after they were married then he headed southwest towards Port Friada. He was flooded with emotions that were both happy and sad. And a part of him was in disbelief of all that had happened so quickly. Archetenus was normally a wary man but his thoughts and emotions so distracted him that he did not see the two men riding towards him until they were almost parallel in the road. Both of the riders were old men, one of them called out to Archetenus, "Where ya headed?"

Archetenus stopped his horse and looked at both of the men; they appeared harmless to him. "Port Friada," he answered.

"Not a good place to be these days. Some rich fellar with one of those fancy houses on the ocean well, it was the damndest thing but he got attacked by an army of Rogetts. Yep people there are pretty damn shook up, you know how bad those monsters can be."

"When did this happen?" Archetenus asked.

The man who had been talking looked at his partner before he answered the question. "Two mornings ago."

"I was in Port Friada two mornings ago," Archetenus said. "Do you know anything else about the attack? Were you in Port Friada?"

"Sam and me passed through there yesterday and all folks was talking about was the Rogett attack. Understand we don't know no one in that city so we're just telling you what we heard. But we heard a lot of people talking when we stopped in for a meal and a drink. Sounds like the guy that got attacked had a damn army of his own, they stopped the Rogetts from getting into the city but from what folks were saying that guy lost a lot of his men. And now folks are wondering why this guy had his own army."

"I know people in that city," Archetenus said. "Did you get the guy's name?"

"It sounded foreign to me," the man said.

"Was it Dieter?" asked Archetenus.

"Well damn yes it was, you know him?"

"I've met him once or twice. Did he live?"

"From what we heard he's alive but his wife and her two body guards didn't make it, those Rogetts they are the devil's spawn."

"I've met his wife too, you say she is dead?"

"Dead or missing, apparently there are a lot of bodies unaccounted for. Those damn monsters must've ate them. So you be careful young fellar there might still be Rogetts on the loose."

As soon as the men were out of sight, Archetenus got off from his horse and called to Miranda. "Is that why I had to get Delilah away from there so quickly, because of the Rogetts?"

"Yes." Archetenus heard Miranda's voice before he saw her standing in a small clearing.

"Wow, thanks Miranda. And Dieter thinks she is dead?"

"Madam Bular told Dieter that Delilah left her store with the two body guards. Their disfigured bodies were found."

"Miranda, why are you helping us like this?"

"I have many reasons but you should be asking me other questions."

"Did you send the Rogetts after Dieter?"

"No and this is the part where you need to listen carefully to me Archetenus. Dieter is a dark lord and a high standing official in the Insidiae organization. He was having great caverns built beneath his house; some were to be used as torture chambers and some were to keep men like you prisoners until you could be auctioned off to demons. He had slaves digging the caverns and they broke through a wall that opened into a nest of Rogetts. This attack has not stopped Dieter but it will delay his plans for a while."

"What is it that you want me to do Miranda? Do you want me to kill Dieter?"

"No. During the Rogett attack Dieter's powers were useless to him. He believes that someone sent the Rogetts after him and blocked his magics, so he is calling together many important members of the Insidiae for a meeting. These are powerful men and women who have kept their identities secret. I want you to spy on Dieter's home, like you were doing before. And I want you to draw the faces that you see."

"Miranda, I am not an artist, I cannot draw these men."

"You will draw with my help. Archetenus this is a very important thing I am asking of you. Before this is done, you will be exposing the faces of darkness and saving many lives. Are you willing to do this?"

"Yes," Archetenus replied without hesitation.

"When you return to Port Friada you will need to buy paper, pens and other supplies. Do not be naïve; Dieter owns much of that city. Do not call attention to yourself and do not try to sell those jewels that Delilah gave to you. Draw the faces and return to the monastery."

"When is this meeting?"

"In four days, But some of the men and women are traveling great distances so they will be arriving over the next few days. You will recognize them. These men have sold their souls for wealth and power which they flaunt. Be careful Archetenus they will kill you if they discover you."

Thaos and Stephan walked into Claudius' study and closed the door. "Father," Stephan said then he looked at Thaos and laughed. "Father," Stephan said again. "We have orders to get you out of the castle and to keep you distracted for a while. Mother has a surprise for you, of course I wasn't supposed to tell you that."

Claudius looked up from his paperwork and smiled. "So how long do you have to keep me distracted?"

"A couple of hours at least," Stephan replied. "I thought we could go riding or go into town for a drink."

"You know I don't think the three of us have gone into the city for a drink together, it's about time," Claudius said as he stood up and the three men left the castle. They rode east towards Langer. "So Thaos, Nikki says the two of you are already working on a second baby," Claudius said cheerfully.

"Yeah, we both want a big family and we've decided to have the babies close together, at least in the beginning."

"Excellent," Claudius said then he turned and looked at Stephan who was riding on his other side.

"Don't look at me," Stephan said with a grin. "Ingr and I just started making love again. I was too afraid to touch her until I was sure all of her wounds had healed."

"Well, that's understandable," Claudius said. "It's remarkable how well she has healed. We have the Sanuri to thank for that."

"Did Ingr tell you that she asked the Sanuri if she would be able to have more children and he told her that she was healing completely so he didn't think that would be a problem?"

"No, she didn't say anything to me about that but I am glad to hear it," Claudius said.

"Father I know I have said this before but I have never seen you or Mother so happy," said Stephan.

"Stephan when you were born we were at war and were being attacked on two fronts. I didn't come home until you were almost two. I always regretted that I missed so much of your life. Having grandchildren is like having a second change. When I look at Marcus I wonder if that is what you were like when you were his age."

Stephan stared at his father because Claudius was not the type of man to open up about things or to be sentimental. "Father I think the babies are bringing out a whole other side of you."

"I can say the same about the two of you," Claudius said. "I am pleased with both of you. You've settled down from your wild ways and become great husbands and fathers. I don't think either of you will regret these changes."

Claudius and his sons rode into Langer, had a couple of drinks and returned to the castle. Nikki and Ingr met them at the front door. "Bella they're home," Ingr called out.

"You girls keep them in the foyer until I get there," Bella said as she rushed down the hallway. Claudius, Thaos and Stephan were all grinning when Bella approached them. "Claudius I know you are not one for surprises but I do hope you like this," Bella said and took her husband's arm and escorted him to his study. Stephan, Ingr, Thaos and Nikki followed them. When Bella opened the door, Claudius stared at the room with amazement.

"Ryan made the desk and chair and that weapons cabinet and that table and chairs," Bella said with pride as Claudius walked around the room looking at his gifts. "Ingr and Nikki upholstered the cushions on the chairs and made the drapes, all I did was buy new carpets. Oh and the boys bought you new weapons and put them in the cabinet."

"Claudius you are so quiet," Ingr said. "If you don't like something we can change it."

"No, no don't you change a thing," Claudius said. "Everything is just perfect. I don't know what to say." He paused. "I am very pleased, thank you all. But what is the occasion?"

"The children wanted to do something for you because you have done so much for them," Bella said. "And I have wanted to redecorate this room for years. And Claudius I would like to take this opportunity to ask for a favor."

As Bella was talking Claudius sat down in his new chair behind his new desk. "When does my wife have to ask me for a favor?" Claudius asked and smiled.

"The favor isn't for me," Bella said. "Claudius look at the beautiful workmanship that Ryan put into your furniture. He really is a talented artist. And well, Claudius, Ryan isn't like you and Stephan and Thaos or even the girls for that matter. That boy just isn't cut out to be a soldier, surely you have seen that. I would like you to release him from his military duties and I thought we could help him set up a shop so he could make a living selling his furniture."

Before Claudius could speak Ingr said, "Claudius you should see Ryan when he works on his projects, it's like something just comes alive in him."

"Is this what Ryan wants?" asked Claudius.

"Oh that boy doesn't even know I am asking you," Bella said.

"So is the whole family in agreement with Bella?" Claudius asked sternly.

"Yes," Thaos said. "And I can help him set up his business."

Claudius looked at everyone with a serious look on his face then he broke into a smile. "Well it's about time somebody said something. That boy would get butchered in his first battle. He isn't even comfortable holding a sword much less using one. He only joined the military to please his grandfather."

"I will draw up the papers tonight. And Thaos, Bella and I can help Ryan set up his shop," then Claudius looked at Bella. "But under one condition. Ryan is a fine craftsman but I don't know if he has a head for business, Bella I will put that in your capable hands. And of course he is going to need a place to live. He might as well move in with us, he is here all the time anyways."

"Oh Claudius thank you," Bella said and walked around the desk and kissed her husband. "You have made me very happy."

"Where is Ryan?" Claudius asked.

"In his woodshop," said Nikki.

"Thaos why don't you bring him here, so I can thank him and we can tell him the news," Claudius said as he stood up and walked over to his weapons cabinet and inspected the weapons that Stephan and Thaos had given him. "Yes, I am very pleased with all of this."

A few moments later, Ryan shyly entered the study with Thaos. Ryan noticed that everyone in the room was looking at him with smiles on their faces. "Ryan I am very pleased with the gifts you have made me," Claudius said. "You are a very talented craftsman and I thank you."

"I am happy that you like them," Ryan said excitedly. "I don't know if you have had a chance to really look at the carvings on the cabinet yet but Bella has been telling me about when you led the army in battle with those creatures from across the ocean so I created the scenes from what she told me."

"Why I didn't even realize that," Bella said as she got up and examined the cabinet. "Ryan this is really incredible. The rest of you have to see this."

"Bella why don't you tell Ryan about what we have been discussing," Claudius said.

Bella walked up to Ryan and talked to him in a motherly tone. "Ryan I hope you don't get mad that I spoke to Claudius before I said anything to you. But I asked him to release you from the military so we could help you open a shop to sell your furniture. And Claudius has agreed, how do you feel about that?"

"Really!" Ryan said. "That would be the most wonderful thing I could ever imagine."

"And we would like you to move in here with us, as family," Bella said. "Now if you don't want to we won't be offended."

"Want to, Bella I feel like all of you are my family, thank you so much," Ryan said and hugged Bella.

Stephan turned, looked at Thaos and winked. "I think we just got another brother," Stephan whispered.

Chapter XIII
The Book of Horror

"We thought we would come out and see how you were doing," Alexander said as he helped Laurel down from the boca.

"Please come in and have some lunch," Zoya said happily as she met them at the front door of the farm house.

"How's Jared doing?" Alexander asked as they walked into the kitchen and saw Jared sitting at the table.

"Frustrated," Jared said with half of a smile. "Now that I am out here I want to do so many things but I can't yet. Glad you stopped by. Zoya is a great cook, join us for lunch."

"But you won't believe how much he has improved," Zoya said as she set more dishes on the table. "He is walking all of the time now and without my help. Hannah comes out every morning to see him and she is amazed at how fast he is healing."

"Do you want some help?" Laurel asked Zoya.

"Oh no, just have a seat," Zoya said as she put a large baked ham in front of Jared to carve. Zoya put bowls of sweet potatoes, beans and a platter of biscuits on the table. Then she filled everyone's coffee cups before she sat down. "Jared tell them the news," Zoya said excitedly.

"As soon as I can get around better, Zoya and I are getting married. And we would like both of you to stand up for us."

"Oh we'd love to," Laurel said sweetly. "I am really happy for the two of you."

"I told Jared that we have to ask the Sanuri soon because he travels a lot."

"Zoya is right," Alexander said. "And I think they are planning another trip to Nora soon. If you want, I can tell him that you want to speak with him."

"That would be fine," Jared said. "I wish I could go with them."

Archetenus rented a room in a boarding house that was a block from Dieter's mansion. Although Archetenus realized that the men he would be spying on were significant threats to him, his only thoughts were of returning to the monastery and getting Delilah.

Archetenus kept thinking about how hard Delilah cried when he was leaving her, an act that touched him greatly. As he was shopping for supplies he tried to avoid places he had previously frequented so that he wouldn't be recognized. Fortunately for Archetenus Port Friada was a huge city and a place where people came to get lost.

The two strangers that Archetenus had met on the road told him the truth. No matter where he went everyone was talking about the Rogett attack at Dieter's mansion. Although Archetenus heard many people say they were relieved that Dieter's men had stopped the Rogetts from attacking the city, many, many other people were now suspicious of Dieter and his activities.

People were speculating as to why Dieter had his own army and why the Rogetts only attacked his place. And Archetenus even heard a few people speculating as to the fate of Delilah. While he was eating lunch in a small restaurant, he listened to the table of older women who were seated next to him.

"That poor girl, she was never allowed out of that house and when you did see her she always had bruises," one woman was saying to the rest. "God knows what he did to her. I know Delilah's folks and she was always a sweet girl."

"Well I never trusted him," another woman said. "We would always see him at banquets and I will tell you he just made my skin crawl. I will bet you anything that he murdered that poor girl and is trying to blame her death on the Rogett attack."

"My Seth says that Dieter must have had his men digging deep into the earth for the Rogetts to come up and attack them. What on earth do you think he is doing? I heard someone say they thought he was digging tunnels under the city."

"As you know Harold is on the City Board," a fourth woman said with an air of self-importance. Then she leaned forward as if she was trying to prevent others from hearing her words. Archetenus laughed to himself because the woman barely lowered her voice. "This afternoon the entire City Board is going to Fort Friada to meet with General Amundsen, they want him to investigate Dieter."

Archetenus lingered over his coffee and listened to the women talk until they changed the subject, then he paid for his meal and left the restaurant. Archetenus felt that it would be too dangerous for him to walk around Dieter's home in the middle of the day and he wasn't sure what to do until it got dark so he decided to go to Madam Bular's shop. Archetenus watched the shop for several minutes before entering. As soon as Archetenus entered he could see there were several customers looking at clothing and bolts of material.

"Well there you are," Madam Bular said and took Archetenus by the arm and escorted him into a back room that appeared to be her office. "How is Delilah?" she whispered.

"She is safe. I wanted to thank you for your help and to ask you why you would stick your neck out like that."

Madam Bular took a deep breath before she spoke. "My first husband was a cruel drunk who beat me daily. I would dream that someone would save me. I saw the look in her. The bruises and it was like her soul was dead. I was glad to help, but you are taking a chance coming back here."

"I will be leaving soon," Archetenus said. "Surely you know what size Delilah wears. I would like to buy a few things so she has a change of clothes."

Madam Bular got a smile that lit up her entire face. "You are a sweet man. You stay here and I will pick some things out and wrap them." Archetenus sat in her office for almost twenty minutes before Madam Bular returned with several wrapped packages.

He handed her a fistful of gold coins. "Will this cover it?"

"It's more than enough," Madam Bular said. "And I put a jacket in the bulkier package. You should leave out the back." She showed him a back door to her office. Before Archetenus walked through the door he paused and looked at Madam Bular.

"How did you escape your husband?"

"I slit his throat one night when he was passed out."

Dieter's normal paranoia was reaching new heights after the Rogett attack on his mansion. Never before had Dieter experienced anything like he felt when his powers were blocked. Dieter knew that only something more powerful than himself; could block his magics.

Dieter had been hearing rumors that there were wars among the demons and he wondered if a demon had blocked his powers; but after some thought, this idea made no sense to him. He was a sort of entrepreneur and many of his clients were demons. Dieter was not aligned with any one particular demon; he maintained a neutral position because that made the most money for him.

He had become very close with some members of the Recupero Sect of the Insidiae because he was extremely interested in the sect's ideas of using humans as vessels for demons. Dieter had no interest in helping Omnibus escape his prison in The Abyss but he feigned interest to get information.

Although Dieter considered many members of the Recupero Sect crazy he was intrigued with their dedication and their experimentations in planting seeds of pure evil into humans. These seeds grew inside their human hosts and were genetically passed through the second son of each generation. Now, in this time they were seeing the results of these experimentations. It took three generations for these seeds of evil to mature and to gain their potency.

The men who were created to be vessels were considerably larger and stronger than normal men. But these genetic experiments had their flaws. The Insidiae were seeing a high level of insanity among the chosen vessels, and now they were seeing a strange disease that was killing many of them.

This disease had not been recorded in normal human beings so there were no known cures. To the Insidiae physicians, it appeared that the bodies of the vessels were destroying themselves. These physicians speculated that the human forms could not adequately house the level of evil that was inserted into them.

Demons could not use the vessels that were infirm because of mental or physical illness so they sought the vessels that were strong and healthy. Dieter had been seeking out and hiring the healthy vessels, because he planned to auction them all off to the demons. He was enraged that so many of his men, who were intended vessels, were killed and maimed by the Rogetts. He estimated that the Rogett attack cost him a small fortune.

Bekka and Joao flew back to the Ice Caves to gather more warriors. Lakin was asking for volunteers to go to Nora and he wanted warriors to watch over Sudfad's castle, the headquarters of the Patronus in Wetpr, Nora and Malga and Gabriel's home. Both of these warriors carried full pack of items that they were to give to Calen's mother.

Natasha and Hannah reluctantly packed for their journey to the Ice Caves. They realized they had lost all arguments with their husbands and the other Rualas about accompanying them to Nora.

"I don't know why you both look so sad," Elan said as the entire group was eating lunch in Gabriel's home. "You are going to love the Ice Caves they are much more beautiful than this world."

"Oh Elan I am sure we will love them too, it's just that Natasha and I want to be at our husbands sides," Hannah said sadly. "All we are going to do is worry about the rest of you."

Gabriel put his arm around Hannah and hugged her. "Calen and I have been talking and we decided to fly to the Ice Caves with you. And once you two are settled, then we will join the rest of the troops."

"Oh, we would like that," Natasha said and hugged Calen. "Your family is so nice but I really don't know them. I would like to have you there, even for just a little while."

"That makes me feel better too," Hannah said and kissed Gabriel on the cheek.

"I wanted this to be a surprise," Lakin said with a smile. "But since you both need cheering up. I sent a message to Mateo; he is the Chief Healer of our people and has incredible powers. Hannah he is going to personally teach you our healing practices."

Calen looked across the table at Hannah. "It is a great honor for Mateo himself to teach you, most of the time he would have one of the other healers teach someone. You know he saved the life of the Sanuri."

"I didn't know that," Hannah said humbly. "Thank you so much Lakin."

"When we were trying to save Jared from the demons," Lakin continued. "Natasha was the only one of us who realized what we were dealing with and gave everyone information on how to proceed. Natasha I also told Mateo about you and he offered to teach you our ways also, that is if you are interested in learning these things."

"Oh, I would love to," Natasha said with great excitement. "But I don't have the medical training that Hannah does, will that matter?"

"Our medicines are very different and you are so bright, I am sure you will learn quickly," said Lakin.

"My family is going to be very proud that you two are going to be students of Mateo," Calen said.

"Hannah and Natasha you keep saying that you don't know anyone in the Ice Caves yet but that isn't really true. Both of you have made friends, perhaps without knowing it. Ever since you have met our people you have been sending gifts and supplies to members of our tribe. And as you know we are a race of warriors. Both of you, as well as Gabriel and Raphael are held in high esteem by our tribe. I have a feeling that you will feel at home very quickly," Misha said.

"Hannah remember when you kept asking us to take much of your family treasures because you didn't want to leave them behind in Nora?" Luca asked. "Well, we did and gave them as gifts to others. When you go to Calen's parent's house, you will see many things that belonged to your parents. All of those beautiful fur coats that belonged to your mother we brought back for the wives of our leaders and Calen's mother. You know that Maxwell and Emeral raised Misha and me too. We told everyone they were gifts from you and Gabriel."

"Luca gave Father that collection of pipes that your father had," Calen said to Hannah. "And it pleased him greatly. What Misha and Luca are trying to say is that our family and many of our tribe already feel like they know you and are looking forward to you coming. And yesterday Simon told me that Annabelle wants to visit us all in the Ice Caves. But he doesn't want to bring all the children because they are so young, so after this baby is born and is old enough to leave with their family they are coming to see us."

"I will admit I am feeling better about this," Hannah said. "You probably think Natasha and I have been silly, it's just that we didn't know what to expect."

"Your lives aren't going to be all that different than they are here," Calen said. "You will just be spending time with different people. In fact Dagon and Koby have already moved into their rooms in our new house."

"Really," Natasha said. "I miss them." Then Natasha looked at Hannah. "Are you thinking the same thing that I am?"

"We need to go shopping," Hannah said and laughed.

"Why?" Gabriel asked.

"So we have gifts to bring."

The night of his first day back in Port Friada, Archetenus discovered a large oak tree on Dieter's property that was growing close to the mansion. Archetenus thought the tree must be almost two hundred years old.

It was tall but it's giant limbs also spread out horizontally and afforded Archetenus perfect views into several rooms on the west side of the mansion.

He noticed that there appeared to be considerably less guards after the Rogett attack; he wondered how many men Dieter lost. Archetenus had heard people in the city speculating on the number of dead and missing body guards that Dieter had employed.

Many of the rooms in Dieter's mansion were illuminated at this time of night, including all of the rooms on the west side of the mansion. Archetenus could not view the front door or foyer from his perch in the ancient tree but he could see into Dieter's study, part of a long hallway, the dining room and most of the kitchen. Archetenus did not have to wait long before Dieter entered his study with another man.

This second man was dressed richly and wore a great deal of jewelry. Archetenus thought it was unlikely that this man was a body guard so he took a journal of paper and a pen from his backpack and started to draw the man's face. To Archetenus' amazement he was actually drawing a realistic likeness of the man. Never before had Archetenus showed any artistic abilities but he remembered that Miranda said she would help him to draw.

A smile came across his face as he remembered Miranda's words when she told him that he was going to be a father; emotions surged through Archetenus that he had never before experienced. Then he paused and wondered if Delilah and the baby were a sort of gift because of some of the decisions he had made. Archetenus knew that Delilah would not be alive if it wasn't for Miranda.

Before he had completed his first drawing another man and a woman were led into Dieter's study. From the way that Dieter treated Delilah, Archetenus thought it improbable that Dieter would allow a woman in their meeting unless she was also a member of the Insidiae. Dieter was pouring drinks for his guests.

The woman took a seat with her back to the window, so Archetenus worked on the drawings of the men, until he could get a better glimpse of the woman. There was something familiar about the frame of the woman. Archetenus completed drawings of both of Dieter's male visitors. Then Archetenus decided to draw a picture of Dieter. It was almost twenty minutes after Archetenus had completed these drawings before the woman turned around. His eyes grew wide as he recognized Sophie; Roch's humble servant was now dressed like a queen.

Gabriel had already taken off his clothes and was sitting in bed reading. "I'm sorry I am late," Hannah said as she hurried into their bedroom chambers. "I was talking with Natasha." Hannah disappeared into the bathing room and reemerged five minutes later. She always liked to prepare for her husband. This night she wore a black satin night gown. Her long blonde hair was flowing over her shoulders as she walked up to Gabriel.

"You look incredible," he said with a smile as he closed his book and put it on the nightstand. Hannah sat on the bed next to Gabriel and leaned forward and kissed him on the lips. "You smell wonderful too, is that a new cologne?" He asked then kissed Hannah again.

"Yes, I am glad that you like it," Hannah said. She started to run her fingers through Gabriel's hair as she spoke. "I can't tell you how happy Natasha and I are that you and Calen are going to the Ice Caves with us. I know we have been difficult it's just that neither of us want to be away from the two of you."

"Hannah don't think that we like being away from you either," Gabriel said as he looked into her eyes. "Natasha looks a lot farther along than she is and it's ridiculous for her to think about going on a mission. And Misha was right, she needs you now. Besides we might not be gone that long."

"I know," Hannah said softly. "But it doesn't make it any easier."

"Hannah I didn't want to say anything before because I don't know what we will find in that tomb in Nora. But you know that Sudfad has given me piles of reports and documentation to review."

"Well, he believes he has a spy in his military named Cedrick T. Kretcher, the Commanding General of Fort Polta. We believe Kretcher is really Cedrick Teivel a dark lord who leads a dangerous clan in the Kingdom of Ryed.

"Do you remember Raul and Simon telling us about how they almost died at the hand of the Hutas? Well, they were on a special mission for Sudfad and only the commanding generals of each fort knew their itinerary. Raul and Simon were ambushed several times before they were almost killed. And there have been some other things that have drawn suspicion to a spy in their military," Gabriel continued.

"As you can imagine Sudfad's investigation is very sensitive. He brought in two generals from the Kingdom of Lentz who uncovered a great deal of the information that he gave to me. I am preparing my plans for this mission. I plan to go to Ryed and I would like you to accompany me." Hannah was about to speak but Gabriel put his finger up to her lips.

"I have not worked out all the details yet; but as you can imagine this will be a very dangerous mission because the Kingdom of Ryed is controlled by dark lords and criminals. When I plan a clandestine mission I do a great deal of research and try to anticipate every possible situation so that my team is prepared. It will be hard work. Do you want to work on the mission with me?"

"Oh yes Gabriel," Hannah said enthusiastically. "What do you need me to do?"

"Good," Gabriel said and kissed Hannah on the forehead. "What I would like you to do now is to take advantage of your time with Natasha and Mateo. As you know, Natasha has trained her entire life for the missions. There are many things she can teach you that will be helpful, also being able to practice the medicines of the Rualas is a gift. Now you aren't coming along just to cook for us, you are going to be an active member of the team."

"Gabriel I feel so honored. I know how close your team is."

The Sanuri sat on his bed in his chambers in the castle of Sudfad. The holy man had been staring at the orb that Jared retrieved from a hell dimension for over an hour. The Sanuri's mind was flooded with thoughts; he was trying to fit the fragmented pieces of information he had into a large picture. He was becoming frustrated at his own inabilities to understand the clues he had been given. So preoccupied was the Sanuri that he did not realize The Lion had joined him.

"You keep staring at that orb, have you seen anything yet?" The Lion asked.

"No, I haven't really asked to see anything in the orb I am trying to understand the information we have obtained and figure out how it all fits together. And I keep having a nagging feeling that something is very wrong. Is that why you are here?"

"I came for several reasons," The Lion replied. "But first you must remember that you are no normal man. When you have strong feelings about something there are reasons for it. Perhaps Angels are whispering to you but you can't distinguish their voices and when that happens you should be asking for guidance."

"You are right my friend have you been whispering to me?"

"That nagging feeling as you call it is your concerns that the mausoleum in Nora is a trap and it is. And as you have suspected it is also a diversion. I do not want you or any of your people to enter that building until I tell you the time is right. I will explain more about the mausoleum later; what you need to concentrate on now is the various things the Insidiae and demons are trying to distract you from." The Lion was walking around the Sanuri's bedroom as he spoke.

"Are the Insidiae and demons working together?

"There are many plans in motion; some the Insidiae and demons are working together and others they are not. So you must understand that you have many who want to throw distractions at you. It has not gone unnoticed by many in the dark worlds that the Prophesy of The Seven Sons is starting to unfold."

"While most do not know who The Seven Sons are, they see a gathering of men and women who bring great light into this world. And all of these men and women are warriors each in their own way. Humans of different kingdoms and different kinds are uniting and they are being joined by the Rualas and the Shettees and this is just the beginning. Many will stand on both sides of the battlefields before this has all played out."

"Before you ask me the questions that plague your thoughts there are some things that I need to share with you. Because the Prophesy of The Seven Sons predicts doom will fall upon the dark worlds, those worlds too are uniting and your foes will be stronger than before," The Lion said. "But some new developments are affecting many things. Jared's escape from hell and his battle against the demons has brought fear to many. The demons realize how strong the humans are when they choose to resist them; unfortunately most humans still have not realized that truth."

The Lion continued, "As you know Miranda has appeared many times to Archetenus in her attempts to stop him from turning into a monster that could destroy much of mankind. They have developed a unique bond so to speak. Although the darkness inside of Archetenus has attacked Miranda and rejected her words, the tiny flickering light that was left in his soul has responded to her. Archetenus has no friends and of all the beings in this world Miranda is the only one he trusts."

"Miranda got Archetenus to denounce some of his demons and to tear off his blood necklace and to crush it. He is actually working on a mission for her. But he still bears the Mark of Satan on the back of his neck, although he does not know it. The demons still have a great deal of control over him."

"How did she do it?" the Sanuri asked in awe.

"The same way I did with Jared and Zoya," The Lion replied. "The most powerful gift that The Great Ruler has given this world is love. And you have seen what it can do. Jared will not return to the demons and he will be a valuable warrior for us. Archetenus on the other hand still has many decisions to make, but for the first time in his life he is starting down the right path. If he continues on this path it will send more shock waves of fear through the underworlds."

"Only three of the intended vessels have been told their destinies and two of them are actively changing their futures."

"And the third?"

"The third is Roch and he has returned from hell as a more dangerous monster than he was before, which is why Ahriman released him," The Lion explained. "Now that Roch has been exposed to hell, he has declared war against Ahriman and he now possesses enough power to carry out some of his ideas."

"Wait, are you saying that Roch returned to this world as a demon?"

"He is transitioning into one. But since he is physically turning into another creature, instead of having a demon use him as a vessel, Roch is going through many painful changes in every aspect of his being. For weeks he has been nothing more than a crippled animal lying on the floor of a forest near his castle. But his mind is starting to regenerate and he is slowly getting his memories back."

"You would be wise to put him as your most immediate mission. You should tell Sudfad's family about him, in addition to Gabriel and the others and I would suggest that you call Ibula and Thedes to the table when you tell everyone. Now for your questions."

"You said you want us to wait on entering the mausoleum; we were going to have some of the Patronus priests and Rualas watch the building; is that alright? Also the spirit that says she is Hannah's mother is she trying to trick us? Or is Zoya misunderstanding the visions?" the Sanuri asked all three of his questions without giving The Lion time to answer.

"It is a good idea to observe the mausoleum but make sure your people understand they should not touch it or even walk close to that building. And as for Zoya, think of her as a gift to both you and Jared. She is the reason Jared changed his life and she will be the reason for many decisions that he makes. Zoya is a faithful servant of The Great Ruler but in the weeks and months to come you must help her to overcome her fears so that her abilities can flourish. Zoya will be more help to you than that orb you hold."

"And that spirit?"

"That is the spirit of Harriet Marcus talking to Zoya, she can get no rest because of the horror her husband brought to this world. Harriet is giving Zoya information about what she sees but remember she is the spirit of a human, not an Angel, her insight is limited."

"This spirit said there were thirteen doors in the mausoleum, during our trials and tests many of us have come upon the number thirteen, we know it has significance. And many of us have been told the phrase 'thirteen levels, thirteen doors', by both Angels and demons. What does that phrase mean and is the mausoleum our final test?"

"First the mausoleum is not your final test; it is but one very dangerous battle in this unholy war. You are correct that the number thirteen has significance. When The Great Ruler created this world He created everything with a balance; with symmetry. Darkness has existed as long as has The Light. The demons and their followers deliberately try to throw the worlds out of balance to cause chaos and fear. That is why The Great Ruler gave The Box of Itifer to the world of man. The number thirteen became the symbol for the dark worlds in their attempts to unbalance creation. The number itself is not balanced, so to speak."

"Actually that makes many things easier to understand but what about the phrase 'thirteen levels, thirteen doors'?" the Sanuri asked.

"Even with all of your wisdom there is still so much you have yet to understand," The Lion said benevolently. "And my statement is said with love because no human should understand the horrors of the hell dimensions. As you know there are many hell dimensions in this world and others. And although they may differ greatly they also have some similarities and they have beliefs which unify them. The dimensions themselves are complicated as are the worlds of man. Each dimension contains its own secrets and mysteries but they all contain different sections to house those they torture."

"I don't understand," the Sanuri said.

"Think of it as a series of prisons where the criminals have been separated because of their crimes. A starving man steals a chicken and is arrested in this world, while that is breaking a law of man is that crime on the same level as a man who tortures and murders others for his own amusement?"

"No, of course not. So are you saying these different sections are called levels?"

"Yes."

"Then what is the significance of the thirteenth level?"

"It has to do with the Prophesy of Isdod," The Lion replied without further explanation.

"I have never heard of that prophesy."

"It is not in the world of man but it is contained in a book of chronicles that the demons worship."

"I didn't think demons worshipped anything."

"This book of chronicles is one of the uniting forces of the underworlds. It is as old as time."

"What is the name of this book?"

"There is no word in the world of man that can directly translate," The Lion explained. "Nor would I utter such a blasphemous word. For the sake of discussion we will call it the Book of Horror. This book contains many things including the history and the future of the underworlds. Whoever is the holder of this book wields great power."

"Is there only one copy?"

"Of the original, yes."

"How can demons predict the future?" the Sanuri asked.

"That my friend is a very long discussion for another time. The reason I am telling you this information is because that book is part of the reason the forces of the dark worlds are uniting and why they are trying to stop the Prophesy of The Seven Sons from being fulfilled. This is enough discussion for now."

"But there is still so much you haven't told me. How does the phrase 'thirteen levels, thirteen doors' fit into all of this and..."

The Sanuri did not finish his question because The Lion interrupted. "Having that information now would greatly affect the choices of many, including you. It is not time for that information to be revealed."

Chapter XIV
Myths and Truths

Archetenus stayed perched in the old oak tree most of the night. Two more men joined the group during the evening and Dieter moved his guests from his study to the dining room. As Archetenus watched these dark lords laughing and talking around the dining room table, he thought no one would recognize them for who they really were.

Now Archetenus understood what Miranda meant when she said he would be exposing the faces of darkness. Archetenus was getting bored after a couple of hours. He didn't know how long he would have his gift of drawing so he decided to draw the faces of everyone he saw at the mansion. He carefully labeled each drawing to avoid any future confusion.

The guests left the dining room around two o'clock in the morning. Archetenus assumed they were retiring to their rooms because he saw new lights in some windows but he stayed in the tree for another hour. Just as he was about to climb down from the tree he heard movement. Archetenus sat motionless as two of Dieter's men walked under the tree towards the back of the house.

No sooner had they passed when four more men walked under the tree in the same direction. These four men were talking loudly. "So the Old Man wants us to go down to the docks and get some more slaves," one of the men said and started to laugh. "Those damn sailors, the last batch we grabbed were so damn drunk it took them two days just to sober up."

"Hell, you'd probably do the same damn thing if'n you spent months on one of them ships. I'll tell you I wouldn't like it. Don't seem natural to me."

"Well, we lost so many to those stinking Rogetts," a third man said. "That Dieter said we might have to go into some of those lowlife taverns near the docks and start grabbing guys. If we do that, we're taking some of the big guys with us cuz those damn bars are rough. Why, every morning there are dead bodies piled up outside the doors."

Archetenus waited until he was sure no one would see him before he climbed out of the tree. He sneaked through the wooded area that was near Dieter's mansion until he came to a city street. Archetenus wanted a drink but he decided to return to his room instead. He flopped on top of his bed, fully clothed. He was tired but he had so many thoughts racing through his head that sleep did not come to him for a very long time.

Archetenus thought about Delilah. He missed her and a part of him was surprised by this admission. He was swept up in the passions and emotions of love. He tried to remember if he had ever felt quite this way before. Although he was enjoying the overwhelming feelings there was a part of Archetenus that was suspicious of everything that was happening to him. How could he fall in love and get married in a couple of days? And now he was going to be a father! His internal struggle finally surrendered to exhaustion and Archetenus fell asleep thinking about Delilah.

"We should do this more often," Vitomas said happily. "I forgot how much I enjoyed riding."

"Simon and I used to go riding every morning," Raul said as they rode across a large field.

"Why did you stop?" Vitomas asked.

"You and Annabelle and the babies," Raul said with a grin.

"I think we should all start going for morning rides again," Vitomas said enthusiastically.

"Annabelle probably won't want to come along, she is getting pretty big," Raul said. "But I will ask Simon. That doesn't mean you and I can't have a date every morning."

"Truly Raul I would love it."

"We should turn around soon. The Sanuri is having a big meeting this morning," Raul explained. "He is having it in the Great Hall and you and Annabelle and Mother are supposed to come also."

"What's it about?"

"All I know is that he is giving us some information from The Lion. It must be pretty important though because he has invited so many people and after the meeting he is leaving for Lentz to meet with the ruling families and the Nordes Tribe."

"Raul do you think there is going to be a war? I mean why would he meet with so many?"

It was the gold that helped Roch recover his senses. Every man has a passion, whether he realizes it or not. Roch was one of the lucky few; he had always known what his great passion was, greed. Roch covered himself with the treasures that he found hidden in the cavern behind the small waterfall. He played with the gold and he slept with the jewels. And on this morning when he awoke it was not to pain and confusion. Roch's eyes popped open and he suddenly sat up and looked around the cavern. On this morning Roch remembered who he was.

When Raul and Vitomas returned to the castle they were shocked to see the courtyard filled with Ruala and Shettee warriors. "Something awful must be happening," Vitomas said with concern.

"Now Honey we don't know that," Raul said. "But look everyone is entering the castle. We should just turn our horses over to the stable boys so we aren't late."

When Raul and Vitomas walked into the Great Hall they saw Simon and Annabelle standing with Ibula and Thedes. "We were just comparing baby stomachs," Annabelle said with a big smile. "Ibula isn't as big as me yet."

"What is this a gathering of pregnant women?" Calen joked as he shook hands with Thedes and kissed his cousin Ibula on the cheek. Ibula's eyes widened when she saw Natasha.

"I know I am getting as big as a house," Natasha said then she winked. "Calen is afraid it's going to take two Ruala warriors to fly me to the Ice Caves." Her comment made the group laugh.

Gabriel and Hannah had joined the group with Calen and Natasha. "So Hannah I hear that you and Natasha are going to be studying with Mateo," Ibula said. "You should feel honored. Lakin told me about the visions you had when Gabriel was on his spiritual journey. In our tribe only Mateo has such visions. You must be special." Hannah blushed at Ibula's words.

"I have heard that you are a very powerful healer," Hannah said. "I am looking forward to learning your ways. Did Lakin tell you that Gabriel and Calen will be coming to the Ice Caves with us?"

Before Ibula could answer the Sanuri said in a loud voice, "Would every one please be seated? And I would like to thank you for coming."

Ibula leaned forward and whispered to her brother Lakin, "Is that the man you spoke of?"

Lakin turned and saw Jared and Zoya enter the room. "Yes," he whispered.

"Sudfad and Renya have been generous enough to provide food and refreshments as you can see which is good because this may be a long meeting." All of the guests were seated at tables and each table contained platters of food and beverages. "As you know I am never at a loss for words but I will admit that this morning I was trying to figure out how to tell you some of the things I was told to say. So I am going to start by telling you some history. At the beginning of time, this world as many others was without darkness."

"I will never understand why the children of The Great Ruler were not satisfied with perfection but as you all know a group of them called out and the Old Ones answered and came to this world and corrupted it. Then more and more demons came because it proved such a rich feeding ground for them. What many of you may not know is that some of those people who originally called to the demons still walk in this world. They were the first to sell their souls, they are called the Grand Masters of the Insidiae organization and they are very powerful."

The Sanuri continue," I believe that everyone in this room is familiar with the Insidiae if not fought against them. There are many secret sects in that organization and they all have private agendas. Most of you are familiar with the Recupero Sect which has been trying to raise the demon Omnibus from his prison in The Abyss. This group believes that the demon will need a vessel to put his essence into once he escapes; so for centuries they have been experimenting on humans to create the perfect vessel."

"They have found a way to insert seeds of pure evil that are passed on through the second sons of each generation. After three generations they thought they had the perfect vessel which many of us thought was King Roch of Stordt. But we have found out that they have been creating many vessels with the idea of auctioning those humans off to the demons. I know this may sound absurd to many of you."

The Sanuri looked through the crowd and smiled when he saw Jared. "Jared I do not mean to embarrass you but will you please stand up?" Jared stood up reluctantly. "This is Jared; he was created to be a vessel for the demons. Jared is not only a physically strong man but he has great will and determination. He decided to change his destiny."

"The demons pulled Jared into hell and were about to auction him off. He not only fought them and returned to us but he retrieved a gift from The Great Ruler that had been stolen hundreds of years ago. Jared has fought his demons and won. He has changed his life and will be working with us on some of our missions."

"Lakin you told me that when you and Hannah and the others were trying to help Jared you heard screams but they were not coming from anyone in the room," the Sanuri continued. "I told you they were screams from hell. And after speaking with The Lion I now understand why. Every man and woman is born with free will, although the demons would have you believe otherwise."

"As powerful as all those demons were that were trying to capture and contain Jared, they lost their power once he made the decision to stand against them. As you can imagine the demons do not want humans to realize the power they possess."

"The Lion told me that another of the intended vessels is standing against the demons although he has not yet come as far as Jared."

The Sanuri looked at Raul and Vitomas. "Vitomas it is Archetenus that I speak of. You said that when he held you captive he kept talking to what seemed to be an invisible person. In reality he was speaking to an Angel named Miranda. It was Miranda who made Archetenus let you go. And it was Miranda who protected baby Jacob and brought him to Matthew and Angelina. Now from the looks on some of your faces I am sure you are wondering why an Angel would appear to a monster."

"If Archetenus would have kept on the path that he was on he would have become a vessel for a powerful demon and would have caused great destruction in this world. Yes, Miranda is trying to save Archetenus from his fate but she is also trying to save all of his future victims. Both Jared and Archetenus are huge and powerful men, which may be a common trait among the vessels. Both of these men were told their destinies and they both decided to change their futures. This freedom of choice cannot be tolerated by the Insidiae and there will be repercussions."

"As you know King Roch was meant to be a vessel also. He disappeared for a while and The Lion told me that Roch had been taken to the hell region of the demon Ahriman. Ahriman and Omnibus were great rivals. Ahriman has released Roch back into this world. He will no longer be a vessel for a demon. The Lion told me that Roch did not crumble under the tortures of hell but fed off from them, which is why Ahriman released him. Roch is now transforming into a demon." Renya gasped loudly when she heard the Sanuri's words.

"The Lion told me that stopping Roch should be our main focus now," the Sanuri continued. "Roch has always been a threat to Sudfad's family and now he is becoming a threat to the entire world. The Lion said that Roch is literally changing into another being and for the last few weeks he has been lying on the floor of the forest near his castle acting like an animal. Roch is slowly getting his memories and strength back and it is only a matter of time before he completes the transformation."

"Now for the second thing I have been directed to share with you." The Sanuri looked at Sudfad and Renya then back at his audience. "As many of you know Sudfad's family has been under attack a great deal and if it wasn't for many of you in this room, Raul, Simon and Petra might not be with us now. The reason for the attacks is that members of the dark worlds suspect that Sudfad's family may be the men spoken of in an ancient prophesy called the Prophesy of The Seven Sons."

"This prophesy is very long so I will summarize it. The prophesy predicts that there will be a time when the forces of darkness gather in great numbers to take control of this world, to destroy all that The Great Ruler has created. The prophesy then tells of Seven Sons of Light, which means they are seven sons of The Great Ruler, not one earthly father. The Seven Sons will lead vast armies against the hordes of demons and will damage them greatly. But the battles will be horrific."

"The prophesy says we will know the time is upon us when good men and women from different backgrounds and worlds come together to stand against darkness," the Sanuri explained. "My friends the night that Sudfad and Renya adopted Thedes and Ibula and united these three races was told about in the prophesy."

"And standing among you are five of The Seven Sons: King Sudfad, Prince Raul, Prince Simon, Prince Petra and myself. Prince Matthew from Lentz is the sixth son and the seventh has not yet been revealed to us. But I have been told that we will know him when we see him and he will bear the scars from demons."

Many of the people in the room whispered and looked around in amazement at the Sanuri's words.

"Darkness has spies everywhere and it has not gone unnoticed that there are now covenants among the Rualas, the Shettees, the Royal Families of both Wetpr and Lentz and the Nordes Tribe. We can expect attacks to increase against us and in addition there are many who are trying to distract us so that we do not interfere with their sinister plans. We will have to be wise in determining what is a threat and what is a distraction. The mausoleum in Nora is such a distraction which we will deal with when the time is right."

"For now we must focus our attention on Roch. We know he is in Taperia but The Lion said that Roch is in a constant state of transitioning which causes his physical form to change, which means we don't really know what he looks like. I have asked you here to share this information; the choice is yours as to whether you want to help in stopping Roch before he becomes more of a monster. There is no dishonor in not working on this mission."

Roch let out a howl that rivaled any animal. He stood up and started to dance around his treasures. Suddenly Roch stopped and stared at his arms and legs which were no longer transitioning from his travel between worlds. His body looked and felt solid, he felt like a human again. It was at this point that Roch realized he was naked. He left the cavern and squatted down by the pond so that he could look at his reflection. Roch did not recognize himself. His hair was long and matted and was filled with burrs and twigs.

Roch had a long beard and mustache that were caked with mud and matted. Roch's normally dark hair had strands of gray. His body was burned from the sun and covered with scratches and bruises. Roch had always been an egotistical man. He had considered himself handsome and was always well groomed. Now Roch sat staring at his image in the reflection of the water. "I look like a mad man," Roch thought to himself and a part of him wanted to cry.

Vitomas was the first person in the Great Hall to stand up and speak. "Obviously I have not spoken with my husband about what I am to say," Vitomas looked at Raul with a look of strength and determination. "I have not been trained as a warrior like most of you in this room. But I was Roch's prisoner and mistress for many years. Annabelle and I are the only two in this room who understand his capacity for cruelty, and that was as a man. I cannot imagine what he will be like as a demon. I would imagine it would be easier for us to destroy him before his transformation takes place. Do you have any idea how much time we have?"

"No," the Sanuri replied.

"Roch was obsessed with me and now he will want to kill me because I betrayed him. For a variety of motivations Roch will want to come after me. I will not allow him to cause any more pain for the family that I cherish. So I propose that we come up with a plan where you use me as bait. I would imagine that it is easier to draw him out than for us to search for him."

"Vitomas no!" Raul yelled as he stood up next to her.

"Honey you have met him, you know I am right. And if I wasn't your wife you would agree with this plan. He's going to come after us all anyways. Let's make it on our terms. So many of you are military strategists I am sure you can think of a way to destroy him."

"Raul, she is right," Gabriel said as he stood up. "I would not want my wife to take that risk either, but we can protect her."

Hannah and Ibula stood up simultaneously but Ibula spoke first, "I have wondered why Vitomas and I are almost perfect images of each other. Sanuri you have said many times there are no coincidences in this world. Now I believe we look as twins to take down this demon. I agree with Vitomas and I will help."

"For those of you who do not know, Roch raped and murdered my nine year old sister in front of my parents and many other people," Hannah explained with great emotion in her voice. "My father committed suicide and my mother died of a broken heart after the murder." Then Hannah turned to Gabriel. "I don't know what I can do but you must let me help, it is the only way that I will be able to find peace."

Before Gabriel could speak, Calen stood up. "Hannah is similar in size and shape to Vitomas and their hair is similar, from the back he might not be able to tell the difference."

"Calen what are you saying?" Gabriel asked.

"Ok I am just thinking here but we have three women who look very much alike, perhaps we could use all of them as bait, because we really don't know where Roch is yet."

"I don't like any of this," Raul said angrily. "I don't want to endanger any of them."

Vitomas turned and looked at her husband. "Raul every day you tell me that our daughter is the spitting image of me. Are we to live in fear that someday Roch will do to her what he did to me and to Hannah's sister? I am not willing to risk our children's safety. Deep down you know this has to be done."

Annabelle stood up. "I don't look like Vitomas and I am very pregnant now, but Roch sent his men after me too and I feel the same way that Vitomas does. I want to help also."

Now Renya stood up and walked to the Sanuri's side. "At this moment I can't tell you how proud I am of my three daughters and my friend. Roch has caused us to live in fear for a long time. And fear is a darkness that feeds upon us all. But Sanuri you have told us in the past that we were not to destroy Roch, are you still telling us that now?"

"No," the Sanuri said.

"Then it is time," Renya said with conviction and looked at Sudfad, who now joined her and the Sanuri in front of their guests.

"I have been waiting for this moment for a very long time," Sudfad said with great emotion. "Roch murdered my parents, raped my daughter and tried to kill my son. I still do not understand why we were told not to go after him before. But we will not fail."

"Thedes, Simon and Gabriel you have not spoken but I am sure you are not pleased with your wives volunteering to help with Vitomas' idea. But all of your wives and families are already in danger simply because Roch exists. I fully sanction this idea. After this meeting I want you to start working on plans. You will have the Wetprian Military at your disposal. And any of you who wish to stay at the castle are our guests for as long as you wish."

Thedes stood up and addressed the group. "I did not speak out in protest because I am proud of my wife and I am proud of Vitomas, Annabelle and Hannah. Our wives trust that we will protect them in this mission and we will not let them down."

After the meeting, Natasha turned to Calen. "Calen you know I want to work on this mission badly and I would like to help in any way that I can. And from the sounds of it Gabriel, Hannah and you will be needed here. I know you wanted me to have our baby in the Ice Caves. Calen what would you think about us staying here until this mission is completed and having your family come and stay with us. You are already building the wing of the house. We can hire extra workmen to get it done faster."

Calen picked up Natasha's hand and kissed it. "I think my parents will understand once I explain everything to them. You are right I should stay here and I don't want us to be separated. I will hire more workmen and why don't you and Hannah start buying all of the furnishings that we are going to need."

"You know from your mother's letters, she and your father really enjoyed building our house in the Ice Caves," Natasha said. "Perhaps they would like to come early and help us with the wing. Joao and Elan or Dack can share a room; that will free up one of the bedrooms in the house. And this way your parents can see what you, Luca and Misha do when you are away from home."

"Zoya, I would like to stay and help with the planning," Jared said. "Why don't you go into town and buy yourself some things. Maybe Laurel will go with you." Zoya did not speak but kissed Jared on the cheek. He reached into his pocket and brought out a leather bag of gold coins which he handed to her. "Make sure you get yourself some things." Then he added with a grin. "Maybe you could stop by a jewelry store and find a ring you like."

After the meeting the people in the Great Hall rearranged the tables so they could form work groups. Jared walked over to the table where Gabriel, Calen and Raphael were sitting. "Mind if I join you?" Jared asked.

"Glad to have you," Gabriel said." But we are waiting on Simon and Raul." Jared looked to his left and saw Simon and Raul each talking with their wives.

"Simon, before you yell at me, I don't know what I can do but I have to do something," said Annabelle.

"I'm not going to yell at you," Simon said and took her hand. "And I'm not going to let anything happen to you and I agree with Vitomas. It's time we stopped him."

"Well then help me figure out what I can do," said Annabelle.

Simon looked at Annabelle for a moment then smiled. "Go get Gala and your parents and bring them to our table."

"I don't like putting you in danger," Raul said angrily. "I can't stand the idea of you being near that monster again."

"Well then my husband, you will have to stop him before he gets close to me," Vitomas said with a flirtatious smile and reached up and kissed Raul on the cheek. "Raul you are a wonderful husband and father but you know that if we are to protect our children we need to do this. I have faith in you that you will keep me safe. Now go use that brilliant mind of yours and start working on some plans." Raul smiled and took both of Vitomas' hands in his and kissed them, then he turned and walked over to the table.

"Before we get started I asked Annabelle to bring Gala and her parents here," Simon said to the men seated at the table. "Where are Luca, Misha and Lakin?"

"They're talking to the Sanuri," Raphael said.

Within minutes Annabelle walked up to Simon's table with Gala and her parents. "Whatever plans we come up with, we will need to get some kind of word to Roch so he knows to come looking for one of the girls. Do you, any of you, still have enough contacts in Taperia and Cana that you could perhaps get some false rumors going?" Simon asked.

"Yes," Gala said and turned and looked at Laurel and Alexander who both smiled and nodded.

"Good, I like this idea," said Gabriel.

Laurel put her hand on Jared's shoulder. "Jared we are all going shopping with Zoya, so you don't have to worry."

"Good, thank you," Jared said. "Maybe you can find some things for the wedding."

Not surprising to either Sudfad or Renya all of their guests for the meeting stayed with them. And as the week wore on more Ruala and Shettee warriors joined them. The Sanuri left for Lentz immediately after the meeting because he had to give the people there, the same message from The Lion.

While many of the warriors were working from dawn to dusk devising various plans to trap and destroy Roch. Luca and Lakin took twenty five Ruala warriors to Nora; their mission was to watch the mausoleum that had been set up as a trap for the Sanuri and others.

On the fifth day after the meeting; Elan walked into the Great Hall and told Calen and Misha they needed to come home at once.

"Is Natasha alright? Is the baby coming?" Calen asked anxiously.

"Everything is alright," Elan said with a grin. "I was just told to bring you home."

Elan led his two cousins into Gabriel's house by the back door which brought them into the kitchen. Seated at the kitchen table with Hannah and Natasha were Calen's parents Maxwell and Emeral and Dagon and Koby, all of whom had smiles on their faces.

"As soon as your mother got your letter we started packing," Maxwell said as he stood up to shake hands with Calen and Misha.

"We love it that you and Natasha want to include us in the building of this home," Emeral said warmly as Calen and Misha each kissed her on the cheek.

"And of course Emeral brought so many baby things that Koby and I had to help carry them," Dagon joked as he and Koby stood up and greeted their adopted brothers.

"Did Mother tell you about the mission?" Calen asked Koby and Dagon as he sat down at the table.

"Of course," Koby said. "Remember we read that book about Roch, that monster needs to be stopped and we are here to help."

"The boys told us a little about what was in that book," Emeral said with disgust. "I think they felt they had to explain why this mission was so important. Especially after meeting Sudfad and Renya's family some of those things just broke my heart. Your father and I want all of you to know how proud we are of you."

"After lunch Natasha and I are going to take your parents to the castle so they can visit Renya and Sudfad unless there is something else you would rather do?" Hannah asked of Calen.

"No, that sounds fine," Calen said. "A lot of us are in the Great Hall working on strategies, you are all welcome to join us."

"Why, I would find that very interesting," said Maxwell.

"Then we are going to take Emeral shopping," Natasha said with a smile.

"Aunt Emeral please don't let them buy anymore pink baby clothes," Elan said kiddingly and everyone in the room broke into laughter.

Roch now recognized his surroundings and knew he was not far from his castle, which he started to quickly walk towards. After almost twenty minutes Roch stopped because he realized he had to analyze his position. He remembered he had been in a hell world but he didn't know how or why he was there. The thought suddenly struck him that if he was not dead and had been in hell, someone had to have sent him there.

"Did this happen to me because someone took my throne?" Roch thought to himself. He knew he was unrecognizable in his current state and badly wanted to bathe and shave but his cunning mind was at work. Roch decided to steal some clothes and to spy on his castle until he could figure out what had happened to him and who was sitting on his throne.

He remembered there had been some small farms outside of his castle walls and now walked in the direction that he remembered them to have been located. As he walked, Roch wondered how long he had been gone. He didn't remember leaving the castle; he mostly remembered being cold and in pain.

Roch remembered hearing constant whispering and he remembered the song that kept playing in his head, the song that tormented him. His body suddenly started to tremble as he remembered waking up in Ahriman's domain. This memory brought such horror to him that Roch stopped trying to remember his past and focused on his current situation.

Within an hour, Roch was standing a few hundred yards away from a small farm. He could see smoke rising from the chimney. He crept closer, concealing himself behind bushes and trees. He watched as a woman was hanging washed laundry on a rope. After the woman returned to the house, Roch crept closer to the laundry. He would have to run across several hundred feet of open area to reach the clothing, so he decided on the things he wanted before he made an attempt to get them.

Just as he was stepping out of the concealment of the bushes, the woman walked out of the house again with another large basket of laundry. Roch jumped behind a bush and patiently waited until the woman returned to the house. Then he bolted from the bushes and grabbed a couple of pairs of pants and some shirts from the rope. Roch ran back into the wooded area feeling exhilarated.

Chapter XV
Patronus

Twelve hundred years earlier the Continent of Opots experienced one of its worse dark ages. War lords and demons were ravishing all of the kingdoms. Strange diseases became another deadly foe and the populace was consumed with fear. When people are consumed with fear they often strike out not only to relieve their anxieties but to help them to feel in control.

And strike out they did but not at their attackers who they felt powerless against. The peoples of Opots struck out at each other, the weak and infirm were the first victims of this new wave of terror. Then the races accused each other of bringing a world of darkness upon them. The horror and the bloodshed knew no relief. The peoples of all the kingdoms of Opots continued to feed their fears which only created more darkness.

A small group of priests from the monastery in Philiste in the Kingdom of Wetpr took a pilgrimage to have an audience with their King. King David was a warrior king and a man reputed to have great integrity and honor. The priests told King David of the horrors they had seen while administering to the peasants. Then this brave group of priests told the King of something that had never before been spoken of. These priests believed that dark lords and demons had infiltrated the Holy Church.

The King would not consider such an idea; but as the priests gave him mounting evidence his opinion started to sway. Then as the ultimate piece of proof, the priests asked the King to accompany them back to their monastery. The King rode with five hundred of his bravest warriors. When they reached the monastery each priest said a small prayer then they led the King and his men into the lower levels underneath the monastery and there the King laid his eyes upon the first unholy altar that he had ever seen.

King David immediately ordered his men to kill the hundreds of snakes that were in the unholy chamber. As his men attacked the snakes, the snakes fought back and the flames from the torches that were affixed to the walls suddenly exploded with light. The demon Ahriman's maniacal laughter roared through the cavern.

King David and his men stood motionless against this unseen horror. In the back of the group stood a tiny priest, he was half the size of his comrades. As fear overtook them all, the littlest priest stepped in front of all the others.

"Great Ruler we need your presence here," the priest called out. Then he took a couple steps closer to the unholy altar. "Demon be gone," the priest yelled. "Only the presence of The Great Ruler has dominion here. Your powers are nothing compared to His and we shall not bow before you."

As the spirit of The Great Ruler entered the monastery; a wind of great fury enveloped the room picking up the snakes and smashing them into the stone walls. The altar and all that desecrated it were destroyed by the fury of this wind. The roar of a single lion filled the cavern as the greatest warrior Angel in the heavens announced to the demon that the humans did not stand alone. The powerful demon Ahriman fought but he was no match for the power of The Great Ruler. The presence of evil left that monastery, never to return.

King David was so moved by what he saw; both the horror of the evil and the miracle of The Great Ruler that he immediately dedicated a portion of his entire army to the Church. These soldiers were to protect all that was holy and to fight the demons of the night. This new army was named the Patronus, which was the word for 'protectors' in the old language.

King David was a warrior and his armies were mighty yet he realized that the tiny, dwarf priest welded more power than all of his men and their weapons. By orders of King David all the men who were to be in the army of the Patronus were to study with the priests of Philiste and to become priests themselves. His hopes were to create an army that was indestructible. An army that could fight both the war lords and the demons and win. King David asked the dwarf priest to return to his castle and to be the King's private tutor.

Over the centuries the Patronus realized they could be the most effective by keeping their true identities concealed. So these warrior priests preformed both clandestine and overt operations. The monastery at Philiste was and remains the main headquarters of the Patronus to this day.

Under the rule of King Sudfad of Wetpr with the cooperation of King Tobias of Puntd the Patronus established headquarters at the monastery at Malga after they drove the demon Ahriman out from that location also. In addition, the Patronus established headquarters in Nora at the estate formerly owned by Gabriel and Hannah and which was now owned by King Sudfad. The Patronus established another headquarters in the Cicero Estate which lies just north of Cicero College outside of Salar in the Kingdom of Wetpr.

King Sudfad purchased a home for High Priest Gabriel, who was a member of the Patronus, and his wife Hannah as a gift for saving the King's son from kidnappers. High Priest Raphael, a close childhood friend of Gabriel's and a member of the Patronus moved into this house also. While these two powerful high priests had studied and fought together; Gabriel specialized in clandestine operations while Raphael shined as a military strategist and led troops in overt operations.

Because of the unwavering faith and courage these two men displayed The Great Ruler led them to what would be their most important assignment. They were asked to work with King Sudfad and his family as Keepers of the Scrolls and to assist Sudfad's family as the prophesized Seven Sons. The home in Salar soon became one of the most important command posts in the history of the Patronus.

"Hello, is this the house of Gabriel?" a woman's voice asked outside of the back door of Gabriel's home. Family and guests were eating breakfast in the kitchen, the back door opened into the kitchen.

"I'll get it," Elan said as he jumped up from the table and walked over to the door. "Cassandra what are you doing here?"

"Hi Elan, those workers told me to come around back," Cassandra said cheerfully. "I have some things for my brother and the others."

Elan stepped back to allow Cassandra into the kitchen. Cassandra was a Ruala warrior; she was shorter than most but just as beautiful and graceful as was common among her tribe.

Cassandra wore her long curly reddish blonde hair in a ponytail and her vibrant blue eyes seemed to dance as Elan introduced her to everyone at the kitchen table. Cassandra was a year older than her brother Joao.

"Joao and the others are with Luca and Lakin on a mission in Nora," Elan explained.

"What are you working on?"

"Calen asked me to watch over Natasha while she is pregnant," Elan said with pride.

"I don't understand," Cassandra said genuinely. "Isn't she a warrior?"

"Thank you Cassandra!" Natasha said loudly. "Perhaps you could explain that to my husband."

"Cassandra once you get to know Natasha you will understand," Calen said with a chuckle. "Sit down and have something to eat." Hannah could not but notice that Emeral, Maxwell, Dagon, Misha, Koby and Calen all seemed to be grinning as if they were aware of a private joke.

"Actually I have some business to discuss with Gabriel," Cassandra said then paused. "Well, perhaps it is with all of you." Cassandra pulled five small rolls of paper from her back pack. Each roll was tied with golden cord. She formally walked up to Gabriel and handed him the rolls.

"What is this?" Gabriel asked as he unsecured the cord on the first sheet of paper.

"My brother Joao, Dack, Bekka, Fala and I are requesting permission to join your team. Those are letters from our parents as well as statements from some of the leaders of our tribe." No one at the table said anything but everyone was smiling so Cassandra continued. "We have all trained our entire lives as warriors but we realize we have much to learn about hunting demons and dark lords. When the others return you can ask them but we all promise to work and study very hard. It would be an honor to us if you would consider our requests."

"I will have to admit," Gabriel said with a broad smile. "I am not used to my Ruala comrades being so formal, Cassandra everyone is family here." Then Gabriel looked at Elan. "Elan why don't you help Cassandra unpack in Bekka and Fala's room. You will probably have to move another bed in there until our construction projects are finished. Cassandra let me talk this over with my team."

"Yell when you want help moving the bed," Dagon said.

After Elan and Cassandra had left the kitchen Hannah asked, "Ok, why is everyone smiling like there is some inside joke?"

"Because Elan has had a crush on Cassandra since he was a little boy," Calen said. "And she seems to have no idea."

"That's sweet," Natasha said. "Why doesn't Elan say something to her?"

"Because he is shy around girls," said Misha.

"Well, he certainly doesn't take after Calen then," Natasha said and laughed.

"Hey, I fell in love with you the second I saw you and I wasn't going to let you get away," Calen said and leaned over and kissed Natasha on the lips.

Gabriel read each letter and then passed them around the table for everyone one to read. "These ties look like they are made of spun gold," Raphael remarked.

"They are," said Maxwell. "It is an honor for the families of these warriors to have their children working with you."

"So what do all of you think?" Gabriel asked.

"This may not be important," Hannah said. "But except for Cassandra they were all with Natasha and me for several weeks before you came home from Nora. They all worked hard and kept asking for more things to do. They are all very pleasant and smart."

"Don't let Cassandra's size fool you," Koby said. "She is a serious fighter and thinks quickly on her feet. And she looks sweet but she doesn't take crap from anyone."

"Well, I guess that is a vote for Cassandra," Raphael said with a grin. "From what I know of them, they all seem like good kids. My only concern and I am probably showing my age here, is that they all seem so young to me. I would feel better if we paired them up with more experienced warriors."

"I agree," said Gabriel.

"My only concern would be Fala," Calen said. "She is considerably younger than the rest and I think a little naïve. But she can fight and use weapons."

"Maxwell," asked Gabriel. "What if we gave them all a try and one or more of them are not up to the tasks, will I be insulting their families?"

"We are all warriors Gabriel," Maxwell replied. "So their parents would understand. But I would suggest you tell all of them up-front that they will be going through a training period and if they can't perform the tasks you will send them home and they can request to be part of your team at another time. That way their dignity isn't hurt as much."

"I like that idea," Gabriel said and looked around the table. "Is there anyone here who is against us accepting any of these kids?" No one spoke so Gabriel continued and looked at Misha, Koby, Calen and Dagon. "Since you know them better, why don't you decide who we pair them up with for training?"

"After Natasha has the baby I think we should pair Fala up with her for a while," Dagon said. "Even if Natasha isn't working on a mission, I just think Fala would feel more comfortable with a woman trainer."

"I have a thought," Elan said as he stood in the doorway of the kitchen. "All the time that Natasha and I spend together she is constantly training me about demons and magics and dark lords. She has loaned me a couple of books to read that are fascinating."

233

"Calen since you won't let Natasha work on any missions right now, why doesn't she give classes to all of us at once. She really is a good teacher. Then that way we will have more knowledge when we go out in the field with you."

Calen was smiling proudly. "I like your idea Elan but it's up to Natasha."

"Oh I would just love to do that," Natasha said happily. "At least I would feel like I was doing something useful."

"Well I'm going to be one of your students," Hannah said and she and Natasha exchanged smiles.

"Natasha your first class show them your bull whip and that jacket that is lined with knives, that will get their attention," Koby said with a laugh.

"So are we in agreement?" Gabriel asked as he looked around the table. "We give them all a try. Natasha starts them out with her classes then you pair them with more experienced warriors."

"Sounds fine to me," said Calen.

"Elan will you bring Cassandra down here?" Gabriel asked.

A few moments later Elan and Cassandra entered the kitchen. "Cassandra take a seat," Gabriel said. "We have decided to give all of you a chance. But you have to understand that these missions are very dangerous and you will be attacked by demons and dark magics."

"So we will put all of you through a training program which will start with classes taught by Natasha; then you will be paired with a more experienced warrior." Cassandra's eyes were wide with excitement as she listened to Gabriel. "If for any reason the team feels that one of you isn't ready for this type of work, we will send you home but you will have another chance to request to be on the team. Does that sound reasonable to you?"

"Oh yes," Cassandra said excitedly. "You won't be sorry. We will make you all proud."

234

Archetenus had spent a week spying on Dieter's home and guests. When it appeared to him that the last of Dieter's guests were leaving the mansion, Archetenus quickly packed his things and rode out of Port Friada, heading to the monastery at Leven. In a way, Archetenus was surprised that everything went so smoothly in Port Friada. The fact that it was all so easy gave him cause for concern.

Archetenus was anxious to see Delilah because of both his feelings for her and his fear for her safety. He rode hard the first day and wanted to ride all night but he knew he had to give his horse a rest. After Archetenus set up his camp he called out to Miranda. When she appeared she was sitting close to him which made him jump.

"Is Delilah alright?" he asked.

"Archetenus I am seeing a whole other side of you as of late, and I like it. Yes, Delilah is fine but very scared for your welfare. Archetenus this girl loves you very much, you would be wise to remember that."

"What are you talking about?"

"Tell me about the last loving relationship you were in with a woman," said Miranda. Archetenus did not answer her. "All I am trying to say is that for a relationship to be successful both people have to work on it. You have the opportunity to be very happy with Delilah."

"You mean I should stop drinking?"

"Well that would be a good start," she said. "But enough of this subject. You did well in Port Friada I am pleased. Did anything surprise you?"

"Hell ya, I couldn't believe I could draw."

Miranda smiled. "If you will only listen to me you will be surprised at the things you will experience."

"I suppose so," Archetenus said with a grin. "So what do you want me to do with those drawings?"

235

"This Archetenus is going to be another test of your faith. Now that Dieter's guests are gone he is going to resume his search for Delilah and the other vessels who are unaccounted for. Not because he is a compassionate man but because he felt that he owned them all and the vessels he was going to make money from. When you reach the monastery do not stay there longer than two days. Take Delilah and head north until you get to the City of Castor in the Kingdom of Lentz. I will provide you with safety unless you fail to follow my directions."

"Do you want us to live in Castor? And what about the drawings?"

"I want you to stay in Castor until I send the one you are to give the drawings to. Whether you and Delilah decide to make that city your home is up to you."

"There is more to this," Archetenus said with a smile.

"There always is. But you have to earn information."

"Why, I got the drawings like you told me to?"

"Archetenus think of all the conversations we have had over the years. Now think of how many times you have actually done what I requested. There are many good people trying to stop Dieter and others from making men like you the slaves of the demons. If I tell you the name of the man you will contact now, well, what if you have a change of heart and align with the demons again; then I have put that man in jeopardy."

Delilah sat on her small bed in her room in the monastery complex. The days since Archetenus left were agonizing for her since she had nothing to fill her time but to worry about him. Delilah prayed for Archetenus' save return. She knew he was a capable man but her knowledge of Dieter's cruelty created a great deal of fear and anxiety within her. It had been a week, since Archetenus left her at the monastery and now a new fear was creeping into her consciousness; what if he never returned for her.

Tears were running down Delilah's cheeks when the door to her room suddenly flew open, which caused her to jump off from the bed. "Archetenus," she cried and ran to him. Archetenus picked Delilah up and swung her around. He was relieved to see that she was safe and unharmed. As they kissed Delilah was crying and laughing. "I was so worried about you," she said.

"And I was worried about you. Have you been alright?"

"Oh yes, the priests have been very kind to me; I was afraid that Dieter would kill you."

"He has been occupied, I will tell you about it later," Archetenus said as he stood Delilah on her feet. He wanted to make love to his young wife but a voice inside of him kept telling him to leave the monastery. When Archetenus entered Delilah's room he had dropped the packages he was carrying; now he stooped to pick them up. "Here I bought you some things," He said as he handed the packages to her, "I am sure you want to change your clothing."

Delilah smiled brightly as she tore open the packages, "Archetenus these things are beautiful; where did you get them?"

"From Madam Bular. Why don't you change while I saddle your horse? We will be leaving right away."

Delilah walked up to Archetenus and took his hand, "Thank you for coming back for me."

Archetenus leaned down and kissed Delilah passionately on the lips, a kiss that stirred their desires. "I couldn't stop thinking about you," he said. "But we aren't safe yet, so I want to get out of this kingdom."

"Where will we go?" Delilah asked as she started to unbutton her blouse.

"We're going to Lentz."

"Do you know anyone there?"

Archetenus looked at Delilah and paused before he answered. "Well, I guess that is hard to say," he said with a grin and walked out of the door.

Roch spent several days stealing items from three different farms. It was starting to become a game to him. He would sneak around the buildings and watch the farmers and their families. When he was feeling particularly bold he stole a blueberry pie that was cooling on a windowsill. At first he would steal little things, like a knife, a rope, some boots, but they were too big for him to wear. He stole a bar of soap, some food and finally a horse.

Roch washed and cut his hair so that it hung to his shoulders. He decided to keep his beard and mustache to help disguise his face but he trimmed them both significantly. He filled his pockets with gold coins and rode into Taperia. The first thing that Roch did was to buy new clothes, boots and weapons. Then he went to the Taperian Imperial Hotel and got a room and a hot meal. Roch bought two fine horses and leather gear then he returned to the cavern behind the water fall and filled his saddlebags with gold coins and jewels. He returned to the hotel and hid his treasure under the floorboards in his room.

Roch had bought a large brimmed hat which he pulled down over his eyes to somewhat hide his face. He walked out of the hotel and stood on the sidewalk for several moments watching people. Then he walked into the nearest tavern, not because he wanted a drink but so he could listen to men talk; Roch wanted to find out what was happening in his kingdom.

"Tell him what you told me," Sabot ordered as he pushed one of the hired men in front of Dieter.

"You don't have to push me," Chalice said angrily. "I haven't done a damn thing wrong." Then Chalice looked at Dieter, who was sitting at his dining room table finishing his breakfast. "I just told Sabot here that yesterday morning I was walking down the street and I saw that big guy that Sabot was supposed to follow. Well, I didn't see Sabot anywhere around so I decided to see what the guy was doing."

238

"He walked into Tabots Jewelers and was looking at jewelry. He was in there for some time then he bought some things and left. I followed him for about two blocks and damn if I didn't lose him in a crowd so I went back to Tabots and asked the jeweler what the guy bought. Two gold wedding rings."

Dieter leaned back in his chair and stared at Chalice and Sabot. "Sabot you have proven to me that you couldn't track a bleeding elk through a ballroom, but at any time that you actually saw Archetenus was he with a girl?"

"No," Sabot replied angrily.

"Chalice did that jeweler tell you what Archetenus said?"

"Yeah, he said the guy didn't talk much, just said he wanted to look at wedding rings. Then he found what he wanted and paid with gold coins. That was it."

"So what do you think this means?" Dieter asked his men.

"Well, it's the first time anyone has seen Archetenus in a while," Sabot said. "He moved out of his hotel room the night before the Rogett attack. And I didn't see much of him for a couple of weeks before that. He mighta been shacking up with some gal. I'll go back to the hotel and see what I can find out."

"He moved out just before the Rogett attack," Dieter repeated suspiciously. "Chalice you did good," Dieter said and took a small pouch of gold coins out of his pocket and handed it to Chalice. "Something just isn't right here," Dieter said. "I can feel it. I want both of you to go out and find out everything you can about Archetenus and where he might be." Then Dieter paused. "I'm going to pay Madam Bular another visit."

"You think Archetenus might have Delilah?" Sabot asked with surprise.

"Well, they both seem to have disappeared around the same time, who knows," Dieter said angrily. "And Sabot don't disappoint me anymore. I am paying you to do a job; do it!"

"I don't like it, it's just too dangerous," Raul said sternly to the men sitting at his table in the Great Hall of the castle. Simon, Gabriel, Calen, Koby and Dagon, were five of the men at the table and all of them had read Sophie's book about Roch. Although they understood Raul's fears about using Vitomas as bait to catch Roch, they were becoming frustrated with Raul. Thedes could see the looks on their faces so he turned to Raul.

"Can we talk privately?" Thedes asked and stood up. Raul didn't speak but followed Thedes out of one of the side doors of the Great Hall that opened into a garden.

"Raul you are my brother but you should leave this planning session. I'm sorry I don't know how to say it softly."

"Now just a minute," Raul started to argue but Thedes cut him off.

"Raul every man and woman in that room is trying to find ways to protect our wives and our families. They are all experienced warriors. And yet you won't even listen to what anyone has to say. You are the one who is going to get someone hurt because you are so filled with fear for Vitomas. Raul you know better than to act like this. The only way we can truly protect our loved ones is to stop Roch and your wife is handling this better than you. Vitomas knows that monster, she understands what makes him tick; she should be at that table not you!"

Raul stared angrily at Thedes for several moments then quickly walked away without speaking. Thedes returned to his table in the Great Hall and looked at the others. "I told Raul to leave, because he is so against everything we are trying to do. He is just too emotional to be a part of this." Then Thedes turned to Simon. "Simon I am sorry."

"Don't apologize to me, you're right. But in Raul's defense, he knows what Roch did to Vitomas and the thought of Roch getting near her terrifies him," Simon said.

Prince Lakin was given orders by the Sanuri to watch the mausoleum. Lakin and his second in command which was Luca, understood that none of their warriors were to go into or even to touch the mausoleum.

Lakin stayed at the Patronus headquarters outside of Nora. Luca organized the twenty-five Ruala warriors into three shifts. Two shifts had eight warriors and one shift had nine warriors, four warriors were to watch the mausoleum itself and the others were ordered to watch the surrounding area. Of these twenty-five warriors, Bekka, Joao, Fala and Dack were in training.

Luca had each of the trainees spend one day with a member of the Patronus, so they could learn about that organization; since Gabriel's team was an extension of the Patronus. Other than discovering the location of the mausoleum, the Patronus had not had any sightings of demonic activity since the battle that wounded Ahriman. The first week none of the Rualas saw any activity in or near the mausoleum, so Lakin sent Luca to Fort Nora to speak with General Colter.

As Luca flew towards the fort he was enjoying the warmth of the morning sun and the cool breeze that was blowing against him. It was relaxing for Luca to get away from everyone else, even for a brief period of time. He believed that Bekka, Fala, Joao and Dack would be worthy members of the team but these four young warriors were so enthusiastic about training they had barely given Luca a moment's peace since the group left Salar.

Luca was flying in a southwesterly direction along the river Nebu towards the fort. He was flying on the eastern side of the river with the wind blowing into his face. Luca started to smell smoke and flew lower to see where the smoke was coming from. Once he cleared a wooded area, Luca heard screaming. He turned eastward towards the sound of the child's voice.

"Let go of them," screamed a young boy frantically as he ran after the two Huta warriors who were dragging his mother and sister out of their burning home. The small boy ran to the barn to get his father and screamed when he saw his father's butchered body hanging from the rafters inside of the barn. The boy was stunned but his mother's desperate screams brought him back to the horror of his reality. Christopher ran into the back of the barn and grabbed a pitchfork then he turned and started to run towards his mother's screams.

Time seemed to stop for Lila as she saw one of the Hutas throw her mother to the ground and start to tear off her clothing.

241

The young girl was so fixated on her mother's rape that she was momentarily oblivious to the fact that the Huta who was dragging her now stopped and attempted to throw her to the ground. At that moment Lila was more afraid for her mother than for herself.

Lila fought with the Huta and kicked him in the groin, as the warrior momentarily slumped forward because of the pain; Lila tried to grab the knife on his belt. The Huta grabbed her with just his right arm and pulled Lila towards him. Instead of trying to pull away, Lila jumped towards the Huta and grabbed his head; she sunk her teeth into his right ear and bite down as hard as she could. The warrior screamed in pain and grabbed Lila with his left arm, pulling her away from him.

In the instant that the Huta pulled her away, Lila saw her little brother running towards the Huta who was mounted on top of their mother. The Huta who was holding Lila saw the look on her face and turned to see the small boy plunge a pitchfork into the back of his comrade. Christopher was only six and did not have the strength to plunge the pitchfork far enough to kill the Huta.

The warrior screamed and fell forward onto Christopher's mother, then he reached around and tried to grab the pitchfork from the lower portion of his back. Meanwhile the Huta who was holding Lila turned towards Christopher. Lila was trying again to grab the knife from the Huta's belt when Luca landed on the ground between the two Hutas.

Luca pulled his knife from his sheath and stared at the Huta in defiance. The Huta smiled to see a hated Ruala standing before him and pulled his knife.

"Get the boy and run," Luca said to the girl as the Huta lunged at him while wielding the large knife.

Luca jumped back to avoid the blade that was aimed at his stomach. The two men crouched slightly as they circled each other with their weapons. Luca could see that the second Huta was bleeding badly but was still trying to pull the pitchfork out of his back. The Huta lunged again and Luca side stepped and leaned towards his adversary and stabbed him in the side just below the ribcage.

242

Luca quickly pulled his knife out and attempted to stab the Huta again but the Huta punched Luca with his left fist. Luca took a few steps backwards to put some distance between him and the Huta when he suddenly saw the girl run past him towards the second Huta. Lila grabbed the handle of the pitchfork and pushed down on it with all of her weight. "I told you to run," Luca yelled as he jumped to avoid another thrust of the Huta's blade.

"No!" yelled the girl defiantly. "He's on my mother."

Luca's momentary distraction caused him to take his eye off the Huta warrior who lunged again and sliced Luca's left side. Luca quickly stepped towards the Huta and encircled the Huta's right arm with his left arm. Luca pulled the Huta towards him and plunged his knife into the Huta's stomach and tore upwards, ripping his stomach open. Still holding the Huta's arm in a lock, Luca stabbed the warrior in the heart, then pulled his blade out and pushed the Huta onto the ground.

Quickly turning around Luca saw Lila struggling with the second Huta who had dislodged the pitchfork and was hitting the girl in the face. Luca grabbed the girl by the arm and threw her behind him with his left arm while simultaneously thrusting his knife into the Huta's stomach with his right hand. The Huta stood motionless for a moment, staring at Luca then he collapsed on the ground. Luca bent down and plunged his knife into the Huta's heart and killed him.

"Mommy, Mommy" Christopher was crying as he knelt over the naked body of his mother. The small boy was rocking back and forth and crying. The girl fell to her knees on the other side of her mother and stared in shocked disbelief. Luca walked behind Christopher and checked the woman for signs of life. Then he put his arm around the boy and looked across the woman's body at Lila.

"Where is your father?" Luca asked.

"He's in the barn," cried Christopher. "They killed him."

"Stay here," Luca said and ran to the barn and saw the father's body. When Luca returned, Lila had her arms around Christopher.

Lila seemed dazed as Luca spoke to her. "My name is Luca I will take you to the priests then come back and bury your parents. I will need you to keep your arms around the boy as I fly with you."

"You're bleeding," Lila said as she saw blood coming through Luca's white robe. "Let me look." Lila looked at Luca's wound then said. "Come in side."

"Did you hear me?" Luca asked. "We should go, there might be more Hutas."

Lila looked into Luca's eyes, then she pulled up her skirt and tore off most of her underskirt." Open your robe," she said and bunched up part of the material and pressed it against Luca's wound. "Hold this," Lila said as she wrapped the rest of the material around Luca's chest to hold the bandage in place.

"Thank you but we need to go," Luca said. "I will hold you with your back against me and you hold onto the boy. Do you understand?"

"Yes," Lila said as tears were filling her eyes.

"What is your name?" asked Luca.

"Lila."

"Lila this is important, can you do this?"

"Yes," she replied in a hoarse whisper, then she turned towards her brother who was kneeling near their mother. "Christopher you need to come here now." Christopher did not move so Lila gently pulled him to his feet and walked him over to Luca.

"Christopher I am going to fly you and Lila to safety, there might be more Hutas near here."

"Ok," Christopher sobbed.

The three had been in the air for only fifteen minutes when Christopher whispered, "Look," and pointed to six Hutas who were riding towards the burning farmhouse.

Luca was surprised that both Lila and Christopher held still as they flew, he was suspecting they both were in shock. Another fifteen minutes and they were landing in front of the headquarters of the Patronus. As soon as Luca set the two down he took them each by the hand and walked them inside of the building.

"What's this?" asked High Priest Rueben when he saw Luca, Lila and Christopher covered in blood.

"Hutas killed their parents. I killed two but we saw more on the ground," said Luca.

"He's hurt," Lila said to Rueben in a dazed manner.

Rueben turned to Padre Cornelius, "Get Lakin, he's out by the barn." Then Rueben stood up and extended his hand to Christopher. "Please sit down, you are safe here." Christopher held Luca's hand tighter and leaned against Luca's leg.

"Christopher this is High Priest Rueben, he will help you," Luca said. But Christopher pushed his body closer to Luca's and shook his head from side to side.

"Would you like a seat?" Rueben asked Lila. She did not let go of Luca's hand either. Lila looked up at Luca and started to ask him a question but Lakin entered the room and she did not finish her sentence.

"This is Prince Lakin of the Rualas," Luca said as he looked at Lila and Christopher. "Their parents were murdered by Hutas a short distance from here."

"I'm a physician," Lakin said as he knelt down before all three of them. "You are all covered in blood. Let me check you for injuries."

"Luca got stabbed," Christopher said and pointed to the bandage on Luca's side.

"We're alright," Lila said. "You need to help him."

"Well, you're going to have to let go of Luca's hands so I can look at his wound," Lakin said with a warm smile.

Lila let go of Luca and reached for Christopher who refused to let go of Luca's hand. "No, I want to stay with Luca," Christopher cried.

"Christopher you can stay with me but you are going to have to let go of this hand for a while," Luca said warmly.

"Ok," Christopher said and walked with Luca and Lakin into the medical room.

"What is your name?" Rueben asked.

"Lila."

"Lila can you tell me where your home is so I can send my men to look for the Hutas?"

Chapter XVI
Horror

"I can't cry, I don't know why I can't cry," Lila said.

"Lila you have seen great horror today, I believe you are in shock," Rueben said gently. "It is a normal reaction." Then Rueben looked up as Lakin approached them.

"Is Luca going to be alright?" asked Lila with concern. "He saved me and Christopher."

"He will be fine," said Lakin as he knelt down by the girl who was sitting in a chair. "The wound wasn't as deep as you might have imagined from the amount of blood. I gave Luca something to make him sleep. He is in his room now, but Christopher wouldn't leave him. I can show you were they are."

"I sent men to their farm," Rueben said to Lakin. "Two Hutas forced their way into the home and set it on fire, then they dragged Lila and her mother outside, where they raped and murdered her mother."

"And your father?" asked Lakin.

"Christopher said he was dead, I didn't see him," Lila said as tears came to her eyes. "But Luca went to look for him. Luca said he was going back to bury my parents."

"My men will do that," Rueben said.

"My mother is naked," Lila said helplessly. "I tried to cover her the best I could."

"Lila do you and Christopher have any other family here?" asked Lakin.

"No, we haven't lived here very long we don't really know anyone," Lila's lip was quivering as she spoke.

"You will stay with us until we can make arrangements for you," Rueben said. "Padre Cornelius has prepared a room for the two of you."

"Lila I know this is the last thing that you want to think about but I will send someone into Nora to buy you and Christopher clothes," Lakin said as he was looking at Lila's torn and blood soaked dress. "Can you write down your sizes?"

"Thank you, you all are so kind," Lila said then she suddenly threw her arms around Lakin's neck and started to cry on his shoulder. Lakin put his arms around her.

"Lila how old are you?" Lakin asked.

"Seventeen."

"And Christopher?"

"He is six," Lila said through her sobs.

Lakin looked at Rueben and said sadly, "I have children these ages."

Archetenus and Delilah traveled all morning and past noon before they stopped to rest the horses and to eat. Archetenus gathered wood as Delilah started to prepare their lunch.

"Archetenus you are so quiet, are you worried?" Delilah asked as they sat near the fire eating.

"I do want to put some distance between us and Port Friada," he answered. "But, well." He set his plate on the ground and put his hand into his pocket. "I bought these for us. I thought we could wear them until you found a ring you liked."

Delilah moved closer to Archetenus and looked at two wide banned yellow gold rings in his hand. "Oh there're beautiful," she gasped and took the smaller ring and put it on her finger.

"Honey they aren't beautiful they are just plain bands," he said. "Does it fit because I tried to measure it with the rings that Dieter gave you?" As he spoke, Archetenus put his ring on his finger.

"It's perfect and it is beautiful," Delilah said as she put her arms around Archetenus' neck. "I don't want another ring."

Archetenus pulled Delilah's body close to his and kissed her on the lips. Their passion burned within them. Both of them were so overwhelmed by their emotions that they did not initially realize they were tearing each other's clothes off.

Lakin smiled when he opened the door to Luca's room. Luca was sleeping on his back and Christopher was curled up and sleeping in Luca's right arm. "I don't want to wake them," Lila whispered. Then she nodded towards a chair in the room. "Can I stay here for a while?"

"Of course," Lakin said. "If you need anything I will be somewhere in the house."

After Lakin closed the door, Lila moved the chair to the side of Luca's bed. She sat on his left side so she could watch his wound for bleeding. Lila felt numb and she was having trouble focusing her thoughts. She too, smiled at the sight of her little brother curled up in the arms of this large Ruala warrior. It was then that Lila noticed that both Christopher and Luca had the same white blonde straight hair; this brought a smile to her face as the tears ran down her cheeks.

Two hours later Raul returned to his table in the Great Hall but he was accompanied by Vitomas and Annabelle. Raul was holding both of their hands as he spoke to the men at the table. "As much as I did not like hearing what Thedes said; he was right. I was allowing my fears to sabotage everything and for that I apologize. But Thedes was also right about something else. He said that no one knows Roch better than Vitomas and Annabelle and that they should be at this table."

Gabriel and Simon both stood up and brought more chairs to the table. "We are most glad to have you join us," Raphael said. Annabelle sat down next to Simon and Vitomas and Raul sat next to each other.

"We believe Roch is in hiding," Gabriel explained. "We have men in Taperia and Rualas and Enrops searching the area. Zoya said she thought he had been released close to his castle. Can you tell us what you think Roch would do or where he would be hiding?"

Annabelle and Vitomas both looked at each other. "I don't know what he is like if he is a demon," Vitomas said. "But Roch the man would never relinquish his throne without a fight. If I had to guess; he is disguised and hiding in plain sight close to his castle and Taperia. He will need to find out what has happened during his absence and who now sits on his throne. Once he finds out who the King is, then Roch will make plans to kill him."

"Vitomas is right," Annabelle said. "And Roch carefully plans out every small detail of his maneuvers. He is probably watching every move that King Hamond makes so he can devise a plan."

"So you think he will be more interested in getting his throne back than in coming after Vitomas?" asked Simon.

"Oh yes," Annabelle said and Vitomas nodded in agreement.

"Once he reclaims the throne then he will turn his eye on Wetpr, especially when he finds out that Sudfad now owns Nora," Vitomas said. "Roch is obsessed with killing Sudfad. He may seem insane but Roch is not stupid; he knows that Sudfad's army is stronger than his."

"I wish we would have invited you two to join us earlier," Gabriel said. "You have good information."

"Is Sophie still in Taperia?" Annabelle asked.

"Yes, she and the warlock have just returned from Port Friada," Raphael answered.

"If Roch doesn't know she is a member of the Insidiae he will contact her, thinking she is an ally," Annabelle said. "After all she basically helped to raise him."

"And if he knows she is a member of the Insidiae he will kill her," Vitomas said.

"So right now Sophie is actually our bait," Calen said. "I will send more of our warriors to the Patronus hiding out in Taperia." Calen stood up and left the table.

Thedes looked at both Simon and Raul and smiled. "The three of us are so much alike," Thedes said. "I too used to underestimate Ibula because she seemed so small and frail to me. And in the Shettee culture the women only took care of the homes and the children." Then he started to laugh. "I was as wrong about Ibula as you two are about your wives. I hope you can see that now."

Bekka opened the door to Luca's room and motioned for Lila to come out into the hallway. "Lila I am Bekka and this is Fala. Lakin had us buy you and your brother clothes, why don't you come with us and we can show you where to change and clean up."

"Thank you so much," Lila said. "You are all so kind." As she followed the two Ruala warriors to their room Lila said, "This all seems so unreal, it's like a nightmare."

Fala put her arm around Lila's shoulder and hugged her. "We will help you," Fala said sympathetically.

"Oh my!" Lila said as she entered their bedroom. One of the beds was filled with piles of clothes. "Why so much?"

"Lakin gave us a bag of gold coins and said to spend it all," Bekka said. "But when we were in the store and told the clerk why we were buying the clothes he went and got the owner and his wife. Well, they started helping us pick things out and they didn't charge us for most of it."

"You know when we first came here we saw the statue of a Ruala warrior in Nora and everyone says you are guardian Angels," Lila said with a smile. "I believe them."

When Archetenus and Delilah finished making love, he was considering staying at their campsite for the night. But as soon as the thought entered his mind he was filled with an overwhelming feeling that they had to keep moving. "Honey wake up," Archetenus said to Delilah as he brushed her cheek with his hand. She woke up smiling and took his hand and kissed it. "We should keep moving," Archetenus said although he wanted to stay and make love again.

"I understand," Delilah said and started to get up.

Archetenus stopped her by gently taking her arm. "Delilah do you want to have children?"

She smiled sweetly and said, "With you, yes."

"Good," Archetenus said and they both stood up and got dressed.

Luca woke up late that afternoon. When he opened his eyes he first saw Lila who was sitting next to his bed and smiling at him. She was a beautiful young woman with long curly reddish hair and large green eyes. She was slender but muscular from doing hard work on the farm.

"How do you feel?" Lila asked and leaned closer to Luca. She placed the palm of her hand on his forehead to check for a fever.

"You look different," Luca said in his still semi-drugged state.

"Lakin, Bekka and Fala bought us new clothes," Lila said. "As soon as Christopher wakes up I will clean him up and have him change." Luca turned his head and looked at the small boy cuddling against him and smiled.

"Luca thank you for helping us."

"Are you alright?" Luca asked as he tried to sit up but winced with pain.

Lila flew to his side. "Let me help you," she said and put her arms around Luca and helped him to a sitting position, then she stacked pillows behind Luca's back to support him. "Actually I don't know how I am," Lila said. "Nothing seems real and I just feel numb." Then she sat down on the side of the bed and looked at Luca. "Are you hungry, I will get you some lunch?"

"I am kind of hungry," he said and looked at Christopher who was still sleeping. "Maybe you should bring two plates."

"Well Master Dieter what a pleasant surprise," Madam Bular said pleasantly as he walked into her shop. "Please tell me have you found Delilah? She is such a precious girl?"

Dieter took his hat off and smiled exposing two rows of golden teeth. "No and that is why I have returned. I wonder if you remember anything else from that day."

"Why no," Madam Bular said. "Delilah was looking at bolts of fabric and one of her guards opened the door and said a horn was sounding and they had to leave."

Dieter walked behind the counter and grabbed Madam Bular's arm roughly. "I certainly hope you aren't lying to me," he said angrily. Suddenly Dieter felt a sharp pain in his groin as Madam Bular pushed the tips of a large scissors against him.

"Dieter don't you try to intimidate me, I will cut your balls off and stick them down your throat. The entire city knows you bought that poor girl and that you beat her constantly. I don't think anyone is going to help you here. You have made enough enemies are you trying for more?"

Dieter let go of Madam Bular's arm and took a couple of steps backwards. His face was filled with anger but he tried to compose himself as he spoke. "What do you mean I have made enough enemies?"

"You are so arrogant and self-serving," Madam Bular said smugly. "Do you think that the city is thanking you for saving them from the Rogetts? Everyone is wondering what you are digging that you unleashed those beasts and why you have a private army. Don't you have a clue as to what is going on around here? You should take heed; the people of this city do not trust you and they don't want you and your army here."

"Lakin gave me some kind of liquid and I washed the blood out of your robe," Lila said as she sat in Luca's bedroom and watched him and Christopher eat their late lunch. "Lakin gave me some special thread and I will mend your robe after it dries."

"Lila thank you but you don't have to do these things," Luca said.

"Yes I do," she replied. "Luca you and I both know that you wouldn't have been injured if I hadn't distracted you and you saved our lives. Christopher and I owe you a great deal." Then Lila paused for a moment. "And to be honest I need to keep busy right now."

"I understand," Luca said. "Those robes are made out of a special material to assist us in flying. And although I have never mended a robe, I am told there is a unique stitch that must be used. So you should ask one of the other Rualas before you start working on it."

"I'm sure Bekka or Fala would know. Do you need more pain medicine because Lakin showed me how much powder to mix with the water?"

"I am about ready for some more."

Lila cleared Luca's and Christopher's dishes away from the bed, as she was mixing the pain medication Lila spoke to her brother. "Christopher this is going to make Luca sleep, so you come with me so I can clean you up and put some new clothes on you."

"No, I want to stay with Luca," Christopher said defiantly.

Lila turned and looked at Christopher with a look of surprise on her face. Before she could speak Luca said. "Christopher do what your sister tells you, then you can come back."

"I can come back, you promise?"

"I promise," Luca said as he tousled Christopher's hair. "I won't be any fun though because I will just be sleeping."

"That's alright," Christopher said and threw his arms around Luca's neck and hugged Luca as tightly as he could. Then Christopher jumped off the bed and walked up to Lila.

"Thanks," Lila said as she handed Luca his pain medicine.

"So are you going to be my private nurse now?" Luca joked.

"I was planning on it," Lila said with a big smile then her demeanor suddenly changed and she said seriously, "Luca I didn't even think, would you rather have one of the other girls taking care of you? I mean, am I intruding on anything because I am sorry."

Luca started laughing. "Lila you aren't intruding on anything, I don't have a girlfriend and I appreciate what you are doing."

"Lila doesn't have a boyfriend," Christopher said with a grin. The look that Lila gave Christopher made Luca laugh so hard that it hurt his side, which he grabbed in pain. Lila turned red with embarrassment.

"We'll let you get some sleep now," she said. "Is there anything else that you need?"

"I bet those priests were lying to us," Sabot said as he mounted his horse.

"Sabot they are priests I don't think they can lie," said Romale.

"Well, if they weren't lying they definitely weren't telling us the entire story," Sabot said. "I could tell from their eyes."

"Quit complaining and tell me what they said to you," Romale snapped as they rode through the gates to leave the monastery at Leven.

"They said they married a young couple a few weeks ago but they didn't fit the description of Archetenus and Delilah. They said they haven't seen any strangers since."

"Well, no one in Leven married them," said Romale. "If I was running away with Dieter's woman I would want to get out of the kingdom as fast as I could. Let's ride towards the border and see if we can pick up any tracks."

It was almost dusk when Archetenus and Delilah made camp. He knew they had to make a fire quickly then extinguish it before it became dark.

A fire could be seen for a long ways and would give away their location. Archetenus gathered wood first and as he was returning to the campsite he heard a familiar voice.

"I am happy that you are listening to the messages I am sending you," said Miranda.

"You mean those feelings that we need to keep moving?"

"Yes. One of Dieter's men saw you in that jewelry store buying wedding rings. They now suspect that you may have run off with Delilah. Madam Bular and the priests have protected you but some of his men will find your trail in the morning."

"How many are there?"

"Five and they are adversaries who should cause you concern."

"Miranda will you watch over Delilah while I fight these men?"

"This is one of the lessons you need to learn," said Miranda as she smiled. "Your question should be to ask me what is next. I told you that I would protect you on this journey and I will. But you must follow my lead."

Archetenus took a deep breath before speaking. "Miranda I have been fighting all my life and it doesn't seem natural for me to be following you on this."

"And that is exactly why you should. Trust me you will get your chance to fight but the men who follow you are no fools and neither is Dieter. Do you want to be on the run your entire life or do you want to end this once and for all?"

"I want to end it."

"There will be times over the next few days that you hear my voice as you do now but you will not see me. Do not speak back to me in front of Delilah." With these words Miranda was gone.

Luca woke up, his room was illuminated by a couple of candles and a fire in the hearth. He looked to his left and saw Lila sitting in a chair next to his bed.

She was leaning forward sleeping with her arms and head resting on his bed. Luca turned and saw Christopher sleeping next to him on his right side. Luca reached over and stroked Lila's hair. "Lila," he whispered loudly.

Lila's head shot up quickly, "Luca are you alright?"

"Yes," he said with a smile. "But why are you sleeping like this, didn't they give you a room?"

Lila straightened herself up in the chair as she started to fully wake up. "Yes, but Christopher won't leave you and I wanted to be here if you need anything."

"I will be alright, why don't you go to your room," Luca said as he looked at the old, hard wooden chair Lila was sitting on. "That chair doesn't look very comfortable."

"I am fine," she said. Luca looked at her as if he was trying to read her face. "Alright, I'm not much better than Christopher; I really don't want to be alone tonight." A look of embarrassment filled Lila's face as she said these words so she changed the subject. "Luca is it alright that Christopher sleeps with you, I think you make him feel safe."

"Actually it's kind of nice," Luca said. "I like kids and haven't been around a little one for a while."

"Well, you tell me when he gets too much for you," Lila said. She was feeling uncomfortable because of the way that Luca was looking at her. "Luca why are you looking at me like that?"

"I am just trying to figure you out. You act so strong and in control but are you afraid to go to sleep?"

"I don't know," Lila said softly. "I know we are safe here. I think I am afraid I am going to see what happened today in my dreams."

Luca paused for a moment. "Lila there isn't a lot of room in this bed but you are welcome to join us if you want. You don't have to worry about anything I won't, well, I won't try anything."

Lila looked at Luca and started to laugh. "Luca are you saying that because you are a perfect gentleman or because you don't find me attractive?"

Luca was surprised at her bold question. He smiled and said, "I certainly find you attractive." Then he became more serious. "Lila I wouldn't take advantage of you, especially at a time like this."

Lila smiled and quickly removed her shoes then she slid under the covers next to Luca. He tried to put his arm up for her to lay in it but the movement caused him great pain. "Well that's not going to work," he said. "Can you squeeze between my arm and my body?"

There was little room in the bed, so Lila lay on her side facing Luca with her body pressed tightly against his. "Tell me if I hurt you," she said.

"Oh I will."

"Somehow I doubt that," Lila said then she leaned up and kissed Luca on the cheek. "Thank you for everything."

Luca looked at Lila for a moment then he kissed her on the forehead.

When Luca awoke in the morning, Lila was gone but Christopher was still sleeping. Luca gently got out of bed trying not to wake Christopher. Suddenly the door opened and Lila walked in with a tray of food.

"What are you doing out of bed?" she gasped. Lila's eyes widened as she looked at Luca who was wearing only a pair of tight white shorts. "I thought you felt muscular," she said with a grin. "But my god Luca, I've never seen anyone with so many muscles."

Luca was clearly embarrassed by her comment. "Where is my robe?" he asked.

"I am mending it. I'm not sure you should be out of bed," Lila said as she set the tray on a small table. "Do you want some help?"

"I'm fine," Luca said as he walked over to the table and sat down. "But I will need my robe; I don't have anything else to wear here." Luca started to eat his breakfast while Lila straightened his bed.

"I will finish it this morning. But I really think you should ask Lakin if you should be up."

"So did you get up early so you could bring me breakfast?" Luca asked kiddingly.

Lila hesitated and Luca could see that she was turning red. "No I couldn't sleep. Let me know if you want more food, I will go work on your robe." As Lila walked past Luca he took her arm and turned her so he could see her face.

"Lila you are bright red," Luca said with a grin. "Why? And why couldn't you sleep?"

"I should go and work on your robe," Lila said but Luca did not let go of her arm.

"Oh no you don't," Luca said as he started to laugh. "You are turning even darker red. What is going on? You know you aren't leaving here until you tell me."

"Luca!" Lila paused then tried to explain. "I'm not used to sleeping with a man."

"Well nothing happened, at least that I know of."

"Oh no, nothing happened."

"Then why are you so embarrassed, you didn't have to come to bed with us."

"Luca I don't want to tell you," Lila said but he kept staring at her and grinning. "I was just sleeping so close to you."

"Why don't you want to tell me?" Luca was enjoying teasing Lila.

"Because, because it's embarrassing and you might thing badly of me."

"Why would I think badly of you?" Luca asked then his eyes grew wide. "Lila you wanted something to happen didn't you? Tell me the truth."

"This is so embarrassing! I'm not going to answer that."

"Is that why you came to bed?"

"No, it wasn't until later. And besides I don't know if I wanted something to happen, I just wanted to kiss you."

"Enough that you couldn't sleep?" Luca asked with a big smile.

"Luca can we please stop talking about this, I'm sorry I said anything. I don't even know you."

"You can kiss me now," Luca said as he gently pulled Lila down on his lap. She did not resist but she looked panicked. "What's the matter are you afraid of me?" he asked.

"No, I don't, oh you are going to think I am so stupid. I don't think I know how," she blurted out.

"Just do what I do," Luca said as he took Lila in his arms and gently kissed her lips. She hesitated before she returned his kiss. Luca kissed her again and again. Each kiss was getting a little longer and more passionate. He could feel Lila getting weak in his arms. She returned Luca's kiss with passion. Luca stopped for a moment and looked at Lila's face. "Is that what you felt last night?" She did not answer but nodded. Then she leaned forward and kissed Luca on the lips again. They started to explore each other's bodies as their kisses became more passionate.

Suddenly Christopher sat up in bed and said loudly, "You're kissing!"

Chapter XVII
Discovery

"What did I tell ya?" Romale said with pride. "Two sets of horse prints heading towards the border and one rider is considerably smaller than the other. Hell Sabot we'll get you back in Dieter's good graces yet."

Romale was an experienced tracker and led the men north towards the border of Zorta. Although Romale and Sabot held the same position in Dieter's organization, Romale was given the lead on this mission. Dieter was extremely unhappy with Sabot, something that could easily cost Sabot his life. The three men who accompanied Romale and Sabot were intended vessels although none of them realized their destinies.

Kraus, Norris and Stone were all genetically altered by the Insidiae to be vessels for demons. All three men fit the physical stereotype of the other vessels. They were larger than most humans and incredibly powerful men. Kraus was starting to experience some of the liabilities of having pure evil planted into his being. Unknown to Dieter, Kraus' brain was deteriorating at a rapid pace. Some of Kraus' co-workers had started to notice his strange behavior but they thought it was a result of his heavy drinking.

Although Dieter had heard stories about the strange afflictions that were attacking the vessels, he neither cared nor gave the stories much credence; because at this point he had not lost any money. If Dieter would have been concerned that his merchandise was damaged, the Insidiae had no reliable tests to determine if a vessel was defective until the man died or showed great signs of insanity.

Lila quickly left Luca's bedroom after Christopher caught them kissing. Christopher on the other hand stayed and ate his breakfast with Luca.

"So what do you think about me kissing your sister?" Luca asked.

"I don't know," Christopher said as he put a piece of sausage into his mouth. He chewed for a few moments then started talking with his mouth full of food. "It's alright I guess. I just never seen either of you kiss anyone before."

"You never saw Lila kiss anyone before?"

"Well, me and mommy and daddy but she wasn't kissing you like that," the boy said with a coy grin.

Luca laughed loudly at Christopher's comment. "Christopher you haven't known me long enough to have seen me kiss anyone."

Christopher looked up from his plate and stared at Luca for a few moments as if lost in thought. "It seems like I have known you a long time, why is that?"

"I don't know," Luca said. "Maybe because we get along so well. Are you finished eating?"

"Yep," Christopher said as he pushed his plate away.

"I think it is time we took a walk," Luca said and stood up. Christopher jumped out of his chair and grabbed Luca's hand and the two walked out of the bedroom and through the house. Luca heard voices coming from the kitchen and headed in that direction.

"Oh thank you, thank you Rueben," Lila said. "You won't be sorry I will work very hard."

"I am sure you will," Rueben said warmly.

"What are you thanking him for?" Luca asked as he sat down next to Lakin at the kitchen table. Christopher climbed onto Luca's lap.

When Lila turned around she saw that Luca was only wearing his white trunks. "Oh Luca I finished your robe I just hadn't brought it to you yet."

"That's fine," Luca said. "But what were you talking about?"

262

Lakin turned and looked at Luca and smiled broadly when he saw Christopher sitting on his cousin's lap. "Lila and Christopher have no family and they just moved to Nora so they don't really know anyone here. Lila asked for a ride into the city so she could look for a job and Rueben just hired her to work here. That way she will make some money and they will have a roof over their heads."

"What kind of work?" asked Luca.

"Cleaning and cooking," Rueben said.

As the men were talking Lila walked up to Luca but her focus was on Christopher. She bent down and said happily, "Christopher we are going to live here with these nice men. What do you think about that?"

Christopher looked at Lila without speaking then he looked up at Luca and asked, "Do you live here too?"

Luca looked at Christopher and then at Lila and for that moment he didn't want to answer the question. "No Christopher I don't live here but I will be here for a while." Christopher didn't say anything but the look of sadness on his face touched everyone who was seated at the kitchen table. Lila too, was unsettled by Luca's statement but she was trying to be cheerful for her little brother.

"Christopher everything is going to be alright," Lila said but Christopher didn't say anything he just looked down at the floor.

"Delilah wake up," Archetenus said softly. Delilah opened her eyes and reached for him; but realized that Archetenus wasn't lying next to her but was fully dressed and squatting in front of her. "I know it's early but I think we should start moving."

"Is something wrong?" Delilah asked as she quickly got up and started to dress.

"No, you might say I just have a feeling."

"Do we have time for breakfast?"

"Yes but we won't take long."

"How long before we reach the border?" Delilah asked as she started to make coffee.

"Another day or two," Archetenus said. "I will feel better when we are out of Ganz."

"Schroeder, I have an assignment for you," Dieter said coldly.

"Sure boss, what is it?" Schroeder did not have the military bearing or the appearance of a fighter that most of Dieter's men had; which is why Dieter choose Schroeder for this job.

"Schroeder you like to talk to people and that is what I need now. I heard a rumor that the people of Port Friada are plotting against me. I want you to go out and see what you can find out."

"Well sure boss," Schroeder said nonchalantly. "Any place in particular you want me to go first?"

"No, but get around don't just go to the taverns because it's probably the people with power who are behind this."

"Lakin said you had to lie down," Lila said as she walked into Luca's room later that morning. "Are you alright?"

"Just tired," Luca said and smiled. "Me and my shadow here decided it was time for a nap." Luca paused for a second. "Lila come over here, sit on the bed." Lila did as he asked. He took her hand in his. "Lila you knew I wasn't from around here didn't you? I mean I wasn't trying to keep anything from you."

"I guess it should have been obvious, I just didn't want to think about it," she said with a shy smile. "Guess that's how I am coping with everything these days, I just won't think about it."

Luca was sitting up in bed and now pulled Lila closer to him. They stared at each other for a moment before he leaned down and kissed her on the lips. "Why don't you stay and I will tell you about the places I live."

"Luca I really want you to tell me about these things but I should probably go, I have a lot of work to do."

"Are you just saying that for a reason to leave?"

"No," Lila said and kissed Luca on the lips. "Rueben is being very kind to me by giving me this job, I want to do good."

"He won't miss you for a few minutes. Where are you sleeping tonight?"

"I guess I hadn't thought about it."

"Stay here with me," Luca said as he stroked her long hair. "Then we can talk."

"Alright," Lila said shyly.

"Do you promise?"

"I promise," she said and smiled.

"Because if you don't come here I am coming to your room."

Lila looked Luca in the eyes as if searching for something. She smiled and nodded. "I will be here. But you do know I will be checking on you before tonight, don't you?"

"Well, I should hope so I might need a nurse," he said with a grin and kissed Lila again. Their one kiss turned into many and after twenty minutes Luca stopped. "Oh I think you should probably go now," Luca said breathlessly.

"I know," Lila could barely get out the words. She stood up and straightened her blouse and skirt, then patted down her hair. "How do I look?"

"Beautiful," Luca said.

Lila blushed. "Thank you I just meant do I look alright to go out there."

"You look fine, they will never guess you were in my bed," Luca kidded.

"Luca, you're awful," Lila said then giggled. As she grabbed for the doorknob to leave, Lila was startled because Lakin was entering the room.

"How's my patient?" Lakin asked Lila.

Lila looked at Lakin and blushed deeply. "He is fine, just tired. I will let you two talk," she said then left the room, closing the door behind her.

"So why did your girlfriend get so red?" Lakin asked as he sat down in the chair next to Luca's bed.

"Because we were kissing," Luca replied with a smile.

"I see," Lakin said as he looked at Christopher who was sleeping on the bed. "You know that boy could pass for your son."

"I know," Luca said as he looked at Christopher. "He has hardly cried and he sleeps a lot, should I be worried?"

Lakin sat back in his chair and stared at his cousin. "The child is still in shock, I wouldn't worry unless this behavior lasts for a long time. From the way Christopher acts around you I will bet he was very close to his father. You do realize that he is looking at you like a father?" Luca didn't say anything so Lakin continued. "I saw the looks on both Christopher's and Lila's faces when they realized you would be leaving at some point. They are both very attached to you."

"I think that is because I saved them."

"Luca that is part of it, I think it is because of the man you are." Lakin leaned forward in his chair. "You have dedicated your life to the missions, I want to remind you that you can have a family and work on the missions too; although I will admit that it is difficult sometimes."

"Are you saying I should marry Lila? I have only known her for a day."

"I'm saying that if the two of them make you happy, don't easily dismiss that. Luca you have to admit that you are just as attached to that boy as he is to you."

"And as far as Lila goes, I like her; I think she is a good person and seems to have many good qualities. And she seems to be quite captivated by you," Lakin said with a grin.

Archetenus had taken great care to conceal his and Delilah's trail between Port Friada and the monastery at Leven. Once they left the monastery his focus was on getting out of the kingdom as quickly as they could. Now that Miranda had warned him that Dieter's men would soon find his trail; Archetenus once again took diligence in concealing their signs.

They broke camp before sunrise and resumed their journey northward. They traveled in a dry creek bed for a while because the bed was mostly stone. Archetenus kept a watchful eye on every aspect of nature to determine if there were other intruders in the area besides him and Delilah.

Delilah noticed that Archetenus seemed more worried than usual but she did not say anything about it. She had great confidence in Archetenus and his abilities to protect them both. They rode until a little past noon, when he found a secluded spot for them to take a break. All morning he had expected to hear Miranda's voice but there were no messages from his holy friend.

"Luca are you two coming out for lunch or do you want me to bring it to you?" Lila asked as she sat next to Luca on the bed and stroked his hair. Luca did not answer her question instead he pulled her towards him and kissed her on the lips. She giggled and kissed Luca again and again.

"How old are you?"

"Seventeen," Lila said nonchalantly then she suddenly looked concerned and asked, "Why is that too young?"

"Well that depends," Luca said with a laugh. "I'm twenty-two is that too old?"

"No silly," Lila laughed. "So are you getting up for lunch or do you want a tray?" she asked and kissed Luca's forehead.

267

Luca stared at Lila for a few moments, "Lila I really like you."

"Oh Luca," Lila said and threw her arms around his neck and hugged him tightly. "I really, really like you too."

"Are you two kissing again?" Christopher asked as he sat up and rubbed his eyes.

"Christopher I think you better get used to it," Luca said with a laugh. "Now let's get up and get some lunch."

"This Archetenus is a smart one," Romale said as he knelt down and looked at the ground before them. "First there is a trail and now nothing, it's like they disappeared."

"Maybe you just lost it," Sabot said sarcastically.

"Well then get your ass down here and look yourself. You're the one who couldn't even keep eyes on him in the city."

Sabot jumped off from his horse and punched Romale in the jaw. Romale was a large man so the powerful blow knocked him backwards but did not take him off from his feet. Sabot quickly moved in and punched Romale in the stomach first with his right fist then with his left. Then Sabot punched Romale in the jaw with his right fist then an uppercut under Romale's jaw with his left fist. Sabot was shorter than Romale but he had a muscular and solid build and Sabot was fast on his feet.

Sabot swung his right fist at Romale's head again but Romale blocked it with his left forearm. Romale punched Sabot in the stomach with his right fist then quickly punched him in the jaw with his right fist. Kraus, Norris and Stone all sat on their horses enjoying the fight between their two bosses. "I'm putting twenty on Romale," Stone said. Kraus and Norris both bet on Sabot.

Romale and Sabot were both hired around the same time frame. These men had more similarities than differences including enormous egos and ambitions. Both men badly desired to be the second in command to Dieter. Romale's and Sabot's long held resentments towards each other were surfacing in this fight. Romale punched Sabot four more times before he could force Sabot off from his feet.

Sabot fell onto his back but quickly rolled to the right and avoided Romale's attempt to kick him in the head. Sabot swiftly moved around Romale and punched him in the kidney then the lower back. Sabot kicked Romale behind his right knee and brought the giant of a man to his knees. Sabot grabbed a garrote from his belt and tightened it around Romale's throat as he stood behind the big man.

Romale was grabbing at the garrote that was choking the life out of him, then Romale grabbed a dagger out of his right boot and stabbed Sabot in the lower leg. This caused Sabot to loosen his grasp on the garrote for just a moment and in that moment Romale turned, while still on his knees, and stabbed Sabot repeatedly in the stomach and chest.

"Pay up boys," Stone said with a grin.

"Archetenus you seem particularly worried," Delilah said as they resumed their journey after their midday meal. "Has something happened that you haven't told me?"

Archetenus knew he couldn't tell Delilah what Miranda had told him. "I just have a bad feeling that we are being followed. Dieter isn't stupid I am sure by now he knows that I am gone too, maybe he's pieced things together."

"But he has no reason to think that you and I have ever met, unless you suspect Madam Bular said something."

"No, that is one tough lady I don't' think Dieter would get anything out of her. If you have to know, I bought the rings just before I left town and well, I've had a bad feeling since then."

"You would tell me if there was something more wouldn't you?" Delilah asked. Archetenus looked at her and smiled. "Archetenus stop your horse," she said with a tone of voice that he had not heard before. He stopped and turned and looked at Delilah who had been riding behind him. "Archetenus I lived with that monster for almost two years. I am not stupid, I heard and saw things. Don't keep secrets from me because I might be able to help you."

"Ok Delilah when I was leaving the jeweler's I saw a man watching me and I've been paranoid about it since."

Delilah stared at Archetenus since she still suspected that he was not telling her everything. "If you really think that Dieter's men are following us then I should show you something. Delilah got off from her horse and took a stick and started to draw a rough map in the dirt. Archetenus dismounted and knelt down to see what she was drawing."

"Whatever criminal business that Dieter is in, he used to do some kind of business with a woman named Juleta who has a castle just over the border into Zorta on the River Toba. I saw a map once. Her castle is south of Sendra. I remembered because he called her a witch and at first I thought he was just being mean but then I realized he meant she was a real witch. So there is a possibility that if he contacts her she could have some of her men along the border."

"Delilah this is good information," Archetenus said as he looked at her map. "Then we should travel farther east and avoid her lands. Once we get to Zorta I planned to travel north up the coast line, we can't do that yet because of those mountains to the east." He looked at Delilah and took her hand. "Honey I don't think you are stupid, I just don't want to worry you, you've already been through so much."

"Delilah kissed Archetenus on the lips and gently placed the palm of her hand against his cheek. "I love you so much," she said. "But remember we are in this together."

"Delilah I am going to tell you something that I probably should have told you before but I didn't want to scare you. Dieter isn't just a criminal he is a dark lord so it makes sense that he would do business with a witch." She stared at him without saying anything. "Did you already know that?"

"No but some things make more sense now," Delilah said thoughtfully, then her eyes grew wide with realization. "Archetenus all of those horrible people that he used to entertain, they must be witches and dark lords too, oh my god!" Then Delilah got a worried look on her face. "Archetenus you told me you were going to try and stop him, what are you doing?"

"Show her the drawings," Miranda's voice whispered in his ear.

"Delilah I hate to tell you because I don't want to put you in any more danger."

"Archetenus I can't be in any more danger, please tell me."

"I have been watching Dieter and trying to get information about him to deliver to a group of people who are trying to stop the dark lords. After I left you at the monastery, Dieter called a big meeting at his house and I drew pictures of his guests, here, see," Archetenus said as he took his journal out of one of his saddlebags and showed Delilah.

"Archetenus these are really good drawings," she said as she turned the pages. "But you don't have the names, do you need the names because I know who all of these people are."

"Yes, would you write the names down and any other names you can think of?" Archetenus walked back to his saddlebag and retrieved a pen for Delilah.

She stood up and hugged him tightly. "You can't believe how happy this makes me," Delilah said. "You told me you worked for Dieter and I know he only hired bad men. Now I find out you were there to spy on him. You are even more of a hero to me now."

After lunch, while everyone was still seated at the dining room table, Luca turned to Christopher. "Christopher just because I am injured doesn't mean that you can't have some fun. If I give you some money can you take Bekka and Fala into Nora and treat them to some ice cream and candy?"

"Ice cream really!" Christopher said as his eyes lit up. "I love ice cream."

Bekka and Fala both laughed at Christopher's reaction. "You can fly with one of us on the way there and the other on the way back. We will have fun," said Bekka.

Luca reached into the pocket of his robe and pulled out two gold coins which he handed to Christopher. "Now put these in your pocket so you don't drop them when you are in the air."

"Thank you Luca," Christopher said with enthusiasm. Then as an afterthought he looked at Lila. "Lila is it ok if I go?"

"Of course and I hope you have fun."

Christopher jumped off his chair and ran towards Bekka and Fala, then he stopped and turned back and hugged Luca, then ran back to the girls. After they left the room Lila turned to Luca. "Thank you so much, you are so good to him. And he just adores you."

"Luca if you are up to a walk, why don't you take Lila around and show her the place," Lakin said with a huge smile. "She has been so busy working and cooking for us that she hasn't seen anything besides the inside of this house. I am sure Rueben can part with her for a little while."

"Of course," Rueben said with a knowing smile. "After such a good meal you deserve some time off."

Luca stood up and extended his hand to Lila, "My Lady shall we?" Lila smiled and blushed and took Luca's hand.

"That was nice of Lakin," Lila said as they were walking out of the house.

"He's my cousin," Luca said. "We have a very close family." Luca held Lila's hand as they walked around the property.

"You tell me if you get too tired; I don't want you to overdo it."

Luca smiled and squeezed her hand. "So how are you doing?" he asked sincerely.

"I'm just trying to stay busy so I don't have to think about it," she said. "It's Christopher that I worry about. He saw father's body, I didn't and he saw that animal rape mother. Luca you saw father's body, what did they do to him?"

Luca stopped walking and turned and looked at Lila. "I really don't want to tell you."

"But I should know so I can help Christopher get through this."

"They skinned him alive then hung him from the rafters," Luca said as he put both of his arms around Lila.

"What!" Lila gasped and started to cry. Luca held Lila close to him as she sobbed.

Dieter was a man of great ambitions and even greater insecurities. He was drawn to the dark arts because he felt it would give him the power and recognition that he so greatly desired. Dieter was the middle child of a family of eleven children; he spent his life feeling faceless and lost. While many of his brothers were strong and handsome, Dieter had such a mundane appearance that people did not seem to see or to remember him. He spent the majority of his adult life trying desperately to be recognized.

Dieter's gold capped teeth and extremely large and gaudy jewelry were results of his need to be noticed and remembered. As a boy he was weak and unpopular; as a man he was a cruel and soulless bully. Dieter cared for no one except himself. His sham of a marriage to Delilah was merely a move to boost his own ego; he wanted to own one of the most beautiful women in the city.

Simply by the nature of becoming a dark lord, Dieter was separating himself from normal society. Yet this insecure egotistical man greatly sought the acceptance and adoration of normal society. Madam Bular's words shook Dieter to his core. He had considered himself a member of high society, a man that others envied and wanted to emulate. Now to find out that the people he sought to impress hated him and were possibly plotting against him, enraged Dieter. He was now consumed with these thoughts and everything else took second place.

Romale's victory over Sabot came with its costs. He had a broken rib, a swollen eye and a mild concussion.

Since Romale was the designated 'tracker' among the group, the decision was made that they would camp until his condition improved. Archetenus was such an experienced warrior that he managed to leave little evidence of a trail even when he wasn't taking great pains to hide his trail. Only a truly experienced tracker could follow Archetenus. Romale's keen eyes and experience were the only reasons the group of killers had found any portion of Archetenus' trail so far.

Romale and the others left Sabot's body where it lay for the animals to eat. The men took everything of value off Sabot and split it among themselves. They rode north a couple of miles until they found a suitable campsite and made an early camp.

"Guess this means you're the number two man now," Kraus said to Romale.

"Sabot was an arrogant ass," Romale spat. "I should have killed him long ago."

"Be that as it may," Stone said as he lay down on this blanket. "Dieter's going to have all of our assess if we don't bring back his lady."

"We're not even sure we're following her," said Norris. "We could be spending all this time chasing the wrong people."

"Will you all just shut the hell up," Romale snapped. "We'll find them. I should be able to see by tomorrow."

That night before Archetenus extinguished their campfire, Delilah had identified all of the people in his drawings. "Do you have more paper?" she asked. He took a second journal from his saddlebags and handed it to her.

"What are you doing?" Archetenus asked and kissed Delilah on top of her head.

"I thought I would write down as many names and things that I can remember that might be important," she said. "I mean it can't hurt."

Archetenus smiled and stroked her hair. He loved Delilah's long hair. "I think that is a good idea but it's getting late, why don't you come to bed now."

Luca was sitting up in bed; Christopher had just fallen asleep when Lila walked into the room. "It took me a while to make the dough for the bread and biscuits tomorrow, I'm sorry if I am late." As Lila talked she took off her shoes and stockings, then her blouse and skirt and set them neatly on a chair.

"You're not late," Luca said and started to smile. "You are going to make it really hard for me to keep focused on what I want to talk to you about." Lila was wearing a thin white camisole that was held together with three pieces of ribbon and a thin white half-slip. As Luca watched her undress he wondered why she was even wearing the camisole since it appeared to be too small and the parts of her breasts that weren't exposed from the neckline were clearly visible through the thin material.

Lila became embarrassed by his statements. "I wouldn't normally wear those things to sleep in," she stammered. "I'm sorry I thought you wanted me to sleep with you, I'll get dressed."

"Lila no!" Luca said. "Please come here, you are just fine. I meant that you look so sexy it will be a distraction."

"Sexy?" Lila said shyly as she walked up to the bed. "I've never thought of myself as sexy."

"Well I do," he said with a grin and gently pulled her towards him and kissed her. "Lila are you alright?"

"I just feel a little awkward Luca, I mean I really want to be with you but I don't know what you are expecting."

"I wasn't lying to you before. I really planned on us just talking and I would like you to sleep here."

Lila smiled and slid under the covers next to Luca. "Lila I want us to get to know each other better so I wanted to tell you about my life and where I live."

Luca told Lila the history of his people. He told her about the Ice Caves, he told her about the missions he works on and his friends. "Luca your life sounds so exciting and so dangerous, now I am going to worry about you even more."

"You worry about me?" Luca asked with a smile.

Lila blushed and nodded. He bent down and kissed her on the lips. "Now tell me about your life," Luca said.

Lila smiled. "Well, I don't know any princes or kings," she said kiddingly. "My life is pretty boring compared to yours. My family had a small farm in the Kingdom of Gandt. My father was a wonderful man but he didn't seem to be a very good farmer. Then there was a drought for two years, then the locust came. We moved to Stordt a few months ago because Father thought the land was better here. We found an abandoned farm and moved in. And I guess you know the rest."

Luca stared at Lila for a few moments before he started to speak. "I don't know how long I will be here."

Lila quickly put her hand over his mouth. "Luca don't talk about it, please I can't think about that." Luca started to speak again but Lila pressed her hand tighter against his lips. "Luca I'm serious, I don't want to hear about you leaving. I am going to miss you so much." Tears started to well in her eyes. "I know you must think I am really silly because we haven't known each other very long," then she paused. "Actually I guess we don't really know each other at all, so I don't know why I am getting so upset."

Luca took Lila's hand away from his lips and kissed it. "I don't think you are being silly at all. I don't want to leave you and Christopher behind but you are right we hardly know each other. So this is what I was thinking but I need you to tell me your feelings about it. I want to bring both of you to Salar. My cousin Calen, who I told you about, is building a huge wing onto Gabriel's house. He is building me very spacious chambers. I thought that you and Christopher could come and live with me and I will take care of you both."

Before Luca could finish speaking Lila threw her arms around his neck and kissed him repeatedly. Then she suddenly pulled back and looked at him. "How do you mean we would live together?"

Luca laughed so loudly that he looked over to make sure he didn't wake Christopher. "Well, that is what we need to talk about. There are several bedrooms in my chambers, you can have your own or you can share mine. Lila if things keep going like they have I can see us getting married but we haven't known each other long enough to make that kind of decision tonight and besides," he paused. "And besides although you seem alright I'm not so sure you still aren't in shock with all that has happened. This is not the best time for you to make decisions like this."

"Luca you are such a good person. I do agree with everything that you have said; it is very logical. But at the same time I have never met anyone like you before. I can't stop thinking about you and when I am with you, well, I don't know how to explain it. I just feel like I want to be yours completely," Lila hesitated as she built up her courage. "Luca I want to share your bed, in fact I would like us to share a bed like that now."

Luca smiled and caressed her cheek. "I like everything you said but honestly I'm not sure you are ready to make love."

"What!" Lila said angrily. She sat up straighter in bed and looked directly into Luca's eyes. "Luca don't tell me what I am ready for. Yes I am still very upset over Mother and Father but that is a separate thing from you and me. Luca I think I am falling in love with you and I want to make love with you," Lila said defiantly.

Luca was grinning the entire time that Lila was talking which was making her angrier. Lila glared at him and was about to speak again when Luca kissed her hard on the lips. He gently laid Lila down and moved on top of her; they kissed passionately for several minutes. "So you think you are ready to make love?" he asked.

"Yes," Lila whispered.

"Well, we can't make love with Christopher here and it's too late to ask someone to watch him."

"We shouldn't just leave him by himself."

"I agree, tomorrow I will ask Bekka and Fala to take him, then if you haven't changed your mind we'll make love."

Lila looked up at Luca and playfully hit his arm. "I'm not going to change my mind." Then she untied the ribbons on her camisole and opened the camisole; exposing her breasts to Luca.

"You are making this so difficult," he said. Lila started to giggle then to moan as Luca kissed and fondled her breasts.

Chapter XVIII
Decisions

"Fala and Bekka have been writing to me almost every day since they have been gone," Natasha said as everyone was taking their seats at the dinner table. "I just got this letter and you can all read it but I want to talk to you about what they wrote."

"A few days ago Luca was flying to Fort Nora and heard a child screaming. He found two Hutas attacking a farm house. One was raping the mother and the other was trying to rape the daughter but she was fighting hard. The six year old boy named Christopher tried to stop the Huta that was raping his mother by stabbing him in the back with a pitchfork."

Emeral gasped loudly, "How awful."

Natasha continued, "Luca fought the Hutas and won but his left side was sliced open. The Hutas stabbed the mother to death then Luca found the father in the barn. The Hutas had skinned him alive and hung him from the rafters. Bekka says that Lakin said Luca's wound was not deep and he will be alright soon. But she goes on to talk about Christopher and his sister Lila. Bekka says that Christopher is so traumatized by what he saw that he won't sleep unless he is with Luca, she said the boy just clings to Luca."

"And Fala wrote that Christopher looks enough like Luca to be his son. Bekka and Fala really like Lila. They said after all she has been through her first thoughts are how she is going to raise her little brother because they don't have any family and they just moved to Nora."

"Rueben hired Lila to cook and clean but Bekka said that Lila is a really good seamstress. She said to tell Emeral that Lila taught herself that special stitch and repaired Luca's robe so well that you can't tell it was damaged. The girls are wondering if we could help Lila find a better job in Salar, maybe as a seamstress."

Natasha handed the letter to Calen, then she gave him a flirtatious smile. "Calen I was thinking that we could let Lila and Christopher stay with us for a while, I mean until she gets a job."

"Salar is so big I am sure she can find work here. And we are building such a large wing onto the house."

Calen did not speak; he looked at Natasha and grinned so she continued pleading her case. "Calen that boy is so attached to Luca; after all they have gone through, why who knows what will happen to him after Luca leaves. And we are so blessed and we have so much. Calen will you stop grinning and say something," Natasha said with annoyance.

Calen turned to Gabriel who was also smiling and winked. Gabriel looked at Hannah and said, "I am surprised, I expected you to be the one to ask that."

"Well I would have but Natasha beat me to it," Hannah said with a warm smile. "I agree with every word that she said. And we are adding on extra rooms here too so there really will be plenty of room for them."

"It is fine with me if Calen approves," Gabriel said.

"Natasha write the girls and tell them to bring Christopher and Lila back with them," Calen said.

"Oh thank you," Natasha said and kissed Calen.

"I'm so proud of all of you," Emeral said. "You are such good people. If you wouldn't have taken those children in I would have asked Maxwell if we could." Emeral looked at Maxwell and smiled.

"Emeral means she would have told me we are adopting two more children," Maxwell said and laughed.

"You know Luca loves children, I will bet he enjoys having that little boy with him," Emeral said. "How old is the girl?"

Calen was reading the letter. "She's Bekka's age and apparently very beautiful. I wonder if Luca is going to adopt her too," he said and grinned.

"Well it's time that boy settled down," Emeral said then she looked across the table at Misha. "And that goes for you too, its time you had a family."

"Yes Emeral," Misha said with a sarcastic grin which caused everyone at the table to laugh.

"Natasha I will help you fix up their rooms. Ask Luca if he wants them to have rooms close to his chambers," Emeral said.

"Sanuri you have given us much to think about," Claudius said at the third meeting the Sanuri had with the ruling families of Lenz and the Nordes Tribe. Although the Sanuri had his own chambers in King Mathas' castle, Claudius had asked that the meetings be held at his home because they had three young babies. Claudius and Bella had also asked the Sanuri to stay at their castle.

"Sanuri I have a question," Ingr said as she stood up. "Why would that demon show me an image of Jared if Jared turned good?"

"Ingr do you mind if I share your story with everyone so they know what we are talking about?" the Sanuri asked.

"No," Ingr said and took her seat next to Stephan.

"You all know that Ingr was savagely attacked by Lazo. What you may not know is that she had actually died just as I entered the bedroom. She had a brief experience of bliss then as her soul was returning to her body the demon Ahriman found a way to speak to her. He sent me a message and showed her three images. Ingr forgot to tell me so Ahriman haunted her dreams until I put a stop to that," the Sanuri explained.

"Ingr is a talented artist and drew the images that she was shown. One was of Jared, the man I talked to you about, one was that of King Roch and the third was Cerephus the man who first took the throne of Stordt after Roch's disappearance."

"In Ingr's visions both Roch and Cerephus looked like they were in pain and were calling for help, while Jared appeared to be riding a horse in this world." The Sanuri now turned to Ingr. "If you still have copies of those drawings you might want to show them to the group. Now Ingr understand that I am just speculating at this answer."

"But first you have to understand that demons do not have the same powers as The Great Ruler or Angels. Demons are not all knowing, they cannot see into the future," the Sanuri continued. "Ahriman was attempting to use Jared as a means to set a trap for me. Ahriman was pretending to be Roch and was contacting Jared, who thought he was being haunted by a ghost. In frustration Jared went to Zoya who is a seer."

"Zoya realized it was a demon tricking Jared. Jared told Zoya about all his contacts with what he believed was a ghost and the two of them realized that Ahriman was trying to set a trap for me. They both risked their lives to come to Wetpr and warn me and to give me a book that Jared had stolen from the Insidiae."

"My best guess is that Ahriman thought he would be successful with his treachery. I believe that if Ahriman had any idea that Jared would conquer his demons and work with us, he would have killed him."

Angelina stood up while holding baby Alexas. "Matthew and I are very concerned for the safety of Vitomas, Ibula and Hannah. Do you know how they are to be used as bait and do they need our help?"

"When I left Wetpr, the Great Hall was filled with warriors who were working on strategies. They have a great deal of help already but you could certainly contact them and offer your services. But I also need to tell you something, something which I did not tell the others in Wetpr and that is because the information was recently revealed to me."

The Sanuri continued, "I told you about Miranda working with Archetenus. As I said he has not conquered all of his demons but he and his new wife are bringing valuable information about the Insidiae to Lentz. We will need to obtain that information and I don't think there is anyone in this room who believes it is wise for Archetenus to take it to Sudfad's family. I may be calling on some of you to meet with Archetenus and get that information."

Before the Sanuri had completed his sentence Sorren stood up, "I will volunteer. Where do I meet them?"

"Well right this moment Archetenus and his pregnant wife are travelling through Ganz; Miranda told them to come to Lentz and she would give him further information once they got here. Archetenus' wife was a prisoner of a powerful dark lord and Master of the Insidiae. He saved her with Miranda's help then married the girl. The man who held her captive is named Dieter. Dieter and Juleta had some business dealings although I do not know what they were. Dieter also has an army made up of men who are intended to be vessels for demons and some of these men are following Archetenus and his wife as we speak."

"Sounds like they could use some help," Sorren said with a grin. "Anyone care to take a ride with me?"

A powerful storm came up that forced Archetenus and Delilah to take shelter. Because of the information that Delilah had given to Archetenus about Juleta, he changed their course and they were travelling northeast instead of a straight northern path. This new course brought them closer to a mountain range which was rich with active gold mines. Archetenus and Delilah were fortunate to find an abandoned miners shack to take refuge in. The shack was small and dirty but there was a hearth and dry firewood.

"Archetenus are our blankets dry because I am afraid to sleep in this bed, it is filthy," Delilah said with disgust.

Archetenus laughed and checked their bedrolls, "Well you are in luck My Lady; we will have dry blankets to sleep on although ours might not be any cleaner than what is on that bed."

"But at least that is our filth," she said jokingly. Suddenly the shack shook as a huge tree was blown over by the storm.

"I'm going to check on the horses," Archetenus said and walked out into the night. The horses were in a small lean-to that was behind the shack. He found them scared but otherwise alright. As Archetenus was returning to the shed he heard Miranda's voice although he did not see her.

"The storm will wash away your trail. But you know one of the men who follows you and he is a keen trails man, he will find your trail again. The Sanuri has sent men to help you but they are coming from Lentz. You are wise to stay here during the storm but after that you will have to decide what you want to do."

"Do you mean fight them or run?"

"Yes."

"How long before help arrives?"

"Two more days, these are the warriors you are to give your drawings to. You can trust these men and women."

"Women?"

"Chief Sorren of the Nordes Tribe and Prince Matthew of Lentz are leading the warriors."

"I want to double back on my trail and ambush Dieter's men."

"With a pregnant wife and valuable information that must be given to the men who come to your aid?"

"Ok Miranda what do you want me to do?"

"And he finally asks. For tonight take shelter with your wife. You will be safe." Archetenus waited for a few minutes in the rain but did not hear any more words from Miranda so he returned to the shack.

When Luca awoke Lila was gone. He knew she had to get up earlier and fix breakfast for the priests and Rualas. Luca lay in bed thinking about the previous night; he and Lila had not made love but it was difficult for both of them. Luca was always a positive person but this morning he realized he felt really happy. He rolled over and looked at Christopher and smiled.

"Christopher it's time to get up."

"Ok," Christopher said as he rubbed his eyes.

"Are you awake, because you don't sound like it?"

"I'm awake Luca," Christopher said and sat up.

"Good because you and I need to have a talk man to man."

"Man to man," Christopher repeated then giggled.

"Christopher you know I am not from around here..."

Before Luca could finish his sentence Christopher started to cry, "Are you leaving?"

Luca picked Christopher up and set him on his lap. "Well, that's what I want to talk to you about. I've gotten pretty attached to you and Lila and I want to take you home with me, what do you think about that? Do you want to come?" Christopher jumped up and put his arms around Luca's neck and hugged him tightly. Luca kept talking. "You and Lila and I will live as a family and you will have your own room."

Christopher sat back down on Luca's lap and gave him a puzzled look. "So are you going to be my new daddy?"

Luca was not prepared for that question. "Well I guess so. But I don't want you to ever forget your other daddy."

"When do we go?" Christopher asked excitedly.

"I'm not sure yet but there is something else. Lila is my girl now and there will be times when she and I want to sleep alone, like your parents did."

"Is that so you can kiss?"

"Yes," Luca said with a grin. "So I was wondering if you would sleep with Bekka and Fala tonight. What do you think?"

"Sure, I like them, I'm going to tell them now," Christopher said and jumped off the bed and ran out of the bedroom leaving the door open. Luca could hear Christopher yelling and Luca laughed as he followed Christopher to the kitchen.

"Bekka, Fala, Bekka, Fala, you'll never guess what," Christopher screamed as he ran into the kitchen and up to the girls. Christopher was breathless and talking very fast. "Luca is taking us home with him. We're all going to live together as a family and I'm going to have my very own room." Everyone in the kitchen was grinning.

"That's great," Fala said. "You know we stay at the same house so we will be able to see you."

"Oh good!" Christopher said then paused and dramatically took a deep breath. "Oh and I am supposed to sleep with you tonight so Luca and Lila can kiss." Everyone in the room broke into hysterical laughter except for Lila who turned red and covered her face with both of her hands.

Luca walked over to Lila and put his arm around her. "Is that alright if he stays with you?" Luca asked Bekka and Fala as he was laughing.

Bekka was laughing so hard that tears were running down her face, "Of course."

"Sorry Rueben but I am stealing your girl away," Luca said with a grin. He had his arm around Lila and she still had not removed her hands from her face.

"I think that is wonderful," Rueben said with delight. "But I will miss her cooking."

As Lakin tried to compose himself he turned to Bekka and Fala who were seated to his left. "You should show him the letter."

Bekka took a letter from the pocket of her robe and held it out to Luca. "Let me explain before you read this, hopefully you won't get mad. Lila we have to talk to you too." Lila put her hands down and looked at Bekka. "Fala and I really like Natasha and we write to her almost every day. So we told her all about Lila and Christopher and you getting hurt. And we probably should have said something to you first but we asked Natasha to help Lila find a good job in Salar."

"Just give him the letter," Lakin said.

As Luca read the letter Bekka kept talking, "Natasha gave our letter to everyone in the house to read."

"Why would I get mad about this?" Luca asked. "It was very thoughtful of you girls and besides you saved me a lot of explaining." Luca handed the letter to Lila. "Everyone in the family wants us to bring you and Christopher home."

"What!" Lila said in disbelief. Tears filled her eyes as she read the letter. Luca watched her and smiled.

"Your family sounds so nice," Lila said with a quivering lip.

"When you write back tell them that Lila and Christopher will be living with me in my quarters," Luca said with a proud smile.

Bekka and Fala both grinned. Lila looked up from the letter and tears were running down her face. "Christopher, Luca's mother wants to know what your favorite color is and what your favorite animal is."

"Why?" asked Christopher.

"Because she will probably have a surprise for you," Luca said.

"Really!" Christopher said in awe.

"Yes really," Luca said with a smile.

"Blue and horses," Christopher blurted out.

"We'll put that in the letter," Fala said as she laughed.

Lakin looked at Luca and said, "Wait until Emeral sees Christopher."

"I know," Luca said.

"What are you talking about?" asked Lila.

"I told you that Emeral is my adopted mother well..." Luca said but Lakin interrupted him.

"Emeral is like the mother of the world," Lakin said. "She is great and she treats everyone like they are her child. She is going to spoil Christopher rotten."

Suddenly Lila got a concerned look on her face. "Luca what will your mother think about us living together?"

"I'll tell you exactly what she will say," Lakin said with a laugh. "It's time that boy settled down then she will tell Misha that he needs to find a girl too."

Archetenus had lain awake a great deal of the night. Delilah lay in his arm, as she usually did and he just stared at her for hours. Miranda was forcing him to go against his natural instincts. Archetenus was not the type of man to run or to be hunted as prey. He wanted to turn around and battle the men who pursued him. But Miranda had a point, he had to consider more than himself.

Archetenus was surprised to hear that the Sanuri was sending men to help him. He was even more surprised to hear that a prince and a chief were leading the men. Archetenus did not know who either Sorren or Matthew were but if the Sanuri was sending such men of high standing; the information that Archetenus carried must be very important.

The rays of dawn were illuminating the small and dirty shack. Archetenus slipped out of bed and got dressed. He walked outside to check on the horses and to feed them, then he walked around the shack to get a better idea of their hideout. The shack was at the foot of a mountain.

Archetenus found a trail and climbed up the mountain until he found a spot where he had a good view of the surrounding land. There were no riders to be seen from any direction. Two days it would take help to arrive, should he keep Delilah hidden in the shack or should they make a run for it?

"That blasted storm washed away their trial," Romale said in frustration as he knelt on the ground in the early morning hours.

"Well let's just keep heading north," Norris said. "We're bound to pick it up again.

"Romale looks like Dieter sent one of his pets," Krause said with a grin as he watched a raven flying towards their location.

The raven landed on the ground near Romale, who took a note from the bird's beak. "He wants to know our status," Romale said to the others who were still sitting on their horses.

"Whatya gonna tell him?" Stone asked.

"The truth," said Romale. "And I am going to tell him to send more men so we can get a couple of search parties going."

"Ok Miranda, what did you want me to do?" Archetenus called out.

"What is your choice?" Miranda asked as she appeared before him.

"I have good views here and if I had to, I suppose I could hide Delilah in one of these mines; that is if there aren't any damn Rogetts around."

"There aren't any Rogetts but in a very short period of time Dieter will be sending more men to look for you."

"Miranda I know you are testing me but I got to tell you I'm just not the kind of man who runs from a fight; this just doesn't feel right to me."

"Which is why it is a test. Tell me about your thoughts about your rescue party?"

"Damn," Archetenus said with a half-smile. "You can read my thoughts. Well, first I was surprised that the Sanuri would send men to help me and then to find out a prince and a chief of a tribe are coming. Makes me think these pictures are pretty damn important."

"You should not be surprised that the Sanuri is sending help. You did not like him because he saw the darkness in you and called you on it. The Sanuri has never been your enemy and you would be wise to remember that. And yes Archetenus the mission you are on is very important, that is why you have to think past your ego and gut instincts. If you let Dieter's men kill you, many more lives than yours will be at risk."

"Ok, you win. What do you want me to do?"

"On the other side of your shack is a small creek and grassy area because of the trees and boulders it is difficult to see. Take your horses there they will be safe. Stay inside of the shack with Delilah. Within the hour Dieter will have ravens searching for you from the sky."

"Ravens?"

"Yes, they are the messengers of the dark lords just as Enrops are the messengers for The Great Ruler. If you try to travel you will be spotted without even realizing it. I have already sent an Enrop to Prince Matthew telling him of your location."

"I guess you were right," Archetenus said. "Thanks."

"What else is on your mind?"

"Will I ever be able to tell Delilah about you?"

"What do you think?"

"Well if I knew I wouldn't ask you," Archetenus said with frustration. "Miranda why do you always answer my questions with a question?"

"To make you think things through," Miranda said. "What would be the benefit of telling her?"

"Well, how am I going to explain Prince Matthew and the others and I really don't like lying to her."

"Archetenus has lying ever bothered you before?"

He thought for a moment before answering, "No."

"Well then I would say that is a very good sign."

"Will she think that I am crazy?"

"Delilah didn't think you were crazy when you told her that Dieter is a dark lord," Miranda said. "Why is it so easy for people to accept demons but not Angels? But the real question Archetenus is once you start telling her the truth how much are you going to tell her?"

"You mean about me being a vessel and all that. You have a point, I probably shouldn't tell her."

"I never said not to tell her those things," Miranda said. "You have chosen this woman to have a family with and to be your partner for life. Do you trust her?"

"Yes," Archetenus said without hesitation.

"Yesterday Delilah told you that she had seen and heard many things while she was forced to be a mistress of a cruel man. She survived for almost two years under awful conditions. Do you think that perhaps she might be stronger than you give her credit for?" Archetenus did not answer. "Well then my next question to you is do you want your wife keeping secrets from you?"

Shortly after noon, Hannah and Emeral were measuring windows in the rooms that were completed in the new wing. Gabriel was paying the workers an extra bonus to get the wing built quickly and their speed and quality of work impressed everyone.

"Hannah, Emeral you've got to read this," Natasha said excitedly when she found them. "I just got another letter from Bekka and Fala, they wrote it this morning. Read it," Natasha said and handed the letter to Emeral. Hannah stood next to Emeral and the two women read it together. They both laughed as Bekka and Fala described Christopher's antics from that morning.

"I know, that Christopher sounds like a cutie," Natasha said.

Emeral gasped and looked at Hannah then at Natasha with joy. "Looks like you are a grandmother again," Hannah said and kissed Emeral on the cheek.

"Girls let's go shopping," Emeral said. "We will fix up their chambers first. Oh this will be so much fun."

Hannah hitched up the small boca and the three women decided to stop at the castle and tell their husbands that they would be shopping in Salar. When they entered the Great Hall they found the men at work researching books and maps. Elan and Cassandra had been invited to join in the research.

"We're sorry to interrupt you," Natasha said as she walked up to Calen and kissed him. Hannah kissed Gabriel and Emeral kissed Maxwell as Natasha talked. "I just got this letter from Bekka and Fala, you all should read it because it's really funny. They wrote to tell us that Luca and Lila are a couple now and he is bringing Lila and Christopher home to live with him in his chambers. Bekka said she has never seen Luca so happy. Isn't that wonderful?"

"I just had a feeling," Calen said with a huge smile as he read the letter.

"We're all going into town to shop for things to fix up their chambers."

Suddenly Calen got a look of concern. "Father come home with me, we may have to make some changes to Luca's chambers if he has a family now."

"Elan, Cassandra you are welcome to go shopping with us," Hannah said. "I don't know if Cassandra has been in Salar yet."

Gabriel looked at the excited looks on the faces of Elan and Cassandra and said, "Go and have some fun."

"Wait," Calen said and handed a pouch of gold coins to Elan. "Here's some money for babysitting my wife, I am sure you earned it." Everyone at the table laughed, including Jared who didn't know Natasha well.

"Calen there is a lot of money here," Elan said with awe as he looked inside of the pouch.

"Take it," Natasha said. "Next he will probably be asking you to babysit Lily." As soon as the words were out of her mouth, Natasha's eyes grew wide and she covered her mouth with her hands. "Calen I'm so sorry."

"Lily," Emeral said with delight. "You're naming the baby Lily?"

"Well, it was supposed to be a surprise," Calen said with a grin. "Lily Irena after you and Natasha's mother." Then Calen looked at the others sitting around the table. "Lily is my mother's middle name and Irena was the name of Gabriel's and Natasha's mother."

"I like that," Gabriel said with a warm smile.

"Oh Emeral I am so sorry to ruin the surprise," Natasha said sincerely.

"Nonsense, I am just as pleased now," Emeral said. "We really have a lot to celebrate today."

"We have company," Sorren said as he pointed to an Enrop that was flying towards them. Matthew held his right fist up in the air as a signal for the troops to stop.

"I have a message for you from the Angel Miranda," the bird said.

"What!" gasped Angelina in amazement.

"Dieter is sending many more men after Archetenus and Delilah. He has dispatched flocks of ravens to search for them from the air. Miranda told them to hide in a miners shack until you come to help. I will take you to them."

"Lead the way," Sorren said.

"Delilah be honest with me, do you still want to be my wife after all that I have told you?" Archetenus asked with concern.

"If I wouldn't have lived with Dieter for so long I might have thought you were crazy," Delilah said. "But everything you have told me about the man who you used to be and the man you are now just makes me even more proud of you. I love you Archetenus." They were still sitting at the table after their lunch. Delilah stood up and walked over to him. Archetenus pulled her down onto his lap and they kissed lovingly.

"Well, since I have decided to tell you the truth about everything there is something more you should know," Archetenus had a huge smile on his face as he spoke. "You're pregnant, we're going to have a baby. Miranda said it happened the first night we made love."

"What!" Delilah squealed happily and kissed him over and over. After a few minutes she stopped and looked at Archetenus seriously. "Now we have to make sure that Dieter's men don't catch us, we have a baby to protect."

Chapter XIX
Surprise

That evening Delilah sat in front of the hearth writing down everything she could remember from her time at Dieter's home. Archetenus had told her that even the smallest detail might be important so she searched the regions of her mind for every memory. Delilah felt content, something she had not experienced for a very long time. She had suspected there was a great deal that Archetenus was keeping from her and to have him voluntarily tell her the truth about his life, no matter how bad it was, made her feel more in love with him than ever.

Once Archetenus started confessing he surprised himself with the things he told his wife. He told her about kidnapping Vitomas because he had to explain how he first had contact with Miranda. However Archetenus did not tell Delilah that his relationship with her was almost exactly the relationship that he had fantasized with Vitomas. Archetenus felt like a great burden had been lifted from him after he explained to Delilah about the man she married. And he felt even more love for Delilah because she accepted him for the person he was.

Both Archetenus and Delilah were ecstatic that they were expecting a baby. But a single thought kept creeping into Archetenus' mind. "What if the evil seed planted in me is passed to my children."

"Sorry dinner is late," Hannah apologized. "We lost track of time." Hannah, Natasha and Emeral were all bringing serving dishes to the table.

"Honey that's fine," Gabriel said and kissed Hannah on the cheek.

Emeral went to the back door and called out, "You boys can bring the rest of those things in after dinner. Food is on the table." Within minutes, Elan, Misha, Koby and Dagon walked into the dining room.

Koby was carrying a large stuffed horse and grinning. "Please tell me this isn't for Luca," Koby said and the others laughed.

"It's for Christopher," Emeral said with a smile. "But I will admit that we may have gotten a little carried away with buying things."

"We were thinking the same thing," Dagon said with a chuckle.

"Well, when you boys settle down we will do the same for you," Emeral said. "Elan where is Cassandra?"

"Elan notice that all came in one train of thought," Misha joked.

"She's upstairs trying on some clothes," said Elan.

"Elan did you buy her clothes with the money I gave you?" Calen asked with a huge grin.

"Just a couple of things," Elan replied with embarrassment.

"Mother I guess we know who is next," Calen teased.

"Hush," Natasha said. "She's coming."

"Cassandra you look so nice," Emeral said. "Turn around so we can see."

Cassandra looked both pleased and embarrassed as she stood in the doorway in a pink silk dress and white sandals. While not revealing, the dress clung to her womanly figure. Koby, Dagon, Misha and Elan all stared at her both with surprise and attraction because the typical Ruala robes concealed her figure.

"God Cassandra you look beautiful," said Dagon.

"No kidding," Misha added while he was staring at her.

Emeral noticed that Elan was looking jealous because of the attention the other men were giving Cassandra. "Elan said he bought that for you," Emeral said. "I think that is very sweet of him."

"I know," Cassandra said and walked up to Elan and kissed him on the cheek. "He even picked it out and he bought me two other dresses too, I'll show them to you after dinner."

"Cassandra did the dress have the slots in for your wings?" Hannah asked.

"No, there was a seamstress at the store. Elan had her make the adjustments."

Calen looked at Elan and smiled, "Must have been a pretty nice store," he said.

"Oh it was," Cassandra said with enthusiasm.

"So how did you like Salar?" Natasha asked Cassandra.

"It is incredible; it's so big and busy. Why, I've never seen such a place," Cassandra said in awe.

"You know Calen with you and me both home, I don't think Natasha needs a lot of babysitting," Gabriel said with a grin. "Maybe you can let Elan off from work and he can show Cassandra around. I am sure there is a lot of the city they haven't seen."

"You heard the boss," Calen said with a laugh. "Have fun."

Elan and Cassandra looked at each other and smiled shyly. "Thanks," Elan said. "How much time should I take off?"

Calen looked at both Elan and Cassandra and grinned, "Well, I guess that is up to you two."

Before sundown, Dieter had two hundred men searching for Archetenus and Delilah. They had orders to meet with Romale. This army was riding hard and fast. Flocks of ravens roamed the grounds between the monastery and the border between Ganz and Zorta. Dieter was not a man to be crossed, his rage was overwhelming him as his head was filled with thoughts that Delilah had run off with Archetenus.

But Dieter had other problems which were also troubling him. He had lost a great deal of his powers. He could conjure some minor spells but he was beginning to have problems with even these.

All of the dark lords and witches who he had called for a meeting at his home could not give him insight about the Rogett attack or his loss of powers. In fact they did not give him much useful information at all except to tell him that never had any of them heard of a dark lord suddenly lose his abilities to perform magics. But they all agreed on one thing; that Dieter must have a very powerful enemy in the dark worlds and that Dieter needed to learn who this demon was.

Dieter did not realize that even before the Rogett attack many of the residents of Port Friada had concerns about him. Although he liked to show off his wealth and power, it was difficult for him to disguise the darkness of his soul. Dieter underestimated most people because he felt infinity superior to others. This character flaw was proving dangerous to his empire. Many citizens had been spying on Dieter and his mansion. This activity greatly increased after the Rogett attack when the citizens of Port Friada learned how large his private army was.

On this night as Dieter paced in his study, swearing and throwing things against the walls, Commanding General Amundsen from Fort Friada was leading an army to Dieter's mansion. Many citizens had gone to Amundsen with their concerns about Dieter and the General too had men watching Dieter's place. After Amundsen received word that two hundred men had left the mansion, he knew the time was right. Amundsen declared war on Dieter.

"I don't know why I suddenly feel so nervous," Lila said as Luca stood in the kitchen waiting for her to finish preparing bread dough for the morning meal.

"You mean because we are going to make love tonight? Are you changing your mind?"

"Oh no Luca, I think it is just all the changes and everything is happening so fast. Actually I think I am nervous about meeting your parents."

Luca walked up behind Lila and kissed her on the back of the neck. "They are going to love you and you will love them."

Lila turned around so she could look at him. "Your family is royalty and your friends are royalty and high priests and the such. I grew up poor on a farm."

Luca put his hands on Lila's shoulders and looked her in the eyes. "Lila my family and my friends don't care about peoples backgrounds or their wealth. What they judge people on is their character. You have nothing to worry about. In fact the day after Lakin met you, he came to my room to tell me how much he liked you and that he thought you and I should become involved."

"Really Luca? Did he really say that or are you just trying to make me feel better?"

"Go ask him yourself. And besides you read that letter from Natasha and Mother. Did they once ask if you came from a wealthy family?"

"No, you are right; that letter was wonderful," Lila said. "I'm sorry I'm acting this way."

"Honey really, everything is going to be just fine," Luca said and kissed Lila on the lips.

"Matthew I know you are still mad at me," Angelina said as she was cooking dinner over a campfire. "But I want you to know that I appreciate you letting me come along."

"The way I remember it I didn't have much of a choice," Matthew said and winked at Stephan.

"You have to admit that the three of you have treated us differently ever since we got pregnant," Angelina said. "You all wanted to marry warriors then you want to chain us to the kitchen."

Sorren roared with laughter as he listened to his daughter talk to Matthew, Thaos and Stephan. "You boys are going to get mad at me," Sorren said with a hearty laugh. "But she does have a point. Why all three of your wives are fierce warriors and you treat them like china dolls."

"You really aren't much of a help here Sorren," Stephan said with a grin.

"Ingr, Nikki and I all promised you that we would not train or do anything dangerous while we were pregnant. And you know we told you that only to make you feel better not because we thought it was necessary."

Thaos laughed, "Ok Angelina what do you girls want, I can tell there is more to this than just a lecture."

Angelina got a big smile on her face. "We want to start training again every day like we used to. Of course Ingr is going to have to take it a little slower but she is healing really well. Now Ingr and Nikki and I have been talking. We can't train all day like we used to because of the babies. We are thinking that we could train for one or two hours every morning right after you leave for work."

"Sounds reasonable to me," Thaos said.

"Thaos do you really mean that or are you just saying that to shut me up?" Everyone broke into laughter.

"Both," Thaos said with a grin.

"Well the three of you could look at how it would benefit you," Angelina said with a coy smile.

"I hate to even ask," Stephan said smiling.

"Well, you would have happy wives and happy wives make happy husbands," Angelina said with a large grin. Sorren again roared with laughter. "And," Angelina continued. "You all want lots of children. Don't you want your wives to keep their girlish figures?"

Matthew, Thaos, Stephan and Sorren were all laughing hard. "Ok, ok you win," Stephan said. "Ingr can start training again."

Angelina looked at Matthew. "Matthew how about you?"

"Well I suppose Ingr can't very well train by herself, go ahead. But the next time you get pregnant I may want you to take it easy again."

"That's fair," Angelina said. Then she walked up to Matthew and kissed him on the cheek. Angelina turned to Thaos. "Thaos what about Nikki?"

"Everything that Matthew said," Thaos replied with a grin. Then he looked at Matthew. "Do you ever win a fight at home?"

"Hardly," Matthew said smiling.

"How do you feel?" Luca asked as he gently moved a strand of Lila's hair from her eyes.

"Wonderful," Lila said with a satisfied smile as she reached up and put her arms around Luca's neck and kissed him. "Now I really do feel like I am yours." Luca started to get off from Lila, "What are you doing? I like feeling you on top of me."

"My weight isn't too much for you," Luca asked and kissed her on the lips.

"No, it feels so good being this close to you," Lila said softly. "Hopefully you didn't hurt your side with all of that."

"A little," he grinned. "But it was worth it." Luca kissed Lila again. "You know we still have a lot of the night left."

"I know," she said and giggled.

General Amundsen was an experienced warrior who learned a great deal during his numerous battles with Hutas and Rogetts. Amundsen knew that two hundred of Dieter's men had left the mansion but he didn't know how many were still on the premises. Schroeder, the man who Dieter sent into Port Friada to spy on the citizens was locked in the dungeons at Fort Friada. Schroeder had given little information to Amundsen's men, other than he was more afraid of Dieter than the soldiers. Schroeder's statement made Amundsen wonder what powers Dieter held over his men.

Before this night, some of the people who complained to Amundsen about Dieter speculated Dieter was involved with dark magics because of things they saw in his house.

Amundsen wasn't sure if he believed in dark magics but he had to admit there was something very strange and secretive about Dieter. Amundsen was not taking any changes. Instead of having his men do an overt charge onto Dieter's property, Amundsen chose guerilla tactics.

Amundsen's men had been spying on Dieters mansion for so long that they knew where the guards were usually posted. Amundsen had fifty of his most experienced fighters dismount and sneak up on the guards and kill them. If the first fifty men did not open the gates to Dieter's compound within fifteen minutes Amundsen planned to send in another fifty. The minutes ticked away and just as Amundsen was about to order a second group of men into the compound the gates opened.

It was very late at night and most of Dieter's men were sleeping. Amundsen himself had seen many of the men in Dieter's army; men of unusual size and strength. Amundsen had no idea that these men had been bred as vessels for demons, but he did know they were a considerable threat to his men. "Show no mercy; Dieter is the only one I want alive," Amundsen said as he led his men into Dieter's compound.

The battle did not go quickly and Dieter's seven hundred men were a formidable match to Amundsen's two thousand troops. The element of surprise gave Amundsen little advantage against these men created by hell.

"What is the meaning of this?" screamed Dieter when he awoke because the tip of Amundsen's sword was pressed against his neck.

"You can come peacefully or I can kill you where you sleep," Amundsen said. "The choice is yours."

Dieter looked at the ten soldiers who stood around his bed. He mumbled an incantation and nothing happened. In fear and desperation he mumbled a second spell and still there were no results. Dieter decided to try another tactic, "I must warn you I am a dark lord. Get back and I won't hurt you."

"Tie him up boys," Amundsen ordered. "Dieter, I don't know much about dark lords but if those were spells you were spouting you aren't very good."

All of the soldiers in the room broke into laughter. Amundsen walked over to a writing desk in Dieter's chambers and scribbled a note. Then he returned to his soldiers who were standing next to the bed with Dieter who was bound hand and foot. "Sergeant," Amundsen said to one of his men. "Take thirty men and deliver this note to King Sudfad's Castle in Wetpr, tell them it is for the Sanuri."

"No!" screamed Dieter.

"Well that struck a chord," Amundsen said with a grin. "Maybe you really are a dark lord. Regardless you are going to hang. We found your slaves in the basement and they've been telling my men a great deal."

"What?" Matthew said out loud and quickly sat up. He looked over at Angelina who was sleeping next to him. Matthew sat up listening to the sounds of the night. "Must have been a dream," he thought to himself but as he started to lay back down he heard the voice again.

"Matthew I am no dream but a friend and I am here to help you."

Matthew was stunned for a moment, then he said in a whisper, "Are you Miranda?"

"Yes, come into the forest so we can talk."

Matthew quietly walked through his campsite trying not to wake the others or to alert the sentries. He was only five yards from his camp when he encountered a woman of great beauty. She had long flowing black hair and a blue dress and she was surrounded by a soft white light.

"Miranda?" Matthew said in awe. As he looked upon the Angel, his knees felt weak; he steadied himself from falling.

"Matthew I have much to tell you and my time with you will be short. But this will not be my only visit to you. Dieter has sent over two hundred men after Archetenus and Delilah. Here is a map that their leader drew." Miranda held out her hand and Matthew stepped forward and took a piece of paper from her.

"The men are being led by a murderous member of the Insidiae named Romale. While he is an enormous man he is not one of the vessels. But the entire army that he is commanding are. Do not underestimate these men they were created by hell beings."

"This map shows me that he has divided his troops and the areas they are searching but it doesn't show me where I will find Archetenus and his wife," Matthew said as he studied the map in the light emitted from Miranda's presence.

"Now it does," Miranda said and an 'X' appeared on the map to indicate the location of the miner's shack. "Matthew rescue Archetenus and take him to the Sanuri. As Jared, Archetenus does not realize that he has been implanted with the Mark of Satan."

"Can I tell Archetenus why?"

"Yes."

"Miranda I understand that Archetenus is carrying important information but why is an Angel going to such lengths to save a man such as him?"

"Matthew everyone is worth saving," Miranda said. "But also you must know that the Insidiae spent years experimenting with humans while they tried to create the perfect vessels for demons. These vessels are not all the same. In Archetenus' case the moment he dies a monster of most evil proportions will be created."

"If the Mark of Satan is removed will that make the difference?"

"It will greatly help."

"Does Archetenus know all of this?"

"He knows that if he does not change his life he will end up a vessel for a demon. He is trying and as of late he is doing well."

"Can I tell him these things?"

"That is up to you."

"Miranda do all the vessels have the Mark of Satan?"

"Yes."

"Then they can be completely controlled by demons."

"Yes Matthew, your army is strong but do you think you can fight an army of demons?"

Matthew looked at Miranda and smiled as he felt he was being tested. "Not without the help of The Great Ruler."

"And would you request such help?"

"Yes," Matthew said and Miranda suddenly disappeared.

"Miranda thank you and thank you for Jacob," Matthew called into the night.

"Matthew you should start out before dawn," Miranda's voice called out.

The next morning as Luca was walking into the kitchen he heard Christopher calling his name. Luca turned and saw Christopher running towards him with Bekka and Fala following. Christopher jumped into Luca's arms and hugged him tightly.

"Did you have fun last night?" Luca asked.

"Yes, Fala and Bekka took me to Nora and bought me ice cream, then we played some games and then we went to sleep," Christopher said with excitement.

"Did you have fun?" Bekka asked sarcastically.

"Yes we did," Luca said with a grin then he looked at Lila, who was blushing deeply.

"This just came for you," Lakin said as he walked into the kitchen. Lakin handed Luca a letter. Luca set Christopher down and read it.

"Lila you need to read this," Luca said and held the letter out to her.

"Luca I need to get these platters on the table."

"We can help with that," Fala said and she and Bekka started setting platters of ham, potatoes, biscuits and eggs on the table.

Lila took the letter and as she read it her eyes grew wide with amazement. "Luca is your mother serious about this?"

"Yes, tell everyone what she says."

"Prince Raul and Prince Simon want us to have our wedding at their castle and Emeral says that many of Luca's friends and family are already in Wetpr working on a mission. She wants to know if she should start planning our wedding."

"Emeral's not really subtle," Lakin said with a laugh.

"Are you getting married?" asked Fala.

"Well we did talk about it," Luca said. "But I told Lila I don't think it is fair to ask her while she might still be in shock. I don't want her waking up some morning and forgetting that she said yes."

"I'll remember that I said yes," Lila said softly.

"So are you saying yes?" Luca asked. Lila nodded and Luca walked up to her and kissed her on the lips.

"Luca that is the most pathetic proposal I have ever heard," Lakin said. "Lila make him do better."

Lila and Luca both started laughing. Luca got down on one knee and took Lila's hand in his. "Lila will you marry me?"

"Yes," she said excitedly. Luca stood up and kissed her again and everyone in the room applauded.

Chapter XX
To Battle

Matthew knew he would not be able to sleep after his encounter with Miranda. He returned to camp and woke Angelina; as he was telling her about Miranda the others sleeping around the fire awoke one by one.

"Ok I heard part of what you were saying," Stephan said as he sat up. "What did she look like?"

"Like a very beautiful woman who was surrounded by light. She had long black hair and a beautiful blue dress on," Matthew said. "At first I was stunned but she was all business, she said what she had to say and left." Matthew handed Stephan the map. "Miranda said that she did not draw the map but when I asked her where Archetenus was that 'X' suddenly appeared. It was the most incredible thing."

"What is this?" Thaos asked and he and Sorren looked at the map with Stephan.

"Dieter sent two hundred men after Archetenus and his wife. They are all intended vessels except for their leader a man named Romale," Matthew explained. "They all have that same Mark of Satan at the base of their necks like Jared did, which means they can be controlled by demons. Miranda said not to underestimate them."

"Then she asked me if I thought my powerful army could battle an army of demons. I had a feeling she was testing me," Matthew continued. "I said not without the help of The Great Ruler. Then she asked me if I was asking for that help and I said yes. Then she disappeared. I yelled after her, thanking her for Jacob and the information. Then I heard her voice telling us to leave before dawn."

"That is something boy," Sorren said. "I wish I could have been there."

"There is more," Mathew said. "I asked her if Archetenus had the Mark of Satan on his neck. Miranda said he does but he doesn't know it."

"She told me to get him to the Sanuri as soon as possible. Miranda knew about Jared and she told me that Archetenus has done well of late, resisting his demons. I asked her why she was going to such lengths to save him. And this is really interesting. Miranda said that the Insidiae experimented on humans for years and not all of the vessels are the same. She said if Archetenus dies before the Mark of Satan is removed that he will turn into an incredible monster."

"So we need to get him to the Sanuri to get that mark removed?" Thaos asked.

"Yes," Matthew replied. "I asked her if Archetenus knew any of the things she had told me. Miranda said he just knew that he is an intended vessel. She told me it was up to me whether I wanted to tell him the rest."

"Matthew I don't know what this Archetenus is like," Sorren said as he threw more wood on the fire. "But I think it is only fair that you tell him."

"So we know that he is a huge and powerful man," Thaos said. "But he is taking direction from an Angel, he saved a woman and got married and he is risking both their lives to bring us information. The guy sounds like he is trying to me. I think we give him a chance."

"Thaos, Stephan you didn't meet Jared," Angelina said. "Once he found out that he was a pawn of the demons; you can't believe what he went through to free himself. I agree, we tell Archetenus everything and let him decide."

"Well whatever he decides," Stephan said. "We have to make sure we keep him alive until we get him to the Sanuri."

"Lakin, Lakin," Dack yelled loudly as he ran into the house. "Where's Lakin?" Dack and Joao had entered the house by the front door which opened to a parlor. As people came running Joao yelled.

"We need help, Fala's been stabbed." Both of the young warriors were in distress to see their friend so badly injured.

The next few seconds seemed like hours to Dack and Joao as Lakin, Luca and the others ran into the room.

"There's a medical room through that door; take her in there," Lakin yelled as Dack carried Fala in his arms. "What happened?"

"Bekka's missing," Joao said. "The others are looking for her."

"Joao go to the barracks and wake all our men and tell them where to look," Lakin ordered.

"My men also," Rueben said as they all were entering the medical room. Lila ran into the room carrying a large bowl of boiling water and towels.

"Dack tell us what happened," Luca said as he helped the young warrior place Fala on a table.

"Well, we get bored watching that mausoleum so we trade off on assignments," Dack said. "Bekka and Fala always work as a team and they were searching the area while Joao and I were watching the mausoleum. Then Trist comes to us carrying Fala, he said he saw signs of a fight on the ground and there was lots of blood. Sahil and Rako are looking for Bekka, Trist gave us Fala and he went back to help find Bekka. Lakin no one is watching the mausoleum."

"Fala!" Christopher screamed and started crying.

"Lila get him out of here, I will help Lakin," Luca said and started to wash blood off from the young warrior so they could identify her wounds.

Joao ran into the medical room and stopped and stared at Fala, who was unconscious and bleeding profusely.

"Lakin I want to go out there," Luca said.

"Go," Lakin said as he was trying to stop the bleeding from Fala's six knife wounds.

"Show me," Luca said to Joao and the two ran out of the house.
"Dack, grab that towel and put pressure over those two wounds," Lakin ordered.

"You'll never be able to hold me," Dieter screamed from his cell in the dungeons of Fort Friada.

"That guy hasn't shut his mouth since he got here," one of the soldiers said. "It's going to be a long day."

"They said he yelled all night too," the second soldier added.

"Hey big mouth," yelled the first soldier to Dieter. "Why can't you be quiet like your friend?"

There was silence. "My friend?" Dieter yelled to the guard. "Who do you have in here?"

"Well if you can be quiet, I'll tell you at the end of my shift," the guard said with a laugh.

Schroeder shrank with horror as he listened to the guard talking to Dieter. Schroeder was infinitely more afraid of Dieter than the soldiers, his mind started to race as Schroeder was thinking of any information he might have that he could use for bargaining his release. Suddenly he had it. "Guard," Schroeder called out. "I need to speak to your General."

"There!" yelled Trist as he pointed to a small clearing. Sahil, Rako and Trist flew downward at speeds they didn't even know they had. Six Huta warriors were dancing around a large fire. Bekka was bound and lying on the ground. These Ruala warriors were experienced. They had fought in many battles with Hutas and they knew exactly what the Hutas were going to do to their comrade.

Bekka saw her rescuers before the Hutas did. She started to yell and thrash around in an attempt to distract the Hutas. Two of them walked over to Bekka, one of the Hutas slapped her hard across the face. Then he picked Bekka up and turned towards the fire. Trist and Rako shot arrows at the Hutas while Sahil dove towards the warrior carrying Bekka.

310

Sahil came from behind and kicked the warrior in the head. The Huta dropped Bekka on the ground and she quickly rolled to her right to get out of the way. "Untie me," Bekka screamed. "And I can fight too."

Rako pulled his knife out of the heart of a Huta and quickly ran to Bekka. In one stroke he cut the ropes that bound her hands. Rako handed Bekka one of his knives and ran towards a Huta who was running towards him.

Bekka quickly cut the ropes that bound her legs. She turned and saw that Trist and Rako were each fighting with two Hutas. Bekka grabbed the knife and flew to Rako, who was the closest to her. She grabbed one of the Hutas from behind and cut his throat. This act momentarily distracted the Huta that Rako was fighting with. Rako plunged his knife into the warrior's heart. Rako ran to help Sahil as Bekka flew to Trist.

Bekka grabbed a Huta from behind but he quickly turned and sliced at her with his knife. Bekka was in the air, not standing on the ground. She flew just out of the reach of the Huta; she moved back and forth to confuse him. He reached up and grabbed at Bekka. She sliced his left arm open with her knife.

The Huta did not drop his knife, he merely pulled his arm back. Bekka flew quickly, dodging his attempts to stab her. The Huta was getting frustrated with Bekka's games; he lunged at her. In that moment he exposed his chest. Bekka quickly flew into him and plunged her knife into his chest. She stabbed him over and over as she thought about Fala.

Trist pulled Bekka off from the dead Huta; she was covered in his blood. "Are you alright?" Trist asked.

"I think so," Bekka said. "Did you find Fala?"

"Yes, Lakin has her."

The four Rualas took to the sky, flying back towards the house. Almost fifteen minutes later they saw other Rualas flying to their left. These Rualas turned and joined Trist and the others. One of the Rualas in the second group said, "There are others searching, also the Patronus we will tell them to turn back." And the second group of Ruala warriors dispersed in the sky.

When Trist, Bekka, Sahil and Rako landed at the house, they landed near the back door. Dack was sitting on one of the steps leading into the house with his head in his hands. As they walked up to him, Dack raised his head and they could see he was crying.

"No, no, no," screamed Bekka as she ran into the house. Lakin was covered in blood and walking out of the medical room. Bekka ran past him, she fell to her knees when she saw Fala's dead body lying on the table. "That should have been me, that should have been me," Bekka cried as she rocked back and forth. Lakin knelt down and put his arm around Bekka's shoulders. "She was trying to save me," Bekka said as she gave Lakin a dazed look. Then Bekka put her hands over her face and began to sob.

Matthew and the others could not return to sleep after Matthew's encounter with Miranda. They talked strategies among themselves while they ate an early breakfast. Matthew and Sorren woke the troops up and they resumed their journey several hours before dawn.

A tributary to the River Toba and the River Shey joined in the Kingdom of Zorta. Matthew and his troops reached the northern shore of this river just as the first rays of dawn were illuminating the sky.

"Matthew that river is really swollen," Sorren said as they looked at the fast moving current.

Matthew sent men both up and down the river to look for a site where they could safely cross. As they waited, Angelina turned to Matthew, "Ask Miranda, if she doesn't answer you nothing is lost."

Matthew looked at Stephan, Thaos and Sorren somewhat sheepishly, then he called out, "Miranda we could use some help down here." The river was deep and the current was moving too quickly to try and cross on horseback. Suddenly they heard singing and saw a huge barge travelling towards them. The barge was on the northern side of the river.

"Stop!" yelled Matthew as he rode his horse to the river's edge.

"Why?" yelled one of the men on the barge.

"I will pay you handsomely to transport my men across the river," Matthew called out.

"How do we know you've got any money?" the same voice yelled at him.

"Can you not see these are royal troops? I am Prince Matthew of the Kingdom of Lentz."

The barge turned towards the northern bank and twenty minutes later was near shore. A burly man with gray hair and a gray beard did the talking. "Can't be too careful these days what with bandits and all. My name is Lester and this is my rig."

"Lester it is nice to meet you," Matthew said and threw a large pouch of gold coins to him. "There's two more of those in it for you when you get everyone across."

"How many you got?" asked Lester.

"A little over two hundred," Matthew said.

"That will be five or six trips," Lester said. "But we can sure do it. Damn, this is more money than I made all last year."

Stephan sent soldiers out to retrieve the others who were looking for areas to cross, while Matthew negotiated with Lester.

"Stephan you go with the first group," Matthew said. "I will be with the last." It took a little over two hours to transport all of Matthew's men to the south shore of the river.

"Lester when are you coming this way again, in case we need to have you take us across?" asked Matthew.

"Well, me and the boys are on our way home to Liza, it's a little village a couple of miles down the river. You show up there and I will take you wherever you want to go," Lester said with a big smile. "The misses is going to be damn happy when I come home this time, sure enough."

When Luca and Joao were running into the house, they first saw Dack on the steps of the porch, then they heard Bekka crying. Luca's heart sank within his chest. The kitchen and parlor where filled with Ruala and Patronus warriors; everyone was somber. Luca ran in the direction of the crying and saw Lakin sitting on the floor cradling Bekka as she sobbed.

Luca walked up to Fala's body. "She was so young," he thought and sadness overwhelmed him. Luca turned and walked out of the room. He looked in Lila's room but she was not there, next he went to his room and saw Lila sitting on the bed rocking Christopher, they both were crying. Lila looked up when Luca entered the room. He put his arms around both Lila and Christopher and kissed each of them on top of their heads. Christopher held his hands out for Luca to take him. When Luca picked him up, Christopher hugged him tightly.

"Can I go see Bekka?" Christopher asked.

Lila stood up and took Luca's hand. Luca carried Christopher and the three walked to the medical room. Lila started to cry harder when she saw Bekka sitting on the floor sobbing. "Bekka!" Christopher yelled and jumped out of Luca's arms and ran towards his friend. Bekka looked up and Christopher threw his arms around her neck; the two of them held each other and cried. Luca grabbed a blanket and covered Fala's body. Then he turned and walked into the parlor.

"Does anyone know what happened?" asked Luca.

"We found six Hutas dancing around a huge fire. Bekka was tied up and looked as if she had been beaten. We got to them just in time to stop them from sacrificing her," Trist said. "Luca, she fought well. Rako untied her and she killed two of the Hutas. But once the battle was over we came here as fast as we could. She didn't tell us anything."

Rueben put several bottles of whiskey and wine on the kitchen table. "I'm sure I'm not the only one who wants a drink right now." Rueben was a tough and courageous man, experienced in battle. But to see Fala's young body and then watching little Christopher trying to console his friend, Rueben was filled with emotion.

Suddenly the crying stopped and within moments Bekka walked into the kitchen. Lila had her arm around Bekka and Christopher was holding Bekka's hand. Lakin was walking behind them and his eyes were red and swollen. "I'm sorry, I know this isn't how a warrior should act," Bekka said as she tried to compose herself.

"Nonsense," Luca said and held a chair for Bekka to sit in. "Bekka can you tell us what happened?"

"That's why I came out here, it just dawned on me they could trick someone else," Bekka said. Trist handed her a small glass of whiskey and Bekka sat down. "Fala was flying behind me and to my left. We were north of a mausoleum; when I saw what looked like a man lying on the ground. The man was dressed in the kind of clothes the people wear in Nora."

"I called to Fala and I flew down. As soon as I turned him over I knew I had been tricked. It was a Huta and he grabbed me by the throat. I grabbed for my knife and someone else grabbed me from behind. I didn't know how many of them there were, I was getting punched and kicked then I heard Fala scream my name."

Bekka had to take a deep breath before she could continue the story. "I couldn't see her at first because I was fighting but all of a sudden I looked up and one Huta was holding her and another was stabbing her. I screamed and one of them hit me so hard I think I blacked out. When I awoke I was tied up and those six we fought were dancing around a fire."

"Lila, would you help Bekka wash up and get her out of that robe so I can check her for injuries?" asked Lakin.

"They know we are in the area," Luca said angrily. Then he turned to Bekka. "Bekka anyone of us would have fallen for that same trick, don't blame yourself for anything."

"From now on I want everyone in groups no smaller than four," Lakin said to his men. "Is everyone accounted for?"

After a few minutes Ardom walked up to Lakin. "Everyone is here except for the nine who are at the mausoleum."

315

"Ardom, take others with you and go to the ones standing guard. Tell them about what happened to Bekka and what my orders are," Lakin said.

Luca looked at Joao and Dack; both young men were crying and looked lost. Luca put his arms around both of them and walked them up to the table. Lakin handed each of them a glass of whiskey. "Is this your first friend to die in battle?" Lakin asked.

"Yes," said Dack. "She was like our little sister. We should never have traded assignments with them."

"Dack you and Joao did nothing wrong," Lakin said in a fatherly tone. "I wish I could tell you that it gets better but it doesn't. It tears me up every time I lose a warrior."

Another hour's ride brought Matthew and his troops to a heavily wooded area. Everyone rode in silence as they were all aware that enemies could be hiding close at hand. The old forest extended southward for several miles. They were almost to the end of the forest when a soldier yelled, "Hutas." An arrow hit a soldier directly behind Stephan and the man fell from his horse. The thud of him falling was obliterated by the war cries of the Hutas.

"Angelina stay behind me," Matthew yelled.

"Matthew we both fight," Angelina yelled as she release an arrow into the throat of a Huta who was running towards her. The Hutas were on foot and were trying to pull the soldiers and the Nordes warriors off of their horses. Sorren let out a war cry and charged his horse at two Hutas; he had a sword in each hand and stabbed both of the warriors. With a powerful sweep of his sword, Thaos severed the head from a Huta. Matthew and Stephan both rode wielding a sword in each hand. They rode through the Hutas, hacking and stabbing.

"Father," screamed Angelina as she saw three Hutas pull him from his horse. Two Hutas were holding Sorren as a third was wielding a battleaxe.

Before the battleaxe could come into contact with Sorren's head the Huta dropped it and clutched at the knife that Angelina had thrown, hitting the Huta in the throat.

Sorren freed himself from the grasps of the Hutas; he threw one Huta to the ground while grabbing his knife from his sheath. Sorren stabbed the Huta who was still standing and ripped the knife upwards exposing the man's organs. The Huta on the ground jumped up only to be taken down by one of Angelina's arrows.

Thaos felt a burning pain in his left shoulder. He pulled the Huta arrow out and charged at the Huta who shot him. Thaos jumped from his horse, knocking the Huta to the ground. The Huta was on his back and was trying to stab Thaos, who grabbed the Huta's arm, turning the knife in the direction of the Huta. The Huta warrior was strong but Thaos had the advantage and stabbed the Huta in the throat with his own knife.

Matthew too had been pulled from his horse and was wrestling with a Huta. Just as Matthew had the Huta on his back a second Huta ran up and grabbed Matthew by the hair. Stephan ran his sword through the Huta's back. As the first Huta jumped to his feet, Angelina shot him with an arrow in the side of the neck. The battle was over as quickly as it had begun.

"Angelina tend to Thaos," Sorren shouted as he was putting pressure on Thaos' wound.

Matthew ordered some of his men to set up a perimeter in case there was a second attack. Other soldiers were ordered to bring the wounded to Angelina and Sorren. Many of the Nordes warriors were healers and they all ran to that location. A third group of soldiers was told to make sure the Hutas were dead.

"You seem uneasy," Delilah said as Archetenus paced from window to window and looked outside.

"Something is not right, I can feel it," Archetenus said. "And I don't like hiding," he added with frustration.

"Archetenus I am sorry that I got you involved with all of this," Delilah said sadly. "I don't want you hurt because of me. Maybe if I go back to Dieter they will let you go."

Archetenus spun around so quickly that Delilah jumped back. "Honey don't ever say anything like that again. We will get out of this." He walked up to Delilah and put his arms around her. "You are my wife and we are having a baby. I love you Delilah, and you certainly didn't drag me in the middle of this. I was already involved when I met you." Delilah leaned her head against Archetenus' chest and started to cry softly.

"I want to hear from Fala's parents before we bury the body," Lakin said as he sat at the kitchen table and wrote a letter.

"But, can you preserve the body?" High Priest Rueben asked.

"I have some things with me," Lakin said. "I can preserve it for a while."

"Lakin, do you want to examine Bekka now?" Lila asked as she walked Bekka into the kitchen. All of the men stared at Bekka in surprise.

"Lila adjusted some of her clothes to fit me," Bekka said and blushed because of the way everyone was staring at her. "Until I can clean my robe."

"I'll clean it," Lila said gently.

"Bekka you look very nice," Lakin said in a fatherly manner. "How do you feel?"

Before Bekka could speak Lila said, "The right side of her body is one huge bruise. I would not be surprised if she has some broken ribs. And she has a large bump on the back of her head."

"Lila you are welcome to come in with us when I examine her," Lakin said as he stood up.

As Bekka turned towards the medical room, Christopher let go of her hand and climbed on Luca's lap.

"Bekka," Joao said softly. "If you want, why don't you sleep in our room tonight? I can sleep on the floor that way you won't have to be alone and look at Fala's things."

"If it is all right with Dack?" asked Bekka.

"Of course," Dack said. "We'll take care of you."

"That room is large," Rueben said. "Just move another bed in there."

Trist and Ardom stood up. "We'll move it," Trist said and Joao and Dack left the kitchen with them.

"What are you doing?" Christopher asked as he watched Luca writing.

"I'm writing a letter to Gabriel, Calen and the others and telling them about Fala," Luca said.

"There are eighty-five dead Hutas," Matthew said as he walked up to Angelina and Sorren.

"That's a pretty big war party," Thaos said as Angelina was stitching his arm.

"I know," Matthew replied. "Makes me wonder if Dieter is responsible for the Hutas."

"Well, that means he would have to know we are coming," Sorren said as he stitched the side of a Nordes warrior.

"How many did we lose?" asked Thaos as he winched in pain.

"Nine dead and I guess you can see all of the wounded here," Matthew said as he looked at the thirty warriors who were being treated for injuries.

"Will you hold still?" Angelina scolded. "Father give Thaos some whiskey."

"I don't want any whiskey, I want to have a clear head," Thaos said. "I think this is just the beginning."

"Your wound is really deep and if I don't stitch it properly you may have troubles with it later on," Angelina scolded then she laughed and said. "And with that second baby coming you are going to need both of your arms."

"What! Angelina what did you say?" Thaos asked as he quickly turned to look at her.

"Oh no," Angelina said and blushed. "I must have ruined Nikki's surprise. I am so sorry Thaos." Sorren laughed loudly as he listened to Angelina.

"Angelina I will act surprised but tell me what you know," Thaos said excitedly.

"Well, Nikki suspected for about a month that she was pregnant and now she is pretty sure; but Thaos she isn't that far along."

"Did she tell you that we have been working on another baby?"

"Yes," Angelina said. "And I am really happy for you."

"Did you hear that Matthew?" Thaos said proudly. "We're having another baby."

With so many of the Nordes Tribe members tending to the wounded, Matthew and his men were able to resume their journey an hour and a half later.

"We've lost almost four hours," Matthew said to Stephan. "I don't like this." Matthew had tripled the scouts as the main body moved southward.

"Let me see that map again," Stephan said. He studied the map for a few moments, then looked at the sky and their surroundings. "I think we will cross the border into Ganz a little after noon, then we should get to Archetenus before dark."

"If nothing else happens," Matthew said uneasily. "Something just doesn't seem right, I can feel it."

"Schroeder I don't trust you," General Amundsen said. "You're coming with us and if you are lying to me I'm gonna hang you on the spot. Do you understand me?"

"Yes General, I'm not lying to you," Schroeder said nervously. "But when we find it you will let me go?"

"Yes, if what you tell me is true," Amundsen said. "So why are you so afraid of Dieter?"

"You'll see when we get there." Schroeder said.

As Dieter paced in his cell he kept trying incantations but his magics were gone. "How can this be?" He screamed out in frustration. Dieter was desperate; he was trying to figure out how to get out of his prison. His brain was flooded with thoughts, then it came to him. He would call upon Petorus, the demon that he sold his soul to. Petorus was one of the original thirteen Old Ones that came to this world. He was an ancient and powerful demon. Dieter knew that if he could just get his powers back he could escape.

Dieter walked to the back of his small cell and quietly called to Petorus. Dieter called and called and each time he made promises to the demon. After twenty minutes Dieter surmised that Petorus was not answering him because he had no offering. Dieter was alone in his cell. He thought about attacking one of the guards but then dismissed that thought as he knew the others would be upon him before he could offer the sacrifice.

Dieter looked around his cell, trying to find something that he could cut himself with. He searched the stone floor and walls for a shard of stone. Finally in desperation, Dieter started to bite through the underside of his right wrist.

Matthew and his troops crossed the border from the Kingdom of Zorta into the Kingdom of Ganz an hour after noon. Matthew ordered a short break so the wounded could get some rest and food. He had guards set up a perimeter around the group.

"I keep looking at this map," Stephan said. "If this was accurate when Miranda gave it to you, I think we should be running into one of Dieter's search parties soon. I figure they should have left the Village of Hadne this morning and if they continue north towards the border as this line indicates, we might have an hour."

"Then let's give them a surprise," Matthew said. "I wonder if they will stay true to these routes. Stephan, Thaos, we'll move the troops west to intersect with this route, then set them up for an ambush."

Archetenus walked around the outside of the miners shack then climbed up the mountain a ways to look in the distance. Everything looked clear; there were no signs of horsemen.

"I told you to stay inside because of the ravens," Miranda said as she appeared behind him.

I feel like a trapped rat in there," Archetenus complained.

"Prince Matthew and his men should be here by nightfall," Miranda said. "They did battle with Hutas this morning and will soon be battling one of Dieter's search parties. Men are dying to save you and Delilah don't let their deaths be in vain, go inside."

"I should be with them," Archetenus said as he started to descend the mountain.

"You will have your chance," Miranda replied.

"Miranda I keep having this strong feeling like something is wrong, am I getting that from you?"

"Archetenus there is much more going on here than you realize. The demon that sent the Hutas after Matthew's men is trying to control you. That is why I am here. Do you wish to be a pawn of a demon or a free man?"

"A free man of course," Archetenus said as he stopped his climb downwards.

"Then I will help you," Miranda said. "But I cannot make your choices for you. You must resist him."

"Miranda please don't let me hurt Delilah," Archetenus said fearfully. "Help me."

Matthew and his men were hidden in a heavily wooded area just south of the border between Zorta and Ganz and north of the Village of Hadne. Seventy-five heavily armed men were riding hard towards the border; their dust could be seen for miles as they were approaching the forest.

"Ravens," Sorren said. Matthew and others looked up and saw a large flock flying overhead.

"I wonder if they can see us," said Angelina.

"Enrops," Thaos said with a grin. The group looked up again as the two large flocks collided in the air; tearing at each other with their claws and beaks.

Dieter's men were riding, two and three abreast. After the first ten men entered the forest Stephan yelled, "Release!" and fifty archers shot their arrows at the riders who were taken by surprise.

"Release!" yelled Thaos and another fifty archers, who were positioned to the left of the first group released their arrows.

The riders who had not entered the forest had no cover to hide behind, many were shot and others were frantically trying to see who was attacking them and where the arrows were coming from. Romale was leading the group that had entered the forest; he did not realize they were under attack until a Nordes spear impaled his right hip. Romale screamed and drew his sword. His horse reared up as dozens of arrows and spears were launched at his men.

Many of Dieter's men were dead, yet not one of Matthew's men had yet exposed themselves. Matthew wanted to minimize the hand to hand combat after Miranda's warning about the vessels being controlled by a demon.

"Show yourselves!" Romale yelled as an arrow entered his chest. Romale managed to stay on top of his horse and turned to run back to his men but four more arrows hit him before he cleared the forest. When Romale reached the clearing he was slumped over his horse and blood was running out of his mouth. He stopped and stared at the sight before him. Almost all of his men were lying on the ground. Hundreds of arrows were sailing through the sky and impaling his men. And the ground was littered with dead ravens.

"What manner of deviltry is this?" screamed Romale moments before he fell dead to the ground.

"Hold your ground!" Matthew yelled then he turned to Angelina who was at his side, "Something is very wrong here, I can feel it." Within moments the ground started to shake as if a great earthquake was underway but the ground did not open up.

"What is happening to them?" Sorren asked loudly as they watched the corpses of the vessels suddenly writhing around the ground.

"Prepare to fire!" Matthew yelled. "I fear the snakes are coming out of them." The army stood in awe as they watched the bodies of men burst open and giant red snakes slither out. Nordes warriors immediately ran forward, with swords and spears and fought the nine snakes that were in the forest.

"Release!" yelled Stephan and a volley of arrows impaled the on-coming snakes.

"Release!" Thaos yelled and another volley of arrows soared through the air.

"The arrows aren't slowing them down," Angelina said.

"Hold your fire!" Matthew yelled as the serpents continued to advance towards the forest. The flock of Enrops attacked the giant serpents, clawing at their eyes.

"Charge!" yelled Matthew as he led the attack against the hellish beasts. Swords drawn the soldiers of Lentz and the warriors of the Nordes Tribe attacked the giant snakes, hacking at their bodies and cutting off their heads.

Angelina's horse reared up as a snake lunge at it and threw Angelina to the ground. The snake lunged at Angelina who was in no stance to strike back. Angelina rolled to her left as Matthew jumped off from his horse and cut the snake's head off with one powerful swing of his sword.

Horses snorted and men screamed as they fought the great beasts. Sorren jumped from his horse and killed a snake that was devouring one of his warriors. Sorren ripped the snake open with his sword but the young Nordes warrior was dead, crushed and smothered as the snake swallowed him.

Chapter XXI
Fire

"By the heavens!" General Amundsen yelled as Schroeder led the General and his men through the caverns underneath Dieter's mansions. "I thought the slaves had shown us all of the torture rooms." Lit troches were attached to the stone walls, their flickering flames enhancing the eeriness of the tunnels.

Schroeder stopped. "General you better have your men draw their swords cuz this room is filled with snakes."

"Why?" Amundsen asked

"Not sure but I think their guarding the thing I got to show you," Schroeder replied. Schroeder was carrying a torch, he opened the door then immediately looked down at the floor; no snakes were in the immediate vicinity of the doorway so he walked in. The smell of decaying flesh attacked their nostrils as Amundsen and his men entered the secret chamber.

"Check to see if any of those people are still alive," Amundsen ordered when he saw countless bodies shackled to the stone walls. "And kill those damn snakes." As the troops followed his orders, Amundsen looked around the room which contained a large unholy altar at the far end and a large fire pit in the middle of the floor. "Schroeder what the hell is this place?"

"It's where Dieter sacrifices people to demons," Schroeder said. "Now do you see why I'm damned scared of him?"

The blood poured down Dieter's wrist and ran onto the floor. "Petorus, your humble servant calls to you. Petorus help me; restore the powers that have been stolen from me." Dieter repeated the same chant over and over. He was starting to get dizzy and nauseous. His blood was pooling on the cold stone floor. "Petorus I offer you my blood, help me."

Suddenly Dieter heard a loud commotion as ten soldiers marched through the dungeons, opened his cell door and dragged him out by his arms.

"What is the meaning of this?" Dieter screamed. "Where are you taking me? Do you know who you are dealing with?" Not one soldier said a word to Dieter. The bright sun momentarily blinded him as the soldiers dragged him from the dark dungeons onto the formation area of Fort Friada.

"Stand him up!" ordered General Amundsen. It was at that moment that Dieter realized there was a large crowd of people in the area, many of whom were not soldiers. "We found your altar where you have been sacrificing the good people of Port Friada to demons." When Amundsen said these words, people in the crowd stared to yell and jeer. "I believe in an eye for an eye," Amundsen said. "Since you like to burn people alive, what better way to send you back to hell with your demon friends."

Dieter looked around and fear gripped his heart when he saw a large wooden stake that was partially buried and surrounded by piles of wood. "No, you can't do this?" he screamed hysterically.

"Tie him up and douse him with oil," Amundsen ordered. The crowd cheered as Dieter was dragged to the stake and tied. Dieter tried to fight the soldiers but he was greatly outnumbered.

"Burn him, burn the demon," the crowd started to chant. The crowd cheered again when soldiers drenched Dieter and the wood he was standing on in oil.

"Dieter do you have any last words?" asked Amundsen.

"I curse you, I curse you all."

"Fire!" ordered General Amundsen.

The crowd cheered as the soldiers lit the stacks of wood that surrounded Dieter. The crowd grew silent as the flames quickly engulfed his body and Dieter screamed in agony. The crowd was filled with horror as they watched a man burn to death.

Archetenus grabbed the back of his neck and fell to his knees in pain.

"Archetenus what has happened?" Delilah screamed and ran to him.

"Delilah stop, don't come near me," he yelled. She stopped momentarily but then took another step towards him. "Delilah I mean it please don't come near me. I don't want to hurt you."

"Hurt me? Why would you hurt me?"

Archetenus doubled over in pain; sweat was pouring down him. "Delilah, my sword is on the table, grab it and stand in the corner."

"Why?" she asked fearfully.

"Just do it!" Archetenus yelled as he tried to stand up.

"Let me help you," Delilah cried.

"Delilah a demon is trying to get control of me," Archetenus said through gritted teeth. "Take that sword and if I try to hurt you kill me."

"Archetenus I can't kill you," she said as tears streamed down her cheeks.

"You're never going to get me you bastard," Archetenus yelled as he writhed on the floor in pain. Delilah ran to a corner of the one room shack and watched with horror as Archetenus rolled around the floor with blood and green foam coming out of his mouth and nose. She ran to the table and grabbed the sword then she returned to the corner and prayed.

After the wounded were cared for and the dead buried, Matthew and his small army headed east towards a line of mountains that sat along the eastern coastline in Ganz. According to the map that Miranda had given Matthew, the shack where Archetenus was hiding was north of the Town of Agger and at the foot of one of the mountains. Agger was a small mining town which consisted of temporary shacks, a general store and four taverns.

A flock of Enrops flew overhead as the army moved forward. All of the warriors were vigilant for attack as they traveled through the mostly forested area.

"Matthew, there's another group of men headed to Agger," Stephan said. "We may have another battle yet today."

"I'm just hoping that no one in Agger knows Archetenus," Matthew said. "Unless the ravens spotted them, I don't think Dieter's men know where he is hiding."

Angelina had been riding in silence. "I keep thinking about what happened to Jared. You saw what happened to those corpses back there. If Archetenus is hiding in a shack with his pregnant wife and the demons come after him," Angelina paused. "Right now I am more concerned for her."

Matthew stopped his horse and called to the Enrops. Several of the giant birds came to him. "Tell the Sanuri all that you have seen here. Tell him that Archetenus bears the Mark of Satan and that we are trying to save him and his wife. Tell him we are concerned that the demons are after Archetenus."

The Sanuri had awaken in the middle of the night because he had a vision of fire. He jumped out of his bed, in the castle of Mathas, packed his things and left a note for the King. The Sanuri was unaware that General Amundsen had sent riders to King Sudfad's castle with a message about Dieter. Amundsen's men were riding north on the western side of the River Toba. The Sanuri was now travelling south along the coastline of the Sea of Grevdt. Their paths would never cross.

Dieter died never knowing who betrayed him or who blocked his powers. He had many faults and one was arrogance. He had started thinking of himself as being invincible and thus he underestimated his rivals and let down his defenses. Dieter managed an area of Opots that was desired by many in the Insidiae.

Cisero had been a dark lord for centuries. A small and somewhat rotund man with gray hair and a large bald spot in the back of his head; he looked more like a kindly grandfather than he did a murderer and butcher. Cisero and Dieter had been rivals for decades. He despised Dieter as a person; he thought Dieter was too flashy and self-promoting.

Cisero hated how Dieter sought for the admiration and approval of normal humans. But it was the proof that Cisero had been compiling to show that Dieter was less interested in the laws of the Insidiae and more interested in wealth and power that allowed Cisero to get the aid of the Grand Masters in disempowering Dieter.

Cisero worked closely with the demon Demanko to bring Dieter to ruins. It was Demanko who ordered the Rogetts to attack Dieter's mansion. And it was Cisero's men who flamed the fears and suspicions that the people of Port Friada had about Dieter. Cisero petitioned for a meeting with the Grand Masters, something that was not often done. Although there were many Grand Masters in existence in the world, only a quorum of thirteen were required to deal with investigations into the members of the Insidiae.

Cisero delivered his petition to Grand Master Emmon, who gathered twelve other Grand Masters from his original tribe. Before the demons came to this world, all men lived together as one. There were no kingdoms, boundaries or walls, because people were not filled with hatred and suspicions of others. There was no intolerance or greed.

The word tribe originally meant family, as all extended family members lived close to each other. But some people carried a seed of darkness and it was these people who originally called to the demons. It was these people who first sold their souls to the Old Ones who answered their calls and it was these people who became the Grand Masters of the Insidiae.

The people who originally called to the Old Ones were rewarded greatly by the demons because the demons could not come into this world unless the humans desired them. Thus the people who became known as the Grand Masters had powers that other humans did not possess. It was the Grand Masters who stripped Dieter of his powers.

Cisero showed the Grand Masters that Dieter had been going behind the backs of the Old Ones and calling to demons from other worlds. Dieter betrayed the Old Ones because he thought he could get more money for the human vessels. And it was Dieter's treacherous actions that were now responsible for some of the wars among the demons.

The Grand Masters swore loyalty to the original Old Ones that came to this world and watched out for the interests of those demons. They condemned Dieter by taking away his powers. Petorus, one of the Old Ones, was the demon who owned Dieter's soul, the same demon that Dieter called to for help. In the instant that Dieter died, Petorus pulled Dieter into his hell region for there is a particular area of hell for betrayers.

Archetenus lay on the floor for almost an hour fighting against the will of the demon Demanko. Demanko was not one of the Old Ones but he was a powerful entity. Demanko was an auctioneer of both men's souls and the bodies of the humans created to be vessels. Demanko was enraged when he lost Jared and humiliated when Jared not only escaped his fate but stole the precious orb from Demanko's altar. Demanko was not going to let Archetenus get away.

Delilah sat in the corner of the shack crying and praying, holding Archetenus' sword. She was afraid to go near Archetenus and afraid to leave him. "Miranda," Delilah called out. "I don't know if you can hear me but please help him somehow."

Archetenus suddenly heard Miranda's voice in his ear. "The demons have no control over you if you refuse to give them the power. Your fears are feeding him. Free yourself and will yourself to come back to your wife and child." Although Archetenus was greatly fighting the powers of Demanko, Archetenus was afraid of what was happening to him and what could happen to Delilah.

Archetenus continued to fight bravely but for all his skills and intelligence he could not figure out how to let go of his fears. "Miranda help me, I don't know how to do this," Archetenus screamed. Miranda grabbed Archetenus' spirit from the demon and returned it to his body in the miners shack.

Delilah heard Archetenus gasping for air. Then he slowly sat up. Archetenus saw the blood and green foam on his body and he felt it on his face. He was wiping his face when his consciousness completely returned and he remembered Delilah. He tried to stand but he could not. He turned his body until he saw her. Archetenus' heart sank in his chest when he saw the terror in her eyes. "Delilah did I try to hurt you?"

"No," she answered in a shaky voice.

"I am so sorry to scare you."

"Is it over?"

"It seems to be, Miranda helped me. But why don't you stay there for a little while until we are sure."

"Archetenus you stopped breathing and you looked like you were in so much pain," Delilah said as she cried. "I called to her to help you. What happened to you?"

Archetenus reached up to the table and grabbed a crock of water and drank it down. Before he answered Delilah's question. "Well, I'm not really sure I understand it. I was in another world fighting with a demon and it was a hell of a fight. Then it must have been after you called to Miranda that I heard her voice. She told me that the demons have no power unless you give it to them and that my fears were feeding the demon. I tried to stop my fears but I couldn't so I called out to Miranda to help me and she brought me back here."

"Your body never left here Archetenus," Delilah said in bewilderment.

Matthew was relieved that he and his men were finally making good time because they ran into no further obstacles as the afternoon wore on. Now they were heading due east towards the mountains. Twice they saw ravens circling over them and each time the birds were killed by Enrops. Matthew wondered how the birds communicated with their dark masters and if the birds had somehow communicated the location of his army.

"Unless someone tips off Dieter's men to Archetenus' location, when they leave Agger they will travel around the west side of the mountains then head north for the border. And they may intercept our path," Stephan said.

"Try to figure out the possible times that we could run into them," said Matthew. "I would like to get Archetenus and his wife and leave immediately. So we could possibly cross paths with them coming or going?"

Archetenus was amazed at how weak he was after his altercation with Demanko. Delilah helped him to a chair and started to wash the blood and foam off his body and hair.

"You said your fears were feeding the demon," Delilah asked. "What were your fears?"

"Losing you and the baby. And I am very afraid that I will turn into a monster and hurt you myself."

"You said you were in another world fighting a demon; didn't that scare you?"

"A little because I didn't understand what was happening which was giving the advantage to the demon and I didn't know how I was going to get back to you. But I have fought many monsters in my life, that demon is just another. And doing battle is part of who I am."

Delilah put the palms of her hands on Archetenus' shoulders and stared into his eyes. "We don't know if this is over. That demon may come back for you so let's prepare. Now you know how to come back; just ask Miranda to help you, so that should take away the advantage that the demon had. You said you have been talking with Miranda for a long time and that you trust her."

"Archetenus you said that Miranda said she would protect us on this journey and that she was going to test you. I think the answer to defeating that demon is pretty simple. Just believe that Miranda is true to her word. And then, my hero, go onto the battlefield and defeat him." Archetenus took Delilah's hand and kissed it.

Romale had put Danar in charge of the sixty-five men heading towards Agger. Like all the rest of the men created to be vessels, Danar was large both in height and build. His body was covered with tattoos, including his face. Danar had wanted his handsome face transformed to look demonic. He took great pains in choosing his tattoos and he got the results that he desired. Danar was greatly stimulated by creating fear in others which his appearance always did. He was a very sadistic man, who took pride in his ability to create great pain in those whom he tortured.

Danar was driving his men hard; he wanted to be the one to find Archetenus and Delilah. Long had he desired Delilah; he knew that Dieter was through with her and wanted her dead. Danar was scheming as to how he could take Delilah for himself.

It was late afternoon when Matthew and his men reached the miners shack. Matthew, Angelina, Sorren and Stephan dismounted. But Matthew told the others not to approach the shack. "Archetenus it is Prince Matthew from Lentz, Miranda sent us to help you."

"We are glad to see you," Archetenus said as he stood in the doorway and looked at the army before him. "We will be right out."

"No," Angelina said. "I am Matthew's wife and a healer. We were with another of your kind when the demons tried to take him. Please let us come in a moment." Archetenus moved to the side to allow them to enter. Angelina was relieved to see that Delilah was unharmed.

"Archetenus please sit down a moment," Angelina said. "The man I spoke of is named Jared, we discovered that he had a tattoo on the back of his neck that allowed the demons access to him. I just want to see if you have the same tattoo. I will merely lift your hair and look." Archetenus sat down in one of the two chairs in the shack. Delilah walked up to Angelina so she could see the tattoo.

"Not sure how to explain it but a demon did take me to another world," Archetenus said. "I was battling him and Miranda helped me to come back."

Angelina looked at Matthew, "It is here. Archetenus the demons branded you with the Mark of Satan."

"I have seen that mark before," said Archetenus.

"When we placed a holy crystal on the tattoo that was on Jared's neck the snake came alive," Angelina said.

"What happened with Jared?" asked Archetenus.

No one said anything for a moment then Sorren spoke, "Son, Jared is one tough man; he didn't want the demons controlling him so he took a handful of crystals and pressed them against the tattoo. That snake can't stand anything holy and it grew to about eight feet as it tore its way out of Jared's body. He was pretty tore up for a while but he is just fine now."

"Do you have some of those crystals?" Archetenus asked.

"No," Matthew said. "Miranda wants us to take you to the Sanuri; he can help you."

"Archetenus you don't want to be tore up now, we're expecting to run into another band of Dieter's men soon. We should be leaving," said Stephan.

"How do you know they are coming this way?" Archetenus asked as he and Delilah gathered their things.

"Miranda gave us a map of their routes, and that is how we found you," Matthew said and turned to walk out the door.

"Wait," Archetenus said and took two journals from his saddlebags and gave them to Matthew. "Delilah and I can explain these later. Our horses are around back."

"One of the Enrops just said that Dieter's men are entering Agger," Thaos said as Matthew and the others walked out of the shack. They'll be heading this way soon."

"We'll use the same tactic that we did with the first group of his men," Matthew said. "Prepare the soldiers."

"When we killed the first group of Dieter's men," Sorren explained to Archetenus and Delilah. "After they were dead those Satan snakes broke out of the bodies and came after us."

Archetenus grabbed Matthew by the arm causing Matthew to turn around. "Delilah is pregnant," Archetenus said. "If that demon comes after me again, promise me that you will protect her."

"I promise," Matthew said. "Are you up to a battle?"

"I've been wanting to turn around and fight them for days," said Archetenus.

Some of the soldiers and Nordes warriors were concealed in the thick forest which extended to the foot of the mountains, while others took higher ground on the mountain itself. Enrops flew overhead, there were no signs of ravens. Archetenus rode up next to Matthew, "What is your plan?"

"All the men who are looking for you were created as vessels," Matthew said. "So they can be controlled by demons. Our archers took out the first group of men. I would prefer to avoid hand to hand combat with them."

"And the snakes?" Archetenus asked.

"The arrows didn't stop them so that was hand to hand combat."

Danar and his men terrorized the small town of Agger during their brief time there. Danar's men pulled people out of buildings and beat them on the streets, trying to get information about Archetenus and Delilah. But none of the townspeople had any information to give them. Frustrated, Danar ordered his men to mount up and they rode out of the town and headed north towards the border. The demon Demanko was not going to lose again; he warned Danar about the ambush he was riding into.

Danar stopped, he didn't understand that Demanko was sending him a message he just knew they were riding into trouble. Before they got to the forest, Danar had his men spilt up to surround whoever lay in ambush.

"Remember the woman is mine!" Danar yelled then ordered his men to battle.

"The men stopped and are splitting into two groups," an Enrop told Matthew.

"They know we are here," Matthew yelled. "They are coming around us." Thaos, Stephan and Sorren moved their men so there were no gaps in the perimeter.

Danar did not have archers among his men; they rode into the forest with swords and battleaxes drawn.

Stephan, Sorren and Thaos waited until Danar's men were just to enter the forest and they had their warriors release the first volleys of arrows. Since Danar's men were in the open without cover, the arrows struck many of them. Horses snorted and reared as hundreds of arrows sailed through the air. Men were yelling and cursing at their unseen enemies.

"They won't run, they will charge us," Matthew said to Angelina. "Prepare for a direct attack," Matthew yelled to the troops. Another volley of arrows was launched from the forest and Danar's men ran towards their attackers.

Delilah was seated on her horse near Archetenus, Matthew and Angelina. She gasped, "I know that man in the lead, his name is Danar he is a monster."

"The one with the tattoos?" asked Angelina.

"Yes," Delilah said. "He told Dieter that he wanted to be a demon that is why he got those tattoos."

Danar stopped his horse and faced the forest. "Archetenus I know you are in there. Give me the woman and I will spare your life," Danar yelled as he was trying to taunt Archetenus.

Danar's men charged into the forest and many of them died quickly. The warriors of Lentz were well concealed in the brush, trees and rocks. And Danar's men made no attempts to conceal their positions.

Danar alone stood in the open facing the forest. Archetenus drew his sword and started towards him. Matthew grabbed Archetenus' arm. "You cannot do this."

"It is my fight, you have done enough," Archetenus replied.

"No you don't understand," Matthew continued. "Miranda said that if you died before we got you to the Sanuri you would turn into a monster."

"Then Prince Matthew I trust that you will slay the monster."

"Archetenus I understand why you stole Delilah. I too have wanted her for my own and after I kill you, she will warm my bed tonight," Danar yelled.

"Archetenus no," Delilah said as Archetenus rode forward to do battle with Danar. Danar smiled when he saw Archetenus riding towards him. Danar dismounted and grabbed his shield and sword.

Danar's men broke through the line of archers under Thaos command first. The archers shouldered or dropped their bows and pulled their swords. Thaos jumped off from his horse and ran his sword through the back of one of Danar's men who was on top of soldier and choking him. As soon as Thaos pulled his sword back, the man stood up and started towards Thaos, who lunged forward and ran his sword through the man's stomach. The man did not falter but kept coming towards Thaos.

"Matthew they are under demon control," Thaos shouted while the soldier who had been lying on the ground jumped on the back of the man and cut his throat. Finally the vessel collapsed to the ground.

"Stay behind me," Angelina said to Delilah as they watched Archetenus dismount and face off with Danar.

Sorren was fighting on the ground with one of the vessels, they both had knives drawn. The vessel lunged and cut Sorren's right arm which held his large knife. Sorren quickly reached down and pulled a smaller knife from one of his sheaths and threw it at the vessel with his left hand. The knife impaled in the vessel's throat, then Sorren charged forward and stabbed the man repeatedly with the knife in his right hand.

"The corpses are turning into snakes," Stephan yelled as he rode among several bodies and cut the heads off from the snakes as they were emerging from their hosts.

Archetenus and Danar had both dismounted and now circled each other, while they sized up their opponent. Archetenus was too experienced in battle to let Danar distract him as Danar continued to make salacious comments about Delilah.

"Miranda help him," Delilah prayed under her breath. "Help them all."

The Enrops were attacking the snakes as they emerged from the corpses. The bodies of the vessels themselves were more difficult to kill but they were dying at the hands of Matthew's army. Matthew and Angelina stood watch over Archetenus for they both knew that if Danar killed him; Archetenus would be their most dangerous enemy on this battlefield.

Danar lunged at Archetenus with his sword. Archetenus quickly stepped to the right and lowered his body. Archetenus swung his sword and hit Danar in the back of the knee, a blow which knocked Danar to the ground. Danar screamed in pain as blood gushed from his wound.

"Get up and tell me again what you want to do to my wife," Archetenus said solemnly. Archetenus could have run in for the kill but he wanted to hurt Danar before he killed him.

"Your wife," Danar spat as he stood up. He could not put pressure on his left leg, so he was trying to balance on his right. Archetenus kept moving, he wanted to make Danar work for his strikes. Danar stared at Archetenus, trying to take in every movement. Then Danar lunged again. Archetenus did a forward roll and came to his feet behind Danar. Archetenus stabbed Danar in the kidneys. Danar screamed and fell to his knees.

Archetenus walked up to Danar. "I'm sending you back to the demons," Archetenus said as he swung his sword and cut Danar's head off.

Demanko screamed with rage, a scream that transcended his hell region until it was heard by the combatants. "It's the demon," Angelina said and they saw Archetenus suddenly fall to the ground. Angelina tore her crystal off from her neck and raced towards Archetenus with Matthew and Delilah close behind her. Angelina jumped off her horse as she saw blood and green foam coming from Archetenus' mouth.

Angelina put her crystal into Archetenus' left hand. "This is holy use it against the demon." She grabbed Archetenus' sword and put the hilt in his right hand. "Use this in your battle." Then Angelina started to pray over Archetenus.

"What should I do?" cried Delilah.

"Pray," Angelina said to Delilah then Angelina turned back to Archetenus. "Archetenus you can bring yourself back." Archetenus started to thrash around violently. Blood and green foam were now coming out of his ears and nose.

"Release him demon, you have no power here," Matthew said. "By The Great Ruler I order you to release him." They heard more hellish screaming and Matthew turned to see if it was coming from the battle. But when he turned he saw Stephan, Thaos and Sorren riding towards them. Matthew knew that battle was over. He turned back to Archetenus who appeared to have stopped breathing. "Is he dead?" Matthew asked.

"He stopped breathing before when he was fighting with the demon," Delilah cried.

"Matthew give me your crystal," Angelina said and as she put it in Archetenus' left hand she said. "Archetenus may you be surrounded with the holiness of these crystals. Again they heard hellish screams. Then Archetenus was still. He wasn't moving. He wasn't breathing.

"Is he dead?" asked Stephan.

"Archetenus come back to me," Delilah screamed.

Suddenly Archetenus bolted up to a standing position and looked around him wildly. He did not recognize his surroundings or the people. "Archetenus its Delilah, and Prince Matthew and Angelina," Delilah said quickly for she feared Archetenus would try to fight with the others. Archetenus stared at them all as his consciousness was returning to him. He dropped his sword then fell to his knees. Delilah and Angelina ran to him.

"I'm alright," Archetenus said as he was trying to catch his breath. "At least I think I am."

Delilah was wiping the blood and green foam off from Archetenus. "Jared was covered in that green foam when he too fought the demons," Angelina said.

"Archetenus can you tell us what happened to you," Stephan asked after he saw that Archetenus was breathing normally again.

"In some ways I'm not really sure what happened," he said and spit out a mouth full of blood. "I felt like I was falling down a great tunnel, everything was pitch black then I heard screaming. The screaming seemed to come from hundreds of voices and they all sounded like they were in great agony."

"Then I heard laughter; I have never heard anything as evil as that laughter. And then I'm not sure but I think two demons were fighting. There were great, well, I really don't know how to explain it except if you have ever witnessed a great funnel cloud that is tearing up everything in its path and turning it inside out then throwing it."

Archetenus stood up as Angelina and Delilah were examining him for injuries. "Then I heard yelling, not the voices in pain but powerful voices that sounded like thunder and they were angry. Then something grabbed me from behind like a great hand. I don't know how but I had my sword in my hand and I stabbed it many times but it kept squeezing me, like it was trying to squeeze the life out of me. I could hear all of your voices."

"Matthew when you commanded the demon to let go of me, he suddenly dropped me and screamed as if he was in great pain."

"I fell into something that seemed like a swamp but it had the most retched smell and the muck that I fell into was very thick. I landed on my feet and immediately I could feel hands upon me."

Archetenus spit out another mouth full of blood. "Then Angelina gave me the second crystal with her words I was suddenly surrounded by light. The kind of light I see around Miranda, then I could see the monsters that surrounded me but they fell back from the light. I felt that I had an advantage so I ran my sword through the monster closest to me. My sword too was surrounded by light and the monster screamed in agony and fell over. So I turned and attacked the rest of the monsters. When I destroyed the last one I was back with you."

Chapter XXII
Reunions

"What's happened?" Gabriel asked earnestly when he saw Elan and Cassandra standing at their table. Neither Elan nor Cassandra spoke for several moments and they both looked like they had been crying.

"Is Natasha alright?" Calen asked fearfully and started to stand.

When Elan spoke he was choking on his words, "Fala was murdered by Hutas and Bekka is injured. Emeral, Hannah and Natasha want you all to come home now so they can read the letter to everyone at once."

Calen slammed his fist on the table, "I knew she was too young I should never have let her go."

"We all decided to give her have a chance," Gabriel said although he felt just as guilty as Calen. "It is not your fault."

"Do you know how it happened?" asked Raphael.

"No, we haven't read the letter," Elan said. "We found everyone crying and they asked us to bring you home."

Misha, Koby and Dagon stood up and started to leave the Great Hall in Sudfad's castle in silence. Vitomas was sitting at the table next to Gabriel and she now touched his arm. "Is there anything we can do?" Vitomas asked.

"No, but thank you," Gabriel said solemnly.

"Well, please let us know," Raul added.

"How old was she?" asked Simon.

"Fifteen," Calen said emotionally as he left the table.

"Thank you for returning I have something I need to tell you," Lakin said to his Ruala warriors who now gathered in the parlor of the house owned by the Patronus. "I just received word from Fala's parents; they want to bury their only daughter at home. I have preserved her body the best that I can with what I have here but I need some volunteers to take her body home."

"I should take her home," Luca said. "I was her supervisor."

"While I would normally agree," Lakin said. "You are still healing from your wounds and you have much to take care of here."

"Dack and I should take her home," Joao said. "We have been her friends since we were children."

"I would like to go also," Bekka said.

"I will go," said Trist.

"As well as I," Rako said.

"All of us who were on duty with her should go in case the family has questions," Sahil said.

"I agree," Lakin said. "I will write another letter to their family that I would like you to deliver. Trist you are the senior warrior in this group you will be in charge."

"I will pack food for you," Lila said as she stood in the doorway listening to them. "When do you plan to leave?"

"Lakin will the body and letter be ready, say in two hours?" Trist asked.

"I will make sure," replied Lakin.

Christopher had been standing with Lila, holding her hand; now he pushed through the crowd and looked up at Trist. "I have a letter too," Christopher said and handed a clumsily folded piece of paper to Trist."

"Is this for her parents?" Trist asked as he bent down and took the paper.

"Yes," Christopher said. "Thank you." Then he ran over to Bekka and climbed on her lap.

Luca looked at Lila, "Can he write?"

"I wrote the words that he wanted and he drew the pictures," she replied with tears in her eyes. "You should read it."

"Christopher can I read your letter?" Luca asked.

"Sure," Christopher said as he was stroking Bekka's hair.

Luca walked up to Trist and took the letter, he read it silently then he looked at Christopher. "Christopher can I read this to everyone here, they were all Fala's friends too?"

"Sure, Lila had to help me with the words."

Fala was my friend. I liked her very much. We had fun. My sister said that Fala is in heaven with our mommy and daddy now. I am sure they will take very good care of her so you don't have to worry. Christopher.

Luca was choking up as he read the letter to the group. Bekka started to cry.

"Bekka why are you crying?" Christopher asked. "Didn't you like it?"

Bekka hugged Christopher, "I liked the letter very much."

Sophie and Erebus had just returned to their room in the Taperian Imperial Hotel. They had finished dinner in the dining room of the hotel and Sophie was pouring two glasses of wine, while Erebus changed his clothes.

"I'll get it," Sophie called out to Erebus when she heard a knock at the door. She opened the door and gasped.

"Hello Sophie, I didn't expect to see you here," Roch said.

"Roch, come in," Sophie said and stepped aside so he could enter. "Where on earth have you been I was beside myself with worry and why do you look like that?" Sophie's voice did not betray the concern she had that Roch might know about her involvement with the Insidiae.

Roch smiled and took off his hat, "I'm not sure you would believe me if I told you."

"Well sit down," Sophie said. "Would you like whiskey or wine?"

"Whiskey," Roch said. "I saw you and Erebus in the dining room. I have a room here too."

Erebus entered the parlor and stared at Roch for a moment. "Sophie and I are married. She left the castle after you disappeared. Roch where have you been; people were looking all over for you?" Erebus asked. Erebus had always been able to see a dark aura surrounding Roch but now Erebus was seeing something that he did not understand.

Sophie handed Roch a glass of whiskey then sat down next to him on the sofa. "Roch do you remember what happened? You were so sick and then you were unconscious for days and..." Sophie paused.

"And what?" Roch asked because he had no memory of what Sophie was talking about.

Sophie looked at Erebus who spoke, "Roch your body started to change both in color and in form. You didn't look like a man any more, then you just disappeared. Cerephus had soldiers looking for you and we were doing spells to help find you. I called to another sorcerer to help us."

Roch looked confused as he listened to Erebus, then he said sincerely, "I don't remember any of that. Will you tell me what happened and how long I have been gone?"

Erebus and Sophie looked at each other with amazement then Erebus said, "Roch let me fill your glass this is going to be a long night and I know you will want that drink."

Matthew and his men did not want to stay in Ganz any longer then they had to. Since they still had a few hours of daylight left they started their return trip to Lentz after they had taken care of the wounded and buried the dead. Matthew, Stephan, Thaos and Sorren were all large men but they had concerns about Archetenus who was considerably larger and stronger. They saw how easily he killed Danar and they were concerned about him turning into a demon.

When they made camp for the night they asked Archetenus and Delilah to stay with them. It was Archetenus who brought up the subject. "I can tell from the looks on your faces that you have concerns about me," Archetenus said. "Let's get it on the table."

"I think I speak for all of us," Thaos said. "We're just concerned about the demons controlling you. I mean as a person you are alright."

"I too have those concerns," Archetenus said. "I don't want to be controlled by the demons and I don't want to turn into a monster. I already asked Matthew this, but if something happens to me I want you to protect Delilah, she is carrying my baby. And I want you to kill me."

"Not that we want to kill you," Sorren said. "But if you turn into a demon can we and is there a special way?"

"I have no idea," said Archetenus.

"I wish you all would stop talking like this," Delilah said emotionally. "Archetenus may have been marked by the demons but he is a good man and he has been fighting them so hard." Then she turned to Archetenus, "What on earth makes you think you are going to lose the fight? Do you ever lose battles no matter who you are against? I think you should put your energies against fighting Dieter's men not each other."

Angelina and Delilah were near the fire cooking and Angelina smiled as she listened to Delilah scolding the men. "I agree with every word she said," Angelina said.

"Matthew you had an Angel appear to you just so we could help Archetenus so he wouldn't turn into a demon. And Archetenus the same Angel said she would protect you. Now for the rest of us, I would be so honored to have an Angel appear to me. Why don't you listen to her?"

"Angelina is right," Delilah said. "Your letting your fears get out of proportion. So to change the subject, after we eat why don't I start explaining some of the things in those journals to you."

The men all looked at each other and smiled because of what the women were saying but it was not easy for them to let go of their fears.

Christopher was asleep when Luca and Lila walked into the bedroom. Luca covered the boy up then turned to Lila, who was undressing. He watched as she took off everything but a thin slip, then he took her into his arms and kissed her. "I will be so glad when we have our own room," Luca said with a chuckle and kissed Lila again.

"Luca it is so wonderful that you let him sleep with you. Christopher is afraid to sleep by himself and he feels so safe with you, as do I," Lila said and stretched up and kissed Luca. "Since he is asleep we could go to my room for a while."

"And if he wakes he will wonder where we are," Luca said. Then he let go of Lila and took off his robe. "In the letter I sent home I told mother to start planning our wedding, but I am sure that the news about Fala greatly upset everyone."

Lila walked up to Luca and put the palms of her hands on his cheeks. "You can't feel guilty for what happened, it wasn't your fault."

"I should have been with them," Luca said and sat down on the edge of the bed.

"You are injured," Lila said as she sat near him. "And besides you don't go out with every shift of warriors. I didn't know Fala long but she was my friend and I miss her terribly," Lila said. "But I don't want you beating yourself up over this."

"You and Lakin and the others were trying to prepare her for your team, which is what she wanted more than anything. She died as a warrior and with honor; she died saving her friend. From what I know of Fala, that is exactly how she would have wanted to die." Luca grabbed Lila and hugged her tightly.

The mood was solemn in Gabriel and Hannah's house that evening. Everyone stayed home but there was little talking. To lose a comrade was devastating. To lose one so young filled all of the warriors with guilt. Finally it was Cassandra who broke the silence.

"Fala was a very close friend of mine; she was like my little sister. She; like all of us who are in training wanted nothing more than to be a worthy member of your team. We wanted to see battle and we wanted to do good. I see the pain all of you are carrying because you feel guilty that you gave her a chance to realize her dreams. Don't you understand that you would have crushed her if you sent her home? We are in pain because of her death but she died fulfilling her dreams. In a way she was lucky, I certainly hope that I have such a death."

Everyone in the parlor stared at Cassandra in silence as her words started to heal them. Gabriel stood up and walked over to Cassandra and hugged her. "Thank you I think we all needed to hear that," he said. "Let's all have a toast, not to the life that was lost but to the life that was."

Roch sat up talking with Sophie and Erebus until the first rays of dawn peeked through the drapes of the hotel room. Neither Sophie nor Erebus trusted Roch and they were not sure if he intended them harm. Although Erebus had not said anything yet to Sophie he was concerned about the unusual aura he was seeing around Roch. Erebus wasn't sure if Roch was already a vessel for a demon.

Roch told Sophie and Erebus the truth as he remembered it for he was hoping they could give him some answers. Roch was trying desperately to regain his memories; memories that contained the answers he sought.

"So what are you going to do about General Hamond?" Sophie asked.

"I intend to get my throne back," Roch said with determination.

"Roch remember that both Cerephus and Hamond assumed the throne because it was vacant. They did not take it by force. Perhaps if you talked to Hamond." Sophie was saying until Erebus interrupted her.

"Sophie don't kid yourself Hamond is not going to hand over the throne. Roch is right to go in disguise until he has a workable plan." Then Erebus looked at Roch, "I am not trying to offend you but you always chose your officers from men who were almost as cruel and cunning as you. If you try to have an audience with Hamond he will have you killed and you know it."

"I know you are right," Roch said. "And I feel that I can trust you that is why I am here."

"Well, we're certainly not going to tell anyone," said Sophie.

"Actually I was hoping you could help me," Roch said to their amazement.

As everyone in Gabriel's house was sitting down to breakfast and Enrop flew into the dining room with a letter. Hannah always left at least one window open in the house so the Enrops would have access. Raphael took the letter and read it. "It's from Lakin," Raphael explained. "He says that Fala's parents wanted to bury her at home so six of his warriors are taking her body to the Ice Caves. He would like us to ask for volunteers to replace these six since they work in shifts to watch the mausoleum.

"I can certainly go," Koby said.

"I'll go too," said Dagon.

Gabriel looked at Calen before he spoke. "Maybe we all should discuss this. The Sanuri said that the mausoleum is a trap for us and that we should concentrate on finding and destroying Roch. Since everyone at this table has been working on strategies and research for Roch I kind of hate to have you reassigned."

"I agree," said Raphael. "And Koby and Dagon you know quite a bit about Roch from your previous assignment. There are hundreds of Rualas at the castle I would think we could get six volunteers. But I will put it out to you."

"What you are saying makes sense," Koby said.

"Well, if someone were to ask me what I think," Emeral said with a coy smile. "I think the two of you should fly out to Nora and bring back Luca and his new family. Lila and Christopher just lost their parents and days later they lose a friend. That little boy is only six; this has to be affecting him. And if Luca is still healing from his injuries he may not be in any shape to fly the two of them back here."

Dagon looked at Koby and Misha, "We can certainly do that. We would be gone less than a week if that is alright with everyone."

"I should go to," Misha said. "In case Luca isn't strong enough to fly this far."

"Sounds fine to me," Gabriel said and looked at Calen and Raphael.

"I think it sounds like a good idea," Calen said. "But you know how dedicated Luca is and perhaps now after Fala was murdered he won't want to leave Nora. I think you should ask him first."

"Well, he is going to have to think about Christopher and Lila now too," Emeral said. "I will send him a letter today. Perhaps he will just send them home and we can take care of them until he returns."

Stephan was studying their map as everyone was eating breakfast. "According to this, the third search party was travelling along the western bank of the River Toba and crossing the border. If they follow this course we shouldn't run into them." Then he looked at Archetenus. "If that demon knows where you are I am sure he knows we are here too. Did you get any idea if he is directing these search parties?"

Archetenus seriously thought about the question as he tried to remember every detail of his experience. "I believe he knew I was fighting Danar because he said something like you aren't getting away that easy. I don't remember hearing anything that directly linked him to the search parties but I would expect the worse."

"That's what I was thinking," Matthew said, then he turned to Stephan. "Try to figure out their location at the time we were fighting with the last group. Then figure out some intercept points."

To everyone's surprise Archetenus looked at them and said sincerely, "I am sorry that all of you had to get involved in this mess and I am sorry that you have lost men trying to help us."

"Well the way I see it," Sorren said. "You are helping us a great deal. There is a lot of information in those journals. King Sudfad and his sons are actually leading the fight against the Insidiae and they will find that information very useful."

"King Sudfad?" Archetenus said. "His son is Prince Raul?"

"Well, I guess now is as good a time as any to tell you," Matthew said. "Prince Raul and Princess Vitomas are my cousins. Our families are very close. When the Sanuri told us about your situation we volunteered to come and help you because we felt it might be awkward for Sudfad's family to come. Just so you know, they know you were intended to be a vessel and they know you have been battling the demons. They also know..." Matthew stopped talking as he realized that Delilah might not know that Archetenus had kidnapped Vitomas.

"Matthew, I told Delilah what I did; you can finish your sentence," Archetenus said.

"They know that Miranda was talking to you when you had Vitomas."

"Do they know that I am married now?"

"I don't think so," Angelina said. "Archetenus, Raul and Vitomas are happily married with three children. And you and Delilah certainly seem happily married. I want you to tell us honestly. Would there be problems if you all met again?"

"Not for my part," Archetenus said. "But if I was Raul I would want to kill me. I hope Vitomas told you that I kidnapped her and wanted to marry her but I didn't hurt her. But I think I sure scared her. I thought she loved me and when I found out she didn't I had all I could do to control my anger around her." Archetenus turned to Delilah looked her in the eyes and could not tell her the truth. While he did become violent when he drank, Archetenus did not drink whiskey when Vitomas was with him.

"I know what I am about to say may scare you but you should know. Miranda made me realize that when I drink I can get very violent. I didn't believe her at first and then you might say she showed me things that I didn't remember that I did when I was drunk. I haven't gotten drunk since and I don't intend to. But when I found out that Vitomas didn't love me I was getting drunk every night that she was with me. And now that I look back, I think if it wasn't for Miranda I might have hurt Vitomas."

No one said anything so Archetenus kept talking. "Delilah in the last few days you have seen and heard some horrible things. I hope you want to stay married to me but if you are changing your mind I would understand."

Delilah looked at Archetenus with shock at his words, then she smiled and kissed him on the cheek. "I'm not changing my mind," she said softly.

"Archetenus your honesty I believe surprised us all, but we welcome it," Angelina said. "Now I have a question for you. King Sudfad's family is leading the battle against the men who turned you into a vessel and the demons. And all of us sitting here with you are related and we are related with Sudfad's family. We too are in the fight. Jared, the other man who was like you is now working with us in this battle. If you wanted to join us, I am sure you would be welcomed but you would have to prove to Raul that you could be trusted. Do you think this is something you would be interested in doing?"

"If I was unwed I would say 'yes' in a second," Archetenus said. "But Delilah and I have no idea where we are going to live and with a baby coming; I don't want to leave her alone and go off to battle."

"Everyone here is married and has small babies," Stephan said, then he started to laugh. "Except for Sorren but he is the grandfather of all our children. We feel the same way. But this is not like being in the army. You don't have to leave your wife."

"What Stephan is trying to say Archetenus is we saw you fight Danar and we would rather have you with us than against us," Thaos said in a joking manner.

"Archetenus you have all kinds of information that could be useful to us," Matthew said. "Not just what is in those journals."

"I don't understand what you mean," Archetenus said as he could tell Matthew was keeping something from him.

"Matthew just tell him," Sorren said. "Or I will."

"Roch was created to be a vessel like you, only his creators had already chosen the demon who would take control of him," Matthew said. "You may think some of what I am going to say sounds crazy but basically there are wars going on between demons. A powerful demon named Ahriman stole Roch so he couldn't be used as a vessel for this other demon. Ahriman recently returned Roch to this world and right this moment Roch is in the midst of transforming into a demon. Sudfad's family is looking for him so they can kill him before he turns into a demon."

"You worked for Roch most of your life," Sorren said. "You might have information that could help them. I can understand if you don't want to be around Sudfad's family son. But you know what Roch was like as a man, think of what he would do as a demon."

"Archetenus, Matthew and I have two small children," Angelina said. "Do you want to bring your child into this world with the Insidiae after you and Roch as a demon? It would benefit you too, to help us."

Archetenus looked at Matthew and grinned, "Your wife certainly has a way with words."

"You have no idea," Matthew said then started to laugh.

"There is no love lost between Roch and me," Archetenus said. "He tried to have me killed a couple of times. I am in agreement with all that you have said but I have two concerns. Delilah and I have no family other than each other. Where ever we go I want to make sure that she and the baby are safe. And for all the effort you have put into talking me into to this. You really need to talk to Prince Raul and the rest of his family. They may not want my help and I can't say I would blame them."

Roch, Sophie and Erebus continued talking until midmorning when they decided to go to the dining room in the restaurant and eat. Sophie and Erebus listened with amazement as Roch told them about his return to this world and the things that had happened to him.

"Roch you were in a hell dimension why did the demon send you back?" Erebus asked. "What does he want you to do for him?"

"Send me back," Roch said. "I escaped."

"Roch no one escapes from hell," Erebus said. "Now let's just say you did, how did you travel through different worlds to get back to Taperia?"

Roch stared at Erebus then said angrily, "You don't have to believe me."

"Oh I believe you," Erebus said. "I just think there is a lot more to this than maybe you remember. And if I were you I would try to remember."

"Well, why would a demon send me back?" Roch asked. "That doesn't make any sense."

Erebus laughed. "Roch none of your story makes sense but it happened. You probably made some sort of deal with the demon and he may leave you alone until he wants to collect. Making deals with demons is very dangerous. You should really try to remember."

Roch lowered his voice as he talked. "I don't have all my memories back. Sometimes it's like I remember just bits and pieces of some things. Like the things you just said to me, you have said similar things in the past haven't you?"

"Yes," Erebus said. "When that demon Demetries was always talking you into things." Since Roch's disappearance Erebus learned that it was Meekos, Sophie's brother who hired Demetries to spy on Roch. Erebus did not want Roch to learn of Sophie's involvement with the Insidiae. Erebus quickly changed the subject. "Roch do you want me to research spells on getting your memory back?"

"Yes, that would be very helpful."

"It's almost noon and none of us have had any sleep," Erebus said. "I propose we all go back to our rooms get some sleep and meet down here for dinner, say at seven. Would that work for you Roch?"

"Yes, I will have to admit that it is nice to have someone to talk to. I'm glad I saw you last night," Roch said.

"Well, I am just so relieved that you are alive and well," Sophie said in a motherly manner. "But what you have been through sounds so horrible."

"Seven then," Erebus said and stood up from the table.

Later that afternoon Matthew and his men were just miles from the border between the Kingdoms of Ganz and Zorta when they heard a loud commotion and looked up to see a flock of Enrops doing battle with a flock of ravens.

"That's not a good sign," Stephan said.

They were travelling through a thick forest. "Ready your men for attack," Matthew said as the hair on the back of his neck began to rise.

"Did you see something?" asked Thaos.

"No, I can feel it," Matthew said. "I don't know how but I know we are riding into a trap."

Matthew had his army take positions where they were. The area was defensible and now they were forcing the enemy to come to them. Archetenus rode close to Matthew and said in a low voice, "I have learned that sometimes when you get really strong feelings and just know things, its Miranda sending you information. Don't ask me how."

Sorren rode up to Matthew and Archetenus. "It's quiet, too quiet. I think you are right." Suddenly a dead raven fell from the sky just missing Sorren but scaring his horse. The horse jumped and snorted. And in that instant an arrow just missed Sorren's arm and impaled a tree.

"Hutas," Sorren yelled. "Hutas."

"Lila I need to talk to you," Luca said as he walked into the kitchen with a letter from his mother.

"Just let me get these pies into the oven; it will be just a moment."

Lila put four berry pies into the oven then walked over to Luca. "More warriors are coming to help us here and when they come, Mother thinks that I should bring you and Christopher home. She thinks the two of you have seen too much tragedy and she is especially concerned about Christopher losing your parents and now Fala."

"I have to agree with your mother, I have been wondering how Christopher is handling all this," Lila said but she saw a strange look on Luca's face. "Luca what is wrong?"

"I just feel like I should stay here and avenge Fala's death."

"Have you talked about this with Lakin?"

"Yes, he thinks I should take you home."

"Luca, I hope you aren't thinking of sending us to your home and staying here. Your family sounds wonderful but we don't know them."

"I was thinking that."

"I would rather stay here with you."

"But you are both right about Christopher, I should get him home," Luca smiled again. "Here you can read the letter, but Mother says now that I have a family I have to start thinking differently."

"Why don't we all go to your home, then after we are settled, if you really want to return to Nora, well I don't want to be separated from you," Lila said, then she paused. "Luca I would rather be with you but I won't try to stop you if you need to return here."

Luca kissed Lila on the lips. "I think you are going to make a good wife."

Erebus and Sophie got little sleep after they left Roch. "He doesn't seem like the same person," Sophie kept repeating. "He almost seemed pathetic."

"Sophie, don't fall for this," Erebus said. "He needs answers and perhaps this is all an act. I told you about the strange aura I saw around him. I have never seen anything like it before. And remember if he made a deal with a demon, it was probably to do something awful. I don't want him to find out about your involvement with the Insidiae."

"Well, it doesn't sound like he even knows about the Insidiae and their plans for him."

"Not yet," Erebus said. "Sophie you are feeling sorry for him. But Roch has always been a cruel and cunning man, he will get the answers he is looking for and then he will have his revenge."

"So what do you want to do?" Sophie asked. "He wants us to help him."

"And we will," Erebus replied. "I would rather have him close than sneaking up behind me."

"Are you going to try and help him get his memories back?"

"I don't know. I can't decide if that would put you more at risk or if that would answer many of our questions also. I don't want you telling anyone in the Insidiae about Roch. At least not yet."

"Erebus I wasn't planning on it," Sophie said. "But having him with us might give us an upper hand."

No sooner had Sorren's warning cry been heard by the warriors from Lentz, than hundreds of Huta arrows flew at the army.

"Shields up! Shields up!"

"They're giving us a taste of our own medicine," Stephan yelled at Thaos. Within moments Huta war cries filled the air as dozens of Hutas attacked Matthew's army.

"Where's the rest?" Matthew said. Then he yelled out, "We are being surrounded."

Sorren called to his warriors and they turned their focus on the rear of the army. Archetenus joined Sorren. Within moments the majority of the Huta warriors were attacking from the rear. Matthew called more of his soldiers from the front lines and sent them to the rear.

The first wave of Hutas who attacked from the rear were on foot and running towards the army. Sorren ordered the archers to release the first, second and third volleys of arrows into the oncoming swarms. The Hutas who were not killed or injured by the arrows continued to charge towards the army from Lentz.

A second wave of Hutas charged towards the rear of the army on horseback. "Release!" Sorren ordered again and again.

"Something isn't right here," Archetenus yelled to Sorren. "We're killing them too easily. I think this is a diversion."

"Talmuth!" yelled Matthew as the shadows cast by the demonic creatures darkened the ground. "Miranda we need help," Matthew yelled.

"Miranda help these men," Archetenus called out. "They should not die to save me."

The giant dragon-like creatures swooped down at the combatants but the trees acted as barriers. The momentary distraction by the Talmuth allowed the Hutas to gain ground as they attacked the army. The archers shouldered their bows and drew their swords and battleaxes.

Archetenus charged forward with a sword in one hand and a battleaxe in his other. He rode through a group of Hutas on horseback stabbing them and beating them. A Huta jumped on the back of Archetenus' horse and grabbed his hair. When the Huta saw the Mark of Satan on the back of Archetenus' neck, he hesitated giving Archetenus the seconds that he needed to dislodge the Huta.

Stephan rolled to his left and avoided being impaled with a Huta spear. Thaos rode up to Stephan with his horse. As Stephan mounted, Thaos grabbed the spear and threw it at a Huta; the spear hit the Huta with such force that the entire head of the spear came out of the Huta's back.

Matthew and Angelina were fighting on their feet, standing back to back. Once Stephan was on his horse, Thaos rode towards Angelina and Matthew. Thaos had his battleaxe drawn and with one mighty swing he crushed the skull of one of the three Hutas running towards Angelina. Then he turned his horse and hit a second Huta in the face. That Huta fell to the ground and never got up. Angelina ran her sword through the third Huta then quickly turned to help Matthew who was more concerned with keeping the Hutas away from Angelina than he was in protecting himself.

Angelina screamed with rage when she saw Matthew's shirt covered in blood. She swung her sword and hit one of Matthew's attackers in the lower back, severing his spinal cord. When the Huta fell to the ground, Angelina ran her sword through his spine just below the neck.

Thaos literally grabbed one of the Hutas away from Matthew and slit the Huta's throat. Angelina was running her sword through the back of another Huta who was attacking Matthew when she heard Stephan scream her name. Instinctively Angelina ducked and rolled forward as Thaos ran his sword through the back of the Huta that was almost on top of her.

Suddenly screeching that was louder than the sounds of war filled the forest, as the Talmuth realized their ancient enemy was upon them. Giant Blue Hengers filled the skies and savagely attacked the demonic Talmuth. The Hengers were smaller than the Talmuth and could maneuver better around the trees. Hengers grabbed Huta warriors off from the ground and crushed them with their powerful claws.

Sorren turned and realized that the Sanuri was fighting next to him. "Glad to see you," Sorren yelled to the Sanuri as he ran towards an oncoming Huta. The roars of hundreds of lions resounded with such power that the forest ground shook.

"Do not hurt the lions," the Sanuri's message rang through the battlefield with clarity. The lions surrounded and attacked the army of Hutas from the rear and it was at that moment that the warriors from Lentz realized they were surrounded by thousands of Hutas.

Demanko screamed with rage. His anger only fueled his insanity and he left his hell dominion and transported to the battlefield. The ground shook and trees toppled over as the ancient demon took form. "Stay back from him," yelled the Sanuri as he moved towards the transforming demon.

"Certainly you don't plan on fighting him alone," Miranda said as she appeared at the Sanuri's side. The Sanuri smiled when he saw the Angel. "Hold out your sword," Miranda said and touched the blade of the Sanuri's sword. "For your courage you have just received a gift that will not leave you when this battle is over," Miranda said as she watched the giant demon taking form.

The Sanuri was momentarily stunned as he could feel a pulsating energy flowing through him. "What have you done?" he asked.

"The blade of your sword is consumed with holiness, no demon can withstand it."

"Demanko you have no power here," Miranda said in a voice so loud that all combatants heard her. The lions and Hengers were destroying the Hutas and now this small army of men and women from Lentz set their eyes upon the battle of the ancients.

Miranda had arrived on the battlefield in the form of a human; a form that all the warriors could see. She carried a sword and a shield that both appeared to be made of light. Demanko roared when he saw her. "I should have known, you have no right to interfere with my affairs," the demon yelled down to the tiny figure of an Angel standing before him.

"The world of man is not yours," Miranda said and started to step towards the demon. With every step she took Miranda grew in size and her body became less dense. "You will not win this battle and you will not win this war Demanko. I will give you a chance to repent."

The enormous demon laughed hysterically at the Angel's words. Then in the midst of his laughter he threw fire at Miranda, who blocked it with her shield. Miranda continued to walk towards the demon as the warriors from Lentz walked closer to the battle of life and death. Demanko cursed Miranda and all that was holy as he threw more fire upon her. Demanko created a wind of staggering proportions. The Army of Lentz clung to trees so as not to be blown over.

Miranda advanced on the demon. Lightening shot out from the hands of the demon and surrounded Miranda but she was not phased and continued forward. The battlefield darken as dozens of demons started to take form around Miranda. She continued towards Demanko who laughed insanely as all of the demons attacked Miranda simultaneously.

"Miranda!" screamed Archetenus and ran towards his friend as did Matthew, Stephan, Sorren, Thaos and Angelina. The other humans stood back stunned in awe but soon they too ran towards the battle, except for Delilah who was struck immovable by her fear and awe.

The Sanuri was already in the midst of the battle by the time the humans joined them. Every time the Sanuri thrust his sword through a demon it screamed in agony and vanished. The humans were not so lucky and they fought the demons the best they could; but not one warrior retreated from that battle.

Suddenly the group of demons screamed and disappeared as Miranda ran her sword through their numbers, until only Demanko was left. "Demanko the humans have turned against you," Miranda said. "You have no power here." As the last of Miranda's words rang out, she thrust her sword through the giant demon, destroying him. A white light surrounded the warriors, blinding and warming them. Some wondered if they had just died, so surreal was the feeling they had of floating.

The warriors regained consciousness and realized they were back on the battlefield but all of their wounds had been healed. Miranda appeared in the form of a human again, standing before them.

"You have been healed because you passed the tests," Miranda said. "Go home now there will be no more battles on this journey. Stephan lift up Archetenus' hair and look at the back of his neck."

"The Mark of Satan is gone," Stephan said with great surprise.

"There are no more monsters among you, go in peace."

Chapter XXIII
Missions

No shortage of Ruala warriors volunteered to go to Nora to work with the Patronus. Calen chose twenty warriors in addition Koby, Dagon and Misha flew with the others to bring back Luca and his new family.

Hannah, Natasha and Emeral worked diligently to prepare Luca's new home and to make preparations for the wedding. Although Elan and Cassandra offered to help, Emeral kept sending them on their own to enjoy their time together. Losing Fala reminded them all how quickly life can be taken. Emeral wanted the two young warriors to enjoy their time together before the warriors left to find Roch.

Hannah was in the kitchen ironing drapes when she heard a familiar voice that shocked her. She walked into the parlor and saw Queen Renya, Princess Vitomas, Princes Annabelle and her mother Laurel walking through the front door.

"Oh my, you should have told us you were coming," Hannah said. "I would have had something prepared."

"Nonsense," Renya said sweetly. "This is a girls outing today. We came to visit. I have heard rumors there has been some conflict. We wondered if we could help."

Natasha and Emeral were walking down the steps from the second floor when they heard voices. They walked into the parlor and they too were surprise to see the Queen in their home. Hannah regained her composure and asked, "Emeral and Natasha would you give our guests a tour of the house including the new wing, while I fix some refreshments?"

Emeral and Renya were the same age and had become friends on Emeral's first visit to Wetpr. Emeral and Natasha told their guests about Fala and about Luca, Lila and Christopher as they gave them a tour of the home. When they finished the tour, Hannah asked them to go into the dining room where she had the table set with a variety of delicacies and beverages.

"Your home is not only beautiful but functional," Renya said. "I particularly like the weapons room."

"I just love this house," Annabelle said. "It's both beautiful and homey."

Once the women were seated Renya started talking. "Hannah, Emeral and Natasha just told us the details about Luca's new family and Fala's death. I want to apologize that our family has not been with you through these struggles. Everyone, your husbands included, have been so immersed with the search for Roch that it was not until this morning that I learned of Fala's death and found out that my son's offered to hold Luca's wedding in the Great Hall."

Vitomas looked embarrassed. "Raul told me he was going to tell Renya and well, I guess it slipped his mind."

"Renya we are warriors that is understandable," Emeral said. "Would you prefer we have the wedding here?"

"Of course not," Renya said with a gracious smile. "I know we are not blood but our families have been so intertwined and have fought side by side in many battles. And for that matter if it wasn't for your family we wouldn't have some of our sons with us today. As far as I am concerned we all are family. So I am offering you much more than use of the Great Hall and my daughters and friend and I are offering our help if you would like it."

"There is a little more to this," Vitomas said. "Now that we are finalizing our plans to destroy Roch we thought it might serve us all to have a fine feast and bring everyone together."

"Well, I love the idea," Emeral said with pleasure.

"You should know that Lila grew up poor and is already intimidated to meet many of Luca's family and friends," Natasha said. "She might be overwhelmed by much of this."

"From what Emeral said she sounds like a lovely girl," Renya said. "And we will work to put her at ease."

Sophie, Erebus and Roch spent long hours together over the next few days. Sophie visited friends at the castle so she could bring information back for Roch. Erebus and Roch talked strategies of how Roch could take back his throne. Roch needed to raise an army but he did not want King Hamond aware of what he was doing. Roch rarely left the hotel because he did not want to be recognized, so Erebus and Sophie preformed many errands for him.

Members of the Patronus had taken over the same abandoned hotel that Gabriel and his team had used when they were spying on Sophie and searching for Meekos. These priests were spying on both Sophie and Erebus but they had not yet seen Roch, who had changed his appearance significantly. High Priest Aaron was in charge of this elite group of Patronus who were working clandestinely. Aaron and his men were aware of the increase in activities by both Sophie and Erebus and suspected that Roch might be in the area.

As Miranda had predicted the journey home for Matthew and his army was uneventful. The awe that struck the warriors at seeing an Angel stayed with them for days. In the evenings, Delilah and Archetenus explained the information in their journals to the Sanuri, Matthew, Angelina, Sorren, Stephan and Thaos. As they talked sometimes Delilah would remember other details and added them to the journal.

"I have seen some of these men," the Sanuri said as he looked at the journal of drawings. Matthew stood up and walked over to the Sanuri.

"There is a picture of a man that I am sure I saw in the castle when Raul and Simon were married," Matthew said as he took the journal from the Sanuri and looked for that particular drawing. "Here," Mathew said and pointed to a picture of an older man, who had a short beard and small eyes that were almost hidden by his thick eyebrows. Previously Delilah had written the man's name under his picture. "Delilah says he is Gregory Bancar."

"I have heard Sudfad mention his name," the Sanuri said then he put the journal down.

"The Great Ruler tests me as He does us all and a while ago I was shown a series of what seemed like unrelated visions. In one such vision I saw glimpses of that wedding reception, I saw a hand wearing a blood ring put a gift on one of the tables. I also saw a man try to break into Sudfad's study, when we were all distracted by the attack on the castle. Marie suddenly appeared in the hallway and the intruder left."

"Do you think that attack was a diversion for something else?" Matthew asked the Sanuri.

"I have wondered about that for some time," the Sanuri replied. Then he suddenly looked at Archetenus. "We will arrive in Castor tomorrow morning. It is a beautiful city. A great place to make a home."

"Archetenus have you decided what you are going to do?" Matthew asked. "You are certainly free to make a home anywhere in the Kingdom of Lentz."

Archetenus paused and looked at Delilah, who held his hand. "Delilah and I have talked this over. And last night after all of you went to sleep I walked out in the forest and called to Miranda. I owe Miranda greatly and I don't like my debits to go unpaid. I would like to work with you and Delilah said it doesn't matter to her where we live as long as we are together."

"And what did Miranda say?" the Sanuri asked.

"As usual she told me to do something I really didn't want to do," Archetenus said and paused. "She told me to go to Wetpr and help in the efforts to bring down Roch. While I would have no problem with such a mission, I have told you my concerns with Sudfad's family."

"And your concerns are?" the Sanuri asked.

"If I was Raul I would kill me, why would they accept my offer to help them?"

"Sanuri we discussed this at length," Angelina said. "Archetenus is happily married to Delilah and promised he would be no trouble to Raul and Vitomas."

367

"Is that true Archetenus?" the Sanuri asked.

"Yes."

"Then I will take you to Sudfad's castle and we will all discuss this," the Sanuri said.

"Do you think Angelina and I should come along?" Matthew asked.

"It would not hurt," the Sanuri replied.

Matthew turned to Angelina and asked, "Can you spend a couple more days away from the children?"

"I never dreamed it would be this hard to leave them," Angelina said. "But I think we should go."

"I think I will ride along with you," Sorren said with a grin. "This might be interesting."

"I am so nervous," Lila said as they landed in the front yard of Gabriel's house. Misha landed next to Luca and set Christopher on the ground.

"That was really fun," Christopher said. "Are we here?"

Koby and Dagon landed within the moment; they were carrying Lila's and Christopher's clothes.

"You look so scared," Luca said to Lila.

"I am and I'm not sure why."

"Everyone will love you," Koby said. "Don't worry about anything."

Lila took Luca's right hand and Christopher took his left and the three walked into Gabriel's house together.

"We're home," Misha yelled as he walked through the door. Immediately people started to come into the parlor from various rooms within the house.

Natasha was the first to greet them. "Luca are you alright?" she asked and gave him a hug. "And you must be Lila." Natasha could see how nervous Lila looked and gave her a hug, then Natasha turned to Christopher. "Christopher wait until you see what we have for you."

"What?" Christopher said with wide eyes.

"Oh, we have so many surprises," Natasha said enthusiastically.

Luca introduced, Natasha, Calen, Raphael, Gabriel, Hannah, Elan and Cassandra. "Where are your parents?" Lila asked.

"Just putting a few things in your chambers," Maxwell said as he and Emeral walked into the parlor.

Luca picked Christopher up and said, "Christopher these are my parents Emeral and Maxwell which means now they are your grandparents."

"Really?" Christopher said with surprise. "I don't think I have ever had grandparents before." Christopher's statement made everyone laugh.

"Christopher can you give us a hug," Emeral asked warmly. Christopher reached his hands out to her. Emeral hugged and kissed the boy then handed him to Maxwell.

"And you must be Lila," Emeral said sweetly and hugged her. "Child you look scared to death."

"I don't know why I am so nervous about meeting all of you," Lila said and blushed.

"Well, let's take them to their chambers before we do anything else," Hannah said and they all walked up the stairs and into the new wing of the house.

"I can't believe this is already built," said Luca.

"Gabriel paid them extra to get the job done quickly," Calen said. "It's good to have you home."

Maxwell was leading the group and carrying Christopher. When Maxwell opened the double doors to Luca's chambers both Lila and Christopher gasped and Lila started to cry.

"Father and I changed the design now that you are a family man," Calen said with a grin and slapped Luca on the back.

They entered a foyer that opened into a large parlor. There were tables of refreshments and tables of gifts set up in the parlor. Luca put his arm around Lila as tears ran down her face. "This is so beautiful," she whispered to him.

"Are these presents for us?" Christopher asked with excitement.

"Yes they are," Emeral said. "But let's see your room before you open the gifts." Emeral opened the door to a room that was decorated in shades of blue and filled with stuffed horses. Maxwell set Christopher down. The small bed had a blue quilt and stuffed toys sat on top of the pillows. The small dresser was covered with toys as were the little table and chairs in the room. The curtains had pictures of horses in the material.

"I've never seen him speechless before," Luca said and laughed as Christopher walked around his room and gently touched things. Then Christopher turned and ran to Emeral and hugged her tightly, then he hugged Maxwell.

"And this is your room," Natasha said with a coy grin as she opened the doors to a beautifully decorated room with a large bed.

"That sure beats the bed you were sleeping in," Koby said with a grin.

Luca looked at Calen and explained, "The three of us have been sleeping in this tiny little bed; this is going to be such a treat. Thank you so much for everything."

"Oh there is more," Hannah said and showed them two more bedrooms, a dining room and a kitchen. "Just like Calen's and Natasha's chambers you have a kitchen, but usually we all eat together in the main dining room."

"Well, let's all go to the parlor and have some refreshments," Emeral said.

"We already started," Misha said with a grin as he and Dagon each walked out of the parlor with a glass of whiskey and a plate of food.

"What do you think?" Luca asked Lila.

"Why, I've never seen anything so beautiful before. I can't believe it is really ours."

The next morning Luca and Lila entered the dining room with their arms around each other and Christopher walked beside Luca carrying a large stuffed horse.

"Grandma," Christopher shouted and ran and jumped into Emeral's arms, which brought tears to her eyes.

"From the way you two are smiling I guess you liked your new bed," Calen said jokingly as he took a seat at the table.

"Yeah, it kept us awake all night," Luca said with a grin.

"Luca!" Lila said and blushed then she laughed. "I should go help them," Lila said and turned towards the kitchen. Luca pulled her back to him and kissed her on the lips.

Lila walked into the kitchen, "What can I do?"

"You can start taking platters in," Hannah said as she was stacking pancakes on a large platter.

"Luca I have never seen you look so happy," Gabriel said. "It is good."

"And what is better is that Luca can't tease me anymore about getting married after knowing Natasha for three days," Calen said. "I think all the men in our family work fast."

"Well then you take after your father," Emeral said as she sat down at the table and Christopher climbed onto her lap.

"Really?" Calen said with a grin. "I don't think you ever told me how you met."

Emeral spoke to everyone seated at the breakfast table, "I don't know if you know that when our people lived in the Kingdom of Norkv they were mostly farmers and not as united as our people are now, which is how the Hutas almost destroyed our race."

"The Ice Caves are unimaginable. They are literally worlds within worlds. When my great, great, great grandfather arrived at the caves he chose a plot of land and built a small farm like he had when he lived in Norkv. And generation after generation of his children lived and worked on that farm. The farm's location was beautiful but very isolated."

"I grew up on that farm and when I was a very young girl my father was seriously injured in an accident, which meant that the majority of work had to be done by me and my brothers and sisters. We spent all our time farming and did not socialize," Emeral continued. "We had heard that many others of our tribe had decided that we would never be victims to demons again and had asked the Sanuri to train them as warriors. But my father had no time for such training."

"One day we received word that there was going to be a huge celebration for the Sanuri to thank him for helping our people. Well, my father couldn't very well make excuses not to attend." Emeral looked at Maxwell and smiled. "My parents never left the farm so all of us were in awe when we arrived in a beautiful city. The celebration was held in the Hall of Light which is incredible. I had never seen anything so beautiful and I just couldn't stop staring at, well, everything. And as we listened to the people talk; it was at that moment I realized how isolated my life had been."

"The celebration lasted for days but the one event I will never forget happened on the third day. A dozen young Ruala boys walked into the center of the room and battled, they were showing the Sanuri how they had learned the moves he taught them. And when that competition was over, one of the elders held up your father's arm for the group to recognize that he was the winner. I do believe I fell in love with him at that moment, of course I was only ten, so it took some years before I even got a chance to speak to that handsome young warrior."

"Emeral, that is a wonderful story," Natasha said. "So tell us, how did you finally meet?"

"After that competition, we found out that a small school had been built. I begged father to allow me to attend. I said I would do double chores if he let me go to school."

"I was the first in my family who wanted to attend school. Eventually all my brothers and sisters got an education," Emeral said. "But part of the education was training to be a warrior. And I loved it. Well, I can't even tell you how I felt. It was, I don't know, like freedom. I excelled in all my studies and training and did double chores on the farm. I worked very hard at home because I was always afraid that my father would make me quit school."

"What your mother didn't know," Maxwell said with a grin. "Is that I had been watching her for a long time. You boys all look at Emeral as your mother but she is a fierce warrior and when we were in school she was the only girl who was beating all the boys in training. And beautiful, your mother took my breath away."

"Really," Cassandra said. "That is so wonderful."

"We usually trained with classmates our own age until the final competitions," Emeral said.

"Your mother beat all the competitors until she worked her way up to my age group," Maxwell said. "The next thing I know I am on the match floor facing the girl I have had a crush on for years."

"Did you fight?" asked Natasha.

"Oh did we fight," Emeral said. "I was afraid that I would look bad in his eyes if I didn't fight well."

Both Emeral and Maxwell started to laugh. "By the time that competition was over, we both were covered in bruises and blood and as we walked off the floor I asked Emeral to be my girl."

"And we were married before all of our bruises and cuts healed, what a sight we were," Emeral said laughing. "But we didn't care we were so in love."

"I love that story," Hannah said. "You have to tell us more."

Although it was early morning when Matthew and his army reached Castor they stopped for the day. Castor was one of the largest and richest cities in the Kingdom of Lentz. It was built on the coast of the Sea of Grevtd. And its port received ships from all over the world.

"After all we have been through, I believe everyone deserves a break," Matthew announced. "Spend the day enjoying the city and we will meet back here at seven and make camp just north of the city."

The Sanuri decided to go sit on the beach. He found a secluded spot and sat in the sun enjoying the beauty around him. Within moments the Sanuri heard the fluttering of wings and saw six Enrops swooping down to land. "King Sudfad has sent two messages for you," one of the giant birds said, while two birds carrying notes stepped forward. The Sanuri read the notes then stood up and walked back to the city.

After listening to Emeral's story Gabriel said. "Now I understand why you and Renya get along so well, I never realized how much alike you are."

"Who is Renya?" Lila asked.

"The Queen of Wetpr," Luca replied.

"The Queen!" Lila's eyes grew wide.

"My dear you will meet her today," Emeral said with a proud smile. "Renya, Vitomas, Annabelle and Laurel came here a few days ago and wanted to help with your wedding."

"Why?" Lila asked in astonishment.

"Our families have fought in battles together and I am proud to say that my sons and daughters who are seated around this table have saved the lives of her sons," Maxwell said.

"We have a lot of stories to tell you," Natasha said to Lila.

"But, but," Lila started to stammer. "Emeral I don't know if Luca told you that I too grew up on a farm, my family was very poor. I never met royalty until I met Prince Lakin and well, I just don't' know about such things."

Calen looked at Lila, "Renya and Mother will plan everything just tell them what you like."

Lila gave Luca a panicked look. He laughed and put his arm around Lila and kissed her. "Luca what do you want in the wedding?" asked Lila.

"I really don't care; whatever you want."

"I have no idea what I want," Lila said fearfully.

"Well then that is perfect," Calen said. "Just let Renya and Mother plan everything that's what they did for our wedding and Gabriel and Hannah's."

Koby started to laugh, "Lila you are getting that look again, like you had yesterday when you were afraid to meet Emeral and Maxwell."

"Lila don't listen to him, I was really nervous about meeting Calen's parents too and now I wish they lived with us all of the time," Natasha said. Calen turned and looked at Natasha and grinned. "Calen don't give me that look," Natasha said and laughed. "I am telling the truth. You know that Gabriel, Hannah and I don't have parents so your parents seem like ours."

"I feel the same way," Hannah said warmly. "I just love having Emeral and Maxwell here."

Calen looked across the table at Gabriel, who was grinning. "Gabriel do you feel the same way?" Calen asked.

"I'm not disagreeing with anything the girls have said."

Calen turned to his parents. "Would you like us to change your chambers to more permanent living quarters and this could be your second home?"

Emeral and Maxwell looked at each other and smiled then Maxwell said. "We both would like that very much. Last night your mother and I were talking about how glad we are that we came and can see what your lives are like when you aren't at home. And we both are so very proud of all of you for the work that you do."

"Oh this is wonderful," Natasha said happily. As Natasha was talking an Enrop flew into the dining room and gave a note to Raphael.

"Aaron and the others have been watching Sophie and Erebus. Aaron says that within the last ten days those two have greatly changed their behavior," Raphael said to the group. "He says that both Sophie and Erebus suddenly seem very busy. He suspects that Roch may have contacted them."

"How close do his men get when they are following them?" Natasha asked anxiously. "Calen if I wasn't pregnant I would want to go back there. Simon and I were able to get close enough to listen to her conversations."

Calen was starting to speak when Hannah interrupted him. "I know Natasha is great at getting information and she has been teaching me a lot of her tricks. Gabriel why don't we go to Taperia and spy on them. You are so much more experienced than the men who are there now," Hannah said excitedly.

Gabriel looked at Hannah and grinned, "Sophie would recognize me, but I like your idea."

"Well, would she recognize Raphael?" Hannah asked. But before Gabriel could answer Hannah said to Raphael. "Simon and Natasha pretended to be a couple and they would spy on Sophie. They gathered a great deal of information."

"We've only been married for a few months and already you want to go out with my best friend," Gabriel teased.

"I think it's a great idea," Raphael said. "But remember she met me at the monastery in Malga some months ago and I believe I made an impression on her."

"Well can't you wear disguises?" Natasha asked. "You know like we did when we were after those demons in Calix?"

"What are you talking about?" Calen asked.

"They got beards and wigs from a theatrical group," Luca said. "They looked pretty good, I wouldn't have recognized them."

"It may take us a while to come up with those things," Raphael said.

"My dear boy, you are working for the King and Queen," Emeral reminded him. "I am sure they can get you anything you want."

"Gabriel has always been the one to use disguises," Raphael said. "I might need some practice."

"I can give you the pointers you will need," Gabriel said. "Tell Aaron we are coming to help." Then Gabriel looked at Calen. "You will be in charge of running things here." Calen got a proud look on his face for it was the first time that a Ruala warrior was put in-charge of a Patronus headquarters.

"Koby and I should go with you because we know that area well," Dagon said.

"You'll need one more to fly you across the border," Misha said. "I'll go too."

"I am going to the castle to brief the others," Gabriel said. Then he turned to his sister. "Natasha can you help Hannah pack since you know what we will need?"

"Of course," Natasha said. "I so wish I was coming with you."

"There will be other missions," Calen said.

Natasha turned quickly and looked at Calen, "So you aren't going to stop me from working on other missions?"

"I don't want you working on missions when you are pregnant and you aren't working on any missions without me," Calen said and smiled.

"Everyone you are my witnesses," Natasha kidded. "Calen's going to let me work on missions again."

"Natasha he just knows he couldn't stop you," Koby said with a grin.

Chapter XXIV
Dark Lords

Two hours after receiving the note from Aaron, Gabriel and the others were on their way to Taperia. Misha carried Hannah, who was exhilarated to fly. Koby carried Gabriel and Dagon carried Raphael. Elan and Cassandra begged to come along as trainees and their request was granted; with the strict understanding that they work with the experienced warriors and did not go off by themselves.

"It's not just for your protection that I am making these rules," Gabriel said as they flew over Wetpr. Stordt is filled with dark lords, warlocks and witches and if they see a Ruala warrior they will know that followers of The Great Ruler are in the area. You will expose the mission as well as the rest of us. Do you understand how important this is?"

"We understand Gabriel," Elan said sincerely. "We just want to start being useful."

"When Hannah, Raphael or I are in the city, in disguise, we will have Enrops acting as our eyes for trouble," Gabriel continued. "We may go days without any trouble or anything interesting happening for that matter, but you have to be available. If we need help the Enrops will be coming to get you."

"One thing you have to understand," Dagon added. "Gabriel and the others can handle just about any situation that comes up, so if they need help it's bad. And you have to get to them as quickly as you can."

"So then if it's an emergency it doesn't matter if we are seen?" asked Cassandra.

"When a group of men tried to attack Natasha in Taperia, she led them out of the city so we could get them," Koby said. Then he started to grin. "Of course Natasha had killed most of them before we got there, that girl is something."

"But we were all so damn scared," Dagon said. "She is like our little sister and those men were after her because they wanted to rape her."

"Basically what we are saying," Koby continued. "Is the members of Gabriel's team will usually think of something to help us hid our identities. But their lives are what is the most important. If we have to expose our presence here to save them, then that is what we do."

"So then basically our role is to protect Gabriel and the others as they have more direct contact with people in Taperia," Elan said.

"Exactly," Dagon said. "Unless you are given another assignment."

The Sanuri walked around Castor until he found Matthew and some of the others. Matthew, Angelina and Sorren were sitting at a table in an outdoor café. "We were wondering where you were," Sorren said with a smile when he saw the Sanuri.

"I went down to the beach," the Sanuri said. "Do you know where Archetenus and Delilah are?"

"Shopping for rings," Angelina said. "But they are supposed to meet us here for lunch."

"Is something the matter?" asked Matthew.

"I got two messages from Sudfad but they raise many questions so I wanted to talk to all of you together."

"Well take a seat," Sorren said. "They should be here soon." Moments after the Sanuri sat down at the table, Sorren said, "Speak of the devil, here they come." Then Sorren saw the look on Angelina's face and laughed loudly, "Ok that may have been a poor choice of words."

Delilah ran ahead of Archetenus and held out her left hand so that everyone at the table could see the diamond and ruby ring she was wearing. "Look what Archetenus bought me," she said excitedly."

"It's beautiful," Angelina said.

"She still wanted to keep the same wedding bands," Archetenus said as he sat down at the table. "I told her I would buy her something better."

"I love these rings," Delilah said. "Which reminds me while we are here you should sell that jewelry that Dieter gave me. I don't want anything that reminds me of him."

"Do you have it with you?" the Sanuri asked.

"Yes," Archetenus said and pulled a leather pouch out of an inside pocket of his vest.

"May I see them?" the Sanuri asked to everyone's surprise since he was a man who placed little value on material things. The Sanuri poured the jewels onto the table, then he held his right hand close to the jewels but he did not touch them. Soon smoke started to rise towards his hand.

"What is happening?" Delilah gasped as the others stared at the jewelry with amazement.

"This may be how Dieter's men were tracking you," the Sanuri explained. "Dieter was a powerful dark lord, he put some kind of a spell on these jewels but I don't know what it is."

"Archetenus throw them away," Delilah said in horror.

"The spell is broken now," said the Sanuri.

Archetenus was staring at the Sanuri. "You said Dieter was, not that he is a powerful dark lord. Was that a mistake in words or has something happened?"

"Well, that is what I wanted to talk to all of you about," the Sanuri explained. "A little while ago I received two messages from King Sudfad. Actually the messages were written by General Amundsen from Fort Friada; but they were delivered to Sudfad's castle. The first message is asking me to come to the fort because Amundsen has imprisoned Dieter, and suspects Dieter to be a dark lord."

"The second message is telling me not to come, because Amundsen found a room with an unholy altar and human sacrifices so he had Dieter burned at the stake."

"I feel relieved," Delilah said. "He was a monster."

"Doesn't this strike any of you as curious that a powerful dark lord is not only captured by men but executed by them? Delilah did anything happen to Dieter that might have affected his powers?" the Sanuri asked.

"I may have an answer to that," Archetenus said. "I was spying on Dieter's place when I saw Delilah. I set up a meeting with her and asked her to spy on Dieter for me and I told her that in exchange I would help her to escape. That same night Miranda came to me and said that I had to get Delilah out of the mansion and out of Port Friada first thing in the morning. In fact, Miranda gave me directions on what to do. As we were riding out of Port Friada we heard a horn blowing, the type of horn that soldiers use."

Archetenus continued, "I took Delilah to the monastery at Leven, where we married and I left her there for over a week. I returned to Port Friada because I had work to do for Miranda. I found out that the morning that Delilah and I left Port Friada, Dieter's mansion was attacked by Rogetts and many of his men were killed and many were missing."

"Dieter's men stopped the Rogetts from getting into the city, but by doing so, the people of Port Friada realized that Dieter had a private army. With my own ears I heard people talking. Many thought Dieter was building tunnels under the city and that is how the Rogetts came to his place. And many people were saying that he murdered Delilah. People were suspicious of him and members of the City Council were going to talk to General Amundsen."

"Miranda said that Dieter was paranoid and thought that someone had used the Rogetts to attack him. She also said that his powers were blocked. So he was calling a meeting of many important members of the Insidiae to find out what was going on. She wanted me to draw pictures of these people. I'll be honest I can't draw worth a damn, but Miranda said she would help me."

"When I realized I was drawing such good pictures, I drew everyone I saw, the help, the guards, the guests. I left Port Friada when the meeting was over, it lasted for days."

"This is all very interesting," the Sanuri said thoughtfully.

"I assumed it was Miranda who blocked his powers and sent the Rogetts," Archetenus said.

"No that is not how she works," the Sanuri said. "It would take a Grand Master of the Insidiae or a demon to be powerful enough to block Dieter's powers. I am suspecting that one of his rivals set Dieter up to get him out of the way, so they could have the region he ruled. And that means whoever has that position now may be more powerful than Dieter was."

Cisero did not lose any time taking over Dieter's territory. The day after Dieter was burned alive Cisero and a large contingent of his men arrived at Dieter's mansion. Cisero's second in command was a man named Canton, a large burly man with a long scar that ran from the top right of his forehead to his left jaw.

Canton was a merciless man. He was not one of the men who were created as vessels but Canton knew about that plot and had no qualms about selling off his fellow humans to make money. Greed is what motivated Canton more than any other desire and Cisero knew what motivations would keep his men loyal to him.

Cisero knew that many of the men who were employed by Dieter were created to be vessels. When Cisero and his men arrived at Dieter's compound it was not as a conquering army but as a new employer. Cisero was not surprised to find that Dieter's staff were more interested in a paycheck than loyalty to Dieter. But what did surprise Cisero were the stories he was hearing about one of the vessels stealing Dieter's wife.

Cisero was told that Dieter sent a small army after the two, but that there had been no word from any of the men in days. Cisero immediately dispatched flocks of ravens to look for Dieter's men. After several days when not one raven returned with a message, Cisero sent out more ravens.

In the meantime, Cisero had unexpected problems with the people of Port Friada. No sooner had he arrived at Dieter's mansion than citizens of the city were knocking at his door. Cisero, like Dieter, was so consumed with his own self-importance and power that he greatly underestimated most people. The first visitors to the mansion immediately alerted the rest of the city that it appeared that another man like Dieter was taking over the compound.

When the citizens of Port Friada first learned of the horrors that had taken place in Dieter's mansion, they were both appalled and frightened. But it was not a crippling fear; it was the kind of fear that motivates good men to stand up against tyrants. Before Cisero's first day in Dieter's compound had ended, the citizens of Port Friada had organized groups to spy on Cisero and his men and all information was to go to Commanding General Amundsen at Port Friada.

The citizens of the city started to keep record of the number of men at Cicero's compound and the numbers and types of provisions that were purchased. Then unbeknown to General Amundsen some of the citizens decided to take matters into their own hands.

A compound as large as Cisero's required a great deal of food and supplies all of which Dieter had purchased locally and Cisero was continuing that practice. The first act of sabotage was to start poisoning Cisero's food supplies. The citizens suspected Cisero might be a dark lord so they did not want to do any overt actions. The first poison they chose was made from the cava plant; it was called demosa and was a slow acting poison with few obvious signs.

Port Friada was a city of incredible size and diversity. But the stories of dark lords, kidnappings, murders and human sacrifices spread through that city in just a matter of days. The dock workers and sailors tended to frequent the taverns in the dangerous part of the city, where the majority of the criminal element resided.

When these men learned that Dieter had been sending his thugs to the docks and taverns to kidnap their kind for slaves and sacrifices, they did something they had never done before.

384

Instead of brutalizing and killing each other they turned their attention to the men who now worked for Cicero. Every night Cicero would send men out to gather more slaves and every night his men disappeared.

Cicero was unshaken by what he considered pranks by the local citizens. But when the ravens brought back news that the army Dieter had sent after Archetenus and Delilah was dead, as were the flocks of ravens; Cicero realized he was dealing with more than just pranks. And when the ravens told him, they did not find any dead bodies other than Dieter's men; Cicero went to his unholy altar for help.

Every man has his own way of dealing with his demons; while some people were poisoning Cicero's men and others were attacking them, there were citizens who rode to the monastery at Leven for help. These citizens requested an audience with High Priest Barnabas and the other priests. Prayer is a powerful tool when one voice is raised; when hundreds of voices are raised to the heavens incredible miracles take form. And all the voices asked for the same thing, "Help us to conquer the darkness here."

The Angel Urian begged The Great Ruler to allow him to go to the World of Nunc and to help the people there. The Angel's request was granted. Since men are not prepared for the holiness of heaven, Urian took a form that was more understandable for the peoples of Nunc. Like the Angel Miriam who takes the form of Miranda and the Archangel Michael, the most powerful warrior Angel in the heavens, who takes the form of a lion; Urian chose a form common to that world.

By nightfall, Raphael, Gabriel and Hannah had not only unpacked their things and settled into the abandoned hotel, which they used as a headquarters but Raphael and Gabriel had gotten adjoining rooms in the Taperian Imperial Hotel. There were no rooms available on the fifth floor where Sophie and Erebus were living, so Gabriel and Raphael got rooms on the third floor of the hotel. They wanted rooms that had balconies that opened to the rear of the hotel so the Rualas and Enrops could enter without being seen.

Raphael and Gabriel posed as brothers and business partners. Their story would be that they were looking for land that was rich in minerals to develop mining. They believed that this story would give them a reason to search the countryside without question. Hannah pretended to be Raphael's wife, in hopes that she and Raphael could become acquainted with Sophie and Erebus. Fortunately for them, Natasha still had the keys she had stolen from that hotel months earlier, so they had access to all of the hotel rooms.

With Sudfad's help, Gabriel, Raphael and Hannah were able to procure a variety of wigs, false beards, mustaches and eyebrows. Both Gabriel and Raphael were normally clean shaven, so they both choose beards and mustaches. Raphael's beard was shorter than Gabriel's but he also chose to wear thicker eyebrows and an eye patch.

"It's taking me a little while to get used to your new looks," Hannah said as the three of them were preparing to go to the hotel dining room for dinner. "But I must say both of you look as handsome as ever."

"Thank you my dear," Gabriel said and kissed Hannah on the cheek. "Hopefully we will see them in the dining room tonight. I want you to get a good look at both of them. From what Aaron said, it sounds like Sophie still enjoys her shopping. I think it would be opportune if you two met in a store."

"Gabriel you know that Jared and Zoya met when he walked into her shop; did you know that he saw Sophie go into that shop first, that is how he found it?" Hannah asked.

"No," Gabriel said. "Do you know the name of the shop?"

"I don't think it has a name," Hannah said. "It is on one of the side streets off the main business street. It is across from a tobacco shop and it has a large sign with a crescent moon and an eye. Apparently the store sells things for healers and for magic."

"This is good information," Gabriel said. "I will look for that store tomorrow morning. Why don't the two of you plan to have breakfast in the dining room then follow Sophie. I know that this type of work is new for both of you."

"If Sophie and Erebus have indeed made contact with Roch, they may be paranoid about being watched. If you walk into stores and restaurants and don't purchase items you will look suspicious. Also you have to act like a real married couple which means you have to argue or yell at each other once in a while."

Hannah stared at Gabriel for a moment as she remembered how they acted when they pretended to be a couple in Nora. "I know exactly what you are about to ask," Gabriel said with a smile. "Yes at times you will have to be affectionate with each other."

Hannah suddenly felt embarrassed and looked at Raphael. "When Gabriel and I first met we pretended to be a couple while his was looking for those horrid priests in Nora. Gabriel was very affectionate. I had forgotten about that," Hannah said as she blushed uncomfortably.

"Gabriel, I am not sure I feel comfortable even pretending to be affectionate with Hannah," Raphael said then he looked at Hannah. "Please don't take offense to what I just said."

"Oh no, I feel the same way," Hannah said then looked at Gabriel.

"Well, the two of you better decide if you can do this before we go down for dinner," Gabriel said.

Hannah and Raphael looked at each other for a few moments, then Hannah turned to Gabriel. "As much as I want to be on this mission I just can't kiss another man. And now I am remembering how difficult it was for Calen to watch Simon and Natasha pretend to be married. I don't think we should risk that kind of conflict between any of us."

"I am glad to hear you say that," Raphael said. "Hannah you are one of the most beautiful women I have ever met, both inside and out; but you are Gabriel's wife. I would feel very inappropriate getting affectionate with you."

"I can't say I am disappointed in what I am hearing," Gabriel said with a grin. "Raphael when you signed for your room did you include Hannah's name on the ledger? Or talk about your wife?"

"No."

"Then there shouldn't be a problem with us switching roles," Gabriel said. "I had assigned both of you to watch Sophie and Erebus because honestly, that is the easiest part of the job. Raphael if you and I switch roles there is much more that I will need to cover with you now, but I know you will do well. To begin with I was planning on searching the hotel and doing research while you two kept Sophie and Erebus distracted. Raphael know that when we have searched hotel rooms in the past, we encountered demons in Nora and deadly spells on objects here in Taperia so you must be very careful."

Daniel appeared to be an unassuming man, tall and muscular he did not boast the bravado of most warriors. His power did not reside in the strength of his physical body; his power came from his faith and grace. Urian chose a form of a simple man because he believed that The Great Ruler's power was more evident when what appeared to be impossible became truth.

Daniel's blonde hair and blue eyes disguised him well as he walked into a meeting of the citizens of Port Friada. He stood in the back of the crowded room and listened to the fears and to the courage of the citizens.

Daniel studied the people in that room, as an Angel he could see into their souls. While he applauded their strength and desire to rid themselves of a dark lord and his madness; Daniel knew that fear caused such darkness in a human heart that it could consume and destroy. Daniel planned to help these people before their fears became distorted illusions. At the end of the meeting Daniel spoke with many of the citizens in the room. They had no idea why they felt better in his presence. They had no knowledge that an Angel walked among them.

That night as Matthew and the others were eating dinner in their camp north of Castor, Delilah looked at Archetenus then at the others and asked, "Am I a bad person because I feel nothing but relief that Dieter is dead? I should think that I would feel bad." The men looked at Delilah but no one spoke.

"You said he bought you, raped you and beat you," Angelina said. "Why would you feel anything but relief? Did you ever develop feelings for him?"

"No," Delilah said. "It's just that hearing that any person was burned alive should at least make me feel sorry for them."

"A great evil was eliminated from this world," the Sanuri said. "You should not feel guilty that you are now free and safe. And starting a new life with the love of your life."

Delilah smiled warmly at the Sanuri's words, "You are right, I don't know what I was thinking. I have lived in fear for so long; sometimes I cannot believe this is real." Delilah squeezed Archetenus' hand when she spoke.

"Sanuri can you tell us if that evil seed will be passed on to our children," Archetenus asked. "I got Delilah pregnant while I still had the Mark of Satan upon me."

"I was wondering when you were going to ask that question," the Sanuri said. "I do believe that Miranda healed you completely. But of course you can always ask her."

"Sanuri I know you are used to seeing Angels," Sorren said. "But I have to tell you seeing Miranda was the most incredible thing I have ever experienced. I mean I have seen demons and too damn many for that matter but to actually see an Angel, well, that is a story I will be telling the grandchildren."

"The fact that Miranda allowed you all to see her was a great gift, I hope you realize that," the Sanuri said. "There is so much darkness in this world and people hope there is a heaven and help from above. Well now you know for sure there is."

"Why did she give us that gift?" Stephan asked. "And what did she mean that we passed the tests?"

"Because you are the men and women who will be leading the armies against the demons and the dark lords. And when they try to corrupt you with fears and insecurities to weaken you, you will have this gift to keep you strong."

As part of their disguise, Hannah, Gabriel and Raphael dressed as people of wealth. They knew that if Roch was to attempt to take back his throne he would need an army and perhaps he would need money and help in raising that army. They were hoping to draw Roch out of hiding by being seen as possible benefactors.

Gabriel squeezed Hannah's hand as Sophie and Erebus walked past their table in the dining room. Hannah glanced at the couple then looked back at Gabriel; she did not want to appear obvious. Like many people, Sophie and Erebus were creatures of habit and always sat at the same table by the front window of the dining room.

The table that Gabriel and the others were seated at was on the opposite end of the large dining room. Gabriel was seated in the middle of the table so he was facing Sophie and Erebus. Hannah sat to Gabriel's right and Raphael to his left.

"Natasha and Simon said that Sophie, Meekos and Erebus always sat at the same table in this dining room," Gabriel said. "We will have to get tables closer to that spot. And we are in no rush here tonight. I would like to stay in the dining room as long as they do." Gabriel motioned for a waiter and ordered a bottle of wine for the table.

The Taperian Imperial Hotel boasted one of the finest dining rooms in the Kingdom of Stordt. The dining room quickly filled with people. Hannah's view of Sophie's table was blocked, but both Gabriel and Raphael were tall men and could see over the crowd. "When Sophie was here waiting for Meekos she had a very regimented routine. I would assume that has changed since she is living with Erebus now but that type of behavior is beneficial to us," Gabriel said quietly.

Just after Sophie and Erebus had been served their wine, Roch entered the dining room. His long hair and beard hid his face as did the wide brimmed hat that he always wore. Roch joined Sophie and Erebus at their table and sat with his back to Gabriel's table.

"That has to be Roch," Gabriel whispered. "He is the only man in here wearing a hat, which is most inappropriate in this type of dining room and his hat certainly does not go with his manner of dress. He is trying to hide his appearance."

Hannah took a deep breath, as her hatred for Roch surged through her. "Hannah are you going to be able to do this?" Gabriel asked. "You can't let your emotions hinder this mission."

"I will be fine," she said. "I was just overwhelmed for a moment. He must be staying here because he walked down the steps then entered the dining room instead of coming in from the street."

"First we have to verify that is really him," Gabriel said. "If we move too quickly and show our hand we may lose him."

"Isn't there something we can do, like pouring blessed water on him to tell if he is turning into a demon?" asked Hannah.

"This is Stordt," Raphael said. "Who knows how many people in this dining room alone are witches or warlocks, you would have the same reaction from them. We have to think of something more conclusive."

"I would like to find out what he is up to also." Gabriel said. "He could have some fiendish plots in the works."

Cisero tried to contact his longtime partner the demon Demanko. It was unlike Demanko not to answer a summons. Cisero was an impatient man and did not like to wait for anyone, after two days of trying to contact Demanko, Cisero decided to try and find out what had happened to Dieter's army on his own. When Cisero moved into the mansion he set up a small unholy altar in his bedroom, while he had his men rebuilding the large altar in the cellar.

General Amundsen's soldiers had torn apart and burned everything that they found in the cellar chambers. But Amundsen was not a holy man and did not realize he could not destroy the darkness in those chambers by such human means. To destroy such a place of horror that had been surrendered to demons, one had to call in holiness to cleanse it.

"How are you feeling?" Sophie asked as she sipped her wine.

"Every day I remember more," Roch said then ordered a glass of whiskey from the waiter. "Did you go to the castle today?"

"Yes I did," Sophie said with pride. "And I got you some gifts." Sophie handed Roch a box.

Roch took the box and peaked inside of it, a smile crossed his face when he saw that the box contained rings of keys to the castle doors. "Things are surprisingly the same since you left," Sophie continued. "Hamond is sleeping in your old chambers. The back staircase that leads from the kitchen to the upper floors has not been locked and appears to never be used. And I was told the secret tunnels under the castle; the ones that the Hutas came through to attack us that time, are still there. They have not been destroyed but there are two guards by each door at all times.

"Thank you Sophie, you have done well," Roch said. "And security, has Hamond increased it?"

"Honestly it looks the same as when you ruled," Sophie said. "While I was at the castle I walked past the war room. The door was open so I looked inside and it looks the same. If Hamond has made any changes since he took the throne I did not notice."

"Erebus, how have you fared?" asked Roch.

"I have learned that Ahriman, the demon who took you, was somehow greatly weakened. Rumors in the underworlds are that The Lion of The Great Ruler weakened him because Ahriman kept trying to trap the Sanuri. This news has spread throughout the underworlds and Ahriman is fighting demons on every front trying to maintain his power. I have heard rumors that he is even being attacked by demons from other worlds."

"Well, he will feel my wrath too," Roch said angrily.

"Roch, Ahriman is one of the Old Ones, what can you do against him?" Sophie asked.

392

Roch looked at Sophie and grinned. The glint in his eyes made her shudder. Whatever Roch was planning he was not sharing the information so Sophie decided to pursue the issue. "Roch we said we would help you but neither Erebus nor I want to go to war with Ahriman or any of the other Old Ones."

"I haven't asked you to," Roch said, then he looked at Sophie suspiciously. "How do you know so much about the Old Ones?"

Although Sophie was taken by surprise by both the question and the look on Roch's face, she had always been one to think quickly on her feet. "Why Erebus has been teaching me all about the underworlds."

"Why did you ask her in such a suspicious manner?" Erebus demanded of Roch. "You know we are only trying to help you."

"I know and I didn't mean anything by it," Roch said. "Let's change the subject and I will tell you about the news I heard when I was having a few drinks. Apparently there was a dark lord in Port Friada named Dieter who had a huge fortress and his own army. From what I heard he had a lot of enemies too."

Roch paused to look at the faces of Erebus and Sophie, "Well, his place gets attacked by an army of Rogetts and someone took his powers from him. The people of Port Friada were scared when they found out he had a private army so they went to the Commanding General at Fort Friada, who ended up attacking Dieter's place and burned him at the stake. Have you ever heard of such a thing?" Roch said with a laugh and left the table.

Erebus and Sophie stared at each other in silence.

As Roch was walking out of the dining room, Gabriel stood up and walked behind him. But when they got to the lobby, Gabriel bent over and pretended to pick something up from the floor. Gabriel gave Roch enough time to climb several flights of stairs before he approached the desk clerk.

"Excuse me," Gabriel said. "But I believe that man that just walked through here dropped a note on the floor."

"Do you mean the one wearing the hat?" the young clerk asked.

"Yes, that's the man," Gabriel said. "Would you be kind enough to tell me what room he is in?"

"He's in room 419," the clerk said without looking at the ledger.

"I'm impressed," Gabriel said. "Do you have everyone's room memorized?"

"No," the clerk said with a slight laugh. "But Master Peters has been here for a while. Do you want me to give him the note?"

"No I will and thank you so much for your help," Gabriel said and handed the clerk a gold coin. Gabriel returned to his table and sat down. "He's in room 419 and he signed in as Peters," Gabriel said as he quickly scribbled some words on a piece of paper. "I told the clerk that that man dropped a note. I am going up to his room to deliver it. Hopefully I can get a good look at his face."

"Gabriel be careful," Hannah said and put her hand on his arm.

"Do you want me to go with you?" Raphael asked.

"No, that would look suspicious, besides we still have to watch the other two," Gabriel said and walked out of the dining room.

Daniel walked along the street that ran in front of Cicero's compound. He made no attempt to hide his presence as he carefully studied the security measures that Cicero had in place.

"You, what are you doing?" a guard called down from his position on the top of the high fence that surrounded the compound.

"I'm taking a walk," Daniel called back in a friendly manner. "Why is this private property? I thought it was a city street."

"Now you just hold on there," the guard yelled. He was trying to distract Daniel as three of Cicero's men were going through the gate. "It is a city street but you sure seem interested in this place."

"It's a beautiful mansion," Daniel said in a friendly manner. "I am sure many people look at it as they pass."

"Well, we don't care much for strangers around here," one of Cicero's men said as he grabbed Daniel's right arm from behind. A second man closed in and grabbed Daniel's left arm in an attempt to control him.

"What the hell! How'd he do that?" The first man yelled as Daniel slipped out of their grasps and turned and faced the three men.

"Why do you put hands on me?" Daniel asked calmly. The three men stared at him with a bit of confusion. Daniel neither ran nor attempted to fight with them. The two men who had grabbed Daniel now moved towards him again.

"I asked you a question," Daniel said with a voice of authority. The two men lunged at Daniel, they tried to grab his arms but it was as if there was an invisible barrier that prevented them from making direct contact with him.

"What the hell!" exclaimed the third man and drew his sword from its sheath.

"Is this some sort of damn magic?" the second man asked as he continued to try and grasp Daniel's arm. Daniel did not move.

"Are you trying to put hands on me because I looked at your mansion or to take me as a slave for your underground caverns?"

"Just who the hell are you?" the first man asked.

"Well, whoever he is he ain't stupid," the third man said as he spit a wad of tobacco on the ground then wiped his mouth with his sleeve. "Mister we is putting hands on you for both reasons. Now I don't know what is going on here but if you don't come with us we're gonna have to kill you."

"You would kill me for walking down the street?" Daniel asked as he stared into the eyes of the men. "Tell me, are you some of the men who Cicero plans to auction off to be vessels for demons or are you just his regular hired thugs?" Daniel already knew the answer to this question.

"Now what the hell are you talking about?" the first man asked as he had stopped his attempts to touch Daniel.

"Many of the men here have the Mark of Satan on the back of their necks. That is no coincidence. Have you not wondered why so many of you are larger and stronger than most men and why some of you are becoming ill and showing signs of insanity?" Daniel asked.

"Don't listen to him," the third man said.

"Jeb doesn't want you to listen to me because he does not bear this mark but he knows that both of you do."

"I never told you my name. How do you know my name?" Jeb asked suspiciously.

"What the hell is going on here?" the second man asked in frustration as he too, realized he could not touch Daniel.

Daniel looked at the man who was standing to his right. "Look at the back of your friends neck and tell me what you see."

"Why should I?"

"Because I am saving your life."

"Hold still Inon, let me have a look."

"Do you see a tattoo of a red snake poised to strike?" Daniel asked calmly.

"Damn, Inon the feller's right."

"I don't have no damn tattoo," Inon snorted.

"You sure as hell do, now check me."

"You've got one too," Inon said in amazement. "What the hell is going on here?"

"That is not a tattoo that is how the demons mark you," Daniel said. "Dieter called you here using his magics because he planned to sell you to demons and now Cicero has taken Dieter's place."

"You know I speak the truth, you have seen the chambers and the unholy altar. If your kind stays here you will soon be imprisoned in one of those underground chambers and held until the auction starts."

"Shut up!" Jeb yelled and ran towards Daniel. Daniel did not move as Jeb ran his sword through him. Nor did Daniel bleed or collapse.

"What the hell!" Jeb exclaimed as he pulled his sword back. "It's like it went through smoke."

Now all three men stepped back from Daniel as fear surged through them. "Are you a ghost?" The first man asked.

"No," Daniel replied calmly. "Go tell the others what I have said. And tell them there are men who bore that mark but got rid of it. It is not an easy journey but it is better than being tortured in hell for eternity."

"Well how do we get rid of it?" Inon asked.

Daniel smiled. "Call out to the heavens for help." Then he vanished before their eyes.

The three men stood speechless, first staring at the place where Daniel had been standing then they stared at each other.

"One of you guys come up here and check me for that mark," the guard on the wall called out fearfully.

"Who is it?" Roch asked suspiciously as he put his hand on the hilt of the dagger in his belt. "My name is Geoffrey," Gabriel said as Geoffrey was the alias he had chosen for this mission. "I was walking behind you in the lobby and saw a piece of paper on the floor. I don't know if it belongs to you." When Roch did not respond, Gabriel continued. "I could just slip it under the door if you like." Roch remained silent so Gabriel slid the note under the door and started to walk down the hallway.

Suddenly the door to Roch's room opened. Gabriel turned and saw Roch glaring at him. "How did you get my room number?" Roch demanded.

"The desk clerk," Gabriel replied nonchalantly. "Listen if that paper isn't yours I am sorry for disturbing you."

Roch was sizing Gabriel up and wanted to make conversation. "I saw you in the dining room; you were sitting with a woman and another man."

"Yes, that's my wife Hannah and my business partner Morgan." Morgan was the name Raphael was using on this mission.

"What sort of business are you in?" Roch asked as he stepped into the hallway.

Now Gabriel walked towards Roch. "We operate gold and silver mines. We're here looking at land. When we were in Nora we heard there were some rich gold veins around here. Here's my trade card," Gabriel said and handed a small piece of paper to Roch. Then Gabriel turned and walked away. Gabriel knew that Roch was still watching him as he walked down the hallway.

When Gabriel joined Hannah and Raphael at the table he kissed Hannah on the cheek. "First contact is made," Gabriel said softly. "I will tell you about it when we return to the rooms."

"Is that him?" Hannah whispered.

"I have no idea," Gabriel said. "But he seems paranoid. If it isn't Roch it is a man who has a great deal to hide."

Fear gripped both Sophie and Erebus as Roch was talking about Dieter. They realized that Roch knew a great deal more than he was telling them. "If he knows about Dieter, he must know about the Insidiae," Sophie whispered as she leaned across the table towards Erebus.

"I don't care what he knows about the other members I just don't want him to find out about you," Erebus said. "I told you we shouldn't trust him. I think we should leave for Ryed tomorrow."

"Let's think about this," Sophie said. "If what he said about Dieter is true then someone else has taken that territory. That could possibly be to our advantage. Also maybe it is time to tell the Insidiae that Roch is here. We may be in a stronger position then you think."

"The only thing I am concerned with is your safety my dear," Erebus said as he gulped down his glass of wine. "You know what he is like, if he feels you betrayed him, he will kill you."

Chapter XXV
Confessions

"You don't think Raphael can hear us do you?" Hannah asked breathlessly as she and Gabriel finished making love in their hotel room.

"All I can say is he can't hear me," Gabriel said with a grin as he rolled off from Hannah and lay on his back. "You know with Christopher running around the house I realized that I have not lived up to my promise of spending more time working on a baby."

Hannah propped herself up on her left elbow and looked at Gabriel. "Honey we both want a family but I don't think we should even consider one until Roch has been destroyed. We have the ability to take him down. I can't even imagine bringing a child into this world if Roch is running wild as a demon." Gabriel gently pulled Hannah towards him and kissed her on the lips.

"You know watching Luca and Christopher together gave me an idea," Gabriel said. "You spend so much time at the orphanage perhaps when things settle down we should consider adopting a child or two." Hannah's eyes widened as she stared at Gabriel. "I mean I still want to have babies of our own what do you think?"

Hannah hugged Gabriel tightly. "I don't know why I thought you wouldn't want to adopt any children, this is so wonderful. There are two children in particular that I have become very attached to. In fact both Natasha and Emeral have met them. They're a brother and sister and their parents were killed by Hutas so they were brought to Wetpr to live with their great aunt but she passed away."

"Nicholas is about Christopher's age and his sister Cerey is only three. They are so adorable. They both have dark hair and huge brown eyes. And they are just the sweetest children but they seem so lost now. I've been afraid that if they are adopted they will be separated."

Gabriel watched the light in Hannah's eyes as she spoke about these children. "Do you think there is a good chance that they will be separated?" he asked with concern.

"Oh yes, unfortunately it happens all of the time and it is so sad to see what happens to the children."

"Why don't you send a letter to Natasha and Emeral and see if they would mind getting the children and watching them until we get home?"

"Oh my god! Are you serious? Don't you want to meet them first? Are you really serious Gabriel?" You will just love them, they are so sweet."

Gabriel was laughing as he listened to Hannah. She was so excited she wasn't taking a breath as she talked. "I am serious," Gabriel said. "But you will also want to look for a nurse for the children; that is if you are serious about helping on some of these missions."

"I will, oh Gabriel I am so happy," Hannah said and hugged him tightly then she jumped out of bed. "I'm going to write the letter now so they will get it in the morning."

"I have never been so happy," Lila said as Luca returned to bed.

"Me too," Luca said and kissed her then slid under the covers. "Christopher is sleeping. He seems really happy here too."

"Oh you should have seen him at the castle, well, I guess you know because he wouldn't stop talking about all of Petra's pets," Lila said. "I thought he would have been shy but as soon as Petra and that little girl walked in with three puppies, well that was the last we saw of Christopher for a while."

"I would like to start a family right away," Luca said as he caressed Lila's hair. "What do you think?"

"Oh yes," Lila said enthusiastically. "I love children."

"I mean I would really like to start a family now. Perhaps we should ask Emeral and Maxwell to watch Christopher for us so we can spend more time making love."

Lila started to giggle. "I could spend all day making love to you. But are you going to tell them why we want them to watch Christopher?"

"Oh course," Luca said and laughed at her embarrassment. "My parents love grandchildren, it will make them happy."

"Sophie I don't want to lose you," Erebus said and kissed her lips. "I think we should leave here in the morning. I just have a bad feeling about all of this."

"And if Roch wants to kill me, do you think he will stop because we have moved?"

"He was a soulless animal as a man. I don't know what he is now or what he is turning into but that aura about him is sinister. I am wondering if he is already a vessel for a demon, just not Omnibus."

"Do you really think so?" Sophie asked as she sat up straighter in bed. "Wouldn't we be able to tell?"

"Perhaps we are seeing the signs but we just don't realize it," Erebus said. "I do believe Roch has lost some of his memories and that could be because he is sharing his body with a demon. I also saw the glint in his eyes, tonight, when he told us about Dieter. He knew exactly what he was saying and he was looking for our reactions. Sophie it is too dangerous to stay here any longer."

Archetenus and Delilah cuddled together underneath their blankets by the campfire. They were whispering as to not wake the others. "I don't really know what to expect when we get to Wetpr, so I don't know if that is where we will live permanently. But Matthew did say that we were welcomed to live anywhere in Lentz, so I can't even guess at this point when we will really settle down. How do you feel about that?" Archetenus asked.

"I just want to be with you," Delilah said and kissed his lips. "I really like the people we are with now, I wouldn't mind keeping them as friends."

"But if you are going to be working with them I would suspect we will have to live somewhat near where they meet."

"When we go to Wetpr don't expect a warm reception," Archetenus warned.

"Archetenus you keep apologizing for all the things you have done in the past but honestly I am so proud of the things you have done now that none of that matters to me."

"Why of course we can watch Christopher," Emeral said with a huge smile as they were all gathering around the breakfast table.

"You are sure you don't mind?" Lila asked as she blushed.

"My dear, Christopher is such a sweet boy and we are so incredibly happy that you two are trying to start a family, it is no trouble at all."

"Emeral!" Natasha screamed from the kitchen. Calen jumped up so quickly that he knocked over his chair.

"Natasha are you alright? Is the baby coming?" Calen yelled as he started towards the kitchen door.

Natasha ran into the dining room and giggled. "Calen you are so nervous about this baby, she isn't due for two months yet. I am alright. We just got a letter from Hannah and Gabriel."

"Natasha you really don't know when the baby is coming, you are just guessing on the date," Calen said with a grin. "So please don't scream like that. What's that exciting anyways?"

"I'll give it to you in a minute," Natasha said. "They found a guy they think might be Roch but they don't know yet. But the reason I screamed is Hannah and Gabriel want to know if Emeral and I will go to the orphanage and get Nicholas and Cerey and bring them home and watch them until Hannah and Gabriel return. They are afraid the children will be separated. And Hannah said it was all Gabriel's idea." When Natasha saw the smile on Emeral's face she said. "You said something to Gabriel didn't you?"

"I might have," Emeral said slyly.

Natasha started to laugh, "So did I. I'll hitch the boca as soon as I am done making breakfast."

"Ok, let the rest of us know what you two are talking about?" Calen said.

"Hannah fell in love with these two adorable little children at the orphanage. Nicholas is close to Christopher's age and his little sister Cerey is about three," Natasha explained. "Their parents were killed by Hutas so they were brought up here to live with an old aunt and she died. Calen they are so cute they both have dark curly hair and big brown eyes and they both seem so sad."

"I don't understand why Hannah was so scared to ask Gabriel if they could adopt them," Emeral said.

"Neither do I," Natasha said. "But I think she thought he only wanted children that were his own blood."

"I'll finish breakfast," Lila said and walked towards the kitchen. "You two go."

Emeral sat down on one of the chairs surrounding the table. "Christopher come here please." He climbed onto her lap. "You know Nicholas and Cerey haven't had anyone to watch over them like you have so they might be a little sad and frightened. Would you like to come with us and bring them home?"

"Sure, is Luca going to be their daddy too?"

"No," Emeral said with a laugh. "Gabriel is going to be their daddy and Hannah their mommy. Christopher would you mind sharing some of your toys with them until Natasha and I buy them some of their own. It won't be for very long?"

Christopher stared solemnly at Emeral for a moment, then he said in an adult manner, "Grandma why don't you put them in my room? Then we can play while you go shopping." Everyone in the room started to laugh.

"That sounds like a wonderful idea," Emeral said and kissed Christopher on the forehead. "You are such a good boy." Christopher jumped off Emeral's lap and held out his hand to her. "Well I guess we are going," she said with a smile. "Maxwell do you want to come too?"

"Wait," Calen said as everyone was leaving the dining room. "I can start moving furniture, what room do you want them in?"

"Well, I suppose the one closest to Hannah and Gabriel's bed room," Natasha said.

"That would be the one that the girls are in," Calen said. "I'll move them to one of the new rooms."

"We got two letters this morning and I want to discuss them with all of you," Sudfad said as his family was taking their seats around the breakfast table. The many Ruala warriors who were staying at the castle ate their meals in the Great Hall, while the Royal Family enjoyed some private time together. "One letter is from the Sanuri and the other from Matthew and Angelina. They are all on their way here to see us. I will pass the letters around for you to read after we discuss some things," Sudfad said solemnly.

"As you know, the Angel Miranda has been talking with Archetenus a great deal. Apparently they have formed a bond and he is working for her now. She sent Archetenus on a dangerous mission to gather the identities of many high ranking members of the Insidiae. While Archetenus was spying on these people he met a girl who was in almost an identical situation as Vitomas was. Archetenus helped this girl to escape; they got married and are expecting a child." No one spoke at the table but many raised their eyes at the news.

Sudfad continued, "Miranda told Archetenus to take the information he had compiled to Lentz, but the dark lord who had owned the girl sent an army of vessels and demons after Archetenus and Delilah. So the Sanuri asked Matthew and others to go help them."

"I will skip a few parts, but on their journey Miranda appeared to Matthew. Matthew, Sorren, Stephan, Thaos and Angelina were among those who went and they fought many battles. When they found Archetenus he had been battling a demon who was trying to take him to hell, like what happened with Jared."

"I will skip a few more parts as you can read about them. But during their last battle they were surrounded by thousands of Hutas and Talmuth. The Sanuri and Miranda both came to their aid on the battlefield and the Angel appeared to them all as she battled many demons. At one point in the fight Miranda was overwhelmed with demons and Archetenus and the others fought at her side. For their courage she healed them all and she removed the Mark of Satan from Archetenus' neck."

"Now," Sudfad continued. "Don't anyone start yelling until I finish my words. Apparently Matthew, Angelina and the others like Archetenus and Delilah and have asked them to help us take down Roch. Archetenus said he would but he is concerned, and he should be, if we want his help. Apparently he said that Raul had every right to kill him. He has promised that he would be no problem to any of us and Angelina says that Archetenus and his wife seem very happy together. Now you can voice your opinions."

To Sudfad's surprise no one yelled, in fact no one talked they all stared at him. "Is your silence a good or bad sign?" Sudfad asked.

"I am sure that Raul and Simon will get mad at what I have to say," Annabelle said. "But Archetenus is a powerful warrior and if he is good, well, couldn't he help us without coming near Vitomas?"

"Archetenus became a hero to the people of Stordt because of his feats at the Gefrey Games. He became so popular that Roch and many of his generals were feeling threatened by him and were devising plots to have him killed. Archetenus and I talked about this as we traveled. He was aware of one instance but not the others," Vitomas explained.

"He and Roch hated each other. Archetenus not only knows Roch as a man but he knows his military strategies. I think we would benefit by having him on our side in this." Vitomas turned and looked at Raul.

"Raul, I am not afraid of him and I will stay away from him if you want but you and Simon need to use your heads and not your hearts on this one."

Simon and Raul looked at their wives then at their parents. "I know you are all expecting me to yell against this," Raul said with a laugh. "I agree we could use him. Now I am not saying that he and I will get along at all but he would be useful for this mission."

"Well for one, having two ex-vessels on our side pleases me," Simon said. "I was with Jared when he battled the demons and if Archetenus went through that and is working for an Angel now he must have really changed his ways. I say we give him a chance and if it doesn't work out, we tell him to leave."

"Luca, Calen they're home," Lila called as she saw Natasha drive the boca into the yard.

Calen and Luca came down the steps to the first floor just as Maxwell was walking into the house. Christopher was holding Maxwell's left hand and Nicholas was holding his right. Emeral was walking behind them holding Cerey and Natasha walked in behind them all. "Aren't they cute," Natasha said with a big smile.

Calen, Luca and Lila were all smiling, not only at the children but at Maxwell and Emeral with all their adopted grandchildren. "Natasha they have the same hair as you and Gabriel," Luca said as he walked up to Nicholas and squatted down.

"Nicholas this is my new daddy," Christopher said proudly. "His name is Luca." Then Christopher looked at Luca. "Nicholas is a little shy." Everyone in the room smiled at Christopher who was acting like the older brother.

"Are you hungry Nicholas because Lila made blueberry pancakes?" Luca asked. Nicholas nodded.

"Nicholas sit next to me," Christopher said enthusiastically and ran towards the table. Nicholas paused then let go of Maxwell's hand and ran after Christopher.

"I think they are going to be just fine together," Emeral said as she handed Cerey to Calen. Cerey reached up and stroked Calen's wing.

"Natasha I think these two kind of look like Gabriel and you, sure they aren't relatives?" Calen asked with a grin.

"Well they are now," Natasha said. "At least they will be when Gabriel and Hannah finalize the paperwork. Emeral and Maxwell signed for them so the priests would release them to us."

"We decided to wait on breakfast until you returned," Lila said as she started to carry platters of food into the dining room. As everyone sat down at the table, Natasha poured glasses of milk and cups of coffee, while Lila brought the food in.

"Natasha we are going to have to buy a little chair for Cerey," Emeral said as she put her hands out to take the toddler from Calen.

"I can feed her," Calen said. "I need the practice."

"This I have to see," Natasha said sarcastically.

Both Christopher and Nicholas were devouring their plates of pancakes and Christopher talked constantly to Nicholas as they ate. "You're going to like it here, everyone is really nice. And you can stay in my room while they fix yours up."

"Emeral, I know you haven't read the letter yet," Natasha said. "But Hannah wants us to ask Renya about a good nurse for the children, for when they are on missions."

"Well, they don't need a nurse as long as Maxwell and I are here," Emeral said.

"Mother are you telling us that this is going to be your permanent home?" Calen asked with a grin.

"Well, your father and I really love it here. And at home our children are all grown and the girls don't really need our help. It's nice feeling useful again."

Both Luca and Calen stared at their mother. "We never knew you felt like that," Calen said. "Father do you feel like that too?"

"Don't get us wrong," Maxwell said. "It's not that we feel totally useless but we had such a houseful of children for so many years and now everyone has moved out. We have a lot of time on our hands these days."

"That's why we were so excited when you asked us to come and help with the new wing and the baby," Emeral said. "Then once we got here, there is so much going on and everyone seems like one big family. We are really enjoying it here. And now with the children and all three of them are so precious, well, it is just really nice."

"What your mother is trying to say is even those who aren't our children, seem like they are. We've become very attached to everyone in this house. And honestly I find your missions intriguing; I wish I could help you more."

"Well, we love having both of you here," Natasha said and walked up behind both Emeral and Maxwell and hugged them.

"We can certainly put you to work," Calen said with a grin. "We've been taking it easy on you because we thought you were on holiday."

"You know you may regret saying all that," Luca said smiling. "You have three grandchildren here now and Lily will be born soon and Lila and I want to have a baby right away. You may find yourselves wanting to go back to the Ice Caves to get some rest."

The next few days Gabriel, Hannah and Raphael paid close attention to the actions of Erebus and Sophie. Roch on the other hand only left his room to come to the dining room for meals. Using the keys that Natasha had previously stolen, Raphael searched Sophie and Erebus' room one morning while they were eating breakfast in the dining room. Other than some spell books and a few objects to be used in incantations, Raphael found little of interest. He was surprised that he didn't find any signs of demons or an unholy altar in their room.

At times Hannah was finding it difficult to stay focused on the mission as she was sending and receiving daily letters about Nicholas and Cerey.

Almost a week passed before Gabriel decided to try another approach, so he wrote a letter and sent it to King Sudfad.

"Raul you are being ridicules," Vitomas said. "You are going to hide me and Annabelle when we are the only two here who can tell you if Archetenus truly seems to have changed. He will be in our castle what on earth do you think he will do?"

"She has a point," Simon said. Simon knew that Raul's fears for Vitomas had greatly escalated after he read Sophie's journal about Roch. Neither Vitomas nor Annabelle knew that the book existed and wondered why their husbands had become so overly protective of them. Raul did not speak but stared at Vitomas, Annabelle and Simon as they sat around the parlor table in Raul and Vitomas' home.

"Well, you better make your minds up soon," Annabelle said. "The letter said to expect them around mid-morning."

"Raul you look so angry," Vitomas said. "What is going on? What have you not told us? You've been acting so strangely ever since..."

"Ever since they returned from that last mission," Annabelle said. "Both of you changed but Raul you seem so angry and controlling all of the time now. What happened on that mission that affected you both so much?"

"There was something," Vitomas said when she saw the look in Raul's eyes as Annabelle spoke. "Please tell us what happened to you."

Simon and Raul looked at each other but neither of them spoke. "We are your wives," Annabelle said. "What could be so bad that you can't tell us?" Raul and Simon remained quiet.

After a moment Vitomas asked, "How would you like it if we kept secrets from you?"

"Some things are left better unsaid," Raul said.

"Not when they change your personality and affect our lives," Vitomas said. "Raul, Annabelle and I are not the only ones who have noticed a change in you. If you don't tell us, well, I suppose we can ask the others who were on that mission. You all seem so close, I am sure they know."

There was awkward silence between the two couples for almost two minutes before Simon said. "You are right, something did affect us but the reason we haven't told you is that we don't think you want to hear it."

Now it was Vitomas and Annabelle who exchanged glances and sat in silence. "We are only trying to protect you," Simon added.

"Protect us from what?" Vitomas said in a voice that was almost a whisper.

Raul reached over and took Vitomas' hand in his. "Honey if we tell you it will upset you both."

"Raul your behavior has been upsetting both of us, please tell us," Vitomas said.

Raul and Simon looked at each other solemnly. "When I was in Taperia with Natasha and Calen and the others, Natasha and I were spying on Sophie. One day we searched Sophie's room and took several books," Simon hesitated.

"And," Vitomas said fearfully.

"And there was one that we thought was her diary," Simon said. "But then we realized that Sophie had been sent by the Insidiae to observe Roch; in order to make sure he was evil enough to be a vessel for Omnibus. She chronicled all of his actions for years."

"Everything?" Vitomas asked as tears started to well up in her eyes.

"It appears so," Raul said softly. "Now I understand why you never wanted to tell me about your past." The tears started to stream down Vitomas' face.

"Why did you read it?" Annabelle asked almost angrily.

"Because we were trying to understand the man, trying to find his weaknesses and his routines," Simon said.

"The book was so awful that none of us could finish reading it," Raul said. "Except for the Sanuri."

"Did everyone read it?" Vitomas asked in horror.

"No, a few of us tried," said Raul.

"Oh I am so sorry, please excuse me," Hannah said as she deliberately bumped into Sophie in the General Store. When Sophie looked at Hannah, she said with feigned surprise, "I know you, you are staying at the same hotel we are."

Sophie looked blankly at Hannah and said, "The Taperian Imperial Hotel."

"Yes; my husband and I and his brother who is also his business partner, have rooms on the third floor. It's my first time staying in that hotel it is really quite lovely."

"Yes it is," Sophie said as she tried to remember Hannah's face. "My husband and I have a room on the top floor; we very much enjoy the view. What type of work does your husband do?"

"They run mines, mostly gold and silver but sometimes they buy land with other minerals. We are here looking for land."

"Your husband believes there is gold or silver here?"

"He bought some mines in Nora and the people told him about some rich mineral strains in this area."

"Really," Sophie said. "I have never heard of any and I have been here for many years."

"Well, I should get what I need, my husband is waiting," Hannah said. "It was so nice to meet you." As Hannah walked away she could feel Sophie's eyes upon her. Hannah's assignment was simply to make friendly contact with Sophie.

Hannah found herself wanting to shake the woman and to demand to know where Roch was hiding. The entire time that Hannah spoke with Sophie, all Hannah could think about was the journal that Sophie had written about Roch.

The journal where Sophie documented Roch's cruel and sadistic behavior, the journal where Sophie herself wrote that she stood by and watched Roch rape and torture women, children and men. The journal where Sophie applauded Roch's behavior as a befitting vessel for the demon Omnibus. It was at that moment that Hannah realized how talented Gabriel and Natasha really were, that they could look into the faces of darkness and play their roles without faltering. And it was at that moment that Hannah realized how important their work was.

"Nonsense, we will have refreshments in the parlor," Renya said. "Sudfad we all want to meet this Archetenus but remember that whatever criminal he may have been, apparently his wife is not and we will not treat her as such. Now Marie is already preparing delicacies for our guests. When they arrive we will take them into the parlor."

"Very well," Sudfad said. "But I don't expect things to go well between Raul and Archetenus, so be prepared for anything."

"Have you discussed Gabriel's letter with the children yet?" Renya asked as she fluffed pillows on the sofa in Sudfad's study.

"No, actually I was waiting for Archetenus to get here. I thought he might be able to give us the information without us upsetting the others."

"Sudfad our mission is to find Roch before he turns into a demon. The girls are more than willing to help yet you and the boys keep shutting them out. Those two girls may be the keys to finding Roch; you are being foolish. You must tell them all about the letter."

Roch's transition was not easy; even though his body was maintaining a solid and dense form he was still undergoing many painful changes on a regular basis.

413

Roch did not understand what was happening to him but almost daily he was regaining his memories about his former life and his time in Ahriman's hell dimension. There were some memories in particular that were filling Roch's mind as of late. When Ahriman gave Roch the choice to become the torturer or the tortured, Roch jumped at the chance to stand alongside of the demons. Ahriman told Roch that his first two victims had special meaning for him.

Ahriman had allowed Roch to see that Pravis and Tenebrae had been high priests in the religion of The Great Ruler but that they had sold their souls to the demons. Roch initially had no idea how these acts had any significance to him. Now as Roch lay on the floor in his hotel room writhing in pain, shreds of his memories about his torture sessions with Pravis and Tenebrae were haunting him. "What was so damn important about those two?" Roch growled between clenched teeth. "What the hell did they say?"

"Sanuri it is always good to see you," Renya said as the Sanuri kissed her on the cheek. "Matthew, Angelina, Sorren," Renya called out as she looked behind the Sanuri and saw her adopted son, his wife and her father enter the parlor. As Renya was hugging Angelina she saw a handsome, giant of a man and a beautiful woman walk into the parlor. Renya's posture stiffened.

"Renya this is Archetenus and his wife Delilah," Angelina said as she was hoping to diffuse a tense situation. "They have been fighting at our side in battle. They are no threat to this family."

Renya walked up to Archetenus and said, "I will not lie to you, your presence here has caused anxieties among my family. Vitomas is our beloved daughter and we are very protective of her. But we have also been told of your battles against the demons and your work with Miranda. You and your wife are guests in our home and will be treated as such but I cannot guarantee your stay here will be without conflict."

"I understand," Archetenus said. "And now that I am married I cannot imagine what I would do if someone stole Delilah. Raul has every right to hate me. But I am not here to cause conflict and if it will help, Delilah and I can stay in the city."

"That will not be necessary," Raul said in a stern voice. Archetenus and Delilah turned to see Raul and Vitomas holding hands behind them and Simon and Annabelle standing behind Raul and Vitomas.

"Archetenus introduce us to your wife," Vitomas said sweetly.

"Delilah this is Vitomas, the woman that I kidnapped and her husband Prince Raul and that is Prince Simon and Annabelle who I also knew from Stordt. This is my wife Delilah."

Delilah and Vitomas walked up to each other and looked searchingly into each other's eyes. "My husband has told me about the man he was; I want to assure you that I have never seen that man in him. Give him a chance to prove to you that he has changed," Delilah said with great sincerity in her voice.

"Archetenus had battles with his demons much in the same manner that Jared did," Matthew said. "And he has risked his life to obtain valuable information for us. I don't expect any of you to become friends but it benefits us all to work together. Since he has turned against the demons and dark lords, I believe he is in as much danger as Jared. I told Archetenus and Delilah they are welcomed to live and to raise their family in Lentz."

"The King is here," Renya said as the family moved out of the doorway to the parlor to allow Sudfad entrance.

"Father this is Archetenus and his wife Delilah," Raul said.

"I have heard a great deal about you, both good and bad," Sudfad said as he shook Archetenus' hand. "But I am anxious to see the journals you have brought us. Please everyone be seated and help yourself to refreshments, we have much to discuss." Marie carried a tray filled with delicacies into the parlor and stared sullenly at Archetenus. After Marie left the room Sudfad said, "I must apologize, Marie is part of the family and she is as protective of the children as we are."

"Both the Sanuri and Matthew have written to me about your work for Miranda," Sudfad continued. "As I said I am anxious to see your journals but before we get into that matter I want to say a few words."

"I did hear a great deal that was being said as I was walking down the hallway. Archetenus you and your beautiful wife are welcome to stay here as our guests. If you are uncomfortable here of course you many go to Salar but as Matthew said we have concerns for your safety and would prefer that you stay here. And my sons will treat you as our guests," Sudfad said as he looked at Raul and Simon. "We are at war and we cannot let our emotions deter us; do we all understand that?"

Both Raul and Simon looked at Sudfad and nodded. "Good," Sudfad said. "Now I have a matter that I want to discuss. I have been waiting for Archetenus to arrive so I could speak with all of you about this at once. We have members of the Patronus spying on Sophie and her new husband the warlock Erebus in Stordt. We suspect they have been in contact with Roch. Gabriel, one of the leaders of this mission, says they have seen a suspicious man meeting with Sophie and Erebus."

"Gabriel himself has spoken with this man but they don't know his identity. He dresses in a manner to hide his face. He is tall and muscular with long black hair that hangs past his shoulders and a full beard and mustache. There are streaks of gray in his hair that can be seen under the large wide brimmed hat that he always wears. Gabriel is wondering if any of you can give him information to help better determine if this man is Roch and not some other criminal. Do you remember any tattoos or scars or anything?"

"Roch has been injured many times in fights," Vitomas said. "He has scars on both his sides and stomach from knife wounds. And a long scar that runs down the outside of his left leg. I don't remember him ever having tattoos."

"Roch has been returned from hell," the Sanuri said. "He is in a different form than he was before Ahriman took him, so his body may not have the same markings on it."

"I will go to Stordt," Archetenus said. "I will be able to recognize him. Can we still kill him as a man?"

"That depends on how far he is with the transformation," the Sanuri said. "But I believe Vitomas has something she wants to say."

"Archetenus you are so big that you can be clearly seen in a crowd. Which means that Roch may recognize you before you see him. I want to go back to our original plans of using me as bait to draw him out," Vitomas said.

"I think that is too dangerous," Archetenus said. Then he looked at Raul. "You approve of this?"

"No," Raul said. "I don't like it at all but it may be the only way we can catch him."

"For a couple of weeks we have had teams of warriors working out different strategies," Simon said. "We believe we can protect Vitomas and the others."

"Others?" asked Archetenus.

"There are two other women who resemble Vitomas who have also volunteered to act as bait," Simon continued.

"Archetenus, I believe that Roch's hatred for me is so strong that once he sees me he will focus on nothing else, which will leave him open to attack," Vitomas said.

"While I agree with you I still think it is dangerous," Archetenus said.

"Archetenus, Roch has sent his men after us, he knows we live here. Some of his men tried to kidnap us when Vitomas was pregnant; she was injured and we almost lost her and the baby," Annabelle said. "We have families now and we don't want our children to become his victims too."

Archetenus looked at Sudfad. "I think I should go."

"I think Raul and Simon should review the plans with you," the Sanuri said to Archetenus. "Then I think you all should go. And you should take Jared with you."

"Is he able to fight?" Angelina asked.

"He will be," the Sanuri said. "Jared and Zoya should meet Archetenus and Delilah; united they will be stronger than they realize."

Chapter XXVI
Brothers

"I have to show you something," Natasha said with a warm smile as she walked into the parlor holding Cerey. "Follow me but be quiet."

Calen, Luca, Lila, Emeral and Maxwell all stood up and followed Natasha to the room they had fixed up for Nicholas and Cerey. Everyone broke into broad smiles when they looked into the room and saw Christopher and Nicholas sleeping on the floor surrounded by their toys. Cerey held out her hands for Calen to take her, which made Natasha laugh. As they all left the room and preceded down the hallway Maxwell said, "I'm not surprised at how fast they have bonded. They have so much in common."

"I think Christopher will bring Nicholas out of his shell," Lila said. "Christopher is so outgoing. Have you noticed how protective he is of Nicholas?"

"Yeah but neither of them seem to have time for Cerey," said Calen.

"Well, it was the same with you two boys," Emeral said then she looked at Natasha and Lila. "You know Calen has three older sisters; well, he was our baby when Luca's parents were killed in a battle. Luca came to live with us and he is just a little younger than Calen."

"The two boys really didn't know each other well before that and the first few days Calen seemed a little jealous that he was no longer the baby. But by the end of the first week, those two boys were so close you would have thought they had been together forever. And they remained that way their entire lives." Lila smiled and held Luca's hand as they listened to Emeral.

"How old were they then?" Natasha asked as she walked with her arm around Calen's waist.

"Calen was five and Luca four," Emeral said with pride. "They looked so much alike some people mistook them for brothers."

Maxwell started to laugh, "Two years later Misha came to live with us and those three boys just terrorized their sisters. Whenever it was quiet in the house we knew they were up to something."

"Did Misha's parents die too?" asked Natasha.

"Well, Misha's father had been killed by Hutas and his mother was trying to raise ten children by herself so we took Misha in. Misha would come over to play with the boys and they got along so well that he just became part of the family," Emeral explained.

"Misha was always staying at our house with the boys so it wasn't a big transition when he came to live with us permanently," Maxwell said as they entered the parlor.

"I have never heard Misha talk about his other family," Natasha asked. "Does he spend time with them?"

"No," Calen said. "Once he came to live with us it was like he disowned them. He doesn't talk about them, even with us."

"Dagon and Koby talk like they lived with you too," Natasha said. "Did you adopt them also?"

"Not officially," Maxwell said with a grin. "They were just always at our house with the boys; they would stay for days at a time. Emeral made me build an extra bedroom for them and after that they never seemed to leave."

"You must have had a wonderful home if everyone wanted to live with you," Lila said.

"We did," Luca said but stopped talking as he watched an Enrop fly into the room.

"It's so kind of you to have us over for dinner," Delilah said. "Can I help with anything?"

"Why don't you take that bottle of whiskey and a couple of glasses to Archetenus and Jared," Zoya said. "And tell them that dinner will be ready in fifteen minutes."

When Delilah walked out onto the porch where Archetenus and Jared were sitting, they stopped talking. She looked at them both and smiled. "Zoya said dinner will be ready in fifteen minutes."

"Delilah, we were just talking about our experiences," Archetenus explained.

"I understand," she said and kissed Archetenus on the head before returning to the kitchen.

"Our husbands are talking about their experiences with the demons. They stopped talking when I went out there."

"I'm glad," Zoya said. "Jared doesn't really tell me much about it. He says he doesn't want to worry me. But I know that entire thing had to be worse than he said."

"Did you see him go through it?"

"Yes and it was terrifying. I couldn't believe how brave and strong he was."

"I was really scared too," Delilah said. "We were hiding in a miner's shack the first time it happened and Archetenus told me to take his sword and kill him if he tried to hurt me. All I could do was to pray and cry. I felt so helpless."

"I was luckier," Zoya said. "The first time the demons came for Jared a physician and a Ruala healer helped him. Then other healers came and Natasha, who is a demon hunter; she is the one who figured out what that Mark of Satan was on his neck. It was awful to watch. I am so glad I wasn't alone with him."

"Tomorrow when they leave are you going to stay at the castle?"

"Yes, Jared wants me to but I hate to leave the farm. I do love it here so; and the Sanuri has Blue Hengers and Enrops watching us."

"If you would like, you could stay in our room with me. Everyone there is so nice but it is awkward because they don't really trust Archetenus."

"But the Mark of Satan is gone."

"It's not that," Delilah said with embarrassment. "Archetenus was in love with Vitomas and even though they had never spoken he thought she was in love with him too. She was a prisoner of Roch's, well, Archetenus stole her and thought she would be happy, he didn't know she had fallen in love with Prince Raul and planned to marry him. Archetenus never hurt Vitomas but I guess he really scared her several times. But he brought her back to the Prince."

"I can understand how you would feel uncomfortable, but give them a chance the Royal Family are really good people. I think there will be much less tension when Roch is destroyed."

"This is difficult," Elan said as they sat around the kitchen table. "I mean the waiting."

"You should have been with us before," Dagon said. "Calen was losing his mind staying back here while Natasha was in Taperia. He was so worried about her. I felt sorry for him."

"And we were all worried about him," Koby added. "You have to be thinking sharp to do this and Calen was so distracted all the time. We're lucky they both didn't get hurt more than they did." Elan and Cassandra looked at each other shyly as they listened to Dagon and Koby.

High Priest Aaron walked into the room, followed by the other members of the Patronus who were in the hotel. As soon as everyone was quiet he spoke. "As you know, Raphael and the others have seen a man who they suspect is Roch but they don't yet know his true identity. Gabriel contacted King Sudfad and the plans are being put into action. They are leaving Wetpr tonight and will be here by morning. Two of the men who were vessels are also coming to help. Once they get here I suspect things will start moving quickly so I would like you all to prepare for their arrival."

"Amos pick five other priests and go into the city in small groups and start buying supplies," Aaron said. "I don't want anyone getting suspicious that we will be feeding an army. I would like the rest of you to start preparing rooms; we may actually fill this place up."

"This is incredible," Vitomas said excitedly as she flew through the sky in the arms of a Ruala warrior. "I like this very much."

"Some people get dizzy or sick when they first fly," Tambor said. "Let me know if you aren't feeling well. But at night it is easier because you can't see the ground."

"Actually I am jealous now, to think that you can travel like this all of the time, it really is a wonderful gift. When the children are older I would love for them to fly too."

"Well, I will certainly take them up if I am around," Tambor said. He was a male Ruala warrior in his mid-twenties. Although he had heard a great deal about the Royal Family of Wetpr he had never met any of them until he volunteered for this mission. He had been staying at the castle for the previous two weeks working on strategies to find Roch. "This is my first time in Wetpr and working with your family," Tambor said. "I have very much enjoyed my stay here and will volunteer for more missions."

"You know that Sudfad and Renya adopted Ibula and Thedes," Vitomas said. "So whenever your warriors come here it just seems like more family. Are you staying for Luca's wedding? They are waiting until we return to set a date. We originally wanted to have a huge celebration and their wedding before everyone left for Stordt but then things changed."

"I would like to stay for the wedding, but I hadn't heard much about it."

"Well, Renya and Emeral are planning it and both of them are incredible at organizing things. All of you will be invited to stay at the castle for as long as you like."

"Can I invite my wife?"

"Of course and I would love to meet her."

"We are crossing the border into Stordt now."

"How can you tell Tambor? I can't see a thing down there."

"All Rualas have great vision; you know they say our race was created by humans and great eagles."

"Is that really true?"

"Much of our history, the paintings and the scrolls were destroyed by the Hutas, so I cannot tell you if that is the truth but it would explain the wings," Tambor said and laughed.

"I spoke with Simon," Thedes said as Ibula carried him through the skies. "I told him to make sure that Raul doesn't hinder us."

"Are you sure you should have said that?" Ibula asked.

"Simon wasn't offended. He understands the situation," said Thedes. "We all understand why Raul is so scared for Vitomas but no one should go into battle being that emotional, someone will get hurt."

"This is the damndest thing," Jared exclaimed to Sar the Ruala warrior who was flying with him. "I mean to travel above ground like this is really something but I can't believe you can carry me so easily, I weigh a lot."

"This is how we carry everything," Sar replied. "Our people are very strong. Have you seen Ibula? She is tiny yet she carries her Shettee husband always and he is very big."

"Well, I will tell you I thought that I had seen and done just about everything but this is really something."

Simon, Raul and Archetenus all flew in silence. Simon was concerned that Annabelle would have the baby while they were gone, although Ibula assured him that someone would return him home as soon as they received word.

Archetenus was concerned about leaving Delilah in a strange place, although he felt better knowing that she and Zoya were sharing a room. King Sudfad's family had been surprisingly gracious to them but the tension was still there and Archetenus felt that Delilah was suffering for his sins.

Raul, a man who had never backed down from a fight; a man known for his courage and skill as a warrior was terrified; not for himself but for his wife. He knew she was the perfect bait to draw Roch out of hiding but Raul could not tolerate the thought of Roch even speaking to Vitomas much less touching her. He had to find a way to kill Roch before he came close to her.

Ahriman was no longer blocking Erebus' attempts to contact the spirits and demons of the underworlds. Erebus felt panicked, a feeling he was not use to. He spent his life loving a person who he thought was lost to him and now that he and Sophie were finally together Erebus didn't want anyone to threaten their relationship.

Erebus did not trust Roch and it dismayed him that Sophie seemed to want to trust him. Erebus started to leave Sophie for periods at a time as he went to a nearby cave and performed incantations. He was seeking information about Roch's time in hell, why Roch was released and what that strange aura was that surrounded Roch. Erebus knew this information would be costly but he was prepared to pay any price.

With Gabriel, Raphael, Simon and Raul gone, Calen and Luca were attending the morning meetings at the castle as well as watching over the families. While many Ruala warriors flew to Taperia there was still a small army at the castle at Wetpr waiting to be either dispatched to Nora or Taperia. Sorren, Matthew and Angelina flew to Taperia hoping to assist with the destruction of Roch.

Delilah and Zoya shared a great deal about their experiences with their unusual husbands and both found comfort in being able to talk to someone else who understood the horrors they felt watching their husbands being pulled into hell. To Delilah's surprise and appreciation Renya, Annabelle and Laurel treated her as a friend.

While few spoke the words, everyone at the castle and at Gabriel's home were concerned for their loved ones on this mission. Although the warriors had tried to plan for every conceivable variable in their strategies to find Roch, they were all experienced enough to know that many things could go wrong.

And they all feared that Roch would complete his transformation into a demon before he could be destroyed.

   Sudfad increased the guards around the castle and greatly increased the number of soldiers patrolling along the borders of the kingdom. In addition, soldiers were stationed outside of Gabriel's home as well as hundreds of soldiers standing prepared to be sent to Taperia to assist the Patronus. Raul and Simon handpicked several dozen experienced soldiers to fly to Taperia with them. These men wore civilian clothing and not the military uniforms of Wetpr.

   With the rays of a new morning sun, hundreds of Ruala warriors descended on the abandoned hotel in Stordt that had become an outpost for the Patronus.

   "This brings back memories," Simon said as he, Raul and Vitomas all walked into the hotel.

   "Something smells really good," Vitomas said as High Priest Aaron met them at the door.

   "We have breakfast prepared and your rooms ready," Aaron said. "After everyone has eaten and settled in we will have a briefing."

   "Is there room for us all?" asked Vitomas.

   "This is a huge building," Aaron said. "I believe everyone here will fit into the main dining room of the hotel without eating in shifts."

   Elan and Cassandra walked up to Simon, Raul and Vitomas. The young Ruala couple now felt brave enough to hold hands in public. "We chose two really nice adjoining rooms for you," Elan said. "Where are your things?"

   "Were you able to get the dresses made in time?" Cassandra asked as they all walked up the stairs to the top floor of the hotel.

   "Laurel sat up all night but she was able to finish them," Vitomas said. "I think that is such a clever idea."

"From Gabriel's letter," Raul explained. "Ibula will put one of the dresses on and fly outside of Roch's window, that way she can spy on him and hopefully he will think he is either dreaming or seeing images of Vitomas. Then both Vitomas and Hannah will walk in the hotel and various other places wearing the same dresses. If nothing else they are hoping this will either annoy Roch or make him so curious that he exposes himself."

"And if the man in the hotel is not Roch what then?" Elan asked.

"The next step is to pull the same tricks on Sophie, hoping she will try to contact Roch about Vitomas," said Simon. "And if neither of these plans work; well, we have a variety of others to test out."

"Gabriel has disguises for you to wear," Elan said. "It is not safe for any of you to show your true faces around here. Also, he has already reserved you rooms on the third floor of the hotel. I believe your rooms are directly across the hall from Gabriel's and Raphael's. He has identification papers and other things in your rooms."

"Sophie's staying on the fifth floor of the hotel and the man they believe is Roch is on the fourth floor, Elan continued. "They have balconies that face the street as do you. Gabriel and Raphael's rooms have balconies that face the alley behind the hotel, so our people and the Enrops will be entering through their rooms. There are many Enrops here and you will be watched constantly."

"I am really impressed," Vitomas said. "You have thought of everything."

"It's Gabriel," Elan said. "But we are learning a great deal. Also Gabriel knows that Annabelle may go into labor and since there are so many of us here, I am the one who is to receive any messages for you Simon and I promise you I will take you home quickly if need be."

"Thank you, I appreciate that," Simon said. "I missed the birth of Arianna and it tore me apart." Then Simon grinned, "So tell me are you two a couple now?"

"Yes," Elan said with a bright smile.

"Good," Simon said. "Calen told us that you have had a crush on Cassandra since you were a child."

"He told me that," Cassandra said with a huge smile. "And I never knew. But I did wonder why everyone was grinning when I arrived in Wetpr. It wasn't until Gabriel told us to spend time together instead of working that Elan finally told me. I wish he would have told me sooner because I have always liked him."

"So you two liked each other for a long time and neither of you knew it?" asked Vitomas.

"Yes," Elan said. "I wish I would have had the courage to say something to her but every time I was around Cassandra it seemed like I couldn't talk." Everyone laughed at this comment.

"Well, you are together now and that is what counts," Vitomas said.

"Here are your rooms," Elan said. "Aaron sent an Enrop to Gabriel to let him know you arrived. Gabriel will send a message when he wants you to come to the hotel."

"What is this?" Vitomas said as she saw a black outfit lying on the bed in their room.

Simon started to laugh. "When Natasha and I were spying on Sophie I bought her that outfit so she could walk around the hotel without being recognized. I believe that is what you are going to wear when we first arrive at the hotel. Gabriel wants to control the times that you are exposed."

"Raul you have been so quiet," Vitomas said as they unpacked their things in their room in the abandoned hotel. Raul did not speak. "Honey if this mission is successful we will be free. I have never been entirely free of my fear of Roch since the day he stole me. Whatever we have to do it will be worth it."

Raul walked across the room and took Vitomas' hands in his. "I have never felt anxiety like this before any battle. I would rather fight a legion of demons myself than to put you in harm's way."

"Raul if it was Gabriel or Simon or Calen feeling like you are; what would you say to them?"

Raul paused before he spoke, "I would tell them not to participate and to leave it to the rest of us."

"Raul, I am not afraid. I trust all of you and know you will protect me and Hannah and Ibula. In fact you may think this is crazy but I have been looking forward to this. Roch has been my nightmare for so long; I am looking forward to my freedom. And think of what a wonderful feat this will be to stop such a monster."

Raul pulled Vitomas to him and hugged her tightly. "He is such filth I don't even want him talking to you."

"Raul you are letting him get to you. Don't let him win this battle. I always remember how you stood up to him. You were so injured but you stood before him and stared into his eyes. Never had I seen a man do that before. And do you remember what Roch did? He backed down from you. Raul that is what you must do again. Let me bring him to you."

Gabriel, Raphael and Hannah had seen little of the man they believed to be Roch for several days. Gabriel had Enrops following Erebus so they knew he was going to a cavern outside of the city and performing rituals; they just didn't know what kind of rituals. Sophie was spending more time in her room in the hotel, which was a change from her normal behavior.

"Something isn't right here," Gabriel said as they sat in the dining room. "I can just feel it."

"Gabriel we are assuming that Roch doesn't know the role Sophie played in his development as a vessel for a demon," Hannah said. "Erebus and Sophie look very much in love. I am sure Erebus wants to protect her. Is it possible the rituals he is doing are some kind of protection spells?"

"I have thought about that too," Raphael said. "I wonder why Erebus and Sophie stay here, surely they fear what Roch will do once he learns about the Insidiae."

"The Sanuri said that Roch was greatly damaged when he was put back into this world. Perhaps he doesn't remember some things," Gabriel said. "If I were Erebus I would be trying to learn what Roch was up to."

"Maybe they plan to kill Roch," Hannah said. "And that is why they are with him. Maybe Erebus is trying to find out how powerful Roch is."

"There are many things that could be going on here," Gabriel said. "But I think we all agree that Erebus is the weak link in the chain. Now we have to find a way to use that to our advantage."

"Gabriel I just saw an Enrop fly past the window," Raphael said. "I'll go up to the room and see if there is a message. As Raphael was walking out of the dining room he passed Roch in the doorway. The two men stared at each other.

"Look," Gabriel said to Hannah. "It's unusual to see Roch in the dining room for lunch."

Roch did not join Erebus and Sophie at their usual table but walked across the room and sat down with Gabriel and Hannah. This was the first contact that Gabriel had with Roch since he delivered the note to Roch's room.

"Mind if I join you?" Roch asked as he was already sitting down at the table.

"So you never told me," Gabriel said nonchalantly. "That note I found was it yours?"

Roch laughed. "I believe it was deliberately discarded. Some poor fool has a wife who is really angry at him." As Roch spoke he stared admiringly at Hannah. "Geoffrey you are a lucky man your wife is very beautiful." Gabriel could feel the hair rising on the back of his neck as Roch spoke. Hannah looked at Roch and smiled at his compliment.

"My name is Hannah," she said sweetly. "I am sorry I didn't catch your name."

"Peters," Roch said. "And I believe I owe your husband an apology. I was very rude to him the night he brought that note to me. I am a man with many enemies and I was not happy that the desk clerk so easily pointed my room out."

"You need not apologize," Gabriel said as he was trying to figure out what Roch really wanted. "This is our first time in Taperia and we have heard stories about the dangers here. Your reaction was understandable."

The waiter brought three plates of food to the table. "My brother had to go to his room for a few minutes," Gabriel said. "Can you bring the food when he returns?"

"Of course, My Lord," the waiter said. Then he turned to Roch. "Would you like to hear our menu?"

"No, I will just have a whiskey," Roch said. After the waiter left the table Roch turned to Gabriel. "I read the trade card that you gave me. I was wondering if you were successful in locating any areas rich in minerals?"

Gabriel knew that Roch was testing him. Gabriel stared at Roch before speaking. "My brother and I do a great deal of business in Nora, are you familiar with that city?"

"Yes," Roch said with a sly smile. A smile that made Hannah want to slap him.

"Then you know that city is built on gold mines. We bought and sold a great deal of property there," Gabriel explained. "The members of the City Council spent a large sum of money to have studies done of the mineral deposits in this kingdom so they would know where to mine. I happened to get a copy of one of those maps. So far we have found the maps to be very accurate. We know where the deposits are here, we just have to locate the landowners and work out the purchase price."

"Honey, Mr. Peters looks so skeptical," Hannah said as she touched Gabriel's arm. "Would you like me to go to the room and get the map?"

"Yes," Gabriel said. He waited until Hannah left the table then he turned to Roch. "You don't strike me as the kind of man who visits people to make friendly conversation," Gabriel said as he stared at Roch. "What is it that you want?"

"I like a man who is direct," Roch said with a grin. The waiter set Roch's drink in front of him and Roch waited for him to leave before speaking again. "You dress like a gentleman yet you carry yourself like a warrior."

"As do you," said Gabriel.

Roch laughed again as he stared at Gabriel. "Are you a warrior?"

"Are you challenging me?" Gabriel asked with an unwavering stare.

"Well, I guess you just answered my question," Roch said as he took a gulp of his whiskey. "I couldn't help but notice that your brother carries himself like a warrior also."

"You are an observant man," Gabriel said. "Are you this interested in all the guests in this hotel?"

"I like your attitude," Roch said. "The truth is I too am here on business and depending on how it goes I might have need for a couple of warriors, who can easily fit in with any group of people."

"My brother and I are not body guards," Gabriel said as he took a sip of his coffee.

"I don't need body guards," Roch said as he stared at Gabriel.

"Then what do you need?"

"I might need someone to hire men for me. Someone who recognizes a warrior when he sees one."

"And you cannot do this yourself?"

"As I said I have many enemies."

431

"And I take it you don't want them to know that you are in the city."

"Something like that," Roch said with a grin. Then he looked up as Raphael and Hannah returned to the table. Hannah handed Gabriel the map and he handed it to Roch. "Well I will be damned," Roch said. "You were telling the truth."

"My husband does not lie," Hannah said with indignation.

"Your wife is beautiful and loyal," Roch said with a grin. "You are a lucky man."

"I will speak with my brother about your concerns," Gabriel said. "We expect to be here for several weeks. Does that time frame work for you?"

"Perfect," Roch said and gulped the rest of his drink. He stood up from the table and tipped his hat to Hannah then walked over to the table where Sophie and Erebus were seated.

"What was that about?" Raphael asked as he watched Roch.

"I do believe Mr. Peters wants us to help him raise an army," Gabriel said with a grin. "I think he is our man."

"But why did he ask you?" Hannah said. "Are you sure it isn't a trap?"

"He recognized that both Raphael and I carry ourselves as warriors and yet we blend in with the crowds of people. He wants someone who can determine if someone is a warrior for hire."

"Well the timing is perfect," Raphael said. "They all arrived this morning. Aaron wants to know when Raul and Simon should come here."

"I think they should come this afternoon," Gabriel said. "We can start tonight. I think I will send Sudfad another letter, telling him to send more soldiers. If Roch wants an army we will give him one."

Chapter XXVII
Nightmares

Matthew, Angelina and Sorren stood in the lobby of the Taperian Imperial Hotel waiting in line to register for a room. Gabriel was sitting in the lobby reading a book and watching which of the crew entered the hotel. Aaron had given everyone on the mission the hotel room numbers of Gabriel, Roch and Sophie. It had been decided that members of their crew would try to get rooms on each of those floors.

Roch had room 419, Matthew and Angelina got room 412 and Sorren room 408. Gabriel was sitting close enough to the desk that he could hear the conversations of the guests who were registering for rooms. The book that Gabriel was holding had blank sheets of paper, on which Gabriel was documenting everyone's room numbers as they registered.

Aaron had also given everyone descriptions of what Gabriel and Raphael looked like in disguise and the information that Gabriel would be in the lobby. But everyone was instructed to walk past him as if he was a stranger. Jared entered the lobby almost five minutes later. He got a room on the fifth floor. Sophie and Erebus lived in room 517, Jared registered for room 518. Jared wanted to watch the woman who helped set up men like him to be vessels for demons.

Before Jared started to walk up the stairs to his room, Raul, Simon and Vitomas entered the lobby. Both Raul and Simon were wearing beards and mustaches as disguises and Vitomas wore a black dress with a wide brimmed hat and a long black veil which was customary for women who were mourning the death of a loved one. Gabriel had previously registered room 305 for Raul and Vitomas and 307 for Simon. Gabriel and Hannah were in room 302 and Raphael in 304.

High Priests Amos and Caleb shared room 421. High Priest Gregory registered for room 510. Padre Augustus got room 505 and Padre Darius got room 403; all of these men were members of the Patronus. Archetenus entered the hotel with the priests. He got room 310. Neither Erebus, Sophie nor Roch were in the hotel dining room or lobby when Archetenus entered.

433

Gabriel saw eight clean shaven men walk into the hotel and enter the tavern area, one of the men nodded to Gabriel as a signal that they were Wetprian soldiers. Additional soldiers entered the dining room and others sat in the chairs which were on the street, in front of the hotel. All of the soldiers were dressed in civilian clothing. Gabriel knew that Roch, Erebus and Sophie were not fools and would quickly identify any one person who was seen following them frequently. The Wetprian soldiers and the Patronus priests had assignments to discretely follow the three.

As Gabriel sat in the lobby he made copies of the lists of room numbers for his team members and for High Priest Aaron. Shettees and Rualas were never seen in most of Stordt. Gabriel did not want these warriors to draw unwanted attention so he was assigning them to more clandestine duties.

"Get out of here!" demanded Cicero as his study was filling up with his men; the men who were created to become vessels for demons.

"Not until we get some damn answers," Paulas yelled.

"I pay you well, that's as much as you need to know," Cicero yelled arrogantly. "Now leave my office and return to work."

Cicero was considerably shorter than the men standing before him, suddenly the crowd parted and four men pushed Canton onto the floor. Canton was tied up, bruised and bleeding.

"Boss, they freed the slaves," Canton said angrily. "But I didn't tell them nothing."

"And what didn't he tell us?" a voice yelled from the crowd. "That those rooms down there were meant for us. That you're planning on auctioning us to demons, is that what he didn't tell us?"

Cicero got a panicked look on his face for a moment. Then he looked at Canton and mumbled a few words. The ropes that bound Canton fell away and the huge man jumped to his feet and stood next to his boss.

"That doesn't impress us," Paulas said. Paulas appeared to be the self-appointed leader of the group. "Boys destroy everything that looks like it is for magic." Paulas ordered. There were hundreds of men in the mansion, although only twenty five could fit into the study. Many of the men who had been standing outside of the study now started to destroy everything they could get their hands on.

"You're not answering our questions," an angry voice yelled in the room. "Why do we all have the same tattoos on the back of our heads?"

"Honest boss I don't know how they found out," said Canton.

"Will you shut up," Cicero snapped. He was the type of man who planned every detail of his actions well in advance of the situation. Cicero was not the type of man who thought quickly on his feet. Now he was trying to figure out how to rectify this situation. Never did he imagine that the vessels would find out about their destinies.

"What's the matter Cicero?" Paulas asked mockingly. "You're always so full of big words, cat got your tongue?"

"He's just trying to figure out some more lies to tell us," Cleo yelled as he pushed his way to the front of the crowd. "I was there, I talked to the man we couldn't kill and he told us about your plans. He showed us the Mark of Satan you put on us."

"What man are you talking about?" Cicero demanded. He was trying to maintain his authority over the vessels.

"A man came here and told us all about you and Dieter and your plans to auction us off. And he told us how you use that damn tattoo to control us. Remove the tattoos!" Cleo yelled.

"Who was this man?" Cicero asked as he continued to evade the questions.

"Someone who didn't bleed when Jeb ran his sword through him," said Inon with a smug grin as he pushed Jeb through the crowd. "And someone who disappeared before our eyes. Tell him Jeb." Inon pushed Jeb down onto the floor. Jeb was not bound but he was bleeding.

"He's right My Lord, everything he said." Jeb said then spit a mouth full of blood onto the floor.

"That's preposterous!" shouted Cicero.

"As preposterous as you and Dieter sacrificing people to demons?" Cleo asked. "Inon tell him what else that man said."

"He said that if we needed help removing your hold on us to call to the heavens. So we're figuring we got an Angel here," Inon said with a grin.

"Look at the big man now," Cleo mocked. "He's white as a sheet."

"Canton where are the rest of our men?" Cicero asked quickly.

"They done killed them all, excepting for me and Jeb."

"Remove the tattoos," yelled Cleo.

"It's not that easy," Cicero said hesitantly. "I didn't put those damn tattoos on you a demon did. And you don't think you're gonna scare a demon do you?"

"Yes," said a calm but strong voice in the crowd. Although the voice did not try to rise above the din and chaos suddenly every man in the mansion stopped what he was doing and they all returned to Cicero's study. The men in the study quickly looked to see where the voice was coming from, then suddenly Daniel was walking through the crowd towards Cicero.

"That's him, that's the fellar," Jeb said as he pointed at Daniel.

Cicero knew he had to assert his powers now or lose this situation. Cicero threw fire at Daniel. The men in the study backed up but Daniel kept walking towards Cicero. The flames did not harm the Angel. Cicero spoke again and the room filled with large red snakes that lunged at Daniel. Without speaking a word, the snakes turned into ashes by the strong presence of holiness in that room. Suddenly a sword of light appeared in Daniel's right hand.

"Gentlemen," Daniel said softly. "You are going to receive a gift. Cicero has called to the demons and an army is on the way. You have the choice; you can stand up to your demons, denounce them and fight them or you can be their slaves through eternity. The choice is yours." Instantly the room started to fill with dark smoke as demons of all manner started to materialize in the mansion. Daniel never yelled but his voice was heard by every man in that building.

There was only one large staircase that went up to all the floors in the Taperian Imperial Hotel. At the top of each level the room numbers started on the right side of the hallway near the stairs. The odd numbered rooms were located on the right side of the hallway and those rooms all had balconies that faced the main street of Taperia. The even numbered rooms were located on the left side of the hallway and they all had balconies that looked over the rear of the hotel. There was a service alley behind the hotel that could clearly be seen from the rear balconies.

Gabriel wanted Vitomas and Archetenus on the third floor near his room, since these were the two people who Roch would recognize. Gabriel wanted to make sure he controlled the situations as much as possible to minimize injuries. Roch was in room 419. High Priests Caleb and Amos were in the room next to Roch's; this was no accident since the two priests were blessing the area to prevent demons from intruding.

Matthew, Angelina and Sorren had rooms across the hallway from Roch but their rooms were closer to the staircase. Angelina and Sorren were both dressed in a manner to avoid suspicion. Instead of the traditional Nordes warriors outfits they were wearing clothing that made them blend in with the people of Taperia. Padre Darius' room was on the same side of the hallway as Roch's but considerably closer to the stairs.

On the fifth floor Sophie and Erebus lived in room 517. Jared's room was directly across the hall from them, he was in room 518. High Priest Gregory's room was on the same side of the hallway as Jared's but closer to the staircase and Padre Augustus' room was on the same side of the hallway as Sophie's but much closer to the stairs.

Before Gabriel's much expanded team, arrived at the Taperian Imperial Hotel, High Priest Aaron briefed them about the mission and their roles and assignments. There was some concern that Sophie might recognize Jared but Aaron thought that could possibly work in their favor. Recognizing Jared might force Sophie to make a move that would lead Gabriel's team to either more members of the Insidiae or to Roch. Thus it was decided that Jared would get a room close to Sophie's. Aaron stressed again and again that every member of the team must watch out for the others.

Many of the men in Cicero's mansion were filled with fear when they saw the demons start to take form in the study. Cicero grinned at the looks on the faces of his men; he knew he had them back under his control.

"You can defeat them," Daniel said as he stepped towards the dark clouds. "They control you by your fears."

"Damn!" Cleo yelled and jumped over Cicero's desk and plunged his sword into Cicero's chest. Cleo's action caused many of the other men to let go of their paralyzing fear. Canton and Jeb were fighting for their lives as they battled with the men who would be vessels. Many of the demons were destroyed as soon as they took form but others were holding their ground as they battled this army of the damned.

While many men fought, many others could not overcome their fears and they fled from the mansion. It was the demons, not Daniel who called these men back. The men who listened to the demons now fought against the other vessels. The choices had been made and the lines were drawn. The battle took on incredible proportions.

Roch was not seen until dinner time. When he walked into the dining room to join Sophie and Erebus he had no idea that most of the people seated at the tables were part of Gabriel's team. Gabriel wanted his team to get a good look at the three before Vitomas and Archetenus made their presence known.

Vitomas wore the veil and coverings of one in mourning as she entered the dining room with Raul and Simon, both of whom were in disguise. They joined Gabriel, Hannah and Raphael at their usual table. "The three people seated at the middle window table are the ones we are watching," Gabriel said in a low voice. "The man wearing the hat is the one we suspect to be Roch."

Raul briefly turned and looked at the table. "I recognize Sophie; I've never seen the man sitting across from her. The one in the middle could be Roch by his size."

"Aaron said that he spends days in his room," Simon said. "What does he do?"

"We don't know," Gabriel said. "That time I went to his room he wouldn't let me look in. I hope that Ibula will be able to tell us when she starts to haunt him tonight."

Fear gripped Vitomas' heart as she slowly turned and looked at the table by the window. She squeezed Raul's forearm as she spoke in a whisper. "That is him, I am sure of it," Vitomas said and quickly turned so that she was facing the rest of the people at her table.

"How can you be sure?" Gabriel said. "You can't see his face."

"But I can see the way in which he is sitting. He never sat up straight like, well, like all of you do." Vitomas was looking around the table as she spoke. "He always slumped forward, like there was something wrong with his back. Look at the way that man is sitting. And he is holding his glass in his left hand. Roch could use both his right and left hands equally well. But since he was always drinking, he always held his drink in his left hand so he could grab a weapon with his right."

"Vitomas you have done very well," Gabriel said. "It is little details like that, that one forgets to disguise."

Raul put his arm around Vitomas and hugged her tightly. "Are you alright?" he asked.

"Yes, I am now, but for just a moment all of the old fears came back."

The battle did not end with the day, long into the night the vessels fought each other and the demons. Daniel fought at their side as the seemingly unending army of demons appeared inside of the mansion. Few of the vessels who were called by the demons had the courage to release the hold of their dark masters. And those who made the choice to stand against the demons found themselves feeling energized and lighter during the agonizing battle.

"Roch, Roch," Ibula called as she flew outside the balcony of his hotel room. To her surprise Roch was sleeping on the floor instead of in his large bed. Ibula was not wearing the normal robe of the Ruala warrior, but a light blue dress which Laurel had made. Laurel made three sets of identical dresses for all of the women who would be bait for Roch.

The balcony doors to Roch's room were opened as he often left them. Ibula landed on the balcony and peered into the hotel room. There were three candles that were still lit in the room. These candles gave off enough light for her to read the grizzly messages that Roch had written on the walls of his room. The letters of the words were large and appeared to be written in blood.

Ibula doubted that Roch used his own blood because of the amount that was not only used for the words but had also dripped down the walls. She studied the words so she could memorize them as she was not familiar with the language. "Roch, Roch what has happened to you?" Ibula called from the balcony. Now she heard movement within the room. It sounded as if Roch whimpered then growled then he shot up to a sitting position and looked around.

Roch was lying on the floor on the side of the bed that was away from the balcony doors, so he could not see Ibula immediately. "Roch," Ibula called again. She saw as Roch attempted to stand up but then fell to one knee. The face Ibula saw was not that of a human. It was hollowed and covered with open running soars and great lesions. The creature before her growled like an animal.

"Roch," Ibula said again. As the creature stared at her, his appearance started to transform. Ibula was not sure which was more horrifying, seeing the face of Roch's demon or seeing him resume the mask of a human.

"Vitomas," Roch whispered. "Is that you?"

"Yes," Ibula said softly. Gabriel had warned Ibula about entering Roch's room. She was told to stay on the balcony where the others could watch her.

"Vitomas," he said as he was now able to stand up. "Are you dead? Am I dreaming?"

"Would you not have me dead?"

"For your betrayal," Roch spat with a savage intensity.

"You never loved me; how could I betray you."

"You were mine," he said angrily as he started to walk towards her. "And of all the men you had to run off with it had to be the son of my brother. You betrayed me and humiliated me, you should be punished."

Ibula took a couple of steps backwards as Roch stepped towards her; not out of fear but to get him to walk through the balcony doors so the others could see him without his hat hiding his face. "Roch what has happened to you?" she asked softly.

"What do you mean?" Roch asked gruffly as he continued towards her.

"That was not your face that I first saw."

Roch stopped walking and gave her a blank look. "What are you talking about? Is this some sort of riddle?"

"Roch what is that writing on your walls?"

"It's none of your business," he growled. The closer that Roch got to Ibula the more he was convinced that he was speaking to Vitomas. "You don't seem to be a dream," Roch said then there was a sadness to his voice.

"But you must be dead. I am not surprised that you became an Angel, you always were one. Why do you come to me now?"

"To help you," Ibula said. "You are so lost in the darkness. What happened to you?"

"I'm not sure actually," Roch said in a manner that took Ibula by surprise for he seemed to be speaking sincerely. "So much has happened since you left me. And there is so much I can't remember." As Roch said this he suddenly grabbed his head as if he was in great pain.

"Are you alright?"

"No," he growled. "Does it look like I am alright?"

"Can I help you?"

"Come back to me, Vitomas," Roch said sincerely then he paused and a low maniacal laugh rose within him. A laugh that made Ibula shutter.

"Roch, look for me," she said then quickly flew away.

The next morning Enrops flew outside of Roch's room. One of them reported to Gabriel that Roch was awake and pacing in his room. Ibula had already told the rest of the team about her experience with Roch the previous night. While Raphael researched the words that Ibula saw written on Roch's walls Gabriel planned the next move.

Gabriel told both Hannah and Vitomas to wear the same dress that Ibula had worn the night before. Then Gabriel grabbed a handful of forged deeds, a map and a bag of gold nuggets and walked to Roch's room. Gabriel had barely knocked on the door before it flew open and Roch looked as if he was in a rage.

"I am sorry if I woke you," Gabriel said as he stood in the hallway and Roch stood in the doorway preventing Gabriel from looking into his room. "I wanted to tell you as soon as possible that my brother and I were able to obtain most of the deeds that we wanted and we will be finishing up our business here sooner than we planned."

"Of course we will be returning in a month or two to start the mining process. If there was still that matter you wanted..." Gabriel did not finish his sentence before Roch pushed him out of the way and ran towards Vitomas as he saw her walking further down the hallway towards the steps.

"What is going on?" Gabriel demanded and grabbed Roch's arm. Roch turned and looked at Gabriel and in that moment Vitomas ran into Padre Darius' room which was near the staircase. Roch pulled his arm away from Gabriel and ran down the hallway then down the steps. It was the first time that Roch had been out of his room without wearing his hat. Jared stood at the bottom of the staircase on the first floor. The lobby and dining room were filled with members of Gabriel's team.

Roch ran past Jared and wildly looked around the front lobby of the hotel then he searched the dining room. While he was on the first floor, Vitomas ran down the steps into her room on the third floor. Jared's job was to detain Roch long enough to give Vitomas time to hide.

"What are you staring at?" Roch demanded when he turned around and saw Jared approaching him. Jared was considerably larger than Roch and walked up close to him in an intimidating manner.

"I've been looking for you," Jared said. "You're the face that damn demon kept showing me. What the hell was going on?"

Roch was stunned and a little frightened by Jared's comments. "What are you talking about?"

"Roch you mean you don't recognize me?" Jared asked tauntingly. "Don't give me that crap you haunted me for weeks."

"How do you know my name?" Roch asked before he realized he had exposed his identity.

"You told me; well, it was either you or that damned Ahriman who kept pretending to be you. I don't know what kind of games you are playing but I have half a mind to kill you just to get this over."

"Keep your voice down," Roch said. This giant man knew Ahriman's name and that he was a demon. Roch hoped Jared could give him some answers; answers that would help Roch regain his memories. "Let's talk," Roch said in a low voice and turned and walked into the dining room of the hotel. As Jared walked behind Roch he nodded to Simon who was sitting at one of the tables.

After the waiter left their table, Roch said in a low voice. "Really I don't know what you are talking about but I was a captive of Ahriman's. There are many things that I do not remember. I will pay you to tell me all that you know."

Jared sat back in his chair and stared at Roch as if he did not believe his words. Jared had been instructed to tell Roch everything about the episodes of Roch haunting him, the priests who hired him and his visions of the men who would be vessels. But Jared was not to talk about his contact with the Sanuri or any of Sudfad's family or other members of the team. "I think you're telling the truth," Jared said after a brief pause. "Maybe if I tell you, you can explain to me what the hell was going on."

While Jared talked to Roch in the dining room, Gabriel and Raul quickly searched his hotel room. They found little of significance other than the bloody writings on the wall. "This place really stinks," Raul said as he wrinkled his nose.

"Remember that smell," said Gabriel. "That is the smell of demons, the stench from hell."

"Are you telling me the truth?" Raul asked.

"Yes, you can always smell a demon before you see them," Gabriel said. "Interestingly when Roch appears as a human he does not have that smell."

"As much as I hate him," Raul said as they left Roch's room. "After Ibula got done telling us about what happened. I kind of felt a little sorry for him. Do you think he knows what is happening to him?"

"A person just doesn't get turned into a demon. Roch made his choices. He is responsible for what is happening to him now. Don't let your pity cause you to hesitate if you are in battle with him." Gabriel said as he and Raul walked down the stairs into the front lobby of the hotel. They entered the dining room and Gabriel boldly walked up to Roch. "What the hell happened up there?" Gabriel demanded.

"I thought I saw someone I knew and I wanted to catch up with her," Roch replied.

"In the hallway?" Gabriel asked with a quizzical look on his face.

"Yes," Roch replied tentatively. Roch appeared distressed by the information that Jared was telling him.

"You must be drinking, there was no one in the hallway besides you and me," Gabriel snorted and turned towards Raul. "We can complete our business at the land office." Both Gabriel and Raul walked out of the dining room and out of the hotel. No sooner had they stepped onto the street than Roch pushed passed both of them and ran down the street towards Hannah who was turning a corner, wearing her hair like Vitomas and the same blue dress.

As soon as Hannah disappeared from Roch's sight, Koby picked her up and flew to the top of a building where they both hid. Within moments Roch appeared at the corner. Hannah and Koby watched as he looked around the streets. Roch appeared both panicked and frustrated. Jared laughed as he watched Roch from his seat at a window table in the hotel dining room.

"Gabriel, I am truly impressed," Raul said as they watched Roch. "I knew you were good but I never realized how good at this sort of thing."

"My goal is to get rid of that monster with as few lives lost as possible," Gabriel said. "After seeing that writing on his wall I fear we have a long ways to go yet."

"He must have killed something to get all that blood," Raul said. "But hopefully the men will find out if there have been any suspicious murders lately."

"This is Taperia Raul. There are probably dozens of suspicious murders every day that have no connection to Roch. My concern is the bounty he must pay to complete his transformation. Nothing is free in the underworld. We could likely find a cavern filled with victims for sacrifice."

Chapter XXVIII
Destinies

By midmorning thousands of citizens of Port Friada were filling the streets around Cicero's mansion. Flames and lightening had been seen around the building during the night. But it was what the people saw in the morning light that made them summon Commanding General Amundsen and his troops to the city.

"Never seen anything like this," a man in the crowd said to a woman standing next to him. They were looking at the giant crater in the ground where Cicero's complex once stood.

"Do you think the demons pulled him back to hell?" the woman asked.

"Maybe he can get us some answers now," the man said as he saw the crowd parting to make room for General Amundsen to ride through.

"By the heavens!" Amundsen exclaimed when he saw that the ground around the crater was still smoking. "When was the explosion?"

Many people in the crowd tried to answer Amundsen's questions at the same time. All the people said the same thing; that no one heard an explosion but they saw great bolts of lightning and flames around the complex all night.

Amundsen ordered some of his troops to search the area of the compound for survivors. He ordered other soldiers to speak with the people of Port Friada and to gather as much information as they could. Then Amundsen led a third group of soldiers to the crater. All of the caverns and torture chambers were gone; it appeared that the ground had devoured the entire complex. So massive and deep was the crater that Amundsen ordered a fence to be built around it to prevent anyone from falling in.

"There is nothing left," said a soldier as he reported to Amundsen. "There are no bodies, or weapons, there isn't anything that would show people ever lived here. I've never seen anything like this Sir, why it's the damndest thing."

As large as the crowd was around the complex, everyone was quiet, so quiet that it added to the eeriness of the scene. Suddenly whisperings could be heard in the crowd, then it parted again as High Priest Barnabas and twelve other priests walked up to General Amundsen.

"Do you have any idea what happened here?" Amundsen asked as he saw the smile on Barnabas' face.

"The people of Port Friada came to us," High Priest Barnabas said. "We prayed to The Great Ruler to send us an Angel to rid us of these demons. I believed our prayers were answered."

No sooner had Barnabas said these words than white flower petals rained down upon the crowd. The people were in awe. Then excitement filled their beings and they started to shout, laugh and cry.

"Your Excellency," Amundsen said. "I am not sure that I believe in demons or Angels; but I don't know how to explain any of this either." As the General spoke, a single white feather floated in the air descending past the faces of these two important men. As the feather fell to the ground General Amundsen and High Priest Barnabas stood in awed silence.

"Now you look like the one who is being haunted," Jared said with a laugh when Roch returned to the table in the hotel dining room. "Did you find what you were looking for?"

"No," Roch growled. "Now finish telling me your story."

As Jared and Roch talked in low voices Sophie and Erebus entered the dining room. Sophie stopped in the middle of the dining room and stared at the table, as she recognized Jared.

"What is the matter?" Erebus asked when he saw the look on her face.

"That man that Roch is talking to is one of the vessels," Sophie said frantically. "In fact he had been hired by Meekos. This is a bad sign, Erebus. I'm going to Malik right now and tell him that Roch is here."

"Sophie, calm yourself," Erebus whispered. "If you go now, Roch may suspect your involvement. Let's go to our table and pretend everything is normal then we will go to Malik after lunch."

Roch did not see Sophie's reaction because his back was to her, but Jared did and a grin crossed his face. Sophie and Erebus saw Jared grinning which caused them both to feel uneasy.

"He's not wearing his hat," Sophie whispered to Erebus as they sat down at their usual table. There were only two empty tables that separated the table that Sophie was sitting at and the one that Roch was at. "Why is he not in disguise?" Sophie asked as she felt this too was a bad sign. Erebus and Sophie tried to listen to the conversation between Roch and Jared but the two men were speaking too quietly to be overheard.

"Now you understand that we don't have the books here that we need for this kind of research," Raphael said to the members of Gabriel's team who filled Raphael's and Gabriel's adjoining hotel chambers.

"Also the blood that Roch used to write these words was running down the wall as he wrote," Ibula said so hopefully I read the words correctly.

"Ibula said she saw the word Arimanius written in many areas of the walls," Raphael explained. "This is another name for Ahriman. Remember that the demons, especially the Old Ones have been in existence for centuries. So they have many names by the different peoples of the worlds. Gabriel and I specialized in ancient languages at the monastery and neither of us have seen the next few words before. We believe them to be older than the texts we are familiar with but there still are similarities to other words."

"Ryvviow is similar to the word Ryvow found in the ancient texts of Semalia," Raphael continued to explain. "That word means devastation. Another word that Ibula said was written in particularly large letters is Zaarond. This word has similarities in many ancient texts and they all mean roughly the same thing, the endless darkness. But it is this word that I found particularly interesting," Raphael continued. "Sertaz. In the texts of Semalia this word means betrayer."

"Of course I am just speculating here," Raphael said. "But we know that Roch flourished in Ahriman's hell, which means that he acted in accordance with the demons. This word Sertaz makes me wonder if Roch was told about the Insidiae and their plans for Roch to become a vessel for Omnibus. Perhaps Roch made a deal with Ahriman to come back to this world and wield revenge on the members of the Insidiae.

"But the Insidiae worship the demons, why would Ahriman allow that?" Jared asked.

"The Recupero sect of the Insidiae swears allegiance to only Omnibus, which was an old rival of Ahriman's," said Raphael. "Also demons are empowered by fear and chaos; I would greatly doubt that they feel any loyalty to the humans who worship them."

"I know that Roch is probably a great liar," Jared said. "But damn, the look in his eyes when I was telling him about Ahriman haunting me; I believe he really didn't know some of that stuff. Except for when I talked about Pravis and Tenebrae, he said he didn't know them but the look on his face told me different."

"You all have done well," Gabriel said. "But this is just the beginning of this mission. Now that we have identified Roch, we need to find out if he has a special place planned for the final transformation and if he does, I'll bet we will find people intended for sacrifice. So far everything is going according to plans," Gabriel continued. "Sophie recognized Jared so we believe she will make contact with other members of the Insidiae. Aaron has men following her. Archetenus you're next; do you have any questions before you go down to the tavern?"

"Is it alright if Sophie sees me?"

"Yes," Gabriel said. "In fact it might be rather interesting to see her reaction."

"Does Roch know she is a member of the Insidiae?" asked Archetenus.

"Jared didn't tell him," Gabriel said. "Why?"

"Well as far as we know, Sophie and Erebus are the two closest things Roch has to friends," Archetenus said. "If he finds out that they betrayed him too, well, it just might set him off good."

"I agree with you," said Gabriel. "But while that may work in our favor, we all know that Roch will kill Sophie. We would like her to lead us to other members of the Insidiae before that happens."

"Sophie what are you doing?" Malik asked angrily as she barged into a meeting being held in his office at the Taperian Fortress Bank.

"Malik this is an emergency, we need to talk at once," Sophie said earnestly.

Malik saw the distressed looks on the faces of both Sophie and Erebus and ended his meeting. Sophie did not speak until the people from Malik's meeting left the room and closed the door.

"I am sorry to interrupt your meeting," Sophie said. "But Roch has been returned from Ahriman's hell dimension. He has contacted Erebus and me. We had not said anything because we were trying to figure out what happened to him and what is still happening to him. Then this morning we saw him meeting with one of the vessels, this could be very bad for all of us because Erebus believes Roch made some kind of deal with Ahriman to return here."

Malik was about to speak when Erebus interrupted him. "There is a strange aura around Roch, the likes I have never seen before. I think Roch is either turning into a demon or is already a vessel for a demon."

Malik stood up and walked over to a side table and poured three glasses of whiskey. He looked pale when he turned around and handed Sophie and Erebus each a glass. "Tell me everything," Malik said. "Even the slightest detail." The three became so engrossed in their conversation that they did not notice the Enrops outside of Malik's open window.

Gabriel was expecting Roch to be upset enough about seeing Vitomas and meeting Jared that he would want a drink. After the meeting, Archetenus walked down to the tavern which was on the first floor of the Taperian Imperial Hotel, just off from the dining room. Archetenus chose a table that gave him a good view of the entire room and the only entrance to the tavern.

Although it was early afternoon, most of the tables in the tavern were filled and men were standing along the bar. As Gabriel predicted, it wasn't long before Roch entered the room. He initially stood in the doorway and surveyed the room before walking up to the bar. Roch was wearing his hat that was pulled down tightly over his head to conceal much of his face.

Roch did not notice Archetenus the first time he looked over the patrons in the crowded room. Roch ordered his drink then turned around to look at the people again when he saw Archetenus staring at him. Roch quickly turned back towards the bar as he was deciding his next move. After a few moments Roch picked up his drink and turned and walked to Archetenus' table.

"Roch I hope you don't think that damn hat hides who you are," Archetenus said smugly.

"Who says I am trying to hide who I am?" Roch asked as he sat down at the table across from Archetenus.

"Well, I've been hearing a lot of different stories about you for some time. Some say you are dead, some say you are a demon now, but they all say you lost your throne. I will say I never thought you would give up that throne without a fight. And now I see you sneaking around in disguise; I guess you aren't the man I thought you were." Archetenus smiled because he could see the anger in Roch's face. But Roch did not speak. "So just for curiosity which story is true?"

"You know I always hated you because of your feelings for Vitomas. When she disappeared I thought you had her."

"I did. So why didn't you come after us?"

"I had men searching for her," Roch replied angrily.

"Well, Prince Raul searched for her himself and found her, guess that shows the difference between the two of you." Archetenus was deliberately trying to irritate Roch.

"So he took her from you?" Roch asked in disbelief.

"No, once I got alone with Vitomas she told me how much she loved Raul and I was taking her to Wetpr when he found us. In fact Vitomas told me quite a few things while we were traveling. Like of your conspiracies to have me murdered. She said you were jealous of my popularity among the citizens and the loyalty the men had for me. I'll tell you I am not sad at seeing you now," Archetenus started to laugh. "The powerful dictator, you've lost everything and you are too afraid to show your face in the city you once ruled."

Roch jumped up and bumped the table so hard that he spilled the drinks. Roch lunged at Archetenus who had anticipated this move and already had a knife drawn from its sheath. Archetenus grabbed Roch by the throat and pushed the tip of his knife against the corner of Roch's left eye socket. "Do you want to be a blind beggar too?" Archetenus asked through clenched teeth. Roch stood motionless. "Now why don't you just take your seat and order us a couple of more drinks," Archetenus said.

Archetenus was getting great satisfaction from humiliating Roch, who returned to his seat without speaking. "You were never man enough to kill me yourself," Archetenus said. "That's why you had to conspire behind my back."

Roch stared at Archetenus angrily; then after a few moments Roch's demeanor changed. "Everything you have said is true, except for the reasons I conspired to have you killed. And you are correct I won't give up my throne without a fight. You and I have always hated each other and probably always will; but we know that we are both fierce warriors. I am making plans on getting my throne back and I need men who can fight. And you could probably steal many of the soldiers away from Hamond. I will pay you a fortune for your help."

Archetenus stared at Roch for a few moments. "First of all would I have to be worried that you would stick a knife in my back and secondly you lost your fortune."

"I have funds. And I have access to the castle. Sophie stole keys for me. And as for the other, perhaps we could make a truce. We could both benefit from this and when it's over we both go our separate ways."

"You mean you would be kicking me out of the kingdom once you regained control," Archetenus said with a grin.

"Would you really want to stay here?" Roch asked slyly.

"No, you've got a point there," said Archetenus. "Let me think about it. But first I have a couple of questions. I don't really give a damn about what you do with Hamond or even if you get your throne back. But while I was traveling, let's just say I met some interesting beings; and I heard that not only were you under the control of a demon at the castle but that you had become a demon. Roch as much as I hate you as a man, I hate demons more. You might say I have met more than I care for; so tell me up front if I agree to work for you am I working for a man or for a demon?"

"I've sent for more troops from the monastery at Philiste to assist with capturing members of the Insidiae," Raphael told Gabriel. "The Sanuri is at our headquarters in Nora and wants our prisoners transported there. King Sudfad will have troops waiting at the border to help our men transport the prisoners."

"Has Malik called a meeting yet?" Gabriel asked.

"Not that we know of," Raphael said. "But we are expecting him to soon. The Enrops said that he appeared very upset at what Sophie and Erebus were telling him about Roch."

There was a knock at the door to Gabriel's room. Gabriel opened the door and allowed Simon to enter the room. "Well, everything seems to be going as you thought," Simon said with a grin. "Roch is sitting with Archetenus in the tavern and Roch does not look happy."

"Wouldn't you think Roch would question all of these things happening in such a short period of time?" Raphael asked.

"Vitomas said that although he would carefully think out his plans he rarely questioned anything else that happened around him," Simon said. "Guess he is too self-absorbed."

"I am just hoping he still reacts as the man he was before," Gabriel said. "He may change greatly as the transformation progresses."

"Can I help with anything now?" Simon asked.

"Raphael is taking over the mission of tracking down the members of the Insidiae and I will continue to run the mission for Roch. Since you are more familiar with this area and Sophie than Raphael is, perhaps you can help him now. Raphael is trying to determine likely meeting places of the Insidiae so he can set up ambush sites," Gabriel said.

"Right up my alley," Simon said. "Saddle up and we'll go for a ride."

"Just stay out of that cave where Ahriman has torn a hole between the worlds," Gabriel warned. "I don't want the two of you sucked into hell."

As Gabriel started to knock on the door to Raul and Vitomas' hotel room he heard laughter. "A, its Gabriel is this a good time?"

"Come in," Raul called out.

When Gabriel entered the room he saw Raul and Vitomas dancing. "You two look like you are enjoying yourselves," Gabriel said with a smile as he closed the door.

"Oh, we are," Vitomas said. "This is a little like a second honeymoon."

"Honey that sounds kind of pathetic," Raul said. "Guess I need to take you on a real second honeymoon when all of this is over."

Raul and Vitomas stopped dancing and walked up to Gabriel. "First Simon and Raphael are riding around the countryside looking for possible sites where the Insidiae might meet then ambush sites near those locations."

"Secondly, Archetenus is talking with Roch in the tavern downstairs and Simon said that Roch certainly did not look happy. And thirdly, do you think you are up for another sighting?" Gabriel asked.

"Yes," Vitomas said happily. "I know this mission is dangerous but truly I am having fun."

"Raul you really have to take your wife out more," Gabriel joked.

"I am realizing that by the minute," Raul said as he hugged Vitomas.

"The fact that Ibula saw Roch's demon face concerns me," Gabriel said. "So I am expediting our schedule a bit. I told Archetenus that I might have you make another appearance while he is with Roch. Roch is seated so he has a view of the lobby. I will go down to the lobby and if Roch is still in the tavern, I would like you to walk out onto the street and turn left and Koby will grab you as soon as you are out the door."

"What about people on the street seeing Koby?" Raul asked. "Unless it is Sophie or Erebus I don't think I care anymore. I am just concerned in finding Roch's lair before the transformation is completed."

It was obvious to Archetenus that Roch was trying to contain his anger and choose his words carefully; which made Archetenus realize that Roch must be really desperate for his help. "There was a demon at the castle for a while," Roch admitted. "He took over Jonas' body for a long time before his true identity was revealed. And as for your other question do I look like a damn demon?"

"Roch you have always acted like one, it's hard to tell," Archetenus said with a grin. "I will help you but the first time you betray me I will kill you, do you understand?"

"As I will you," Roch said. "I need an army if I am to retake my throne. As you have guessed I am trying to keep my identity a secret until..." Roch did not complete his sentence.

456

He stood up and ran out of the tavern, through the lobby and out of the front door of the hotel. Roch looked both ways down the street but no longer saw the woman he thought was Vitomas so he returned to his table in the tavern.

"What the hell was that about?" Archetenus asked gruffly. Then when he saw how white Roch's face was he added, "You look like you have seen a ghost. Are you sure you are alright?"

"It's nothing," Roch said. "Maybe I am seeing ghosts."

Archetenus poured more whiskey into both of their glasses and asked, "So tell me how the hell did Hamond get your throne anyways? I know Cerephus had raised an army and was planning to kill you but I never heard about Hamond doing anything."

"What did you say?" Roch was choking on his whiskey as he spoke.

"I said Cerephus was plotting to overthrow you for years, in fact a lot of the guys, me included were waiting for him to do it. He had more than half of your army willing to follow him."

"What!" yelled Roch.

"Hell, you were gone all of the time and left him in charge; he had plenty of time to work on getting allies. And Vitomas told me he was stealing from you all of the time and you never realized it."

"She never told me."

"Why the hell would she," Archetenus said with disgust. "You should have been killed a hundred times for the way you treated that girl. She was the best thing that ever happened to you and you were too damn arrogant to realize it. You should have seen it when Raul found us. I won't lie to you I was in love with Vitomas but the look in her eyes when she saw him. I didn't like it, but later I felt good that for the first time in her life she was happy and safe. I heard they got two sons and a daughter now and I am damn happy for them."

"Archetenus I know you are just talking about her to anger me," Roch said. "So change the subject. I want to hear more about Cerephus."

"He came to many of the men and offered them more money to work for him."

"But my men were loyal to me," Roch said angrily.

"You really are crazy," Archetenus said. "Most all of them thought you were insane but they stayed for the money. You know the reason I asked you about that demon was I have run into some of the men in my travels. Several of them told me they left you because you were riding with a slimy demon and that none of them trusted you at all. I'm telling you this because it may be harder to raise an army than you think. Your boys may just a soon stay with Hamond."

As Archetenus was talking Roch appeared deep in thought. "Erebus, I should have known." Roch said angrily.

"What are you talking about?" Archetenus asked.

"Cerephus brought Erebus to the castle; they were close friends, now he pretends to be my friend."

"Face it Roch you have no friends, the way you treat people," Archetenus said. "I'm serious; people are around you for two reasons, fear or profit; certainly you know that."

Roch looked up as he saw Erebus and Sophie walk into the dining room. "That's him," Roch said.

"Archetenus turned and looked into the dining room. "You mean the guy with Sophie?"

"Yes."

"Well that makes sense," Archetenus said then took a gulp of his whiskey.

"What do you mean?"

"It's just amazing that you had no idea what was going on around you. I'm not going to spoil the surprise, why don't you ask Sophie who she really works for." Archetenus said and stood up. "I told a lady I would meet her for dinner, I will see you around."

Archetenus left the tavern and walked up the stairs to Gabriel's room. When he entered the room he found it full of people who were talking and laughing. "Well, he didn't change in front of me," Archetenus announced as he took a seat. "But I sure went out of my way to piss him off."

"It's just a theory I have," Gabriel said. "The farther he gets in his transformation I believe it will be harder for him to maintain his human appearance. I am speculating that he has to concentrate on keeping that appearance and if he gets upset he may show his true self."

"Well, we started out with him trying to attack me; I pulled a knife on him. Then he offered me a job to help him raise an army. We talked a lot and just about everything I said made him mad but he was trying to hold his temper. I thought it was because he wanted my help but maybe you are right," Archetenus said, then he started to laugh. "You should have seen his face when he saw Vitomas; he turned white as a sheet."

"Yeah as quickly as he came out of that tavern I was afraid he might see Koby grab her from the street," Gabriel said. "I was watching from the lobby."

"He almost did," Koby said. "Fortunately Vitomas was moving quickly."

"Roch told me something that I didn't know," Archetenus said. "I asked him how Hamond got the throne when it was Cerephus who spent years plotting to get it. Well, Roch didn't know anything about that then he gets mad again and says that Cerephus brought Erebus to the castle and they were close friends."

"You mean Sophie's husband?" Gabriel asked.

"Yes, then Roch says that Erebus is acting like his friend. I told Roch he has no friends and that Sophie wasn't who he thought she was either. So I would expect some fireworks now."

Roch gulped down his drink then marched over to Sophie's and Erebus' table. "I just had the most interesting conversation with Archetenus," Roch said as he sat down at their table.

"Archetenus, he's alive?" Sophie asked with surprise.

"He looked damn alive to me," Roch said. "I just hired him to help me raise an army. While we were taking he tells me that Cerephus was plotting to overthrow me for years. Is that true Erebus?" When Roch saw the look in both Erebus' and Sophie's eyes he knew Archetenus was telling the truth.

"I don't know anything about that," Erebus said.

"You're a damn liar," Roch roared. Then he turned to Sophie. "And Sophie don't you think it's time you told me who you really work for? Were you a spy in my castle all those years?"

Sophie's face turned white, she composed herself then looked Roch in the eyes. "Now you will find out who I work for." As Sophie said this a group of men grabbed Roch. Two men slipped a noose over his neck and pulled it tightly as others tied his hands and legs. Roch yelled and cursed as they dragged him out of the hotel.

One of the Wetprian soldiers burst into Gabriel's room. "A group of men have Roch and they are dragging him out of the hotel."

"Don't stop them, follow them," Gabriel said. "I'll bet they're Insidiae." Several Ruala warriors flew out of the room to follow Roch. Gabriel called to some Enrops and told them to follow Roch also. "I'm going down to the dining room to find out what happened," Gabriel said. Raul, Jared and Archetenus all stood up. "I don't want you coming with me, we can't look like we know each other. Wait and then come down individually," Gabriel said.

"I can come with you," Hannah said as she grabbed her shawl and the two walked out of the hotel room.

460

"Let go of me," Roch screamed as the group of men carried him to a covered boca that was outside of the hotel. The driver of the boca was waiting and as soon as Roch and six of the other men were in the back of the boca the driver sped through the streets of Taperia. The rest of the group of men followed the boca on horseback.

The boca and riders were moving quickly as they left the city; they almost ran over Simon and Raphael who were returning to the hotel. When Raphael and Simon saw Enrops and Ruala warriors following the group, they turned their horses around and also followed the boca, but they were careful to keep enough of a distance as not to appear suspicious.

When Gabriel and Hannah arrived in the dining room, Sophie and Erebus were still seated at their table, acting as if nothing had happened. Because few people were in the dining room at that time of day, Gabriel and Hannah were able to get a window table near Sophie and Erebus.

"Are you alright?" Erebus asked Sophie with concern.

"Yes, yes," Sophie said as she appeared to be catching her breath. "You were right I should have gone to Malik sooner. Well now he knows, we will have to leave here soon."

"Sophie I suspect that Roch has known for a while but he was waiting until he no longer had a need for us," Erebus said. "Tomorrow get Malik to write a new letter for Teivel and we will leave for Ryed as soon as possible."

Gabriel was listening to their conversation and his interest peaked when he heard Erebus mention Teivel's name. "Why do you think we need another letter?" Sophie asked.

"I want Malik to include that you helped to capture Roch and hopefully Teivel will leave you alone. If that doesn't work, then perhaps Malik is right and we will have to live someplace else. After all that you have done you would think they would let you out of that damn organization," Erebus said angrily.

461

"Well if they kill Roch right away we could stay here too," Sophie said. "Or Port Friada was a beautiful city."

"Sophie are you sure you are alright?" Erebus said. "You aren't looking well."

"I'm fine," she said. "I feel relieved and guilty at the same time." Sophie's attention was drawn to movement at the front of the dining room as people were entering. Raul and Vitomas were both in disguise and joined Gabriel and Hannah at their table. "Erebus something isn't right here," Sophie said in a lowered voice. "There's Archetenus and Jared. They don't seem to be together but why would two vessels show up here on the same day and both talk to Roch?"

An Enrop flew down to Raphael and Simon and said. "Dagon says you should stay back. Those men just dragged Roch out of the hotel. Gabriel thinks they are Insidiae. We will follow them."

"You're right," Raphael said. "We will return to the hotel and wait for word of their location." Raphael and Simon turned around and resumed their journey to Taperia. "This may be the most fortunate stroke of luck yet," Raphael said. "To get Roch and a sect of the Insidiae."

"I hope you are right," Simon said. "But I have to tell you that I have a bad feeling about all of this."

Malik's men traveled fast, they rode straight north from Taperia, crossed the River Neior then entered the Mangee Forest, where the density of the trees and brush forced them to slow down. Once they entered the forest the Ruala warriors flew much lower to the ground and concealed themselves in the canopies of the trees. Malik's men continued to travel in a northerly direction for almost twenty minutes before they stopped at a huge log cabin.

462

Dagon, Koby and the other Ruala warriors and Enrops watched as the men carried Roch out of the boca and into the cabin. Roch appeared to be unconscious; not only did Roch have his ankles and wrists bound but Malik's men had wrapped chains around his entire body while he was in the boca. There was also a rope and a chain around Roch's neck.

"Arie go to Raphael and Gabriel and tell them this location and what you have seen. We will stay here," Dagon said to a large Enrop who was perched in the tree next to him. Arie and a dozen other Enrops left for Taperia. Koby did not want the remaining Enrops to fly too close to the cabin, since members of the Insidiae would recognize the significance of Enrops in the area.

After five minutes all of the members of the Insidiae had gone inside of the cabin. They did not post any guards around the perimeter of the structure. Koby now told a few of the Enrops to peek into the windows of the cabin. Four Enrops quickly flew past the windows and returned to the Ruala warriors.

"They have Roch chained to the wall," Uma said. "From what we could see it looked as if the others are just sitting around and talking."

"They must be waiting for a superior to arrive," Dagon said.

Almost an hour passed before Arie returned. "Raphael, Simon and Aaron are on their way with an army of Patronus priests but there is a carriage travelling on the road between them and you. Raphael believes the people in the carriage are coming here and he does not want to alert them, so he and his men are not travelling quickly."

Matthew, Angelina and Sorren stayed at the hotel to protect Vitomas. Jared and Archetenus were within eyesight of Sophie. Jared sat at a table in the dining room and stared at her, while Archetenus sat at a table in the tavern that gave him a good view of Sophie's table. Gabriel wanted the men to stare at Sophie; Gabriel was hoping this maneuver would upset her and she might reveal some information.

Gabriel, Hannah, Raul and Vitomas sat at a table near Sophie and Erebus so they could listen to their conversation.

"Sophie you are being silly," Erebus said. "Why would two of the vessels be interested in you?"

"Well, if they know I am a member of the Insidiae that created them, they might be," she said nervously. "What if they are working with Roch and planning revenge on the Insidiae?"

"First do you even know if those two men are aware they are vessels? And secondly the Insidiae is such a secretive society it is unlikely any of them know about it," Erebus said. "Now have another glass of wine to calm your nerves."

"I wish I never would have joined the Insidiae," Sophie said as she took a sip of her wine.

"So do I my dear, so do I."

Dagon, Koby and the other Ruala warriors and Enrops remained hidden in the foliage of the forest that surrounded the log cabin. Almost twenty minutes after Arie's message, an elegant carriage stopped in front of the cabin. There was a man who looked like a hired fighter sitting in the passenger seat next to the driver. Another man who also looked like a body guard stepped out of the carriage and looked around before he allowed Malik to exit.

"That makes twenty-two, not counting Roch," Koby whispered to Dagon. "And some of those guys look like vessels." Koby left the tree top he had been sitting in and flew down to the road to meet Raphael and his men.

"You were right, that carriage came here. Looks like one of the men in it is important and the others were his body guards," Koby said. "So far we have counted twenty-two men, about half look like vessels, and Roch. They have Roch tied up with ropes and chains and they chained him to the back wall of the cabin. He was unconscious when they carried him in, he might be drugged."

Raphael ordered his men to surround the cabin but to stay out of sight. "Have you heard anything in there?" Raphael asked.

"No, it's been completely quiet," Koby responded.

"Maybe they have moved him underground," said Raphael. "Have a couple of Enrops look into the windows. I don't want to advance on them without knowing where they are."

Arie flew to Raphael and Koby, "Something is going on inside of the cabin; it sounds like a fight."

"Sound the horn," Raphael ordered. And the priest behind him blew the Horn of Asher, signaling the Patronus warriors to attack. Simon and Raphael charged at the front door of the cabin with swords drawn. Ruala warriors and Enrops descended on the cabin. Patronus warriors kicked in the front and back doors of the cabin almost simultaneously, while Ruala warriors and Enrops flew in through the windows. As one they stopped and stared at the carnage before them.

"Is he here?" Raphael yelled as they turned over the remnants of bodies.

"How could he get out of here?" Simon asked loudly as he too was sorting through the corpses to find Roch.

"He's transformed," Raphael said. "We are too late."

"The hotel," Simon said. "He will go after Sophie now." The Patronus and Ruala warriors ran out of the cabin and raced towards Taperia.

Chapter XXIX
Dues

"Great Ruler be with us," Raphael prayed as they sped back to the Taperian Imperial Hotel. Raphael sent Enrops ahead to warn Gabriel and the others that Roch had transformed into a demon. Simon sent Enrops to his father to warn the family about Roch.

"I don't understand how we didn't see him," Simon said. "Is he invisible now?"

"Who knows," said Raphael. "We don't know what kind of demon he is or the powers he possess. If Ahriman sent him back to this world to create chaos and destruction, Roch might be very powerful."

"And how does Ahriman benefit from that?" Simon asked with disgust.

"Demons are empowered by fear," Raphael said. "Ahriman has lost much of his power; perhaps he thought this would help him."

"But didn't Ahriman release Roch before The Lion attacked Ahriman?"

"Yes, but Ahriman has not lost control of Roch just because he is in this world."

Arie flew into the lobby of the Taperian Imperial Hotel, then he turned to the left and flew into the dining room and landed on Gabriel's table. The room was filled with various members of Gabriel's team, all of whom were seated at tables. The fact that the Enrop had made such a blatant entrance gave all of the team members cause for concern.

"Is Raphael alright?" Gabriel quickly asked.

"Yes, none of his army was hurt, but all the Insidiae are dead and Roch is missing," Arie said. "Raphael believes that Roch has transformed and is heading back to this hotel for Sophie. Raphael and his men are on their way here."

"Thank you," Gabriel said. "Please tell as many of my team as you can find." Then Gabriel stood up, the urgency of the situation far surpassed the need for secrecy now. "Roch has transformed, he murdered the Insidiae and Raphael believes he is headed back here. Matthew, Sorren, Angelina and Raul, take Vitomas and Hannah to our room and be prepared for anything. Do not leave that room unless Raphael or I send you word," Gabriel announced loudly.

Erebus entered the dining room. Sophie was not feeling well so he had walked her to their room and returned to the dining room to eat his meal. Gabriel quickly walked up to him. "Erebus, Roch has transformed into a demon and has killed the men who took him, we believe he is headed back here to get Sophie," Gabriel said earnestly.

"Who are you and how do you know these things?" Erebus asked suspiciously.

"I am High Priest Gabriel of the Patronus and my team and I have been hunting Roch to stop him from turning into a demon. Now take me to your room." Erebus did not move. "Erebus there is no time to waste." Gabriel yelled with frustration. Then Gabriel turned back to the dining room and called, "Jared, Archetenus, Amos and Caleb come with me." Gabriel pushed past Erebus and ran up the stairs to the fifth floor of the hotel. Erebus now ran behind them.

"Betrayer," Roch spat angrily.

Sophie was lying down on the bed and jumped up when she heard Roch's voice. She looked around the room but did not see anything. An overwhelming presence of evil filled the room and fear gripped Sophie's heart.

"You spied on me for the Insidiae," Roch yelled. "All of those years you lived in my castle and acted like a friend. And now you have betrayed me again. I will send you to meet your brother and those two other hypocritical priests."

"Roch what are you saying?" Sophie wanted to stall for time as she was mumbling a protection spell.

"Turn around woman and see your judgment," Roch growled. Sophie spun around and gasped. Roch stood before her covered with the sediment of hell. A foul smelling black tar-like substance dripped from his body. His head was enlarged and his body was covered with long hair like an animal. His limbs were gnarled and his fingernails were so long they were curling under.

"When my master gave me a choice I was no longer the victim in hell. I tortured the others, a job I relished. Ahriman gave Pravis and Tenebrae to me; he said I would find them interesting. They told me everything about you and Meekos and the Insidiae. Now let me show you how I paid them back." Roch held out his arms exposing web-like flaps of skin between the sides of his body and his arms.

These pieces of skin resembled wings and suddenly openings appeared in them; openings into hell. Sophie stood in horror as she watched images of her brother Meekos and his associates High Priest Pravis and High Priest Tenebrae screaming in agony as their bodies were being torn apart.

"Roch no, please I can explain," Sophie begged.

"Sophie let us in," Gabriel called through the closed door. Erebus was trying desperately to unlock the door to his hotel room without success. When the key would not release the lock, Erebus tried a spell. Sophie screamed, and Jared pushed past Erebus and kicked the door open.

Roch stood over Sophie's dismembered body with the wildness of an animal that has just killed its prey. "No! No!" Erebus screamed and started to run forward but Gabriel held him back. "Everyone stand your ground," Gabriel said as he stared into the eyes of the monster.

"Great Ruler we need your presence here," Gabriel said and High Priests Amos and Caleb began to pray out loud and in unison. Roch laughed a loud, maniacal laugh then he began to growl. "Demon you have no power here," Gabriel said sternly. "You are just a puppet of Ahriman's and he is powerless against The Great Ruler as are you."

Suddenly the room filled with laughter, but it was not Roch who was laughing. "So we meet again priest," Ahriman said. The demon that Roch had become knelt down before the unseen presence of the demon Ahriman.

"What, you are not impressed with my creation?" Ahriman asked mockingly.

"Ahriman you will not win this battle," Gabriel said. "Be gone and take your play thing with you."

"Play thing, my you speak boldly," Ahriman said. "Perhaps you won't be so cocky when I tell my play thing that you have Sudfad's family and your lovely wife hidden in your hotel room. Your wife helped you escape from me before; that will not happen again."

"Roch, Vitomas and her husband are in the priest's room. And the priest's wife is the sister of that little girl who gave you so much pleasure in Nora. I told you I would reward you for your services." In an instant Roch disappeared and Ahriman's laughter followed Gabriel and the others as they ran out of the room and down two flights of stairs.

"Lion help us," Gabriel screamed with fear as he ran, never had he felt fear like this before. Although Gabriel was moving quickly he felt as if he was in a dream moving in slow motion. Archetenus, Jared and High Priests Amos and Caleb followed Gabriel. Erebus fell to his knees and wept over the bloody body of his wife.

Vitomas screamed when she felt an unseen hand touch her. When she looked at her right arm it was bleeding. "He's here," Vitomas screamed again as she saw Raul fly through the air and hit the wall. Raul was pressed against the wall and blood was running from his mouth and nose. "Roch it is me that you want, leave the others alone," Vitomas yelled.

Sorren, Angelina and Matthew had swords in their hands but they could not see their enemy. "Roch be a man and show yourself," Hannah said with hatred in her voice. "Long have I waited to look upon you." Roch materialized and when he did Raul fell to the floor.

"Finally your true self is revealed for all to see," Hannah said tauntingly as she was trying to distract the demon.

"Miranda please we need you," Angelina prayed as she stared in horror at the hideous monster before them.

Vitomas ran to Raul, "He's dead," she screamed and grabbed Raul's sword. Before anyone else could move Vitomas turned and plunged the sword into Roch. Sorren, Matthew and Angelina all ran forward as one and attacked Roch, who laughed at their ignorance.

Gabriel and the others barged into the room and saw the battle before them. They too, grabbed their swords and attacked the monster from hell. Ahriman's presence filled the hotel. Doors were opening and closing. Pictures were flying off from the walls and dishes off from shelves. People were running out of the hotel screaming when Raphael, Simon and the others rode up to the front door. Simon and Raphael jumped off from their horses and ran into the hotel.

Hannah ran to Raul, who suddenly opened his eyes. He grabbed for his sword but Vitomas had it as she repeatedly stabbed the monster. Ahriman's laughter was getting louder and louder as the fear of many empowered him. When Simon and Raphael entered the room, the doors and windows suddenly closed and locked. Raul ran forward and pulled Vitomas away from Roch, pushing her behind him. Raul took his sword from her hands and just as he was leaping at the demon, the air in the room became thick, a thickness that was so intense that it stopped the movements of all including the demon Roch.

"It must be my birthday," Ahriman said happily. "I have three of The Seven Sons in my trap, and two powerful priests. I could not have planned this any better. Let me just relish the moment," Ahriman said and laughed loudly.

Members of Gabriel's team were pounding on the door and windows to the room but they could not get in. Gabriel and the others could not speak to warn them. "Your friends think they can save you," Ahriman said sarcastically. "I've always admired loyalty. You are such ignorant fools to think you can defeat me, me! The Master of Demons, The Originator of Darkness. There is no escape for your world. You are mine now and forever."

"How you like to talk," The Lion said as he materialized in the hotel room. Miranda and Daniel also materialized and softly touched each person in the room breaking the demon's spell. Ahriman screamed with rage. So powerful was his anger that the entire hotel shook to its foundation. "Ahriman have you learned nothing?" The Lion asked with great authority. "You instill an illusion of power and fear in a war you will never win."

"You cannot stop me!" Ahriman screamed. "Leave here now, they are mine."

"Make me," The Lion said and started to glow with a transparency only known in heaven.

Roch growled at the Angel; Miranda and Daniel drew their swords and stepped forward.

"Please," Raul yelled. "He is mine."

"Very well," Miranda said and touched the tip of Raul's sword. Raul felt as if he was losing consciousness for a moment as the holiness surged through him. "Now it is an equal playing field." Miranda said. "But there are many more demons in here than the one standing before you."

"Then touch us all," Sorren said and tightened his grip on the hilt of his sword.

Daniel smiled, "It is done." And with his words the doors and windows unlocked; and the army of demons in the hotel were exposed by the light. "Fight with courage," Daniel said. "For you have holiness in your hands."

Ten thousand demons filled that hotel; Gabriel's team numbered five hundred human, Shettee and Ruala warriors. But not one warrior relinquished to the fear in their hearts. They charged the demons and the holiness of their swords destroyed the darkness.

"He is mine," The Lion said of Ahriman. The great demon materialized before them. As Ahriman grew in size he burst through the ceiling and the roof of the hotel. Plaster and boards rained down on the combatants.

471

The Lion did not increase his size; he leaped and grabbed the demon by the throat. The worlds shook with their fury.

Miranda and Daniel fought at the sides of the children of The Great Ruler. The hell dimensions quaked with the intensity of the fight. When other Old Ones realized what was happening they sent their minions to join the battle, to overthrow the Angels and the meager army of beings.

Raul and Roch eyed each other as they both crouched and circled around the other. Their hatred was overwhelming. Like Ahriman, Roch started to grow in size, a trick to intimidate his opponent. As a man Roch was a powerful warrior but his strength was his rage. Raul was trained well in many disciplines, he was strong, fast and he thought quickly on his feet.

"I have waited a long time for this; when I have killed you I will rape your mother and kill your father," Roch said tauntingly as he was trying to force Raul to lose his concentration.

"You have obviously never met my mother," Raul said. "She would kill you with the ease of a warrior."

Roch lunged at Raul, who did a forward roll to the right and missed being gouged by the claws of the great beast. Raul thrust his sword into the leg of the demon and black tar oozed from the wound. Roch had not lost any of his speed with his increased size; he spun around and sliced the air with his fingernails as Raul jumped backwards.

"The only reason my father has allowed you to live," Raul taunted. "Is because The Lion would not let us kill you before this day."

Roch snorted and growled, suddenly his tongue sprang out of his mouth and enveloped Raul, picking him up and pulling him towards the demon's mouth. Roch was squeezing the life out of Raul who was losing consciousness.

"Raul!" screamed Vitomas.

Archetenus was fighting near the leg of the great beast, he now turned and leapt into the air and sliced Roch's tongue with a single blow of his sword. Roch screamed in pain. Raul regained consciousness when he hit the floor. The end of Roch's tongue which was still wrapped tightly around Raul's body did not immediately die when separated from its master. Archetenus ran his sword through the remnant of the tongue multiple times, until Raul could free his arms. Raul too stabbed the tongue and it finally released its grip upon him.

With Archetenus and Raul's focus on the tip of his tongue, Roch bent down and grabbed at Archetenus. Simon jumped onto the arm of the great beast and plunged his sword into it. Matthew and Sorren turned from the demons they were fighting and ran up to Roch. Matthew jumped up and grabbed onto one of the large folds of skin that connected the demons' arms to the sides of his body.

Roch shook his arm trying to dislodge Simon who was repeatedly plunging his sword into Roch's arm. When Roch raised his arm, Matthew swung himself off the flap of skin and grabbed a tuff of the demon's hair. Matthew climbed up the left side of the demon's body towards the demon's head.

Roch shook his arm again and Simon flew off and fell to the ground. Raul was now free of the tongue and he ran to Roch's right leg and started to climb up the demon. Sorren was already racing up Roch's left leg. Simon was momentarily stunned from the fall. Archetenus helped Simon to his feet and the two warriors charged at the demon Roch. They grabbed onto the huge tuffs of hair that covered the demon's body and climbed upward.

Elan and Cassandra fought side by side. Since they could not enter Gabriel's room by the locked balcony doors; Cassandra and Elan burst their way through balcony doors on the fourth floor and fought their way down a landing of stairs to the third floor and to Gabriel's room. Both were well trained fighters but neither Elan nor Cassandra had fought against demons before. Elan continuously shifted his attention to Cassandra because of his feelings to protect her.

"Use your swords," Gabriel yelled into the hallway. "They have been blessed."

Cassandra had dropped her sword and was fighting with her knife before Gabriel yelled out. Elan quickly grabbed Cassandra's sword from the floor and threw it to her. A demon tried to grab the sword but quickly pulled its arm back in pain. The demon's hand started to smoke from the touch of holiness. In that moment when Elan was throwing the sword to Cassandra, a demon sliced Elan's left arm off at the shoulder.

"Elan!" Cassandra screamed and flew to his side. "She pulled her crystal necklace off from her neck and pressed it against Elan's wound. Then she cut Elan's crystal necklace off his neck and pressed that against his wound also. Elan's robe was soaked with blood, as Cassandra picked him up and flew above the battle into Gabriel's room. "Hannah!" Cassandra screamed. "Help me!"

Hannah could hear the fear and panic in Cassandra's voice but she could not immediately see her in the chaos. Then out of a cloud of smoke Hannah saw Cassandra carrying Elan's bloody body and Hannah's heart sank in her chest. "Put him on the bed," Hannah screamed as she ran for her medical bag. A demon lunged at Hannah but Gabriel cut its head off before Hannah realized she was being attacked.

"Vitomas help me!" Hannah screamed as she ran back to Elan.

"Go!" Jared shouted as he plunged his sword into the demon that Vitomas had been fighting with. Vitomas ran through the crowd.

"I'm going back for his arm," Cassandra cried hysterically and disappeared into the battle.

"Vitomas press this against his shoulder," Hannah said as she handed Vitomas a thick bandage that contained holy crystals. A demon lunged at the bed; Koby tackled the demon and plunged his sword into its back.

"I'll stand guard," Koby yelled to Hannah as he pushed the demon's body away from the bed. "Dagon," Koby yelled through the din. "Dagon, the bed."

Dagon heard Koby's voice and rose above the demon he was fighting. Dagon quickly moved behind the demon and cut its throat then he flew to Koby. Anger welled in Dagon when he saw Elan's unconscious and bloody body. "Ibula! Ibula!" Dagon screamed as he fought with a demon that was trying to grab Vitomas. "Ibula! Ibula!"

"Ibula and Cassandra arrived at Elan's bedside simultaneously. Cassandra was crying so hard that she did not see the demon that plunged his knife into the calf of her right leg. Ibula spun around and cut the demon's head off.

"Can you help him?" Cassandra cried as she placed Elan's severed arm on the bed.

"Vitomas take care of Cassandra's leg," Ibula said. "Let Hannah and me work on Elan."

Matthew, Sorren, Simon, Archetenus and Raul climbed up Roch's body as the demon kept growing in size. All five of the men stabbed Roch repeatedly as they climbed. Matthew was the first to reach Roch's neck and he plunged his sword into Roch's neck several times then jumped up and grabbed Roch's ear and climbed up the ear. Matthew then plunged his sword into Roch's left eye and the demon screamed in pain and rage. Matthew pulled his sword out and plunged it two, three, four more times into the demon's eye.

Sorren hung on to the demon's hair with his left hand and plunged his sword into Roch's lungs with his right. Raul quickly climbed past Sorren. Roch attempted to grab Raul with his right hand but Simon and Archetenus both stabbed Roch repeatedly in his right arm and hand, giving Raul time to ascend up the monster.

Matthew was climbing up the back of Roch's head. Raul now reached the demon's right shoulder, which he ran across and plunged his sword into Roch's neck. Roch was writhing in pain as holiness surged through him every time he was impaled with the holy instruments. Archetenus reached Roch's heart first and stabbed him again and again. Simon climbed past Archetenus and followed Raul, who plunged his sword into Roch's right eye. The room shook with the intensity of Roch's screams.

"His head," Raul yelled to Simon as the two brothers climbed up the face of the demon. Roch heard Raul's words and tried to shake the men off from him; but Matthew, Raul and Simon maintained their holds on the demon's body and continued to climb.

Thedes burst through the crowd, looking for Ibula. He stabbed and sliced demons as he bolted through them. Relieved when he saw Ibula bending over Elan, Thedes turned his back to her and helped Koby and Dagon as they fought the demons that would attack Elan and those caring for him.

Gabriel and Raphael fought back to back as they defended themselves from attack. "I think they have singled us out," Raphael said sarcastically. Both men were injured but they continued to battle the demons. Suddenly Daniel appeared next to them, inside of the circle of demons.

"Glad to see you," Gabriel said as he raised his sword and sliced a demon's head off. With Daniel, the three formed a triangle and the battle took on a heightened intensity. Never would Gabriel or Raphael be able to explain what happened the moment the Angel joined them. They would reflect that perhaps they became intertwined in Daniel's presence, as the three seemed to become one and they vanquished the legions of demons that surrounded them.

"Miranda thank you for coming," Angelina said as the Angel fought at her side.

"I can't let anything happen to Jacob's parents," Miranda said and smiled. Both Miranda and Angelina were being attacked by hordes of demons. The light emitted from the Angels led the demons to their most desired targets. "Tell me Angelina, do you trust me?"

"Yes, of course," Angelina said breathlessly as she was tiring.

"Then turn towards me and hand me your sword."

Without hesitation Angelina turned her back on the demons and handed Miranda her sword. But instead of taking the weapon Miranda kissed Angelina on the forehead. To be kissed by an Angel is like no other experience a being outside of heaven can understand. In that instant Miranda's light surrounded Angelina and renewed her, restored her and saved her. In that instant a demon's sword sliced down towards Angelina's head. Angelina reached up and grabbed the wrist of the monster and he dropped his sword at her touch.

"Can you stop the bleeding?" Cassandra cried as she watched Hannah and Ibula working on Elan. Koby, Dagon and Thedes could not turn to look at their comrade as the demons swarmed around them.

"Vitomas!" Hannah yelled.

"Vitomas grabbed Elan's sword and threw herself to her right as a demon tried to grab her hair. Vitomas plunged the sword into the demon's stomach, then into his head as he fell to his knees. "Cassandra help me push him back," Vitomas said as the two women rolled the demon's body away from Elan's bed.

Matthew, Raul and Simon stood shoulder to shoulder on the head of the great beast. "In the name of The Great Ruler," Simon said as the three plunged their swords into the demon's brain. Again and again they thrust their swords into Roch's head. The holiness of the swords disconnected Roch from his master Ahriman. Without Ahriman's power Roch started to shrink and to flounder. He weaved back and forth as his body quickly reduced in size.

"Jump off," Raul yelled to the others. First Archetenus, then Sorren jumped off the great beast. Simon and Matthew followed. "This is for Vitomas," Raul yelled and plunged his sword into Roch's brain again. Then Raul jumped off the demon, hit the ground in a roll and stood up facing Roch.

Roch as a demon did not have the power to maintain the illusion he presented. As Roch stumbled and fell forward he returned to his human form. He landed hard on his face. With one mighty swing, Raul cut Roch's head off and watched as the now red blood spurted out.

"What's happening?" screamed Hannah as the room started to shake violently. She and Ibula both threw their bodies over Elan to protect him from falling plaster and timbers. Combatants fell and rolled across the floors as the entire hotel was crumbling from its foundation.

Raul fell several times as he made his way through the throng to find Vitomas. She was clutching Elan's bed as her feet kept going out from under her. Fires had started in the building and the rising smoke added to the chaos. Above the screams and battle cries, above the sound of a building tearing at its seams a lion roared and for just a moment, an instant in time, the world stood still.

Chapter XXX
Tears

Lila and Natasha finished setting the platters of breakfast food on the table, then took their seats next to their husbands. As soon as Lila sat down, Christopher looked at Lila and asked.

"Lila what did Luca do that made you so mad?"

Lila and Luca looked at each other with confusion then they both looked at Christopher who was sitting on Luca's left side. "Luca hasn't done anything to make me mad," Lila said. "I don't know what you are talking about."

"Well you kept screaming his name this morning, I heard you," Christopher said as he put a fork full of eggs into his mouth. When Luca roared with laughter and Lila turned bright red, the others at the table realized what Christopher was talking about and they too laughed.

Lila looked at Luca for help. "I don't know what to say," she gasped.

"Luca tell him the truth," Emeral said as she was feeding Cerey. "He's a smart boy.

Luca paused for a moment as he regained his composure then he turned to Christopher. Both Christopher and Nicholas were staring up into Luca's face. "Christopher you know that Lila and I are going to get married right?" Christopher nodded and put another fork full of eggs into his mouth. Well, we are trying to make a baby like Calen and Natasha and sometimes when grown-ups are doing that they make strange sounds and call out each other's names."

Both Christopher and Nicholas looked confused, they stared at Luca and Lila, then at Calen and Natasha, then Christopher and Nicholas looked at each other. Without speaking both boys returned their attention to their plates of food. After a few moments Christopher said, "Make a boy," and continued eating. Luca laughed and ruffled Christopher's hair as three Enrops landed on the dining room table.

Arie stepped forward. "Everyone is coming back they will be here in a few hours. They sent us ahead because everyone is wounded and will need care."

Natasha gasped and grabbed Calen's forearm. "Is Gabriel alright?"

"They are all wounded but Hannah said to tell you she is the most worried about Elan. They saved his life but he lost his arm." Tears ran down Natasha's cheeks as she listened to Arie speak.

"Can you tell us what happened?" Calen asked as he put his arm around Natasha's shoulders.

"Roch transformed into a demon and killed many men and Sophie. The demon Ahriman was Roch's master and came to the hotel. There was a great battle with thousands of demons."

"How did they live through that?" Emeral gasped.

"The Angels came and fought with them," Arie said.

"Angels?" Maxwell repeated in disbelief.

"The Lion, Miranda and Daniel. The Lion fought Ahriman and put him in a prison in The Abyss. I must go to tell the King now," Arie said and the Enrops flew out of the house.

"Emeral can you watch the children?" Natasha said as she cried. Without waiting for Emeral to answer Natasha said, "Lila we need to prepare food and make soup for those who are too weak to eat. And we need to prepare the rooms."

As Natasha stood up, Calen took her hand. "Luca and I can prepare the rooms, what do you want done?"

"Put water, cups, extra blankets and extra chairs in each room for now," Natasha said.

"What can I do?" Maxwell asked.

"Go into Salar and buy trays, we may be serving meals in bed." Natasha turned towards the kitchen then grasped her stomach.

480

"Natasha are you alright?" Calen asked anxiously.

"I'm fine," she said and walked into the kitchen.

"Come we must prepare for wounded," Renya said as the Enrops left the castle. "Laurel get Gala and Philip and tell them both we have many wounded warriors arriving here in a few hours. Ask them if they need us to purchase any supplies."

"Zoya and Delilah help Annabelle prepare rooms. I'll go to the kitchen and get the staff started on food," Renya continued. She saw the looks of concern on the faces of the women. "Ladies it is much better to keep busy at a time like this, trust me I have been through this many times." Then as an afterthought Renya added. "Gala and the Court Physician may not be enough, Laurel ask Alexander to go into the city and bring more physicians here. I am sure that Hannah will also have a house full of wounded."

When the women left the parlor, Renya returned to Sudfad's study. The King sat alone in the room pondering the information they had just received. "It's over Renya, can you believe it?" Sudfad asked. "Roch is finally dead. I only wish I was the one who killed him."

Renya put her arms around Sudfad and kissed him on the forehead. "Our sons are alive and that monster is dead, this is a time of great celebration for our household, our prayers have been answered," she said.

Sudfad kissed Renya's hand. "It is so strange, long have I dreamed of the moment when Roch was destroyed, yet," Sudfad paused. "I know this sounds crazy; he was my only brother. I am surprised at the sadness I feel."

"They're here, they're here," Christopher yelled as he ran through the house with Nicholas behind him.

Calen was the first one out the door as the Ruala warriors were landing. Koby was the first to the house, he was carrying Elan, who was unconscious.

"Elan," Natasha cried when she saw her friend.

"I'll take him," Calen said.

"I've got him," Koby replied. "Help the others." Koby walked into the house towards Elan's bedroom.

Hannah was helping Gabriel into the house. Natasha ran to them. "Put him to bed," Hannah said. "While I help the others." Hannah turned and put her arm around Raphael to help him walk. "Misha I will take him you can barely walk yourself," Hannah said. Within moments, everyone in the household was outside helping their wounded comrades to come home.

Christopher, Nicholas and Cerey stood wide-eyed as they watched the bandaged people being brought into the house. "Nicholas that's your daddy," Christopher said loudly when he saw Gabriel.

Hearing Christopher's words Gabriel stopped and looked at Nicholas and Cerey who were standing together holding hands. Gabriel smiled warmly. "Let me put you to bed first then I will bring the children in," Natasha said as she led her brother to his bedroom.

"We received word that Renya set up a makeshift hospital with extra physicians at the castle," Hannah said wearily to anyone who would listen. "The others have all gone there."

"Hannah, stop," Raphael said. "I don't want to go to my room now; I would like to sit with Gabriel."

"I'll help him," Luca said and took hold of Raphael.

Hannah stood still for a moment, lost in her thoughts. Weariness overwhelming her; when she realized that Christopher, Nicholas and Cerey were looking at her. "Oh my god!" Hannah said and ran up to the children. She hugged all three of them tightly. "I am sorry I was gone," Hannah said. "But we were at war."

"That's alright," Christopher said. "We've been having lots of fun."

"Have you?" Hannah asked and Nicholas looked at her and nodded. "Good, I'm so glad. Come, I will introduce you to my husband Gabriel." Hannah picked Cerey up and took Nicholas by the hand. Christopher held Nicholas' other hand and they walked down the hallway.

"I told Nicholas that Gabriel was his new daddy," Christopher said.

"Thank you Christopher I appreciate that," Hannah said as she entered the bedroom. Gabriel was sitting up in bed talking with Raphael who was seated in a chair and Natasha who was standing next to the bed.

"Look at this," Raphael said with a broad smile.

"Gabriel I would like you to meet Nicholas and Cerey," Hannah said with a smile that consumed her face. "Christopher has been taking good care of them while we were gone."

"Nicholas why don't you come up here and sit next to me," Gabriel said warmly, then he looked at Hannah and said, "I can hold her." Hannah put Cerey in Gabriel's right arm while Nicholas crawled up and leaned against Gabriel's left side. Christopher climbed on the bed and sat next to Nicholas.

"Christopher and Nicholas are inseparable," Natasha said with a warm smile.

"We're best friends," Christopher said to Hannah then he turned to Gabriel. "Nicholas is kind of shy, he talks to me a lot now but he didn't at first. I told Nicholas you are his new daddy." Everyone in the room smiled.

"Nicholas I am so glad to meet you and Cerey," Gabriel said. "Hannah has told me so much about you. I hope you will be happy living with us." Nicholas smiled but did not speak. "This is your uncle Raphael," Gabriel continued. Both Nicholas and Cerey looked at Raphael as Gabriel spoke.

"I'm sure we will become good friends," Raphael said.

"Gabriel they look just like you," Calen said as he walked into the room. "They are really good children."

Gabriel put his arm around Nicholas and hugged him and Nicholas leaned harder against Gabriel; which melted his heart.

"I'll let you get acquainted with your new family, we can talk business later," Calen said. As Calen spoke he was looking at Hannah's, Raphael's and Gabriel's faces. "You all look like you could use some sleep."

"I need to check on the others," said Hannah

"I can do that," Natasha said. "Why don't you stay here? I will get you if something comes up that I can't handle."

"Thank you," Hannah said as the exhaustion took control. She sat down on the bed next to Gabriel and the children.

"Lila and I have made a lot of food, if you are hungry I can bring some trays in to you," Natasha said.

"I'm too tired to eat," said Hannah.

"I don't want anything," Gabriel said as he kept staring at his new son and daughter."

"Neither do I," Raphael said to Natasha, then he looked at Gabriel. "Do you want me to leave?"

"No," Gabriel replied. "We are all family."

Emeral walked into Elan's room and saw Cassandra sitting by his bed crying. When Cassandra saw Emeral she ran to the older woman and threw her arms around her. "He got hurt because of me," Cassandra sobbed. "I dropped my sword and as he threw it to me the demon cut his arm off."

Emeral hugged Cassandra tightly and stroked her hair. "It's not your fault dear," Emeral said soothingly. "But know Elan is really going to need you now. He is not good about expressing his feelings. You know he has been in love with you for a very long time; now he may feel that you don't want him because of his injury."

Cassandra looked up at Emeral. "Well that is just stupid," Cassandra said. "His injury isn't changing my feelings for him."

"And that is something you are going to have to tell him," Emeral said. "Elan is a wonderful boy, he is bright, courageous and he has a gentle heart, but he feels he is not as good as his cousins because he hasn't had the experience in battle that they have. I fear this injury will only increase his insecurities. Tell me Cassandra do you love him?"

"Yes," Cassandra said as the tears ran down her cheeks.

"I know my nephew; he will withdraw because of this. If you truly love him you are going to have to take the lead in this relationship for a while."

"Thank you Emeral," Cassandra said as she wiped the tears from her eyes. "I am going to move my things in here so I can take care of him."

"Good," Emeral replied with a warm smile. "I will have Luca move another bed in here. His bed is too small for the two of you."

Renya hired nurses, physicians and cooks to help with the wounded warriors. The entire family waited nervously for their loved ones to return. A trumpet sounded signally the army was home and everyone in the household, including Marie ran out to the front lawn. The physicians and nurses ran to the warriors as they entered the courtyard, there was not a warrior among them who was not injured. The women looked anxiously at the many faces, trying to find their husbands.

"Simon," yelled Annabelle and ran to him as a wounded Ruala warrior landed with the Prince. They hugged and kissed for several minutes. "Come in," she said.

"No, not yet we have to help the others," Simon said as he turned to the many warriors behind him. Simon and Annabelle started to help others into the castle as Ruala warriors landed with Raul and Vitomas.

After Renya and Sudfad hugged Simon they found Raul and Vitomas. "Vitomas you are injured too," Renya gasped as she hugged them both."

"She fought well mother, you would be proud; Simon's lessons paid off," Raul said and put his uninjured arm around his petite wife.

"Oh wait until we tell you what happened," Vitomas said as Sudfad hugged her. "Never in my life have I seen such things. Roch turned into a giant monster, it was unimaginable."

"There is so much we have to tell you," Raul said. "But first we need to get these others into the castle, then Vitomas and I both want to hug our children."

"Archetenus!" Delilah screamed when she saw her husband in the crowd. She ran to him, then stopped in horror when she saw his bandages. "You are hurt," she cried.

"Honey we are all hurt," Archetenus said and pulled her close to him. "But we are alive," he said and leaned down and kissed his wife passionately.

"Have you seen Jared?" Zoya asked frantically as she ran up to Archetenus and Delilah.

"He's here," Archetenus said and looked around until he saw Jared. "Jared," Archetenus yelled. "Zoya is here."

"Thank you," Zoya said as the tears ran down her face. Zoya was having difficulty seeing through the crowd because of her size. She stood near Archetenus until Jared found them.

"Jared, look at you," Zoya cried as she ran to him. "You're so hurt."

Jared hugged and kissed Zoya. This was the first time that Jared ever returned from battle and had someone who greeted him and cared if he survived. "If you think we look bad, you should see the other guys," he joked and winked at Archetenus.

"Well, let's get you inside," Delilah said.

"We will be in shortly," Archetenus said. "There are others who cannot walk; we need to help them in."

"Gala, I need help," Angelina yelled as she was bending over a Patronus priest and trying to stop the bleeding from a stomach wound. "I am out of supplies." Gala ran to her friend with a medical bag.

Because of their close association with the Rualas, Gala and Angelina routinely carried holy crystals with them. Gala put crystals on the warrior's wound while Angelina cut a bandage and placed it on top of the crystals. The two women put pressure on the wound until the bleeding stopped. "We need help carrying this man in," Angelina yelled into the crowd.

"Sorren go inside, you can barely stand," Matthew yelled as he carried one of the Wetprian soldiers inside of the castle.

"I will not lie down until all of the warriors are cared for," Sorren yelled with indignation and turned to help a Ruala warrior carry another more wounded warrior inside of the castle.

The Queen, herself helped to care for the wounded as King Sudfad carried warriors into the makeshift hospital they had created. "It is a miracle that as many of us survived as did," High Priest Aaron said to Sudfad as the King helped him into the castle. "There were tens of thousands of demons, if it wouldn't have been for the Angels we all would have perished."

"You and your men will stay with us until you all have healed," Sudfad said. "We have the finest physicians and healers in Salar here. My family and my kingdom owe you a great debit."

All of that day and late into the evening both Gabriel's and Sudfad's families were busy tending to the wounded. Elan awoke late in the evening and when Emeral went to his room to visit him she found it filled with visitors.

"Aunt Emeral, Cassandra has moved in here with me," Elan said with a mixture of pride and shock.

"I can see they moved the smaller bed out of here," Emeral said as she looked around the room.

"He is so stubborn that he had to walk to the bigger bed, he wouldn't let us carry him," Luca teased.

"Can't imagine where he got that from," Emeral said with a grin as she looked at Calen, Luca and Misha.

Cassandra walked into the bedroom, "Elan I hope you have another robe here because I can't get the blood out of this one."

"In the closet," Elan said. "This is very strange having you wash my clothes."

"Well, you are going to have to get used to it," Cassandra said and kissed Elan on the cheek.

"Mother I told you they would be next," Calen said with a grin. "So do you want us to build you family chambers in the new wing?"

Elan's face suddenly showed the terror and hopelessness he was feeling. He didn't speak for several moments and when he did it was haltingly. "I don't really know what is going to happen now," Elan said. "I expect that Gabriel will send me home." The sound of Elan's voice and the look in his eyes greatly touched all in the room. Everyone sat in silence for a moment.

"Would you let Elan and I talk in private for a few moments?" Emeral asked. Everyone stood up and walked out of the room. Emeral closed the door then walked over to Elan's bed and sat down next to him. "Elan, you know you don't have to be strong for me." Elan was sitting up in bed and leaned forward and put his arm around Emeral and started to sob.

"I wish I would have died," Elan cried.

"Why?"

Elan took his head off from Emeral's shoulder and looked into her face. "Why?" he repeated incredulously. "Look at me! I'm not a warrior anymore; I'm not even a man." Elan was crying so hard that he couldn't see Emeral.

"Tell me Elan, did your left arm give you courage?"

"No," Elan said as he wiped the tears from his eyes.

"Did your left arm give you that brilliant brain you have or your gentle heart?"

"No," he said angrily. "But, I am a cripple now."

"Elan you are only crippled if you will yourself to be," Emeral said. "You were gravely wounded protecting the woman you love. There is great honor in that." Elan started to speak but Emeral interrupted. "Please let me finish?" She said. "Elan you are so much more than your one arm. You need to realize that. The loss of your arm will not change the man you are. But if you allow yourself to be filled with fear and anger, well then you just let that demon win the battle. And the Elan I know is stronger than that."

Elan stared at Emeral but did not speak so she continued, "Cassandra and I had a long talk while you were asleep. She loves you very much. Cassandra told me that your injury could never change the way she feels about you. And I am going to let you in on a little secret, it doesn't change the way any of us feel about you. You are a courageous warrior and I know you will be a good husband and father some day. Elan remember who you are, don't let the demon beat you." Elan stopped crying and hugged Emeral tightly. As Emeral hugged him back she did not want Elan to see the tears in her eyes.

There was a knock at the bedroom door, "It's Gabriel, is this a bad time?"

"No, Emeral called out and walked across the room and opened the door. "Well if you two aren't a sight," Emeral said with a grin as she saw Calen helping Gabriel to walk and Luca holding onto Raphael.

"Yeah, I suppose we look pathetic," Raphael said and laughed as they all walked into Elan's bedroom.

"Should you be out of bed?" Elan asked. "You both look awful."

"Well, we got some disturbing news," Gabriel said as he sat down in one of the chairs next to Elan's bed. "Is it true you just requested permission to leave the team?"

Elan was shocked by Gabriel's question and looked at both Calen and Luca who had serious looks on their faces. "No," Elan said. "I said I thought you would send me home because I am a, because of my injury."

"The four of his here are the ones who determine who is on the team," Gabriel said. "And not one of us planned to send you home or to replace you with someone else. Of course if you don't want to be on the team you should tell us now."

"Oh I want to be on the team," Elan said eagerly. "But what can I do?"

"Elan the question should be what can't I do," Raphael said. "Honestly we know you won't be able to shoot a bow but think about it. Is there anything else you won't be able to do?"

Elan looked at the four men before him, four men he admired greatly. "Are you serious?"

"Yes," Calen said. "You're staying on the team. Now back to the question you didn't answer before. Do you want Father and me to build chambers for you that are large enough for a family?"

"I haven't even talked to Cassandra about getting married," Elan said with embarrassment.

"Elan that girl has already made up her mind," Emeral said with a smile. "Just ask her, then we can start planning the wedding."

Chapter XXXI
Renewal

"I can't believe they can sleep through this storm," Hannah said to Gabriel as she walked into their bedroom and shut the door. Hannah started to change into a nightgown and brush her hair as Gabriel sat up in their bed and watched her.

"Why didn't you think I would be willing to adopt children?" Gabriel asked. "After one day I am already in love with those two little tykes."

Hannah turned and looked at Gabriel with a guilty smile, "Who told you, Natasha?"

"And Emeral; they both fell in love with Nicholas and Cerey and said that I would too."

Hannah slid under the covers and cuddled up to Gabriel. "I don't know I just thought you wanted your own children only. I should have talked to you about it but honestly when Nicholas and Cerey were brought to the orphanage you were so busy with the mission that I didn't want to bother you."

"Bother me, Honey our family life has priority over the missions." Gabriel said as he put his arm around Hannah. "Please don't ever hesitate to talk to me about things again."

"Simon wake up," Annabelle said as she got out of bed. "Simon."

"What darling?" Simon asked sleepily as he reached for her. When Simon realized that Annabelle was no longer lying beside him he propped himself up on one arm. "Annabelle is something wrong?"

"It's the baby," Annabelle said as she smiled through gritted teeth. "I think it's time."

"What!" Simon yelled and jumped out of bed.

"Simon you always panic so," Annabelle said. "I am going into the guest room, will you get Angelina and the others?"

"Of course," Simon said as he frantically looked for his pants that were lying at the foot of the bed.

"Simon calm down," Annabelle said and laughed.

"I'm calm," Simon said as he tried to walk and put his pants on at the same time. Simon started out the bedroom door then turned back to Annabelle and kissed her. "I'll be back in just a few minutes," he said and ran out of the bedroom.

"Hannah," Calen yelled as he burst through the bedroom door. Both Hannah and Gabriel jumped up. "Hannah the baby is coming."

"Calen, move Natasha to one of your guestrooms so she doesn't soil the bed and I will get dressed and be there in a moment," Hannah said.

"It's too late for that," Calen said nervously. "Her water broke, she said she's had contractions all day but didn't say anything."

"Calen she will be alright. Now you are going to have to leave the room so I can get dressed."

"Oh, I'm sorry," Calen said and walked into the hallway, closing the door behind him.

Hannah jumped out of bed and ran to her closet. Then she realized that Gabriel was trying to get out of bed. "Where do you think you are going?" she asked.

"With you," Gabriel said. "She's my baby sister."

"Gabriel it could be many hours before she has the baby, you are too injured to even walk by yourself. Please stay in bed and I will send someone for you when we know it's close to the time of birth." As Hannah spoke there was a weak knock at the door. When Hannah opened it she saw Nicholas and Cerey holding hands and standing in the hallway.

"Cerey is scared of the storm," Nicholas said. "Can we sleep with you?"

Hannah smiled warmly and knelt down. "Honey your aunt Natasha is having a baby now, I have to leave."

"Nicholas, Cerey you can sleep with me," Gabriel said with a big smile. Both children ran into the room and jumped onto the bed. The movement caused Gabriel to slightly moan in pain.

"Gabriel are you sure?" Hannah asked with concern. "They might kick your wounds."

"Honey our children are scared. I'll take care of them, don't worry."

Hannah smiled as the children slid under the covers on either side of Gabriel and huddled next to him. Gabriel put his arms around Nicholas and Cerey and hugged them tightly. "You know they really do look like they could be your natural children," Hannah said as she put on her shoes and grabbed one of her medical bags. She walked over to the bed and kissed Gabriel, then Nicholas and Cerey. Hannah's heart swelled as she looked at her family.

Elan awoke when Cassandra slid into bed next to him. He was still amazed that the girl he had been in love with all his life was now sharing his room.

"I'm sorry that I woke you," Cassandra said apologetically. "Do you need some more pain medicine?"

"Not yet," he said. "I want to stay awake a little while. You look so beautiful Cassandra." Elan had never seen her in a nightgown before. Cassandra was wearing a pink silk gown with a plunging neck. Elan put his right arm around her and kissed her. "Cassandra did you move in here because you wanted to or because you feel sorry for me?"

"What!" Cassandra said and quickly sat up in bed. "Elan if you weren't hurt I would slap you for asking something so stupid. I moved in here because I love you and I want to take care of you and," Cassandra grinned. "And Emeral said I would probably have to make the first move."

"She did not," Elan said in amazement.

"She did too," Cassandra said and laughed. "Ask her yourself."

Elan started to laugh. "I didn't want to scare you off by acting too fast," he explained.

"You're not going to scare me off," Cassandra said. "Elan you and I have cared about each other for years and neither of us had the courage to say anything, look at all of the time that we wasted. I don't want to waste any more time."

Elan looked seriously into Cassandra's eyes as if searching for an answer. "Are you sure?"

"I have been sure for a long time," she said and kissed Elan on the lips.

"Cassandra go into the top drawer of my dresser, there's a box with a ribbon around it."

Cassandra jumped out of bed and ran over to the dresser. As soon as she opened the top drawer she saw a beautiful red velvet box with a gold bow. "I found it."

"Bring it here," Elan said as he sat up in bed.

Cassandra sat on the bed next to Elan and handed him the box. "No you open it," he said with a proud smile.

"Elan it's beautiful," Cassandra said excitedly as she took the diamond ring out of the box and put it on her finger. "I love it."

"Do you really?"

"Oh Elan, I really do."

"Well, this certainly wasn't how I planned to ask you to marry me. I wanted to do something really romantic for you."

"Elan we have the rest of our lives for that."

"Cassandra I have been in love with you since I can remember. I can't imagine life without you. Would you marry me?"

Cassandra started to cry and threw her arms around Elan's neck and kissed him over and over. "Yes," she whispered into his ear.

In less than one half hour the entire Royal Family of Wetpr, including Thedes and Ibula were gathered in the parlor of Simon's home. Marie was bringing trays of refreshments into the parlor as the men were rearranging the tables so they could play cards.

Angelina, Vitomas and Ibula were in the bedroom with Annabelle. "That storm sounds awful," Vitomas said as she held Annabelle's hand.

"You've got a while," Angelina said after she examined Annabelle. "Do you want me to get Simon?"

"Yes," Annabelle said then started to laugh. "You should have seen him when I woke him up. He was trying to run out of the room and put his legs into his pants at the same time, I was waiting for him to fall on the floor."

"Well at least he remembered his pants," Vitomas said and laughed. "I can't remember now, it must have been when Ariel was coming that Raul ran out of the bedroom and into Matthew's and Angelina's chambers without his pants on."

"Thank goodness he put them on before he burst into our bedroom," Angelina said and laughed. "Isn't it funny how nervous they get?"

"Simon, sit down and let us deal you in," Sorren said. "It will get your mind off things."

"Yeah, before he wears a path in that rug," Raul teased.

"And you should talk," Simon said. "I think you are the worse of the lot of us." Simon stopped pacing and listened by the door. "It's been hours, Gala said that the fourth baby would probably come fast."

"I doubt if anything is wrong," Sudfad said. "Angelina would have told us."

Suddenly everyone turned and looked at the front door of the parlor as Luca walked into the room. He was soaked with rain water from flying in the storm.

"Luca its three o'clock in the morning," Simon said. "Did you come because Annabelle is having the baby?"

"No," Luca said earnestly. "Marie just told me when she let me in. I came for Ibula. Natasha is having her baby too and Hannah is worried that something is wrong."

"I'll get her," Simon said and walked into the bedroom.

"We thought she was at least a month behind Annabelle," Renya said.

"I don't think she really knows when the baby is due," Luca said. "That may be one reason Hannah is worried. Natasha is delivering the first baby in maybe centuries that is half human, we don't really know what to expect."

"Luca, just let me get some more supplies," Ibula said as she ran out of the bedroom. Then as an afterthought Ibula looked at the room full of people. "Annabelle is doing just fine. There is no need to worry about her."

"I'm coming with you," Thedes said to his wife and the three quickly left the parlor.

496

Lila was bringing in pots of coffee as the entire household was sitting in the parlor outside of Calen and Natasha's bedroom. Christopher, Nicholas and Cerey were all covered with blankets and sleeping on the sofa. Emeral, Hannah and Calen were sitting in the bedroom with Natasha when Ibula entered the room.

"You're soaking wet," Emeral said.

"I didn't want to take the time to dry off," Ibula said as she put her medical bag on the floor and walked towards the bed.

"Natasha I asked for Ibula to come," Hannah explained. "Because I have never delivered a Ruala baby before and we don't know if you are going into labor early."

"That's fine," Natasha said as the sweat was running down her face.

"She seems to be in a lot of pain," Calen said with concern.

"I can give her something for that," Ibula said, then she looked at her cousin. "Calen have you ever seen a woman give birth before?"

"No," he said with a shocked look.

"Well, pain is part of the process so don't get too worried," said Ibula.

"I really didn't want to give her anything until you got here," Hannah said.

"I helped deliver a human baby in Lentz," Ibula said as she felt Natasha's stomach. "It's pretty much the same. But I think Ruala women open wider to allow for the wings, if anything is going to be a problem I would imagine that would be it." Ibula was examining Natasha when she said, "Annabelle is having her baby tonight too."

"What!" Calen said nervously. "Natasha how can you and Annabelle be delivering at that same time?"

Natasha scowled at Calen. "Are you really asking me that?"

497

"Calen why don't you step out for a minute and talk to Thedes," Ibula suggested. "And maybe you should have a whiskey to calm your nerves," Ibula added with a grin.

"Will you be alright?" Calen asked as he was squeezing Natasha's hand.

"Yes, I think it's a good idea for you to have a break," Natasha said. "You're starting to make me nervous." Calen kissed Natasha and left the room.

"Emeral have you ever seen Calen like this?" Ibula asked with a grin and Emeral laughed. "I have fought in many battles with your husband," Ibula said to Natasha. "I have never seen him like this before. He loves you very much."

"Ibula he has been so protective of me during the whole pregnancy that I was feeling smothered," Natasha said as she tried to reposition herself in bed. "I certainly hope he isn't like that with every child."

"I just walked through your parlor and they were all acting like they could be the father," Ibula said and laughed again. "Natasha everything looks normal to me. As big as you are I am suspecting you might be further along than you thought. But even if the baby is early, don't worry Hannah and I can take care of it."

The night seemed overwhelmingly long for both families. Just as the morning sun was starting to show its face over the land, criers rode through the streets and country side announcing that a prince had been born.

"Did you hear that?" Maxwell said as he stood near an open window. "Simon and Annabelle had a boy. We will need to buy a gift."

"I am going to start breakfast," Lila announced wearily and stood up from the overstuffed chair she had been sitting in. "If some of you want to push some tables together I will bring the food up here."

"We'll take care of it," Luca said and kissed Lila on the cheek. "Let me know when you need help."

"I would like you to meet David Matthew Calen," Simon said with pride as he carried his new born son into the parlor. The family gathered around him.

"Oh he's beautiful," Renya said. "And look at that curly dark hair."

Vitomas came out of the bedroom with her arms full of soiled bedding. "He is a big baby," she said with a smile.

"And with good lungs," Laurel said. "I'm surprised you picked Calen for one of his middle names."

"Well, we have Alexander Raul and Anthony Sudfad," Simon said. "Calen and I got really close on that mission. He seems like a brother."

"Well, you got the important name," Matthew said kiddingly as put his arm around Angelina, who now entered the parlor.

"The room is cleaned up," Angelina said with a yawn. "So you can visit Annabelle now."

"How are you doing?" Renya asked after she kissed Annabelle on the forehead.

"I'm fine now," Annabelle said. "But it was a long night. And I can't believe how hungry I am."

"Marie has been up all night too," Sudfad said as he proudly held his new grandson. "I'll bet she has breakfast ready."

"I'll get you some food," Vitomas said as she and Raul stood next to the bed with their arms around each other.

"Has anyone heard if Natasha had her baby yet?" Annabelle asked.

The sound of a baby crying brought everyone to their feet in the home of Calen and Natasha. Calen ran to the door and knocked. "Can I come in?"

"Calen why don't you wait a moment for us to clean up." Ibula said as she peaked out the door. "Your wife and daughter are doing just fine." Ibula disappeared back into the bedroom. Calen turned to the others and grinned. It was now midmorning and no one had slept but the excitement of the arrival of the baby reenergized everyone in the room.

"You can come in now," Hannah said with a happy smile as she opened the door. Natasha was sitting up in bed holding her daughter and smiling.

"She looks just like you," Natasha said as Calen knelt next to the bed.

"Does she have wings?" Misha asked.

"Yes," Natasha said then laughed. "So you all are going to have to help me catch her."

"She looks just like a normal Ruala baby," Ibula said as Thedes hugged his wife.

"Take her," Natasha said to Calen, who instantly got a look of terror on his face.

"She's so little," he said.

Emeral took the baby from Natasha and put her in Calen's arms. Emeral adjusted his arms so Calen was supporting the baby's head. "That's how you hold a baby," Emeral said with a proud smile.

"Calen I don't think you will ever get that smile off your face," Luca said as Calen showed everyone the baby.

"Can we see her?" Christopher asked.

Calen knelt down and showed the baby to Christopher, Nicholas and Cerey, all three of the children stared at it without saying anything. Gabriel walked to the bed without assistance and kissed his sister. "I can remember when you were that small," he said with a grin.

"I'm really glad we are all together," Natasha said and kissed Gabriel on the cheek.

"It's a Ruala tradition that everyone kiss the new mother," Misha said with a grin and kissed Natasha on the cheek. Koby and Dagon followed him as did Luca and Maxwell. Elan and Cassandra walked up to the bed together. As Cassandra was bending down to kiss Natasha on the cheek, Natasha asked excitedly, "Cassandra is that an engagement ring? When did Elan give it to you?" Now everyone in the room turned and looked at Elan who was beaming with pride and Cassandra.

"Elan gave it to me just before Luca came and told us you were having the baby. We didn't say anything because it was your night."

"Emeral did you see this ring?" Natasha asked. "It's beautiful."

"Elan picked it out himself," Cassandra said warmly as the family now gathered around them to see the ring and to shake Elan's hand and kiss Cassandra.

"We have much to celebrate," Maxwell said. "Emeral since the girls are always cooking for us, why don't we make a traditional Ruala meal for the family tonight?"

"I think that is a wonderful idea," Emeral said. "But we will need to go shopping right away."

"Maxwell you cook?" asked Hannah.

"Oh, he is a wonderful cook," Emeral said.

"Will you be getting a lot of things?" Hannah asked. "Because I can drive the boca."

"Emeral will you make your special cake?" asked Koby. "Maybe make two of them."

"If I can find all of the ingredients I will. We really should get going," Emeral said. "This will be fun."

After Emeral, Hannah and Maxwell left the room Natasha said, "I never even thought that your food would be different from ours. I feel silly now. I would certainly be glad to fix the food of your tribe."

"It's not all that different," Calen said as he continued to carry their baby. "And besides you, Hannah and Lila are all such good cooks it's not like we are missing anything."

"So what is Emeral's special cake?" asked Lila.

"It's incredible," Cassandra said. "It is made with three different kinds of chocolate, then served with heavy cream and more chocolate poured on top."

"I think she is going to need to make more than two," Gabriel said with a grin.

The children had previously left the bedroom to play; now Nicholas ran into the room and up to Gabriel, who was seated in a chair. "Papa, Grandma Emeral said to tell you that Christopher and Cerey and me are going shopping with them." Gabriel was so stunned that Nicholas called him papa that he didn't say anything for a moment. Nicholas jumped up and hugged Gabriel and started to run out of the room.

"Nicholas," Gabriel called. "Come back here a moment." Nicholas ran back to Gabriel. "Here's some money for candy for you and Christopher and Cerey." Nicholas smiled brightly as he took the coins. He hugged Gabriel again and ran out of the bedroom. Everyone in the room was watching Gabriel and smiling.

"I can't believe he called me papa," Gabriel said warmly.

"I can't believe he talked that much," Calen said. "In case you hadn't noticed, Christopher is really protective of Nicholas and often does his talking for him."

"For so long it was just Gabriel and Raphael and me," Natasha said. "Then after their missions changed it was just me and Gabriel for years. Now look at us, we both have children and all this family. Isn't it something how life changes."

Natasha paused then quickly looked at Raphael. "Raphael, now it's your turn. We need to find you a wife," Natasha teased.

"That was an incredible meal," Gabriel said as he finished his second piece of desert. "Emeral you could make that cake every day and I wouldn't get tired of it."

"Everything was good," Raphael added. "And I will admit Maxwell I was surprised with your cooking skills. You're both a seasoned warrior and an excellent chief; not many men can say that."

"Well, we are glad that you enjoyed it," Maxwell said as Emeral, Hannah, Lila and Cassandra cleared the dishes from the table. "Emeral and I have been wanting to do something for you."

"Well, you can cook anytime," said Gabriel.

When the table was cleared of dishes, Hannah, Lila and Cassandra carried out trays of wine glasses with bottles of fine wine. "Please fill your glasses we are going to have a toast," Maxwell said. When everyone's glasses were filled Maxwell and Emeral stood up.

"When most of you were in Taperia, Emeral and I told Calen and Luca some things that surprised them very much," Maxwell explained. "Emeral and I have been warriors and parents for most of our lives. After years of having a house filled with children and commotion we suddenly found ourselves alone. Our daughters are busy with their families and although they and their husbands are trained as warriors they rarely volunteer for battle. And they rarely have time for us and for the boys."

"Our sons, and that includes you Koby and Dagon, because we feel like you are our sons also, are always gone working on missions for The Great Ruler. Emeral and I will admit we were starting to feel a bit useless. Then Calen and Natasha wrote us a wonderful letter asking us to come and stay with them for a while. Although we were greatly excited by the invitation, we have spent little time out of the Ice Caves, except for when we have fought in battle."

Maxwell continued, "Emeral and I really weren't prepared for what we found here. All of you have worked and lived together for so long that you are a family. And you all welcomed us with open arms and adopted us as your parents and grandparents." "We now understand what our sons and daughters work at and we are so proud of all of you. Calen is redesigning our chambers for a permanent home. We would like to spend more time here to help you with your work and families. So let's have our first toast to family."

After everyone had taken a drink from their wine Gabriel said. "You are both welcome to help us with any of the mission work also, I am sure that your experience is invaluable."

"Thank you Gabriel and I for one will take you up on that," Maxwell said. "But now my beautiful wife has some things that she wants to say."

"First I want to tell Elan that Maxwell did not mean you aren't like a son to us," Emeral said. "Koby and Dagon have lived at our home since they were small boys." Emeral now looked at everyone sitting at the table. "When Maxwell and I came here for the weddings that Renya prepared in your honor, Sudfad showed us their family rings. That man is the King of the wealthiest kingdom in Opots yet his greatest possession is the ring his daughters designed for him. We very much liked the idea of a family ring, so Maxwell and I designed our own."

"We had the jeweler who made the King's family rings make ours. Now mind you, it was not easy to find a design that we felt was beautiful and practical because our family is so large. But we hope you like them. Hannah will you pass out the boxes?" Hannah opened the door to one of the cupboards in the dining room and took out a large tray that was covered with small boxes.

"I will wait until all of you open your boxes before I explain some things," Emeral said and paused for a few moments as she watched the looks on the faces of her family. "Hannah didn't know about these until today. We had the jeweler add Cassandra's and Lily's stones just this morning and picked the rings up on our way home from shopping for groceries."

"These are beautiful," Natasha said as she took her ring out of the box.

"I know," Hannah said as she walked up and hugged both Emeral and Maxwell. "I couldn't believe it when we stopped at the jewelers."

"For us too," Elan said with pride as he opened his box.

"I have never had anything so beautiful," Lila said. "I'm not as eloquent with words as Maxwell and Emeral but it has been unbelievable to me, how all of you have accepted Christopher and me into your family. You have shown us so much love and kindness and..." Lila stopped talking because she was crying. Luca hugged her, then Lila walked over to Emeral and Maxwell and hugged both of them. Within moments everyone was out of their seats and thanking Emeral and Maxwell for their gifts.

Emeral waited for everyone to stop talking before she spoke again. Both Emeral and Maxwell were happy with how pleased everyone was with their gifts. "Now that you all have your rings," Emeral said. "I want to explain the meaning of them. The main setting is a golden sunburst; that is a common symbol of our people. When the Sanuri saved our people and brought us to the Ice Caves, we realized the gift we had been given. We were given a second chance at life and we vowed to always be grateful to The Great Ruler for His mercy."

"Unlike Sudfad's family," Emeral continued. "We don't have a family crest. So Maxwell and I chose diamonds as our family stone because they resemble the healing crystals in our world; each of your rings has a large diamond in the center. The small stones that surround the diamond and run along the split bands are birthstones for each one of us. There are stones for our daughters and their families, our son's and their families, Gabriel and his family and Raphael."

Then Emeral turned to Elan and Cassandra. "We weren't originally planning on adding stones for the extended family, well, because there are just so many of us. But, Elan you have always been close to Maxwell and me and our time here has only made you seem more like one of our sons. We have stones for you and Cassandra in the rings and we will add the stones of your children."

505

"Since our family is growing; Maxwell and I will have smaller bands made up to hold the additional stones. We thought the bands could be worn above or below the original rings." Emeral turned to Christopher, Nicholas and Cerey who were still eating desert. "When you are older we will have rings for you also."

"Ok," Christopher said nonchalantly as he took another bite of chocolate cake.

Gabriel now stood up and held his glass in the air. "Emeral and Maxwell this is not only an honored gift but it solidifies the bonds between us all. We are one family and nothing will ever come between us."

Chapter XXXII
Repercussions

"Listen fella, you've had enough," the bartender said.

"Give me another bottle," Erebus demanded.

"I don't mind ya getting drunk but ya keep crying and it's disturbing the others," the bartender continued.

Erebus looked around the crowded, smoky tavern. "There isn't a damn person looking at me," he said angrily. "Now give me another bottle." Erebus threw a handful of gold coins on the bar so hard that some of them bounced onto the floor. The bartender reluctantly handed Erebus a bottle of whiskey, then picked up the money. Erebus grabbed the bottle and his glass and walked unsteadily over to one of the few empty tables in the room. "Damn bastard," Erebus said as he sat down.

There were five men playing cards at the table next to Erebus. Another four men were standing near the players watching them. "Heard they're tearing down that hotel," one of the players said. "I can't believe that last bit was even standing. Don't cha all think that was the damndest thing?"

"What that there was a fire?" another card player asked.

"That was more than a fire," the first player replied. "Did ya really look at what was left? Why it looked more like there had been an explosion that tore the place apart. I used to be a miner; I know what an explosion can do. Mark my words, when they finally figure out what happened they won't be saying it's a fire that destroyed that place."

Erebus listened to the men talking and tears ran down his face.

"Jared, it's good to see you," Gabriel said as he stood up behind the desk in his study. "Please have a seat," Gabriel added as he and Jared shook hands.

"I talked to Simon this morning," Jared said as he put his hat on the chair next to him. "Sounds like the Sanuri isn't coming back for a while; so I was wondering if I could get either you or Raphael to marry me and Zoya. I'll pay you of course."

"Raphael is at Sudfad's castle checking on some of his men, who are still healing," Gabriel said. "But I feel I can speak for him. Both of us would be honored to perform your ceremony and neither of us will take a cent. What day are you planning on?"

"Well, we were waiting for some of the guys to heal up too," Jared said. "It's not going to be a big thing; just a small wedding at our place. Would two weeks from Saturday work for you?"

"What time?"

"Last Zoya told me, we were thinking mid-morning," Jared said with a large smile. "Of course she'll be getting an invitation to you and your family."

"Well, we would love to come," Gabriel said. "How's the arm?"

"Healing fine, but my ribs are taking a little longer," Jared said with a grin. "Guess I'm getting old."

"Jared I know we just got back home but I am planning another big mission; this one will take us to Ryed. I could use a good man like you."

"When are you going?"

"Well I am still planning things out. I won't lie to you it will be dangerous. We will be going after the dark lord who tried to have Raul and Simon killed."

"He is a member of the Insidiae?"

"Yes and if my information is correct he pretty much controls that kingdom. We suspect he has spies in Sudfad's military so we will need to find out who those men are."

"Well, you can count me in. Of course Zoya's not gonna like it. I mean me being gone again. Do you want me to say anything to Archetenus? He and Delilah are coming for dinner tonight."

"Yes I would. I wasn't sure if they were going to stay in Wetpr."

"I don't think they have figured that out yet. Things are going a lot better with them and the King's family than they expected; so I think he and Delilah are trying to decide if they want to live here or in Lentz. I'll be honest, Zoya and Delilah are getting real close and I think that is influencing their decisions."

"Don't get me wrong; King Mathas and his family are great people. But Sudfad's family and mine have made arrangements so our wives and children will always be protected if any of us are on a mission. That would certainly extend to Zoya and Delilah."

"Well, Sudfad and the Sanuri made arrangements to protect me and Zoya, but I will tell Archetenus."

The loud voices of children were heard in the hallway and within a moment Christopher, Nicholas and Cerey ran into the study and up to Gabriel. "Mama says it's time for lunch," Nicholas said to Gabriel.

"Jared, I would like you to meet my new son and daughter Nicholas and Cerey and this is Luca's son Christopher. Nicholas and Cerey did not speak; they leaned against Gabriel and looked at Jared.

"They're pretty shy," Christopher said as he stared at Jared. "You only have one ear, did you know that?"

Jared laughed, "Yep it got cut off by a Huta."

"Did you kill him?" Christopher asked in a softer voice.

"Yes, he and his friends killed my first wife."

Christopher was quiet for a moment before he spoke. "Luca saved me and Lila from Hutas but they killed our mommy and daddy. And different ones killed their mommy and daddy," Christopher said as he nodded towards Nicholas and Cerey.

"I'm sorry to hear that," Jared said sincerely. "But I don't think any of you could be in a better home."

"Hannah after lunch would you mind watching Christopher for a while?" Lila asked as they were putting food in serving dishes.

"Certainly," Hannah said. "With that smile on your face I am guessing you are doing something for the wedding?"

"We're going to pick up our rings and I can't wait to see them," Lila said excitedly. "Luca designed them and I saw the drawings but that's not like really seeing them." Hannah smiled at the excitement in Lila's voice.

"How are the plans going?" Hannah asked.

"I have to admit that I am a bit overwhelmed. Emeral and Queen Renya are planning such fancy things and they are inviting so many people. Hannah my family was so poor that some years we barely had enough food to eat. I am just not used to all of this," Lila explained. "And Luca is so generous; he keeps telling me to buy clothing and such. Hannah I'm not used to store-bought clothes and everything seems so expensive to me."

"Which is why we are going shopping today," Luca said with a smile as he stood in the doorway of the kitchen.

"How long have you been there?" Lila asked as she blushed.

Luca walked across the room and put his arm around Lila and kissed her on the cheek. "Long enough," he said. "Mother says you haven't picked out a wedding dress yet; is that because you are afraid to spend money?"

"Luca do you have any idea what those dresses cost?" Lila asked. "I don't feel right about spending your money."

"Well that's a relief," Luca joked. "I thought you were marrying me for my money." Lila playfully hit his arm. "Seriously Lila it is our money and you don't have to worry about going hungry anymore. Right after lunch we are going shopping and I don't want you to look at the prices on anything."

By lunch time Erebus could barely walk. He stumbled out of the tavern and walked across the street to his hotel. His room was on the second floor; Erebus tripped and fell as he was walking up the stairs. "Damn it!" Erebus yelled as he hit his nose on one of the wooden steps. Blood started to gush from his nose and dripped on the steps as he walked. Erebus pulled a soiled handkerchief from his pocket and held it against his nose as he made his way to his room.

It took Erebus three tries to open the door to his room. Suddenly memories flooded his mind of the day Roch murdered Sophie. Guilt filled his consciousness. Erebus kept thinking that they would have been able to save Sophie if he only could have opened the hotel door faster. But a new thought entered his mind, as Erebus lay down on his bed. When Roch was in the room with Sophie, Erebus couldn't get the door open with the key; Erebus later thought that was because he was upset. Now Erebus remembered that his spells would not open the door either.

"What was blocking me?" he thought. "Was Roch strong enough to block my spells? Probably not; it must have been Ahriman or the Insidiae. Those damn Insidiae they are responsible for my Sophie's death."

"I'm so excited," Lila gushed as she and Luca walked into Andrew's Jewelry store in Salar. Andrew recognized his customers as they walked in.

"Luca they are in back, I will get them," Andrew said and walked into the back of the store. While they waited, Luca and Lila looked at other pieces of jewelry.

"Mother says you need a necklace and earrings to go with your dress," Luca said as he looked around the store. "She said pearls are traditional." Lila didn't get a chance to say anything before Andrew returned to the front of the store.

"I hope you like them," Andrew said as he placed a velvet cloth on top of the counter. He unfolded the material and exposed four rings. "I like your idea of the child's ring."

511

"Oh Luca they are beautiful," Lila said as she looked at the ornate silver bands that contained rubies and diamonds. "Did you make one for Christopher too?"

"Yes," Luca said with a broad smile. "I think we should have him at the altar with us and we can all put on our rings at the same time."

"You are the sweetest man I have ever met," Lila said and stretched upwards and kissed Luca on the lips.

"You can wear your engagement ring now," Luca said as he picked up a silver ring with a large ruby setting.

"Luca an engagement ring!" Lila said excitedly. "I never saw a drawing of this."

"I know," he said as he slipped the ring on her finger. "I have a lot of surprises for you today."

The loss of Dieter, Cicero and Malik in a matter of weeks spread fear throughout the Insidiae. Rumors spread wildly within the organization that they were being attacked by all manner of adversaries. Questions were being asked and clandestine meetings were held throughout Opots. At these meetings word started to filter out that the vessels were turning against their creators and refusing to accept their intended destinies. The members of the Insidiae knew that these humans needed help to relinquish the holds that the demons had upon them.

The Insidiae were aware of the wars raging between demons; Ahriman's defeat at the hands of The Lion opened up a vast territory and the demons of this world were fighting savagely for it. But many were not aware that for the first time in the history of Nunc, demons from other worlds were launching attacks against the holders of this world. The underworld was in complete chaos as the demons fought to maintain their power and domains. The dark ones were turning their attention towards each other, thus giving the humans a momentary reprieve.

Although the members of the Insidiae were worshippers of demons they were not confidants of their masters. Some dark lords were better than others at obtaining information but the many questions and rising fears of the Insidiae brought many of them to one conclusion; they needed to find the Grand Masters.

"What's all of the commotion?" Natasha asked as she walked into the dining room carrying baby Lily. When she saw others sitting at the table she said jokingly, "I want you all to notice that Calen is actually letting me hold the baby for a few minutes." Everyone laughed as Calen had been holding and caring for the baby since she was born.

"I'm not really sure," Hannah said. "Luca wanted us all here, including the children."

Within minutes the entire family was seated at the table. Luca and Lila walked out of the kitchen carrying trays of treats and wine glasses. As Lila filled the table with plates of delicacies, Luca carried bottles of fine wine from the kitchen and handed them to his father to open.

"Are we celebrating something?" Misha asked as he filled his plate with food.

"Yes," Luca said smiling. When all the food and refreshments had been served Luca and Lila stood at the table holding several baskets. "Lila and I made great headway with our wedding plans today. So we are now ready to share them with all of you."

"Before Luca tells you the rest," Lila said. "I have to tell you that Christopher and I grew up in a family that often could not afford food. I have been feeling too guilty to spend money on the wedding so everything you are about to see, Luca picked out and had made before today. I was so surprised."

"Child did you find a wedding dress?" Emeral asked.

"Yes, Luca picked it out and it is so beautiful," Lila said excitedly. "The dressmaker will deliver it tomorrow I can't wait for you to see it."

"I thought the groom wasn't supposed to see the dress before the wedding," Raphael joked.

"Either I picked it out or she wasn't going to be wearing one," Luca said. "We picked out the bridesmaid dresses too and you will have to go to the dressmaker tomorrow."

"Who are the bridesmaids?" Natasha asked.

"Well, I guess we are getting a little ahead of ourselves," Luca said. "Raphael we would like you to perform the ceremony."

"I would be honored," said Raphael.

"Calen I would like you to be my best man. And I would like Gabriel, Misha, Koby, Dagon and Elan to stand up for me. Natasha will be the maid of honor and we would like Hannah, Cassandra and Bekka to be bridesmaids. Obviously we are short two women so mother has, well, I will let her explain that part," Luca said.

Emeral smiled, "I invited a couple of young ladies from the Ice Caves to be in the wedding, they are not relatives but daughters of friends of mine."

"Does this mean you are trying to marry us off too?" Koby asked with a grin.

"No, well yes," Emeral said with a laugh. "But you don't have to marry these girls, just walk down the aisle with them. But I will tell you they are quite beautiful."

"I'll walk down the aisle with Bekka," Koby said. "Nothing against these other girls," he added. "I just like Bekka and I want to be there for her incase this is all too much, I mean after Fala."

"I think that is wonderful," Emeral said.

"Well, now that we have that worked out," Luca said with a laugh. "I want to show you our rings." Luca took a small box out of one of the baskets and passed it around the table. "I had one made for Christopher also and I want him to stand in front of the altar with us."

514

"Oh that is the sweetest thing," Hannah gushed.

"Luca designed all the rings himself," Lila said with great pride as the family was looking at them.

"I'm impressed," said Calen.

"We would like Nicholas and Cerey to walk down the aisle and throw flower petals," Luca said. Then he turned to both those children. "Would you like to be in our wedding?" Nicholas looked at Christopher as if getting approval then he nodded his head. "Good," Luca said. "Father, Lila would like you to walk her down the aisle."

"I would be honored," Maxwell said with a proud smile.

"Lila do you want to start handing out the gifts?" Luca asked. Lila picked up both baskets which contained boxes and each box had a name written on it. "The bridesmaid dresses are light blue," Luca continued. "As we said earlier we picked them out and you will need to be fitted."

"The dresses are so beautiful," Lila said as she walked around the table handing everyone two boxes.

"We picked a dress out for Cerey," Luca said then turned to Emeral. "And mother I picked a dress out for you also."

"What!" Calen said with a laugh.

"Wait until you see it," Lila said. "It is a one of a kind and Luca didn't want anyone else to buy it."

"None of my sons have ever bought me clothes before," Emeral said emotionally.

"Emeral it is so beautiful," said Lila. "It is perfect for you."

"Well girls, I think we are all going to the dressmaker's tomorrow," Emeral said with a proud smile.

"Now that everyone has their gifts you can open them," Luca said.

"Luca!" Natasha gasped when she opened a box that contained a light blue sapphire necklace and earrings.

"These are beautiful," Cassandra said as she put her necklace on.

"All of the women have matching jewelry including Cerey," Luca said.

"Oh Luca, she is so little she might lose them," Hannah said as she opened Cerey's boxes. "Look," Hannah said as she held up a little necklace and earrings.

"Well I like my gift," Dagon said as he pulled out a dagger with light blue sapphires in the hilt.

"All the men will wear those daggers on their belts and you have matching stones for the cuffs of your shirts," Luca said. Then he turned to Christopher and Nicholas. "I have daggers for you also but I am going to wait to give them to you when you are older."

"You got the boys cufflinks too!" Hannah said as she watched Nicholas and Christopher open their boxes.

"Emeral, Luca did all of this," Lila said. "I am so proud of him."

"Lila, Luca has never really spent money because he has always lived the life of a soldier," Emeral said. "I am proud that he is doing all of this."

"That's not all," Lila said. "Today he bought me so much clothes, I have never had such beautiful things." Lila walked up to Luca and kissed him on the cheek.

"Elan you look like you are in shock," Misha teased.

"I guess I am. Cassandra and I haven't even started to make plans for our wedding; I guess I didn't realize there was so much to it."

"Lakin go," said the Sanuri. "He is family. I will stay here and monitor things."

"Are you sure?" Lakin asked. "With the increased numbers of Hutas in this area something is going on. Besides didn't Luca want you to perform the ceremony?"

"I told him I needed to stay here so he is going to have Raphael perform the service. I really don't want to leave until I figure out the meaning of the symbols that we found on the mausoleum."

"Well if you are sure," Lakin said. "My wife and children will be attending the wedding; it will be nice to spend some time with them. I will return after the wedding."

"Lakin, spend some time with your family, that's an order," the Sanuri said with a grin.

"Hello is anyone home?" a woman's voice rang out in the front foyer of Gabriel's house.

"Bekka," screamed Christopher as he ran towards the voice. "Bekka. Nicholas, Cerey you have to meet my friend."

Bekka dropped her bag on the floor when she saw Christopher. He ran and jumped into her arms. Christopher and Bekka hugged and kissed each other. "Bekka these are my friends Nicholas and Cerey," Christopher said as Bekka set him on the floor.

"It is very nice to meet you," Bekka said as she shook hands with both of the children.

"They are kinda shy," Christopher said exuberantly. "Their parents were killed by Hutas too and Gabriel and Hannah adopted them."

"I am sorry to hear about your parents," Bekka said and hugged both of the children.

"Well, it's about time you showed up," Luca said as he walked up to Bekka and kissed her on the cheek. "Everyone's out being fitted for clothes; I'm minding the fort and the kids."

"Life is really changing for you," Bekka said with a smile. "And you look so happy Luca."

"Bekka you've got to come and see my room," Christopher said as he grabbed her hand. "You can stay with me if you want."

"Thanks but I think I still have a room here," Bekka said.

"We moved you to a larger room in the new wing, so Nicholas and Cerey could be closer to Hannah and Gabriel," Luca said as he picked up Bekka's bag.

"I heard about Elan," Bekka said in a lowered voice. "How is he doing?"

"Physically well," Luca said. "He was very depressed at first. But now that he knows he is staying on the team and getting married; we hope he realizes he has much to live for."

"He and Cassandra are getting married? Did he ask her or did she ask him? It was always so cute how he got tongue-tied around her."

"He asked her," Luca replied with a grin. "But that was after she told him she was moving in with him."

The gangs of demons in Nunc were not the only ones consumed with power struggles; as fearful as some of the members of the Insidiae were, they too had battles over the new territories that had opened up. Both Malik and Cicero had been masters over large and very rich regions of Opots. Power hungry dark lords were both waging wars against their rivals and trying to seduce demons to be their allies. This conflict created an increased need for soldiers. Some dark lords were calling out to vessels while others were using a more creative approach.

From the stench of hell; from the black tar that covered the hell regions rose a new creature. A creature that walked like a man. A creature with the strength and size of the vessels. A creature that was made out of the waste and decay of tortured souls. The demons named their new foot soldiers the Amulth because this word in the language of the demons meant filth.

The Amulth were soulless creatures so they would not be tempted to abandon their demon masters and turn to good as were the humans. Their composition made them worthless as vessels for demons in the human dimensions; instead the Amulth would act as extensions of the demons. Because these creatures were made out of the essence of hell itself, the demons could transport them through dimensions. Several dark lords paid dearly for these soldiers of hell. A new terror was coming to the World of Nunc; a new terror to control the world of man.

Chapter XXXIII
A Rough Night

"You could go to the castle and visit your namesake," Gabriel said with a grin as he took his seat at the dinner table.

"What are you talking about?" Calen asked when he realized that Gabriel was looking at him.

"Simon's son is named David Matthew Calen," Gabriel said. "And he is a beautiful baby. He has Annabelle's hair and Simon's build."

"He named his baby after you!" Emeral said with pride. "I think the entire family needs to visit the castle. And we need to bring gifts."

"I don't know what to say," Calen said with a mixture of surprise and pride. "I guess I haven't gone to the castle because Lily is so young." Then he looked at Natasha. "Do you think she is old enough to take out?"

"The castle is a short distance from here," Hannah said. "It shouldn't be a problem."

"So both the babies were born on the same day?" Bekka asked.

"Yes," Natasha said. "David is just hours older than Lily."

"You have a beautiful little boy and a beautiful little girl born hours apart," Bekka said with a grin. "It will be interesting to see what happens when they grow up together."

"I don't understand what you mean," said Natasha.

"You might be holding the next princess of Wetpr," Bekka said with a laugh.

The next afternoon Erebus stumbled into the Taperian Fortress Bank, "Who's replaced Malik?" Erebus yelled with slurred speech. People in the bank stared at Erebus; a male teller came from behind the counter and walked up to Erebus.

"My Lord, please keep your voice down," the teller said in a low voice. "Malik owned this bank and no one else has bought it yet."

"You mean the Insidiae aren't going to use this place as a ruse anymore?"

"My Lord, please you are drunk, perhaps you should sleep it off."

"Perhaps my ass," Erebus shouted indignantly. "I want to talk to whoever is the head of the Insidiae because they are responsible for my wife's death."

"My Lord, I have no idea what you are talking about," the clerk said nervously. "Please leave now; you are disturbing the other patrons."

"It's good to see you," Zoya said as she walked out onto the porch, drying her hands in her apron. "I have pies in the oven; you are just in time."

"I hope you don't mind us just dropping in like this," Delilah said as Archetenus helped her off her horse. "We were out for a ride and thought we would stop by."

"Where's the old man?" Archetenus kidded.

"Jared's next to the barn," Zoya said with a laugh at Archetenus' comment. "He's building tables for our wedding celebration.

"I suppose he could use some help," Archetenus said and walked their two horses over to the barn.

"So have you decided where you are going to live yet?" Zoya asked as she set a cup of coffee on the table for Delilah.

"Actually that is why we were out for a ride," Delilah said. "We were looking at land. Archetenus met with Gabriel, Raphael and King Sudfad this morning. They would like him to continue to help with missions. Archetenus said he would consider it only if he knew his family was safe and cared for while he was gone."

"Gabriel has already asked Jared to be on another mission," Zoya said. "I'm not really sure how I feel about that. On one hand I am proud of him and the work he is doing and on the other hand I greatly fear for his safety," Zoya said as she sat down at the table with Delilah.

"You and I are of the same mind," Delilah said "If Archetenus agrees to work with them, I suppose we will live here; otherwise we will probably move to Lentz."

"Well, I hope you stay here. You know you could stay here with me when Archetenus is gone. The Sanuri has the Hengers watching this place and the army stops by on patrols every day. I would enjoy the company."

"So what did you decide?" Jared asked as he was cutting lumber.

"Haven't yet," Archetenus said. "Tell me what you need me to do."

"Those over there are the table tops," Jared said. "And the legs are over there. You could start putting them together. They aren't fancy cuz we will have cloths over them. We're setting them up outside for the food and drink."

"Jared you and me, we've been fighters our whole lives; how does being a farmer suit you?"

"Well I was a farmer once before. Problem was I was also a mean drunk who spent more time in the taverns than at home. That's why my first wife died. I just couldn't leave a card game. When I finally got home I found her body."

"Hutas?"

"Yep, it took me six months but I tracked every one of those bastards down and skinned them alive, just like they did her." Jared stopped sawing and looked at Archetenus. "The way I look at it I got me a second chance on life and I'm not going to make the same mistakes. I got me a beautiful young wife and a nice spread, I'm gonna do it right his time. What about you?"

"All I've ever been is a soldier," Archetenus said. "I'm afraid I don't have a lot of other skills. Delilah loves your place and would like a little house in the country."

"Well, you've got money don't you? Get a couple of hired hands to do the work. And I will certainly help you. It wasn't that I was a bad farmer before, I was a bad drunk."

"Well, that is something else that you and I have in common. I can handle a couple of drinks and I am fine. But when I was drinking heavy I would black out and, well, kill people. Did some prison time for it. I didn't even remember what the hell I did to land in prison; that was until Miranda showed me. She said that if I didn't stop getting drunk that Delilah would see Dieter in me, well that was enough to sober me up."

"Have you seen Miranda lately?"

"Not since the last battle. I haven't heard her voice either. I'm thinking that's because I am making better decisions."

Archetenus and Delilah left Jared and Zoya's home late in the evening. "You are welcome to spend the night," Jared said.

"It's only five miles to the castle," Archetenus said with a grin. "I think we can make it."

As Delilah left she squeezed Zoya's hand. "Remember what we talked about," Delilah said and smiled, then she and Archetenus walked out into the night.

"Everyone is finally asleep," Vitomas said as she slid under the covers next to Raul. "What are you reading?"

"You know we suspect there is at least one spy in our military," Raul said. "Well, Mathas loaned Father a couple of his top officers to help us with an investigation and this is part of their report. It substantiates our fears. Father has put this into Gabriel's hands now."

"You're talking about when you and Simon were almost killed and only the generals knew your travel plans aren't you?"

"Yes, it appears the Insidiae was behind those attacks on us," Raul said as he put the report on his bedside table and put his arm around Vitomas.

"So they will be going off on another mission?"

"Eventually."

"Are you and Simon going with them?"

"One of us may have to but we don't know yet so don't start to worry," Raul said and kissed his wife on the lips. "But there is something I need to talk to you about."

"I really like them," Zoya said after Delilah and Archetenus left their house.

"So do I," Jared replied. "Why don't you leave the dishes and come to bed."

"Jared, you look exhausted," Zoya said nervously. "But can we talk for a few moments?" Zoya had a worried look on her face and she was acting uncharacteristically agitated.

"Sure," Jared said suspiciously and sat down at the table. Zoya started to pace back and forth in the kitchen. "Zoya what is the matter? Is something wrong?"

"Jared you know there is so much we don't know about each other."

"Zoya if this is about my past," Jared said. "Ask me anything, I will tell you."

"No, no," Zoya said. "It's just well there is so much we haven't talked about."

"Zoya what is wrong? Is this about your past?"

"No."

"Zoya come over here and sit down. Now tell me what is going on. I have never seen you act like this before. Does it have something to do with Archetenus and Delilah?"

"Raul is something wrong, you have that look again?" Vitomas asked and sat up straighter in bed.

"Well that depends. This next mission that Gabriel is working on sounds pretty dangerous."

"More dangerous than the one with Roch?" Vitomas asked in amazement.

"Well perhaps just as dangerous as that one," Raul said. "He needs good men and he asked Jared and Archetenus to go with him."

"And?"

"Well, Archetenus hasn't committed yet because he wants to make sure that Delilah will be taken care of while he is gone."

"I can understand that," Vitomas said. "He seems to love her very much. But what are you getting at Raul?"

"They haven't decided where they are going to live yet," Raul continued. "And if Archetenus is going to be working with Gabriel on a regular basis they should probably live in Wetpr."

"Well that makes sense. But you don't want him living here, do you?"

"That is what I wanted to talk to you about. How do you feel about him now?"

"I'm not scared that he is going to do anything if that is what you are asking. I really think he is a changed man and he seems devoted to Delilah. But can you ever forgive him for what he did?"

"I'll tell you I didn't want him on that last mission, but he saved my life. Matthew, Angelina and Sorren like him and think he is good man to have on our side."

"But what about you?"

"I'm beginning to feel the same way but I don't want him around here if it is going to upset you."

"Raul," Vitomas said as she brushed his cheek with her hand. "I knew the missions were dangerous but now that I have been on one, well, it was so much worse than I expected. I want you to be safe and if you and Archetenus can get along, I agree he is a good man to have on our side. I have seen him kill monsters with his bare hands. He is a brave warrior."

"So then you don't mind if he and Delilah build a home here?"

"I never thought I would say this, but no."

Jared pulled one of the kitchen chairs up close to his. "Zoya please come here and sit down." Zoya sat down and looked at Jared. "What are you so upset about?" he asked with great concern.

"Jared do you want to have a family?"

Jared stared at Zoya for a moment, then he started to smile. "Zoya are you pregnant?"

"Well I'm not sure but I think I am." Jared stood up quickly picking Zoya up and twirled her in the air.

"So you aren't mad?" Zoya asked.

"Mad, why would I be mad?" Jared said and kissed her on the lips.

"This is beautiful, riding in the moonlight," Delilah said. "Don't you think it is romantic?"

Archetenus looked at Delilah and grinned. "I have to admit I have ridden in the moonlight a lot but it is different when you are with a beautiful woman. "Delilah I know I have asked this before, but I really want an honest answer. "Do you want to live in Wetpr or Lentz?"

"Archetenus," Miranda's voice suddenly filled his head. "Turn your horses around and quickly ride back to Jared's home. You're riding into an army of demons."

"Delilah turn around and ride back to the house as fast as you can," Archetenus said as he drew his sword.

"What is going on?"

"Just do it, now!"

"I don't understand why you thought I would be mad," Jared said as he set Zoya's feet on the floor.

"Well I didn't know," Zoya said "I thought you would either be really happy or really mad."

Jared laughed loudly. "I am really happy." He bent down and kissed Zoya again but half way through the kiss he stopped and his body stiffened. "Horses," he said and walked to the door.

"Jared it's us," Archetenus called out. "Let us in."

Jared opened the door and Delilah and Archetenus ran inside of the house. "Miranda said to come back here, that we were riding into an army of demons," Archetenus said.

"Bolt the shutters on the windows and doors," Jared yelled to Zoya and Delilah as he ran to his weapons chest. "Help yourself," Jared said to Archetenus as he grabbed a couple of knives, a battleaxe and a sword from the chest.

"Luca!" Christopher screamed loudly. "Luca!"

Luca and Lila were lying in bed kissing. Luca jumped out of bed and started to run towards the door. "Luca, you're naked," Lila said and threw a folded blanket to him. Lila jumped out of bed and picked her nightgown up from the floor. She quickly pulled it over her head and followed Luca into Christopher's bedroom.

"What is it?" Luca asked as he ran into Christopher's room.

Christopher was sitting up in bed crying. Luca quickly looked around the room then sat on the bed next to Christopher. Lila knelt down by Christopher's bed. "Christopher what is the matter?" she asked.

"I dreamt about them," Christopher cried hesitantly. "Mommy and Daddy and the Hutas."

Luca hugged Christopher tightly then picked him up. "Why don't you sleep with us tonight," Luca said and carried Christopher into their bedroom.

"What is that sound?" Jared asked. "Does anyone else hear it?" Loud squawking sounds filled the night air.

"It's the Hengers," Zoya said. "They must be attacking the demons." Suddenly they heard screams as well as shaking at the doors and windows.

"I don't like feeling like a sitting duck," Archetenus said as he walked towards one of the shuttered windows.

"What did Miranda tell us to do?" Delilah asked.

"She just told us to ride here as fast as we could and to lock ourselves in the house," Archetenus said. "She said we were riding into an army of demons."

They heard loud banging against the front door as if the demons were using something strong to try and break the door down. "Miranda do we fight?" Archetenus yelled out loud as the screeching of the Hengers grew louder.

Miranda's voice was now heard by all within the house. "Just stay where you are. I will tell you when to come out."

"I don't like this," Jared said.

"I know," Archetenus replied. "Is there a place the women can hide if they get in?"

"There's that false wall in the back of our bedroom closet," Jared said. "Not sure if there is enough room for them both."

"Well let's see," Archetenus said and ran to Jared and Zoya's bedroom with everyone following him. Zoya opened the latch and exposed a hidden compartment.

"We would both have to sit down," Zoya said.

"Both of you; just see if you can fit in there," Archetenus said. Both Zoya and Delilah crouched down and walked through the closet to the hiding place. They both sat on the floor in the secret compartment.

"We can fit but there isn't a lot of room," Delilah said.

"It those bastards get in here, you two hide in there," Archetenus said as he checked the shutters to the bedroom windows. Jared ran back to the kitchen door where there were still sounds of loud pounding.

"Just seems like we should be fighting," Jared said with frustration.

"I know, but Miranda has never given us bad information," Archetenus said.

Suddenly the pounding sound against the door stopped. They all listened to the eerie silence. "I think they are on the roof," Archetenus said.

"Miranda please help us," Delilah said out loud.

The next morning Luca was the last to walk into the dining room. He was carrying Christopher who had his head lying on Luca's shoulder. Lila had gotten up much earlier to help Hannah fix breakfast.

"Is Christopher sick?" Emeral asked. "I've never seen him so quiet."

"We had a rough night," Luca replied. "He was having nightmares about what happened to his family."

Emeral got out of her seat and walked up to Luca and Christopher. "Christopher do you want to come to grandma?"

Christopher reached out to Emeral who took the boy and hugged him tightly. Emeral kissed Christopher several times and said, "I can't imagine what kind of memories you have but know that you are safe here. None of us will let anything happen to you." Christopher hugged Emeral tightly and started to cry.

"He needs to let this out," Emeral said to Luca. She turned and walked into the parlor and sat down in a rocking chair. Emeral held Christopher tightly as they rocked back and forth.

"She's amazing," Natasha said as she first looked at Calen then at Maxwell. "Emeral always knows the right things to say."

"I know," Maxwell said with a soft smile. "That poor boy has been through a lot."

Nicholas and Cerey were sitting at the table when Nicholas looked at Gabriel and asked, "Papa is Christopher going to be alright?"

"Yes," Gabriel said. "He is sad today."

"That's because his parents are dead," Nicholas said with a sad look on his face.

"Nicholas and Cerey come here," Gabriel said. Both children jumped off from their chairs and ran to Gabriel who picked them up and set them on either side of his lap. "We are sad that your parents are dead," Gabriel said as he hugged the children. "We don't ever want you to forget them. But know that Hannah and I and everyone here loves you and we are glad that you came to live with our family." Hannah and Lila were both standing in the doorway with tears in their eyes.

"Where is Christopher?" Lila asked Luca.

"He and mother are in the parlor." Lila walked behind Luca and kissed his head.

Just as Hannah and Lila were sitting down three Enrops flew into the dining room. "Miranda sent us," one of the giant birds said. "She wants you to come to Jared's house; they were attacked by demons last night." Everyone jumped up from the table except Natasha who was holding Lily and Lila.

"I'll get my medical bag," Hannah said and ran out of the room.

"Everyone go ahead," Cassandra said. "I'll bring Hannah."

"Mother," Luca called.

"Go, I'll stay with the children."

Three Enrops flew through an open window in the dining room of the castle. Sudfad's family was seated at the breakfast table, while their many guests were eating in the Great Hall. "Miranda sent us," one of the birds said. "She wants you to come to Jared's farm, they were attacked by demons."

As the men jumped up from the table Raul asked, "Is the battle still going on?"

"We don't know," the bird replied. "We weren't there, Miranda called to us. Miranda said the King should come also."

"I'm going to the Great Hall to get the others," Simon said as he ran out of the dining room.

"I'll ready some troops," Raul said as Sudfad ran to get weapons.

"You can come out now," Miranda called.

Jared opened the door to his house just as the first rays of dawn were illuminating the land. His eyes opened wide as he saw the scene before him. "Oh my god!" Zoya gasped as she walked out onto the porch of their house. "There must be hundreds of them."

"There were two thousand of the monsters," Miranda said as she appeared to them. "Jared what did you learn from this?" Jared looked around and saw that all the buildings on his farm were still standing and intact. Then he looked again at all of the dead bodies lying on the ground.

"That I should trust you," Jared said sheepishly. "Just so you know Archetenus told me all about you and him. It's not easy for men like us to trust."

"Which is why I sometimes have to be more dramatic in my approach," Miranda said.

"You mean you caused this?" Archetenus asked as he walked around the grounds looking at the demons.

"Of course not," Miranda scolded. "The Great Ruler and His holy messengers never send demons upon people. I could have destroyed the demons before they got here, but all of you had lessons to learn. Jared and Archetenus you have been making good decisions that have greatly altered the paths your lives were taking. And many of your decisions were influenced by your love for your wives."

"You have both said that you want to continue to help Sudfad and Gabriel and the others save this world from the plague you see before you. If indeed you are men of your word and you do these things you will need my help and the help of other Angels and The Great Ruler. There is more to these worlds than your limited sight can see; you must learn to trust us."

"You are both men of battle," Miranda continued. "You know that in the midst of war you do not have a great deal of time to mull things over. Jared two thousand demons attacked your home last night yet not one of you are injured and there is no damage to your land. How can you explain that?"

"It was Delilah wasn't it?" Jared asked. "She asked you to help us."

"A few simple words and this is the result," Miranda said. "Archetenus you should have known to ask and Jared you will now know." As soon as Miranda finished speaking the sky filled with Ruala warriors who were carrying human and Shettee warriors. In the distance a large dust cloud could be seen, the result of an army of men riding to Jared's farm. "I have sent for the others," Miranda said. "The lessons are not over."

Ibula was the first to land because she was carrying King Sudfad. Both the King and the Princess stood in awe before the Angel, then they both fell to one knee and bowed before her. "You do not bow to anyone besides The Great Ruler," Miranda said. "Please rise."

"I have heard the others speak of you," Sudfad said humbly. "But in all my days I never thought I would receive such a gift as to actually see an Angel." Sudfad's voice shook with emotion as he spoke. Sudfad's' act of honor and humility was seen by all of the warriors.

Miranda waited a few moments as all of the warriors gathered around her, their eyes expressed both the horror and the miracle that lay before them. "I sent for you because I wanted you to see the new horror that the world of darkness has inflicted upon man. Three masters of the Insidiae have fallen and others battle over their territory. The demon Ahriman has fallen and the demons too battle for territory. Jared you were the first vessel to renounce the Mark of Satan, Archetenus you were the second, others followed your lead in the battle that destroyed Cicero's compound."

"The world of darkness shook with fear for they do not want men to realize that The Great Ruler gave them freedom of choice and this my children is an incredibly powerful gift. The demons would have you as hopeless slaves to their madness. But with freedom of choice you can rise above anything in this world of man."

The warriors stood mesmerized as Miranda spoke, no sounds other than her voice could be heard. "So great was their fear that some dark lords sold their souls and fortunes to have an army created that would never leave the darkness. An army of soulless creatures who would never make the decision to renounce their demon masters. And this is what they created," Miranda said as she waved her hand at the demon bodies that littered the ground.

"These are called Amulth, in the language of demons that word means filth; because these creatures are literally made from the filth and decay that covers hell. These creatures are made of the decay of tortured souls, souls of some of the most heinous creatures in the worlds. Feel free to look upon them, for they will be the armies you will be battling."

"They all look exactly the same," Archetenus called out. "Why is that?"

"Every creature, no matter how small, that is created by The Great Ruler has a uniqueness that is both a gift and an expression of love. The demons want to control their slaves, they do not want individuality or distinctiveness; they want unconditional fear and servitude. Look upon these creatures for you will recognize the same plight of many men."

The soldiers dismounted and joined the Rualas and Shettees as they walked around the bodies of the demons. "Miranda there does not appear to be a mark upon them," Raphael asked. "How do we destroy them?"

Miranda said, "I believe Jared can answer that question for you."

"I had a lesson to learn last night," Jared said. "While Archetenus and I would have fought this army and lost, Delilah called out to Miranda and the army was defeated." Then Jared looked at Miranda. "I will not forget what I have learned this night, you have my promise."

"Miranda," Simon asked. "We feared retribution from the demons and have tried to protect Archetenus' and Jared's families. Now that the demons know where they live, should we move them?"

"Archetenus, Delilah, Jared and Zoya come before me," Miranda ordered. "Would you choose to live lives of fear or enjoy the love that The Great Ruler has given to you?"

"We do not want to live in fear," Delilah said. "If we need help we will call upon you."

"Simon you have your answer," Miranda said.

"Miranda I have known you for years," Archetenus said. "And there is always more to what you say. You called them all out here for more than to see these demons didn't you?"

Miranda explained, "This is a time of great darkness for the world of man. Times like these are always pivotal in the history of a world. The decisions and choices that you make will sway the course of history. Remember this day when an Angel came before you. Many of you here have had Angels fighting at your side, but what you may not know is that we were always there; we are just allowing you to see us now. Raul tell them how we helped you in Taperia."

"They touched our swords with holiness so we were stronger than the demons and they fought at our sides," Raul said emotionally.

"The strongest weapon you can have in this world is faith," Miranda said. "Never forget that lesson."

Chapter XXXIV
Venator

"I'm glad that Miranda got rid of all those damn demon corpses," Jared said as Alexander and Archetenus helped him set up the tables. Zoya and Laurel were in the kitchen cooking while Delilah and Gala were setting the tables and putting bouquets of flowers around the area designated for the wedding party. Jared had built a small platform for Gabriel to stand on. The platform had three steps, Jared and Zoya would kneel on the middle step during the ceremony. The platform was painted white and decorated with flowers and candles.

"Jared," Laurel called out as she walked onto the porch. "You and Zoya need to start getting ready; we can take care of the rest of this.

"Go!" Archetenus said as he and Alexander lined up several large tables.

"Zoya's getting dressed in your guest room," Laurel said. "You shouldn't see her until the wedding. Jared grinned and walked through the house to their bedroom and closed the door.

"What the hell!" Erebus mumbled as he awoke and looked around at his surroundings. He was cold and he felt a dampness creeping through his body. Erebus did not wake easily because of the amount of whiskey and drugs in him. It took him a few moments to comprehend his plight. He realized he was tied at the wrists and the ankles and lying on a stone floor. Erebus maneuvered his body to a sitting position and looked around; he appeared to be in a cave.

Adrenaline started to pump through Erebus's body and brought him out of his confused state. "The bank," he thought. "The last place I remember is being in the bank." Erebus was now convinced that the Insidiae had him. He mumbled a chant to free himself from the ropes that bound him but his incantation was unsuccessful. "Of course," Erebus said out loud.

"They would put a spell on the ropes," Erebus thought to himself. Erebus was a powerful sorcerer and he knew he was dealing with powerful dark lords. Erebus sat quietly trying to think of the types of spells they would use.

As he looked around his location he saw two torches fastened to the stone walls; their light illuminated only a small area around him. Erebus saw nothing else, no chains, no other prisoners, no bodies. Suddenly fear surged through him. "What if they are going to sacrifice me?" he thought.

"Those bastards," Erebus said out loud. And suddenly a change occurred within his being. Erebus's brain had been clouded and consumed with his grief for the loss of his wife and the whiskey that he drank to try and dull his pain. But now, Erebus was thinking clearly. At that moment with calm resolve, Erebus declared war on the Insidiae.

"Oh excuse me," the young woman said as she bumped into Raphael at one of the refreshment tables. "Oh I am so sorry," she gushed as Raphael wiped the coffee off from his black jacket. "Please let me clean that for you it is the least that I can do," the woman said.

"No, no that is not necessary," Raphael said as he stared at the beautiful woman standing before him. The woman appeared to be in her late teens. She had straight black hair which she wore in double twists on top of her head. Her brilliant blue eyes seemed to dance as she looked at Raphael.

"Please I insist," she said with a laugh. It was then that Raphael realized he was staring at her.

"Forgive me for staring," he said. "The jacket is fine."

"Well then I will owe you," the woman said with a flirtatious smile. "Please may I know your name so that I might repay my debt one day."

Raphael laughed and responded to her teasing. "My name is Raphael and yours?"

"Vivian," she said with a coy smile.

"Well, Vivian it is an honor to meet you. Are you here with anyone?"

"Some friends but I seem to have lost them in the crowd."

"This crowd is very small," Raphael said with a grin. "It would be difficult to lose anyone here."

Vivian paused for a moment then laughed. "How you tease."

Suddenly everyone's attention was drawn to two carriages that stopped in front of the group. The carriages bore the emblem of the King of Wetpr and they were escorted by twenty soldiers.

"The King is here?" Vivian gasped.

King Sudfad stepped out of the first carriage, then he turned and helped Queen Renya out. The Queen turned around and took Arianna from Simon. Simon got out of the carriage and helped Annabelle out. She was holding baby David. Once Annabelle had her feet firmly on the ground, Simon turned and took Anthony and Alexander out of the carriage.

In the meantime, Raul got out of the second carriage. He helped Vitomas out, she was holding Ariel. Then Raul helped his sons Sudfad and Samuel out of the carriage. Petra jumped out without assistance. Christopher, Nicholas and Cerey ran up to the carriages to greet the other children.

"I will watch them all," Lila said as the boys immediately started to chase each other around the tables.

"Don't ignore Cerey," Calen called out as he and Natasha walked up to the Royal Family.

"I can't believe they came," Zoya gasped as she peaked out of the bedroom window. Delilah looked over Zoya's shoulder to see who Zoya was talking about.

"Did you invite them?" Delilah asked.

"Of course but I never thought they would come," Zoya said. "I mean the princes, well, they have been here before but the King and Queen, I am shocked."

"Well, it looks like they brought you plenty of gifts," Delilah said. "Now get away from that window and let me finish your hair or you will be late for your own wedding." Delilah was forming some of Zoya's long hair into ringlets. "So did you tell Jared?"

"Yes, I was so nervous and you were right, he was very happy at the news."

"I told you," Delilah said. "I think both our husbands are tired of living on the road. They are ready to settle down and have families. Archetenus is very excited about our baby and I bet Jared is just the same way."

Erebus sat in the cavern, for what he believed to be hours. He tried a variety of incantations but nothing loosened the ropes that bound him. He had heard no other sound than that of his own voice, he believed he was alone; but suddenly there was movement. Every fiber of Erebus's body stiffened as he listened for sounds in the darkness.

Erebus mumbled a new incantation and the flames of the torches cut through the air as if a great wind had affected them. In the increased light Erebus saw little, only that he was in a cave. Erebus closed his eyes and concentrated and suddenly balls of fire filled the air. Erebus quickly looked around his surroundings and still he saw nothing but rock walls. Another sound, movement; and Erebus looked up and saw eyes looking at him.

"That was a beautiful ceremony," Vivian cooed as she and Raphael walked towards one of the refreshment tables. Vivian had not left Raphael's side since they met. The two sat together during the wedding ceremony.

"Yes, Gabriel always has a way with words." Raphael picked up a glass of lemonade and handed it to Vivian, then he took one for himself. "So where are your friends?"

"Why I don't know," Vivian said as she looked around at the faces of the small crowd attending the wedding. "I certainly hope they didn't leave, I came here in their boca."

"Why would they leave?" asked Raphael.

"I have no idea," Vivian said sweetly. "But if they did could you possibly give me a ride back to my hotel?"

"Certainly," Raphael said as he stared into Vivian's large eyes. "Zoya and Jared are new to this area, how do your friends know them? How do you know them?"

"Well, I really don't know them," Vivian said. "I am visiting here in Salar and my friends invited me along. He is their physician."

"I see," Raphael said with a smile. "Come I would like to introduce you to some of my friends." Raphael held out his arm for Vivian and they walked over to Gabriel and Hannah who were talking with Raul and Vitomas, all of whom smiled as Raphael and Vivian approached them.

"Vivian I would like you to meet Prince Raul and his wife Vitomas and my closest friend Gabriel and his wife Hannah." Vivian smiled sweetly. She had her right arm wrapped around Raphael's left arm. Raphael now put his right hand on top of Vivian's right hand. "Vivian suddenly appeared at the ceremony with a story that her friends had abandoned her here." Raphael could feel her body stiffening as he spoke. "She says her friend is Jared's and Zoya's physician."

Gabriel quickly moved to Vivian's left side and grabbed her arm. "Hannah search her for weapons," Gabriel said.

"I am their physician," Hannah said with deliberation as she pulled a dagger from the inside lining of the jacket that Vivian was wearing. Natasha saw what was happening.

"Wait!" Natasha yelled then she turned to Calen. "Here take Lily." As soon as Calen took the baby Natasha ran over to Gabriel and the others. "Hold her tight," Natasha said as she started to search Vivian for weapons. Annabelle, Lila, Laurel and Delilah took all of the children inside of the house as the rest of the wedding guests now surrounded Gabriel and the others.

Vivian remained silent as Natasha took two darts from the decorations in Vivian's hair and handed them to Raul.

"Be careful they have been dipped in something." Natasha pulled a second dagger from a sheath in the back of Vivian's dress, just under the neckline. Natasha found a third dagger in a sheath on Vivian's right leg and a garrote wrapped around Vivian's waist.

"Well, now that we have established that you are an assassin," Gabriel said. "Who sent you and who are you here to kill?" Vivian looked at Gabriel and smirked.

"Luca, Calen check on the others," Raphael said. "She could be a distraction."

"I have seen her before," Zoya said as she walked up to Vivian. "Yesterday she was watching us as we were buying some things in Maggie's General Store." Now Zoya directed her question to Vivian. "Did you follow us out here?" Vivian did not speak.

"She doesn't have the Mark of Satan on her neck," Natasha said as she looked under Vivian's hair.

"We didn't see anyone else," Koby said as he and Dagon returned to the group.

"Jared, Archetenus do either of you recognize her?" Gabriel asked.

"No," Archetenus said. "But I saw her latch onto Raphael as soon as she appeared here. I never saw her ride up on a horse or in a boca."

While Natasha was searching Vivian, Hannah ran to their boca and grabbed her medical bag. She returned to the group and handed a bottle of blessed water to Gabriel. "Why don't you do it?" Gabriel said. Hannah poured a little of the water onto Vivian's hand but nothing happened.

"Hold out her other hand," Hannah said and poured some of the blessed water on it. To everyone's surprise when the water touched her skin it did not smoke.

"Well you aren't a witch, demon or dark lord," Gabriel said. "So I am to assume you are an assassin for hire. This is most interesting."

Vivian had not uttered a word since Raphael exposed her as an imposter. "Gala do you still have any of that special potion?" Sudfad asked loudly.

"Yes, My Lord at my home. I will get some," Gala said and started to walk towards her boca.

"I'll take you," Dagon said and picked Gala up and ascended into the air.

Simon walked up to Gabriel, Raphael and Vivian carrying a chair and some rope. "We don't want her inside near the children," Simon said. "So we can interrogate her out here."

"Raul and Simon want you to keep the children in the house," Hannah said to Annabelle "They just gave that woman the truth potion. Is everyone alright in here?"

"Yes," Annabelle said with a laugh and led Hannah into the kitchen where all the children were seated around the table eating."

"Hannah this cake is really good," Christopher said. "You should try some."

"I hope we will all be eating with you soon," Hannah said with a warm smile, then she turned to Annabelle. "I am going back out there I want to see how this potion works."

"The children are alright," Hannah announced as she returned to the group. "Has she talked yet?"

"I was waiting for you to return," Gabriel said. "Before I started."

"Zoya gave me some paper so I can write down what she says," Natasha said.

"She looks drunk now," Simon said. "You could start."

"What is your name?" Gabriel asked.

"Vivian," the woman said then giggled.

"Are you an assassin?"

"I only kill when I have to."

"Why were you carrying so many weapons?"

"A girl has to be prepared," Vivian said then giggled again. Gabriel and Raphael both looked at each other with confusion because she was not presenting herself as they expected.

"Why are you at this wedding?"

"I've been tracking some creatures and their trail stopped a few miles from here. When I was in the city yesterday I saw the woman, the one who talks to spirits. I heard her talk about the wedding and I thought I would come out here and talk to people. I thought I might get some information about the creatures."

"Why have you been tracking creatures?" Gabriel asked.

Suddenly Vivian held her head up proudly, "Because I am a Venator of the Clan Gesmal, for centuries my people have hunted the monsters."

"Venator means hunter in the old language," Raphael said to the crowd.

"I know," Vivian said. "It is an honored position among my people."

"Are you a demon hunter?"

Vivian smiled proudly, "We call them monsters but yes."

"Where is your tribe from?"

"The Kingdom of Ryed," Vivian said. "There are many monsters there and now the creatures from the sea are walking upon the land, they are assassins for the monsters."

"Why wouldn't you tell us this before?"

"Who would believe me?" Everyone in the small crowd now smiled at Vivian's comment.

"Why did you single out Raphael?" Gabriel asked. "Do you know of him?"

"He is very handsome and he did not seem to be with anyone," Vivian said with a smile.

"How did you recognize Zoya as a seer?"

"We have many such women in our tribe; the light around them is different."

"Who are you traveling with?"

"I travel alone; all Venators travel alone."

"You have been tracking demons from Ryed by yourself? Why have you traveled so far?"

"They are not demons, but the creatures from the sea. I told you they are the assassins and I want to see who they are after. If they fail in their mission others will be sent. I need to warn the people."

Sudfad pushed his way up to Vivian. "When you say creatures from the sea are you talking about the Kingdom of Ogg?"

"Yes."

"You have seen these creatures?" Sudfad asked.

"Yes, many times."

Sudfad now turned around and said, "Raul send a letter to Mathas immediately and tell them about this." Natasha handed Raul the paper and pen that she had been holding. Sudfad turned back to Vivian. "Young lady, we might know who the creatures are after. Will you help us?"

"Tell me where they are going and I will kill them."

"I didn't realize that Natasha had a sister," Koby said as a joke.

"Sudfad how long does this potion last?" Gabriel asked as he and Raphael untied Vivian.

"We've never given it to a woman before," Raul said. "The few times we used it we gave it to large men and then killed them afterwards."

"You will not kill me," Vivian said as she tried to stand up then her knees buckled. Both Gabriel and Raphael caught Vivian before she fell.

"Since you are the handsome one," Gabriel said kiddingly to Raphael. "Why don't you take care of her until this wears off?"

"Oh you two," Hannah said with a huff and took Vivian's left arm. "Vivian would you like some coffee and something to eat?"

"Yes," I am very hungry," Vivian said. Natasha took hold of Vivian's right arm and they started to walk her into the house.

"My weapons," Vivian said. "I need my weapons."

"We'll give them back to you when you sober up," Natasha said. "Now come in the house, we have all kinds of good food in there."

A small flock of Enrops landed and took the letter for King Mathas. "Father I am writing a letter for the Sanuri also, I wonder what he can tell us about the Clan of Gesmal." Raul said.

Erebus' heart started to race as he saw the Raftifa above him. These ancient bat-like creatures were known to devour human flesh. He quickly said a protection spell, then he wondered why the Raftifa hadn't attacked him.

Erebus concentrated on fire and soon several more balls of fire appeared in the cavern. He quickly positioned himself so that the ropes that bound his wrists behind his back were over one such fiery orb. Erebus winced with pain as the fire burned his flesh but within moments he was able to break his wrists free. He untied his ankles then a new fear filled him.

Erebus had no idea where he was or how to get out of the darkness. He closed his eyes for a moment and tried to determine if he could feel any air moving in the cavern; he could not. Erebus sent more fireballs into the air and saw that there were five tunnels leading from the chamber he was in.

Erebus made a split second decision and stood up and ran into the tunnel that was closest to his left. The tunnel was dark; he produced more fireballs. The air burst through his lungs as he ran, his chest hurt and his heart was pounding then he heard them; the sound of wings.

An hour later, Vivian sat at the table in Zoya's and Jared's kitchen. "What did you give me?" she asked. "My head is killing me." Vivian held her head in both of her hands.

"Here take this for the pain," Hannah said and handed Vivian a glass of liquid. Vivian stared at the glass suspiciously. "I am a physician," Hannah said. "This really will help your headache." The rest of the guests had resumed the celebration of Zoya's and Jared's wedding. Hannah and Vivian were the only two people inside of the house. "Do you remember anything from when you were under that truth potion?"

"Truth potion! Is that what it was? I felt like I was drunk."

"Well you acted like it too. I'll be honest I have never seen anyone take a potion like that before. How do you feel other than your headache?"

"My stomach is queasy but I think I am alright. Why would you give me a truth potion?"

"Well, we are all demon hunters too and lately the demons have been coming after us. We thought you were a witch or a demon at first," Hannah said as she felt Vivian's forehead.

"You are Venatores?" Vivian gasped. "I didn't realize there were others than my clan."

"Oh there are many of us," Hannah said. "And we are afraid that those creatures you have been hunting are going after the Royal Family of Lentz. So when you are feeling better the King and the others would like to talk to you."

"Is everyone at this wedding a demon hunter?"

"Well, most of us are."

"That is incredible; my people will never believe this."

"You never told me if you remembered my husband asking you questions."

"Oh I think I remember everything," Vivian said. "This is the first time I have ever been caught by anyone. I am fortunate you are hunters too."

"How are you feeling?" Raphael asked as he piled Vivian's weapons on the table in front of her.

"Like someone kicked me in the head repeatedly," Vivian winced with pain when she spoke.

"How did you really get here?" asked Raphael.

"I have a horse that I left not far from here, he is grazing."

"So why did you tell me you would need a ride?"

Vivian smiled although that act also gave her pain, "Why do you think?"

"I don't know that is why I am asking," Raphael said seriously.

Vivian looked at Hannah who smiled and said "Raphael and my husband are priests."

"You don't look like any priests I have ever seen," Vivian said with surprise. "You look like warriors."

"Well we are that too," Raphael said. "But I don't understand what being priests has to do with your answer."

Vivian and Hannah looked at each other and smiled. "She wanted to spend time with you," Hannah said with a grin.

Now Raphael looked embarrassed, "I guess I do work too much, I didn't see that."

"Raphael as embarrassed as you look, I am not sure what you are thinking," Vivian said. "Honestly I have been hunting those creatures for over two months and this was the first time I have been at a gathering with normal people for a while. You are an extremely handsome man; I just wanted to talk with you for a while and maybe have a dance; nothing more. And as soon as I can stand up I need to be going."

"King Sudfad and his family have returned to the castle," Raphael said. "When you are well enough they want us to bring you to them. They think those creatures are after some of their family."

"Oh I do remember him saying something," Vivian said. "Alright." She started to stand up then quickly fell back to her seat. "It might be a few minutes," she said weakly.

"You turned completely white and looked like you were going to pass out," Hannah said. "I rather think it will be more than a few minutes. Vivian where are you staying?"

"I have a camp about four miles from here."

"Raphael I think she should stay with us," said Hannah.

"I agree," Raphael replied then he turned to Vivian and said. "Tell me where your camp is and I will get your things."

"You can't go there; I have several traps set up. I will be alright."

"Vivian less than a week ago an army of demons came through here. It is not safe for anyone to be alone," Raphael said. "Tomorrow when you feel better we will get your things. Where is your horse?"

"He will come when I whistle but I am not ready to ride yet."

"Raphael will you stay with her for a few minutes?" Hannah asked. "I am going to find Gala and talk to her about that potion. Hopefully I can find something to counteract the effects."

"Certainly," Raphael said and sat down at the table.

When Vivian heard the door close she said, "I am sorry that I embarrassed you in front of your friend; that was not my intent. I have been alone for so long it was just nice to be around people again."

"You did nothing wrong," Raphael said with a laugh. "I was embarrassed because I realized how long it has been since I was in a social setting with a beautiful woman; I guess I just forgot some things."

"You have been hunting demons for a long time also?"

"Yes."

"I understand. It gets lonely sometimes and at times I forget how to act around other people too."

"So tell me how is it that a beautiful young girl is hunting demons by herself?"

"I am of the Gesmal Clan. Our people have been demon hunters for as long as anyone can remember. From the time we are young children we train but not all of us are chosen for this honored position. I worked very hard to become a Venator."

"Why do you hunt alone?"

"That is how we have always done it."

"Are the hunters both men and women in your clan?"

"Yes but as I said not everyone is a hunter."

"Since you hunt alone, do Venators live very long in your clan?"

Vivian smiled, "The good ones do. I have been hunting on my own for three years now."

"How old are you?"

"Eighteen, why how old are you?"

"You mean to tell me you started to hunt demons on your own when you were fifteen?"

"You act so surprised," Vivian said trying to smile. "That is normal for our people. You didn't answer my question."

"I am twenty-five," Raphael replied.

"Then you must be a very good hunter," Vivian said. "Raphael I think something is wrong." Raphael could see that she was turning white. "I think you should get Hannah." Vivian had barely completed her words before blood started to run from her nose and she started to shake.

Raphael ran to the door, "Hannah quickly," he yelled and returned to Vivian. Now there was blood on her face and dress. "I need water," Vivian said and tried to stand up but she collapsed. Raphael caught her just before her head hit the floor.

Erebus could feel the rush of wind as the huge Raftifa flew around him. They seemed to be playing with him; diving at him but not attacking. Sweat poured down Erebus' body as he ran; he knew he had to rest soon. He continued to light the darkness with fire balls. He tried to see if there was a small place for him to hide in the tunnel. Suddenly a Raftifa flew close to Erebus' left side, hitting the warlock with his wing and knocking Erebus to the ground.

Erebus quickly rolled onto his back and shot fire balls at the Raftifa that was rapidly descending upon him. The creature emitted a high pitched scream that hurt Erebus' ears as the fire burned its neck and wings. "Of course," Erebus said out loud. He took a deep breath and conjured dozens of balls of fire that flew at the soaring monsters. The tunnel filled with shrill screams and the stench of burning flesh. Erebus jumped to his feet and started to run again.

"Where am I?" Vivian asked as she saw Raphael sitting in a stuffed chair near her bed. But before he could answer she continued, "Is this your room?"

"You're in one of the guest rooms in our home," Raphael said as he set the stack of papers he had been reading on his lap. "Hannah has been sitting with you but she just left so she could put the children to bed."

"Is it night? How long have I been out?" Vivian asked as she tried to sit up.

"You have been sleeping for about six hours. How are you feeling?" Raphael asked as he walked over to the bed to help her.

"I'm not really sure," Vivian said as her movements were making her dizzy. "The room is spinning." Raphael helped her to a sitting position and placed a couple of pillows behind her back. "Could I have some water? I am very thirsty." There was a pitcher of water and glasses sitting on one of the side tables. Raphael poured a glass of water and handed it to Vivian. He noticed that her hand was shaking as she took the glass.

"Thank you," Vivian said before she slowly drank the water. "Is this Hannah's?" Vivian asked as she realized she was wearing a nightgown.

"I have no idea," Raphael said with a laugh. "The girls changed you."

"Girls?"

"There are a lot of us in this house."

"Are you family?"

"We have become family," Raphael said. "These are good and courageous people."

"Do you have a family here?"

"I am not married if that is what you are asking."

Vivian paused for a moment then asked, "That potion you gave me; was it poison?"

"Honestly we are beginning to wonder the same thing?" Raphael said. "The Princes and Gabriel have only used it a few times and that was on large men, who they killed after the interrogation. We don't know if the dose was too strong for you or if these are typical side effects."

"Raphael, Hannah must give me something to help. I have to find those creatures," Vivian said earnestly.

"We have Enrops searching for them; they will notify us when they find the creatures."

"Enrops, birds?"

"Yes, they work with us and can speak many human languages."

"I have heard such stories about them but I did not think there was any truth to them."

"We have warned the people who we think the creatures are after so they can be prepared for attack. They are all warriors," Raphael said. "So you just concentrate on getting better, we will take care of the creatures."

"I have never had others do my work," Vivian said. "May I have more water? What are you reading?"

"I am preparing for our next mission," Raphael said as he refilled her water glass.

"You study for the missions? To hunt demons?"

"Some of our missions are very complicated," Raphael said with a laugh when he saw the look on Vivian's face. "There are groups of men who employee and work with the demons and we try to get them also."

"In Ryed, the Teivel Clan are all witches and dark lords, we usually do not fight with them, just the demons."

"Those are exactly the type of people we fight, what can you tell me about this clan?"

"A great deal what do you want to know?"

Chapter XXXV
Strange Allies

"I was just coming to check on you," Hannah said as she saw Raphael and Vivian walk into the dining room for breakfast.

"She wanted to get out of bed," Raphael said as he had his arm around Vivian to steady her. "But I am not convinced that is a good idea."

"What are you wearing?" Emeral asked when she saw that Vivian had on a robe that was extremely too large for her.

"I couldn't find my clothes so Raphael gave me his robe," Vivian said as she sat down at the table.

"Your dress was full of blood," Natasha said. "So we washed it for you."

"She did not get much sleep last night because we spent the night talking," Raphael said as he sat down next to Vivian. "She knows a great deal about the Teivel Clan."

"Really?" Gabriel asked with heightened interest. "Raphael did you tell her why we are interested in them?"

"No, only that we fight dark lords and witches."

Vivian looked around the table at the people, "Are you of the Ruala Tribe?" she asked Emeral.

"Yes we are."

"I have heard of your people but I have never met a Ruala before," Vivian said. "I have heard that you are some of the most fierce warriors in all of Opots. I am honored to be among you. Is it true that your tribe saved the people of Nora from thousands of Hutas?"

"Yes," Calen said "And I am proud to say that almost everyone in this room was at that battle. There were more than Hutas in Nora, there were many demons and dark lords. The Lion, the emissary of The Great Ruler helped us greatly."

"Do you know of the Sanuri?" Vivian asked.

"Yes," Gabriel said. "We work with him. He has a home at the King's castle."

"Really?" Vivian asked in awe. "He has not visited our clan for a very long time. He is the only emissary of The Great Ruler that I know of."

"The Great Ruler has many emissaries," Gabriel said. "The Sanuri has never spoken of your clan. Which I find interesting since we will be going to Ryed for our next mission."

"If you are planning on fighting with the Teivel Clan you must bring many warriors," Vivian said. "They have an army. In fact they own King Nehmota so they have control over his army as well. All the citizens who are not dark lords or witches are terrified of the Teivels and do their bidding."

"And your tribe?" asked Gabriel.

"We live in the southern portion of the kingdom so that we do not have as much interaction with the Teivels. My clan has been fighting demons since our early ancestors walked in this world but we have no armies."

"We do," Gabriel said. "Will you help us fight against the Teivel Clan?"

"Of course," Vivian said haltingly.

Hannah stood up from the table. "Vivian I think you need to return to bed, you look like you are going to pass out again," Hannah said then she turned to Gabriel. "You can talk business later this girl needs some rest."

"I agree," Vivian said as she started to stand up. "What are you doing? I can walk," Vivian said to Raphael as she picked her up and started to carry her out of the dining room.

"Yes I am sure you can," Raphael said sarcastically.

"Raphael you should have let her get some sleep last night," Hannah scolded.

"I am sorry but she did seem alright."

After they left the dining room Christopher looked at Luca and asked, "Is that girl going to die?"

"I sincerely hope not," Gabriel said guiltily.

"Gabriel you didn't know the potion would affect her like it has," Natasha said. "It is not your fault."

"I beg to differ," Gabriel said solemnly.

"I am truly sorry to call you all together at this time of night," Mathas said as the families of Fahron, Claudius and Sorren joined King Mathas' family in the royal parlor. "But I felt that what I have to tell you cannot wait." Rosa entered the room holding baby Sarah. "The refreshments will be served in just a moment," Rosa said.

"Thank you dear," Mathas said to Rosa then he turned to the entire group of people. "I have received several letters from Raul and Sudfad in the last few hours. I will let all of you read them but first I will tell you what they said. Without going into a lot of detail, Sudfad's and Gabriel's families were attending Zoya and Jared's wedding when a strange woman showed up. She raised some suspicions so they put blessed water on her but she was not a demon or dark lord."

"They then gave her some of that truth potion that Gala makes. It turns out the woman is a demon hunter from the Clan of Gesmal in the Kingdom of Ryed. She was tracking two creatures from the Kingdom of Ogg and lost their trail around Salar. She said that the creatures from Ogg are assassins for the demons and if they don't complete a job others will be sent. Sudfad fears the creatures are coming after us."

"When did she lose their trail?" Claudius asked.

"Yesterday," Mathas replied.

"This doesn't make sense," Stephan said. "A lone woman is tracking them. Are they sure she is telling the truth?"

"Stephan I have heard of that tribe," Thaos said. "They are fierce warriors who train since childhood for their roles as hunters. Only the best of the warriors are allowed to hunt the demons and they are called Venatores, that word means hunter. They all work alone. I have never met any of them though."

"One interesting thing is the woman, her name is Vivian has been tracking them across the ground, they haven't used the waterways as we thought they would. Sudfad said that Vivian has no information about who these creatures are after, but she said that they only leave their kingdom to do work for the demons. Apparently once Vivian spotted them she followed them to Wetpr," Mathas said.

"That woman has to have guts," Sorren said approvingly. "Is she coming here?"

"Well, that brings me to the last letter I received from Sudfad," Mathas said. "Because of their suspicions, they gave Vivian the truth potion. Sudfad has only used that potion a few times on large men who were killed immediately after the interrogation. Vivian is a young girl, the age of our daughters here, and she is violently ill. Sudfad said that Hannah is concerned Vivian might die. They have sent Enrops out searching for the creatures and will notify us as soon as they have any information."

Shara and Angelina looked at each other. "Dear do you have any aplewort here?" Shara asked.

"Yes," Angelina said. "Mathas we have an herb which may help this girl, but we have to mix it with water and let it set for a day. Can one of your soldiers take it to her?"

"Of course," Mathas said. "Matthew will you make the arrangements? In the meantime I have extra security patrols around all of your homes. The soldiers that escorted you here will also escort you home. You will need to be prepared for anything until we receive more information.

"You've had us worried," Emeral said when she saw that Vivian was awake. "We've been taking turns sitting with you."

"How long have I been sleeping?" Vivian asked groggily.

"All day and half the night," Emeral said. "You must be starving, would you like me to get you something to eat?"

"Yes please," Vivian said as she sat up in bed. "I am hungry but my stomach is still sick."

"We made soup for you," Emeral said as she stood up. "Now stay in bed, I will be back shortly."

"You can go in," Emeral said to Raphael as she passed him in the hallway.

"Don't you ever sleep?" Vivian asked with a smile when she saw Raphael in the doorway of her room.

"I feel guilty," he said as he walked into the room and sat down in the stuffed chair near her bed. "Gabriel and I gave you that potion then I kept you up talking all night. I really am sorry about all of this."

"You didn't know," Vivian said. "If I live through this, perhaps we can have a dance sometime that is how you could pay me back."

"I'll look forward to it," Raphael said with a smile. "I might have some good news for you. We received a letter from the people we think those creatures are after. There are two powerful healers in that family and they are sending some medicine that they believe will help you. They were going to have soldiers bring it here, but Koby and Dagon flew to Lentz to get it. They can travel faster by flying."

Vivian stared at Raphael. "I am surprised you are going to so much trouble for someone you don't know."

"Why?"

"I guess I don't know," Vivian said. "I just would not have expected it."

"Here is some soup, bread and milk," Emeral said as she carried a tray to Vivian. "If you can keep that down there is pie in the kitchen."

"Thank you, it smells good." said Vivian.

"Well, I will leave the two of you to talk," Emeral said and smiled at Raphael.

"Would you like me to leave too?" Raphael asked.

"No stay and talk to me," Vivian said then chuckled. "Although I may tell you to leave if I can't keep this food down. Did the Enrops find the creatures?"

"Not yet."

"I lost their trail just before I reached Salar. I started to wonder if they went underground but I couldn't find any tunnels. They can swim underwater. If there are waterways by those people, you might want to warn them."

"Is there a special way to kill them?" Raphael asked as he walked over to the desk in Vivian's room and picked up paper and a pen.

"They aren't magic," Vivian said as she sipped her soup. "I have killed them with a sword or knife before. What are you doing?"

"I am writing down this information to send to King Mathas, why?"

"I just thought of something," Vivian said. "Would you please get me some paper and a pen also?"

Vivian wrote on both sides of the paper without speaking to Raphael. When she was done Vivian looked at him and asked. "Raphael do you have a knife on you?"

"Yes."

Vivian moved her food tray and pushed the covers off her. "Are you getting out of bed?" Raphael asked.

"No, I need you to cut that bracelet off my ankle," Vivian said as she swung her legs around so they hung off from the bed.

"What is this?" Raphael asked as he looked at the unique leather bracelet that had rough precious stones embedded in it.

"It is a lamsman," Vivian explained. "Every stone represents a major feat I had to perform to become a Venator; my name is also on it. Raphael cut the bracelet off and was examining it as Vivian started to write on a second sheet of paper. "When you and Gabriel go to Ryed you can trust no one for the Teivels' own everyone except for my clan. I will help you but if I die from this poison I want you or Gabriel to take this letter and the lamsman to my tribe. Here you may read it," Vivian said as she handed the first sheet of paper to Raphael.

"Vivian you aren't going to die."

"Raphael you don't know that and all of you are looking at me like you fear I will. My father's name is Joshua, he is a good man and a brave warrior, the name of our chief is Duncan. You should meet with both of them. I am writing down their names and drawing a map so you can find my village. Raphael do you know where my horse is?"

"He followed you back here," Raphael said as he read the letter. "We have him in the stable; he is being cared for."

"If I die return him to my village. We are a poor people and another warrior will need him."

"Vivian look at me," Raphael said seriously. "If you die I will personally go and tell your family." Vivian smiled but did not say anything; she turned back to the map she was drawing. "You're telling your father that you died of a wound." Raphael said as he read the letter.

"Well I am certainly not going to tell him you poisoned me," Vivian said with a grin. "He might not be as willing to help you; after all I am his only daughter."

"If you die I will tell him the truth."

"That is up to you but you might want to wait until after he helps you."

Raphael handed the lamsman to Vivian. "Someday I would like you to explain those symbols to me."

"No keep it," Vivian said and shoved it back to Raphael. "I want to make sure you have it because it may be the only thing that keeps you safe in Ryed."

"I'm going to send this information to King Mathas, I will be right back," Raphael said. He stood up and to Vivian's surprise Raphael kissed her on the top of her head.

"Now the handsome warrior kisses me when I am dying," Vivian teased.

"You're not dying so stop talking about it."

"Well I might be and I might not," Vivian said with a grin. "But at least I got a kiss out of it; although I think you could do better."

Raphael laughed. "Well, stay alive long enough for me to bring you some pie," he said and left the room.

Raphael gave the note to an Enrop then he walked into the kitchen where he found Emeral working. "How is our patient?" she asked.

"Look at these," Raphael said as he handed Emeral the letter that Vivian had written to her father and the lamsman. "Every stone on that bracelet signifies a feat she had to accomplish to become a hunter." Raphael sat down at the kitchen table while Emeral read the letter.

"It's a very touching letter although I can't help but notice she says she is dying of a wound."

"She is afraid for Gabriel and me when we go to Ryed. She promised to help us and if she dies from that potion we gave her she wants her father to honor her promise. She doesn't want to tell him that we may be responsible for her death. Now I feel even guiltier than before."

"Raphael neither you nor Gabriel knew what affects that potion would have on that girl; it was not like you were deliberately trying to hurt her. Now tell me why you have that bracelet."

"To give her father as proof that the letter is from Vivian. She says her clan are the only people not controlled by the dark lords in that kingdom. She said we shouldn't trust anyone who is not a member of her clan."

"So you are feeling even guiltier because she is trying to protect you when you couldn't protect her."

"Yes, I think you said it exactly."

"Do you think she is trying to make you feel guilty?"

"No, she is cracking jokes while she is drawing maps for us."

"I suspect she is frightened of dying but she is a trained warrior and will not let you see that side of her. The fact that she is doing all of this to honor her promise only goes to show what an exceptional warrior she is."

"Raphael I know I am not your mother, but I guess I feel like everyone's mother here. You lead an unusual life. You are a good man; you are extremely dedicated to your missions and The Great Ruler. Gabriel told me he never thought he would meet a woman who could live in his world and then he met Hannah. I think you have met your Hannah. It's obvious that you are both attracted to each other. Why don't you let your guard down and see where this relationship goes."

Raphael was quiet for a moment then he said, "If she lives."

"Oh I suspect she will live," Emeral said. "That girl tracked two monsters across the continent I don't think she is going to let some poison kill her."

"I'm going to take her some pie," Raphael said as he stood up. "I can watch her the rest of the night so you should get some sleep."

"Why did I have the feeling you were going to say that?"

When Raphael walked into Vivian's room he saw that she was sleeping. He removed the tray from the bed and put her drawings on his chair. Raphael pulled the covers over Vivian then he prayed for her healing.

"I hate living like this," Angelina said to Matthew as they were walking with their children to the main dining room for breakfast. "I would rather be in battle then to be constantly looking over our shoulders and jumping at shadows."

"I agree," Matthew said. "But for now it is the best that we can do. Last night I sent a letter to Gabriel asking for more information about the creatures. For one it would be nice to know what language they speak. I would rather capture them and get some information from them."

"If they are trained assassins as Vivian says, they will not give up information easily."

"I know that is why I asked Raul to send us some of that truth potion," Matthew said. "Hopefully the Enrops will see the creatures before they get close to any of us."

Christopher walked into Vivian's room while the others were preparing for breakfast. Raphael was sleeping in the chair next to Vivian's bed. Christopher stopped and looked at Raphael then he jumped onto the bed and stared at Vivian until she woke up.

"Well, who are you?" Vivian asked. Raphael awoke when he heard her speak.

"I am Christopher, Luca saved me and my sister Lila from the Hutas and now we live with him. He is my new daddy," Christopher said proudly. "My friend Fala was killed by the Hutas too. Are you going to die?"

"Well I don't know, I hope not," Vivian said and grinned as she sat up in bed.

"I hope not either," Christopher said. "Here I brought you one of my horses to keep you company until you get better." Christopher handed Vivian a large stuffed horse.

"Thank you, that is very generous of you Christopher. I will take good care of him," Vivian said with a warm smile. Christopher jumped off the bed and ran out of the room. Vivian looked at Raphael and they both smiled. "He is a cute boy," she said.

"All three of the children here have lost their parents to Hutas. Christopher is just now starting to have nightmares. I would imagine you have encountered Hutas in your travels."

"Yes but I try to avoid them because they travel in packs like wild animals," Vivian said with disdain. "Tell me Raphael did you sleep well in that chair?" she asked with a grin.

"It's a bit small," he replied with a laugh.

"I appreciate what you are doing but I don't need people to watch over me. You should sleep in your bed."

"Are you just saying that to get rid of me?" he asked with a grin.

"No, I like your company but you are such a big man and that is such a small chair."

"Perhaps I will find a larger chair."

Vivian grinned at Raphael's comment. "So why do you sit there?" she asked.

"Hannah wants you watched around the clock."

"I see, is that the only reason?" Vivian asked with a coy smile.

"Well, I am partially responsible for your condition."

"Oh, so it is guilt that makes you suffer in that small chair?"

Raphael leaned back in his chair and smiled at Vivian for several moments before speaking, "Luca and Lila are getting married at the end of this week. The wedding will be held at the King's castle and there will be a ball. Would you like to accompany me? We could have that dance that you want."

Vivian's eyes lit up and for the first time Raphael saw her act like a young woman instead of a warrior. "Really," she said excitedly. "I would love to; oh I hope I am better by then." Vivian paused. "I don't have that kind of clothes with me, do you think Hannah would loan me a dress?"

"I will buy you a dress," Raphael said as he stood up.

"No, I could not take such a gift from you."

"Why not? It is the least I can do; I almost killed you," Raphael said as he stood next to her bed. "Do you feel up to going downstairs for breakfast? Hannah brought you a robe that should actually fit you."

"I would like to get out of this bed," Vivian said giddily. "I am very excited about that wedding but I don't know who Luca and Lila are."

Raphael helped Vivian out of bed and held the robe for her as she put it on. "I will be performing the wedding ceremony so you will have to sit with the other wedding guests at that time. Will that be a problem?"

"Oh no," Vivian gushed as she took her long hair out of a pony tail so it could hang down her back. "I am honored that you asked me. Wait," she said as Raphael started to help her out of the room. "I can't forget Christopher's horse," Vivian said with a laugh and grabbed the toy.

"It concerns me that we know these creatures are in the area and the Enrops have not spotted them," Stephan said at the morning meeting in King Mathas' study. "From the description Zoya gave us they certainly can't blend in a crowd.

"Perhaps we should get another description from that warrior who has been tracking them," Sorren suggested as he filled his cup with coffee. "Maybe they somehow disguise themselves when they are on land."

Mathas always kept a window open in his study so that Enrops could enter the castle. "As Sorren was speaking one of the giant birds flew into the room and landed on the King's desk with the note from Raphael. Mathas took the note and read it. "It's from High Priest Raphael. He says the girl Vivian is still gravely ill but during the moments when she is awake her mind is working and she has been giving them a great deal of information about the Teivel Clan in Ryed and the creatures she was tracking."

"She lost their trail just before Salar," Mathas explained. "The trail was so completely obliterated that Vivian thought the creatures went underground but she could not find any tunnels. She says they can swim underwater so we need to be concerned about waterways near our castles. She has killed these creatures in the past with a sword and a knife, so they can be killed like any human. Raphael also asks when they can expect the medicine we are sending."

"Koby and Dagon arrived late last night," Matthew said. "After a meal and a short rest they returned to Wetpr."

"Shara says that aplewort works quickly. It draws the poison from the body and eliminates it. The girl will be vomiting for a while but after that she will be alright. That is if we caught it in time," Sorren explained. "I think she could be very valuable to us. If Vivian lives I would like her to meet with us."

"I agree," Claudius said. "We could send a troop escort."

"I sent a letter to Gabriel yesterday," Matthew said. "To get more information about these creatures, such as what language they speak. I also sent a letter to Sudfad asking for some vials of that truth potion. I think it would be in our best interest to try and capture at least one of them."

"Nikki and Ingr and I am sure Angelina," Thaos said as he looked at Matthew, "Have really had it with all of these threats that Juleta has sent against our families. I certainly can't blame them. But at the same time I am concerned they may take some sort of action on their own."

"Did Nikki say this to you?" Stephan asked with concern.

"No but I found our wives whispering together yesterday. They looked very serious and I didn't believe the story they told me as to what they were discussing."

"Why not?" Sorren asked with a grin.

"Those girls looked mad and serious and they said they were discussing baby clothes," Thaos said with a laugh.

Stephan chuckled, "Yeah, our wives really aren't good liars."

"With all the flocks of Enrops we have encountered," Koby said to Dagon as they were returning to their home in Wetpr. "You would think they would have spotted those creatures by now."

"I was thinking the same thing," Dagon said. "Makes me wonder if something else is going on."

"What do you mean, like magics?"

"Yes after all Juleta was a dark lord, but have we considered that Vivian isn't telling us the truth?"

"I don't know if anyone can lie once they have been given that potion."

"Well, I mean she seems alright the little I have seen her," Dagon continued. "But I am going to talk to Gabriel about it just the same."

"Vivian after breakfast draw me a map to your camp and I will retrieve your things?" Raphael said as the family was sitting around the dining room table.

"Oh my god, how could I have forgotten," Vivian gasped. "I have traps set up around my camp. I need to disable them before someone is killed."

"What sort of traps?" Gabriel asked.

"Trip wires and poison arrows," Vivian said then she turned to Raphael. "Let's leave soon, I have a bad feeling about this."

"You're in no condition to travel," said Hannah.

"Hannah I am good at my traps and I don't want anyone here to get hurt."

"I'll take her in a boca," Raphael said.

"Cassandra and I will go with you," Elan said. "It will be good to get out of the house."

"I'll go too," Luca said. "I would like to see her traps."

"Vivian I have some clothes you can borrow," Natasha said. "Do you want to wear a skirt or riding pants?"

"Riding pants please."

Natasha handed Lily to Calen and helped Vivian to stand up. The two women walked out of the dining room.

"Now that she is gone," Raphael said. "I want to show you something. Emeral saw it last night." As Raphael spoke he took the lamsman and letter from his pocket and handed it to Gabriel along with the maps. "Vivian is concerned that we will be killed in Ryed. She says the dark lords own everyone except for her clan. If she dies from the potion we gave her she wants us to give this letter to her father and the chief of her tribe, so they will honor her promise to help us."

As Gabriel started to read the letter Raphael continued, "This is a lamsman, every stone indicates a feat she had to conquer to become a hunter, she wants us to give this to her father so he knows the letter is really from her." Raphael handed the lamsman to Calen who was sitting to his right.

"Why is she telling her father she is dying of a wound?" Gabriel asked.

"Because she is afraid he won't help us if he believes we are responsible for her death. But if that girl dies I am telling her family the truth," Raphael said. "She also wants us to return her horse so that another warrior can use it."

"I agree," Gabriel said as he studied one of the maps.
Everyone was taking turns reading the letter and looking at the lamsman and maps when Natasha and Vivian returned to the dining room. Emeral smiled when she saw Raphael's face as he looked at Vivian, who was wearing tight riding pants, a white blouse and boots. "I'll get the boca," Raphael said and left the room.

"Raphael showed us the letter you wrote to your father, it was very generous of you," Gabriel said. "Vivian I am truly sorry that we gave you that potion and I have been praying that you will be healed. But if you do die, Raphael and I will tell your family the truth."

Cassandra, Luca and Elan were flying over the boca as Raphael drove it. "Stop just ahead," Vivian said. "My camp is in that thicket. Please let me go in first." Luca and the other Rualas flew over the thicket to check for dangers. "Don't land," Vivian called to them. "There are four traps."

"Well, you only need to disable two," Luca called down to Raphael and Vivian as they were walking towards her camp. "We found the creatures you were hunting."

"They doubled back to kill you," Raphael said with concern.

Vivian smiled when she heard the fear in Raphael's voice. "That is why I set traps. Stay here now. Don't anyone enter until I tell you it is safe," Vivian called out and walked into the thicket. "You can enter now," Vivian yelled after a few minutes. When Raphael entered the thicket he found Vivian and the Rualas looking at the bodies of the two dead creatures.

"They've been dead for a couple of days," Luca said to Raphael.

"Are they human?" asked Cassandra.

"They were once," Vivian said as she searched the clothing on the bodies of the corpses. "I found something," she announced as she pulled a small pouch out of the pocket of one of the creatures. Vivian dumped the contents of the pouch on the ground and explained. "Never stick your hand into a pouch, sometimes they are traps, always empty them on the ground."

Raphael picked up the folded piece of paper that fell out of the pouch.

"What is it?" asked Elan.

"A map," Raphael said. "But I will have to study this as it does not have the normal indicators on it."

"It could be a map of just waterways," Vivian suggested.

Raphael smiled, "I think you are right."

"I think we should take these creatures back with us so Gabriel and the others can see them. Elan can you bring the boca closer?" Luca asked.

After Elan left Cassandra said, "That might be too much for him now."

"He wants us to treat him like an equal not a cripple," Luca said then he turned to Vivian, "Show me how you set up your traps."

"Gabriel, Calen, Maxwell, Misha we have the bodies of the creatures," Elan called out as he entered the house. "Come see them."

Raphael tied the horses in front of the house and helped Vivian down from the boca. "You're not looking good," he said as he set her on the ground.

"I just need to lie down, I am alright," she said weakly.

"Do you want me to carry you?"

Vivian grinned, "I don't think that will be necessary."

Raphael put his arm around Vivian and helped her into the house. As they passed the open door to Gabriel's study both Vivian and Raphael looked into the room. Suddenly Vivian pulled away from Raphael and grabbed the knife from its sheath on his belt. Vivian ran into the study. "Gabriel get away from him he is a dark lord," she yelled.

Gabriel jumped up from his desk, "Vivian stop. I know he is a dark lord."

"What!" Vivian gasped as she looked at Erebus. "You associate with dark lords?"

"We have a common enemy, which killed his wife. He is here to offer his services."

"Don't trust him," Vivian said.

"You move quickly for a girl who is dying," Raphael said sarcastically as he took his knife from Vivian's hand.

"Do I know you?" Erebus asked as he stood up and walked towards Vivian.

"I am Vivian of the Clan of Gesmal and I am a Venator," Vivian said with pride as she stared challengingly into Erebus' eyes.

Erebus smiled, "Gabriel the Venatores are the most vicious warriors in Ryed. I must say you are gathering a group of unlikely allies."

Chapter XXXVI
Fears That Bind Us

"I'm getting so excited I can't even sleep at night," Lila said as she danced around Luca in their bedroom. "In a few days I am marrying the most wonderful man in the world." Luca gently took hold of Lila's shoulders and pulled her towards him. He kissed her passionately on the lips.

"Do you have any place to be in the next couple of hours?" Luca asked with a grin.

"No and Hannah has Christopher," Lila said smiling.

Luca picked Lila up and carried her to their bed.

"I have to admit that I am both excited and embarrassed," Vivian said to Raphael as they were riding in a boca to Salar. "I've never had a man buy me clothes before."

"That's nothing to be embarrassed about," Raphael said with a grin. "I think you would be more embarrassed showing up at the ball in Natasha's riding pants."

Vivian laughed, "You do make a good argument. Raphael I told you before that my village is poor; when I am home I do not dress like Hannah and Natasha."

"That was a beautiful dress you had on when I met you."

"It was a disguise."

Raphael turned and looked at Vivian, "Why do I have the feeling you are trying to tell me something?" She did not answer his question but looked both sad and guilty. "Vivian, a few days ago you could have died and now, well, that tonic that Shara and Angelina sent certainly worked miracles. I can't tell you how guilty Gabriel and I have been feeling for forcing you to drink that potion."

"As far as I am concerned we have a great deal to be grateful for and to celebrate. You are well, you saved our friends from the creatures and my longtime friend is getting married. Please Vivian just enjoy all of this."

"I felt like I was going to die after I took that tonic," Vivian said and laughed. "But it got all of the poison out of me." Then she paused and asked softly, "Raphael why are you really doing all this?"

"What do you mean?"

"Being so nice to me? Is it because you feel guilty?"

"That was a little part of it," Raphael said as he looked at Vivian. "Vivian you are a beautiful, captivating woman and I believe you stole my heart that first day at Jared's wedding. I will tell you it took me by surprise when you suddenly appeared and started flirting with me."

"It took me by surprise when I walked into that wedding celebration and saw the most handsome man in the world," Vivian said with a grin. "I watched you for a while because I couldn't believe you weren't with another woman. Imagine my surprise when you thought I was a demon." They both laughed. There was another long pause then Vivian said softly, "Raphael I like you very much, much more than I should but you understand that I am a Venator don't you?"

"Everyone in that house is a hunter, why?"

"My people hunt differently than yours."

"Vivian there are many ways to hunt," Raphael said. "What are you really trying to say?"

"You know I will have to leave."

Raphael turned and looked at Vivian. She looked sad and serious. "When?" he asked fearfully.

"I don't know yet."

"Is there any place you have to be in the near future?"

"No," Vivian said softly.

"Then plan on staying here, with us and we can get to know each other better."

"And what then?"

"Vivian I don't think it is fair to either of us for you to condemn this relationship before it has even started," Raphael said. "Let's spend time together and learn about each other's lives, then have this conversation again later. Does that sound fair to you?" Vivian didn't speak. "Is there something else you aren't saying?"

"I have trained all my life to be a Venator; Raphael that is all I know."

"Are you telling me that the Venatores don't marry and have families?"

"No, some of them do."

"Then is it that you are afraid of a relationship?"

"I don't know," she said in almost a whisper.

"Vivian you have seemed very happy with us. The family loves you and you fit in, which is not an easy thing since we are all hunters. Tell me the truth do you really want to leave now?" Raphael was not sure he wanted to hear the answer to his question.

"No," Vivian said. "And I think that is what scares me."

"Vivian please, I am asking you to stay for a while," Raphael said sincerely. Vivian didn't speak but after a few moments she moved closer to Raphael and put her arm through his.

"What is happening Claudius?" Bella asked as she entered his study.

"I am calling the family together because I have some news," he replied. Nikki, Thaos and Ryan entered the study and sat down.

"Stephan and Ingr will be here in just a minute," Nikki said. And no sooner had she spoken the words than they walked into the study.

"You know we received that note a couple of days ago that said the creatures were dead, well, we just received more information. Natasha made copies of a map that was found on one of the creatures and drew pictures of them. Of course, they had been dead for a couple of days but the likeness is very similar to the drawings that Ingr did from Zoya's vision." Claudius handed the pictures and maps to Stephan. "And look at that map; it is identical to the one you took off Lazo."

"Has Mathas seen these?" Stephan asked as he handed the papers to Thaos.

"Gabriel's letter said he sent the same drawings to each of our families," Claudius said. "We also know now how they were killed. Vivian had set trip-line traps around her camp. While she was at Gabriel's house the creatures must have backtracked and entered her camp."

"Well, it's a good thing she was with Gabriel and Hannah," Bella said.

"I'm looking forward to meeting her," Ingr said to Nikki.

"What type of weapon was released by the trip-lines?" Thaos asked.

"Poison arrows," Claudius said. "And Gabriel added a little note here. Vivian said that these creatures often put traps in any pouches or bags that they carry so we shouldn't put our hands in such things if we come across them."

"I think it is very fortune for us that Vivian followed them," Nikki said. "Did Gabriel mention if she was improving from the tonic Shara sent?"

"Yes he did," Claudius said. "She got very sick after taking the tonic as the poison was being driven out of her body but she is doing well now. Gabriel also reminded us of Luca's wedding. Vivian will be there if you want to meet her."

"Stephan the children are big enough to travel now and those creatures are dead: do you want to go to the wedding?" Ingr asked with a big smile.

"There will be more creatures," Stephan warned.

"But it will probably take a while for them to get here," Ingr persisted. "We haven't been to anything since I was injured. Stephan I refuse to live the life of a prisoner and I don't want us to raise our children to fear shadows."

Stephan put his arm around Ingr and kissed her on the cheek, "I know and agree with you, it's just after seeing you injured and the babies are so small," Stephan paused. "I guess I am being over protective."

"And this from the man who never wanted to get married," Ingr said with a grin. Then she took Stephan's hand and kissed it. "So can we go to the wedding?"

Stephan smiled and looked around the room, "Does anyone else want to go?"

Claudius smiled, "I too would like to meet the warrior who killed our assassins and your mother and I haven't danced in a while."

Nikki looked at Thaos who grinned and asked, "Do you want to go?"

"Yes, I love going to Wetpr, we should tell Sorren and Shara also because they always enjoy the celebrations that Renya has."

"Raphael this place looks very expensive," Vivian said as they entered a shop on the main business street in Salar. Raphael did not respond to Vivian's comment but walked directly up to the woman behind the counter. "Prince Raul and Prince Simon suggested we come here," Raphael said.

"We will be attending a wedding and a ball at the castle and my friend will need a couple of dresses."

"A couple!" Vivian said.

"That's what Hannah said," Raphael replied with a laugh.

"Yes the Royal Family shops here a great deal, we are honored that you have chosen us," the woman said as she walked from behind the counter. "Was there a particular color you were interested in or did you want to look around first?"

Vivian motioned for Raphael to come to her. "If the Royal Family shops here, the clothing must be very expensive. Raphael I barely know you; I cannot let you spend this kind of money."

"Vivian I want to do this for you, please just allow me." Vivian didn't say anything. "Are you afraid that I will expect something from you?"

"Oh no," Vivian said. "I know you are not that kind of man. Raphael look around you. I could probably feed my village for many months for what you will be spending on one dress."

Raphael kissed Vivian on the forehead, "Please just do this for me."

She nodded. "Alright but know now that I am the one who feels guilty."

Neither Vivian nor Raphael liked the first three ball gowns she tried on but when Vivian came out of the dressing room in the fourth dress Raphael caught his breath. "That is it, what do you think?" he asked of the emerald green silk dress. It was strapless and very form fitting.

"I feel like a princess," Vivian said in awe as she looked at herself in the mirror.

Raphael walked up behind her and put his hands on her shoulders. "You look like a princess," he said to Vivian, then Raphael said to the clerk, "She will need shoes and whatever else to go with this dress."

"Yes My Lord."

Raphael picked out a pale pink dress for Vivian to wear at the wedding ceremony. Vivian said little while they were in the store or as they walked out onto the street. Raphael put the packages in the back of the boca and turned around to help Vivian into the front seat. "Would you please bend down?" Vivian asked. Raphael smiled and did as she asked.

Vivian put her arms around his neck and kissed Raphael on the lips tenderly at first but within moments their passions ignited; Raphael pulled her into him and kissed her with all the emotions in his heart. Vivian became weak in his arms so Raphael held her more tightly. After several minutes they stopped and stared at each other. Both of them stunned by the electricity that surged between them.

"Now I know what scares me," Vivian said breathlessly.

"Are you sorry that happened?"

"No," Vivian whispered. "Please kiss me again."

That evening as everyone was gathering around the dinner table in Gabriel's home, Christopher was watching Vivian and Raphael with a mischievous grin. "We saw you today," Christopher loudly burst out. "You were kissing."

Raphael and Vivian laughed. "Yes we were," Raphael said. "Vivian was thanking me for the dresses."

"She must have really liked them," Christopher said with a grin. "Cuz you were kissing for a long time." Everyone in the room broke into laughter.

"He wanted to go over to you," Hannah said as she laughed. "But I stopped him."

"I'm glad I'm not the only one he embarrasses," said Lila.

"You should see the beautiful dresses Raphael bought me for your wedding," Vivian said. "I felt like a princess."

"Did he pick them out or did you?" Emeral asked.

"He did," Vivian said. "I didn't want to spend his money."

"Well, I am becoming more proud of my sons all of the time," Emeral said. "Lila was the same way so Luca picked out all the dresses for the wedding and I might say they are just beautiful."

"I grew up on a farm and we were very poor," Lila said. "I just feel like I need to save every cent in case we need food."

"I know," Vivian said. "My village too is very poor besides I never had a man buy me clothes before."

"Well, the two of you have more in common than you think," Luca said to Lila and Vivian. "Sometimes Lila feels a little out of place because she is not a warrior."

"Lila you shouldn't feel that way," Hannah said. "I'm not really a warrior. I know I was intimidated by Natasha when I first met her because everyone kept talking about what a fierce warrior she was and how many men she had killed."

"I didn't know that," Natasha said. "Now I feel bad."

"You are a warrior?" Vivian asked Natasha.

"I have been hunting demons with Gabriel since I was small. He raised me and I would beg him to come on his missions. But Calen didn't want me to work on any missions while I was pregnant and unless there is an emergency I don't want to work on any until Lily is a little older."

"Natasha show Vivian your jacket with all the knife sheaths," Koby said. "I still can't get over that. Vivian the first time I worked on a mission with Natasha one of the Enrops told us she was in trouble and a group of men were after her. Between her bullwhip and knives she had killed four of them by time we got to her."

"Yes, my wife almost died twice during that mission," Calen said. "And she wonders why I am protective." Everyone could hear the emotion in Calen's voice so no one said anything for a few moments.

"Calen, I have heard that the women in your tribe are all warriors," Vivian said as she was trying to break the tension. "Is that true?"

"Yes but they are also mothers and wives," Calen said.

"Yes we do it all," Cassandra joked. "What about your tribe?"

"The men and women that are chosen to be Venatores usually concentrate on hunting. We are taught that it is dangerous to have distractions, a Venator must focus on their job."

Gabriel saw the look on Raphael's face as Vivian spoke. "While that is one way to look at it," Gabriel said. "I have found that having Hannah in my life has helped me greatly in my work. She is brilliant and resourceful. I think a couple needs to work out what they want their relationship to be."

"Why don't you show me where you live," Vivian whispered to Raphael as they were leaving the dinner table.

"Almost immediately after Gabriel and Hannah got this house; most of us left for a mission. Hannah and Natasha were very mad that their husbands would not take them along. So it was a great surprise to all of us that while we were gone Hannah and Natasha had the house rebuilt so that it fulfills the needs of our work. There is a huge weapons room and a large medical area. Hannah changed Gabriel's study so it is better set up for our work and she built these chambers for me," Raphael said as he opened the door.

"This is very beautiful," Vivian said as she walked into his parlor area. "Did she decorate it or did you?"

"She and Natasha did. Gabriel and Calen have been adding many bedrooms and chambers to the house to hold other warriors also. So besides being a beautiful home this has become a headquarters for the Patronus."

"Hannah told me about the Patronus," Vivian said. "I had never heard of you before. I must say I was impressed and Hannah is so proud of you both."

"Hannah is a good woman," Raphael said. "It makes me happy that my friend found such a wonderful wife."

"You must read a lot," Vivian said as she walked around his rooms and saw all of the book cases.

"Yes I do but many of those books are for research not pleasure reading."

Vivian suddenly spun around and looked at Raphael. "I don't want to fall in love with you Raphael; I can't." Raphael stared at her, he didn't know what to say but he was aware of the painful sinking feeling in his chest. "I don't mean to hurt you," Vivian said when she saw the look on his face. "I have never thought about a man the way I do you and it is so confusing. My whole life I have trained to be a Venator. I never considered anything else."

"And you are considering other things now?" Raphael asked as he walked up to Vivian and stood very close.

Vivian looked up at Raphael, "I can't focus on anything else but you. This has never happened to me before. When you kissed me today, it was like I became someone else."

"What do you mean?"

"I don't even know how to describe it without sounding crazy. Raphael a Venator is taught to always be in control of each and every situation. We are trained to always be at least one step ahead of the monsters. When we kissed today, it was, I felt like we became one; I felt so weak in your arms and it scared me. Do you understand what I am trying to say?"

"I too felt it Vivian and I believe that is what falling in love is like. It has never happened to you before?"

"No," then Vivian got a strange look on her face. "Have you felt that way before?" she asked jealously.

"Yes," Raphael said and laughed. "But I was eight so I am not sure that really counts." Vivian laughed.

"Raphael I just realized I was jealous of the idea of you with another woman; this is just all so new to me."

"Come and sit by the fire," he said as he took Vivian's hand and led her to the sofa in his parlor. They sat close to each other. "I hope you are learning that you can be a hunter and have a happy life also," Raphael said. "In the Ruala and Nordes tribes the women are warriors and yet they have husbands and families and it is very normal for them. Are you afraid I am going to want you to stop being a warrior?"

"I didn't even think about that."

"Well, the answer is no, I am not going to ask you to give up who you are."

"The problem is that I am not sure who I am anymore," Vivian said as she put her arms around Raphael's neck and kissed his lips.

"I'm really excited," Nikki said to Thaos as she was packing baby clothes. "This will be so much fun."

"I'm glad you are excited," Thaos said and kissed her on the forehead.

"Aren't you?"

"Honestly I don't get excited about balls," he said with a grin. "But I admit that Sudfad and Renya do throw great celebrations."

"You're worried about those creatures, aren't you?"

"I just have a bad feeling. I know those two creatures are dead but I think this is long from over."

"I'm not sure we should have let that happen," Raphael said as he lay on top of Vivian and stroked her hair. "But I am glad we did."

"I know," she whispered as she was ran her fingers through his hair. "Raphael you are the most handsome man I have ever seen. I just never realized how dangerous you were."

"What do you mean?"

"I could get lost in you and it scares me so."

Raphael kissed Vivian's forehead, then the tip of her nose, then her lips. She wrapped her arms around him tightly and let her fears go.

Raphael and Vivian walked into the dining room for breakfast the next morning holding hands and smiling; the kind of smiles that true love making brings to the soul. Everyone in the room noticed but no one said anything. After several minutes Misha's curiosity could no longer wait for he too found Vivian desirable. "So are you two a couple now?" Misha asked. While Raphael smiled at the question, Vivian's face showed the fear that filled her being.

"A couple? Why did you ask that?" The fear in Vivian's voice took Misha by surprise.

"I didn't mean anything by it," Misha said. "I just meant you two are holding hands and you look really happy."

Vivian looked at Raphael and panic overtook her. "We can't be," she whispered and got out of her chair and ran out of the dining room. Raphael quickly followed her out of the room.

"What happened?" Misha asked. "I really didn't mean to insult anyone."

"That girl has trained all her life to be a lone warrior," Emeral said. "And from the little I know of her I believe she excels at her role. It's obvious that she and Raphael are falling in love. And while that can be terrifying for some people for her it would mean a change of everything she is and stands for. I am not surprised she is so conflicted."

"So you think they are falling in love?" Misha asked in a tone that caused the rest of the family to look at him.

"Misha are you interested in her?" Calen asked with surprise.

"I don't know why you asked it like that," Misha said a little defensively. "She is a beautiful woman."

No one spoke for a few moments then Cassandra tried to change the subject, "But she can be a warrior and have a husband and family too; doesn't she understand that?"

"We have been raised to understand that, she has not." Then Emeral turned to Calen. "Calen, my son you know I love you dearly and I respect you as the man and warrior that you are. But your fears for Natasha's safety are imprisoning her and we all see it. Vivian too saw it last night and I believe it only exasperated her own fears." Calen's face turned white as he listened to his mother.

Emeral felt that she opened a door that too long had been shut. "Calen, Natasha is a loyal and loving wife to you yet you do not seem to accept her for who she really is. If you would have married a Ruala girl I doubt if I would be saying these things to you. My son I don't mean to embarrass you but you need to think about my words. The only difference between Natasha and a Ruala wife is that she does not have wings and for that you would change her?"

No one at the table spoke and the silence was deafening. Finally Natasha put her hand on Calen's arm and said, "It's alright Honey." Her words jolted through Calen with a new realization.

"So you agree with what Mother is saying?" Calen asked Natasha. She said nothing and looked down at the table.

"Calen we all agree with Emeral," Koby said. "But it is your marriage and not our place to interfere."

Silence again filled the room. Cassandra decided to try to change the subject again. "Where is Bekka? Has anyone else noticed that she seems to be avoiding all of us?"

"She's been doing a lot of work for me on the wedding preparations," Emeral said. "It's obvious she is trying to keep busy."

"Has she talked to any of you about Fala?" Maxwell asked. Everyone at the table looked at each other and then at Maxwell.

"Bekka cries a lot," Christopher said. "Just go to her room you will see." The words of the child filled them all with guilt. Koby got up from the table and walked out of the room. Everyone sat in silence again.

Natasha turned to Christopher. "Have you been visiting Bekka?"

"Yes, I gave her one of my horses to make her feel better."

Koby knocked on the door to Bekka's room, when she did not answer he turned the doorknob and slightly opened the door. "It's me, Koby can I come in?"

"Yes," Bekka said.

When Koby entered the room he saw Bekka sitting up in bed clutching a pillow, her face was red and swollen from crying. Koby shut the door and walked over to the bed and sat down across from her. "We've missed you," he said softly.

"I'm sorry," Bekka said. "I just can't seem to get over this. I wish the Hutas would have killed me instead." Koby put his arms around Bekka and hugged her tightly. She started to cry again. "I miss her so much Koby, we did everything together."

"Let it out," he said as he stroked Bekka's hair. "I am going to tell you something that you probably don't want to hear. You will never truly get over this. There isn't a warrior in this house who still doesn't hear the voices of their dead friends. But Fala wouldn't want this for you. She was so full of life; she would want you to go on living."

Vivian quickly ran from the dining room to her bedroom and closed the door. "Vivian can I come in?" Raphael asked.

"I don't think that is a good idea," she said. "I need some time to think." Now it was Raphael who felt panic.

He opened the door and saw Vivian lying across the bed on her stomach with her hands over her face. She heard the door open. "Raphael I don't know what you are doing to me but I feel like I can't think anymore."

"I know," he said as he sat down on the bed. "I have been feeling the same way."

"Then what is happening to us?" Vivian asked as she sat up and looked into Raphael's face.

"You know what is happening?" he said softly.

"Well, is this supposed to be what it is like?" Vivian asked with frustration. Then to Raphael's surprise she started to cry. He pulled Vivian to him and hugged her tightly.

"Vivian most of my life I have avoided relationships because I thought they would interfere with my work for The Great Ruler. In your tribe hunters are well known, it is not the case in my world. I was afraid that any woman I met would not understand what I do."

"I have never told anyone else this but when Gabriel wrote to me and said he had fallen in love and married, I really thought I had lost my friend. Then I came here and met Hannah and now that I am living with the Rualas also I realize my fears were that, nothing more than fears." Vivian pulled away from Raphael so she could look into his face as he spoke. She said nothing but kept wiping the tears from her eyes.

"Hannah is not trained as a warrior but did you know that she created explosives that helped Gabriel and the Rualas in that battle in Nora? She has killed men and stood up to demons and I have seen my friend become stronger and happier with her in his life. Vivian I have never asked you to give up hunting and I never will. I respect your training and sacrifice."

"But you are a very intelligent woman and you know there are many ways to hunt. You don't have to be alone; we can hunt together."

"I never cry," Vivian said with frustration as she wiped the tears from her cheeks.

Raphael laughed and kissed her on the forehead, "Come let's go back downstairs."

Koby and Bekka walked into the dining room holding hands. Everyone smiled but no one commented on the fact that she looked like she had been crying. Misha took one of the empty chairs and put it next to Koby's chair for her to sit in.

"Bekka we are sorry that we haven't been there for you," Luca said. "We have no excuses. Apparently Christopher is the only one who has thought about you more than other things in his life. Please let us make up for it."

"It's alright," Bekka said as she wiped tears from her cheeks. Vivian and Raphael entered the room and Vivian was surprised to see Bekka crying, this now drew Vivian's attention. "It's silly I should be getting over this."

"Bekka don't expect yourself to get over this," Maxwell said. "We have all lost loved ones in battle the best you can do to honor their memories is find a way to go on."

"But she died saving me. I'm the one who should have died that day."

"There are many things in this world we do not understand," Emeral said softly. "And maybe we are not meant to. Just know that for whatever reason The Great Ruler spared your life that day and you are a blessing to us all." Bekka did not say anything but the tears started to run down her cheeks. Koby put his arm around her and hugged Bekka tightly.

"May I ask what happened?" Vivian asked. "Or is it too painful to talk about?"

"We found a mausoleum in Nora that may be an opening to a hell dimension," Luca explained. "The Sanuri sent some of us there with the instructions to watch it only."

"I can tell the rest," Bekka said as she tried to compose herself. "We knew there were Hutas in the area because Lila's and Christopher's parents had been murdered."

"While we are all trained as warriors there is special training if you are lucky enough to be selected for Gabriel's team. There were four of us in training in Nora. Dack, Joao, Fala and me. Fala was much younger than the rest of us and she was like everyone's little sister. She was so much fun and full of life."

"We were out on patrol one morning and I saw a man's body on the ground. He was dressed as the people of Nora dress so I flew down to check on him. As soon as I knelt over him he turned and grabbed me and I realized he was a Huta, suddenly other Hutas came out of hiding and they started to beat me. Fala flew down and fought with my attackers but one of the Huta's held her arms while another one stabbed her over and over."

"I tried to get to her but one of them hit me so hard that I blacked out. When I woke up I was bound and the Hutas were dancing before a fire. I knew they were going to sacrifice me to one of their demons and that thought filled me with rage. Suddenly I saw some other Rualas in the sky; they were looking for me. I tried to distract the Hutas. When my friends came they cut me loose. All I could do was see Fala's face; I went crazy I kept stabbing the Hutas over and over."

"Bekka had many injuries," Lila said. "But she still killed two Hutas. She never thought about herself she only thought about Fala." Lila turned to Luca. "I didn't tell you this before but when we were in Nora I asked Bekka and Fala to be in our wedding. They were both very excited."

"Bekka as painful as that was," Maxwell said. "I think it was good that you finally told us. Now you can unlock those memories instead of holding them in."

Chapter XXXVII
Songs of the Heart

Erebus still had the jewels he had stolen from Roch and now that both Meekos and Sophie were dead he had their family money also. Sophie meticulously set up her will so that Erebus would never want for anything. Erebus swore to himself that he would never return to the Kingdom of Stordt. After he left his meeting with Gabriel, Erebus hired two men to drive a large covered boca which contained what was left of his and Sophie's belongings. He hired a carriage and two drivers for his personal transportation and he hired ten men for protection.

Erebus was travelling west to his castle in the Kingdom of Ryed. He sat alone in his carriage and cried at the loss of his wife. Erebus was no longer using whiskey to drown the pain and grief; he was trying to keep his head clear so he could plot against the Insidiae. Erebus told Gabriel every shred of information that he knew about that organization.

Erebus promised to provide Gabriel with any additional information that he uncovered. Sophie had previously shipped much of her belongings and the belongings of Meekos to Erebus' castle. Erebus did not know what was in the many crates that Sophie shipped but he hoped to find more useful information about the Insidiae, information that he hoped would help him destroy that diabolical society.

Erebus was also filled with unforgivable quilt. When Gabriel was trying to save Sophie from the demon that Roch had become; Erebus delayed in telling Gabriel where Sophie was. For the rest of his life Erebus would wonder if in those few seconds that he hesitated, they could have saved Sophie's life.

Fahron once again volunteered to stay in Lentz and to oversee the kingdom while the families of Mathas and Claudius traveled to Wetpr for Luca's wedding. Many of them did not know Luca well but they all loved the celebrations that Renya organized. Chief Sorren of the Nordes Tribe, his wife Shara and their two young sons also traveled in the royal caravan. Besides enjoying the festivities, Sorren had developed a kinship with King Sudfad.

These two older warriors found they had much in common and they greatly enjoyed their talks together. In his youth, Sorren was a rebel leader who fought against King Mathas for control of the kingdom. Now, because of the marriages of their children, they were all family. Sorren, Claudius and Mathas all powerful warriors and strong leaders were now more interested in their children and grandchildren than they were in waging wars or seizing power and land. These former enemies now enjoyed each other's company and they formed an alliance to protect their families at all cost.

As the family gathered around the dinner table at Gabriel's home Emeral made an announcement. "Misha and Dagon, the girls will be arriving first thing in the morning. I am surprised that they are waiting until the last minute like this but that is neither here nor there. The question is when do you want to meet them?" Neither Misha nor Dagon answered her question.

"Is she getting them wives?" Vivian asked Raphael.

"No!" Misha said emphatically. "Luca has so many of us in the wedding party that we needed more girls to walk down the aisle with so Emeral sent for a couple for us."

"Dear, the boys are always afraid that I am trying to marry them off," Emeral said to Vivian. "And they are right," she added with a laugh.

"Koby if you want to walk with one of these other girls, that is alright with me," Bekka said.

"No, he claimed you right away, we get the surprises," Misha said sarcastically.

"Emeral who did you ask?" Cassandra asked.

"Mia, the daughter of Tyron and Elsa and Melanie the daughter of Casey and Tasha. They are beautiful young girls. I don't know what all the fuss is about," Emeral said with a grin.

"I know both of them," Bekka said. "And they are really pretty. And they are friends of your sisters."

"I know them too," Cassandra said. "You two are going to like them."

"We'll see," Dagon said. "Emeral you didn't tell the girls that we were going to marry them or anything did you?"

"Of course not," Emeral said teasingly. "You boys just don't appreciate my hard work."

"If they are friends of our sisters," Misha said with disdain. "I assume they are like them."

"Boys give them a chance," Emeral said.

"Misha why did you say that about your sisters?" Natasha asked.

Everyone at the table was quiet for a few moments before Misha spoke. And it was obvious to everyone that he was choosing his words very carefully. "Our sisters are nothing like Emeral or even all of you women here. In fact, now that I think about it all of you girls are like Emeral; you act more like her daughters than her blood daughters do." Misha hesitated.

"Our sisters are more concerned with money and status than anything else," Luca said. "And how they turned out like that with Emeral and Maxwell as their parents I will never understand." No one spoke for several moments.

"Changing the subject," Gabriel said with a grin. "Vivian the families that we believed those creatures were after are coming for Luca's wedding. They would very much like to talk with you and to show you some documents that they have."

"I would be happy to meet with them."

"You'll like them," Raphael said to Vivian. "The Nordes Tribe, like the Rualas train all of their men and women to be incredible warriors. Three women from the Nordes Tribe have married sons of the ruling families of Lentz. They are all good people but King Mathas' oldest daughter was an insane dark lord and she has repeatedly put bounties on the heads of all these families. The Sanuri destroyed her but apparently she had plans set up to still pay assassins if she died."

"Why did she do that?" Vivian asked.

"Juleta planned to kill her father to take his throne," Gabriel said. "And she had her little sister kidnapped and was going to sacrifice her to a demon. And there is more, you will meet a man named Claudius, he is one of the ruling members of that kingdom. He has a son named Stephan and an adopted son named Thaos; turns out that Juleta desired both of these men and neither of them wanted anything to do with her. Juleta became jealous when she found out they both had married and she has repeatedly tried to have their wives killed."

"I hope you told these people that King Douma will keep sending assassins until the job is completed."

"They know and that is one reason they want to talk to you," Gabriel said. "Those families are all warriors but they all have young babies and fear for the safety of their children."

"Perhaps they should offer Douma more money than Juleta paid to stop the attacks," Vivian said.

"These men are warriors," Calen said. "I don't think they would pay off an enemy."

"Calen this is a different situation which is probably why Juleta hired Douma's men. The Kingdom of Ogg exists on the floor of the Schenomi Sea, so they cannot be attacked as other kingdoms."

"How can that be?" Maxwell asked. "I mean I have heard stories about the Kingdom of Ogg but until you came here and I saw those creatures you killed, I never believed any of those stories were true."

"I can only tell you what I was taught," Vivian said. "It was said that centuries ago the Valdees Tribe, that is the tribe that lives in the Kingdom of Ogg, once lived in the lands that are now called the Waste Lands of Manod. But in those days they were not waste lands but lush fields and forests."

"Legends say that the Valdees were such a cruel people that their gods punished them and their king who was named Douma declared war against these gods."

"Douma lost the war and his people had no place to go so he formed an alliance with a powerful demon who gave the Valdees the ability to live under water. Douma ordered his tribe into the sea and created a kingdom that he named Ogg."

"Has anyone ever seen this kingdom?" Luca asked.

"All I can tell you is that no one from my clan has. But since we live close to the Schenomi Sea we do see these creatures often. They have to pay a bounty to the demon they serve, so they come to land to steal people for slaves and to kill."

"How do you know if this is true?" asked Misha.

Vivian paused for a few moments, "Because we have taken captives and tortured them for information."

"So they speak the same language as you?" Gabriel asked.

"No, not as we are speaking now. They speak a variation of an old language that was once common to our region; it is called Kaladac."

"And you can speak this language?" asked Raphael.

"Yes," Vivian replied. "All the Venatores learn that language."

"Gabriel and I both studied ancient languages at the university," Raphael said. "I have never heard of this language can you translate it for us?"

"Do you mean write it down for you?"

"Yes."

"Of course, I would be happy to."

"Do you know who the demon is that the Valdees pay tribute to?" Gabriel asked.

"Baal, he is said to be one of the oldest demons in this world."

"Just a minute," Raphael called out when he heard someone knocking on his door. Raphael got out of bed and put on his trousers then walked to the door. When he opened it he smiled. Vivian was standing in the hallway looking embarrassed. She was holding several sheets of paper. Raphael moved so she could enter his room.

"I have been working on that translation for you and I wanted to know if this is how you wanted it," Vivian said and handed the papers to Raphael.

"Come, sit by the fire," he said and led her to the sofa that was in his parlor. Vivian didn't speak as Raphael looked over her work. "This is excellent thank you," Raphael said as he set the papers on a table near the sofa. "But is this the real reason you came to my room at this time of night?"

"I know I should stay away from you but I can't," Vivian said with a panicked look on her face. "Raphael I don't know what I am doing anymore and I always know what I am doing. Do you have any idea how this makes me feel?"

He smiled and pulled Vivian close to him. "I have been feeling the same way but I am not letting it torture me like you are. Vivian you are at war with your emotions."

"But Raphael," Vivian paused for several moments then continued. "I feel weak when I am in your arms and I like it. I am a Venator I can never feel weak."

"Honey you are talking about two very different things," Raphael said soothingly. "If a demon came through that door right now, you would most likely be attacking it before I even had my weapon drawn and you know it." Vivian laughed. "The weakness you feel in love making is not the same as having weakness on the battlefield," Raphael paused then said. "You know Emeral might be a good person for you to talk to."

"Why?"

"She is a fierce warrior and seems to have adopted all of us as her children," Raphael said. "She is a wise woman. I am sure she can explain these things to you better than I can."

"Perhaps I will," Vivian said more to herself than to him.

"Did you come here because you wanted to spend the night with me?" Vivian nodded but did not speak. "You don't need to make excuses to be with me," Raphael said and kissed Vivian on the forehead. "I would very much like it if you stayed with me every night."

"Would you really?"

"Yes but I think you are too scared right now to consider that."

"I have slept with you the last two nights and tonight as I was writing in my room, it did not seem right. I realized that I needed to see you. Raphael this is all so new to me. I spend months by myself when I am hunting and now I can't be away from you for more than a few hours."

"I have to admit I am very happy to hear you say that."

"Raphael in my clan if two people sleep together always they are husband and wife."

"Some people feel like that here too but usually the man gives the woman a ring and asks her to marry him and then they have a ceremony like Luca and Lila will tomorrow." Raphael stared into Vivian's eyes. "Vivian you have been so frightened of our relationship that I have not wanted to tell you what was in my heart for fear it would scare you even more."

"Raphael do you want me to be your wife?" Vivian asked in a whisper.

"If I tell you the truth are you going to run out of here?"

"No," she said hesitantly.

"Yes."

Vivian looked at Raphael then looked at the floor then looked back at him. "My heart is racing with both excitement and fear, I must think about this."

"Please don't run away."

Raphael's voice had such fear and sincerity in it that it touched Vivian's heart. She caressed his cheek with her hand then kissed him on the lips. "Let's go to bed," she whispered.

"Natasha are you awake?" Calen asked as he looked at his wife who was sleeping in his arm.

Natasha jumped up to a sitting position. "Is it the baby?" she asked wearily.

"No, Lily is sleeping. I am sorry now that I woke you."

"Calen is something wrong?" Natasha asked.

"I wanted to talk."

"Well this must be serious," Natasha said half kiddingly. "What do you want to talk about?"

Calen now propped himself up on his left arm and looked at her. "For the last couple of days I have been thinking about what Mother said about how I treat you. At first I was really angry at her words but then after what Koby said, well, I started really thinking about it." Natasha didn't say anything but she took Calen's right hand into hers.

"I know you are a fierce warrior; that is one of the things that attracted me to you. But when those men were after you and later when you almost died from that demon snake; Natasha I have never felt fear like that before. I just love you so much I don't know what I would do if anything happened to you and now that we have Lily. Mother said I don't accept you for who you really are. I do, I just don't know if I can explain it."

Natasha caressed Calen's face then kissed him on the lips. "I have known this all along that is why I never said anything. And I too, have been torn apart with fear for you my husband. Calen I will be honest I greatly miss working on the missions but also having a baby is so much more work than I ever imagined. Right now I just want to stay with our baby but there will be times when I want to work on the missions too. I understand what Vivian is going through because being a demon hunter is part of who I am also. So what do you want to do about this?"

"I don't want you going on any missions without me," he said.

"So there will be missions?"

"Yes."

"I can accept that."

Calen started to laugh, "Or I could just keep you pregnant all of the time."

"Why did I know you were going to say that?" Natasha said with a grin and leaned forward and kissed Calen. He took her into his arms and kissed her passionately on the lips, then down her neck and shoulders. Natasha moaned as he climbed on top of her.

Vivian lay in Raphael's arm and watched him sleep. Love poured through her like the blood in her veins. "I have never seen anyone so beautiful," she thought as she now propped herself up on her elbow.

Vivian's head had been spinning since Raphael said he wanted to marry her. While Vivian's heart said 'yes' her fears were screaming through her being. "I don't know what to do," Vivian thought as tears started to stream down her cheeks. She reached up and caressed Raphael's hair; Vivian loved his thick, straight black hair.

Suddenly she realized Raphael was looking at her. Vivian smiled with embarrassment. "So you have been watching me sleep?" he asked and smiled as he put his arms around her and pulled her down on top of him.

"I can't sleep I have so much on my mind," Vivian said and softly kissed Raphael's cheek.

"Do you mean about us?"

"That is part of it," she said. "I just have been thinking about so much." Raphael started to gently rub her back which made Vivian melt into him.

"Raphael I realized I do love you," Vivian said softly. "But I am scared and I still have so much to think about."

"I love you too," Raphael said and gently kissed Vivian on the lips. "I think that the fact you told me how you feel is a sign that you are coming to terms with your fears."

"I don't know," she said. "I still feel so confused. But I know I love being with you like this." Vivian softly kissed Raphael's chest. He smiled and caressed her long hair, then he put his arms around her and rolled them both over so Vivian was on her back.

"I love being with you like this too," Raphael said and kissed her passionately on the lips.

The next morning was chaotic in both the castle of Sudfad and the house of Gabriel as guests arrived and everyone prepared for the wedding of Luca and Lila.

"I am so nervous, I couldn't sleep all night," Lila said to Luca as they returned to their room after breakfast.

"Perhaps this will help," Luca said as he handed Lila a small box.

"Oh Luca it is beautiful," she said as tears came to her eyes. "This bracelet matches my necklace and earrings. Luca I have never had such beautiful things I am almost afraid to wear them."

"Nonsense," he said. "Here let me help you put it on."

Lila kissed Luca over and over as she admired her gift. Then she ran to the dresser and took a velvet box from one of the drawers. "I hope you like it," she said. "It is very difficult to buy for someone who has so many things."

"Honey how did you pay for this? You won't let me give you money."

"Gabriel and Hannah gave me quite a bit of money to buy you a gift. I didn't even spend it all," Lila said excitely. "But I might have to explain what this is."

"I know exactly what this is," Luca said with a big smile. "I have seen Raul's and Simons. I love it."

Luca opened the large golden locket and found a wisp of Lila's hair and a wisp of Christopher's. Each strand of hair was tied with the tiniest of bows. "I had just diamonds put on the front because they are your family stone but if you want more stones let me know."

"No this is beautiful and I love it," Luca said as he kissed Lila.

"Luca turn it over."

Luca read the inscription on the back of the locket; *Our hearts are always with you.* And he could feel his heart swell within his chest.

"Do you need help getting into your dress?" Raphael called through Vivian's bedroom door.

"Actually I do, come in. There are so many little buttons on the back of this," she said with a laugh.

"First let me look at you."

Vivian turned and faced Raphael. She was wearing her long black hair in one large twist with ringlets flowing down her back. The pale pink dress had a low neckline and puff sleeves. Her athletic and womanly figure was flattered greatly in the bodice and skirt. "Raphael is something the matter?"

"No, you just took my breath away for a minute. You look incredibly beautiful. Now turn around and I will button you."

"And you look very handsome in that suit. Is that what you will wear during the ceremony?"

"I will put my priest's robe over this when I conduct the ceremony. You are right there are a lot of buttons back here," Raphael said as he laughed. "Now hold still," he said when he finished buttoning her dress.

"What are you doing?" Vivian asked with a smile then she realized Raphael was putting a necklace on her.

"Look in the mirror."

"Raphael this is too beautiful," Vivian gasped as she looked at the pearl necklace that had a pink sapphire in the middle. "But I cannot accept this it is too expensive."

"Does that mean you have already made your decision?" he asked solemnly.

"No it does not," she said. "I am just not used to such things. Please don't be hurt by what I said."

"Here are the earrings and I have jewelry for your gown tonight, so you will just have to get use to this," Raphael said and kissed Vivian on the cheek. She stretched up and kissed him on the lips which he returned hungrily. After a few moments Raphael said, "We have to stop now or we will never make it to the ceremony."

Hannah and Gabriel had Christopher, Nicholas and Cerey in their chambers as they were trying to dress the children as well as themselves for the wedding. Both Gabriel and Hannah were laughing at the antics of the boys.

"I love this," Hannah said to Gabriel.

"So do I," he replied as he was trying to get Nicholas to wear a tie.

"Hannah do you have my gift?" Christopher asked excitedly.

"Yes dear, now hold still and I will give it to you as soon as I button this."

"I want to show it to Gabriel," Christopher said with a grin.

Hannah walked over to the desk in their bedroom and took a small box out of one of the drawers. She gave it to Christopher and explained its contents as Christopher ran up to Gabriel.

"Lila had one of those lockets made for Luca like Raul and Simon have. Christopher wanted to get Luca a gift so he had this disk made to put on the chain of the locket.

"Read both sides," Christopher said proudly.

Gabriel picked up a smooth round golden disk that had *you are my hero* engraved on the front and *Luca I love you* engraved on the back. After Gabriel read the inscriptions he looked at Hannah who was smiling proudly then back at Christopher.

"Christopher," Gabriel said. "Luca has been my friend for many years and I can tell you he will love this; it is very beautiful." Hannah smiled at how touched Gabriel seemed as he read the inscriptions.

"When should I give it to him?" Christopher asked.

"We are all meeting in the parlor before the wedding I think that would be a fine time," Gabriel said and grinned.

"Nicholas will you come here?" Hannah asked. Nicholas ran to her. "Now you give this to Papa. Cerey go with him."

Gabriel knelt back down as all three of the children gathered around him. "Is this from you?" Gabriel asked as Nicholas handed him the box.

"It's from all of us Papa, even Christopher."

Gabriel smiled broadly when he saw his family locket. He hugged all three of the children before he took the locket from its box. Then he stood up and kissed Hannah, "Thank you dear, I love it."

"Gabriel there's writing on the back," Christopher said enthusiastically. Tears came to Gabriel's eyes as he read, *So we can always be with you.*

"Everyone looks wonderful," Maxwell said as the family gathered in the parlor for a glass of wine before the ceremony.

"Oh my!" said Emeral when she saw the children enter the room. Everyone smiled as the children walked in.

"They are adorable," Natasha said.

"We've had a little trouble getting the boys to keep their ties on," Gabriel said and winked. "Are Luca and Lila still planning on joining us?"

"Yes," Emeral said. "Since he picked out her dress he has already seen her in it."

"Did you two ever meet Mia and Melanie?" Elan asked Misha and Dagon with a grin.

"No," Misha said. "We've been too busy."

"Well then you have a surprise coming," Emeral said.

"Hannah look what Raphael bought me," Vivian said as she showed Hannah her necklace and earrings.

"They are very beautiful," said Hannah. "And so are you. I love how you fixed your hair."

"Here they come," Calen announced as Lila and Luca entered the parlor. Everyone applauded.

Maxwell handed them each a glass of wine, "To Luca and Lila, may they have a long and happy life together."

As everyone was taking a drink of their wine, Christopher's voice rang out. "Now Gabriel?"

"I think now would be perfect," Gabriel said with a smile and looked at Luca.

Christopher ran up to Luca and handed him a small box. "I picked the words," Christopher said excitedly as Luca knelt down and took the box from him.

"He really wanted to get you a wedding gift," Hannah said to Luca. "It's to go on the chain of your locket."

Luca was speechless as he read the front of the disk; his emotions were welling within him. "There's more on the back," Christopher said. Luca looked as if he was going to cry as he read the back inscription; Luca grabbed Christopher and hugged him tightly.

"Why don't you read it out loud," Bekka said when she saw the look on Luca's face. The room stood silent as Luca read the words that Christopher had engraved on the disk and silent they remained for several moments afterwards.

In royal grandeur, Renya sent carriages to pick up the wedding party and guests at Gabriel's home. Everyone was filled with excitement especially when they arrived at the castle; for Emeral was the only one in Luca's family who knew what was planned.

The wedding ceremony was to be held on the royal grounds and the King and Queen opened the festivities to the citizens of their kingdom. The smell of thousands of flowers filled the streets of Salar as the carriages rode in the grand procession. "Is this what all weddings are like?" Vivian whispered to Raphael as they rode in a carriage with Elan and Cassandra.

"Oh no," Raphael said. "Queen Renya loves to have celebrations. This is a wedding befitting a prince."

Vivian watched Elan and Cassandra; they seemed very much in love. But she could see the sadness in Elan's eyes and his self-consciousness about his amputated arm. "Elan have you been training since you lost your arm?" Vivian asked to everyone's surprise.

"No," Elan said. "Honestly I am just trying to get use to functioning without it."

"Because demons are so powerful and can do such damage, part of our training as a Venator is in preparation for losing an arm or a leg and still conquering in battle. If you would like, we could train together some time."

Cassandra smiled and looked at Elan who asked. "Do many Venatores lose limbs?"

"Oh yes," Vivian said. "Mostly they lose their lives but they often lose limbs too."

"Does it stop them from being a lone hunter?" asked Elan.

"In most cases no, the choice is up to the hunter. Is your injury going to stop you Elan?"

"No," he replied with determination.

"Good then perhaps tomorrow we will start training."

"I would like to join you," Raphael said as he hugged Vivian.

"As would I," said Cassandra.

"Elan would you prefer to start training alone?" Vivian asked.

"No," Elan said with a smile as the idea of this training was exciting him.

"I don't know this area as well as you," Vivian said. "So can you find a good location?"

"Gabriel's property backs up to the River Nebu, there is a sandy area where we train," said Raphael.

"Perfect," Vivian said. Then she paused for a few moments. "Raphael when we get home I would like to look at the map we took off those creatures again."

"Why is something wrong?" Elan asked.

"I didn't realize Gabriel's property is on the water. I was so sick when I first looked at that map that I might have missed something."

"I'm glad you said 'home'," Raphael said with a grin, then he turned to Elan and Cassandra and said, "I'm waiting for Vivian to decide if she wants to be my wife."

"Really?" Cassandra said with an excited smile. "I hope you say 'yes'."

"Vivian I don't know if anyone has told you that the Ruala people hold Gabriel and Raphael in very high esteem. They are well known as hunters besides being courageous warriors. It is a great honor for any Ruala warrior to be chosen to work on the team," Elan said.

"It's not only an honor for the warrior but the for the warrior's family," Cassandra said. "I know that our style is different from yours but you should be very proud to become a member of this family; I know I am."

During the wedding ceremony Vivian and Emeral sat together as everyone else in the household was in the wedding. Emeral held Lily, who did not cry, even when the trumpets were blowing. Vivian had never witnessed such a grand event. The excited crowds and the soldiers in their dress uniforms seemed to make the event more spectacular. But it was when Raphael spoke to the wedding couple and to the crowds that Vivian's heart melted. As soon as Raphael started to speak, silence fell so only his voice could be heard and Vivian suddenly felt as if she was listening to an Angel speak.

Raphael's voice rang out as if carried by the wind. The guests, the soldiers, the spectators listened in awed silence to his words. Vivian suddenly realized she was crying and when she turned she saw that Emeral too had tears running down her cheeks. Christopher stood at the altar with Luca and Lila and when the bride and groom exchanged rings they gave one to Christopher also, to signify his importance in their marriage; an act which also brought tears to the eyes of many.

When Luca, Lila and Christopher turned and faced their guests and the crowds, doves were released into the air and Vivian had made her decision.

Chapter XXXVIII
Threats

After the wedding party got into their carriages and started the procession through the streets of Salar, Vivian quickly walked up to Raphael. "You were wonderful," she gasped. "I can't believe how you can speak; you had us all crying."

Raphael smiled, "Well, I am a priest."

"I have heard other priests speak Raphael and you truly have a gift." Vivian walked closer to him and squeezed his hand. "I am so proud to be with you," she said emotionally. Raphael leaned down and kissed Vivian on the forehead but just as quickly stood up as they heard approaching footsteps.

"I'm sorry," Raul said smiling. "I didn't mean to interrupt."

"You weren't," Raphael said. "Vivian do you remember Prince Raul?"

"Yes," she said and smiled.

Raul walked up to Vivian and took her hand and kissed it. "I want you to know that we are truly sorry for how sick you got from that potion; we had no idea it would affect you like that."

"I know," Vivian said. "But perhaps if I wouldn't have gotten so sick I would not have met Raphael and the others; I believe it was worth it." Vivian gave Raphael a coy smile as she said these words.

"Raul I have asked Vivian to marry me," Raphael said. "She is trying to decide if she can give up the life of a lone hunter."

"Say yes," Raul said. "You couldn't be marrying a better man. And I must say you look beautiful."

"Raphael bought me all these things," Vivian said with pride.

Raul looked at Raphael and smiled then Raul said to Vivian. "Our family from Lentz is gathering in the parlor and would very much like to speak to you."

"Let me just finish up here and we will be right in," Raphael said, then he looked at Vivian. "Or do you want to go ahead?"

"No, I will wait for you. Can I help?"

As Raphael was removing the cloths and candles from the wedding altar he said, "I am very glad about what you said to Elan. He has seemed so lost after his injury. If it wasn't for Cassandra I don't know what he would do. I think he now doubts himself because it was his first big mission and he got hurt watching over her."

"What were you doing?"

"It's a long story which I can tell you later but when Elan got hurt we were in a hotel in Taperia fighting thousands of demons."

"Thousands! Raphael are you telling me the truth?"

"Yes and there was only a couple of hundred of us, if the Angels hadn't joined us we would have lost."

"Angels," Vivian gasped. "Now you are teasing me."

"No I'm not," Raphael said with a grin. "Just ask the people from Lentz, they were there. Vivian I hope you stay long enough for me to tell you about all these things."

Raphael and Vivian walked into the parlor in the castle holding hands. To Vivian's surprise the room was filled to capacity with people.

"I am sorry we are so crowded in here," Sudfad said. "But Renya has the Great Hall prepared for the ball and won't let anyone in there." Sudfad took Vivian around the room and introduced her to King Mathas and his family, Claudius and his family which now included Ryan, and Sorren and his family. "And I believe you have met the others," Sudfad said.

"She wasn't introduced to anyone at that other wedding," Simon said.

Sudfad then continued introductions with Raul and Simon, Jared and Zoya and Archetenus. "Before we get started," Sudfad said. "First I would like to explain to Vivian that we are all fighting demons and the people who call to them. And as family and friends we are very close and communicate often, so our family from Lentz knows about your tribe and the creatures that you killed."

"Also as you know Vivian when we first met you we thought you might be a spy for the Insidiae so I sent a letter to the Sanuri. He says he knows your family but has not seen you since you were a little girl. He also told us that he believes your sudden appearance here is a gift to us and that we should all work together."

"Vivian first I would like to express our gratitude for killing those creatures and helping us," King Mathas said. "My family is in your debt. Have you been told about my daughter Juleta?"

"Yes, Gabriel and the family told me so I would be prepared to meet you. I cannot understand a daughter turning against her father like that. I am sorry for your family."

Mathas paused, so Matthew spoke. "Vivian, Juleta has broken my father's heart so at times it is difficult for him to speak of her. We are families of warriors yet we are families and as you can see we have many babies. Juleta's hatred knows no bounds; she tries to inflict the most pain that she can which causes us to fear she will strike against our children. She already tried to kill her little sister: the Sanuri helped us attack Juleta's castle and save Margarit. Afterwards in the ruble a man found this letter and map." Matthew walked up to Vivian and handed her the papers.

"What is the matter?" Claudius asked when he saw Vivian frown as she read the letter.

"While the words seem straight forward, this is not the language of the Valdees Tribe but they do come to the mainland to steal slaves; perhaps a slave translated this." Vivian said then looked at the map.

"A few months later," Stephan explained. "The bodies of three men were found hidden in one of the mines. The bodies were stripped naked but from their appearances they had greatly fought their attackers. Another map, identical to the one in your hand was found in the clenched fist of one of the bodies."

"Were there any attacks against your families?"

"No," Claudius said. "We found no bodies of the creatures and there were no sightings of them."

"May I make a copy of this letter to study?" Vivian asked. "I don't want to alarm you but something really is not right with all this. This is not the normal behavior of the Valdees. They are aggressive and savage warriors and they always fight to the death. These creatures work for a powerful demon; if they fail at their duties they know there will be grave consequences. If creatures were already sent to attack your families they would have."

"Which means they could have been here for another reason," Thaos said. "Juleta was extremely cunning and had many well planned attacks against us."

"You are warriors, I am sure you have fought Hutas," Vivian explained. "The Valdees and the Hutas are very similar."

"So there could be someone near us who is controlling them," Claudius said. "It happened once before with a different type of demon that Juleta sent after our families."

"That is a possibility. If I would not have seen the creatures with my own eyes, I would wonder if this was a trap or a distraction," Vivian said.

"We have considered that also," said Matthew.

"Vivian has written down the language of the Valdees and translated the words for us," Raphael said. "We can make copies for you."

"We can help with that," Angelina said. "If you want to give us just one copy we will make the rest."

"Vivian, do these creatures wear any tattoos of the Mark of Satan?" Archetenus asked.

"I am familiar with that mark," Vivian said. "I have never seen that tattoo on any of them. But they do cover their bodies with tattoos so I could have missed it."

"Or they wear some other mark," Sudfad said. "Vivian has anyone told you about Jared and Archetenus being created as vessels for demons?"

"No!"

"Don't worry we aren't any more," Archetenus said. "But you should know about this."

"Archetenus do you want to tell her and I will make a copy of this letter for her," Ingr said. The meeting went on for another hour and ended when the wedding party returned to the castle.

"Lakin," Christopher screamed as he ran through the crowd of guests in the Great Hall and jumped into Lakin's arms. Lakin laughed and hugged Christopher tightly. Luca and Lila followed Christopher. Lila kissed Lakin on the cheek. "We are so glad you could make it," she said then gave Lakin a second kiss on the cheek.

"Lila, Christopher I would like you to meet my family," Lakin said as he set Christopher down. "This is my beautiful wife Zada."

"Lakin has told me so much about you and Christopher I feel like I already know you," Zada said with a warm smile.

"I can't begin to tell you how kind your husband was to us after our parents were murdered; it meant a great deal," said Lila.

"And the children I will introduce by ages, my son Jacot, my daughter Abella, my son Tavin, another beautiful daughter Isla and our youngest son Brik," Lakin said with a father's pride.

Christopher walked up to Brik, who was close to his age. "I've never seen a boy with wings before. Lily has wings but she is a baby." Christopher turned to Luca. "Can I get wings?" Christopher asked seriously.

"I'm pretty sure you have to be born with them," Luca said as everyone laughed.

"You want to meet my friends?" Christopher asked Lakin's children. "Luca can I take them to meet Nicholas, Cerey and Petra?"

"Yes," Luca said "But keep Cerey with you." Christopher turned and ran and Brik and Isla followed him.

"Luca I have never seen you look so happy," Zada said as she kissed him on the cheek. Then Zada looked at Lila. "You married a good man."

"I know," Lila said. "He makes me so proud. But I must admit that this ceremony was a bit overwhelming. I never expected anything like this."

"Renya does love to do things right," Lakin said.

"So what is going on in Nora?" asked Luca.

"Oh no you don't," Zada scolded. "You aren't talking work at your wedding; that can wait."

After the meeting with the families from Lentz, Vivian asked Raphael to take her back to Gabriel's house so she could write another translation of the language of the Valdees. She also wanted to study the maps and letter that these families had. Vivian and Raphael agreed that she would stay at the house and work and he would come back for her, in the early evening so they could attend the ball. Raphael returned to the castle.

"It's Elan and Vivian," Elan called out as he knocked on the door to Sudfad's study. Jared was closest to the door and opened it. Almost all of the men who were at the morning meeting were in the study and Gabriel had joined them.

"We are sorry to interrupt," Elan said. "But Vivian has some things she should tell you."

"Were you out riding?" Raphael asked Vivian because she was wearing Natasha's riding pants and blouse.

"I was going to ride to the river but Elan flew me," Vivian said as she walked across the room and handed some papers to King Mathas. "Here is your translation."

There was another knock on the door, when Jared opened it Angelina, Nikki and Ingr came into the crowded study. "We saw the serious looks on Elan's and Vivian's faces so we followed them," Angelina said. "Is something wrong?"

"She was just about to tell us," Sudfad said.

"While I was working at home I kept thinking about all you told me this morning. And the more I thought about everything the more I realized something was very wrong with how we were looking at these threats against your families." Vivian turned to Elan, "Would you move a table so I can lay the maps out?" Stephan and Archetenus helped Elan with the table as Vivian continued.

"The Valdees Tribe is well known in Ryed for coming to land and capturing people to use as slaves. There have been ships found off the coastlines with the entire crews missing and people believe the Valdees took them. This morning you told me that Juleta was cunning and that she tried to find ways to hurt you the most which is why you are concerned about your children." As Vivian spoke she placed the two maps that the families from Lentz had next to the map taken from the creatures she killed on the table. "What is worse than having a loved one die?" Vivian asked.

"To have them stolen and not know if they are alive or dead," Raul said.

"Exactly," Vivian replied. "Look at these maps. While they look the same there are small differences. The 'X' that marks the location where you thought the payment was to be placed is in a different location on each map."

Everyone in the room now gathered around the table. "Look, there are dots along the boundaries of each body of water. "At first I thought the dots were the result of sloppy drawing but then Elan took me to the river behind Gabriel's property and that is exactly where this dot is located," Vivian pointed to the newest map they had obtained. "I think Juleta wrote that letter herself, knowing you would find it and focus on the area that was marked near her castle."

"That sounds exactly like something Juleta would do," Matthew said as he studied the maps.

"You should look at the maps and see if you can identify the other locations that have dots," Vivian continued. "I think those dots signify some kind of underwater cages or tunnels."

"What do you mean?" Sorren asked.

"If those creatures stole one of your family members you would have the armies of two kingdoms, the Rualas and the Enrops searching for them. They would have to find a way to travel without being seen," Vivian said.

"They may be able to breathe under water," Stephan said. "But how do they keep their captives from drowning?"

"I do not know the answer to that question but I too have wondered about it."

"One of these dots is right behind our castle," Thaos said and showed the map to Claudius.

"They could also be escape routes," Gabriel said. "I think Vivian is right and we should examine these maps with new eyes."

"Young lady, you have done a great deal to help us," Mathas said to Vivian. "Tell us a way we can repay you."

"You already have," Vivian said with a grin. "You sent me that awful medicine. For a while I didn't know if that was worse than the poison."

"If there is ever anything you want, let us know," Claudius said. "And know you will always have a home in Lentz."

Vivian turned to Raphael, who was standing at her side. "Is there anything you want?"

"Not from them," Raphael whispered into Vivian's ear as he grinned.

"Vivian; Nikki and Ingr and I would very much like to talk to you about your tribe and your training," Angelina said. "Are you coming to the ball?"

"Yes, I 'm coming with Raphael."

"I would like to sit in on that conversation too," Sorren said. "That is if you don't mind an old man joining you."

"That old man can out fight three younger ones," Matthew said and grinned.

"Speaking of the ball," Sudfad said. "Renya will have my head if all of you are late, we can continue this meeting later."

"Did you get any rest? "Cassandra asked Elan after she saw him walk out of Sudfad's study.

"No, I was helping Vivian; she noticed some things on those maps that may be important." Cassandra smiled at Elan's words since it was the first time he sounded interested in a mission since his injury.

"You will have to tell me about it," Cassandra said as she took his hand. "But before that, come to the Great Hall with me." When they entered the Great Hall, Cassandra pointed at Misha and Dagon. Both men were standing together with the women they had as companions in the wedding ceremony. "Look at them," Cassandra said with a laugh. "After all that complaining, they haven't left Mia and Melanie for a moment."

"I have never had such beautiful things," Lila said and kissed Luca. They had returned to their home to prepare for the ball. "You didn't have to buy me another dress for the dance," she said excitedly has she held up the pink ball gown.

"Help me out of this dress," Lila said and turned so Luca could unbutton the many buttons on the back of her wedding dress.

"What do I have to wear?" Christopher asked as he walked into their bedroom and jumped on the bed.

"You don't have to wear that suit, but you should look nice," Luca said. "What do you want to wear?"

"What are you wearing?"

"I'm staying in my suit," Luca replied as he continued to work on the buttons on Lila's dress.

"Then I will stay in mine," Christopher said and jumped off the bed. "I'm going to tell Nicholas to stay in his suit," Christopher yelled as he ran out of the room.

"Can I come in?" Raphael asked as he knocked on Vivian's bedroom door.

"Of course."

Vivian walked over to the dresser and was taking something out of a drawer when Raphael asked angrily, "Vivian are you leaving? We have to talk about this." He was staring at Vivian's bed. All of her belongings were packed and piled on top of the bed. "Vivian I don't want you to go," he said in a hoarse whisper.

Vivian walked up to Raphael and stood very close to him. "My things are packed because I was hoping you would help me move them to your chambers; I don't know where you want me to put my things." She could see the fear draining from his face.

"Does that mean you have made your decision?"

"Yes," Vivian said with a smile. "My handsome warrior priest, I am taking you for my husband." Raphael tried to kiss her but Vivian stopped him. "No first let me do this. In my tribe it is customary that when a man and a woman decide to marry that the woman's family gives a gift of great significance to the man's family. I have nothing to give you but this," Vivian said as she handed her lamsman to Raphael.

"I cannot take this."

"Yes you can, we are one now," Vivian said. "But it is your decision if you want to wear it."

"Will it fit?"

"Elan gave me some leather to extend it."

"I will wear it," Raphael said proudly.

"Then my husband please sit down and pull up your right pants leg." Vivian knelt down in her ball gown and fastened the lamsman on Raphael's ankle. He kissed Vivian on the lips then set her on his lap.

"I came in here to give you these," Raphael said as he handed Vivian a box.

"Raphael! I can't."

He interrupted her, "Don't say you can't accept it because we are one now." He lifted the emerald and diamond necklace from the box. "Turn around and I will put it on you. Do you like it?"

"I love it, but it must be so expensive."

"Turn around and let me see," Raphael said. "You look incredibly beautiful." As Vivian took the earrings out of the box and was putting them on Raphael continued. "Do you remember when we gave you that potion and you told us you carried many weapons because a girl always had to be prepared?"

"Yes," Vivian said as she laughed.

"Well I feel the same way," As Raphael spoke he took another box from his coat pocket and opened it, exposing an emerald and diamond engagement ring. "It is our tradition that a man gives a woman a ring when they decided to marry." Vivian stared at the ring but could not speak. He took it out of the box and placed it on her finger. "If you don't like it I can get something else."

"Raphael it is so beautiful I couldn't even say anything." Vivian threw her arms around his neck and kissed him on the lips again and again.

As their passions were rising Raphael stopped kissing Vivian. "We really need to leave for the ball now." She started to stand up but Raphael pulled her back down onto his lap. "Vivian I can't tell you how happy you have made me."

When the guests and wedding party were allowed to enter the Great Hall they stood in awe at the regal elegance before them. Gold was the theme; the color was accented by thousands of white flowers and white candles. The Royal Family and the wedding party were seated at the front table which faced the rest of the guests. Dancers, jugglers and musicians were hired to entertain the guests as they dined.

Because Raphael had performed the wedding ceremony he and Vivian were told to sit at the front table, something which made Vivian feel uncomfortable. She had never attended a banquet like this and often looked at Raphael for clues as to how she should respond to different things. When the speeches were finished; Luca and Lila were the first couple on the dance floor, followed by Sudfad and Renya then Emeral and Maxwell. The rest of the wedding party and guests soon followed.

"So we finally get our dance," Vivian said as she leaned her head against Raphael's chest.

"You're the most beautiful woman here."

"And you the most handsome man." Vivian now pulled her head back so she could look into Raphael's eyes. "Is this the kind of wedding ceremony you want for us?"

He smiled, "What kind of ceremony would you prefer?" Vivian hesitated. "Be honest," Raphael said.

"I hope you won't get angry," she said. "But now I understand why Lila was so nervous about this. I would not feel comfortable being the center of attention for hundreds of strangers. I have lived in the shadows; this is beautiful yet very strange to me."

"You didn't answer my question," Raphael said. "If we planned our wedding tonight what would you want?"

"Something small for just you and me."

"Why are you so hesitant to tell me?"

"Because I think you would enjoy a wedding such as Luca and Lila are having. I would rather be married at Gabriel's house with just the family. In my tribe we also have a banquet but it is usually a pig roast instead of something this elegant. We have competitions during the day and we too dance at night."

"Why would you think I would want a wedding like Luca's?"

"Because you fit into this world so well, and the jewels and fine clothing you have bought me. Raphael until I came here I have never seen such beautiful things much less worn them."

"Well, I must say you seem to fit into this world yourself. How is that since you come from a poor village?"

"I have traveled greatly hunting demons and as you know they can be found any place. Like you and Gabriel I sometimes go in disguise to blend in with the people in the area I am hunting."

"I think we are going to work very well together. You should know that I too came from a poor family. My father saved every cent he had to send me to the monastery at Philiste to study. Then my mother became ill and he had a poor crop year and could no longer afford to send me to school."

"Gabriel's family was incredibly wealthy although I did not know that when he and I first became friends. When Gabriel found out that I was going to have to leave school he went to his parents and asked to use his own money to pay for my education. They were so touched by his generosity as a boy that they paid for my education and brought me into their home as another son. They were killed in an accident and Gabriel and I both raised Natasha. Just the three of us living in a huge castle."

"You lived in a castle?"

"Before his parents died, we usually stayed at the monastery but Gabriel did not want to raise his little sister in a monastery with all of those men and I must say I agreed with him. Now that I look back at it, we really didn't know what we were doing, but we tried to replace her parents."

"So that is why she is such a powerful warrior. I think that tells a lot about you and Gabriel, not every boy would take on such noble responsibility. Is that also how you are so rich?"

"Yes, they left me a fortune in their will as they did Gabriel and Natasha. And honesty Vivian I have dedicated my life to my work and have spent little money on anything else. Which is the same for Luca and that is why he is having such an extravagant wedding."

"So then you would like a wedding such as this?"

"No," Raphael said. "I would prefer a small wedding with the family also. I would be very happy with the wedding you described. But since Gabriel is like my brother I would like him to stand up for me. Since the Sanuri is not here that would leave Prince Lakin to perform the ceremony. Would you like to marry while Lakin and his family are still in Wetpr?"

"I would marry you tonight," Vivian said softly.

"We should not detract from Luca's and Lila's wedding," Raphael said. "How about the end of the week? That would give us five days to prepare?"

"Whatever you want my husband."

"Emeral thrives when she takes care of her children, I would like to ask her to help us with the wedding."

"I would be happy with that," Vivian said and kissed Raphael.

Raphael danced Vivian across the floor to Emeral and Maxwell, "Can we change partners for this dance?" Raphael asked. "As Emeral and Raphael glided across the dance floor he asked, "Emeral would you be up for planning another wedding?"

Emeral smiled warmly, "You and Vivian?"

"Yes, we would like to marry at the end of the week, just something small at the house with the family and a pig roast."

"I am so happy for you Raphael I think you and Vivian are perfect for each other," Emeral said happily then her demeanor changed and she was all business. "You aren't giving me much time, you know you will have to invite the Royal Family don't you?"

"Emeral, enjoy your son's wedding we can talk about ours tomorrow. Besides, so far you are the only one who knows."

After several dances with his wife, Sorren asked Sudfad if he could go into the King's study to review the maps that they had obtained from the Valdees Tribe. Like Vivian, Sorren too was greatly disturbed and felt they were missing something which was just before their eyes. The River Shey flowed on the western boundary of the lands owned by the Nordes Tribe. The Village of Tyger, which is where Sorren and his family lived was built on the shores of this river as was the castle of Claudius.

"Just as I thought," Sorren said out loud to himself as he studied the maps. Sorren saw a dot indicated on the map next to Tyger and another just north of that village along the river. Many of the inhabitants of Tyger fed their families with the fish and creatures they took from the river.

Sorren decided to have his best divers investigate the areas that had dots drawn on the map. As he studied the maps, Sorren realized that the last map they had obtained had many more dots drawn on it than the previous maps. He now surmised why the creatures they suspected to be in Lentz months earlier had stolen clothing and not attacked their families.

The next morning at the breakfast table in Gabriel's home Hannah said to Christopher. "Why don't you plan on staying with Nicholas and Cerey the rest of the week that will give Lila and Luca some time together?" Christopher looked confused by Hannah's statement. "Christopher don't you want to stay with Nicholas?" Hannah asked.

"Oh yes we had a lot of fun last night but I don't understand why Luca and Lila need time together they are together all of the time."

As Hannah was about to answer Christopher's question Gabriel asked her, "Do you really want to start that conversation?" Hannah laughed.

"Christopher we will move more of your toys into their room after breakfast," said Hannah.

Emeral and Maxwell were already in the dining room when Raphael and Vivian walked in. "You will need to tell everyone at breakfast," Emeral said. "So I have time to organize things."

"What are you talking about?" Gabriel asked then he noticed the ring on Vivian's hand. Gabriel stood up from the table and walked over to Raphael and hugged him then kissed Vivian on the cheek.

"What is going on?" Natasha asked as she carried a tray of food into the dining room.

"Is everyone here?" Raphael asked as he looked around the table.

"I wouldn't wait for Misha and Dagon," Koby said as he and Bekka walked into the dining room holding hands and smiling. "Neither of them came home last night."

"I see," Emeral said with a grin as she looked at Koby and Bekka. "I do believe romance was in the air last night." Calen too, saw Vivian's ring but he did not say anything, he just smiled.

"Luca and Lila are sleeping in this morning," Hannah said as she walked into the dining room with platters of pancakes. "So we won't wait for them."

"Well I guess everyone is here," Maxwell said with a smile.

Hannah was turning to walk back into the kitchen when Emeral stopped her. "Hannah wait a moment Raphael and Vivian have something to tell us."

Raphael put his arm around Vivian, "We are getting married and if it is alright with you Gabriel and Hannah. We would like to have the wedding here, something small with the family." Hannah and Natasha both ran up to Raphael and Vivian and hugged and kissed them both.

"Of course it is alright," Gabriel said. "We would be honored."

"They would like the wedding at the end of this week so Lakin can perform the ceremony," Emeral said. "So I will need help with the preparations."

"In Vivian's village they organize competitions during the day then they have a pig roast and dancing at night," Raphael said. "We would like the same thing."

"Oh that sounds like fun," said Natasha.

"Gabriel and Hannah and Natasha and Calen you are my family and we would like you in the wedding," Raphael said.

"Cassandra and Elan I would like you to set up the games and competitions," Emeral said. "And Koby and Bekka I want you to help me get the furniture and everything we will need for the ceremony and banquet."

"I would rather help with the competitions," Koby said with a grin."

"Ok, you work with Elan and I will work with Bekka," Cassandra said as she and Elan walked up to Raphael and Vivian to congratulate them.

"That was easier than I thought," Koby kidded as he and Bekka stood up from the table and walked towards Raphael and Vivian.

"You will have to plan some games for the children too," Emeral said with a grin.

"And Maxwell we would like you to walk Vivian down the aisle," Raphael said.

"Two beautiful brides in one week; I am a lucky man," Maxwell said with a pleased smile.

"Elan you have the skill you just seem to have lost your confidence," Vivian said as they took a short rest from training.

"Vivian if I tell you something don't tell the others," Elan said. "Since I was small I have looked up to Calen, Misha and Luca. They had such exciting lives. They have fought in many battles even before they joined Gabriel's team. I wanted to prove to them I could be as good as they are. This was my first big battle and this happens."

"I was told you lost your arm while protecting Cassandra. There is honor in that," Vivian said but Elan did not seem to take comfort from her words. "Elan I certainly don't know Gabriel, Calen and the others as well as you do. But they strike me as the kind of men who would be honest and tell you if they thought you couldn't do the work or you would get others hurt."

"Elan don't get mad but right now you are your own worst enemy. That demon took your arm; don't let him take your life. You and I are going to train hard every morning and I want you to participate in the competitions. And you don't want to let your teacher down on her wedding day."

"Last night I left the dance so I could come in here and study these maps," Sorren said to the morning meeting of leaders in Sudfad's study. "There are dots near Tyger and a little north of our village. Then I realized that the map we just got from those creatures has many more dots than the first two. We wondered why those creatures would kill men and steal their clothes. I think we have had creatures in our kingdom for a while and they have been spying on us and making preparations for something." Sorren turned to Raphael. "Is Vivian at the castle?"

"She is training with Elan," Calen said. "He seems to respond better to her than to us."

"I think that is understandable," Sudfad said. "I think part of Elan's problem is that he feels like he let you down."

"I have some more questions for her," Sorren said. "Do you want to bring her here or I can come to your house?"

623

"I can bring her here," Raphael said as Gabriel and Calen smiled at him. "Well, I was going to wait until after the meeting, but Vivian and I are getting married Saturday. The ceremony will be in the morning, games and competitions in the afternoon and a pig roast and dance in the evening. You are all invited. We will be at Gabriel's house."

"That sounds like a good time to me," Sorren said. "And congratulations she seems like a fine girl."

"I think we could stay a few more days," Mathas said. "What about you Claudius?"

"I agree."

"Not to change your plans," Sudfad said. "But you know you are welcome to have it here at the castle."

"Thank you, but we would prefer something a little smaller," Raphael said. "Last night Vivian told me that as a hunter she has always been in the shadows and to be the center of attention for all those crowds, like Luca and Lila were, rather horrified her."

"Trust me," Simon said as he looked at Raul. "We understand."

Chapter XXXIX
War

"Take this to Claudius he is at the castle of King Sudfad," Fahron said to the Enrop. As soon as the giant bird flew out of his office Fahron turned to the soldier standing before him.

"Lieutenant Carlsman I want men patrolling the bank of the River Shey south to the Monastery at Tufold and as far north as the boundaries entering the lands of the Valdore Tribe. Troops from Fort Castor will be conducting the patrols from the monastery southward to our border with Zorta. I want the men prepared for invasion. The patrols are around the clock; do you have any questions?"

"No My Lord."

"That will be all then," Fahron said. "Will you send in Sergeant Ferguson, he should be in the hallway?"

"Yes My Lord."

"Sergeant please close the door," Fahron said. "I have written letters to the families, I would like you to deliver them as well as a bag of gold coins for each family. As the letters state we will take care of the families so they will not want." Fahron opened his desk and took out ten bags of gold coins all equal in size and placed them on his desk for Ferguson to take. "I trust that all of the bodies have been delivered to their homes."

"Yes My Lord but the condition some of those bodies were in it might have been better if we buried them here."

"I understand what you are saying," Fahron said. "Actually after I saw the bodies I thought long and hard if we should return them to their families.

"This week has gone by so quickly," Vivian said nervously. "I can't believe, well, I have never been this nervous in my life." Both Hannah and Natasha laughed as they helped Vivian into her wedding dress.

"Did you get any sleep at all last night?" Hannah asked.

"Not a wink and Raphael slept like a baby. I was so nervous I was afraid that I would wake him."

"It's different for men," Natasha said. "Now turn around so we can make sure it is perfect. You look absolutely beautiful. When Raphael sees you in this dress I bet he won't be able to talk."

"You haven't let him see the dress yet have you?" Hannah asked.

"No, only because he wanted it to be a surprise," said Vivian.

"Gabriel picked up the watch," Hannah said as she opened a velvet box that exposed a gold pocket watch on a golden chain."

"I can't believe I forgot about that," Vivian said frantically. "Thank you both so much, I had no idea what to get him. When am I supposed to give it to him?"

"Any time you want," Hannah said. "Do you want me to put it on the dresser?"

There was a knock on the bedroom door, "Its Maxwell are you ready?"

Natasha opened the door and laughed. "Vivian is so nervous you might have to hold her up walking down the aisle."

"Well you all look so beautiful," Maxwell said. "Everything is ready; they are just waiting for us." Maxwell walked up to Vivian and extended his arm. "It will be alright dear just think about Raphael and nothing else."

"Oh my," Vivian said as they were now standing in the doorway of the foyer looking out at the yard. "I really didn't expect all of this."

"Well we may have gotten a little carried away," Hannah said and hugged Vivian. The front yard was filled with even rows of chairs that all faced a large arbor that was covered with white and yellow roses. There was a long white carpet leading to the arbor that the wedding party would walk down.

Dozens of large bouquets of white and yellow roses decorated the area. And a group of musicians were sitting to the far side of the arbor playing soft music. Hannah and Natasha wore light yellow dresses that were fitting for a garden wedding.

"That's our cue," Maxwell said as the music changed. Hannah, then Natasha walked out of the house and started their walk down the white carpet. Vivian clung to Maxwell's arm as they started to walk towards the arbor. Fear gripped her heart and she had an overwhelming feeling to flee until she saw Raphael. The look on his face when he saw her warmed Vivian's being.

"Come in," Fahron called. It was only mid-morning and there had been a constant stream of people in his office.

"My Lord," the young sergeant said as he waited for Fahron to look up from his paperwork.

"Sergeant Tanner, what is it?"

"Some of the men found a campsite not far from the King's castle. It looked to be a day or two old. Whoever was staying there brushed the ground to cover their tracts."

After the wedding ceremony almost everyone, including Raphael and Vivian changed their clothing so they could participate in the games and competitions. "Mother you should join some of these," Raul said as he kissed Renya on the cheek. "I would love to see the faces in the crowd when you show off your skill with a sword."

Renya laughed, "I am not sure the people are ready for that."

"To have a queen that is such a warrior as you," Angelina said. "I think it would be an inspiration."

Renya looked at Emeral, "Do you want to show the children that we are more than mothers?"

"Really you are going to do this?" Raul asked as the two woman stood up. "Do you want to change your dresses?"

"I have some things that will fit you," Emeral said and the two women went inside of the house.

"Mother and Emeral are going to join the competitions," Raul said to Simon who was standing with Jared waiting for their turn at the knife throwing competition.

"I have to see this," Simon said with a grin. "Which competitions are they entering?"

"I don't know yet," Raul said.

Twenty minutes later Renya and Emeral both came out of the house wearing riding pants, boots and blouses. Both women had belts which held several knife sheaths and a sword and they both were carrying bows and quivers of arrows. "They had this planned all along," Raul said in shock. Simon, Calen and Luca all stopped what they were doing to stare at their mothers. Sudfad and Maxwell were standing together with grins on their faces.

The two matriarchs of their families chose the bow and arrow competition first. This competition required teams. "I want to be on Renya's team," Angelina yelled and ran towards that area. Ibula too joined that team as did Nikki, Ingr and Vivian. "Who will play against us?" Angelina yelled.

"It should be our husbands," Ibula said. "Who will oversee the game?"

"I will," Claudius yelled with a large grin on his face.

Each team had to shoot at a variety of targets while both standing and riding. Within minutes of the start of the completion all the guests left the other competitions to watch this unusual sight. Two players would be up at a given time, one from each team. Renya had not shot from a riding position for a number of years and failed to hit as many targets as Sudfad. But from a standing position the Queen was unbeatable.

None of Emeral's sons had ever seen her in battle or in a competition. They stood speechless as they watched both of their parents shoot with skill and accuracy. The game lasted an hour and the men won by only one point.

"I am sorry ladies," Renya said. "I have not shot from a horse in many years."

Renya, Emeral, Sudfad and Maxwell entered all of the competitions and drew crowds wherever they played. When it was Renya's turn at the sword fighting competition, no one wanted to fight against her initially. Then Sorren stepped onto the field. "I have never fought against a queen before," Sorren said. Then lunged at Renya, who side stepped his blow and kicked him behind the knee.

As Sorren momentarily stumbled he realized the queen wanted a real competition. The crowd cheered as these two old warriors exchanged blows. Sorren was more powerful but Renya was agile and fast on her feet. This was a timed event and when the trumpet blew, both contestants were still on their feet. The crowd roared.

Not to be outdone, Emeral was next in the arena and again there was hesitation. "Fight with her," Natasha said to Calen.

"I can't fight my mother," Calen replied as he watched with horror as King Mathas joined Emeral in the arena. Koby, Dagon and Misha pushed to the front of the crowd and stood in awed silence next to Luca and Calen. "I don't know if I can watch this," Calen said nervously.

Emeral had a different fighting style than Renya, Emeral was much more aggressive and time was called when she accidently cut Mathas on the arm. The injury was minor. But the fight stayed with her sons for the rest of their lives. Maxwell and Sudfad were doing well in the competitions but they too found that their children did not want to fight against them.

When Renya, Sudfad, Emeral and Maxwell had finished the sword fighting competition, Vivian and Elan walked into the arena holding hands. The crowd remained and all knew this was the first time Elan had entered a competition since his injury.

Vivian started off as the aggressor; she was fast, powerful and skillful and Elan proved a worthy opponent. He utilized the tricks for using his leverage and maintaining his balance that Vivian had taught him. They fought hard and when the trumpet was blown they both were standing.

Vivian grabbed Elan's arm and held it up in the air and the crowd roared and applauded. Tears ran down Emeral's face as she watched Elan, she knew he had his confidence back.

It wasn't until the evening dance and banquet that Claudius and Mathas received the messages that Fahron sent. Claudius and Mathas showed Sorren and Sudfad the messages but they all decided to let the rest of their families enjoy the evening.

"I've never been to anything like this before," Delilah said. "I am so glad that we came."

"I too have enjoyed this day," Archetenus said. "I would never say anything but Luca's wedding was too fancy for my taste. I like this much better."

"I know, I was thinking the same thing," Delilah said with a warm smile. "Archetenus I really like the people here and I think we are making good friends. Would you consider settling down here, or do you think things would be too uncomfortable?"

"Well, I wondered when Raul and I first started out in the sword completion if we were really going to fight," he said with a laugh. "But I agree with you. I think this will make a good home for us."

Raphael and Vivian were dancing slower than the other couples because they were oblivious to their surroundings. They held each other tightly and felt the love that overwhelmed them.

The next morning Sudfad's usual meeting was moved from his study to the Great Hall because so many people were invited. Breakfast was served to the participants as they started the meeting by listening to King Mathas, Claudius and Matthew talk about the Valdees Tribe. They gave as much information as they had prior to receiving the latest messages from Fahron.

To Vivian's surprise she was called in front of the room to talk about her tribe, her role as a demon hunter, the creatures she had been following and the Valdees Tribe. Sorren asked Vivian to remain in front of the room and he joined her to explain the three maps they had in their possession.

Before Vivian returned to her seat, Sorren announced that Vivian and Raphael had married the day before and she would now be living in Wetpr. The audience applauded the married couple which greatly embarrassed Vivian but Raphael was beaming with pride when she joined him at their table.

Claudius and Mathas returned to the front of the room. "Now that all of you have been caught up on the information we had prior to yesterday Mathas and I will share with you messages that we received from General Fahron, who is running the kingdom in our absence. Mind you that Mathas and I have briefed Fahron on all the information that you now possess and Sorren has sent the same information back to his tribe."

"When we first received information about Vivian and the creatures she stalked we increased the number of guards around our castles and we had our soldiers include the shorelines of the River Shey on their daily patrols," King Mathas explained. "Three days ago, one of these patrols found the dead bodies of two men near the river; both bodies had been greatly mutilated and stripped of their clothing. We believe these two men were local fishermen."

"Their bodies were found close to the border of the Nordes Tribe; this area is also close to the castle of Claudius. In the past couple of days a total of twelve bodies have been found, ten of them belonging to our soldiers. The horses and uniforms of these men were missing and these bodies were also mutilated. All of the bodies were found in various areas near the river."

"Yesterday, some of our men discovered an abandoned camp site near my castle; they believed the site to be only a couple of days old." Mathas continued, "At this point we suspect the creatures of the Valdees Tribe have killed these men, but we have no proof of that. Fahron has ordered constant patrols along the entire river that flows through our kingdom."

"Soldiers from both Fort Langer and Fort Castor are patrolling these areas. Instead of sending two or three soldiers on patrol we now have entire platoons patrolling day and night. Whoever is attacking us, we are taking it as a declaration of war."

"Has anyone tried swimming in the areas where the dots are located to see what they might contain?" Calen asked.

"Many of my people are fine divers," Sorren said. "They will be searching the area near the Village of Tyger when I return."

"Have you been sending this information to the Sanuri also?" asked Lakin.

"Yes," Claudius said. "We have also sent him copies of the maps and the letter that was found in Juleta's castle."

"If it is not the Valdees Tribe who is attacking your men," Luca asked. "Who else would you suspect?"

"A couple of years ago," Matthew explained. "Juleta hired men to kill some of our soldiers and wear their uniforms when they attacked innocent villagers in the lands of the Valdore Tribe; she was trying to start a civil war. "But in those instances the bodies were not mutilated."

"I have seen the work of the Valdore tribesmen," Thaos said. "They like to tie a man's limbs to four different horses so their bodies are pulled apart. Is that the type of mutilation they have seen?"

"No," Claudius said. "According to Fahron each man's lungs were cut out."

Vivian quickly stood up. "We have found bodies like that also in Ryed."

"We've wondered how these creatures could transport others under water," Stephan said. "Is it possible that they can somehow use the lungs of others for this purpose?" The room grew silent.

Sudfad ordered five hundred soldiers to join the two hundred soldiers from Lentz in escorting the families of Lentz back to their homeland.

"Matthew I owe you a great deal," Archetenus said as the people of Lentz were preparing for their journey. "If you need anything I will be there to help you."

"I appreciate that Archetenus; hopefully there will be no need."

The party from Lentz left the royal castle at Wetpr amidst tears and handshakes. Twenty Ruala warriors, including Ibula and Thedes, volunteered to fly along with the caravan. Thedes had become close to Matthew, Sorren, Stephan and Thaos on a previous mission. These men shared a strong bond as warriors and friends. Ibula had become particularly close with Angelina, which did not surprise anyone since these two women shared such similarities.

Shortly after the people from Lentz left the castle, Sudfad called another meeting. Since his castle was still filled with Ruala warriors and their families who had attended Luca's wedding; Sudfad decided to call everyone together as a group to work on ideas and strategies concerning the Valdees Tribe.

"Elan we have thirty minutes before dinner," Gabriel said. "Would you take me to the river and show me the areas you and Vivian were examining?"

As soon as Elan and Gabriel left the house, Emeral went up to Raphael's study where he and Vivian were working on the translation of the Valdees' language. "Would you two come down to the parlor for a few minutes?" Emeral asked. When they entered the parlor they found most of the family in the room. Within moments Calen and Luca walked in. Both men were carrying large stacks of boxes.

"More wedding gifts?" Vivian asked with surprise.

"No," Calen said as he put his stack of boxes on a table near Vivian. "It's our way of thanking you for what you did for Elan."

"This isn't necessary," Vivian said. "Elan is a good man, most of his problem was that he admires all of you so much he was filled with guilt because he thought he let you down."

"We know," Luca said. "But he wouldn't listen to us."

"And he was avoiding us, except at meal times," said Misha.

"He's got that fire back in his belly and he isn't withdrawn anymore," Calen said. "And we appreciate what you did."

"I didn't really do all that much," Vivian said. "You are all so close, I think he felt comfortable talking to someone he didn't know."

"Elan was afraid that I would get jealous because you were holding hands yesterday," Cassandra said with a grin. "He said you practically had to drag him into the arena."

Vivian smiled and nodded. "We trained hard all week, I knew he was ready but he didn't think so. As soon as he focused on the fight, well, you saw how well he performed."

"Open your gifts," said Natasha.

"There are so many," Vivian said.

"There are a lot of us," Maxwell said with a warm smile.

Vivian opened the first box and took out a blouse, "This is so beautiful, thank you so much."

"The girls said you didn't have a lot of clothing so that is what we bought you," Luca said.

Vivian turned to Raphael, "Did you know about this?"

"Someone had to tell them what size you wore," he said and kissed Vivian on top of her head.

"You are the most wonderful people," Vivian said emotionally. "I have only known you for a few weeks and I feel so much a part of your family."

"We found two more bodies," Fahron told Mathas and Claudius as soon as they returned to Lentz.

"Are they our soldiers?" asked Mathas.

"No, we believe them to be local fishermen," Fahron said. "Not that it makes it any easier."

"Were they mutilated in the same fashion?" Claudius asked.

"Yes, the physician still has the bodies because I wanted you to see them," Fahron said. "Perhaps you can see something that I haven't."

"I would like to have the boys come with us," Claudius said. "Extra eyes cannot hurt."

Stephan, Thaos and their families had barely unpacked before soldiers came for them, requesting their presence at the King's castle. "I would like to go too," Nikki said.

"As well as I," said Ingr. "It will give us some idea of what we are dealing with. The two young couples rode to the King's castle with a military escort. When they entered Mathas' study they also found Matthew, Angelina, Sorren, Fahron and Claudius waiting for them.

"I have to warn you it's a gruesome sight," Fahron said as he led them to the physician's office.

"I thought you said those creatures took the lungs," Thaos said as he examined the bodies of the two men. "These men look like they have been torn apart by wild animals."

"They all looked like that," the physician said wearily. "The lungs were the only organs I found missing in all of the bodies. Whoever is doing this must be insane and they certainly have no skill as a surgeon."

"But even a skilled hunter could remove certain organs without tearing a body apart like this," Stephan said. "Do you think those creatures are doing something else with the bodies also?"

"What do you mean?" Mathas asked. "You mean besides torturing these poor victims?"

"You said everybody looked the same," Stephan said. "And these two are opened up so all of the organs are exposed. Maybe their bodies are different from ours."

"And they either don't know where the lungs are," Angelina interrupted Stephan as she took a closer look at one of the bodies. "Or they are looking at how we are made."

"It could be ritualistic too," Nikki said. "They do work for a demon."

"Was there anything else that was similar between all of these bodies," Thaos asked. "Any kind of marks?"

"They were all found in different locations along the river," Fahron said. "And whatever killed them brushed the ground so there would be no footprints."

"Then we ruled out wild animals," Claudius said.

"Fahron can you chart along a map where the bodies have been found?" asked Sorren.

"I already have, and I compared it to the maps we have from the Valdees," Fahron said. "After you wrote to me about the dots on the map I have been charting the deaths. I will show you but the bodies and dots do not line up."

"All of the bodies, showed signs of fighting like bruised knuckles," the physician said. "They were all men," then the physician paused. "Fahron am I mistaken or were all these bodies about the same height and weight?"

"You mean they are attacking a certain size of man?" Claudius asked in disbelief.

"Well they could be practicing for us," Stephan said as he and Thaos started to turn one of the bodies so they could see its back.

"Or maybe they need lungs that are a certain size," Ingr said.

"Look at this," Stephan said. "There are little circles all over this man's back and the back of his neck."

Matthew and Sorren quickly rolled the second body over, "Also on this one," Sorren said.

The physician closely examined the back of one of the bodies, "I did not see these on the others but I have kept these bodies longer so you could examine them. The others were buried quickly."

"We aren't finding any circles anyplace else," Angelina said as she, Nikki and Ingr were examining the bodies.

"I just keep staring at these bodies," Matthew said. "And I know there has to be more to all of this. Juleta had such fiendish plans; I feel like we are looking at a puzzle and all of the pieces are before us but we can't see them."

"I don't like it," Hannah said. "You don't know what is down there."

"Well, that is exactly why we are going down there," Gabriel said as he fastened a knife sheath to his ankle.

"We'll stay together Hannah," Vivian said. "And the others will be on shore to help us."

"Hannah if there is significance to that dot on the map" Raphael said. "That is on your property. You have children here. We can't put the family at risk."

"I know," Hannah said I just wish there was some other way."

"Here," Luca said as he landed on the shoreline of the river. "I bought these in the city, who knows what you might find down there."

"Spears," Gabriel said with a grin.

"Actually they may be very useful," Vivian said.

Natasha and Lila stayed in the house with the children while the rest of the family congregated in the rear of Gabriel's property that backed up to the River Nebu. Bekka flew up to them from the southern side of the river. "I didn't see anything unusual," she said.

Koby landed a few moments later. He had been following the river north for several miles. "Everything looks normal," Koby said. "Good luck."

Gabriel kissed Hannah, then he, Raphael and Vivian dove into the river. Hannah clutched Emeral's hand as they watched the ripples in the calm water. After several minutes all three came up for air then they went back underwater.

"Oh my god is that one of them?" Hannah gasped as a lifeless body rose to the surface. Luca grabbed Hannah as she started to run into the river.

"It's not Gabriel or Raphael, I don't know who it is," Calen said as he flew over the water and picked up the corpse.

"Look there's another," Emeral said and pointed to the right of the first corpse. As Koby flew after the second corpse, a third, fourth and fifth appeared. Gabriel, Raphael and Vivian all came to the surface gasping for air.

"There's a few more bodies down there," Gabriel said and after they caught their breath all three returned to the underwater cemetery. Four more bodies floated to the surface, the Rualas pulled them out of the water and lined them up along the shoreline.

"I'm sorry to interrupt your meeting," Sorren said as he walked into the study of King Mathas. "But I have something you must see." Claudius, Fahron, Mathas, Matthew, Stephan and Thaos followed Sorren out of the front door of the castle where they saw four bodies draped over horses. "Some of my best divers searched the water where the dot was indicated near my village and this is what they found. All the bodies were locked up in some kind of underwater cage."

"Are they from your tribe?" Thaos asked as he was walking closer to the bodies.

"No, we don't know who they are and as you can see they have their clothes and their bodies have not been mutilated."

"Dagon is already going to get Raul and Simon," Calen said as Gabriel, Raphael and Vivian came out of the water and looked at the grizzly sight before them.

"They were all tied to rocks, we had to cut them loose," Gabriel said.

"It's hard to tell how long they have been dead because the fish have been eating them," Misha said.

"Have you seen anything like this in Ryed?" Raphael asked Vivian.

"No."

"Vivian what do the Valdees eat?" asked Misha. "I hope this wasn't a feeding ground you just disturbed."

"When I have tracked them, they eat meat and fish just like we do," Vivian said as she stared at one of the bodies. "What if they are a sacrifice to a demon?"

"Well, every one of them has their left ear cut off," Luca said as he walked among the corpses. "Perhaps they have to bring back proof that they killed someone."

"Or maybe they just keep trophies," Gabriel said. "I think we should go back in and search along the shore line." Within moments Gabriel, Raphael and Vivian disappeared into the river.

"I have more divers searching that area north of our village where there is another dot on the map," Sorren said.

"These bodies have been in the water so long we can't distinguish their faces," Claudius said as his soldiers took the bodies off from the horses and lined them up on the ground. Stephan and Thaos started searching the bodies and piling the belongings next to each body.

"Well, whoever killed them wasn't interested in money," Stephan said as he pulled a handful of gold coins out of the vest pocket of one of the corpses."

"They still have their weapons on them," Matthew said. "All their knives are still in their sheaths and this one has a knife in his boot."

"They must have been taken by surprise," Claudius said. "Sorren what was the cage like?"

"I didn't see it but the divers said it was about eight feet by eight feet and made of wood. They said it was roughly made."

"Why would they store bodies in the water?" asked Mathas.

"We didn't find anything else," Gabriel said as they returned to the group on the shoreline.

"We searched them," Luca said, talking about the corpses. "They all had money in their pockets and most of them still have their weapons in their sheaths."

"Here's the King," Hannah said as Sudfad, Raul, Simon and six soldiers rode up to the shoreline.

"Nine bodies, all tied to rocks," Gabriel said. "We looked up and down the shoreline and didn't find anything else."

Vivian held up a piece of cord. "This is what they were tied with. The Valdees make this type of rope, it is thin so it probably doesn't weigh them down when they are swimming."

"So we know the creatures were storing bodies in the river but why?" Sudfad asked as he dismounted to look at the corpses.

"Sergeant go back to the fort and bring more men and a wagon to put these bodies in," Raul said to one of the soldiers.

"They are all missing their left ears," said Luca.

"I am going to send a letter to the Sanuri," Sudfad said. "Maybe he can help us figure out what is going on here."

"I don't like it," Claudius said at King Mathas' morning meeting. "It's been almost two weeks since the bodies here and in Wetpr were discovered; and nothing since. I tell you Mathas it's too quiet, the hair on the back of my neck is on end something is going to happen soon."

"Did you ever think that maybe we were supposed to find those bodies?" Thaos asked. "I mean all we did was follow the dots on that map."

"But what would be the purpose?" Mathas asked.

"What was the purpose of putting all those poor men in the water?" asked Claudius.

"My Lord," yelled a soldier as he ran into the King's study.

Everyone jumped up when they saw the look on the soldier's face. "What is it Jackson?" Mathas asked.

"The soldier was out of breath, he was trying to talk as he gasped for air. "My Lord, Princess Angelina's horse just returned to the yard without her and there is blood on the saddle."

"Raphael, Gabriel," screamed Cassandra. "Raphael, Gabriel." Both men ran out of the house when they heard Cassandra's screams. Calen, Luca and Misha were running behind them.

"We found Vivian's horse by the river," Cassandra said as she picked Raphael up. "There are three dead creatures and blood everywhere but we can't find Vivian."

They took his gun and crossbow
And tried to make a cross
To signify the dead
Another life was lost

And the wars go through the ages
So many lives are lost
As their comrades take their weapons
And try to make a cross

The wind blows sand forever
And covers bodies where
No one will ever find them
Or know that they were there

Souls On Fire © 2008

By

Sandra J Yearman

Glossary of Characters

Aaryan: a male Grand Master of the Insidiae

Abaddon: an ancient demon/one of the Old Ones

Abella: daughter of Prince Lakin and Princess Zada/Ruala

Abigail: sister of Marie/ nurse for grandchildren of King Sudfad

Adi: son of Elen and Batya/ Ruala

Adrone: youngest son of Joshua and Iris/younger brother of Vivian/Clan of Gesmal

Adwell: Prince/ son of King Zachariah and Queen Noella of New Samona/husband of Nada/father of Misha/ Adwell was killed in battle leaving Nada to raise ten children/Ruala

Ael: an ancient demon/ one of the Old Ones

Ahriman: an ancient demon/ one of the Old Ones

Akasha: former king of Ryed/grandfather of Nehmota

Alexander: former servant of King Roch's parents/ father of Annabelle

Alexander: one of the twin sons of Simon and Annabelle

Alexandras: King of Wetpr/brother of Jaretta/uncle of Sudfad and Roch

Alexas Rose: daughter of Matthew and Angelina

Alexis: son of Usman, the leader of the Valdore Tribe

Alice: and her husband find Jorge near death in Nora

Amundsen: Commanding General of Fort Friada in the Kingdom of Ganz

Ana: Princess/daughter of Zeman and Oda/niece of King Manu of New Samona/Ruala

Anda: one of Chief Romogi's three wives/Huta

Andres: Princess of Ryed/daughter of Oren and Astrel/ has twin sister Jorga

Andrew: jeweler in Salar

Andrus: father of Rabi/Ruala

Angelina: daughter of Sorren, Chief of the Nordes Tribe/female warrior

Annabar: daughter of King Sharonne

Annabelle: handmaid and best friend to Queen Vitomas of the Kingdom of Stordt

Anthony: one of the twin sons of Simon and Annabelle

Arca: Enrop leader who protects King Mathas' family

Archetenus The Brave: Captain in the Taperian Army

Arianna: daughter of Simon and Annabelle

Ariel: daughter of Raul and Vitomas

Armstrong: soldier and scout in the army of Wetpr

Arthur Marcus: father of Hannah

Asher: male Ruala warrior

Asmodeus: an ancient demon/ one of the Old Ones

Astrel: former princess of Ryed/daughter of Akasha and Norah

Atomos: Elder of the Centras and Keeper of the Box of Itifer

Augustus Endleson: a wealthy businessman who owned part of the City of Nora

Baal: an ancient demon/ one of the Old Ones

Babu: Enrop

Bac: male Ruala warrior

Bachnenus: warrior guarding refugees/Shettee

Bali: Enrop leader of the flock that does battle at Juleta's castle

644

Balin: Prince of Norkv/son of Thaddius and Omara/grandson of Benjeman and Esther

Banacus: General in the army of King Tobias of Puntd

Banaka: a female Grand Master of the Insidiae

Barak: Prince of Norkv/grandson of Benjeman and Esther

Barak: Prince/son of King Neputa and Queen Tiara/Shettee

Barid: Prince of Ogg

Barid: Prince of Ryed/son of Nehmota and Vasart

Bastra: Huta captain

Batya: wife of Elen/Ruala

Beatrice Endleson: wife of Augustus

Becca: Princess of Norkv/daughter of Thaddius and Omara/granddaughter of Benjeman and Esther

Behtay: Princess/daughter of Segal and Cahina/niece of King Manu of New Samona/Ruala

Bekka: female Ruala warrior

Bella: wife of Claudius and mother of Stephan

Benedict: Prince of Norkv/son of Benjeman and Esther

Benjeman: vicious rebel leader who overthrew the government of Samona

Bentra: an ancient demon/ one of the Old Ones

Berta: Queen of Stordt/wife of Micha/grandmother of Roch and Sudfad

Bertha: an elderly woman from Nora

Betty: a woman from Nora

Betu: male Ruala warrior

Black Jack: a regular patron at the Ghost Ship Tavern in Port Friada

Brik: son of Prince Lakin and Princess Zada /Ruala

Brina: Princess of Norkv/daughter of Valor and Cai/granddaughter of Benjeman and Esther

Cabal: son of Karzman and Nadia

Cacu: Enrop leader that joined Raul and Simon on a mission

Cade: son of King Pergo and Queen Vinus/ Kingdom of Gandt

Cadi: daughter of Prince Hadar and Princess Paj/ granddaughter of Manu/Ruala

Cael: Shettee boy who is adopted by Thedes and Ibula

Cahina: Princess/ married to Segal son of King Zachariah and Queen Noella of New Samona/Ruala

Cai: Princess of Norkv/wife of Valor who was the son of Benjeman and Esther

Calen: male Ruala warrior/cousin of Luca/son of Maxwell and Emeral

Calla: female Ruala warrior

Calvin: a desk clerk at The Captain's Retreat Hotel in Port Friada

Campbell: one of the spies at the Castle at Wetpr

Canton: Cisero's second in command

Cara: Princess of Ogg

Carlsman: a Lieutenant in the Army of Lentz

Carson Dormors: a wealthy landowner in the Kingdom of Ganz

Carston: member of the governing body of Nora

Casey: male Ruala warrior/father of Melanie/husband of Tasha

Cassandra: female Ruala warrior

Cassandra: daughter of King Friada and Queen Marla of the Kingdom of Ganz

Cedrick Teivel: a ruthless, powerful man in the Kingdom of Ryed

Celo: Prince of Ryed/son of Oren and Astrel

Cere: daughter of Tristt/Shettee

Cerephus: General in the Taperian Army

Cerey: orphan girl/sister of Nicholas

Ceria: Princess/daughter of Gunnel and Uma/niece of King Manu of New Samona/ sister of Elan/Ruala

Chaez: son of Fahron

Chaladrone: an ancient demon/ one of the Old Ones

Chalice: hired fighter for Dieter

Chalta: daughter of King Pergo and Queen Vinus/ Kingdom of Gandt

Chance: works with the Patronus

Charlene: a woman from Nora

Charles: hired farmhand of Arthur Marcus

Chief Romogi: leader of the Hutas/ Kingdom of Marba

Christopher: six year old boy who Luca saves from the Hutas/brother of Lila

Ciao: female Ruala warrior

Cisero: a member of the Insidiae

Clair: a woman from Nora

Claudius: General in the Army of Lentz

Cleo: a man who works for Cicero/a vessel

Cobren: Prince of Norkv/son of Grace and Makalo/Grandson of Benjeman and Esther

Compro: Taperian soldier injured at Wall of Dorath

Corwin: son of King Fahra and Queen Sitha of Zorta

Crater: a soldier in the army of Wetpr

Crispus: a guard at King Roch's castle

Dack: male Ruala warrior

Dacron: former prince of Ryed/is murdered by his younger brother Nehmota for the throne

Dael: an ancient demon/ one of the Old Ones

Dagon: a male Ruala warrior

Dagor: son of King Fahra and Queen Sitha of Zorta

Dai: son of Gael, grandson of Manu/Ruala

Damas: an ancient demon/ one of the Old Ones

Danar: a man created to be a vessel for demons

Daniel: an emissary of The Great Ruler who takes on the disguise of a human man

Danilla: mother of King Mathas

Darius: Prince of Samona/son of Thomas and Rewel/brother of Varden

Delilah: wife of Dieter

Delilia: Queen of New Samona/mother of Ibula, Lakin, Gael and Hadar/ wife of King Manu/Ruala

Demanko: a demon

Demetries: a demon

Denise Froush: wife of Martin who is a wealthy ship builder in Port Friada

Denks: a soldier in the army of Wetpr

Denton: one of the spies at the Castle in Wetpr

Derek: friend of Thaos

Derlock: Huta warrior

Dieter: member of the Insidiae

Dion: Princess of Samona/wife of Yorggi who was the son of Thomas and Rewel/brother of Varden

Dixon: a Taperian soldier

Dominic Petlov: was the senior High Priest at the monastery at Malga before he was murdered

Dorme: Prince of Ogg

Doros: works for High Priest Meekos

Douma: King of Ogg

Duncan: Chief of the Clan of Gesmal in Ryed/ husband of Liza

Duran: father of Nikki/Nordes Tribe

Edith: wife of Lloyd a banker in Nora

Elan: male Ruala warrior/son of Gunnel and Uma

Eldridge: works with the Patronus

Elen: son of Andrus and Naomi/ brother of Rabi/ Ruala

Elexas: a female Nordes warrior

Elsa: female Ruala warrior/mother of Mia/wife of Tyron

Emeral: mother of Calen/Ruala

Emeric: a male Grand Master of the Insidiae

Emmet: worker for Gabriel

Emon: a male Grand Master of the Insidiae

Erebus: sorcerer from Ryed

Esser: Prince/son of Segal and Cahina/nephew of King Manu of New Samona/Ruala

Esteban: a member of the Insidiae

Esther: Queen of New Norkv/wife of rebel leader Benjeman

Fabron: Prince of Ogg

Fadil: a male Grand Master of the Insidiae

Fahra: King of Zorta

Fahron: General in the Army of Lentz

Fala: female Ruala warrior

Farnsworth: General in charge of building Fort Serpha in Wetpr

Fatima: Prince of Ryed/ son of Oren and Astrel

Fatronas: an ancient demon/one of the Old Ones

Fengu: Enrop leader who helps Gabriel and his group against Omnibus

Ferguson: a Sergeant in the Army of Lentz

Fraisier: a businessman and member of the Insidiae in Nora

Friada: King of the Kingdom of Ganz

Gabriella: sister of Marie/nurse to grandchildren of King Sudfad

Gad: male Ruala warrior

Gael: Prince/son of King Manu and Queen Delilia/Ruala

Gala: a healer from the Kingdom of Stordt

Galen: male Nordes warrior

Geoff: Prince of Lentz/son of Princess Isabella and Captain Josef

Geoff: Prince of Norkv/son of Benedict and Sasaha/grandson of Benjeman and Esther

George: an advisor for King Fahra of Zorta

George: middle son of Chief Duncan and Liza of the Clan of Gesmal in Ryed

Gita: wife of Hadi/ Ruala

Gladys: member of Nordes Tribe/ mother of Nikki

Glenda: great, great, great grandmother of Gala/ a healer from the Kingdom of Stordt

Grace: Princess of New Norkv/daughter of Benjeman and Esther

Gracie: cook for the Arthur Marcus family

Grady: worker for Gabriel

Great Ruler: God

Gregory Bancar: a wealthy landowner in the Kingdom of Wetpr and member of the Insidiae

Gunnel: Prince/ son of King Zachariah and Queen Noella of New Samona/husband of Uma/father of Elan/Ruala

Hadar: Prince/son of King Manu and Queen Delilia/Ruala

Hadi: son of Andrus and Naomi/brother of Rabi/Ruala

Hadu: female Ruala warrior

Hamon: one of the members of the Nordes Tribe who was injured in an attack at Snakes Crossing

Hamond: General of the Taperian Army who declares himself king

Hanger: one of the spies at the Castle at Wetpr

Hannah: physician in Nora/ Roch murdered her sister

Harold: owner of the general store in Nora

Harriet Marcus: mother of Hannah and Laurabelle/wife of Arthur

Hatus: General in the Army of Lentz/on loan to Sudfad

Hector: fighter hired by Juleta

Hector: Prince of Samona/son of Varden

Henry: and his wife Alice find Jorge in Nora

Henry: husband of Noreen/father of Jacob

Hermanas: second in command to Archetenus at Wall of Dorath

High Priest Aaron: member of the Patronus

High Priest Amos: a member of the Patronus

High Priest Barnabas: most Senior High Priest of the monastery at Leven

High Priest Caleb: member of the Patronus

High Priest Ephraim: a member of the Patronus

High Priest Gabriel: member of the Patronus/demon hunter

High Priest Gideon: a member of the Patronus

High Priest Gregory: member of the Patronus

High Priest Joseph: member of the Patronus, in charge of the Cicero Headquarters

High Priest Josiah: member of the Patronus

High Priest Meekos: priest at the monastery at Malga

High Priest Nicholas: most Senior High Priest of the monastery at Philiste and most Senior High Priest of the Patronus

High Priest Paulas: member of the Patronus

High Priest Phanuel: member of the Patronus

High Priest Philetus: member of the Patronus in charge of Malga Headquarters

High Priest Pravis: priest at the monastery at Malga

High Priest Raphael: a leader of the Patronus

High Priest Rueben: member of the Patronus in charge of Nora Headquarters

High Priest Silas: a member of the Patronus

High Priest Tenebrae: priest at the monastery at Malga

High Priest Timothy: was murdered by Meekos, Pravis and Tenebrae

High Priest Tyrus: a member of the Patronus

High Priest Uriel: member of the Patronus

High Priest Vincent: assigned to the monastery at Malga before he was murdered

High Priest Zophar: priest at monastery at Malga/ trained as a healer

Hores: son of Chief Romogi and Anda, Kingdom of Marba/Huta

Horta: Prince/son of Gunnel and Uma/nephew of King Manu of New Samona/brother of Elan/Ruala

Hunter: Prince of Samona/son of Varden

Ian: husband of Mia/ brother-in-law of Calen/ Ruala

Ibula: warrior princess and healer of the Ruala Tribe/daughter of King Manu and Queen Delilia

Iden: warrior guarding refugees/Shettee

Igor: brother of King Sharonne

Imad: a male Grand Master of the Insidiae

Ina: daughter of Mia and Ian/ Ruala

Ingr: female warrior of Nordes Tribe

Inon: one of Cisero's men/a vessel

Ipos: an ancient demon/ one of the Old Ones

Iris: mother of Vivian/wife of Joshua/Clan of Gesmal in Ryed

Irit: daughter of Hadi and Gita/ Ruala

Isabella: Princes of Lentz, sister of Mathas, Renya and Tasha, married to Captain Josef

Isadore: wife of Fahron

Isla: daughter of Prince Lakin and Princess Zada/Ruala

Isla: female warrior of Nordes Tribe

Ivan: youngest son of Chief Duncan and Liza of the Clan of Gesmal in Ryed

Jace: husband of Oda/ brother-in-law of Calen/Ruala

653

Jack: member of governing body of Nora

Jackson: a private in the Army of Lentz

Jacob: boy who Angelina found in the woods

Jacot: son of Prince Lakin and Princess Zada/ grandson of King Manu/Ruala

Jaden: Sergeant in the Army of Lentz

Jago: son of Elen and Batya/ Ruala

Jake: works for Talverson Transport Company in Port Friada

Jakiv: Prince/son of Segal and Cahina/nephew of King Manu of New Samona/Ruala

Jama: Enrop leader who protects Chief Sorren's family

James: Taperian soldier

Janja: Princess/daughter of Gunnel and Uma/niece of King Manu of New Samona/ sister of Elan/Ruala

Jared: hired fighter

Jaretta: King of Stordt/husband of Queen Lillian/ father of Roch and Sudfad

Jarrod: works for Pravis/leads attack on castle in Wetpr

Jasper: Prince of Lentz/son of Princess Isabella and Captain Josef

Jatu: Enrop leader who protects Fahron's family

Jeb: friend of Thaos

Jeb: one of Cisero's men

Jela: Queen of Samona/wife of Varden

Jeremy: cousin of Andrew the jeweler in Salar

Jerik: a male Grand Master of the Insidiae

Jess: a soldier of Wetpr

Jillian: Queen of Ogg/wife of King Douma

Jinn: an ancient demon/ one of the Old Ones

Joao: male Ruala warrior

Jonas: Captain in the Taperian Army

Jorga: Princess of Ryed/daughter of Oren and Astrel/ has twin sister Andres

Jorge: a cook who is kidnapped from Endleson Hotel in Nora

Josef: Captain in the Lentz military/ married to Princess Isabella, sister of King Mathas

Joshua: father of Vivian/husband of Iris/Clan of Gesmal in Ryed

Juleta: cousin to Raul and Simon/daughter and oldest child of King Mathas and Queen Rosa

Kadin: a member of Valdore Tribe

Kagen: a man who kidnaps and exploits children

Karta: male Ruala warrior

Karzman: leader of Kozach Tribe/ stepfather of Michael

Kasper: Prince/son of Zeman and Oda/nephew of King Manu of New Samona/Ruala

Kata: Princess/daughter of Gunnel and Uma/niece of King Manu of New Samona/ sister of Elan/Ruala

Khryriss: an ancient demon/ one of the Old Ones

Kiana: Princess/daughter of Gunnel and Uma/niece of King Manu of New Samona/ sister of Elan/Ruala

Klass: Lieutenant in the Wetprian Army

Koby: male Ruala warrior

Koh: son of Prince Gael and Princess Mada/grandson of King Manu/Ruala

Kora: Princess/ married to Raphael son of King Zachariah and Queen Noella of New Samona/ mother of Luca/ Raphael and Kora were killed in battle when Luca was a small boy/Ruala

Korth: son of Tristt/Shettee

Kraus: hired fighter and intended vessel, works for Dieter

Kretcher: Commanding General of Fort Polta in Wetpr

Krister: Princess of Samoan/daughter of Thomas and Rewel

Kyra: young sister of Marie/ friend of Petra

Laban: Prince of Samona/son of Yorggi and Dion/grandson of Thomas and Rewel

Lael: daughter of Nina and Rhea/ Ruala

Lakin: Prince/son of King Manu and Queen Delilia/husband of Zada/Ruala

Lala: Princess/daughter of Adwell and Nada/niece of King Manu of New Samona/ sister of Misha/Ruala

Lana: female warrior of the Nordes Tribe

Lana: Princess/daughter of Segal and Cahina/niece of King Manu of New Samona/Ruala

Lani: daughter of Mia and Ian/Ruala

Lara: one of Usman's wives

Larson: a fighter hired by Juleta

Laurabelle: Hannah's sister who was murdered by Roch

Laurel: Annabelle's mother and former servant of King Roch's parents

Lazo: fighter hired by Juleta

Lea: Princess/daughter of Adwell and Nada/niece of King Manu of New Samona/ sister of Misha/Ruala

Leo: Prince of Samona/son of Darius and Rebek/grandson of Thomas and Rewel

Lila: seventeen year old girl who Luca saves from the Hutas/sister of Christopher

Lilian: female warrior of the Nordes Tribe

Lillian: Queen of Stordt/wife of Jaretta/ mother of Roch and Sudfad

Lily: daughter of Calen and Natasha/Ruala and human

Liza: wife of Duncan the Chief of the Clan of Gesmal in Ryed

Lloyd: banker in Nora

Loftus: Commanding General of Fort Styls

Loni: daughter of King Friada and Queen Marla of the Kingdom of Ganz

Louie: works for Talverson Transport Company in Port Friada

Luca: male Ruala warrior

Lucifer: an ancient demon/ one of the Old Ones

Luque: Prince/son of Segal and Cahina/nephew of King Manu of New Samona/Ruala

Mab: a female Grand Master of the Insidiae

Mabon: warrior guarding refugees/Shettee

Mada: Princess /wife of Prince Gael/Ruala

Madam Bular: owner of a dress shop in Port Friada

Maggie: elderly store owner in Salar

Mahon: son of King Neputa

Makalo: Prince of Norkv/husband of Grace who was the daughter of Benjeman and Esther

Malana: daughter of King Neputa

Mali: Princess of Norkv/daughter of Makalo and Grace/granddaughter of Benjeman and Esther

Maligma: an ancient demon/ one of the Old Ones

Malik: member of the Insidiae

Malus: sorcerer from Ryed

Mandrake: Taperian soldier

Manu: King of New Samona/The Chief of the Grand Council made up of Rualas and Shettees/ father of Ibula, Lakin, Gael and Hadar/husband of Delilia

Marcia: friend of Hannah's/ Roch's men murdered her family

Marcus Stephan: son of Stephan and Ingr

Margarit: daughter of King Mathas and Queen Rosa of the Kingdom of Lentz/ cousin of Raul and Simon

Margolia: girl from Nora who was sacrificed to a demon

Marie: a cook for King Sudfad and Queen Renya

Markus: a soldier in the Army of Wetpr

Marla: High Priest Meekos' housekeeper

Marla: Queen of the Kingdom of Ganz

Martha: a cook for Cerephus

Martin Froush: wealthy ship builder in Port Friada/husband of Denise

Mary: Jared's young wife who was brutally murdered by Hutas

Mata: Igor's wife

Mateo: Chief Healer of the Ruala Tribe

Mathas: King of Lentz/ brother to Queen Renya

Matilda: one of Usman's wives

Matthew: son of King Mathas and Queen Rosa of the Kingdom of Lentz/ cousin of Raul and Simon

Maxwell: father of Calen/ Ruala

Maxwell: infant son of Nina and Rhea/grandson of elder Maxwell/Ruala

Melanie: female Ruala warrior/daughter of Casey and Tasha

Melina: mother of Thaos

Melinda: grandmother of Misha

Mia: daughter of Maxwell and Emeral/ Ruala

Mia: female Ruala warrior/daughter of Tyron and Elsa

Mica: Princess of Norkv/daughter of Benedict and Sasaha/granddaughter of Benjeman and Esther

Micha: oldest son of Joshua and Iris/older brother of Vivian/Clan of Gesmal

Micha: son of King Sharonne/ grandfather of Sudfad and Roch

Michael: ancient king of Wetpr/father of Queen Sumona

Miranda: emissary of The Great Ruler who takes on the disguise of a human seer

Miriam: a friend of Hannah's/works at Endleson Hotel in Nora

Misha: male Ruala warrior/lieutenant

Molach: a member of the Insidiae

Moloch: an ancient demon/one of the Old Ones

Morris: member of governing body of Nora

Myla: wife of the owner of the Dragons Inn in Salar

Naal: warrior guarding refugees/Shettee

Nabi: male Ruala warrior

Nada: Princess/ married to Adwell son of King Zachariah and Queen Noella of New Samona/ mother of Misha/ Adwell was killed in battle leaving Nada to raise ten children/Ruala

Nadia: wife of Karzman

Naomi: mother of Rabi/ Ruala

Napo: Enrop leader who protects Claudius' family

Natasha: sister of High Priest Gabriel

Nathaniel: Sorren's oldest son/ Nordes Tribe

Nebula: son of Chief Romogi and Anda/ Kingdom of Marba/Huta

Nehmota: King of Ryed

Neputa: leader of the Shettee Tribe when it was conquered by the Hutas

Nestor: a demon that specializes in procuring things for a price

Nica: Enrop leader who protects Sudfad's family

Nicholas: orphan boy /brother of Cerey

Nicolas: Prince of Puntd/son of King Tobias and Queen Tasha

Nieatzae: an ancient demon/ one of the Old Ones

Nikki: female warrior of Nordes Tribe

Nina: daughter of Maxwell and Emeral/Ruala

Nina: youngest daughter of Karzman and Nadia

Nita: Princess/daughter of Adwell and Nada/niece of King Manu of New Samona/ sister of Misha/has twin brother Waed/Ruala

Nobel: former prince of Ryed/son of Akasha and Norah/father of Nehmota

Noella: the first Queen of New Samona/wife of King Zachariah/mother of seven sons/Ruala

Norah: former queen of Ryed/grandmother of Nehmota

Noreen: mother of Jacob/ wife of Henry

Norris: hired fighter and intended vessel, works for Dieter

Nyla: oldest daughter of Karzman and Nadia

Oda: daughter of Maxwell and Emeral/ Ruala

Oda: Princess/ married to Zeman son of King Zachariah and Queen Noella of New Samona/Ruala

Odam: male Ruala warrior

Odell: one of the spies at the Castle at Wetpr

Omar: Prince/son of Zeman and Oda/nephew of King Manu of New Samona/Ruala

Omara: Queen of Norkv/wife of Thaddius who was son of Benjeman and Esther

Omnibus: an ancient demon/ one of the Old Ones

Omoria: former queen of Ryed/wife of Nobel/mother of Nehmota

Opago: an ancient demon/ one of the Old Ones

Oren: former prince of Gandt who marries princess Astrel of Ryed

Ottillia: Princess of Lenz/daughter of Princess Isabella and Captain Josef

Padre Augustus: a member of the Patronus

Padre Bartholomew: survives the massacre at the monastery at Avaide

Padre Cornelius: a member of the Patronus

Padre Darius: a member of the Patronus

Padre Dibon: a priest at the monastery at Malga

Padre Dominick: priest at monastery at Malga

Padre Edgar: member of the Patronus

Padre Edward: a member of the Patronus

Padre Francis: priest at monastery at Malga

Padre Joram: member of the Patronus

Padre Lucas: a member of the Patronus

Padre Octavos: runs orphanage in Salar

Padre Philip: a member of the Patronus

Padre Philip: a priest at the monastery at Malga

Padre Simpson: priest at the monastery at Malga

Padre Sorben: a member of the Patronus

Padre Stephens: priest at monastery at Malga

Padre Thomas: priest at the monastery at Malga

Padre Tobias: a member of the Patronus

Padre Xavier: priest at monastery at Malga

Paj: Princess/wife of Prince Hadar/Ruala

Pata: daughter of Chief Romogi and Trina/Huta

Paul: third son of Joshua and Iris/younger brother of Vivian/Clan of Gesmal

Paulas: a man who works for Cicero/a vessel

Paulas: Sergeant under Archetenus in Taperian Army

Paullo: works for High Priest Meekos

Pearl: eldest daughter of King Tobias and Queen Tasha of Puntd

Pergo: King of the Kingdom of Gandt

Peter: Sorren's second son/Nordes Tribe

Peters: member of the governing body of Nora

Petorus: an ancient demon/one of the Old Ones

Petra: peasant boy from Ort who saves Padre Bartholomew

Philip: Prince of Puntd/ son of King Tobias and Queen Tasha

Phillip: Court Physician to the Royal Family of Wetpr

Polgate: one of the men who kidnapped Petra

Potomas: warrior guarding refugees/Shettee

Powell: a lieutenant in the Military of Lentz/stationed at Fahron's castle

Prescott: a hired killer

Rabi: male Ruala warrior

Radnor: a male Grand Master of the Insidiae

Rael: Prince of old Samona/husband of Krister who was the daughter of Thomas and Rewel

Rahi: a female Grand Master of the Insidiae

Rakio: Prince/son of Adwell and Nada/nephew of King Manu of New Samona/brother of Misha/Ruala

Rako: a male Ruala warrior

Raphael: Prince/ son of King Zachariah and Queen Noella of New Samona/husband of Kora/Ruala/father of Luca/ Raphael and Kora were killed in battle when Luca was a small boy/Ruala

Ratri: male Ruala warrior

Raul: Prince/son of King Sudfad and Queen Renya of the Kingdom of Wetpr

Raum: an ancient demon/ one of the Old Ones

Rebek: Princess of Samona/wife of Darius, who was the son of Thomas and Rewel

Renya: Queen of Wetpr/ wife of Sudfad

Rewel: Queen of Samona/wife of Thomas/mother of Varden

Rex: a notorious pick pocket in Port Friada

Rhea: husband of Nina/ brother-in-law of Calen/ Ruala

Riftca: male Ruala warrior

Roch: King of the Kingdom of Stordt/brother of King Sudfad

Rogers: one of the men who kidnapped Petra

Rolif: son of Chief Romogi and Silva/ Kingdom of Marba/Huta

Romale: member of the Insidiae

Romos: an elder of the Centras

Rosa: Queen of Lentz/wife of King Mathas

Rosalie: a dressmaker in Nora/wife of Peters

Ryan: grandson of Jeb/friend of Thaos

Sabot: member of the Insidiae

Sahil: a male Ruala warrior

Samara: wife of Tristt/Shettee

Samat: son of Chief Romogi and Silva/ Kingdom of Marba/Huta

Samos: Prince of Norkv/son of Thaddius

Sampson: oldest son of Chief Duncan and Liza of the Clan of Gesmal in Ryed

Sampson: Sergeant in the Taperian Army

Samuel: a high priest at the monastery at Malga who was murdered

Samuel: Prince of the original Samona/grandson of Thomas and Rewel

Samuel: second son of Raul and Vitomas

Sanuri: a holy man/emissary of The Great Ruler/warrior

Sar: an Enrop

Sar: male Ruala warrior

Sara: daughter of Usman

Sarah: baby granddaughter of Mathas and Rosa

Sarah: housekeeper for Claudius and Bella

Saran: daughter of Karzman and Nadia

Sasaha: Princess of the original Samona/granddaughter of Thomas and Rewel

Sasha: female warrior of the Nordes Tribe/wife of Galen

Satan: an ancient demon/ one of the Old Ones

Saunders: a Taperian soldier

Schroeder: man who works for Insidiae leader Dieter

Segal: Prince/ son of King Zachariah and Queen Noella of New Samona/husband of Cahina/Ruala

Seguna: former princess of Ryed/daughter of Akasha and Norah/ committed suicide

Selen: house keeper for Juleta

Shara: wife of Sorren/Nordes Tribe

Sharonne: King of Stordt; great, great, grandfather of King Roch and King Sudfad

Shon: son of King Fahra and Queen Sitha

Shone: Princess/daughter of Zeman and Oda/niece of King Manu of New Samona/Ruala

Sicily Bella: daughter of Stephan and Ingr

Sila: Princess of Ogg

Silva: one of Chief Romogi's three wives/Huta

Simmons: Commanding General of Fort Nir

Simon: adopted son of King Sudfad and Queen Renya of the Kingdom of Wetpr

Sinclair: King of Lentz/father of King Mathas

Sirius: works for High Priest Meekos

Sitha: Queen of Zorta

Smoking Joe: a regular patron at the Ghost Ship Tavern

Sonja: female warrior of the Nordes Tribe

Sophie: cook and servant of King Roch

Sorren: leader of the Nordes Tribe

Sporos: priest turned demon

Stephan: Captain in Army of Lentz/son of Claudius and Bella

Stiller: a fighter hired by Juleta

Stolas: an ancient demon/one of the Old Ones

Stone: hired fighter and intended vessel, works for Dieter

665

Sudfad: King of the Kingdom of Wetpr and brother to King Roch of Stordt

Sudfad: little Sudfad is grandson of King Sudfad

Sumona: Queen of Wetpr/wife of Alexandras/aunt of Roch and Sudfad

Syrius: a Bakken hired by Juleta

Tabeth: daughter of Fahron

Tabith: son of Tristt/Shettee

Tabitha: Princess of Lentz/daughter of Princess Isabella and Captain Josef of Lentz

Tadeo: Prince/son of Adwell and Nada/nephew of King Manu of New Samona/brother of Misha/Ruala

Tafer: a warlord who drove the Hutas out of the Kingdom of Norkv after years of wars and rebellions

Tahira: a female Grand Master of the Insidiae

Tahira: Princess of Samona/granddaughter of Thomas and Rewel

Tal: son of Oda and Jace/ Ruala

Talmai: Shettee boy who Thedes and Ibula adopt

Tambor: male Ruala warrior

Tamour: General in the Army of Lentz/on loan to Sudfad

Tanner: a Sergeant in the Army of Lentz

Tapster: a demon who works for Meekos

Tarig: a lieutenant in the Huta army

Tarin: son of King Neputa and Queen Tiara/Shettee

Taron: Prince/son of Adwell and Nada/nephew of King Manu of New Samona/brother of Misha/Ruala

Tasha: female Ruala warrior/mother of Melanie/wife of Casey

Tasha: Queen of Puntd/ married to Tobias/ sister of Renya and Mathas

Tate: a Lieutenant in the Wetprian Army

Tavin: son of Prince Lakin and Princess Zada/Ruala

Tega: housekeeper for the cabins of the captains of the Taperian Army

Tegman: soldier of Wetpr

Temark: villager of Neva

Thadddius: Prince of the new Kingdom of Norkv/son of Benjeman

Thaddies: member of Nordes Tribe/ father of Ingr

Thanatoes: an ancient demon/ one of the Old Ones

Thaos: a hired fighter

Thatcher: Prince/son of Zeman and Oda/nephew of King Manu of New Samona/Ruala

Thatus: Taperian soldier

The Lion: emissary of The Great Ruler who takes on the appearance of a lion when he is in the world of man

Thedes: warrior guarding refugees/Shettee

Thomas: King of the original Kingdom of Samona/father of Varden

Thomas: second son of Joshua and Iris/older brother of Vivian/Clan of Gesmal

Thomas: the young husband of Zoya who was murdered in Taperia

Thompson: Wetprian soldier

Thronson: one of Meekos hired killers

Tiara: Queen of Shettee Tribe when it was conquered by Hutas/wife of Neputa

Timothy: son of Fahron

Tito: member of Valdore Tribe

Titus Derek: son of Thaos and Nikki

Titus: a lieutenant in the Taperian Army

Tobart: a member of the Nordes Tribe

Tobias: King of Puntd.

Tomas: works for High Priest Pravis

Tome: a businessman and member of the Insidiae in Nora

Tomi: son of Usman the leader of the Valdore Tribe

Toomback: Huta warrior

Torance: father of Thaos

Torin: oldest son of Karzman and Nadia

Tratz: one of the men who kidnapped Petra

Travor: Taperian warrior who was injured at the Wall of Dorath

Tresdore: son of King Sharonne

Trevor: Prince/son of Zeman and Oda/nephew of King Manu of New Samona/Ruala

Tria: daughter of Oda and Jace/Ruala

Trina: one of Chief Romogi's three wives/Huta

Trina: Princess/daughter of Zeman and Oda/niece of King Manu of New Samona/Ruala

Trist: a male Ruala warrior

Tristt the Horrible: Shettee warrior

Tye: Prince of Norkv/son of Princess Grace and Prince Makalo

Tyron: male Ruala warrior/father of Mia/husband of Elsa

Tyson: Wetprian soldier

Ulger: a demon

Uma: Princess/ married to Gunnel son of King Zachariah and Queen Noella of New Samona/mother of Elan/Ruala

Umar: Prince/son of Adwell and Nada/nephew of King Manu of New Samona/brother of Misha/Ruala

Uri: son of Nina and Rhea/ Ruala

Usman: leader of the Valdore Tribe

Valor: Prince of the new Kingdom of Norkv/son of Benjeman and Esther

Vandrew: Petra's male tutor

Vania: Princess of Samona/daughter of Yorggi and Dion/granddaughter of Thomas and Rewel

Varden: last king of Samona/he and his family were murdered by rebels

Vardin: one of the men who kidnapped Petra

Vasart: Queen of Ryed/ wife of Nehmota

Vinca: Queen of Stordt, wife of Sharonne

Vincent: Prince of Ryed/son of Nehmota and Vasart

Vinus: Queen of the Kingdom of Gandt

Vitomas: Queen of Stordt

Vivian: a demon hunter from the Clan of Gesmal

Voltar: Prince of Samona/son of Darius and Rebek/grandson of Thomas and Rewel/later becomes King of Wetpr

Waed: Prince/son of Adwell and Nada/nephew of King Manu of New Samona/brother of Misha/has twin sister Nita/Ruala

Wallis: member of governing body of Nora

Wilard: Captain at Fort Polta

Willis: son of King Pergo and Queen Vinus/ Kingdom of Gandt

Xeni: a female Grand Master of the Insidiae

Yara: daughter of Nina and Rhea/Ruala

Yorggi: Prince of Samona/son of Thomas and Rewel/brother of Varden

Yori: son of Usman the leader of the Valdore Tribe

Yuri: Prince/son of Adwell and Nada/nephew of King Manu of New Samona/brother of Misha/Ruala

Zac: one of the men who kidnapped Petra

Zachariah: first King of New Samona/husband of Queen Noella/father of seven sons/Ruala

Zada: Princess/wife of Prince Lakin/Ruala

Zadok: a male Grand Master of the Insidiae

Zede: an ancient demon/ one of the Old Ones

Zehmann: an ancient demon/ one of the Old Ones

Zeman: Prince/ son of King Zachariah and Queen Noella of New Samona/husband of Oda/Ruala

Zorda: Taperian soldier injured in battle at the Wall of Dorath

Zoya: a seer from Taperia

Glossary of Terms

Aboultis: the calling cards of demons

Abyss: a vast void used to imprison demons

Acura: the whispering shadows/are in the inner circle of demons that directly serve the Old Ones

Amark: ancient language of The Great Ruler

Amulth: means filth in the language of demons/these monsters are made out of the waste of tortured souls from the hell dimensions

Anewa: one of seven continents in the World of Nunc

Aplewort: an herb when mixed with water purges poisons from a body

Asherane: ancient tribe that lived in the northern regions of the Kingdom of Lentz

Astras: the ancient underground city of the Centras

Beltrad: a species of lower level demons

Blood rings: Large red rubies set in silver with markings of the Old Ones

Boca: a covered wagon pulled by horses

Box of Itifer: a gift to the world of man from The Great Ruler; this gift affects the balance of creation

Bozie: a game of skill played by the Nordes Tribe

Cava plant: a poisonous plant that grows freely near bodies of water

Centras: ancient race of creatures who have the responsibility of protecting the Holy Box of Itifer

Chalice of Ascension: a gift from The Great Ruler, this gift contains unimaginable powers

Cicero College: in Wetpr, outside of Salar, where Raul, Simon and Hannah attended college

Clan of Gesmal: a tribe of demon hunters who live in the southern region of the Kingdom of Ryed

671

Crystal pillars: in the Ice Caves of Mordv/are blessed by The Great Ruler and filled with spiritual life force

Czarsta: one of seven continents in the World of Nunc

Demalogs: an inferior species of demons

Demosa: a slow acting poison from the cava plant

Diamond of Cazo: a gift from The Great Ruler, this gift can unleash powers from the center of the world

Durisks: large demonic birds/their elongated beaks contain rows of fangs

Engas: a wild cat that inhabits the Vandrew Mountains

Engor: a small pack animal that lives in trees

Enrop: a large species of bird that can speak many human languages

Farduth: a Shettee necklace that symbolizes a male has completed his rite of passage to become a warrior

Gafet: an ancient Shettee weapon

Gants: large apelike creatures/Watchers of the Caves of Muldun

Gate of Isula: the only opening in the great Wall of Dorath

Gefrey Games: games of sport where men fight each other and great beasts to the death

Grand Masters: the first people to call to the demons and invite them into this world

Great Ruler: God

Hall of Antiquities: a giant hall located in the monastery at Malga/ a sanctuary for holy items and manuscripts

Hall of Light: the Great Hall in the Ice Caves of Mordv

Hengers: giant blue eagles/ birds of war

Highland Pass: the only passage through the Rosu Mountain Range

Holy Scrolls: gifts given to each kingdom by The Great Ruler, these gifts contain powers, wisdom and immortality

Holy Vault: a secret vault under the King's study in the castle in Wetpr designed to protect holy objects

Horn of Asher: a horn used by the Patronus warrior priests to signal each other

Horn of Cass: a horn used by the Wetprian soldiers to signal each other

Horn of Cornwell: a horn used by Dieter's men to signal each other

Horn of Eel: a horn used by the Ruala warriors to communicate with each other

Horn of Esker: a horn used by the Valdore Tribe to communicate with each other

Horn of Ire: a horn carried by the Taperian soldiers to communicate with each other

Horn of Shana: a horn carried by the soldiers of Lentz to communicate with each other

Horn of Tula: a horn used by the members of the Nordes Tribe for communication

Horn of Vamont: a horn used by the Kozach Tribe for communication

Horn of Xepoltr: a horn used by the Shettee warriors to communicate

Huta: a race of humans that is driven by hatred and ideas of racial superiority who live in the Kingdom of Marba

Insidiae: means conspirators/a highly organized secret group of humans who have sold their souls to demons

Jacar: giant leech-like creatures

Jacept Plant: a plant that a powerful poison is made from

Kafer: a small crescent shaped knife carried by the Beltrad

Keepers of the Scrolls: the Royal Family of the Kingdom of Wetpr entered into a covenant with The Great Ruler to protect his gifts until a time when they can be safely given back to the world of man

Kozach: a tribe that lives in the far north central regions of the Kingdom of Wetpr

Lamsman: an ankle bracelet worn by Venatores/stones in the bracelet signify great feats they had to accomplish to become a demon hunter

Linges plant: a plant that grows in damp, swampy regions in Opots/the white berries are used to make the drug Melanwhop

Mark of Satan: a coiled red snake with green eyes and a yellow tongue

Matu potage: a food staple of the Shettee Tribe

Mayka: one of seven continents in the World of Nunc

Melanwhop: a drug made from the linges plant, causes lethargy and apathy

Mordov: the special place in hell for hypocrites

Motfer: the land of the dead

Nefandus: a secret sect within the Insidiae

Nordes: a tribe of fiercely trained warriors who live in the northern region of the Kingdom of Lentz

Nunc: the world where this story takes place

Old Ones: the original demons that came to the World of Nunc

Opatu bread: a food staple of the Shettee Tribe

Opots: one of seven continents in the World of Nunc/the continent where this story takes place

Oran: a tobisk that is filled with a mixture of ramni oil, buruto powder and meno salts, designed to explode on impact

Patronus: an elite group of men who serve as the protectors of the church

Porto: one of seven continents in the World of Nunc

Prophesy of Isdod: is contained in the demonic Book of Horror/this prophesy explains the significance of the thirteenth level.

Prostras: an ancient tribe that once inhabited the Ice Caves of Mordv

Raftifa: ancient bat-like creatures that devour human flesh

Ravens: messengers used by the dark lords

Recupero: a sect within the Insidiae that worships the demon Omnibus

Rogetts: a tribe of humans that have digressed into murderous mutant monsters

Rualas: an ancient tribe of warriors said to be half human and half bird

Salszar: one of seven continents in the World of Nunc

Salts of Envoy: a sleeping potion

Scio: a crystal ball

Scroll of Imari: a gift of The Great Ruler, a scroll that unleashes the power of the Box of Itifer

Seal of Natun: a gift from the Holy Ruler that can open doors to other worlds

Serpents of Satan: can only be called forth by dark lords and demons, large red snakes with green eyes and yellow tongues

Seven Sons Prophesy: an ancient prophesy about seven sons who stand up against the demons and dark lords

Shesone: an ancient fighting style of the Shettee Tribe

Shettee: an ancient tribe of warriors said to be half human and half lion

Solv: a specific prison within the Abyss

Song of the Second Son: an ancient prophesy about an evil that is passed between second sons of a family resulting in a monster that brings terror and darkness to the world of man

Sundra Templer: a gift from The Great Ruler that was stolen by dark lords/an orb with extraordinary powers that can be used in multiple ways such as transporting humans through other worlds

Tabutu: an ancient form of fighting developed by the Asherane Tribe of the Kingdom of Lentz

Talisman: an object with magical or supernatural meaning

Talmuth: giant red dragon-like creatures

Tangers: large wild, grazing animals that travel in herds

Tansof: one of seven continents in the World of Nunc

Telgras: a hell beast that looks like it is half wolf and half panther

Teragon: death terror/a monster created as a result of diabolical acts

Terbot bear: a bear that roams in the northern regions of the Continent of Opots

Tervator: fourteen foot monster that walks like a man with long dark hair over its entire body and bull-like horns protruding from its head

Texts of Semalia: ancient texts about demonic language and rituals

The Book of Horror: a book that is worshipped by demons/contains prophesies

The Celebration of Days: an annual celebration of the Centras

The Hall of Understanding: the building in Astras where the history of the Centras is documented in drawings

The Hunters: another name for the Shettee Tribe

The Lion: a very powerful messenger of The Great Ruler assumes the form of a lion when he walks in the worlds of man

The thirteenth color: not seen in the world of man it is the color of horror/hell

Timbar: ghost dragons/ demons that can fly

Tinchure water: an herbal pain remedy used by the Nordes Tribe

Tincture of the Redeti Plant: Hutas dip the tips of their weapons in this insect infested liquid. The insects lay eggs inside of the victim. When the eggs are mature and hatch, two inch worm-like creatures are produced and will eat the organs of the victim causing a long and painful death

Tobisks: sphere shaped objects, metal and hollow inside that are designed to be launched from a Trebuchet

Trebuchets: wooden machines used to catapult objects

Tygrus: a ship that docked in Port Friada

Unholy altar: altar used to worship demons

Valdees: the tribe that lives in the underwater Kingdom of Ogg

Valdore: a tribe of merciless separatists who live in the extreme northern regions of the Kingdom of Lentz

Venator: means hunter in the old language

Venom of the Atha serpent: one of the poisons that Hutas put on their arrows

Vessel of Darkness: a human created from darkness to hold the essence of a powerful demon

Wall of Dorath: a giant wall that separates the Kingdoms of Norkv and Xepoltr from the Kingdom of Marba

Willimonns: small furry creatures that are hunted for food and sport

Xelope: the oneness of spirit with all that lives

Zendoti: demons that are distinguished by the geometrically shaped tuffs of hair that protrude from their heads

Glossary of Maps

The maps are displayed in order of relevance

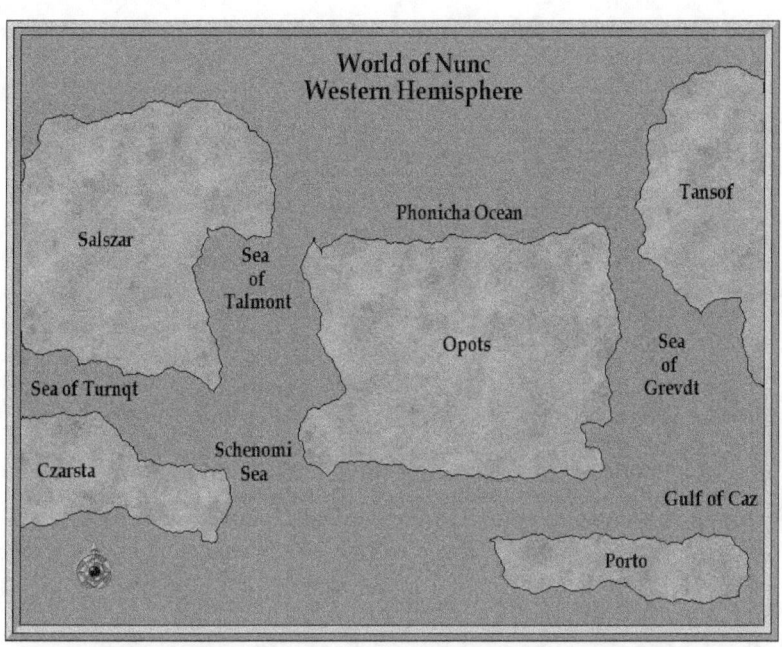

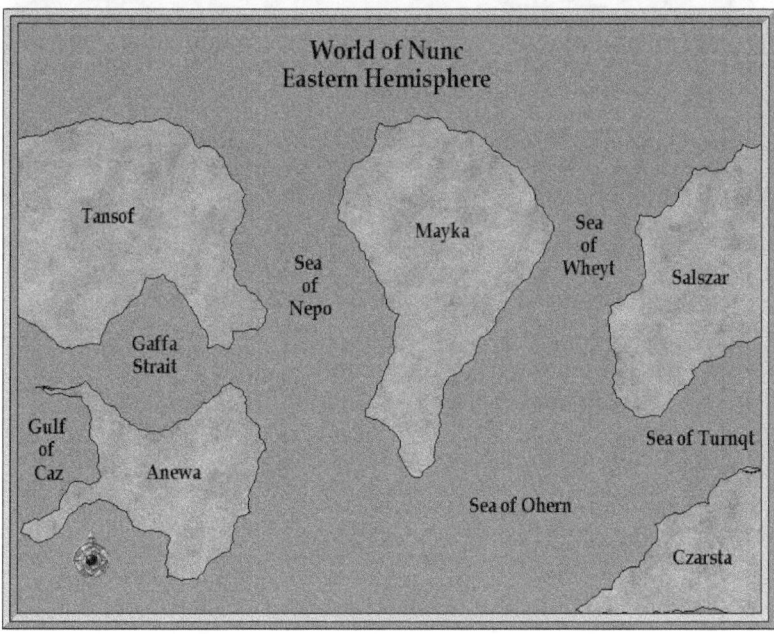

679

Continent of Opots
With new forts

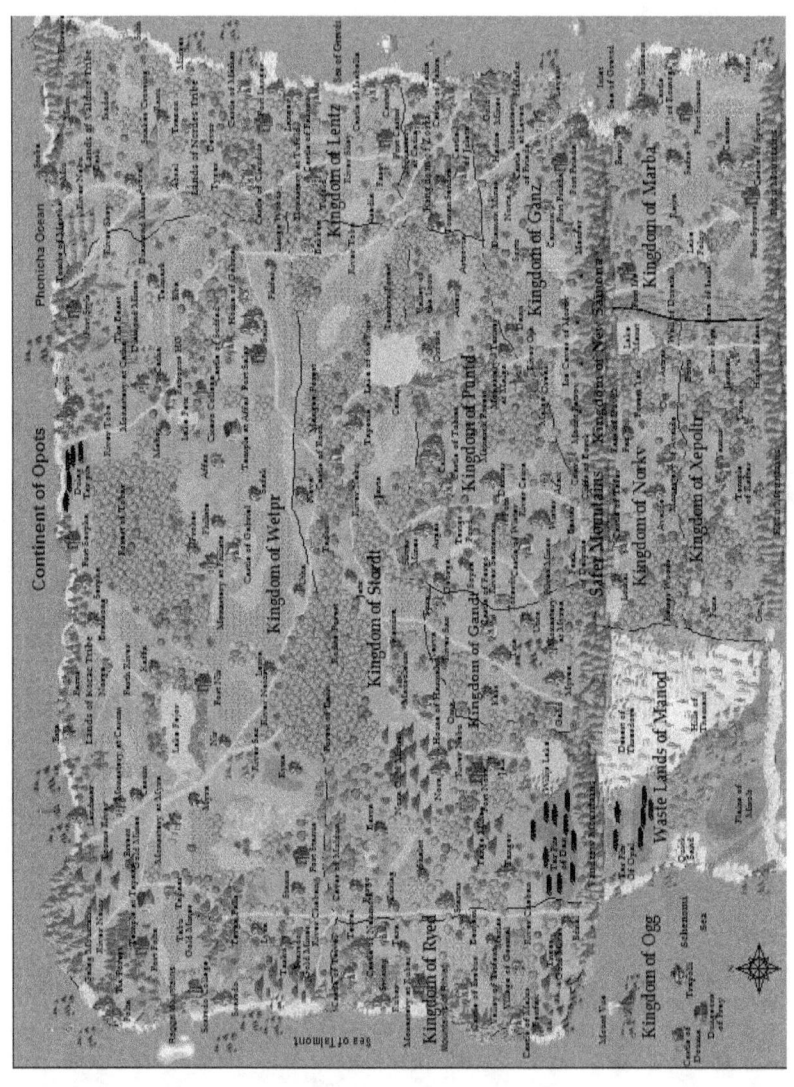

680

Western Stordt
With Fort Nora

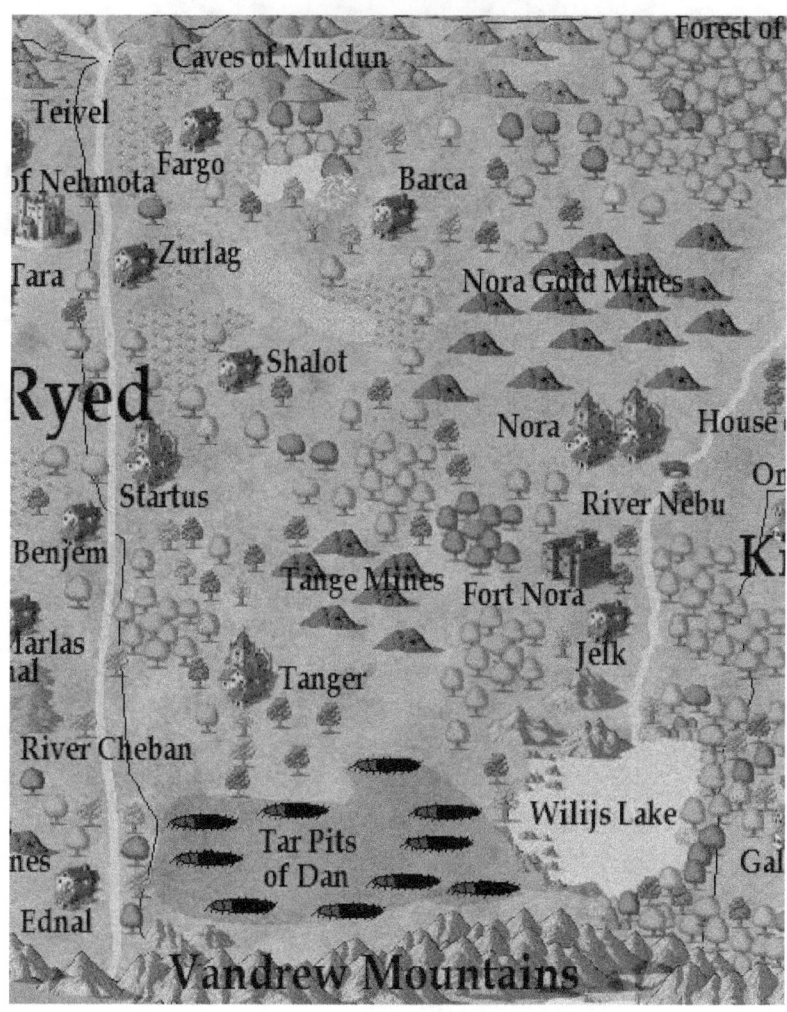

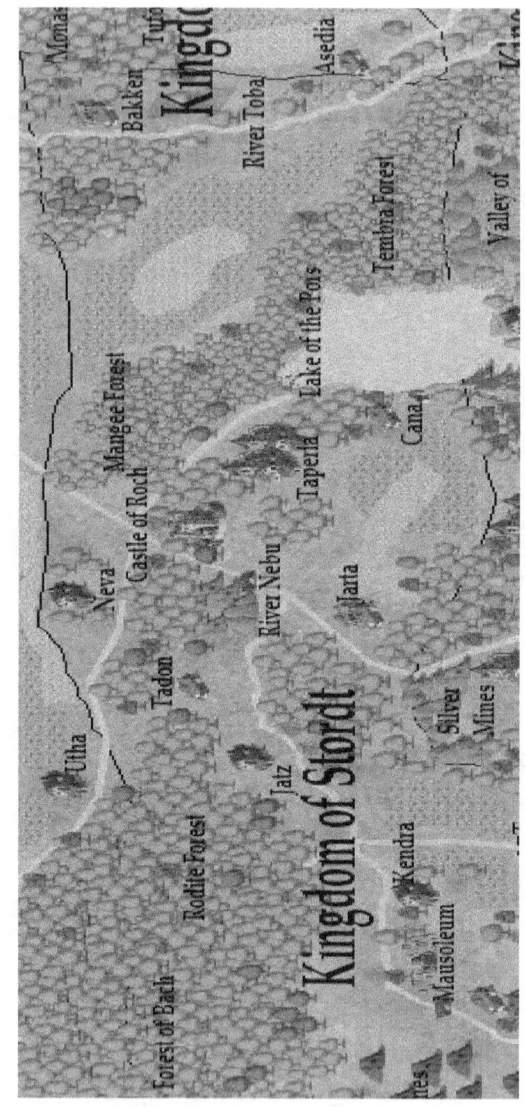

Western Wetpr
With Fort Stanus

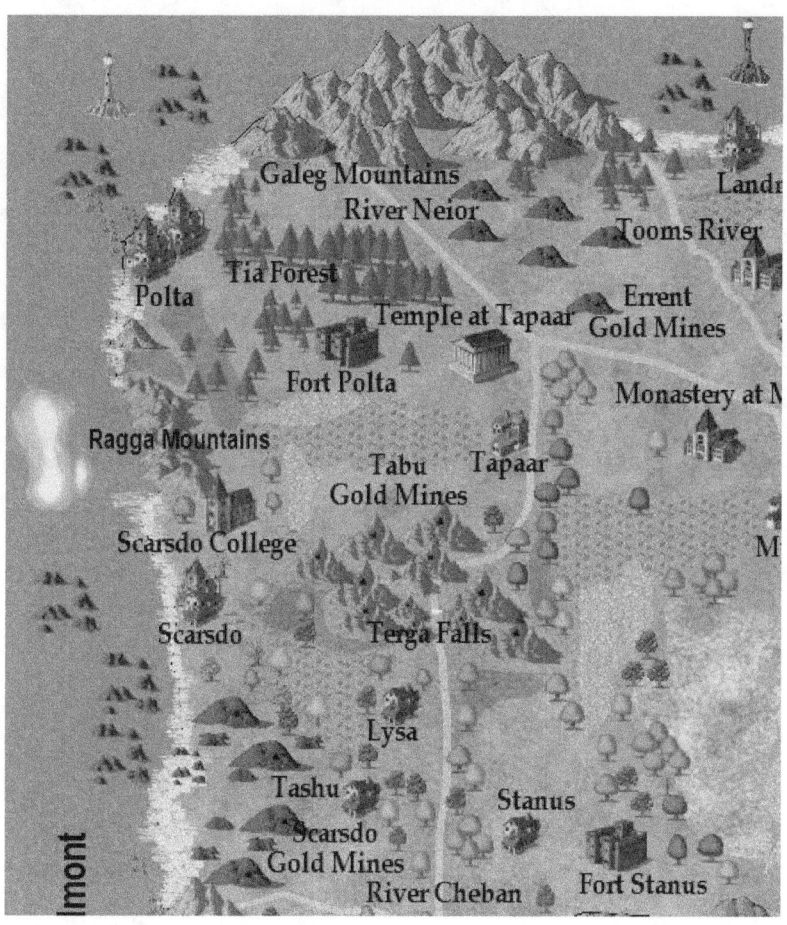

Eastern Wetpr
With Fort Serpha

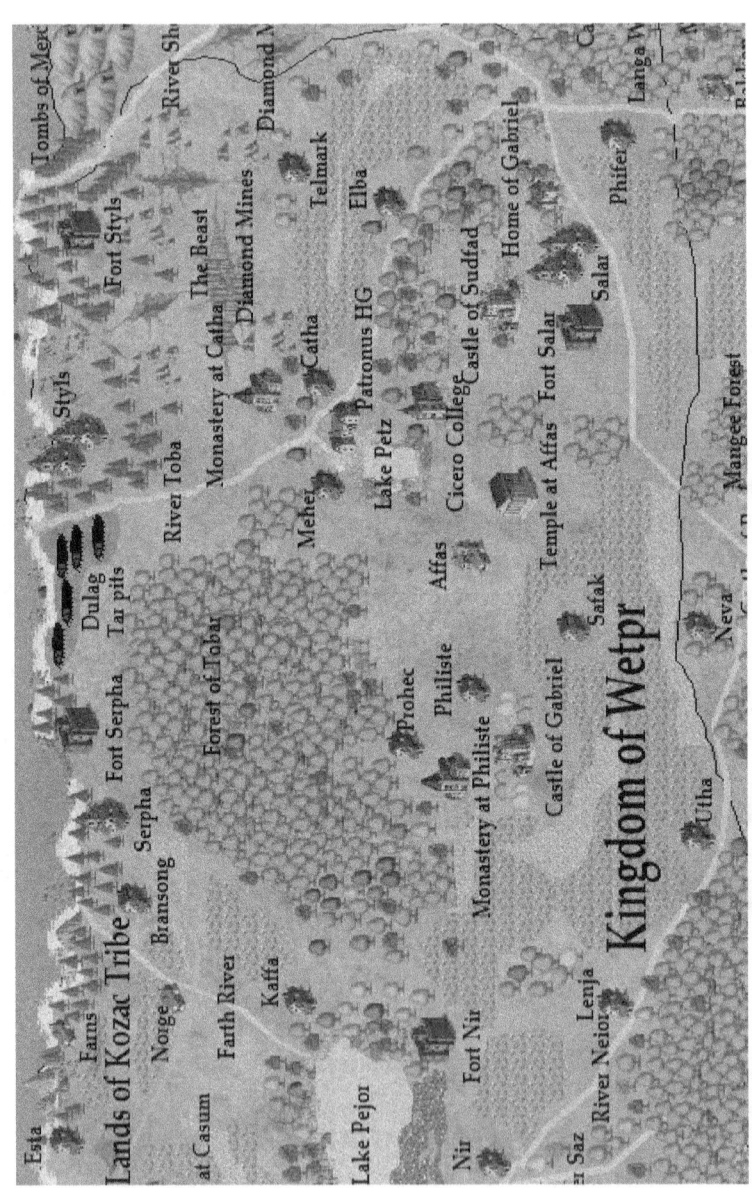

685

Marba

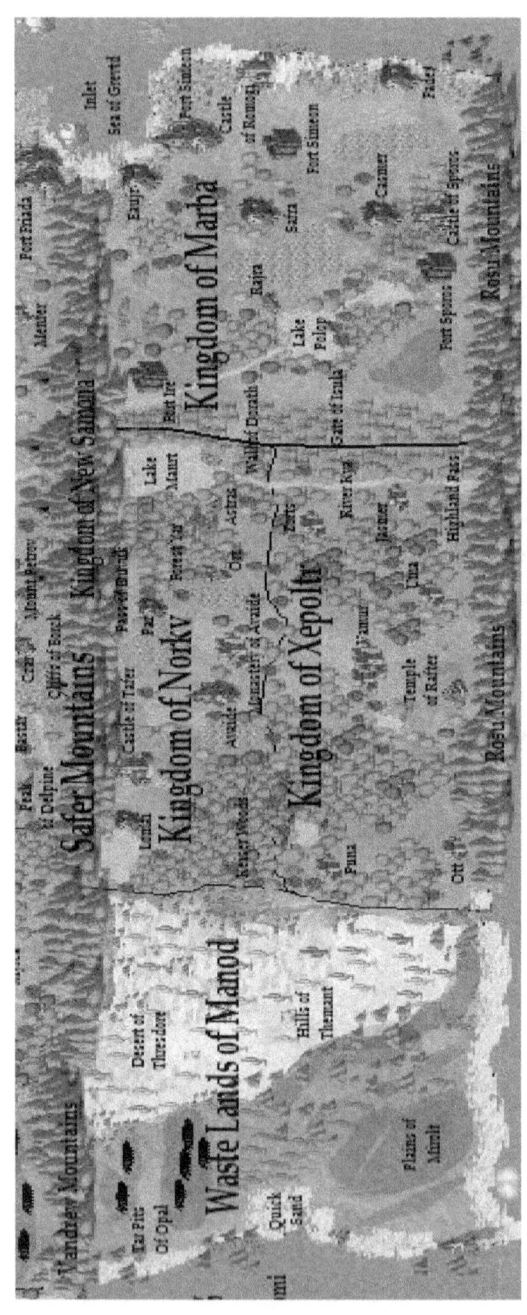

692

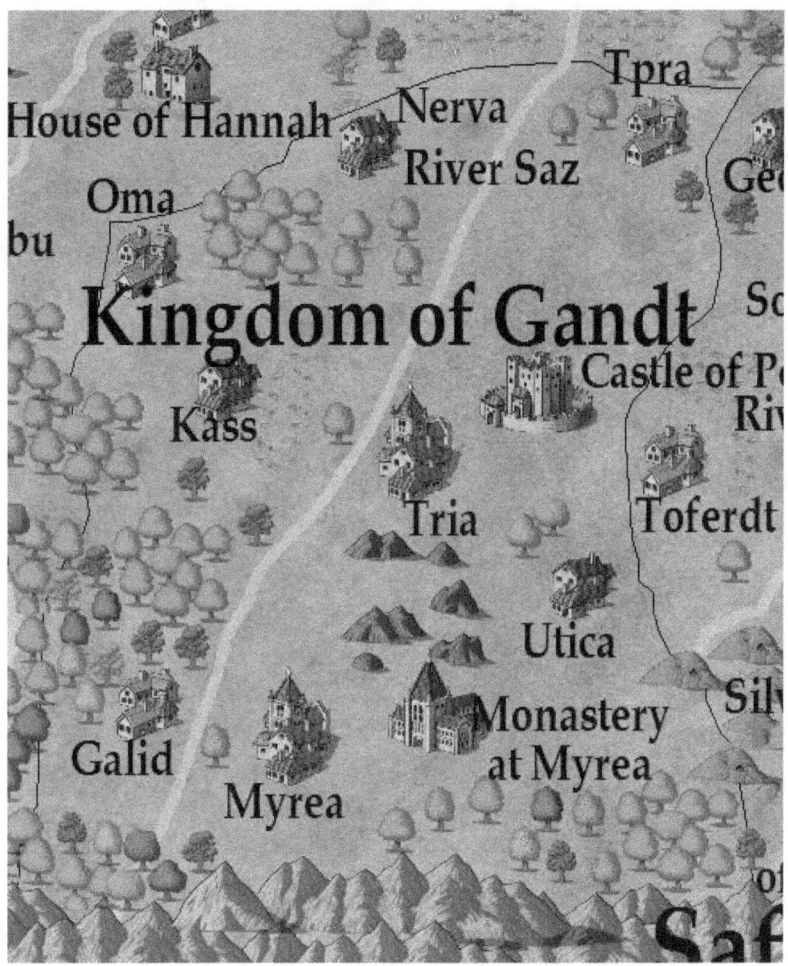

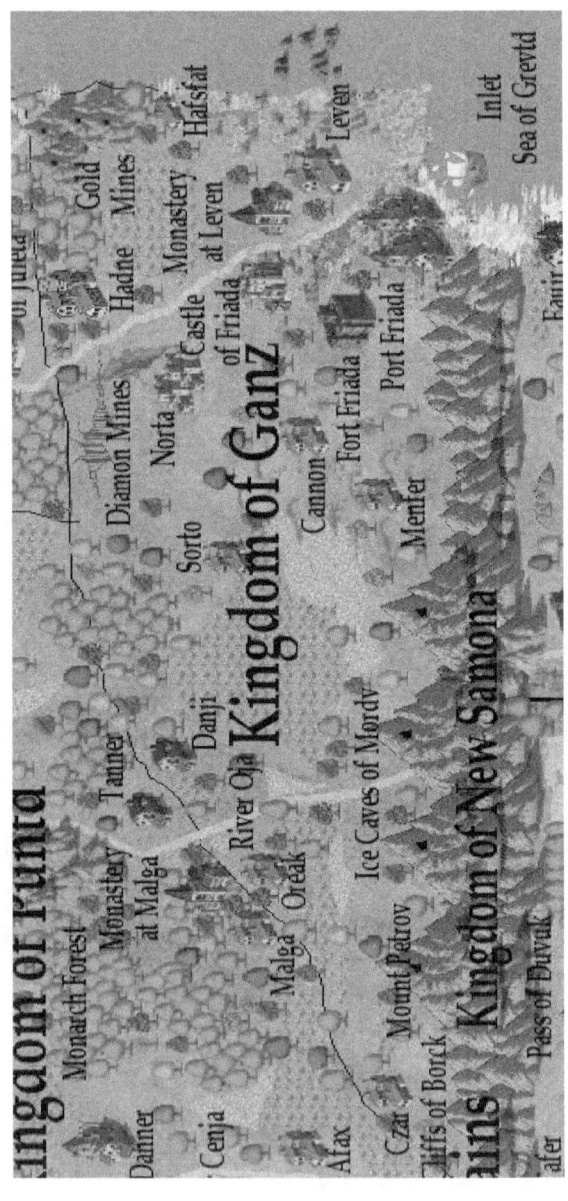

Astrum Solar System

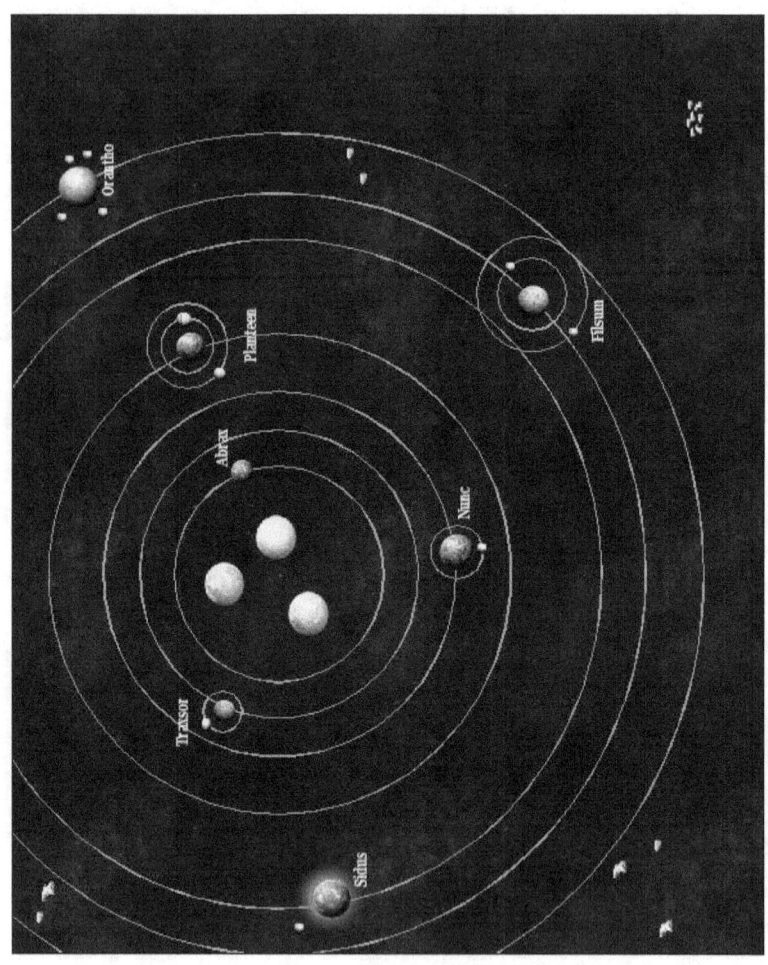